7 3/20

STOP AT NOTHING

STOP AT NOTHING

A NOVEL

MICHAEL LEDWIDGE

HANOVER
SQUARE
PRESS

HANOVER
SQUARE
PRESS™

Recycling programs
for this product may
not exist in your area.

ISBN-13: 978-1-335-04495-2

Stop at Nothing

This edition published by arrangement with Harlequin Books S.A.

Hanover Square Press
22 Adelaide St. West, 40th Floor
Toronto, Ontario M5H 4E3, Canada
HanoverSqPress.com

The author would like to thank the following for their professionalism, advice and belief in this book:

Josh Getzler and everyone at the Hannigan Getzler Agency

And especially Peter Joseph and his excellent team at Hanover Square Press

STOP AT NOTHING

PART ONE

CATCH OF THE DAY

1

When the sun started to go down, Gannon was out alone on his boat in the Atlantic thirty miles northwest of Little Abaco.

His boat was called the *Donegal Rambler*, and it was a forty-foot Delta diving boat with covered seating at the back and tank racks that could hold twenty cylinders. But he'd removed most of the tanks when he'd headed out that morning, and in their place he had seven sea rods set up on outrigger mounts.

Up in the slowly chugging boat's open flying bridge, Gannon stood with his back to the wheel, carefully watching where the rods' green-tinged monofilament lines trailed back into the boat's bubbling wake like the strings of a submerged puppet.

The lines were baited with mackerel and squid and jig lures, and he was trolling them along at a steady nine knots to make them appear to be a swimming school of juicy fish.

Or at least that was the game plan, anyway.

Gannon folded his big forearms as the *Rambler*'s two inboards purred steadily under his Converse low tops.

He'd been out since early morning, stalking the deep Atlantic falloff, and so far hadn't gotten even a bounce on any of the rods.

A dwindling plastic sleeve of sunflower seeds sat in a drink holder at his left elbow, and he lifted it out and shook a few into his mouth. He was half-turned, spitting the shells into a waste bucket he kept beside the captain's seat, when he saw that the falling sun was about to depart behind a bank of dark clouds.

Gannon squinted down at the Simrad depth finder.

The best shot for a sword to hit was at the tide changes, especially high to low like it was now.

He looked back up at the sky and frowned.

Time and light were running out on him.

He was pondering this and just about to spit another shell into the bucket in frustration when the closest of the starboard rods whipped down and bounced back, and the air suddenly filled with the sweet zipping sound of eighty-pound test paying out.

Sunflower seeds went flying as Gannon slipped the boat into Neutral and flashed down the ladder without touching the rungs. As he grabbed the big, frantically unreeling rod up out of the mount, he smiled at the heavy tug on it. Swords usually liked to nibble first, but this one apparently had just gone for it.

He gripped hard on the rod and began reeling, rapidly taking up slack, racing the now-quickly-ascending fish to make sure it didn't get a chance to unhook.

The fish jumped for the first time thirty feet from the boat twenty minutes later. It was a gigantic white marlin, long and shining, with a dark blue bill and a beautiful Mohawk-like blue comb.

Even for an experienced fisherman, it was no small feat to hook a billfish during the day, and Gannon watched in boyish wide-eyed awe as it arced through the gold-tinged air, its body and tail trembling like a sprung diving board.

Then the hundred-pound-plus sport fish slapped back down into a swell with a loud explosion of water, and Gannon got giddily spinning again, sweat pouring off his face, the big rod bowing almost in half as he cranked and yanked.

He was tight on the fish and had it about twenty feet away and closing when it got stupid with panic and ran under the plunging bow. Gannon, pretty hyped up on adrenaline himself, immediately ran forward with the rod so the line wouldn't get tangled.

"Dammit!" he yelled as the bow of the boat bobbed up, and he felt the line immediately snag on something. A split second later, there was a loud crack, and all Gannon could do was watch as his snapped-free UHF radio antenna hit off the bow rail before it disappeared into the water.

Before he could even begin to deal with that, the fish spurted again and came back around to starboard and resurfaced ten feet from the boat. Gannon blinked sweat out of his stinging eyes and then whistled as he got a good look at it. He'd caught bigger sailfish before, but this was no contest the biggest white marlin he had ever hooked.

He was piecing together how to bring the monster around to the boat's port-side diving door when it suddenly twisted and went back under. That was when Gannon dropped the rod altogether. The reel clattered against the deck as he grabbed up the thick monofilament line with his gloved hands and began tugging the huge fish in hand over hand.

He had it just off the hull, holding the banjo-tight line firmly with his left hand, and was kneeling down on the deck lifting the gaff with his right when he felt it give one more mighty thrashing spasm.

"No!" Gannon screamed out as the frenzying line gave a funny jerk and the weight suddenly and completely disappeared on him.

He groaned as he stood and lunged over the gunwale with the gaff. But the huge fish was already gone. Gannon watched brokenhearted as its immense beautiful tail, already ten feet deep and counting, waved bye-bye down in the clear water as it dived.

Spit the hook a foot away! Gannon thought in agony as he slammed the gaff down loudly against the deck.

He glanced forward at the jagged, now-useless piece of metal clamped to the bow rail that used to be his radio antenna.

After busting up his boat!

He lifted the sea rod and reeled in nothing and shook his head in furious disgust as he stared at the empty hooks.

"Fish one. Gannon less than zippo," he said and after a moment began laughing as he looked for a towel.

He'd been a fisherman all his life, and it was either that or weep, he knew.

2

The sunset sky was glowing like a sheet of gold leaf by the time Gannon reeled in everything and got all the gear and tackle packed up and stowed tight.

After he washed up in the head, he went back up into the flying bridge and set the GPS for Cooperstown on Little Abaco to the south. Cooperstown was actually a little out of his way as he lived farther south and east out on Eleuthera Island. But with the radio antenna MIA, he wanted to be near shore by the time it got too dark.

He slipped his face shield up and his Costa polarized shades on and opened the boat wide to about thirty knots. Through the breeze, the sky began to lose its glow, and the endless plain of water took on the dark metallic tone of tarnished silver. Even for a Monday, the fishing lanes northwest of the Bahamas were deader than normal, the horizon empty in every direction. In fact, the only other vessel he got a glimpse of all day was a faint outline of a container heading west to Florida that morning when he started out.

His thoughts drifted to dinner. There was leftover lasagna in his fridge that he could nuke. Instead of fresh-grilled swordfish, he thought, shaking his defeated head in the rush of the wind. Oh, well. At least the beers would be cold.

It was about fifteen miles due east of Cooperstown when he saw something low in the sky off in front of the boat. He thought it was just a shine of light off a cloud. But then he saw that the light was moving, and he jacked up his shades onto his forehead, cupping his hands above his eyes.

Out from the postcard-Caribbean gold of the sky to the left came a plane, a small corporate jet plane, sleek and shiny and pale white. He watched it coming steadily due west at a right angle to the bow. He gauged it to be about four miles to the south. It seemed to be flying quite low. He waited for it to pull up, but it didn't. It kept zipping westward going fast, low and straight as a line drive.

He eased off on the throttle and grabbed his binoculars, putting his elbows up on the console to steady the view. Then he thumbed in the focus and something in the pit of his stomach went cold.

The plane *was* too low, flying maybe a hundred feet off the deck. It was also going way too fast like a stunt jet plane at an air show. It almost looked like a guided cruise missile rocketing just above the surface of the water.

Where had it come from? Gannon wondered, turning at the waist to keep it in the glass. There weren't any airports to the east. Hell, there wasn't *anything* east of the Bahamas. Maybe it had just left out of Marsh Harbour Airport?

It was directly off the front of his bow when he realized he couldn't hear its engines. Instead of a rumble, there was only a kind of whistling, a low whisper very faint in the distance of metal scratching air.

Gannon watched as the plane descended even lower. It had to be twenty feet off the water now. Maybe the pilot was being a hot dog, and in a moment, it would pull up, he thought hopefully.

Then the eerily whispering plane finally ran out of sky.

Its left wingtip touched down first, sending up a huge fountaining spray of water. In another moment, he watched as its belly struck down. Through the white water it threw up, you could see the fuselage vibrating violently. As it skidded along, a rough crunching, grinding sound started in the distance, like denim tearing. Fragments of metal began to shed off into the air behind it.

Even as Gannon watched this, he hoped dumbly that maybe it would be okay.

Like the Sully guy in NYC, he thought, as the back of the plane suddenly began to fishtail.

It swung all the way around backward and kept going. It was about to complete a full three-sixty when there was a rise in the tearing sound's pitch, and the plane went airborne again.

In the frozen silence, Gannon winced as he watched the spinning hundred-foot-long aircraft wobble up through the air sideways like a boomerang flung by a drunk.

Then there was a sound like a bomb going off, and all he could see in the binoculars was a hanging column of pure blinding white.

3

"Mayday! Mayday! Mayday!" Gannon called into his radio as he immediately throttled up, wheeling toward the crash site. "This is *Donegal Rambler, Donegal Rambler, Donegal Rambler.* VA number three eight seven five. I am at GPS heading twenty-seven point one-four-nine by seventy-seven point three-one-five. A plane is down! I repeat. A small commercial jet plane has crashed. How many people involved is unknown. Send help. *Donegal Rambler* is a forty-foot diving boat. Over."

He let off the handset's thumb key. There was nothing but choppy static. He checked to make sure that he was on the Channel 16 distress band then spun the volume dial as high up as it would go. The static only came in louder.

"Mayday! Mayday!" he was saying again when he remembered the snapped antenna.

He cursed as he roughly clipped the useless handset back into its holder. When he glanced forward over the dip and rise of the console, he made out the plane's tail fin on the horizon. Seeing that it was upright, a brief flutter of hope rose in his chest.

Then he looked with the binoculars.

No!

The plane had snapped in half. You could see its pale white tail section with its huge high fin and about twenty feet of it. Other than that, there was nothing. He panned over the water left and right. There was no nose, no wings. The whole front part of the aircraft was completely gone.

He was still trying to reckon this terrible fact when he began to encounter debris. A cluster of water bottles went by. A white garbage bag. A snapped piece of varnished wood paneling with drink holders in it. A man's black Nike sneaker.

On the other side of a swell to starboard appeared a huge white drumlike object. It was bouncing up and down in the water like a giant fishing bob. He couldn't think what the hell it was. Then he came close enough to smell the jet fuel and see the glistening steel turbofan blades still rotating inside of it.

A football field beyond the ripped-free jet engine lay the plane's dissected rear fuselage. Gannon eased the throttle back. He looked up at its aerodynamic rear stabilizers as he came alongside it. *G550* was written in high-sheen blue paint upon its pale side.

He slipped the boat into full idle as he came around to the front, where the cross-sectioned fuselage had breached asunder. From its top hung a spaghetti of aluminum framing and electrical wiring and tattered fiberglass. Yet through these ragged streamers, the rear interior of the aircraft was almost perfectly intact. There was cream-colored carpet on the floor, a window seat covered in bungee-corded luggage, a highly varnished wood sideboard.

Behind the sideboard was the open doorway of a restroom. Gannon stared into it, mesmerized. The white marble sink basin within it looked like something from a five-star hotel.

"Hello!" Gannon called into the fantastic floating ruin. "Hello! Is anyone in there?"

Gannon closed his eyes, listening intently. Thirty seconds passed. A minute. There was nothing. The only sound was the low chugging of his diesels.

He retrieved his binoculars and pointed them to the south. Far off beyond the wreck at ten miles or more, he could just make out the dark coast of one of Little Abaco's tiny uninhabited outer islands.

"What in the hell?" he said angrily as he scanned a three-sixty.

Why were there no boats in the water? he thought. Or choppers in the sky? Hadn't the pilot called in a mayday? Hadn't the airport in Little Abaco seen it disappear off the radar?

He went back up into the flying bridge and did another slower, tighter sweep with the binoculars. About another football field north of the tail section, he spotted a thick clump of objects floating in the water. It was quickly getting darker now, so it was hard to know what they were. Just five or ten black lumps bunched together, rising and falling in the calm swells.

"Please don't be what I think you are," he said to himself as he levered at the throttle and turned the wheel.

He'd chugged the *Rambler* in close enough to see that the items were only a cluster of floating pillows and seat cushions when he spotted something below in the clear water beneath them.

It was something large and pale.

4

Gannon came down the ladder and threw off his shirt and grabbed a diving mask from his equipment locker. The diving door was port side rear, and he swung it open and extended down the telescoping diving ladder with a loud clack and plunged feetfirst into the warm water.

In the darkening water below the hull of his boat there were some undersea limestone ridges at a depth of about fifty feet. In the murk, about fifty feet farther down their crusted slope, was the entire front of the jet with its huge wings and most of its forward cabin resting on a coral plateau.

He searched the plane and the coral all around it through the mask until he couldn't hold his breath anymore. Then he scrambled back up and stripped off the mask and kicked off his wet sneakers as he raced across the deck for his tanks.

It was three minutes later when Gannon plunged backward into the water. He clicked on all his lights and thumbed at the buoyancy compensator as he spun himself around and down into the dim water.

He was geared up with everything he could think of. His double 120 tanks, his flippers and wrist dive computer, his brand-new BCD vest. The light was almost gone now, so he'd also grabbed his powerful hand-strap Sola flashlight along with his GoPro camera diving mask because the camera had another light.

Descending along the crusted ridgeline toward the plane, he swung the powerful flashlight back and forth at the wreck, hoping to see air bubbles. But all he saw were bits of fiberglass and a couple of gray angelfish that came out of the coral, attracted to the light.

He finally came flat and level with the plane two long minutes later. The first object he made out inside the torn tube of its opening was the back of a large beige luxury leather seat. To the right of it across the narrow aisle was an empty leather couch of the same creamy beige color. A few feet in front of the couch beneath a porthole window was a low wood desk with a large black TV monitor on it that blocked his view farther in.

There was a brief moan in the plane's metal as Gannon floated there, considering his options. He checked his depth gauge with his flashlight. It said he and the plane were at one hundred fifteen feet.

He looked back at the plane through his mask. The ripped opening of the front half of the plane was strung with even more tatters of wire and shredded metal than the floating half above. But there was ample room for him to swim in as long as he stayed low.

He trimmed some more air out of his buoyancy compensator to get his horizontal balance even better, then went in slowly, careful of his hoses. He arrived at the beige chair and grabbed on to its armrest to pull himself forward.

He immediately face-planted down into the carpet as the

chair unexpectedly swiveled on him. He lost his balance, and his light and his mask went askew. He had just cleared the mask and was turning, pushing up off his knees, when he bumped into something with his chest, and he swung the light around.

And came nose to nose with the revolting open-eyed corpse sitting in the chair's seat.

Bubbles spewed, and he almost lost a flipper as he reared back in full-blown blind panic and terror. His mask went askew again and completely fogged into a gray mess as he clonked his head off the plane's low ceiling.

He turned and twisted and lunged away out of the plane as fast as his kicking flippers and fear-crazed windmilling arms could take him. He didn't stop swimming until his hand finally found his neon dive rope he'd dropped twenty feet to the wreck's south.

He cleared his mask again and floated there beside the faintly glowing rope. The hiss and gurgle of the regulator loud in his ears, his heart hammering.

Of course the people are dead, you idiot, Gannon thought angrily as he glanced back at the wrecked plane. *What the hell else would they be?*

He needed to stop this silliness, he thought as he looked past the plane into the immensity of the rapidly darkening ocean in front of him.

Diving alone in the open Atlantic was suicidal by itself without going into some coffin-sized wreck filled with who knew what. He was almost certain to get himself killed in another minute if he kept this nonsense up.

The rasp of his breath calmed a little as he fussed with his mask strap. He looked at the time on his dive computer. Then he glanced back at the wrecked plane again.

Oh, whatever. One more try, he thought, already swimming back toward it.

5

The dead man belted into the swivel chair back in the plane was a tall and lean distinguished-looking white-haired Caucasian male somewhere in his midsixties.

He looked polished, Gannon thought. Expensively groomed. With his white dress shirt with the sleeves rolled up and his gray suit slacks, he could have been a doctor from a daytime TV commercial.

When Gannon looked more closely in the flashlight beam, he could see there was actually something wrong with the man's photogenic face. There was a horribly pale bluish cast to his skin especially around his open eyes, and from his nose to his chin, there was a thin stripe of what looked like dried blood.

Behind his diving mask, Gannon squinted, perplexed.

How could his blood already be dry? he thought.

Gannon swam in a little to the right of the corpse. In two

more leather swivel chairs on the left-hand side of the aircraft's tight cabin sat two more dead men.

Like the first man, they were both white, both wearing business clothes. The one closest to him was about thirty-five or so. He had a closely cropped haircut and was stocky and rugged-faced. The other one seated farther toward the front of the plane was younger. He was bony, in his early twenties. He had longish hair and the wisp of a blond beard and was wearing white earmuff-style headphones.

Gannon passed the light from one to the other. Like the first body, they, too, had the same strangely pale bluish tone to their faces.

When Gannon finally turned to the right-hand side of the cabin beside them with the light, it took the entirety of his restraint to not rear back in another panicked bubble-spewing jolt.

In the forward galley before the cockpit was yet another dead man. He was floating upright as if standing. Unlike the others, this dead man was black and was dressed in jeans and a gray hoodie. Gannon watched as the corpse rotated around in a slow, horrid lifelike turn. There was the same blue sickly look to his features as well, and his nosebleed had been so bad, it had stained the top of his sweater black.

When Gannon pointed the light into the cockpit behind the body, he could see that there were two pilots in white-shirted airline-like uniforms still seated at the controls.

He tried to look to see their faces more closely, but the upright floating hoodie-wearing dead man in the galley was blocking the view.

And the chances of him moving the floating dead man out of the way or going any farther into the claustrophobic undersea mausoleum even another inch, Gannon thought, were exactly none at all.

Six dead. No survivors, Gannon thought with a nod. There was nothing to be done.

Time to go, he thought, flippering around in a hectic rush to finally get the hell out of there.

6

After what seemed some very long, slow minutes of following the coral ridge back up through the ten-story depth of the dark water, Gannon finally hauled himself back aboard his boat.

After he pulled himself up through the dive door, instead of sitting on one of the benches, he spit out the regulator and knelt and lay facedown on the deck in the sluice of the water.

He'd shrugged out of his clanging tanks and was still light-headed with the ebullient joy of breathing through his nose and being alive when he finally stood a long minute later.

And still, there is no rescue effort! he thought as he looked over the wreckage to the now-dark horizon.

Nothing. Not a boat. Not an aircraft. Not even a light anywhere in sight.

The boat pitched hard port to starboard in a swell as he peeled off his dripping gloves. As it baby cradled back and forth, he turned to the left and saw that the floating rear tail section of the shattered jet was lower than it had been. It had foundered to one side a tad, its pale cruciform tail fin slightly tilted.

In a moment, it would sink, too, Gannon thought, shaking his head at the absurdity of the whole crazy thing. In an hour, the dark Atlantic would swallow it like it had swallowed the first half of it. And but for Gannon's memory, it would be as if the plane had never existed at all.

Gannon had just pulled up the dive rope and was clacking up the dive ladder a minute later when the boat pitched again, and he heard the clatter to starboard.

He walked over and looked over the gunwale and saw some luggage there in the water, bumping up against the side of his boat.

The first piece Gannon brought aboard with the help of his gaff was a little dark green hard case that looked like something you'd put a camera in. He laid it on the deck and went and got a penlight. He clicked the light on, put it in his mouth, undid the case's clasps and flipped up the lid.

Inside of the case, sunk into the hard gray packing foam, was a gun. He could tell by its distinctive shape and black matte texture that it was a polymer Glock pistol. There were some large magazines and a suppressor half-buried in the packing material beside it. He peered at the length of the magazines then tilted the light at the pistol barrel. A thin number 18 was engraved along the side.

A Glock 18? Gannon thought with a whistle.

He'd heard of them. They looked like a regular pistol but they were actually small yet extremely powerful handheld machine guns with a rate of fire twice that of an Uzi.

A fully automatic machine gun pistol, he thought, looking at it curiously. But weren't only people in law enforcement or the military allowed to legally possess those?

He was still staring down at it with a hand to the back of his wet mind-boggled head a full minute later when he heard some more knocking and clacking against the boat.

The second hard case he pulled aboard was silver and far heavier than the first. He actually had to gaff it around to the diving door and almost threw out his back as he lugged it up over the lip. It had to be about seventy pounds or more, he thought as he brought it over and thumped it onto the deck next to the gun case.

He stood, chewing at his lower lip as he stared at it. Then he finally knelt down and opened it up.

And felt his breath exit his lungs in a mad-dash rush.

Gannon tracked the columns and rows. Right to left and up and down. And then he did it again.

The case was jammed tight with money. They were all hundreds. Packets and packets and packets of United States of America Benjamin Franklin one-hundred-dollar bills.

They were wrapped tight in red rubber bands. He edged one out. He thumbed at the cloth-like paper. He held it up to his face and smelled it and riffled its soft edge against his wrist.

"Seventy pounds," Gannon whispered as he stared.

But that's not all, came a TV game show host voice from somewhere in Gannon's mind as he noticed a huge lump in the cloth webbing on the underside of the case's lid.

Inside the flap, there was a big butter-soft black leather bag about the size of a laptop case. The word *Cross* was embossed along its bottom. He lifted it out and unzipped it and unfolded it on top of the pallet of money.

He was no jeweler, but inside of the leather bag was what appeared to be rough uncut diamonds. Some were grayish and some had a yellow tinge, but most of them were as colorless and clear as broken car glass.

They had been separated into clear plastic sleeves by size. A grouping of about ten of them in one sleeve section along the left side of the sheet particularly captured his attention.

He'd seen diamonds before. Just never ones the size of Jolly Rancher hard candies.

There were about enough diamonds to fill a cereal bowl, Gannon thought, shaking the bag. Hell, more. Several bowls. He bit at his lower lip some more as he began nodding idiotically. He was staring down at the damn entire box of cornflakes, wasn't he?

Seventy pounds of worn US hundred-dollar bills plus a fat satchel of uncut diamonds, he thought as he stood. Plus a fully automatic law enforcement—only machine gun pistol.

He glanced back at the sinking tail section.

Plus six dead men in a multimillion-dollar crashed luxury Gulfstream jet.

He knew what it was now. He had thought it already, but now he knew.

It was a drug deal. Some kind of crazy high-level drug deal. Down in South America. In Colombia or Bolivia or somewhere with the cartels. But it had gone super loco apparently.

Gannon blinked at the piled treasure.

He looked up at the dark vault of the sky, the first faint silver sprinkling of stars that could be seen there.

The opportunity he had here. All that money. Like a Powerball hit.

Only the kind you could never tell anyone about.

He slowly passed a hand over his scruffy jaw. He looked at the water, turned in every direction. All still dark. Still nobody coming. He looked at the cross of the listing tail section about to sink.

What would the Bahamian government do with it? Gannon thought. *Lower the tax rate? Give it to the poor?*

Sure they would, he thought as he took a deep breath.

Then he decided.

Was it even a decision at all? he thought as he went and found his gloves again and pulled them on.

Gannon hurried up to the bow and clicked on the electric anchor winch. As the chain began to chatter against the bow roll, he came back and dumped the money out onto the deck and tossed the bag of diamonds on top of it. He wiped down the empty suitcase with a wet towel before he brought it back to the diving platform and filled it with water and made it sink.

He thought about keeping the gun before he closed its lid and wiped its case down and heaved it into the sea from whence it came.

He tossed the diamonds and money into a dirty blanket he used as a pad when doing engine repairs and locked it in the head before he went forward and secured the anchor.

Gannon could feel butterflies in his stomach and his heart pounding crazily in his chest as he came back and climbed the ladder up into the dark flying bridge.

"Caught something after all," he said to himself with a crazy laugh as he turned off the running lights and slammed the twin diesels to full reverse, keeping his eyes on the dark horizon.

7

Coming on eleven at night, there was an accident on Miami's Palmetto Expressway that was backing up traffic just west of the I-95 on-ramp.

Pressed up against the left side window of the coast guard C-130 Hercules on approach to Miami Coast Guard Air Station, navy lieutenant Ruby Everett squinted down at the commotion.

In the police blue-and-red bubble light glare, she counted three vehicles involved, a pickup truck and two cars. She craned her neck back as the thunderous aircraft zoomed over the highway. She looked for debris, telltale skid marks. But it was fruitless. They were too far away.

Easy, tiger, she thought as she felt the aircraft's landing gear hum beneath her toes.

You'll have more work than you bargained for in about five seconds flat.

"Hey, can I ask you a question?" said the pilot in her earphones.

She turned away from the window and came forward in the jump seat. The pilot was leaning out of the cockpit, smiling back at her. There were two other crew members sitting behind her, but they both seemed to be sleeping.

Ruby listened to the roar of the engines behind her in the big cavernous cargo plane as she looked forward at the pilot and the smile on his face. There was something creepy about the guy that she couldn't quite put her finger on. He seemed normal enough. Plain looking. Midthirties. Very neat.

But maybe that was precisely it. He was too neat, too plain. He looked like one of those blend-into-the-woodwork, plain-looking neat guys from one of those Discovery Channel shows where women ended up floating in the Everglades after the first date.

"What was that?" she said as she pulled her blue camo utility cap down tighter over her dark brown pulled-back hair.

"What division are you in?" he said.

"Office of Naval Safety," she said, tugging at her matching blue camo blouse to make it as baggy as possible.

As usual, she'd changed immediately into her navy blue utility working uniform and boots when she'd gotten the call. She actually had to gun it back to her apartment up in Ensley to change and to grab her gear. She'd only just gotten back in time to hitch this cargo flight out of Pensacola Naval Air Station, where she was based.

"Naval Safety?" the pilot said, glancing at his instruments then back at her.

"I know. It makes us sound like hall monitors," she said. "We're basically the NTSB but for the military. We investigate aviation mishaps."

"Ah, a toe tagger," he said with a nod. "That's wild. You must have seen some real freaky stuff."

Ruby smiled back politely.

She'd been backup for plenty of accidents in the four years she'd worked at Safety but had only been on-site to two real ones. The biggest was an air force cargo plane that had gone down in upstate New York the year before.

It was a NATO base resupply plane coming back from an overseas deployment somewhere. It needed to refuel in Canada, and there had been some screwup with the liters-to-gallons ratio. They'd also eventually surmised that the gas tank low-level alarm never went off due to a burnt-out transducer.

She remembered finding the black box herself on the bank of a frozen creek in Chittenango State Park near Syracuse. She most definitely remembered the pilots' screams from it. Both pilots and the 140-million-dollar aircraft had been completely obliterated on impact.

"You like it?" the pilot said.

She glanced out at the lights of Miami-Opa Locka Executive Airport coming at them hard and fast in the aircraft's windshield.

"It's a job," she said.

That wasn't true. Ruby loved it. The engineering, the math, the detective work, the excitement. Not being chained to a desk.

Well, at least usually, she thought, squinting down at the floor.

For the first time in her professional life, she had been actually disappointed when her boss had called her in for a job.

It was because of her sister. Her little sister, Lori, was due any minute to give birth to her second child. When Ruby's phone rang two hours before, she'd actually been hanging out at Lori's place in Lake Charlene waiting for her water to break so she could drive her to the hospital.

It had been Ruby's hope to ride out her last night of being on call into her upcoming leave. She'd been pretty much banking on it actually. With Lori's husband, Mitch, in the marine corps on active deployment in the Middle East, there was no way Ruby wanted Lori, her only sibling, to have to give birth alone.

Ruby winced as she thought about her sister, big as a house, on the sofa with her little three-year-old son, Sean, running around like a monkey.

Hopefully, she could get the preliminaries started on whatever the hell this was and then pass it off to the other members of her team and skedaddle.

"What kind of plane crash you going to?" the pilot said, absently flicking off the autopilot on the console as he sat forward again. "A navy plane? Some arrogant navy Tomcat pilot seen too many Tom Cruise movies and became tarmac pizza?"

"I don't know yet. We do all branches. They didn't tell me much. They just said they needed me in Miami ASAP."

"One other question," the pilot said, looking back at her with his creepily plain grin.

Oh, boy, here we go, Ruby thought.

"Shoot," she said.

"You married?"

"Engaged," she lied.

She saw the spinning chopper right away as they landed. To the left of the big coast guard hangars was one of their famous rescue helicopters seen in the recruiting commercials, red with the white stripe. There was a crewman in a helmet and a dark blue flight suit sitting in its open side door.

What was it called again? she thought as she unbuckled her seat belt. A Dolphin, she remembered as she stood and shouldered her gear bag. An MH-65 Dolphin.

"Lieutenant, your chariot awaits," said a chief petty officer with a ruddy face and a beer gut on the other side of the Hercules's dropped ramp.

"What's going on, Chief?" she said.

"No rest for the weary, Lieutenant," he said over the wind rush and rotor whine as he led her through the humid night air toward the Dolphin.

"We have a cutter on scene, the *Surmount,* out of Miami Beach. The bird will take you straight out."

"Are there any other members of my team here?" she said.

"No. There's no one. Are you supposed to wait for them?"

"I'm not sure. I keep texting my boss, but he hasn't gotten back. Did you send anybody else out?"

"No, but my orders are to get you out there right away. I recommend you just head out now, and I'll send out your friends later if they show. This one's a four-alarmer, from the sound of my boss."

Ruby looked at the old salty coastie, at the bright blinking lights of the churning chopper waiting for her.

"Let's do this," she said, tucking down her cap as she plunged into the rotor wash.

8

A thousand miles due north of Miami, snowflakes fell steadily against the upstairs window of Robert Reyland's house in Falls Church, Virginia. There was a pretty good wind going as well. Downstairs in the brick chimneys of Reyland's big new house, the whistling gusts of it sounded almost musical.

But Reyland didn't see the flakes, didn't hear the wind.

He was too busy watching it become midnight on his encrypted secure cell phone.

He raised his large bald head and looked around the small silent room. There wasn't much in it. The eyebrow window above the gun safe, the cardboard boxes in the corner they still hadn't unpacked.

The Realtor had told them that the tiny space off the master bedroom suite originally was supposed to have been a nursery for the people who had built the place, but the wife had miscarried, so they'd just left it empty.

Unforeseen botched circumstances, Reyland thought, passing a hand back and forth soothingly over the shaved-smooth skin of his head.

He placed his BlackBerry back down on the top of the gun safe he'd just taken it out of.

My, oh, my, can I empathize.

He shifted his weight on his wife's tiny vanity chair he'd brought in from the bathroom. He was still in the suit and overcoat he was wearing when he'd gotten out of the car from the airport two hours before.

He'd been in London waiting to hear word from his boss when he'd gotten the report about his plane falling completely out of contact. The eight-and-a-half sleepless hours he'd just spent on the British Airways flight back to DC had felt like the most useless of his entire life.

He refused to even consider all the worst-case scenarios. At least not yet. Even for him, some things were just too terrible to contemplate.

He had gone immediately from Reagan International downtown to his office and called everyone he could. Twice. They had done some projections, but there were too many factors. The wind, the orientation of the instruments. It was a needle in a haystack even with the satellites.

Reyland palmed at his head like LeBron on a mid-dunk basketball.

Now he was home to get some sleep.

Yeah, right, he thought as the phone suddenly rang.

He felt his heart thump like a kick drum as he looked at the screen.

It was his right-hand man, Emerson.

Here we go, Reyland thought, closing his eyes as it rang again. In his mind, he pictured a coin flipping.

Heads, you live. Tails, you die.

He forced himself to take a very deliberate breath before he thumbed down the accept button.

"Where?" Reyland said.

"The ocean. Atlantic Ocean, northwest of the Bahamas."

"The Bahamas! What?" Reyland said as he let out a breath. "How the hell did it get there?"

"It must have happened before the second turn in the flight plan," Emerson said. "They never made the turn, and it just kept going till the gas ran out."

"What a damn disaster! Is he alive?"

"No. It got ripped up on impact. Tore in two. Dunning is dead. All of them are dead. No survivors, just like they said."

Reyland pondered that for a long silent beat. His mentor, the great Dunning, was gone. Just like that. It was hard to wrap his mind around. He put it aside.

"How far out from land?" he said.

"Ten, fifteen miles offshore of… Let's see… Little Abaco. It landed underwater on a coral shelf."

"Who called it in? Civilian?"

"No. The coast guard found it. A drug-interdiction cutter out of Miami Beach. They spotted the wreckage with their radar. Thought it was a drug boat."

"Are we lucky it wasn't a civilian. But coast guard, huh? I don't like it. Did they see inside the cabin?"

"No, not really. The bodies are still in the part of the plane that's underwater. We lucked out there."

"Wait, wait, wait. What do you mean by 'not really'?" Reyland said, squinting.

"Well, the coast guard went through standard rescue procedures when they spotted it. One of the rescue divers went down to check for survivors. Don't worry. I'm already getting any and all tape and making plans to isolate the crew."

"We on the way?"

"Yes, Ruiz should be wheels up with our team by now. Luckily, there was a salvage vessel out of Norfolk out training. It's six hours away. Ruiz has some ex-SEALs with him. They'll go under and get everything that needs getting off. All in all, it's looking about as good as we could have hoped."

"I don't like it," Reyland said. "The coast guard is out of our purview. I don't have to tell you the lid we need on this."

"Don't worry. It won't be a problem," Emerson said. "I'll send word again that the coast guard is to completely stand down and babysit until Ruiz and the navy vessel show up, and we get it all the hell out of there.

"By the way, London called again. Twice. But I stalled them like you said. Also, have you figured out how you're going to tell Cathy?"

"Who?"

"Cathy. You know, Dunning's wife."

"Oh. No. I haven't. Not yet. Shit. She thinks he's at a conference in Italy. I mean, imagine? Add telling her the great Dunning is dead to the list of my magic tricks."

"I could do it, boss, if you want," Emerson said quickly.

Reyland's gray eyes squinted as he sat up, suddenly noticing the eager-beaver tone in Emerson's voice.

He was really all over everything, wasn't he? Reyland thought. London. Their military contacts. You bet he was. Trying to use the crisis to climb a rung or two.

What's the expression? Never let one go to waste?

There was a long beat of silence in the cold of the small room. Down in the living room, Reyland heard the wind in the chimney suddenly chime like a bell.

"You're right, boss," Emerson finally said. "I'll leave it to you."

9

After over an hour of monotonous black ocean, the sudden deck lights of the USCGC *Surmount* were as bright as a rock concert.

Ruby's stomach churned in time to the change in pitch of the chopper's turboshaft engines as they came to a hover. She loved flying in airplanes and was actually a licensed pilot herself, but like so many others in the military, helicopters always made her nervous.

As they swung in above the rear flight deck helipad, outside the window she could see several sailors in life jackets and hard hats along the 270-foot cutter's aft rail.

"Okay, Lieutenant, if you're ready, we're going to lower you down in the bucket," the Dolphin crew chief said with his Southern accent in her intercom headphones.

She turned and looked at him in horror as he showed her some kind of harness.

"What?" she shrieked.

"Gotcha," the helmeted crew chief said with a grin. "Don't worry, Lieutenant. Roy will land it. Maybe even on the boat, if we're lucky."

The officer who met her on the chopper pad's edge was fair-haired and clean-shaven and, like almost everyone else in the coast guard, looked young enough to still be in college.

"Welcome to the *Surmount*, Lieutenant Everett. I'm Lieutenant Martin," he said, shaking her hand as he led her up a short set of steps through a doorway.

Inside, there were three blue-uniformed seamen on the bridge. She dropped her bag in an unobtrusive corner, the air-conditioning delicious after the humid heat in the chopper.

"So you're the investigative team," Martin said as they watched out the pilothouse glass where a team of coasties with a hose was already refueling the Dolphin.

"The first," she said. "There are four of us altogether. The others are on the way. So what do you have? A downed aircraft?"

"It's a plane," Martin said, nodding. "One of our guys on watch spotted it on our radar about five hours ago. We do long-range drug-interdiction patrols out of Miami Beach, so we thought it was a boat in distress on the water at first.

"But as we approached, we saw its tail fin barely sticking up out of the water. That was only from its rear section. It's actually broken in two. The front part is under a hundred feet of water. I was about to call the local airport on Little Abaco for any missing aircraft, but then I saw the bulletin. My father's buddy Al Litvak works at the naval safety office, so I called him first directly. You know Al?"

"Yes," Ruby said. "He's one of my boss's bosses. You said there was a bulletin?"

"Yep. It was on our OPREP board. I saw it when I came on watch. It said something about a missing air force jet to be on the lookout for."

She thought about that. No one had told her about a missing jet.

"So it's a jet? What kind? Do you know?"

Martin took out an iPhone and brought up a picture.

"Not a military one, as far as I can tell. It's some kind of corporate jet. Our diver took a photograph of a dataplate on a piece of debris near the tail section. *Gulfstream*, it says. See?"

She looked at the image. *Gulfstream* was *all* it said. There was nothing stamped in the boxes for model and serial number and FAA certification.

Maybe it was an EC-37B, she thought. The EC-37B was the new military version of the Gulfstream 550 that had electronic warfare capability. It could jam radar and other electronic systems.

Perhaps it was on a test flight? Which was maybe why it hadn't been picked up by local airports' radar?

Ruby peered at the photograph again. She had never seen a blank dataplate before. It was like staring at a car license plate with no number on it.

"After we spotted it, we immediately did our rapid emergency rescue response to check for survivors. There was no one in the tail part. Then we saw that the sunken front portion was within diving range, so I had one of our rescue divers go down for a peek. Six aboard it, including the two pilots. All dead."

"That's terrible. Where are they now? Below deck?" she said.

"Who?" Martin said.

"The deceased," she said, blinking at him.

"No," Martin said, looking at her. "We didn't do the recovery yet. I got a call from my base commander to stand down and let you guys take care of it."

She gave him a funny look.

"Is that right?" she said.

"What's the problem? Is that not protocol? With the bodies, I mean?"

"No, it's not," she said. "I've never heard of the deceased being left in place before. We usually get brought in after all remains are recovered from the wreckage."

Martin squinted, puzzled.

"He was pretty insistent about us not going near the aircraft again until you guys showed," he said. "He said a navy salvage vessel is en route."

"My boss didn't tell me that. I thought he was waiting to hear from me first," she said.

"Well, looks like somebody's getting their wires crossed, I guess. What else is new," Martin said.

A burly older man in a bosun's mate uniform came out of a door on the other side of the ship's glowing control boards.

"Hey, Lieutenant, you got a call," he said.

Martin looked at him then back at Ruby.

"Give me a sec," he said.

10

Ruby went to the window. As the Dolphin lifted off, she looked down and saw a diver in a wet suit talking to a seaman along the main-deck starboard rail.

"Hey, guys. I'm Lieutenant Everett from Naval Safety investigating the crash," she said as she arrived in front of them. "Did you go down and see the wreckage?"

The diver nodded. He was a cute kid, lean and blond and green-eyed with a fresh green tattoo of a shamrock on the webbing of his right hand. He was short, about five foot five or six. Sitting gracefully in his Body Glove suit, he could have been a teen surfer resting between waves.

"How far down was it?" Ruby said.

"About a hundred and twenty feet," the blond diver said.

"Can you go deeper?"

"You'd be amazed," said the older deckhand with a wink as the kid blushed.

Ruby glared at the joker, a thick-featured, dark-haired thirty-something with a goatee. She looked at his deckhand's green hard hat. What was the navy term for green hats? Oh, yeah. Deck apes.

"We're trained to go up to two hundred or so or even more, but you need special tanks with added helium," the young diver said.

"Were the deceased in uniform? Air force personnel or navy? Could you tell?" she said.

"Lieutenant?" called a voice from above.

Ruby turned around to see Lieutenant Martin at the pilot-house rail above, waving.

"Excuse me," she said to the diver. "We'll talk later, okay?"

"I'll be here," the diver said.

"Me, too," said the deck ape with a wink.

She went back up the stairs and followed Lieutenant Martin inside. He led her across the bridge through a short corridor into his wood-paneled office.

"Coffee?" he said, closing the door.

"Please. Black."

She stood silently waiting as he poured. The mug he handed her had a picture of a cute little blond boy in a funny puffy Hulk costume on it.

"Please, sit back and get comfy, Lieutenant," Martin said, gesturing at a bench-like padded couch bolted to the wall. "There's been a change in plans apparently."

"What do you mean?" she said.

"We've been advised to completely stay away from the wreckage. We're actually leaving now. We're supposed to babysit at a distance of a quarter mile. We're not supposed to touch any debris. Just keep people away. Starting now. No personnel are to go near the wreckage until the navy salvage ship arrives. Including you."

Ruby's brow wrinkled.

"What? Why?"

"I don't know."

"But how does that make sense?"

Lieutenant Martin leaned forward in his bolted-down office chair and thumbed back his hat as he thought about that. He took it off and began spinning it off a finger.

"I have absolutely no clue," he finally said. "But as it turns out, I shouldn't even have called you. My boss is pissed that I jumped the chain. I should have called him first, he said, even though he's on leave with his family on vacation out in California. You ever see something like this with a crash before?"

Ruby looked down into her coffee and then back at him before she slowly shook her head.

"Not even close," she said.

11

The clock in the dashboard was at 2:53 when the dirt road Gannon was looking for suddenly leaped out of the darkness into his headlights on his right.

His GMC Sierra skidded slightly as he brought it to an abrupt stop on the right shoulder and flicked on the cab light. There was a map of Eleuthera Island's southern end on the passenger seat, and he reached over and lifted it up. He looked at the map then looked back at the dashboard, where he'd been clocking the distance on the odometer. Then he flicked off the dome light and shifted the truck into Reverse.

He'd finally arrived home around ten and put up the boat at his berth in Davis Head Harbor and went back to his house in Tarpum Head.

Weeds leaped and danced in the bobbing headlights as he turned off the asphalt down onto the slightly sloping bumpy dirt drive.

Now it was four hours later, and he was twenty miles south of his house in a mostly unpopulated part of Eleuthera known as Bannerman Town.

After a few hundred yards, he stopped again, shut off the engine, got out and stood looking.

There wasn't much to see. The old road led into fifty or so acres of deserted pineland that had belonged to a run-down resort that had been abandoned years before after hurricane damage had finished it off.

He crossed the rocky, sandy dirt to the rear of the truck and dropped the tailgate. In the bed was another vehicle, a golf cart–like utility quad ATV 4x4 known as a Gator. It, too, had a kind of truck bed that was filled now with diving tanks and coils of lights and ropes.

Gannon dropped the ramp and backed the Gator down. He winced at the tremendous roar of its four-stroke engine as he fired it on.

Not exactly stealth mode, was it? he thought. But there was no helping it.

He went to the back of it. Down between the tanks was a bulging faded-green canvas sea bag and he zipped it open.

Sealed up watertight in thick plastic vacuum-sealed garment bags were the money and the diamonds and his GoPro camera.

He hadn't planned on adding the GoPro to the rest of his salvaged contraband until he'd wisely decided to take a look at it back at the house and realized he'd actually filmed the whole dive into the plane.

It was some pretty creepy footage. Not to mention incriminating.

He certainly hadn't meant to memorialize the event, but he must have accidentally hit the camera's record button when he turned on its light while he was in the water.

He zipped the canvas bag back up again. As he stood there in the dark it occurred to him that he could still cease and desist from what he was doing here. That even now there was still time.

Then the moment passed, and he found himself hopping in behind the Gator's wheel and flicking the lights on.

12

The narrow foot lane he was looking for was another two hundred feet down the pitch-black drive.

It was off to the left atop a thickly overgrown slope, and thistles and sharp pine brush and branches scraped like claws through the Gator's open door as he throttled up to it.

About a football field from the tree line where he'd come in, the path began to slope steeply downward as the pine forest trees began to thin. The trees gave way to a shrubby glade, and he hit the brakes a moment later as the path suddenly ended.

Beyond in the headlights of the ATV was a large depression in the earth about the size and shape of an ice hockey rink. It was rimmed with steep, almost sheer ten-foot-high pale rock walls, and at the bottom of it was a large pond-like body of water.

The large quarry-like opening in the ground was known as a blue hole. All over the Bahamas, blue holes were cave-like water-filled sinkholes that had been formed by eons of rain eroding through the soft Bahamian limestone.

There were several that were famous diving tourist spots but not this one. The only reason Gannon knew about this one out here in the boonies was because he had dived it three years before with a geology professor from Australia who had hired him to watch his back while he did research.

Gannon had thought the old Aussie was a little off his rocker until he dived down with him and saw the amazing subway-like network of corridors and caves with his own eyes. Several channels were almost a mile in length and went down hundreds of feet in depth. Every day for two weeks they had explored and mapped the cave network with guide ropes and radiolocation transmitters.

From behind his seat, Gannon produced a cardboard tube and tipped out the rolled-up laminated map that he and the professor had made of the cave system.

Then he clicked on a flashlight and uncapped a Sharpie marker.

It was almost 3:30 on his wrist dive computer when he finally managed to get his game plan sussed out and all his equipment and the money bag lowered on ropes down to the water.

He had just climbed down himself and was about to get into his tanks when he realized he had forgotten something after all.

"If it's not one thing, it's another," he mumbled to the darkness as he scurried back up the rope and rock in his bare feet.

He went to the Gator and lifted up the green cloth fishing rod bag he'd left in the foot well. He couldn't strap the small cloth bag to his back because of the tanks, so he decided to tape it to his lower right leg with a few wraps of black vinyl electrical tape he'd brought along.

Two minutes later, Gannon was finally back down in the warm water of the blue hole completely geared up.

Here goes nothing, he thought, as he finally untied the heavy money-filled bag and let its weight take him down.

Most of the top part of the hole was like the bowl of a giant wineglass. But at seventy feet, its bottom tapered, and three corridor-like passageways opened up, two to the west and one to the east.

Gannon took the eastern passageway that went another thirty feet down in an angled sort of corridor that was like a steep stairwell with no stairs. At the bottom of the stairwell was a short corridor-like passage that went in two directions, east and west.

Remembering the directions he'd memorized, Gannon went to the left, east, and passed two more branches: one to the left and one to the right, and then a third on the left that he took. A hundred feet in on a level plane, the walls and ceiling of the hotel corridor–like passage began to close narrower and narrower to that of a barely diver-wide pipe.

Just when it looked like it was going to dead-end, the pipe suddenly opened up into a huge rectilinear chamber that rose up thirty or so feet.

Gannon pulled himself in through the manhole-sized opening and swung his light up at the stalactites. The professor had dubbed the chamber "the cathedral" because of its height.

Along the high wall to his right, about twenty feet up, he stopped the light where a horizontal lip of rock jutted out.

Gannon shone the light down onto the sea bag and opened it and took out the twenty-pound weight. Then he adjusted his buoyancy and floated and swam up to the ridge with the bag.

Arriving at the ridge, he peeked over at the shelf of rock he had noticed when he had explored the chamber with the professor. When he placed the heavy sea bag down onto the shelf, it fit almost perfectly, but it kept floating up a little. After a few more failed tries of stuffing it down, he swam down to the cathedral's floor, retrieved the weight, swam up and put it into the bag.

Gannon paddled back a little bit and looked with the light at the almost-invisible ridge of rock. He smiled around the regulator in his mouth.

The money bag was settled now. Invisible.

Better than a Swiss vault, he thought.

Gannon was squeezing into the pipe-sized tunnel out of the cathedral when he realized the green cloth fishing rod bag was still taped to his leg. He backed into the cathedral chamber and cut the tape with a knife from his ankle and held the bag in his hand as he looked around.

Just above the tunnel exit he found a rock ledge, and he took the narrow tube-shaped cloth bag and dug it down into the silt and rocks there.

Now we're done, he thought.

13

"Okay, here we go. Which famous English writer was called 'the prophet of British Imperialism'?" a tall, skinny coast guard sailor at the next table read off a Trivial Pursuit card.

"Harry Potter," somebody called out in the bright sunny bacon-scented room. Then somebody called out "Joe Mama" in a funny voice, and they all cracked up.

Ruby put down the beat-up Nicholas Sparks paperback she'd found in the lounge next to the mess and looked out at the bright light coming through the big window at the other end of the cafeteria.

They were shore bound now, still in the Bahamas on Andros Island on a US naval base called the Atlantic Undersea Test and Evaluation Center.

She had actually heard of it. It had some deep ocean trench close by off its coast where they supposedly tested submarine stuff, sonar and torpedoes and missiles and depth charges and who knew what else.

As if she could care what they did here, she thought, checking her watch and seeing that it was coming on two in the afternoon.

Why the hell was she here?

It wasn't clear. Three hours after Lieutenant Martin had received his babysitting orders, a navy salvage ship called the USS *Recover* had arrived.

When the navy ship had relieved them, she had thought they would head back to base in Miami. Silly her. Lieutenant Martin had been ordered south directly to Andros Island to dock here at the obscure base until further notice and that was all.

Or at least, Ruby thought, that was all she was being told.

She lifted up the paperback again but then put it down, stood, went to the window and looked across the base yard at the USS *Recover.*

It had arrived at one of the deep-sea docks a half hour before. They had some kind of big dividers or something set up on its deck. As if they were actually hiding the damn wreckage or something.

She stared at the boat, trying to decide which pissed her off more: that they'd stuck her here without explanation or that someone else was doing her job.

What was also great was she'd tried to call her boss to get her the hell out of here, but there was no service. There was Wi-Fi, but it was password-only, and what do you know? No one at the base would give any of them the password.

Ruby wanted to find Lieutenant Martin to complain, but he was conspicuously absent.

Out of bitching range, she thought. *He'd move up quickly.*

Just called out here to stand down, she thought as she looked at the stupid navy ship. Which really, really wasn't working for her since she was supposed to be on leave by now helping her sister, Lori, due in less than twenty-four hours.

Ruby shook her head as she pictured Lori by herself out in Lake Charlene, waiting for her water to break. If it hadn't already.

"Screw this," Ruby mumbled as she crossed for the door.

It was incredibly humid outside, the hot air still, the sun beating. She walked down the mess hall's rust-tinged steps and across the bleached concrete base yard. There were some more rust-flaked steps onto the deep-water dock on the other side, and she was already sweating like it was going out of style as she came up them.

As she walked along the three thousand–ton navy ship's looming football field–length of gray steel for the boarding ramp, she could hear some clanking coming from it, faint voices, the hum of equipment.

It sounded like a crane up there or a Bobcat or something moving things around. People working up there, arranging the wreckage.

But not Naval Safety people? she thought, looking up at the ship, huge and gray and still. She swiped sweat off her forehead with her blue camo blouse sleeve. Some other mysterious people up there, the Keebler elves of the navy or the Smurfs maybe, up there stealing her job.

"I'm sorry. You can't be here," called down a sailor way up on the ship in a booming voice as she arrived at the other end of the gangway ramp.

He was a tall blond guy with a goatee and a bullet-shaped head. A petty officer first class, by the three red stripes on his shoulder.

Unbelievable. Why would they put such a heavy hitter at the ramp? she wondered.

"I'm Lieutenant Everett from Naval Safety. Is the plane up there? The jet they found? I'm supposed to be working on it," she called back.

"Sorry," he said. "No one can come aboard, Lieutenant. Captain's orders. Call your CO."

"I can't. I don't have the damn password for the Wi-Fi."

The sailor at the other end of the gangway shrugged his large shoulders.

"No one can come aboard, Lieutenant. Sorry," he said, not sounding very sorry, his face like a slab of stone.

14

Ruby walked across the yard, cursing to herself, sweat dripping down her back. She was slow to anger normally, a get-
alonger by nature. But she'd about had it.

Most of the *Surmount*'s sailors were outside now at the bottom of the mess steps. They were smoking and kicking a hacky
sack around. One of them had a football, and they were laughing and carrying on like middle schoolers with the teacher gone
as they tossed it back and forth.

Beyond them in the shadow of the mess hall was a bleached-
white wooden picnic table next to an old grill that was Cheeto-
orange with rust. Ruby sat down at it, looking out at the endless
turquoise Caribbean behind the building.

How far to Florida, she thought, if she started swimming
now?

"Hey," said a voice behind her.

The short blond surfer kid diver looked even younger in his

ironed uniform. And cuter in a cute little brother sort of way. He looked like a Catholic grammar school eighth-grader on picture day.

"Hey," Ruby said as he sat down across from her.

"This sucks, huh?" he said. "I saw you head over to the ship. What's the story?"

"They won't tell me."

"I'm Steve, by the way. Steve Vance," the diver said, offering his hand with the green shamrock tattoo on it.

She shook, smiling at him.

"I'm Ruby," she said, dispensing with all the navy protocol rank bullshit that she actually despised.

"Hey, Ruby, you want to see something?" he said, waving his phone at her.

"Tell me you got the Wi-Fi password," she said, tenting her fingers in prayer.

"No. Better," he said, handing over his phone.

There was some kind of video queued up on the screen. When she pressed the play triangle, it showed a bright beam of light in dark water. After a moment, coral passed at the edge of the light and then a pale aircraft fuselage appeared along with a porthole plane window.

Ruby hit the screen, pausing it.

"No way!" she said. "But I asked Martin for the dive footage, and he said it was unavailable."

The diver gave her a wink.

"Yeah, well, can't hurt to take a copy for myself, can it?" he said, looking around. "Believe it or not, Lieutenant Martin can be a prick. He got a shippie shit-canned for getting loaded on board last trip out, a good buddy of mine, who was the best sailor in the entire seventh. I tried to tell Martin that he had just found out his girl was leaving him, but he couldn't care less.

"I yelled at him pretty good in front of everyone at dinner about a week later, and since then, he's been busting my chops pretty good. Any screwup, he could just blame me, right? So that's what the folks at GoPro are for. I'm documenting everything I do. I have to cover my ass."

Ruby pressed Play again. She sat up when she saw the first older dead man in the captain's chair.

What in the hell? she thought, looking at the white-haired guy. He didn't look military. He looked like a lawyer or a businessman or something.

The moment she saw the blue patches on his face and the dried blood, she knew what had probably happened to make the plane crash.

There had been a sudden loss of cabin pressure, Ruby realized.

The bluish face on the screen was almost identical to a picture of a plane fatality victim she had seen in one of their training manuals about cabin pressurization system failure.

At high altitude, pressure system failure was extremely deadly. First, the rapid change in pressure often induced nosebleeds. Then because of the low percentage of oxygen at 40,000 feet, a rapid loss of consciousness would almost immediately occur. Even after only thirty seconds of losing oxygen at a high enough altitude, pilots could become completely incapacitated.

A sudden loss of cabin pressure knocking out everyone on board also explained the challenging search for the plane, Ruby realized. If the autopilot was on at the time, the only limit to how far the plane could have traveled was based on how much fuel was in the tank. If the Gulfstream's tanks were even relatively full, it could have come from virtually anywhere, Ruby realized. South America. Heck, maybe even Europe, she thought.

Ruby shook her head when she realized that the plane might have even had military-grade radar-jamming capability.

No wonder they had been so frantically looking for it.

It had been a true ghost plane.

She watched as the camera lit over the rest of them. Still no uniforms. They all looked like civilians, four civilians. Even the pilots' uniforms looked like commercial ones.

She remembered the dataplate again. The blank dataplate.

What in the hell *was* going on? she thought.

She watched it a second time. She had the odd urge to wipe her hand on her uniform shirt after she finally handed back the phone.

"You tell anybody you have this?" she said.

"Just my buddy Matt. The guy I was talking to when you spoke to us last night."

"The deck ape?" Ruby said.

Steve laughed.

"That's Matt," he said.

"Okay, Steve. Listen to me. Don't tell anybody else about this video, okay? And tell your buddy Matt to shut the hell up about it, too. Keep it to yourself."

"Why?" he said.

Ruby turned back to the gray boat looming there. The dividers up there on the deck. The big stone-faced petty officer guarding the rail.

"Silence is golden," she finally said.

15

An hour and a half later, a Chevy Cobalt drove out of the base without incident. Then a Nissan Altima came in. Then a Kia Soul headed out, and the guards by the fence came out of their shack and stopped it.

On the side of the guardhouse were two signs: POSITIVE ID REQUIRED and RESTRICTED AREA AUTHORIZED PERSONNEL ONLY—KEEP OUT.

Keep out? Ruby thought. "With pleasure," she mumbled from where she stood beside a brick barracks two hundred feet to the gate's south. *Hell, I didn't even want to come in here in the first place.*

Her decision to leave after seeing the video had been a no-brainer. It was obvious they were all being detained because of the mystery plane. Some upper-echelon ass-coverer had probably gotten word that the plane had something to do with some classified horseshit and had frozen everyone in place until he figured out which was the best ass to kiss next.

Under normal circumstances, she could put up with the government and the navy's top-down bureaucratic bullshit about things. But these weren't exactly normal circumstances, were they?

Plane or no plane, she was technically on leave now, and if she didn't get back to Florida this afternoon, her little sister, Lori, would have to give birth by herself.

What she needed to do now was get on a plane. She'd learned there was a commercial airport that was actually within walking distance of the base, but the question was, would they let her off?

She didn't know. She certainly wasn't going to ask anyone. She'd been in the navy long enough to know that if you wanted to get something done, you just went for it. It was far easier to ask for forgiveness than permission.

Ruby was still squinting at the gate that she needed to get past a minute later when a white Ford Focus drove onto the base. Its driver showed something to the guard. As it came up the road, Ruby smiled and shook her head when she saw the familiar smiling Asian face behind the wheel.

"Hey, sailor. What's a nice girl like you doing in a place like this?" said her Naval Safety coworker Mark Thanh with a wink as he rolled down his window.

Ruby grabbed her bag and ran over, beaming.

"Mark! Am I glad to see you," Ruby said, chucking her bag into the back of his rental. "I thought everybody died. What the heck took you so long?"

"I just got back from leave and wasn't a minute into the office when El Jefe turned me right around to come down and relieve you. Your sister still hasn't had that baby yet, right?"

"That's what I want to know," Ruby said, glancing at the guard shack. "You need to get me to the civilian airport double time."

They made the U-turn. As they approached the checkpoint,

she stifled a groan as the big sergeant-at-arms at the gate held up a hand for a second.

He peered at Ruby's face, confused. But then he saw Mark's face again and realized he'd just seen him, and then he tentatively waved them on.

As they came out onto the base road, Ruby turned around and looked back. The guard hadn't moved from the spot. He was looking at her again with the same confused look.

Ruby felt weird then, sort of guilty and suddenly and oddly quite afraid.

"Rube, you all right?" Mark said.

"I'm fine. Just worried about my sister," she lied as the gate and the white buildings of the base behind them got smaller and smaller under the hot blue sky.

16

The steel diamond-plate steps rang loudly against Reyland's shoe heels as he came down the steep flight from the top deck of the USS *Recover*.

He was going to need to get some polo shirts or something, Reyland thought, unbuttoning his suit jacket in the Caribbean heat as he reached the bottom of the steel steps. It had actually been snowing at Bolling Air Force Base in DC when he took off two and a half hours before.

He glanced at his encrypted phone as it buzzed in his pocket. London again. Screw them. They'd have to wait. Everybody would have to just back the hell up for five seconds.

"Watch the chrome dome, boss," his tactical team head, Thomas Ruiz, called out as he led Reyland to the right down the hot dim corridor.

Reyland smiled at Ruiz as he ducked under a sharply jutting electrical box.

The short and stocky former Delta Force sergeant didn't walk so much as barrel through the world with a rooster-like strut.

The below-deck corridor was lined tight on both sides with cables and massive pipes and water hoses. They stopped at the end of it, and Ruiz knocked twice on a closed bulkhead door. The metal door squeaked and then opened inward like a bank vault. Just inside stood a very muscular black man wearing sunglasses in the same buff-colored tactical uniform as Ruiz.

The formidable man snapped his heels together as he gave them an ironically formal salute.

"Knock it off, Shepard," Ruiz said, elbowing the man out of the way as they walked past.

The low warehouse-like hold they entered was roofed with steel beams. The bodies were laid out in the middle of it on a blue tarp, two by two. They were in dark green plastic body bags, and as Reyland came closer, over the boiler room smell of the ship's machine oil, he caught the first fecal whiff of their rot.

Ruiz stopped before them and nodded at Shepard, who knelt at the first body bag. The rest of Ruiz's men, a half-dozen veteran professional operators, sat a ways off in a dim corner of the hold. Aloof. Yawning. Not even looking at them. Some standing, some squatting, all in complete monk-like silence. They weren't even talking to each other.

As the bags were zipped open, Reyland watched Ruiz take a cigar from his pocket. The Zippo he lit it up with had an ace of spades engraved in the side.

"Here," Ruiz said as he offered the stogie to Reyland, soggy end first. "You're going to need this."

They went over to the first one.

Reyland let out a breath as he looked down.

His boss, Arthur Dunning himself. *Holy Toledo.*

Even in death, his boss had an austere bearing. Even now his standing expression was that of a crafty old coach about to throw a chair across a basketball court.

A memory came suddenly. Dunning, competitive in all things, was a scratch golfer, and they would play twice a month. He remembered the time he had almost beaten him a few years before on the course out on Griffin Island. He'd been up one on the last tee. Then right in the middle of his back swing, the sly old bastard had actually coughed. Reyland remembered slicing it, burying it in the woods good and deep.

"Shit happens," Dunning had said, giving him a smug little smile.

Reyland fought off the strange desire to smile a little smugly himself as he looked down at his dead mentor laid out on the beat-up below-deck windowless room like a bunch of garbage in a split-open Hefty.

Sure does, boss, he thought, nodding. *It surely does.*

Reyland looked at the other dead men.

"How'd the plane go wonky? The cabin pressure like they said?"

"No clue," Ruiz said, blinking at him. "I'd expect it's something like that because of the blue patches on their faces there. Looks like they suffocated. But there's no way to tell unless we bring in the mechanics and experts. I'm no structural engineer, boss."

"Now tell me, Tommy," Reyland said, looking the hardcase commando in the eye, "we're the only ones to see this abortion, correct? Our team and the coast guard diver and a few coast guard people?"

"Well, actually," Ruiz said, raising a brow.

"Actually what?"

Ruiz folded his stocky forearms.

"They sent an investigator from Naval Safety before we got the call. The cutter captain has an uncle in the navy and went VFR direct to him, jumped the chain."

"No!" Reyland cried.

Ruiz nodded.

"They even flew her out to the cutter. But as far as I know, she didn't see this or anything else. The cutter was ordered away before she could see any of the wreckage. She actually left the base. There's another investigator now. Some navy fool who keeps asking to get on the ship."

"Why bring her up?"

"No reason. I know how thorough you like to be. Especially in a situation of this, um, magnitude. I thought you might want to make a note of who's coming and going."

Reyland nodded at his tough little security man. Ruiz was as sharp as he was ruthless. He never missed a trick.

"Okay, good, Tommy. Noted. Now, where are the packages?"

"Ah, the packages," Ruiz said, gesturing with his chin.

Reyland followed him into the corner of the hold opposite his resting men.

As they arrived, Ruiz kicked at a silver hard-pack suitcase with his tactical boot, sending it spinning. Reyland looked at it. It was open and empty.

"What's this?"

"We found this at the site in some coral thirty feet from the plane," Ruiz said. "Empty just like this."

"No!" Reyland said, staring at the empty case. "You have got to be putting me on. Someone is playing games, huh? Did a little five-finger salvage job? One of the coasties? Or maybe the navy inspector who left?"

Ruiz shrugged.

"Not her. We watched video of her leaving the base. She only took her kit bag."

Reyland pulled his phone out and called Emerson topside on the *Recover*'s deck.

"Yes, boss?"

"Plan B. Call HQ. I want full intelligence jackets on everybody on that coast guard tub from the captain to the guy who scrubs the urinals. Also, tell that peckerhead base commander

who drove us in here we need some rooms to conduct interviews."

"On it," Emerson said.

Reyland looked at Ruiz in the dimness of the hold, looked
at the empty suitcase. A bead of sweat rolled down his hairless
head and neck into the back of his starched shirt collar as he
tucked his phone away.

"Looks like we're doing this the hard way, Tommy," he said.

17

Late Tuesday afternoon just before sunset, Gannon was at his bungalow in Tarpum Head.

In his favorite pair of camo cargo cutoff shorts and the last of his clean button-down shirts, he was out on his covered back porch, lying back on a plastic chaise.

There was a warm bottle of beer in his hand, and he took a sip of it, looking out on things. On his backyard. On the thorny brush that edged it. On the blue glitter of the Caribbean to the south.

He'd come home around dawn and wolfed down the entire half tray of lasagna he had made two days before and proceeded to sleep like the dead. He'd woken up around three in the afternoon and had to call a resort he had just started working for to apologize for the diving appointment that he had missed.

"If this happens one more time, you're fired," the manager had screamed at him.

"You got it," Gannon had said pleasantly before he hung up. "Goodbye now."

He was freed up now, wasn't he? he thought, smiling, as he put his hands behind his head in the warm breeze.

Freed up in a whole entirely new way.

He yawned and listened to the birds chirp in the warmth of the evening. He had just taken a shower, and his hair was still wet. He thought about bringing out the little Bluetooth speaker to get some tunes going, but he was too comfortable.

He looked out across the crabgrass. Alongside the edge of his yard were three chewed-up tennis balls he had forgotten to throw away. They had belonged to his late-departed boxer, Buster, who had died of old age two months before.

For the twentieth time, he told himself that he needed to find a new dog. Fishing, especially, had always been so much finer with Buster beside him. But something always seemed to come up.

He lifted his beer again.

It was probably because his good old Buster was so awesome, Gannon thought. He didn't want to replace him yet. That was it.

He sipped his beer and nodded.

It was out of respect.

He closed his eyes and thought about all the problems he could erase now. The loan on the boat, the one on the house, the costly leak in the line between the *Rambler*'s tank and the fuel pump he was ignoring. Wipe those pesky critters away with one swipe.

Not right away, of course, he thought with a smile. *No, no, no.* He would wait and wait and wait. All he had to do was wait now. He sighed. He had no problem with that. When he put his mind to it, he could be quite a patient man.

He smiled. What was especially delicious was the secret of the whole thing. He had nothing to do with the local area of Little Abaco. He knew no one up there. There was no way to know that he had been there.

Besides, even if they surmised that the money had been picked up by someone, there were what? Five thousand fishing and pleasure boats in the Bahamas? Ten?

It made him giddy how free and clear he was.

18

He was finishing his beer and thinking about walking on down the beach road to his local watering hole to procure an actually cold one when his phone rang.

He smiled as he looked at the caller ID. His son usually took a minimum of twenty-four hours to text him back.

But in this case apparently, he was making an exception.

"Dad? What's going on?" Declan said, sounding stunned. "I just read your text. What are you talking about? You're joking, right?"

Gannon smiled as he sat up under the rusty awning.

"Hi, son. It's no joke. Pack your stuff. When opportunity knocks, you have to answer the door."

"But, Dad, I told you Larry won't give me the time off. He can't. We're already down a guy. He'll go ballistic. I'll lose my job."

"Don't worry about that, son," Gannon said. "You're going,

and that's final. Actually, scratch that. *We're* going. I'm heading over to go with you."

Declan had been an outstanding pitcher ever since Little League, but he'd broken his arm skateboarding in his junior year, and they thought that was that.

But about six months ago, he'd started rehabbing as a goof after work with one of his buddies who'd played a little minor-league ball, and now like some returned gift from on high, he was apparently hitting the midnineties with ease. His friend had arranged a meet with a scout and just like that Declan had actually been invited to a tryout for the Brewers.

The rub was the tryout had to be in the middle of the week, and Declan's boss was a jerk and wouldn't give him any time off. The kid was already living lean with three roommates in a town house in St. Pete and couldn't risk losing his job, so he was up a creek.

When Gannon found out about all of this, he had felt bad for not having even a couple of grand for his son to pursue his dream. With the boat maintenance and his bills, he'd pretty much blown through his entire savings over the last year or so.

That was why he had gone out fishing with close to the last couple of hundred bucks to his name. He thought if he caught something big, he could sell it at the dock market and help out his son like a real father instead of a broke beach bum.

But all that was water under the bridge now, wasn't it? Gannon thought.

He smiled.

He had him covered now.

And then some.

"This is…incredible!" Declan said. "But I thought you said you were broke. That the boat's pump or whatever is on its last legs and that guy screwed you on the money he owes you for that three-day thing you did?"

"He paid me," Gannon lied.

"No! Really? *Really?*"

"Yes. Really. You're going. I got us covered. And if that ass, Larry, cans you, I'll help you find another job. Call me crazy, but I think Tampa probably has more than one air-conditioning and refrigeration tech apprentice position somewhere. I just can't believe your arm is back. That's what's really unbelievable," Gannon said.

"You're telling me," Declan said. "I don't even like talking about it, I'm so afraid it'll crap out again. When will you get in?"

"Earliest flight I can get is Wednesday. I'll meet you at the airport there in Tampa around five or so and then we'll both get a flight to Phoenix."

"But won't that all cost a fortune? Especially last minute?"

"Don't worry about it. It's how these things happen, son. We're just going to go for it."

Gannon smiled again as Declan laughed like an excited little kid.

He was still smiling, enjoying the moment, when he heard the sound from the front of the bungalow. It was the crackle of tires, the sound of a car slowly coming down his little remote cul-de-sac.

Gannon sat up, squinting. He wasn't waiting on any visitors.

When he heard brakes, he stood and peeked all the way around the side of his concrete blockhouse. In the gap between his pickup and the house, he could see the front of a vehicle. It was a Jeep. A white-and-blue Jeep.

A familiar white-and-blue Jeep.

Gannon bit his lip, thinking quickly.

No, he thought.

No way. Calm yourself. It can't be. No way. Not this quick.

"Dad, I'm going to pay you back. I promise. Every penny. Hey, you there?" his son said as Gannon glanced at the back of his pickup in the carport.

The Gator and the tanks were still up there in the bed. Dammit. Why the hell hadn't he put them away?

"Dad? You there?" his son was saying when the doorbell rang.

"Um, bad connection, son. I'll call you back," Gannon said quickly as he hopped off the back porch.

19

"I'm right here, Sergeant Jeremy," Gannon said to the uniformed cop as he was about to get back into his white-and-blue Bahama PD police Jeep. "Right here. No need to call up the SWAT team."

Gannon smiled as he came out into his front yard through the carport, walking unhurriedly. He had undone another button on his shirt and had a fresh beer with him.

"Ah, so you are, Michael," the cop said with a smile back as they shook.

As always, the muscular, handsome black man in his early sixties looked impeccable. His big general's hat was squared neatly on his head and his white-and-blue police uniform shirt was crisp and highly starched.

Gannon had met Sergeant Jeremy three years before working for a small resort on Windermere Island. A tourist kid out sea kayaking had gone missing in the Atlantic, and he and Sergeant Jeremy had gone out in the *Rambler* looking for him.

For hours, they had scoured the entire treacherous rocky east shore. The kid had turned out not to have gone kayaking at all, thank goodness, but during the search, he and the good sergeant had commiserated on everything from fatherhood to eighties music to the current insane state of the world.

Sergeant Jeremy, who was a deacon at St. Anne's up in Rock Sound, often roped Gannon into usher duty during his sporadic church attendance, and they sometimes played poker.

Gannon turned back, checking to see if the sergeant could notice the Gator and tanks back there in the bed of his pickup under the carport.

Maybe, maybe not, he thought.

"You're here early for the poker game. Isn't it at Teddy's next week?" he said.

"No, no. It's not a social visit, Michael. I was wondering if you might be able to help me. Did you hear about the accident?"

Gannon looked at him.

"Accident?"

"You didn't hear?"

"I didn't turn on the radio today. What's up?"

"There was a plane crash in the water on the north side of Little Abaco last night. My son's friend Alan in the coast guard got called in."

"That's terrible. Bad? Was it an airliner or something?"

"I don't know. Probably not or it would be an even bigger deal. Lot of activity, though. I know you fish up around there sometimes. I thought maybe you might have seen or heard something."

Gee, thanks for remembering, Gannon thought.

"That's crazy. No. I didn't see anything," Gannon said.

"You did go fishing, though, yesterday, right? Like you usually do Mondays?"

Gannon looked at him. Sergeant Jeremy seemed cheery and laid-back as they came, but he was nobody's fool. There wasn't much in the island's resorts—and even more so with the island's residents—that happened without his knowledge. Especially on his beat in the lower southern part.

"Yep. I went out in the morning as usual. But I actually didn't go out that far. I tried my spot off Governor's Harbour first and got a hit. It was a white marlin, but it went under the bow and the damn line broke my radio antenna. So I stayed in close to shore here at home."

Sergeant Jeremy tapped a finger against his lip. Then he smiled.

"Any extra fresh swordfish you'd like to share with your good friend?"

Gannon took a hit of his beer and wiped at his mouth with his fingers.

"No. Sorry, friend," he said, swiping his hand on his shorts. "None for me either. After all that, the big nasty son of a gun spit the hook five feet from the boat. You should have seen this thing."

"Ah, yes. The one that got away. Big as my Jeep, was it?"

"No way," Gannon said with another smile. "Way bigger."

Jeremy looked at him. Then looked down his little street.

Gannon looked with him at the palm fronds waving there in the breeze.

"Was that Little Jorge with you?" Sergeant Jeremy said with an eye roll.

As he usually did, Gannon grinned as he thought about his young, somewhat sketchy first mate.

"No," Gannon said, squinting. "First mate Little Jorge is still…on vacation."

"Vacation? A young man of leisure. Very interesting."

"Anything else I can do for you?" Gannon said. "I'd offer you a beer, but with you being on duty and all, I wouldn't want to insult you."

"Always thinking of others, Michael, aren't you? That's probably why I like you so much," Sergeant Jeremy said after he closed his door. "Shall I expect to see you Sunday? It's my turn for the sermon. It's called 'God Has a Mission for You.' I'll even keep it under half an hour this time, I promise."

"Deacon," Gannon said, blessing himself as he backed for his house, "to be present on such an auspicious occasion, I will do my level best."

20

The too-bright cement windowless room Emerson led coast guard rescue diver Stephen Vance into was in the basement of the base's power plant building.

Used as an emergency brig, the walk-in closet-sized room had raw cement block walls and a threadbare linoleum floor that was a pale institutional green. The curtain blocking off the cell's back corner toilet was opaque and yellowing at the plastic edges and seemed in several spots to be coated in black mold.

Beside it in the room were only four other items: a folding table, two folding chairs and a little mirror on the wall opposite the door.

Perfect, Reyland thought, watching through the peep show one-way glass. The toilet curtain especially. Just atrocious.

Reyland smiled at the haughty expression on Emerson's face as the two of them sat. He always loved watching the way suspects became instantly intimidated by Emerson's six-foot-tall height and dark-haired preppy good looks. He had played varsity lacrosse at Boston College, and his resting countenance was still one of pure big-man-on-campus arrogance. The men in the unit actually called him Prep School behind his back.

Emerson had confided to Reyland at the last Christmas party that he could have joined a Wall Street bank like his brother but had chosen the Bureau instead on purpose. In his junior year, he had read a book about the way homicide cops did interrogations, how they were legally allowed to screw with and to bully people, and he finally realized what he wanted to do with his life.

He had drunkenly told Reyland that what he loved most about his job was the back-and-forth of grinding down a subject until he made him, as Emerson put it, "his soft sweet little bitch."

Reyland smiled as he watched Emerson take out a laptop and clack it down and fold it open with slow ceremony onto the table.

Though he was smart enough never to admit it out loud, that was Reyland's favorite part of the job, too.

"Hi, Stephen," Emerson said as he pulled in his chair. "My name is Agent Emerson. Can I call you Steve?"

"No," the little diver said, getting huffy straight off. "You can address me as Petty Officer Third Class Stephen Vance."

Emerson sighed.

"That's not the way you want to play this. This is no big deal. Just some questions for my report, and we're done."

"No big deal?" the diver said. "Why have I been separated from my crew? What the hell do you want from me? I wrote out an incident report of my dive in detail for my commanding officer. Read it. I got nothing more for you or anyone. Bringing me into this disgusting pit. Is this Nazi crap supposed to scare me or something?"

Emerson sighed again.

"All right. Fine," Emerson said as he stood and gracefully crossed the room.

He even moved like he had money, Reyland thought. Tan in his crisp khakis and polo shirt, he could have been a country-club golf pro.

"Have it your way," Emerson said as he casually knocked on the cell door.

"What do you mean? You're acting like I'm not cooperating?" the diver said, getting a little nervous now. "I cooperated. Just read my report."

"Oh, I've read it. Don't you worry about that," Emerson said, smiling, as there was a sound of approaching steps out in the hallway.

"Take off your shirt, please," Emerson said, as there was a loud knock on the door.

"What?" Steve the diver said, screeching back the chair as he stood.

"You heard me. Take off your shirt," Emerson said, unlocking the door. "For your polygraph."

Reyland stifled a laugh at the lie. You didn't have to take off the subject's shirt. Emerson was just brilliant. He really did love this. It was personal with him. You could tell. You couldn't fake being this sadistic.

What an asset.

He was a master.

"Sorry, buddy. That's not happening. I want my CO in here right now," Vance said.

But he was already sweating. You could see it on his brow. See it shining on his upper lip.

Vance jumped, knocking over the folding chair as the door burst open and Ruiz and Shepard came in with the equipment. Huge Shepard with his ever-present aviator sunglasses was especially intimidating in the tight confines of the concrete room.

"Take off your shirt, please," Emerson said again. "Or we will do it for you."

A minute later, the young diver sat shirtless and small on the folding chair. Ruiz put on the blood pressure cuff while Shepard put the two bands called pneumographs around his narrow chest.

Emerson himself attached the galvanometer's two finger straps to the pointer finger of the diver's left hand. He stood looming over him, almost on top of him. Like a daddy putting a bandage on his kid's boo-boo.

"What's this? Some kind of LGBT thing?" he said to the diver, pointing at a thin band of gold on his pinkie as Ruiz and Shepard left.

"It was my mother's wedding band," the diver said. "She died when I was small."

"Take it off," Emerson said. "No jewelry for the test."

"Thank you very much," Emerson said brightly when the diver finally dropped it in his outstretched waiting palm.

Bravo, Emerson, Reyland thought proudly. Skin-on-skin contact, violation of the subject's personal space, forced removal of precious items.

Textbook.

Emerson slowly and meticulously attached all the leads to a little black box that was then connected with a USB cord to his laptop. He turned the laptop's screen around so Vance could see it.

"Pay attention. This is important," Emerson said. "See these? These four moving lines? The upper two are respiratory rate and electrodermal, and these bottom ones are for your blood pressure. These instruments monitor your vitals. Your breathing, your pulse, your blood pressure, your perspiration, and any slight movements of an arm or a leg.

"Now, before we get started, I want you to read something," Emerson said, taking a laminated card out of his pants pocket.

"Do you understand what this document says?" Emerson said after a minute as the diver stared down at the card. "It basically says that if you lie to me during this polygraph examination—if any of your vitals indicate falsehood—you will not just be subject to court-martial, you will be guilty of obstruction of justice, a federal felony punishable by up to five years in prison."

"What?"

"Every time you lie, it will be a felony, *Steve*. Do you understand, *Steve*? Every falsehood you tell is a year in Leavenworth."

"But you can't do this! You can't do this! It's illegal. Please!" the diver said.

"Not only can I do this," Emerson said, turning the laptop back around, "I have to, *Steve*. It's my job."

21

Reyland left after the first hour when the diver began to stutter uncontrollably.

It was a humid night outside in the open shipyard, but there was a nice breeze off the darkly gleaming Caribbean. It was steak night in the officers' mess hall, and there was a pleasant, happy, summer vacation kind of smell of charcoal from the grills.

From the mess, he grabbed a tray and a plate of sirloin and mashed potatoes and took it upstairs to the office space above the mess that they were using as a staging area.

Reyland was sitting at a conference table, sipping a cup of lukewarm coffee with Ruiz, when Emerson came in two hours later. They waited for the interrogator to hit the head and come out and crack a Diet Coke from the fridge.

"So what's the story?" Reyland said.

Emerson put down the soda.

"My first read is that he didn't take it. He doesn't know about the missing money."

"But?" Reyland said, looking at Emerson's clouded face.

"He has a secret," Emerson said. "It's something about the video."

"The video? We got that off Martin first thing," Ruiz said.

"Yes. But there's something there about him handing it over. Every time the video comes up, there's a hiccup. Tiny but there."

Reyland sat up.

"That's the most important thing of all," he said. "Containing and burying the inside of that plane. A video getting out is beyond comprehension."

"I know," said Emerson.

"So bear down," Reyland said.

"What do you think I've been doing, boss? He's digging in. The little prick is actually tougher than I first thought."

"Short and spunky. Terrific," Ruiz said, taking a quarter out of his pocket.

"So you're thinking he might have made a personal copy of the video or something?" Reyland said.

"Maybe," Emerson said with a nod.

"Do you have his phone?" Ruiz said.

"Yes. It's an iPhone, but he won't give me the passcode," Emerson said. "Little Porky Pig was adamant about that. Told me to go f-f-f-screw myself."

Reyland blew out a breath. Here he was thinking they'd have some smooth sailing and now this. He looked over at Ruiz, who nodded. They'd already been going over worst-case scenario contingents concerning the diver.

The B plan was drastic and had its own downsides and risks. But this whole situation was about as desperate as it got.

"Okay, Emerson. Good job," Reyland said. "Why don't you get some sleep?"

"What? You don't want me to try some more?"

"No. Don't worry about it. You've done your part. We'll leave him to Ruiz and his men."

Emerson had a disappointed look on his face as he picked up his soda and left.

"So if the diver doesn't know where the money is, where is it?" Reyland said.

Ruiz brought his right fist up onto the table, walking the quarter back and forth over his knuckles. He spun the quarter on the tabletop and then slapped it flat and peeked at it.

"A local must have taken it," he said. "Saw the wreckage, grabbed a bobbing suitcase before the coast guard found it. A fisherman or a sailboater."

"A local civvie," Reyland ruminated, taking out his phone as he watched Ruiz spin the coin again.

They really would have to do it the hard way, he thought.

22

Sergeant Jeremy made a funny humming sound as he bumped along the uneven field with his grandkids at his farm in Greencastle.

There were six of them altogether stuffed into the tiny cab of the old blue Ford tractor. The two older boys were hanging out the open left side and the two girls out the right. The littlest one, three-year-old George Junior, sat in his lap laughing as Sergeant Jeremy hummed and let him steer.

As usual on his day off, Sergeant Jeremy was "tilling the earth," as his wife sarcastically called his on-again, off-again interest in working their ramshackle farm. He had exchanged his uniform for a T-shirt and jeans and a Miami Marlins baseball cap, and he and the grandkids were coming back from spreading compost at the top field. Now after helping Pawpy, they were taking the long way back before Granmama's Bible class.

He saw the man as they arrived at the end of the field. He

was standing in a patch of sunlight a hundred feet down the old cow path. The man was white and tall and was wearing a dark polo shirt and business khakis.

"Run along now, children," Sergeant Jeremy said as he stopped the tractor and ratcheted on the hand brake.

"Hi, there. Are you Officer Jeremy Austin?" the visitor said as the children jumped down and started running past him for the house.

"I'm Sergeant Austin," Sergeant Jeremy said as he cut the engine altogether and came halfway out of the cab without stepping all the way down. The man was bald and so tall they were still almost eye level. He looked into the man's pale gray eyes.

Like a wolf's, he thought.

"I hear you're the man to talk to in these here parts," the white man said.

"And you are?"

"Me? Oh, I'm from the FBI."

"Ah, an American," Sergeant Jeremy said as if this delighted him.

"Yep. All the way from the US of A," the large bald man said, grinning. "We're looking into that plane crash that happened north of Little Abaco a few days back."

"Oh, I see. We haven't heard much about it after the initial report. Your navy is handling it, I believe."

"Yes, my navy is taking care of it, but you see, we're looking for information, Sergeant. Information about anyone you know who might have been out on the water that evening."

"Is that right?"

"Yes. I know there are a lot of boats on the island, but everybody down here is pretty cozy, aren't they? Especially the fishermen and workers on the boats. Everybody has his personal little fishing spots here and there. At least that's what I hear."

Sergeant Jeremy kicked free a clod of mud that had gotten caught up in the huge tread of the tractor's tire.

"What is it you're trying to find out?"

"You don't have to worry about that. We're just looking for the names of anyone you can think of who might have been out on the water when the crash occurred."

Sergeant Jeremy toed loose some more soil with his boot.

"Which night was this, now? Monday?"

"Yes. Two days ago. Monday night."

Sergeant Jeremy looked as the bald man pulled free a strand of tall dried grass and spun it in his fingers. He was comfortable, serene. Not a care in the world. Like he was on his own land, Jeremy thought. Like everywhere belonged to him.

"What time did the crash occur?" Jeremy asked.

"This would have been probably, oh, around seven or so," he said.

Sergeant Jeremy pursed his lips as if deep in thought.

"No one comes to mind right off. Folks around here rarely go up that far. Even charters. Most of the locals around here are pretty stingy with the gas."

As if I would tell you anything, you arrogant American prick, Sergeant Jeremy thought.

"Well, if you can think of anyone, give me a ring, would you?" the bald man said, smiling as he offered a business card. "I don't know if you've heard, but we're giving out grants now. Expanding our network here in the Caribbean. I would love to get some of those Washington grants out here to you to help you and your station. You could always use new equipment, yes? New vehicles? Perhaps even a boat. We can always use good partners."

Sergeant Jeremy took the card and beamed down at it exaggeratedly. The fake smile on his face like he'd just won the lottery.

Reyland, the card said under the FBI logo. Deputy Assistant Director Robert Reyland.

"If I hear of anything, Mr. Reyland," he said, giving the arrogant American official his best vacant *welcome to the Bahamas, mon* grin, "you'll be the first to know."

Reyland stood there for a moment staring at him, staring at the empty field around.

"Can I give you a lift back to the road?" Sergeant Jeremy said, stepping up into the tractor cab.

"No, thanks," Reyland finally said with a dismissive wave of his hand. "You can go ahead now, Sergeant. I'll find my own way out."

23

There were about a dozen fat gulls atop Mama Lizbeth's grocery store's dried wood awning, and they all seemed to give Gannon the stink eye as he jogged in off the beach the next morning at a little after 8:00 a.m.

As he caught his breath, he spotted an old red Toyota sedan with missing hubcaps and tinted windows at the other end of its sandy asphalt lot.

Gannon smiled as the island beater gave off a brief honk.

As he stepped over, its driver's door swung wide. A thin, smiling, mischievous-looking young black man with long dreads stepped out and gave him a funny little bow. His white wife-beater and khaki shorts were immaculate, pristine.

"Oh, so you really are still alive," Gannon said as he came over and gave his on-again, off-again first mate, Little Jorge, a hand slap and hearty man hug.

Little Jorge laughed.

"Alive and kicking, Captain Mike, always," he said in his musical island drawl.

Gannon shook his head at him.

When he first came down to the islands, Gannon took an instant liking to the cute, funny, hustling kid who hung around the docks with his older brothers. He'd actually been pretty good buds with Little Jorge's whole large family ever since he had taught the motley lot of them how to dive free of charge in an effort to keep them out of trouble.

The sun caught the glint of gold in Little Jorge's pirate's smile. Gannon definitely had his work cut out for him there.

Little Jorge wasn't exactly what one would call a reliable employee, but when the wiry twenty-two-year-old showed up for work, he was actually top-notch. He knew the waters around the Bahamas better than anyone and was one of the most skilled, natural fishermen Gannon had ever seen.

"How'd your, um, vacation go?" Gannon said.

"Just got back this very minute when I saw your text," Little Jorge said.

"Three weeks this time?" Gannon said.

Little Jorge shrugged and laughed again.

His family was originally from San Andrés Island in Colombia, and sometimes, he and his brothers—like other reckless young island men—would try to make a quick and extremely dangerous buck by acting as pilots on the Picuda go-fast drug boats that played cat-and-mouse in the Caribbean with the coast guard from South America to Miami Beach.

Gannon had tried to talk to him about it, about what a .50-caliber bullet could do to a young man's future, but every time he would explain how unwise it was, the amiable young man would just giggle until he stopped.

Little Jorge was giggling now.

"I was actually starting to get a little worried this time," Gannon said.

"Worry? No, no, Captain Mike. About me? Never. Like the man says, 'Don't worry. Be happy.'"

Gannon rolled his eyes then laughed himself at the goofy, crazy kid as he shook his head.

"So tell me, did you replace Buster yet?" Little Jorge said.

"No," Gannon said. "I keep forgetting."

"I miss watching the lines with old Buster," Little Jorge said. "So what is it, Captain Mike? Where are we heading out this morning? The resorts? Is it diving or fishing or both?"

"No, I'm heading to the States for a bit, but I have some fishing appointments coming up, and I was hoping you could cover for me."

"You mean you want me to go out on the *Rambler* on my own?" Little Jorge said, blinking at him in shock.

Gannon blinked back. He was a little wary about it himself, but he wanted things to seem as normal as possible while he was gone.

And who knew? Maybe the responsibility would do him some good, Gannon thought.

"First time for everything, Little Jorge. I thought you could take Peter with you."

"No, my brother Peter is away, but Andre is here."

"Go with Andre, then," Gannon said. "The boat's at Davis Head. We need everything. Water and gas and bait. Oh, and a new radio antenna. I left some money under the seat with the schedule."

A touched expression crossed the young man's face when Gannon handed him the boat keys.

"I'll take good, good care of her, Captain Mike," Little Jorge said, looking down at his hand.

"You damn well better," Gannon said, giving the kid another clap on his back before he went up the steps for the store.

24

Inside the store, Mama Lizbeth's grown daughter, Joni, was manning the cash register. Gannon waved, but as usual, she ignored him as she turned to the little TV that perpetually played from the edge of the beat-up Plexiglas counter.

Joni was usually all smiles with everyone, the locals and the day-tripping boaters who came in on their grocery store's dock, but for some reason, she seemed to hate Gannon's guts with a fierce-burning passion.

Why? he thought for the millionth time as he passed down into the aisle.

What had he done? Run over her dog and not noticed? Looked like someone who'd robbed the store?

He could never figure it out.

He walked to the back. On the shelves, products were laid out in no particular order. Soup cans next to paper plates next to shaving cream.

He saw there were some packages of Oreos on a shelf.

When was the last time he had eaten one? he thought as he picked them up. But then he checked the date on them and put them back.

On the shelf below, there was a box of some desperate onions and a dwindling tray of sorry yams. Getting produce out here in the island sticks was the absolute worst.

He found what he was looking for in the center aisle. A jug of Tide and some Clorox bleach and a package of sponges. He wanted to get his laundry done and tidy up before he left on his afternoon flight.

When he came back up the aisle, Joni was turned almost fully around now, seemingly absorbed in some news on her little TV. He tapped his foot to get her attention, but that did no good, so he watched with her for a minute.

She was watching the BBC broadcast. There was something about a British singer who had OD'd and then something about protests in London over the latest computer hacker, and then there was a lager commercial that made her finally turn around.

He was coming out of the island bodega, blinking at the sunlight, when he saw Sergeant Jeremy. It would have been hard to miss him. His Jeep was parked almost butt up against the bottom of the grocery store's sandy steps and he was sitting on its hood.

"Hello, Michael, my friend," he said.

"Hey, buddy. How's the crime rate?" Gannon said, smiling broadly as he came down the steps.

"Everyone's still looking into that plane crash. I actually got a visit from a US official about it. He came by the farm."

Holy shit, Gannon thought.

"Yeah?" Gannon said, shifting his bag to his other arm. "Somebody from the coast guard?"

"No," Sergeant Jeremy said, folding his arms as he looked him in the eye. "It was a man from the American FBI."

"No way. An actual G-man, huh?" Gannon said, nodding like a fool as he tried to hide his awe and shock.

"Yes. They're asking around about anybody who might have come across anything. They wanted a list of anybody out on the water Monday night."

"Is that right?" Gannon said.

Sergeant Jeremy took off his hat and wiped his brow with a neatly folded white handkerchief he took from his pocket, then meticulously squared his hat back on his head again.

"Yes," he finally said. "I thought about you and your fishing trip, but you already told me you were far away from the crash site that night, so I said I couldn't help him. He said he wished to speak to anybody at all out that evening. But he was a very pushy, very arrogant man. I didn't think you wished to speak to him, so I left you out of it."

Gannon let out his breath as he began to nod.

"Well, thank you for that. I'm glad they got to the man who knows how to, um…properly handle things around here."

Sergeant Jeremy looked at him very closely.

"Tell me, what are your plans this week, Michael?"

"Plans? Oh, I was thinking of giving my boy a visit. I'm flying to the States this very afternoon, in fact."

"Oh, yes, your son. What's his name? David? No, Dean, is it?"

"Declan. Yeah. Haven't seen him in a while, so I'm going to hang out with him for a few weeks."

"That's sort of sudden," Sergeant Jeremy said.

"Yeah, well, I didn't get a chance to see him over Christmas."

"But the tourist season is just picking up for you, yes?" Sergeant Jeremy said, peering at him.

"I'm going to have Little Jorge take out the boat."

Sergeant Jeremy gaped at him for a beat. Like everybody else on the island, he knew all about Little Jorge and his family's sketchy reputation for going on sudden "vacations."

"Time to give that boy some experience out on his own," Gannon added. "Do him some good."

Sergeant Jeremy hopped down from the Jeep's hood.

"That's a good plan, Michael. At least the part about you going away for a bit. That's probably best."

"Best? What do you mean? Why's that?" Gannon said to the sly old codger.

Sergeant Jeremy winked as they shook hands.

"We can never spend enough time with the ones we love," he said.

PART TWO

GIVE MY REGARDS TO BROADWAY

25

Up on the wall behind the counter was the lineup of all the usual suspects. There was Elmo, of course, and Dora and several of the Power Rangers. There were also a few newcomers since last time, a Wonder Woman and PAW Patrol dog and one of those yellow one-eyed Cheez Doodles Minion things.

Then Ruby saw it and smiled because there was obviously no contest at all.

"I'll take that one," she said, pointing at the giant inflated pink baby bootie balloon that said *IT'S A GIRL!* across the incredible length of it.

"Oh, and one of these as well," she said with a yawn as she picked up a bottle of 5-hour ENERGY from the display beside the register.

"Actually, make that two," she said, cracking open the one in her hand and grabbing another.

What a day! she thought.

She'd gotten back to Pensacola at eleven at night, and at a little after three, her sister Lori's water broke. With the jet lag and panic, she'd driven like a nut to Sacred Heart Hospital, almost breaking the mechanical stick that blocked the parking lot entrance.

But it had all worked out. Seven hours later, at 5:11 p.m. Eastern Standard Time, her first and only niece, Alice Wells, a brand-new, healthy tiny human, had arrived on earth only slightly before her scheduled due date.

Lori and Ally were doing great, thank God, and her husband, Mitch, had been able to watch it on Skype from Afghanistan on her phone. If Ruby hadn't already been crying in the delivery room, the enormous roar of Mitch's fellow marines when he screamed "It's a girl!" at them would have done the trick.

Now, exhaustion or no exhaustion, it was crack-of-dawn victory lap time. In addition to the balloon, Ruby was going to grab a bottle of champagne and Lori's favorite roast beef hero from Firehouse Subs and then swing by Lori's neighbor's house to grab her nephew, Sean, so he could meet his little sister.

No rest for the weary, she thought, yawning as she came out into the early morning Party City parking lot.

Or for sisters slash aunts of the year.

She'd just managed to get the hatchback of her Kia Rio down over the pink blimp when her phone rang. She fished the phone out of her purse and checked the caller ID as she pulled the driver's door open.

Wally Derwent? she thought, dropping behind the wheel. He was her cubicle buddy from the naval safety office.

"Hey, Wally," she said.

"Hey, Rube. Sorry to bug you on leave, but I picked up your phone here a minute ago. Some guy is real frantic to get into contact with you. He called yesterday, too."

"That right?" Ruby said, bleary-eyed, as she slammed her door. "Did he leave a name?"

"No, he wouldn't say. All he said was he knew you from the *Surmount*, and he left his number and said he really, really, really needed to get into contact with you."

The *Surmount*? she thought.

Then the 5-hour ENERGY started to work.

She remembered.

The *Surmount*. The coast guard. The crazy plane everyone was being weird about.

Her sneaking off the naval base.

Oh, shit, she thought.

"Guy sounded young," Wally said. "Don't tell me you're robbing the cradle."

She remembered the cute young diver. What was his name again? Steve. Steve Vance. Fan of deep dives and green shamrock tattoos.

And unauthorized GoPro videos.

Oh, shit, she thought again.

"What's the number?" Ruby said.

26

"Hello," said a hushed voice, picking up on the first ring.

"Hi, this is Lieutenant Everett from Naval Safety. My office just called. You wanted to speak to me?"

"Hold up," the voice said.

Ruby ripped open the second 5-hour ENERGY. It was empty when she placed it down into the Kia's drink holder.

"Hello?" the voice said.

"Yes? This is Ruby Everett. Is this you, Steve?"

"No, this isn't Steve. My name is... Screw it, I won't even say in case they're listening."

Listening? Ruby thought.

"Listening? Who's listening?" she said.

"It doesn't matter," the voice said. "We met on the deck of the *Surmount*. You said to Steve, 'Can you go deeper?' and I said like a jackass, 'You'd be amazed.'"

Ah, yes, the deck ape, Ruby remembered.

"Now listen to me very carefully," he said. "They took Steve."

Ruby stared at the steering wheel as she tried to absorb the statement. She glanced at the empty parking lot asphalt, at the traffic going by on Interstate 10.

"Took him?"

"Yes. The government took him. He's been medically quarantined, they said. Whatever the hell that is. But no one knows where he is. It's like he's been swallowed into a black hole."

Ruby held the phone, silently trying to understand. She was having trouble. She tried to think despite her exhaustion.

"Wait. Slow down. Where are you now?" she finally said. "Still at the base?"

"Yes. They have us in a dormitory now. Tuesday, around five, they started interrogating all of us about the crash. Lie detector tests. They were complete pricks. They threatened us with jail time if we failed the test."

"Who were they? Military investigators?"

"No. Some Washington stuffed shirts. FBI agents or something. They wouldn't say. You should have seen how badly they treated us. They took us all into this disgusting prison cell. Asked us if we took anything from the crash site. If we knew anyone who was hiding anything they might have found. I feel like suing them.

"Now they're saying we're all quarantined due to some virus going around. But that's bullshit. None of us are sick. But that doesn't matter. We have to find Steve. Everybody came back except for him. They claim he's really sick and is being treated at a hospital nearby. It's complete shit. It's all lies. He's been secretly arrested or something."

"C'mon," Ruby said. "For real? Is this a joke?"

"I wish. Shit, wait! Someone's coming," the deck ape said quickly. "I have to go. Listen, there's a guy in New York you need to contact for us. An independent investigative reporter.

We told him what's going on, but he needs corroboration, more info from a credible source. Here, take down this number. You got a pen?"

"Wait. No. Listen. You don't want me. I'm actually off this," Ruby said. "I'm on leave now. You need to contact my coworker down there. His name is Mark Thanh. He's in charge now. He relieved me yesterday. Are you in contact with him?"

"What are you talking about? There's nobody here except us. It's just our crew."

Ruby took a deep breath, trying not to lose her patience.

"You need to talk to Mark Thanh. I know he's there. I saw him myself. He drove me to the airport. He's a wiseass Asian guy from New York?"

"I don't have a damn clue who you're talking about," the deck ape said in a kind of plea, emotional now. "Please. We haven't seen him. We haven't seen anyone. There's nobody else down here. Please take down this number quick. I don't know if they're listening."

Ruby rifled through her glove box.

"Okay. Shoot."

"The reporter's name is Eric Wheldon," he said after she had taken the number down. "You can see him on YouTube. He has a channel."

"An internet reporter? You mean like some conspiracy guy or something?"

"He's the real deal, Lieutenant. He works with a lot of whistle-blowers, especially military. One of the guys here had a brother in the merchant marines, and he was screwed until he told Wheldon, who got the story in the *Washington Post*."

"I don't know if I can do that," Ruby said.

"You *need* to talk to him and verify everything you know about the crash and how they got us stuck here on the base and especially that Steve is missing, okay? Contact him, please. I have to go."

"I really don't think I can help you," Ruby said.

"You have to. You're the only one who can," the deck ape said.

Then the line went dead.

27

"Hey, Wally," Ruby said into her phone as she pulled from the parking lot out onto the Dixie Highway.

"What's up, Rube?"

"Have you heard from Mark since he relieved me?" she said.

"Mark? No, not since he got sick down at that base you guys were at."

She stopped abruptly as she almost went through the red light.

"Hey, wait. You feeling okay? You're not sick, too, are you?" Wally said.

What the hell was going on? she thought.

"Ruby?" Wally said.

"No, I'm fine," Ruby said. "What's the matter with Mark?"

"Apparently, he's got a really bad flu or something, they said. He can't even come home because of a quarantine now. Something like that. That's what the boss told me. I thought you knew."

"Did we send another team?" she said.

"No. Jackie and Irrizarri just got back. They wouldn't even let them on the base. They're postponing the entire investigation until after the doctors clear the base."

Ruby remembered the diver's video. The old polished businessman. The tougher-looking middle-aged guy. The younger scruffy kid with the headphones. The black guy with the hoodie.

What in hell was on that plane? she thought as her phone started pulsing with a new incoming call.

"Thanks, Wally. I'll call you back," Ruby said abruptly.

"Hello, is this Lieutenant Everett?" said a new voice.

It was a man's voice. An older man now. Not the deck ape.

A horn suddenly honked from behind her because the light had turned green.

Ruby screeched off the strip road into an empty Chick-fil-A parking lot and stopped.

"Who the hell is this?" Ruby said.

"My name is Eric Wheldon. I'm a reporter. I got your number from the *Surmount* crew. You're in Naval Safety, right? You went to investigate the crash in the Bahamas?"

She suddenly felt dizzy. How could this be happening? What was she supposed to say?

"I don't know how you got my number," Ruby said, "but I can't help you, sir. Please don't call me again."

"Lieutenant," Wheldon said calmly. "Please don't hang up. I know. A reporter calls out of the blue. Panic time. But it's not like that. Let me explain."

Ruby sighed.

"I used to work for the State Department," Wheldon said. "I quit when I witnessed some very corrupt behavior by the federal government. Then I worked as a reporter for a major paper and saw a lot of covering up of that same exact corruption, so I quit that, too. Since then, I've been reporting on my own and helping whistle-blowers to get their stories out to the public."

"I'm sorry," Ruby said. "This is too much. I didn't get any sleep last night. I'm about to drop. I—"

"I understand," Wheldon said. "All right if I call you back this afternoon? It'll give you time to see my work on my YouTube channel. Bottom line, I think something serious is going on with that ship and crew. Especially with the rescue diver who saw the plane. They seem to have renditioned him."

"They what?" Ruby said.

"Taken him off base to a secret black site. A different country, most likely, for forced interrogation."

What in the hell? Ruby thought, struggling to keep up.

"What was up with that crashed plane, Lieutenant?" Wheldon said. "Steve dived down and saw it. Now Steve is gone. I'm thinking there's a connection there."

"Listen, Mr. Wheldon," Ruby said, rubbing at her forehead. "Let's get something straight. I'm no longer assigned to this investigation. I can't be of any help to you."

"Too much too soon," Wheldon said. "Okay, I understand, Lieutenant. If you would just check out my videos and see what I do. Then you can call me back."

"I have to go," Ruby said.

"Just one thing, though. If you talk to anyone, talk to me. Whatever you say to the so-called 'real press' will go straight to the people doing this. It happens every single time. They don't protect sources anymore. Industry wide, they're under pressure from the government. They'll roll on you so quick it'll make your head spin."

"I have to go now," Ruby said again, suddenly desperate to get off the phone.

"Lieutenant, one more thing. If you don't want them to track you, take your battery out of your phone. They can still follow you by the cell towers if the battery is still in it."

"Track me? Me? What did I do? Who would track me?" Ruby said, incredulous.

"They, Lieutenant. There really is a They. You're about to find that out, I think. When you do, call me first thing, okay? I can help you," Wheldon said.

28

Gannon's noon flight out of North Eleuthera was only an hour to Miami. But he had to wait two more hours for the connecting flight, so he didn't get into Tampa until almost five.

At six, he was sitting at a bar in Tampa's Airside C terminal when he saw his son coming through the crowd in front of the food court.

Gannon stood, smiling. Declan was fair-haired like he was but stood several inches taller at an impressive six foot three. He had actually filled out a little, too, Gannon noticed proudly as he came over. He was thicker at the shoulders, at the neck.

Gannon wasn't a hugger, yet he found himself hugging his strapping son right there in the middle of the bright bustling concourse.

He held him for a second after, looking at him. His mother's straight nose, her hazel eyes. Gannon smiled as he remembered him as a hyperactive kid, holding him on his knee for hours at family events so he wouldn't take down the Christmas tree. It had been six months since he'd last seen him.

Then he thought about his wife, Annette, who had died when Declan was just a freshman in high school.

How proud would she be of this solid young man here? he thought. Just beside herself, he knew. Over the moon.

Especially about the tryout. How many times had he come home from work to see them in the backyard hitting Wiffle balls to each other. She had actually been the biggest baseball fan in their family.

"Look at you, huh?" Gannon said, finally letting him go. "You weren't kidding about working out, were you? You're a monster. You're like hugging a soda machine."

"Dad, I can't begin to thank you for all of this," his son said, looking out at the concourse. "I mean, look at us. We're actually doing this!"

"No worries. You just rest that sweet arm," Gannon said, patting it gently.

"Just you wait, Dad. You won't believe your eyes. When do we leave here, by the way? At seven?"

"Yeah, a quarter after. It's a Delta flight. Gate whatever it is over there," Gannon said, pointing at a cluster of seats to the right. "We go to Atlanta first and should get in to Phoenix around midnight. I couldn't get a direct flight."

"No problem, Dad. Are you kidding me? Direct flight. I'd take a Megabus. I'd just about given up and then here we are right out of the blue."

"Yep, it's right out of the blue all right," Gannon said, hiding a smile as he took another pull of his beer.

When Declan left to hit the head, Gannon saw that the gate was filling up with people, so he strolled over to check that their flight was still on time. Declan was already sitting at the bar with two more fresh beers by the time he arrived back.

"Hey, Dad, look," he said, pointing at the TV above the bar. "They're talking about your neck of the woods."

Gannon looked up. A cable news channel was playing. On the screen was a petite blonde female reporter with the sparkling blue Caribbean behind her. Gannon's eyes went wide as he read the caption beneath her.

Plane Crash in the Bahamas, it said along the bottom of the screen.

Gannon waved over the bartender.

"Could you turn that up, please?"

"What's up? Did you hear about this?" Declan asked him.

"A little," Gannon said, straining to listen.

"...fifteen nautical miles off the coast of the Bahamian island known as Little Abaco when the US Coast Guard out on long-range patrol out of Miami Beach came upon it."

Golly tamale, here we go, Gannon thought, holding his breath as they showed footage of a coast guard cutter.

"The plane, a Cessna Denali seen here," the reporter continued as they showed a stock photo of a prop plane, "is a seven-passenger single-engine turboprop with an impeccable service record and a range of eighteen hundred miles."

Gannon's mouth dropped open.

A Cessna what? A little turboprop? he thought. What the hell were they talking about? It was no prop plane. It was a jet. It was a huge corporate Gulfstream 550 jet.

Were they talking about another crash? he thought, completely confused.

"The plane belonged to this couple," the reporter said as the screen changed to show a skinny curly-haired white guy and a pretty East Indian woman.

"Ben and Chandra Tholberg of Miami, Florida."

Who the hell were they? Gannon thought, even more stunned. There was no woman on the jet. It had been men. All men.

"The Tholbergs, who lived in Coral Gables, had a vacation

house in Puerto Rico that they were returning from. Officials said Mr. Tholberg, an account executive at Century Bank and Trust in Coral Gables, had been an experienced pilot, so it will take some time before the mysterious cause of this tragic crash is known. Back to you, Brian."

Gannon kept blinking up at the screen even after it cut back to the studio.

"What's up, Dad? Did you know them or something?" Declan said.

Something, Gannon thought, his mind reeling.

"You okay, Dad?"

Gannon finally pulled his eyes off the screen and looked around at the airport bar. It had a tiki theme. There was straw on the wall behind the bottles and surfboards everywhere.

"No," Gannon finally said, mustering a smile. "I mean, yes. I'm fine. It's the, um, woman. She looked just like this girl I knew in high school. This aggravating Indian girl who used to sit behind me in math class."

He quickly gulped at his beer. He thought about Sergeant Jeremy. What he had said to him about the FBI poking around, asking questions.

He had one himself.

Why would the US government completely lie about a plane crash? he thought, glancing back up at the TV.

29

There was heavy evening traffic on the Beltway, so even with the lead car blooping the siren, it took them almost an hour from Dunning's house to get to the base. The driver had radioed ahead, so the uniformed guards at the gate were at crisp attention as they came right through.

It turned out to be some pretty perfect timing. Through the tinted window, Reyland could see the lights of the AC-130 turning in the dark sky as they came alongside the hangar. As they slowed just beside the tarmac, Emerson, riding shotgun with the driver, turned to see if he should open the door, but Reyland shook his head.

"I've been meaning to ask you something, Mr. Reyland," Dunning's very attractive black-haired daughter, Belinda, said as they stopped.

She was sitting opposite from him across the rear of the limo beside her devastated mother, Catherine.

Reyland folded his hands in the blue serge lap of his Brooks Brothers suit.

"Please, like I said, anything," Reyland said.

"I know you've told Mother here, but I'd like to hear it from you. How was it that my father died exactly?"

Reyland blinked at the thirtysomething. She was tall and chic and stunning in her all-black and sunglasses. Like other rich women, she had been a ballerina once and still retained that thin, gracious, model-like comportment.

A flash of memory came to him. Stopping by Dunning's villa once with some paperwork, he'd come upon Belinda soaking wet in a white one-piece with her other smoking-hot private high school BFFs by the pool.

Reyland swallowed.

"The doctors at the hospital in Rome said it was a massive stroke, Belinda," he said quietly. "They assured me that he wouldn't have felt anything. He just went to sleep and that was it."

Reyland watched Belinda slowly absorb this.

"Will we get a chance to see him?" Belinda finally said.

He glanced at the curve of her *Swan Lake* throat, perfect and smooth and pale between the stark black collar of her coat and the salon-perfect line of her dark hair. She was wearing a most-enchanting scent. A hint of peach over something mysterious and sumptuous that Reyland couldn't quite name.

"At the base here? No. I'm so sorry," Reyland finally said. "The civilian funeral home representatives need to take him straight from the plane in order to make the final preparations."

Reyland glanced over to where the hearse waited. A marine honor guard was standing at attention in the doorway of the hangar beside it, starched white gloves and the black patent leather shining.

He certainly couldn't complain about the optics, he thought.

Even Dunning, who was a hard-ass stickler in just about everything, would have approved.

"C'mon, Mother," Belinda said. "I can see the plane. Father's coming in."

"It's perfectly fine if you need more time. We still have a few minutes," Reyland said, bringing his hands together as if in prayer.

"Okay," Catherine Dunning finally said. "Okay."

The vice president's retinue showed up as the plane made its taxiing turn. The president, still on his Asian trip, couldn't make it, but he would be back just in time for the funeral. The VP came over and gave Belinda a hug and patted Catherine's hand, whispering to her. He smiled at Reyland as they nodded at each other.

"Nice to see you again, Ron," the VP said to him.

"You, too, sir," Reyland said, not correcting him that they had never met before and that his name was actually Robert.

It didn't matter. DC was a kinetic place. Factions were already making movements, readjustments.

He wouldn't make that mistake twice, Reyland thought in the roar of the approaching plane.

The turboprops roared even louder in the cold as the big plane crawled over to where they stood. Its back ramp was already down as it finally stopped before them. The marines, on the march, entered and went up with robotic precision.

The casket they came out with was straight lined and much smaller than Reyland expected. Under the flag, it looked like the kind of cardboard box that ready-to-assemble Walmart furniture came in.

The pallbearers stopped before the widow, and two of the marines from the honor guard marched over, giving the flag the required thirteen folds. As they did this, Reyland looked at himself in the limo's tinted glass and smoothed his black tie. When he glanced over at the photographers in the media pen set up beside the hangar, he could see that they were going stone-cold bat shit.

Roll 'em, boys, and don't forget my good side, Reyland thought, raising his chin high.

And why not? It was a moving performance. Solemn, austere. All of it. A splendorous display of reticence. Emerson had suggested taps, but Reyland had nixed it. Better to save it for the burial.

As the soldiers finally slid the boss into the dead-mobile, Reyland nodded to himself, pleased. There were still some long hard miles to go before he slept, but at least the press was already swallowing the Rome thing like a widemouthed bass. By tomorrow, the arrow of the bullshit wheel would be firmly landed upon one of the grandstanding press's all-time favorite chestnuts, A Nation in Mourning.

As the marines headed back to the hangar, Reyland glanced over at the tears flowing freely past the soft bud of Belinda's brilliant diamond-pierced earlobe a foot in front of him.

As she began to tremble, Reyland leaned ever so slightly forward and placed his hand on her perfect shoulder, careful to keep his chin up for the photographers as he mournfully closed his eyes.

30

It was coming on 3:00 a.m. when the vrooming Honda Ruckus moped slowed and came to a puttering halt on a dirt road on the southeast outskirts of Culiacán, Mexico.

There was a fork in the high-desert country road, and the handsome middle-aged man astride the rumbling bike sat for a moment before it with a ruminative look on his face.

He sat studying the two roads, the moonlit plains of chaparral they carved through, the mountains in the far distance. After a moment, he removed a pair of reading glasses from his crisp shirt's breast pocket and carefully consulted the GPS on the phone in a holder between the moped's handlebars. Then he put the glasses back and kicked up some dust as he rolled up the right-hand branch.

The small up-country compound he stopped before ten minutes later had a solid steel plate gate in the center of its nine-foot-high cement block outer wall. He unlocked the gate with the key from his pocket and squealed it open. Then he rolled in the moped and squealed the gate back and firmly relocked it.

The small building inside had once been a gas station. Before one of its old rusted pumps was a portable gasoline generator with a cord that went in under the station's closed door. He ripcorded the generator on and unlocked the old station's front door and came through its unlit empty front room into the back.

Beneath the tarp he pulled back was a steel cellar door built into the concrete slab floor. It was secured with a thick Master key padlock that he unlocked with his key ring. The well-oiled hinges made no sound at all as he opened the door up and out.

He squatted, looking down into it. Seven feet below was a dirt-walled cell that looked like a large grave dug into the earth. Light from the standing floodlight below fell across just the legs of the prisoner in the corner.

One couldn't tell if it was a man or a woman. It was just a figure, a small pale bare-legged figure with the knees drawn up and the arms hugging the shins. The feet were black with filth.

Good, the torturer thought as he saw how the prisoner was shivering.

He adjusted the floodlight as he got to the bottom of the ladder. As he did this, the figure raised a thin arm up as if to ward off a blow. The torturer looked at the bright green of the shamrock tattoo on the American's hand. He had spent some time in America and knew the symbol was supposed to stand for good luck.

The torturer had to catch himself from tsking at the irony of it, at the cruel difference that often arose between one's hopeful expectations and the actual brutalities of blind uncaring fate and chance.

The torturer stepped over slowly and looked down at the naked man. He had fought them from the very beginning, raged. You wouldn't think a man his size could reach such volume.

Now, after leaving him without food or water here in the dark for twenty-four hours, it was time for a new tack.

"My name is Dr. Segurro. I am here to tend to you. Are you awake? Hello?" the torturer said in his excellent English as he knelt beside the American.

The torturer was wearing a nice dress shirt and slacks and had a stethoscope. He warmed it in his palms before he put it to the man's chest.

"Put out your tongue," he said.

The prisoner did so, snorting and gasping.

"Yes, very good. Very good," the torturer said, shining a pen-light into the man's eyes.

"Listen to me very carefully," the torturer said. "Something in you has ruptured. It's your spleen. Do you understand? You're broken inside, and if we don't get you to a hospital, you're going to die. These men obviously want something from you. If you tell them, I can get you out of here. But if you do not, you will die. This is your final chance."

"Okay, okay," the American said immediately. "I'll tell you."

The torturer smiled at the man's instant reversal. He had seen this happen more than once. Twenty-four hours in the dark with the rats was incredibly effective. One of his very favorite techniques. It was heartening to build up a store of knowledge of his craft.

"I copied the videotape of the dive," he said. "It's on my phone. The passcode is 6543. I showed the video to the lieutenant from the navy. She watched it twice. Now, please, some water. Please."

"I have water outside. I will get it in a moment. Just please speak louder. You're running out of time," the torturer said, putting his recording phone to the American's bruised face.

"The girl fr-fr-from Naval, Naval Safety. The pretty brown-haired girl. I showed her the video," he said again.

"Lieutenant Everett, yes," the torturer said, remembering his memorized notes. "You showed it to Ruby. Yes."

"Yes. Ruby. I showed her. Now help me, please. Please. I don't want to die. Save me. I need water."

"Yes, of course, of course. You have done well. What's your passcode again?"

"6543."

"I will tell them. I will be right back."

The torturer went up the ladder, relocked the cellar door, placed the tarp back over it, went outside and killed the generator.

He had a little kit bag beneath the motorbike's seat, and from it, he removed a sanitary baby wipe that he used meticulously on his hands and face before he took out his phone.

"Mr. Ruiz?" the torturer said, lighting a cigarette as he sat on the moped out in the silent country under the glittering starlight.

"Yes. Good news," the torturer said. "There's been a breakthrough."

31

Out in the cool of the morning off Interstate 10, Gannon watched his son raise his left arm, turning the baseball in his long, graceful fingers.

They were in Arizona now, somewhere west of downtown Phoenix. It was just after sunrise, and they were standing in the open desert a couple of miles from their hotel beside an empty truck stop pull-off.

The early morning workout had been Gannon's idea. In full coach mode now, he had gotten Declan up and moving the second he woke up.

Nothing like getting the blood pumping, to smooth out any pretryout jitters he might be having, Gannon thought.

"Ready, Dad?" Declan said.

Gannon was about to say yes when a car came off the two-lane highway into the strip of truck stop beside them. Gannon watched it. It was a silver sedan.

He kept watching as it pulled to a stop in front of their rented Silverado truck. There was only one person in it. He couldn't tell if it was a man or a woman.

Shit, was it a Ford? he wondered suddenly. Didn't the feds drive Fords?

No, he saw. It was too small. It was some kind of Honda. He stood silently watching it anyway. After a moment, it pulled away again and was gone back onto the road.

"Dad?" Declan said again.

Maybe his son wasn't the only one who needed to work out a jitter or two this morning, Gannon thought as he punched his catcher's mitt.

"Okay, let's go. Batter up! Play ball!" he yelled as he finally crouched down.

They went for almost an hour, then piled back into the rented Silverado. They were heading off the exit ramp back for the hotel when they saw the Starbucks sign.

He'd left Declan in the truck and was inside waiting his turn in the crowded morning rush line when his eyes glanced off the newspaper in the rack by the door.

Gannon stared. When he suddenly realized what he was looking at, he couldn't decide which was making his suddenly kick-started heart beat faster.

The above-the-fold page-wide photograph.

Or the huge three-word headline above it.

He zombie-shuffled numbly back through the people behind him to the rack and lifted up the paper.

He stared at the photograph some more. The thick white hair. The somber and austere expression.

No. There was no mistaking it.

FBI DIRECTOR DEAD, Gannon read again and then stared back at the face of the old white-haired man he'd seen dead under the water on the crashed jet.

FBI Director Dunning Dies of Stroke in Rome.

32

Fenwick's on 13th Street across from Franklin Square had a gleaming mahogany bar and tufted leather banquettes and waiters who wore white tuxedo jackets even at breakfast service.

It was always ranked in the top five of DC's oldest and most highly regarded establishment institutions. The joke was that the old Fenwick waiters had served not just Washington's senators but also the *actual* Washington Senators, the black-and-white-TV-era American League baseball team that had been disbanded in 1971.

At a quarter after nine in the morning, Reyland sat center court, smoothing down his silk Hermès tie between the bespoke lapels of his best Hackett of London navy suit. He glanced to his left, where Emerson sat looking the way he had ordered him to, neat and lean and preppy and highly polished.

Prep School, he thought, glancing at him, pleased. He hired

only people who could pull off that throwback J. Edgar Hoover FBI look.

He looked around the room ever so casually. He usually did his power noshing at the Hayes across from the J. Edgar Building on E Street, but he needed to be seen in the legend seats now that he was a shoo-in for deputy director.

And so far, his PR appearance seemed to be coming off pretty well. He'd been there only ten minutes before the UN ambassador to the Conference on Disarmament had come by to kiss his ring as well as the senior adviser to policy planning at State. Richie Dempsey, the famous four-hundred-pound owner of the legendary eatery, had waddled out of the kitchen to say hello and even his hardcase elderly mother had texted as he was leaving the house to give him a rare upvote for his debut appearance on the front page of the *New York Times*.

That wasn't even the best news, he thought, as he dabbed some country ham into the yolk of his perfectly runny poached egg.

Last night, Ruiz's Mexican contractor had finally broken the diver.

As they had already been theorizing, the diver, Stephen Vance, had in fact copied a backup video of the dive onto his phone. Not only that, as they had also been theorizing, Vance had indeed shown the video to the female naval inspector, Ruby Everett, who had left the base.

That the diver had done this was quite troubling now that the cat had been let out of the bag about Dunning.

But the good news was that Vance hadn't *given* her the video. They had done a full forensic on his mobile phone, and the video of the dive had not been uploaded to anyone.

So in essence, there was no proof. The leak was still very much sealable.

It was now just a matter of picking up the naval inspector, some surprisingly attractive hick nobody out of Ohio coal country named Ruby Everett.

Ruby, the rube, was out on leave to points unknown, but that wasn't going to be a problem since his team had been on it since three this morning.

Speaking of which, Reyland thought, stifling a smile as he saw one of Emerson's zonked-looking computer guys come in and stand at the end of Fenwick's storied mahogany bar.

Reyland touched Emerson's elbow as he stood to leave the banquette.

"Tell that stooge he can't come into a place like this looking like that. He wants to work for me, he better buy a tie, shave, and maybe start eating some salads."

"C'mon, boss, cut him some slack just this once. That's Billy Rayne, my MIT ace in the hole. He's a genius."

"Rayne," Reyland mumbled. "Rain Man is more like it."

Emerson came back to the table three minutes later, all smiles, with a folder in his hand.

"Good stuff, boss. We've found our errant little naval safety inspector."

"Finally! Where?"

"She has a sister that just squatted out a new hillbilly," he said, smiling as he placed the printed Google map onto the table. "The sister's house is here just north of Pensacola Air Station."

"And, oh, look. She even bought some goodies from Party City. Isn't that special?" Reyland said, flicking the report page to her USAA credit card statements.

"The arrest team will be out of where? Jacksonville?" Reyland said.

"No, Mobile," Emerson said, taking out his phone as the old tuxedoed grandfatherly waiter refilled their water glasses.

"Shouldn't take them more than an hour to get there," he said.

33

Sweating under the overcast morning sky, Ruby chugged along doing a long, lazy loop, jogging the Pensacola neighborhoods north of the naval base.

She'd let out an hour before from Lori's house, where she was still staying over. She'd lived in the modest neighborhood when she first joined the navy and could have practically done the familiar five miles past the sunburned bungalows blindfolded. Lake Charlene north to Glendale, Glendale to Fairfax Terrace, then out to the strip of New Warrington Road that they just called Navy Road because it led into the base.

She jogged steadily at an easy pace past the curving blocks, not pushing it. She always loved running in the morning, that pleasant, still half-asleep hopeful feeling of being outside in the freshness of the new day. She'd run cross-country track in high school well enough to get a partial scholarship to the University of Miami and tried to keep it up. She'd sprained an ankle the year before and then work got busy, and she just kind of let it go for a bit. But now she was gradually coming back after the layoff in fits and starts.

As she ran, her mind wandered to all the crazy phone calls she had gotten.

She still hadn't done anything about any of them. What could she do? Were Mark and the diver actually sick? Which seemed fishy. Or had the government gone nuts? Which seemed even fishier. Or was it something else?

She thought about the reporter. His YouTube videos. His advice on taking the battery out of her phone.

No, she thought as she ran. No way.

From personal experience, she knew the government was often careless, often even stupid. But it wasn't crazy. It wasn't actually malevolent. There had to be some rational explanation.

But she had to do *something*, didn't she?

She suddenly stopped and began jogging in place to let a minivan back out of a driveway.

Once she got back, she thought, as she began running again, she'd bite the bullet and call up Wally and ask again about Mark.

Her thighs were starting to burn on an upslope of her return loop five minutes later when her phone vibrated. She took it out of her waist pack and blew her sweaty bangs out of her eyes to look at the screen.

"Hey," she said, relieved to see it was only Lori.

"You okay?" Lori said, sounding sleepy.

"Of course. What's up? Is Ally okay?" Ruby said as she slowed and stopped.

"Yes, yes. Fine. Did you forget your key or something?" her sister said.

"What? No. I'm not home yet. What is it, Lori?"

As she stood listening, she heard baby Alice start crying.

"Somebody is knocking on the door," Lori said. "That's not you?"

Ruby sprinted across Penton and up to Lori's corner on Norton Street.

And saw them—all of them—there in front of the house.

34

Midway down the street in front of Lori's little house were a half-dozen vehicles. They were gray unmarked cop cars, and they were parked sideways out in the street, completely blocking it.

Alongside them stood half a dozen figures in blue raid jackets.

Ruby gasped when one of them turned and she spotted the three impossible-to-miss frightening Day-Glo yellow letters scrawled across the back.

FBI? Ruby thought.

There was a roar of a diesel engine and then from the other end of the street came some kind of armored van. It was a giant gunmetal gray SWAT truck and from its running board hung a team of tactical officers. They had shaved military jarheads and khaki-colored ballistic armor and military rifles that looked like something out of a middle schooler's video game.

Then it happened. As the heavy armored FBI SWAT van

mounted the sidewalk in front of Lori's house, the reality of what she was in the middle of finally slammed into Ruby like a wrecking ball to the chest.

She suddenly remembered the reporter's words.

They are real, Ruby. There really is a They.

"Ruby, what should I do? Someone's knocking hard now. What the hell is this?" Lori said in her ear.

Ruby stood there speechless. She stared mutely at the agents, at the houses around her. There was no one around. No one to notice the world going nuts.

Move, dammit! she thought. *Snap out of it! Do something!*

Ruby ripped her eyes from the cars and mayhem down the block and took a deep breath and quietly crossed the intersection. When she made the other side, she looked at her phone and saw that Lori's call had dropped off.

She ran at top speed into the dead end at the end of the side street. She hopped over someone's short back fence, darted across the yard, came around the house back into another cul-de-sac and made a right down McNeil, the street that ran parallel to Norton.

When she was about halfway down across from Lori's house, she quietly hopped another fence and went into someone else's side yard and crouched by some ornamental grass.

Over the house's backyard fence, she could see onto Norton. There was one of the double-parked FBI cars there with two male agents and a female one.

She looked at the hard expressions on their faces. Their drawn guns down by their legs. Like they were coming after a hijacker. A terrorist holed up with a weapon of mass destruction.

Her fear suddenly flipped to pure anger. What bastards, she thought, looking beyond them at Sean's Playskool scooter and kick balls under Lori's modest brick bungalow's carport.

They couldn't see that there were kids in the house? People's children. They didn't care about that?

She was watching the agents consult solemnly with one another when somewhere off to the left someone yelled out in a football coach roar.

"Open up! FBI! We have a warrant!"

And then there was a crunching boom and a shatter of glass as the sons of bitches actually broke down Lori's door.

Even from a block over, she heard Lori scream as a file of FBI agents ran in over her front lawn.

Ruby stood up breathing hard, a hand to her mouth. She was feeling nauseated now, helpless and numb, like she was coming out of herself.

The sound of little Sean's screaming cries snapped her out of it and she lifted her phone.

"911. What's your emergency?"

She was going to say "There are FBI agents entering my sister's house," then stopped herself.

"Help me! Someone just kicked in my door! A break-in, a break-in! Someone's in my house! 334 Norton. 334 Norton. Help me, please. Send someone, please. They have guns. Help!"

She hung up and stood in the side yard of the house stock-still with her hands clasped in prayer as she waited. When she heard the sirens another long two minutes later, she hopped back out of the person's side yard and headed back into the street.

As she ran out toward the corner, she saw them coming at her up 70th. Two radio cars, Pensacola's finest, roaring up, lights flashing, as they made the left onto Norton.

She speed-walked down to the corner and saw the cops getting out, some of the agents rushing over showing credentials. Lori's neighbors were now out on their porches and scrub grass front yards wondering what the hell was going on.

Then Ruby started running, booking for all she was worth, past Norton and down 70th before they figured out she wasn't there.

35

Ruby ran all the way, a full three miles more, up to the Mobile Highway. The first car rental place she found was on the strip between a mattress store and a Church's Fried Chicken. The bell on its door jangled loudly as she nearly took it off the hinges coming through at an almost dead run.

"Hello and what have we here?" said a guy sitting at a desk behind the counter. He was young and had one of those silly mountain man hipster beards that went to the chest of his corporate polo.

"I need to rent a car," Ruby gasped, red-faced, sweat dripping onto the carpet tile.

"Let me guess. Got tired of running? Figured, let me try this car thing," said the rental clerk snarkily as he laid down the cell phone he was playing with and stood.

"I just got into a damn car accident!" Ruby said loudly, acting only a little more in shock than she actually was. "My Mazda got completely totaled! The fire department had to cut the door off! I almost died."

"No way," the clerk said, wide-eyed, no more snark or irony in sight.

"Yes. Two miles down the road there. Some dumb little twit was texting on her phone and T-boned me. If her front end came in another inch closer, I'd be dead right now."

"I'm so sorry," the guy said. "Are you okay? Can I get you something?"

"No. I'm sorry for yelling. I'm still shook up a little, I guess. I just need a car real quick. My mama just had back surgery over at Sacred Heart. I need to pick her up. She has a bad heart, too, and she worries."

"You poor thing," the clerk said. "We'll get you fixed up. We just got a minivan in, a Honda Odyssey, a nice new one. Would that help you? I'll even charge you for a compact."

"Perfect," Ruby said. "Thank you."

"We'll get you right out of here," he said as he handed her a pen and a clipboard.

She sat in a chair, dripping sweat onto the paperwork, as he left to get the van. The clipboard shook in her hand as the enormity of everything came crashing down around her ears.

She thought about her sister and the children. She thought about Mark Thanh, her coworker, quarantined somewhere. And Steve, the diver, gone missing. He was just a kid.

She looked out at the traffic. On her run, she had been thinking that she would head to someplace safe in order to figure out what to do next. Call some friends. Maybe call a lawyer.

But she knew what she had to do now.

Ruby took out her phone and opened the back and pried out the battery as the guy with the beard arrived outside with the van.

36

Maryvale Baseball Park, Cactus League home of the Milwaukee Brewers, was a sprawling, newly revamped spring training facility in West Phoenix.

Gannon, standing by the third baseline seats, glanced out onto the sunny infield where Declan was demonstrating his bunting skills to some scouts and coaches. He fouled off the first, but then dropped down a beaut up the third baseline as he began to book.

Gannon placed his phone down in his lap and clapped.

"Way to go, son. That's the way," he yelled and immediately lifted his phone back up and went back to reading yet another completely fake news story about Director Dunning's tragic death by stroke in Rome.

"Hey, is that your kid out there?" said a guy from behind him.

"Yep," Gannon said without turning around.

"Wow. That's some slider he has. Just nasty. You have to be pretty proud."

"Yep," Gannon said as he flicked at the screen.

The gaggle of baseball people broke up after a minute, and Declan jogged over to where Gannon was sitting.

"What's up, son?" Gannon said, his eyes still glued to his phone.

"We're still waiting on the assistant GM himself," Declan said. "Then we're going to start the simulated game."

"Is that right?"

"Did you hear me, Dad?"

Gannon looked up.

"I'll be right back," Gannon said, standing.

"Right back? Where the hell are you going?"

Gannon headed back outside the stadium altogether into the truck. He turned it over and cranked up the A/C as he pressed on the video he had just found on YouTube.

He turned up the volume on his phone as a lean middle-aged man appeared on the screen, walking along what appeared to be a New York City street.

The man had neatly cut light brown hair streaked with gray, and he was wearing a nice overcoat over a business suit with no tie. It almost looked like a camera crew was following along with the guy, taping him as he walked, but he was probably holding one of those selfie stick things, taping himself.

The man's name was Eric Wheldon, and Gannon had already quickly learned that he was some kind of alternative news reporter with a YouTube channel.

His channel had hundreds of videos with thousands of hits on each. The videos had all-caps titles like: BREAKING: STATE DEPARTMENT DENIES AMBASSADOR JOYCE'S TIES TO MUNICH HOOKERGATE! And, LATEST NSA HACKER UPDATE: IS MESSERLY STILL IN LONDON? And, CHINESE DELEGATION MEMBER LU DIES IN SUSPICIOUS HEART ATTACK!

What was of special interest to Gannon in his current state of panic was the title of the video he was now watching.

MYSTERIOUS PLANE CRASH IN BAHAMAS. IS IT REALLY WHAT THEY'RE SAYING?

"Hey, everyone, greetings from freezing-cold NYC and welcome to episode 349," Wheldon said.

"What shall we talk of today, my friends?" he said. "How about plane crashes? Yesterday, a little birdie told me about a very curious one down off the coast of sunny Florida. This little birdie works in one of our vaunted armed forces divisions, and said he was recently sent out to a site near the Bahamas."

Wheldon paused, smiling into the camera. Gannon looked at the building he was passing. It had brass doors, and in the granite beside the door, a shining brass plaque said 485 Park.

"Is that right? I said to my friend," Wheldon continued. "I believe I heard about that Bahamas crash on the news. You're talking about that Cessna Denali turboprop that went down, right? About that poor married couple who tragically lost their lives? Well, my friend said. The crash was in the Bahamas, that's true. But it was no prop plane. No? I said. How do you know that?"

Wheldon stopped walking and stared into the camera.

"Because how could it be a prop plane, my little birdie told me, when we fished two Rolls-Royce jet engines out of the water?"

Gannon felt the hair on the back of his neck stand up. He couldn't believe this. The FBI director. Now the crash.

Everything was starting to snowball. It was all blowing up now.

And he was smack-dab dead center in the middle of it.

"That's a pretty darn good question, isn't it?" Wheldon said.

"I'll say," said Gannon, dry-mouthed.

"Anybody out there know the answer?" Wheldon said.

37

Atop the concrete subway steps, Ruby stopped and stood still in the massive flow of hurrying people.

She gaped up at the giant TV screen billboards. The cartoons and lingerie ads. The streaming ABC News electronic billboard beside her that said it was twenty-nine degrees.

She checked her watch. It was almost midnight. Her train had arrived in New York City at eleven fifteen, but it took a little while in the chaotic disorienting swirl at Penn Station to figure out which subway she needed to take to get to Times Square.

Disorienting, Ruby thought, looking around.

Yep. Disorienting was the theme of her week all right.

Even after a full minute, she kept standing there, staring. She knew she looked like a tourist, but she didn't care.

She had one or two other things on her mind right now, she thought.

She found a Starbucks half a block west of the subway and

went in and got a tall black. Looking out through the foggy, greasy glass to get her bearings, she could see there was some kind of frantic commotion going on at the corner. People were stopped and staring and some of them were pointing phones at some other people there on the ground.

She thought maybe it was a fight. But then the crowd parted, and she saw it was a smiling Buzz Lightyear and green-painted Lady Liberty break-dancing together on a flattened cardboard box.

"My, my, my," she said.

On the morning of the day before, she'd left the rental van in the parking lot of a mall near Savannah/Hilton Head International Airport and taken a series of cabs to Yemassee, South Carolina, where she got on the Amtrak to New York.

It was Eric Wheldon's idea that she ditch the van for the Amtrak. She'd called him the moment after she bought a new prepaid burner phone. The first thing he told her was to take out as much cash as she could from an ATM and not to use her credit card.

She had wanted to call her sister, Lori, to make sure she and the kids were okay, but he said no way. That they would definitely be tapping her line. Which thoroughly sucked, but at least her brother-in-law, Mitch, would be home by now.

She slammed back the last of her coffee and dropped the cup into the trash hole and pulled the door back out to the grim, frigid sidewalk. She was supposed to meet Wheldon on the corner of 44th and Broadway, and when she arrived, there was a crowd on the corner. It was some kind of nightclub opening, and there were photographers standing by a red carpet and a velvet rope.

She looked at people, searching for Wheldon as she passed. In his YouTube videos, he was a neatly dressed reporterish-looking middle-aged white guy.

There was no one who looked like that in front of the red

ropes, so she went to the corner and waited on the light. On the opposite side of it, she saw a couple of dog walkers standing there, allowing their dogs to greet each other.

Of course, she thought.

Why not take the dog out for a stroll at midnight in Times Square in the freezing cold? To meet Buzz Lightyear for a break-dancing lesson maybe? Makes sense.

As she arrived at the opposite curb, she realized one of the dog walkers was staring at her. He was a pale, fiftyish man in a long dark overcoat.

Was it Wheldon? Ruby thought. The neat hair and reporterish look were the same, and he seemed to be about the same age. Though he hadn't mentioned any dog.

Or had the FBI found her? Ruby thought, gnawing on her lip. They looked reporterish, too.

They didn't break eye contact as she went past him north up Broadway. She was coming to the corner of 45th when she noticed that he was coming up behind her. She stopped short, freaking out a little. He handed her something before he kept going like a shot with the dog around the corner of 45th.

She kept going straight up Broadway and waited until she got across the next side street before she looked at it.

It was a flyer for an Irish pub on 50th Street.

12:30 was written in Sharpie along its bottom.

38

The hearty, happy smell of steak and Guinness made Ruby smile when she came in out of the cold through the door of O'Lunney's Times Square Pub.

After all the traveling and cold and walking and worrying, she suddenly felt ravenously hungry and very tired.

She looked at the people at the half-filled bar, the jewel-colored rows of shining bottles behind it.

"Hey, there you are. This way, miss," said a pleasant-looking goateed man in a dapper gray suit as he came out from behind the bar.

He led her down some steps to a downstairs bar and past it to a dark booth where the neat man from the corner stood as she approached.

"Welcome to the jungle, Ruby," Wheldon said as she stepped over.

"Where's your dog?" Ruby said.

Wheldon laughed as she sat.

"What dog?" he said with a wink.

"You are Eric Wheldon?"

"At your service," he said.

"An Irish coffee, please," she said to the waitress when she came over.

"I'd also like a menu, too, if we're staying. I'm starving," Ruby said, unbuttoning her coat as the waitress left.

"No, we should actually be leaving in a minute," Wheldon said, glancing at the stairs. "We should keep moving."

"Are you kidding? I haven't slept an hour straight since I called you. I'm about to drop. Is it really necessary?"

Wheldon took out a folded sheet of paper from inside his long coat and put it on the tabletop. He flashed the light from his phone on it to show her.

Ruby swallowed as she looked at her photo from her military ID.

"You tell me," he said.

"What the hell is that?"

"It's the FBI wire on you. You're a hot commodity."

"Oh, no, no, no... Am I like on the news now?"

"No, not yet. That's an interoffice sheet. They want to bag you discreetly, if they can."

"AWOL?" she said as she read the charges. "Bullshit! I'm on leave! And 'Suspicion of Terrorist Activities'! Are they crazy?"

"Yep, that's how they do it. If it's a national security top secret matter, they just go to their rigged secret court and get one of their cronies to rubber-stamp it. They don't need probable cause or to show any evidence. They just say it's a sensitive security issue and, boom, they get the warrant."

"I can't believe this. Are you being watched, too?"

"Off and on," Wheldon said. "They don't seem to like me or my YouTube channel very much. Weird."

The waitress brought her coffee.

"How the hell do you know all this stuff?"

"I told you I used to work in the State Department. I still know a few people, good people, who have had it up to here with what's happening."

"What *is* happening?"

"We'll get to all that. We need to get out of here first. I have a friend. You can crash on her couch. You'll like her. Everybody likes Rebecca."

"Then what?"

"Then tomorrow, we talk. Trade notes. Figure out your situation. How does that sound?"

"Honestly, sort of crazy," Ruby said as she stared at her very first personal WANTED poster there on the paper. "Five seconds ago, I was at my sister's house feeding my new niece. Now the FBI is after me, and I'm here in New York with a conspiracy theorist."

"Not theorist," Wheldon said, smiling as he dropped a couple of bills on the table. "Analyst, Ruby. The conspiracy is real. As you know yourself now."

Ruby took a sip of her coffee as Wheldon stood and yanked open a door beside their booth.

"Are you ready?" Wheldon said.

Ruby looked out the door. Beyond it there was a bunch of garbage bags and beer case boxes and a set of metal fire escape–style stairs heading up. A frigid ear-nipping wind rushed in.

"No, but let's do it anyway, I guess," Ruby said as she finally stood.

39

When Reyland woke it was around midnight and there was a sound of violins.

When he opened an eye, up on the big wall-sized screen, he could see men in Civil War uniforms being carried on stretchers. Scarlett O'Hara appeared, looking to and fro, and then the camera panned back to dramatically reveal a sepia-colored train yard filled with the dead and dying as the music turned to a sad strain of Dixieland.

Reyland yawned. Movie night had been his nine-year-old son Jason's idea. The kids were all off from school the next day because of some teachers' conference, so they'd all come down with popcorn and Mike and Ikes and blankets. They'd decided after several votes on the vintage Disney classic *Freaky Friday*, and then after the kids fell asleep, his wife had put on *Gone with the Wind*.

That had done it for him. He hadn't lasted through the opening credits.

"Okay, you lazybones," Reyland called out, clicking off the projector with the remote.

No one moved. His littlest, Sadie, was closest, and she squealed as he tickled her awake at her bare foot with his toenail.

"Mom, make him stop," she said as everyone finally got up.

At first, he had thought that the theater room the previous owners had done up with red curtains and even a little ticket stand in the hall was the corniest crap he had ever laid eyes on. But even he couldn't deny how much he actually loved it. The sound system especially. He'd never go to a real movie theater again.

As Jason, Tyler and Sadie zombie-stumbled off to bed, he helped his wife, Danielle, collect the popcorn bowls. He smiled, checking out his wife from behind as they came up the stairs. She'd just turned forty, but she worked out like crazy, and she still had a great rack and an ass you could bounce a quarter off.

She was still the hot LSU cheerleader he'd picked up at the Orlando Hard Rock Cafe after the Citrus Bowl back in the roaring nineties. Or at least mostly. He remembered Christmas in St. Barts two years before when they had left the kids in the hotel and gone sailing. How would he ever forget? Shirtless and tipsy, she had climbed to the bow and done a mermaid impression for him in just her Santa-red thong.

He frowned as he thought about work, Dunning, the missing navy girl.

Why? Reyland thought. Couldn't life just always be champagne and sailboats and Santa-red thongs?

"Bring up some bottled water, okay?" his wife called by the back stairs as he clicked off the basement lights.

"Yes, dear," he mumbled into the dark.

He was closing the Sub-Zero when he saw Emerson's three

missed calls on his phone on the charging pad on the other side of the kitchen island.

"Tell me the good news," Reyland said as he stood at his back door, looking out into the dark yard.

"Everett's in New York."

Reyland's face instantly brightened.

"New York? In custody?"

"No. You're not going to believe this, boss. It's not good. She's met up with that internet jackass Wheldon."

"Who?"

"You know. Eric Wheldon. He leaked the Oliveras thing about four months ago. He was the reason the *Post* finally picked it up."

"Oh, no, no, no," Reyland said, knocking at the French door glass with his Notre Dame school ring. "Tell me we have eyes on them right this second."

"No, but we're on this. New York already has a great jacket on Wheldon. We have his apartment and his office. You want me to get a forward team together?"

"Yes. Wake up Ruiz and call aviation. We need a plane three hours ago," Reyland said.

40

The late morning traffic on the BQE outside of LaGuardia Airport was catastrophic. But as the cab glacially got off the BQE onto the LIE, it did the impossible.

It actually got worse.

From the dead-stopped interchange five miles south of the airport, Gannon looked out, amazed at the evacuation-level volume of work vans and big rig trucks and taxis and cars. Then he looked forward at Manhattan, where the machine belts of vehicles were being fed.

The great gray barbed skyline on the western horizon looked like some giant instrument of torture set and ready for fresh victims.

Gannon zipped up the Carhartt coat he had bought from a sporting goods store in Arizona on the way to the airport.

And look who's headed straight into the jaws of it, he thought.

Gannon closed his eyes. Damn did this suck, he thought. Especially leaving Declan flat all by himself back at the stadium in Arizona. He hadn't even had time to stay for the simulated game in order to catch the next direct flight.

But what choice did he have?

What was going on, he didn't know, except that this wasn't a damn game. This wasn't some lucky fantasy scheme where he walked off into the sunset with a secret bag of doper money anymore. He could kiss all that good-night and goodbye.

He needed to get out in front of this and damn quick, he thought as he passed a hand nervously through his hair.

Before he found his sorry ass sitting in a prison cell.

They stopped and sat motionless for so long the cabbie actually put the car in Park.

"It's worse," Gannon finally said. "How could it have gotten worse?"

"What's that?" said the driver, pulling one of the hissing earbuds out of his head.

He was a skinny young Asian dude with a Mets flat-brim cap and a white North Face vest. He looked like a college kid.

"Nothing. I just hate this," Gannon said.

"Hate what?" he said.

"This. This city. It's a crumbling black sinkhole filled with hate and dirt and pizza rats."

"What? Come on, man. How does anyone hate the Big Apple? That's ridiculous. It's the biggest, greatest, most happening city in the world. Like where are you from, bro?"

"Here," Gannon said, staring out. "I'm from right here."

They drove for a bit then stopped again. The kid put his earbud back in, but then after a second, pulled it out again.

"If you hate it so much, why come back?"

"This is a onetime shot, believe me," Gannon said. "I had to come back. I have something to do."

"Must be something pretty important, huh?"

"Yep."

"What?"

Gannon took out his phone and looked at it stupidly for a moment then put it back into his pocket.

"I'm not really at liberty to divulge that information," he said.

"You're a real man of mystery, aren't you?"

"Buddy," Gannon said, looking out at the shark-toothed skyline. "You don't even want to know."

41

Just north of Little Italy, the icy breeze was so strong Gannon had to fight the cab door to get it open.

He'd just made the unmarked Chevy on the northeast corner of Orchard Street when its driver's door opened. The big man who got out of it smiling had shoulder-length dirty blond hair and a black leather jacket.

With his Fu Manchu and big Red Wing boots, he didn't look like a cop. He looked like a Hells Angel trying to find his lost Harley.

"Mickey, you crazy son of a bitch. Look at you. Mr. Winter Tan. You're back!" his old partner, Danny "Stick" Henrickson, said, embracing him.

"Look at me? Look at you. You look exactly the same, well, except for this," Gannon said, flicking at the dusting of white in Stick's mustache.

"Yeah, I know. It's horrible, right?" Stick said, smoothing

at his whiskers. "You know how vain I am. I was heading to Duane Reade for a new tube of Just For Men when you called."

Gannon smiled as he pounded his old linebacker-sized partner on the back. He hadn't been all that great at keeping in contact with old friends after he moved out of the city, but Stick was the exception.

"So should we sit in the car or hit a Starbucks or something?" Gannon said, shivering.

"No, no. For ancient reunions with old maniac partners, I roll out the full red carpet," Stick said. "Like the hick jacket, by the way. Are you a farmer or something now?"

Stick took out a set of keys and opened up the door of a shop across from where the Chevy was parked. Silver Mine Properties, it said on the door.

"Yeah, I'm a farmer, and you're what? Moonlighting as a broker now?" Gannon said as they came into a cozy office space with some cubicles and a reception area.

"Actually," Stick said as he clicked on a light, "my sister's new husband is the manager of the building here. The last tenant just left, so they're still trying to lease it out. I coop in the office here when I'm downtown."

"Oh, I get it now," Gannon said as he peeked in an inner office and saw the drum set.

Before the cops, Stick had his fifteen minutes of fame as a replacement drummer in Cold Iron Mine, a once famous Staten Island heavy metal band that had toured Europe.

Which actually made sense, Gannon thought, shaking his head at Stick. You had to be heavy-metal-drummer crazy to be an undercover cop.

And Stick hadn't been just any undercover cop either but one of the greatest NYPD narcotics officers of all time, Gannon knew. Though Stick looked like a big dumb white boy headbanger, his mom, a pretty Puerto Rican lady, had raised him speaking Spanglish in the Lower East Side projects. None of the dozens of Dominican dealers he put away could ever believe how well he understood what they were saying.

"You're downtown a lot now, huh, with the feds?" Gannon said. "Your last email said you were still with the JTTF, right?"

"Yeah, well, that was like seven months ago," Stick said as he locked the door. He lay back on a couch in the reception area and put his big Red Wing engineer boots up on a motorcycle magazine–covered coffee table. "I actually had me some second thoughts about it."

"I thought you were all over it."

"I was. The OT was great, but two weeks in, you wouldn't believe the bullshit, Mickey. All the politics and crazy shit. They had us following people who had nothing to do with anything, brother. I mean, it was like gumshoe shit for the politicians or something. I didn't know what the hell it was. I like to do like real cop work against, you know, dealers and crooks and killers. So now I'm back where I was before."

"Up in Midtown North?"

"No, I'm at the One Nine," Stick said proudly. "You're looking at the new detective squad coleader."

"The One Nine? The Silk Stocking District? No way!" Gannon said, grinning. "Your mom must be so proud. Drummer boy makes it to Park Avenue! Must be busy with all the drive-bys up there in rich people land, huh? Let me guess. The butler did it?"

"Ha ha. Keep laughing. You'd be surprised how busy it gets."

"Ever think of this thing, um, retirement, I think it's called, Stick? You have what? Almost thirteen hundred years in now?"

"Screw your career advice, jackass. I thought you said the next time you came back they'd be playing the bagpipes out in Brooklyn at Ascension for you."

"Yeah, I know," Gannon said quietly.

"What the hell is it anyway that makes you darken Gotham's doorstep again? The suspense is killing me."

"I won't even get into the particulars with you, man. Less you know, the better."

Stick shook his head and laughed at that.

"So what can I do for you, then?"

"It's going to sound crazy."

Stick grinned as he put his big palms together.

"Then you've come to the right place, brother."

"There's a guy on the internet on YouTube. His name's Wheldon. Eric Wheldon. He's an alternative news independent reporter. Ever hear of him?"

Stick looked at him strangely.

"Wheldon? Who? No."

"He walks around the city. Talks about government stuff?"

"You're trying to contact some conspiracy theory guy?"

"Yes," Gannon said, taking out his phone and showing him a screenshot. "This is the guy. His name's Eric Wheldon. I know you know everybody. I was hoping you would know somebody who knows him."

Because of his legendary undercover status, Stick knew virtually every cop, FBI agent, DEA agent and district attorney from Yonkers to Suffolk County. In addition to a few Yankees and half the cast of the TV show *Law & Order*, where he used to moonlight as security.

"Ever consider emailing him?" Stick said. "Saves on the hotel and airfare."

"I did," Gannon said. "Several times. But he doesn't answer. This is pretty important. I really need to talk to him. Like now."

Stick squinted as he tapped at his mustache with a knuckle.

"I actually know a few computer nerds in the department that might be of some use. You need to sit down with this guy pronto, huh? Is this about aliens or something? Ancient aliens maybe? On your new farm? No, wait. I got it. Crop circles."

"Stick, I just need your help, okay? I didn't come back up here because I miss the dirty snow. It's important. I'm begging you to help me contact this guy."

"Okay. Relax. Relax. Just wondering."

Stick winked as he took his cell phone out of the leather jacket.

"You just sit back and watch the master at work, Mickey, my boy," he said. "Your wish is my command."

42

At only a little over two hundred flight miles from Washington, DC, to New York City, it took the unmarked government Gulfstream twenty-one minutes tarmac to tarmac to land Reyland and his men at New Jersey's Teterboro Airport.

At five after three in the afternoon, they disembarked into the gray and cold and transferred everything off the sleek white jet into the three black Ford Expedition SUVs waiting along the open tarmac side fence.

By 3:10, they were on the Jersey Turnpike eastbound with all the traffic heading into the city. But they didn't head into the city. Right as the traffic began backing up before the Holland Tunnel, the three dark vehicles swerved onto the litter-strewn shoulder one after the other.

Down at the end of a battered off-ramp was a stop sign they blew past into an industrial area called Kearny. Huge chemical tanks went by on their left. A transmission tower. A looming dark steel railroad bridge.

When they came around a bend, a CSX freight train double stacked with rusty shipping containers was rolling out in the opposite direction.

Getting out, Reyland thought, smiling.

While the getting was still good.

A hundred yards farther south down this godforsaken road, the convoy of tinted-windowed vehicles slowed. The potholed drive they pulled onto had a tall razor-wired fence gate across it with a rusted sign that said KEEP OUT New Jersey State DOT.

Reyland's driver zipped down the window. He fished into his pocket as Reyland listened to the terrific ocean-like roar from the rushing traffic on the turnpike above. Then the driver finally laid his electronic passkey to the fob reader and the rusty gate slid sideways with a rattle and a buzz.

Beyond the gate were salt sheds and stacks of cement highway barriers and columns of road plows that they quickly skimmed past on their way toward a half-dozen construction trailers and shipping containers that were set up in a horseshoe pattern at the truck yard's rear.

Reyland stared at the bristle of satellite dishes and cell tower masts rising from the huge trailers' roofs.

Port New York Center 11, as the site was officially known, was one of the very first federal-to-local law enforcement fusion centers set up in the scramble after 9/11.

He had actually attended the not-so-publicized ribbon-cutting ceremony with Dunning and the former FBI director almost fifteen years before.

Up the stairs and through the door of the huge center trailer a moment later, it looked like a war room. There were columns and rows of desks and computers everywhere.

Reyland looked at the huge screen that took up the entirety of the back wall. It was divided up into smaller ones that showed street traffic and various locales. One screen showed New York City's Central Park. On another was Kennedy International Airport.

Center 11 usually had an alphabet soup of JTTF, FBI field agents, NYPD, Port Authority cops and New Jersey state troopers manning it. But today it was staffed with a small group of hand-selected counter-intel agents and contractors for a special covert counterterror training exercise.

Or at least that was what Reyland was describing it as in the official report.

Reyland turned as Emerson brought over a tall balding Hispanic guy wearing steel-rimmed glasses.

"Robert, you know Agent Arietta, right?" Emerson said.

"Of course. Edgar, how are you?" Reyland said, putting out his hand to the lanky Hispanic.

Arietta, who was rumored to be somewhat autistic, didn't even glance at it or him as he called out, "Bring up array one."

The patchwork grid of screens instantly morphed into one big screen that showed the parking lot of a small brick building on a suburban street somewhere.

"Okay. This is Eric Wheldon's apartment building in Pelham, Westchester," Arietta said.

"Where did Wheldon work again?" Reyland said.

"He rode a Middle East desk at Langley," Emerson said.

"Is that right?" Reyland said. "I wonder how much he's going to like getting rode in a Leavenworth mop closet after we get through with him."

"We've been on it since four in the morning," Arietta continued. "We were about to pop in for a peek around five when he came home alone with no girl. But the good news is we were able to get this with a shotgun mic through the crack in a window."

"Okay. I can meet him tonight if it's legit," came a voice over the overhead speaker. "Okay. Okay. Get me a number. I'll call him back with the location."

"What's that supposed to mean?" Reyland said.

"It means he's meeting up with someone tonight," Arietta said. "The New York office has been watching this joker on and off since his last leak came out at the *Washington Post*. We've been watching him for the last three months. Whenever he meets with people, it's usually one of three locations."

Arietta went to a keyboard and the screen suddenly changed into three side-by-side views of the city.

"Here at the Roosevelt Island Tram on the East Side," Arietta said, pointing. "Or this diner here on Tenth Avenue in Chelsea or this hotel here down from Madison Square Garden."

Reyland looked up at the already-congested pre–rush hour New York City vistas, the crush of cars, the stressed-looking people. The resolution of the images was remarkable. It was like he was standing in the flat-screen section of a Best Buy.

"These camera angles seem high. Traffic cameras, right? Are these live feeds?" Reyland said.

"Yes, it's called the 3RT Retina system," Arietta said, heading over to a keyboard. "It's brand-new. We just got it patched into the traffic cameras a month ago. Watch this."

Arietta went over and clicked some more keys. All of a sudden, red computer-generated squares appeared around the license plates of the cars and on the faces of people in the crowd. The squares followed along with the moving subjects as driver's licenses began to appear along the bottom of the screen. One after another after another.

Reyland looked in shock at the smiling driver's license faces that began to line up along the bottom of the screen. The computer was ID'ing everyone, he realized. He felt a fluttery feeling in his stomach as he watched.

"This is live?" Reyland said. "In real time. You're picking all this up live? And ID'ing everyone live? I've never seen this."

"It's the new video analytics platform coupled with the latest in facial recognition. We have the software tapped into that new Cray at the DOE at Oakridge. They just put it online. With our full trunk-to-block fiber-optic linkup, the speed of the processing is mind-blowing. We're talking two hundred petaflops, which is the equivalent—"

Reyland put up a hand.

"Yeah, uh-huh. It's quick and powerful. Great," Reyland said. "Bottom line, if our little navy friend shows her face in one of these locations, we got her?"

"Her face is already in the system," Arietta said with a nod. "If she shows her face, the computer will know in a fraction of a second."

"Ruiz, what do you think in terms of a setup?" Reyland said.

The short, stocky mercenary stepped forward. He'd been watching everything silently from near the rear of the room among his contingent of men. He pursed his lips and squinted his eyes as he slowly looked from one location on the screen to the next.

"Let's get some printouts of these locales," he finally said. "And we'll take a look-see."

43

Gannon got off the train at Pennsylvania Station at 6:45 p.m. and walked through some corridors and came up a set of stairs onto cold Seventh Avenue. On the dark sidewalk in front of Madison Square Garden there were incredible crowds of commuters, and he had to wade against the flow of the massive herd of them to get to the avenue's east side.

The Arlington Hotel that Stick had told him to go to was halfway down 31st, sandwiched between a luxury wig importer and a shuttered Chinese restaurant called Bamboo Lucky 21. He was a little early, so he passed it and walked the rest of the block over to Sixth Avenue.

He stood there on the corner in the steady rush-hour flow of people. He stepped aside for an Asian woman pushing a double stroller as an ambulance with a blaring siren slowly carved a path through the blocked-up intersection.

Across the street, he watched a messenger chaining up his

bike to a bus stop sign pole. Watching the man bend to secure the lock, Gannon immediately picked up the flat bulge in his jeans back pocket that he knew was a box cutter.

He blew into his cupped hands, grinning in the cold as he thought about his previous life as a beat cop. He had actually loved foot posts. Being a sheepdog out among the sheep looking for the wolves.

After another five minutes, he crossed the street and went back up to the old hotel. He thought it would be crummy inside, but the lobby looked newly redone. There was dramatic diffused lighting and maroon-colored wallpaper and a minimalist chunk of pale limestone for a check-in desk.

The pretty young woman behind it had some kind of Rosie the Riveter retro thing going on with her dark hair. She smiled at Gannon as he sat in a chrome Euro-style chair opposite the desk.

He took out his phone and looked at it and watched it trill as it changed the hour.

"This is Eric Wheldon," a voice said.

"Mr. Smith here," Gannon said. "The Arlington, right?"

"Yes. You have some information for me?"

"Yes."

"What's it about?" he said.

"Is it safe to talk on the phone?" Gannon said, looking at the desk clerk. "I thought we would talk face-to-face."

"It's safe," the voice said.

"It's about Dunning," Gannon said quietly. "He didn't die in Italy."

"Many people are speculating that."

"I'm not speculating. I know," Gannon said.

"Interesting," said Wheldon, unimpressed.

"I saw him with my own eyes."

"Saw him?"

"I actually touched him—his corpse, anyway," Gannon said.

"I would love to believe you, Mr. Smith, but in my business, I need proof. All I have is my reputation for truth. Without proof, I cannot use your information."

"I can prove it."

"How?"

"I have a videotape of Dunning dead. As well as the others."

"The others?"

"Yes. There were six dead altogether. Including the pilots."

"Where is this tape?"

"We should talk face-to-face," Gannon said.

There was a pause.

"Then turn around," Eric Wheldon said.

44

The elevator and the hallway were nicely done like the lobby, but the room itself up on the fourteenth floor had faded beige walls and cheap gray office carpet and Walmart furniture. Gannon looked at the old radiator under the yellow-shaded window opposite the door. It looked like a public school classroom with a bed in it.

"We can talk in here, Mr. Smith," Wheldon said, opening an inside door on the left.

The suite's side room had a table and chairs and a little kitchenette in it. Beyond the table was the bathroom.

"Please call me Pete," Gannon said as he sat at the small table.

"Okay, Pete," the reporter said, sitting down opposite.

Wheldon seemed smaller in person than on his videos and his eyes were bluer. He was in the same nice overcoat he was wearing in the video where he was walking up Park Avenue.

"Now, before we get into this, how comfortable are you about disclosing your identity?" Wheldon said.

"Extremely uncomfortable," Gannon said.

"Okay, so I'll hold off taping," he said. "Now, where did you see Dunning?"

"I saw him on a Gulfstream 550 corporate jet that went down fifteen miles north of Little Abaco in the Bahamas," Gannon said. "They said it was a turboprop plane on the news, but that was completely made up."

"How did you see it?"

"I was out marlin fishing on my boat by myself, and I saw it go down and rip in two."

"Was it on fire or something? What was wrong with it?"

"No, it came in almost gliding very low to the water. I'm not an expert, but I think it had run out of gas."

"Go on," Wheldon said.

"I was right on top of it when it ripped into the water, and I rushed over and saw that the front of it had snapped off and sunk down on a coral shelf. I run a diving business, so I suited up and went down to see if there were any survivors.

"I saw Dunning there inside the plane. He was with two other white guys, one older, one younger. They looked like agents maybe. There was also a fortysomething-looking black guy in a hoodie and jeans as well as two uniformed pilots. They were all dead. As in already dead. Their faces were blue like they had suffocated or something."

"Did you report this?"

"No," Gannon said, shaking his head. "I didn't know it was Dunning until I saw his picture in the paper yesterday morning."

"No, I mean the crash itself. You didn't call anyone when you saw the plane go down?"

"No."

"Why not?"

Gannon looked at him.

"Well, I tried to radio it in at first, but my boat radio antenna was busted. Then I...found the money."

"Money?" Wheldon said, squinting.

"Yes. Diamonds and money. In a suitcase. There were several million dollars in one-hundred-dollar bills and a mother lode of uncut diamonds."

The reporter's calm composure evaporated. His mouth gaped open as he sat up.

"Listen, I know it was wrong," Gannon said. "And I'm re-gretting it now, believe me. I should have immediately turned it in. And I would have. But no one came. I was out there for an hour, and there wasn't a soul. I had no idea the damn US government was involved. I thought they were all a bunch of dead dopers or something, so I thought why not exit stage left? No harm no foul."

"This money and diamonds," Wheldon said, staring at him with his intense blue eyes. "You still have them?"

"Yes."

"Both?"

"Both," Gannon said. "It was stupid of me. Say the word, and I'll go get them and give them back. I'll do whatever to get this crazy bullshit to stop. That's why I'm here. I want to make this right. Lying about the death of the FBI director is bananas. Just bananas. They can't get away with it. I won't let them. That's unacceptable. People need to know the truth."

"Where is everything?"

"Back in the Bahamas. I hid everything along with the GoPro footage I took from my dive."

Eric Wheldon stared at him with a dumbfounded look.

"This video. You can tell it's Dunning? Clear video?"

Gannon nodded.

"I can't believe this. Is it somewhere secure?"

Gannon thought of the ridge in the pitch-black, unmarked submerged cave a hundred feet underground.

"Yeah, you could say that. Like I said, I had no idea it was the FBI director until I saw his picture in the *Times* yesterday morning."

"I can't believe this," the reporter said again.

"That makes two of us, buddy," Gannon said. "Now it's your turn. What in the green world of God is going on?"

45

"It was a whisper jet," the reporter said.

"A what?" Gannon said.

"A whisper jet. Tell me, were there any numbers or letters on the tail of the plane?"

"I don't remember."

"How about on the jet engines? Sometimes Gulfstream puts the ID tag number on the engines."

Gannon thought about the giant white fishing bob he'd seen.

"No, there was nothing on them."

"That's why they call it a whisper jet. National secrecy and security. It flies anywhere, and no one knows who or, in this case, what's on it. The plane that went down was probably the FBI director's personal jet."

"No! The FBI director gets his own private rock-star jet? A Gulfstream?"

"Oh, but of course. Not just any kind either. An air force

model with aftermarket add-ons like radar jamming. The attorney general has one as well. The least we could do is have our sworn protectors live as large as possible. It's only taxpayer money after all, right?"

"They can do that? Fly around without markings, jamming radar? Aren't there rules?"

"Sure there are. For everybody but the people who make them. Or in this case, claim to be enforcing them. You read the news today? You hear about Messerly?"

"Messerly?"

"The new NSA defector leaker guy stuck at the embassy in Europe."

"Oh, yeah. Messerly. I remember him. From last year, right? The new Assange. What about him?"

"They just blocked all his social media accounts this morning. Just flat-out blocked them. Said he was too hateful. The single greatest whistle-blower of all time who's trying to expose the illegal surveillance of the entire global population is too hateful? They apparently own the social media companies as well as the mainstream media now. They can do anything they want."

"I don't understand," Gannon said.

"Could you excuse me for one second? I need to make a phone call."

"That depends. Who are you calling?"

"It's okay. A source. I just want to confirm something. Just give me a second, okay?"

Wheldon left the room. Gannon could hear him talking in a low voice. He let out a breath and stared at the grimy bargain hotel room. At the little oven, at the half-open bathroom door. He wondered if coming here was actually a good idea.

"You're right, Pete," Wheldon said as he returned and sat down. "Dunning's plane isn't at its usual hangar at Joint Base Bolling in DC. It never returned from Italy. Not only that, there are rumors that it never actually landed in Aviano Air Base in Italy like it was scheduled to."

"What do you make of that?" Gannon said.

Wheldon shook his head.

"I'm trying to grasp all this," he said. "Dunning's supposed to go to Italy but doesn't arrive. Then there's the diamonds. Uncut diamonds. Sounds like Africa. Has to be. Blood diamonds probably."

"You've lost me," Gannon said.

"This is what I think," Wheldon said. "I think Dunning was running what they call a rat line. Basically, it's smuggling using diplomatic cover. They used them in World War II to get the Nazis out of Germany into South America. They've been using them since probably forever to smuggle drugs or stolen valuables. Whatever you want to wherever you want. Hide it in the diplomatic bag. It's one of the oldest tricks in the book."

"But in America? I don't buy it. The FBI director? You're saying he's secretly a smuggler?"

"That's exactly what I'm saying. I bet the stones from the plane are blood diamonds out of Sierra Leone or the Ivory Coast. Instead of Italy, Dunning went there. I wouldn't be surprised if Dunning was facilitating an arms deal."

"An arms deal?"

Wheldon nodded.

"In the interim between when he was deputy director and director, he was counsel for one of the nation's biggest defense companies. Since it's illegal to sell guns to these rebel groups, they love to use untraceable diamonds."

"Like a secret cash-for-clunkers deal?" Gannon said.

"Exactly. Only in this case, it's diamonds for land mines or maybe attack helicopters. But on the way back, something went wrong with the plane and now their ass is hanging in the breeze."

"That's crazy," Gannon said. "That only happens in the movies."

Wheldon shook his head.

"What do you think makes this world go round, Pete? Truth, justice and the American way?"

"Yes," Gannon said.

"Lucky you," Wheldon said, letting out a breath. "It's power, Pete. Power."

46

Gannon made a pained face.

"So they've just gone crazy? At the top? At the FBI? Full-tilt corrupt?"

Wheldon nodded.

"Bought and paid for. An organization is only as good as the people in it, Pete. You ever hear of a dirty cop when you were on the force?"

Gannon squinted at him.

"On the force?" Gannon said, making a puzzled face. "What do you mean? You think I'm a cop?"

"Let's see," Wheldon said. "Face like the map of Ireland, voice like a Yankee announcer and you actually want to return several million dollars of loot you found while fishing out on your boat. Is it such a crazy guess?"

"No comment," Gannon said.

"Anyway," Wheldon said. "The combination of the global

money and influence and no one checking up on them is like nothing ever before seen on the planet. Now you add the technology, the NSA collection of all the global communication data, and now they have a trove of information and blackmail on virtually everyone."

"The NSA collection of what?"

"You need to get out more, Pete. Since one month after 9/11, the NSA has been collecting everybody's electronic sweet nothings and storing them in their computers for a rainy day. It was supposed to be just for checking on the terrorists, but now they don't give a rat's ass about the law. They're using it against everyone. A blackmail Fort Knox.

"And you can't think of the FBI in terms of being a domestic law enforcement agency anymore. After they signed the Patriot Act, the FBI joined the CIA. Almost all of the alphabet soup agencies are now under the same umbrella."

"Like Big Pharma and Big Tobacco, we've got Big Intelligence now?" Gannon said.

"Exactly."

"That can't be right. There must be something in the Constitution, no? Where's the outrage? Why the hell isn't the press doing anything? Isn't that their job?"

"Pete, pay attention. Most media companies are multinational corporations, too. Everybody has secrets, Pete. All you need is a little dirt on some top key people in each of the media outlets, and every story you want tanked gets tanked."

Gannon looked at him.

"Okay, so while I went out fishing, my country apparently turned into one massive corrupt racket. Now what? What do we do now?"

Wheldon drummed his fingers on the table.

"I think there's someone you should meet. She told me the same story you just told me. Well, not exactly the same. But it all fits."

"She?"

"Yes. She's a navy lieutenant, an accident investigator who was sent out to the plane crash site before the cover-up started. At the site, she met a coast guard diver who showed her the video he had filmed of the inside of the plane. That's why when you told me there were six people, I knew you were legit. She told me the same thing last night."

"So there's another video?"

"No. She doesn't have it. She just saw it. And the diver who filmed it is missing now. The FBI tried to grab her down in Florida as well, but she was just able to get away."

"Holy crap. This is real. A full-scale cover-up. This is really happening."

"You said it. Which is why I'd like to interview the both of you and upload it onto my channel."

Gannon sat up straighter in his chair.

"Now, hold up. I don't want to be on a video."

"Don't worry," Wheldon said. "I won't show your face or anything, and I can mask your voice. I could bring her here and talk to her in the bedroom, and you can stay in this room here so you don't even have to see each other."

"That's how it works? Just put it out there? Shouldn't we get my GoPro tape first?"

"No, the more visible the faster the better. The more visible the less likely they'll target you for elimination. If the truth of Dunning's death is out there, their mission will shift from plugging the leak to spin-doctoring the news narrative. Putting you six feet under after the truth is exposed will make less sense for them."

"Say that last part again?"

Wheldon stared at him steadily.

"There is no organization more deadly than a covert intelligence service. A politician tells a group of government workers to work hand in hand with violent military men to do unaccountable things in secret. Outside of the light of scrutiny, these men are told to eliminate people or to sell arms to foreign militaries. Without inventory or receipts. Without any way to check up on them.

"The National Security Division of the Justice Department is not allowed to be inspected, we are told, because the inspectors don't have the intelligence clearance. You see the problem here? What do you think happens?"

Gannon shook his head.

"We need to do this now, Pete," Wheldon said. "The more hits we get, the better our chance of exposing this corruption to the public."

"You think this will go viral?"

"It should, Pete," Wheldon said, wide-eyed. "This is the biggest bombshell I've ever heard."

47

For how on the ball and techy Agent Arietta seemed, his bare windowless trailer office looked like something out of one of those cable shows about hoarders.

It had a cheap white plastic folding table for a desk and a couple of old gray metal file cabinets in the right-hand far corner. Instead of having a computer, the desk was covered in a mountain of paper, and in the corner opposite the metal cabinets was a big plastic trash barrel filled to the brim with greasy take-out containers and Dunkin' cups.

Reyland was sitting at the paper-covered desk reading the file on Eric Wheldon's daughter away at William & Mary when Emerson popped his head in.

"Boss, we got something."

When Reyland went back into the war room, the lobby of the Arlington Hotel was blown up on the big wall screen. He gazed up at the gold-lit sconces on its brown walls and the people standing by the white marble check-in desk. The feed was coming from one of their agents who'd gone in with a pin camera.

"What's up?"

"The girl on the right. Brown hair. Might be her," Emerson said.

Reyland walked over closer and looked up at a girl in profile there at the check-in desk. He studied the photo that the surveillance team had taken of Ruby Everett in Times Square the day before.

"Didn't the outside camera with the facial recognition see her?" Reyland said.

"Well, actually, only if she came in walking from the Seventh Avenue intersection where the camera is," Arietta said. "If she got out of a taxi in front of the hotel, it's probably too far for the camera to see."

"Now you tell me," Reyland said, rolling his eyes at Mr. Geek Squad.

"What do you think?" Emerson said.

Reyland made a sour face as he stared back at the screen.

"I don't know," he said. "Same eye shape, same nose, but the video quality is garbage. It's too hard to tell. Tell them to get closer."

"You need to get closer," Emerson said into his phone.

They waited. The live feed camera wobbled and swung around the other side of the target.

"Wait a second, Arietta. What the hell are we doing?" Reyland said. "Can't you get this feed into your damn supercomputer ID software to tell us if it's her?"

"Yes, of course. I didn't think of that. Give me a second," he said.

If you want something done, you have to do it yourself, Reyland thought, rolling his eyes again.

He placed his hands behind his back as he watched the target head for the elevator. She was pressing the button when she turned, and the red computer box appeared around her face.

"Okay. We're linked into the computer now. Matching up," Arietta said as the door rolled open, and the woman got on.

"Should they follow her? Get in the elevator?" asked Emerson.

"No. Hold up, hold up. Don't spook her. Take it easy," Reyland said.

The elevator door had just closed when a ping came from Arietta's laptop.

Then Reyland smiled as Ruby Everett's military ID appeared up on the screen as clear as day.

48

Ruby came out of the elevator onto the fourteenth floor into a hallway that smelled like weed and furniture polish. As the elevator door rolled closed behind her, she took out her phone. She checked the room number on the text Wheldon had sent her against the plastic plaque on the wall. Then she made a left down the dark-walled hallway.

She'd just been dropped off by Eric's friend Rebecca. She'd crashed at Rebecca's apartment in Inwood the night before, and her hostess had explained that she had worked with Eric in the CIA when she was younger.

Since then, she'd put up several of Eric's whistle-blowers as they came into town. There were more and more these days, she'd said.

Ruby counted the doors. Making a turn at the far corner of the narrow corridor, she suddenly heard the pornographic sound of a woman coming from somewhere.

She shook her head as she zipped her fleece hoodie up to her chin. She still wasn't sure about any of this. About being up in New York. About going underground like some kind of anti-government nut.

Under normal circumstances, she liked to consider herself a good citizen. She always honestly paid her taxes, always voted, always went to jury duty whenever she was called.

She would have gladly turned herself in to the FBI to work this all out, she thought as she came to the end of the sleazy hall, if it weren't for the fact that it seemed to be the FBI itself that was the problem.

14H was the very last door of all. It opened as she was about to ring its doorbell.

"If it isn't Mrs. Smith," Wheldon said. *"Entrez-vous?"*

The room inside was large but drab. Besides the bed and desk, there were two chairs, one just beside the door and another at the foot of the bed facing the desk. On the desk, there was a smartphone in a little tripod with its camera pointed at the bed.

"I thought you said you weren't going to film me," Ruby said, looking warily at the phone as Wheldon locked the door.

"Don't worry. I'm not. Cross my heart," Eric said. "You're going to sit here by the door. I'm going to sit in the chair in front of the bed with the camera taping just me the whole time. I promise."

Wheldon thumbed at an almost-closed door on the room's left-hand wall.

"Now if I could direct your attention, Mrs. Smith. Like I texted you, there's a man in the sitting room who's also going to be part of this conversation. We'll call him Mr. Smith. Say hello, Mr. Smith."

"Hello," said a man's voice through the crack in the door.

"This is weird," Ruby said, wincing at the almost-closed door. "Honestly, I don't know, Eric. I don't even know if I should do this."

"I know. You're right," Wheldon said. "All of this is an incredibly silly way to do anything. Unfortunately, these are some desperate times we're living in, aren't they? And if we want to get back to a semblance of sanity and normalcy and justice for our families and kids, it's up to regular people like us to do the job.

"Because the FBI apparently isn't in the fidelity and bravery and integrity business anymore, is it? Or even the mainstream media when you consider how they're covering everything up. I think it's important that more and more people know that. But with that said, I can't and won't force you. You're free to go whenever you want."

Ruby sighed.

"You'll disguise my voice like you said?" Ruby said.

"Of course," Wheldon said. "Your own mother won't know it's you once I get done editing."

"Okay, fine," Ruby said, finally sitting in the chair by the door.

Wheldon took his seat.

"We're going to keep it casual and just talk like we've been doing," Wheldon said. "Nothing fancy. I'll ask you guys questions and you answer them to the best of your ability, okay? I just need to set up my laptop, and we'll be ready. Sound good? We're all on the same page?"

"Okay," said Ruby.

"Okay," said Mr. Smith through the crack in the door.

49

Outside in the fusion center's truck yard, the MH-6 helicopter's red running lights pulsed like a campfire ember against the dark.

In the high nails-on-chalkboard turbo whine, Ruiz adjusted his butt on the chopper's ice-cold exterior running board bench and gave a last tug on his safety harness. Then he gave a knock on the curved glass canopy, and he and his men were up, up and away with their feet dangling off the helicopter's skids into the pitch-black freezing open January air.

Ruiz felt his stomach get left behind as the aircraft went out from under the turnpike overpass. Still gaining altitude, they skimmed smoothly up over a traffic-filled road, over a junkyard, then over a river.

On the river's other side was a lightless golf course, and as they turned to the left north over Hoboken, the magnificent sparkling sprawl of Manhattan's night skyline came into view.

Ruiz looked at the lights in the high black towers, the water of the Hudson below them like a plain of brushed steel.

"Look, Paw. Them building scrapers are even bigger than our silo," one of Ruiz's commandos said in a hick drawl.

"Can it, Boyer," Ruiz said.

"Less than ten," the pilot called over the comm link.

Ruiz smiled around the chaw of chewing tobacco in his mouth as they choppered east at about the height of the observation deck of the Empire State Building.

He actually loved this shit. He had always been a daredevil. He was from the South Side of Chicago and used to train-surf the Loop along with his ghetto buds when he was a kid. Twelve years old, speeding out in the cold, holding on for dear life at the curves.

Faster than a speeding bullet, he thought, chuckling as he spit. *Able to leap tall buildings in a single bound.*

There was another crackle on the comm line as they flew over a tourist boat on the Hudson a thousand feet below.

"Where now? That circular building?" the pilot called out.

"That's it," Ruiz said, looking down at Madison Square Garden between his legs as they approached it.

"Why do they call it a square garden when it's a damn concrete circle?" the pilot said.

"Beats the shit out of me," Ruiz said, spitting down at the boat. "Remember, go in high then drop down to about thirty or so midbuilding at the back."

"Hover above the alley in between. Got it, bro. I can see it now."

Ruiz looked down at the old gray brick hotel as they swung downward toward it. He would have loved a fixed position shot at a distance, but Room 14H was in the back opposite a windowless warehouse. At least the FLIR body heat infrared scope on his rifle would be sharp as a razor out here in this cold.

They went even faster as they lost some altitude.

The comm line crackled again.

"Okay, we're a minute now. One minute."

Ruiz held up a finger to his three men beside him on the skids in the buffeting wind like an infielder reminding his teammates that it was one out.

The pilot glanced at Ruiz through the bubble of glass between them and gave him a Tom Cruise smile.

"You guys do realize you're all out of your minds, right?" he said.

The wind snapped at the cloth of Ruiz's black tactical pants as he tugged at the harness and the rappelling rope.

"Just keep the black egg in the air," Ruiz said as he clicked his M4's selector off Safe with his gloved thumb.

50

"Okay. Hello, everybody. Welcome to the latest. What is this episode? Number 352, I believe," Gannon heard Eric Wheldon saying.

Gannon sat there in the side room beside the slightly cracked-open door, fidgeting in his kitchen chair. Even though it wasn't TV and his voice would be disguised, and it wasn't even live, he was still nervous about saying something stupid and screwing it up. A memory of being an altar boy came to him. Standing next to the priest, wide-eyed up on the bright altar with the eyes of the entire parish staring at him waiting for him to trip over his feet.

"Tonight," Wheldon said, "I have a really great info drop for all of you that relates to your favorite new subject and mine. The oh-so-mysterious death of—"

In the suite's little sitting room, Gannon sat up in his chair waiting for Eric to continue.

Then there was a heavy thump through the crack in the door.

"Eric?" he heard the Mrs. Smith woman say. "ERRIICC!"

Gannon went to the door and pulled it open and saw the screaming Mrs. Smith down on the carpet. Eric Wheldon was down on his back beside her with the back of his neatly combed head half gone and the scarlet mush of the inside of it dumped out on the floor.

Even over the woman's screaming, Gannon suddenly heard a slight yet distinct sound in the air on his left.

He'd heard it before.

It was the soft yet unforgettable slight click that a high velocity bullet made when it just missed you.

"Down, down, down!" Gannon yelled and immediately dropped to the carpet as the window above the radiator came in with a crashing rain of glass.

A muffled clatter of silenced automatic fire made a constellation of ripping holes grow across the yellow shade as Gannon crawled low alongside the bed. He reached out and seized the screaming navy lieutenant by the back of her plaid shirt, and she screamed even louder as he yanked her around the other side of the bed away from the window.

A corner of the bed's headboard exploded into toothpicks as he dived with her into the sitting room. As they landed, a dotted line of bullets popped instantly through the Sheetrock wall just above them. Gannon kicked closed the door. Then he flipped the cheap table and propped it against the wall with his back.

In the next room outside the broken window, Gannon could hear the high turbo whine of a helicopter hovering close above the hotel. Then he heard a sound at the window itself. Something was smashing at the glass.

It was a boot! Gannon realized.

Holy shit! There was somebody at the damn window! They must have been on a rappelling rope or something. They were coming in!

Gannon folded into the fetal position as the gun started up again blowing more holes through the wall. Bullets whined and pinged off the small two-burner stove across the room.

Gannon suddenly stared at the stove. He quickly crawled over and turned up the two gas burners as high as they would go. More bullets burst in through the shower tile as he speed-crawled low into the bathroom. He grabbed toilet paper rolls from under the sink and some towels and crawled back out.

The paper wrapper on the rolls caught immediately as he threw all of it up onto the clicking blue-flame stove burners. Then one of the towels began to burn.

The hotel fire alarm that went off a split second later was unspeakably deafening. There were two earsplitting blasts of what sounded like a circus clown slide whistle and then a recording began shouting.

"THE SOURCE OF THE ALARM SIGNAL YOU ARE HEARING IS NOW BEING INVESTIGATED. THE SOURCE OF THE ALARM SIGNAL YOU ARE HEARING IS NOW BEING INVESTIGATED."

As the siren blast whooped twice again, Gannon glanced over and saw that all of the towels were burning now. He crawled over and grabbed one and opened the door into the bedroom. Keeping low, he thrust the burning towel under the edge of the bedspread and set it alight. It caught up immediately in a horrid chemical stink, and there was immediate thick black smoke. He threw another burning towel onto the desk.

When the bed was going pretty good, he peeked out around the burning bottom of it. The entire end of the room by the shattered window was covered in smoke, and the wall behind the desk was catching fire.

Gannon got to his knees, coughing, and grabbed the metal frame of the bed and hurled the whole burning mess of it up and at the window. Then he reached into the sitting room and grabbed the young woman by the hand.

He thought he was certainly going to get shot in the back as they leaped over the murdered reporter a split second later.

But the bullets didn't come, and Gannon got the front door flung open, and they were out in the hallway with the black smoke chasing behind them.

51

They ran down the hall in the terrifying alarm squeal. Very confused-looking people were standing in some of the doorways of the other rooms.

"What the hell is going on?" said one of them, an old hairy guy in a bathrobe.

"The hotel's on fire! Run!" Gannon yelled as he dodged past him around a corner.

On the other side of it was a pretty thirtysomething woman standing beside the stairwell doorway.

In midstride, Gannon registered three things about her almost simultaneously.

She had fear in her face. There was a phone in one of her hands and a semiautomatic pistol in the other.

Gannon didn't break stride as he let go of the navy lieutenant's hand. Instead, he tucked down his shoulder and hit the armed woman a lick at the upper chest that leveled her off her feet and sent both of them into the stairwell and down the stairs.

Gannon rode the woman down the stairs like a toboggan and landed his two-twenty hard on top of her at the bottom of the half-flight floor. As he got up, he could see that the nice-looking honey blond–haired woman wasn't holding anything now and her face was showing pure shock. She was gasping and staring at where one of her broken left forearm bones was sticking up between her elbow and wrist, almost through the skin.

Gannon saw her phone there on the concrete beside her, and he stomped it with his new construction boot in a shatter of plastic and then lifted her fallen gun.

It was a Smith & Wesson stainless-steel .45, the single-stack stippled beavertail grip small in his big hand. He racked the slide and saw that there wasn't even a round in the chamber. Gannon checked the eight-round magazine with a click and put one in the pipe with another. Then he cocked the bobbed hammer all the way back with his calloused thumb as he tucked it into his waistband.

He went back up the stairs into the corridor. For a split second, he gave serious thought to returning to the burning hotel room and killing the son of a bitch in the window who'd murdered Wheldon. Instead, he grabbed the navy lieutenant's hand again and brought her down past the fallen woman.

The alarm was still clown whistling, and there was a pandemonium of people in the lobby when they arrived downstairs two and a half minutes later. Without looking at anyone, Gannon led them behind the empty check-in desk into the back. There were some desks and cubicles there and an emergency fire door in the corner with a push bar that Gannon immediately kicked open.

The eggbeater churning of the low-hovering helicopter above

them was incredibly loud as they came out into the garbage alley on the east side of the building.

Then Gannon pushed through another gate, and they were out on 31st Street in the cold air, heading east down the sidewalk toward Sixth Avenue, running as fast as they could.

52

Reyland, in the fusion center, stood before the war room screen in a frozen rictus of wide-eyed baffled rage. On the screen above, smoke was pouring into what looked like a stairwell as a voice repeated, "The source of the alarm signal you are hearing is now being investigated. The source of the alarm signal you are hearing is now being investigated."

"Emerson, you said we had a team on the floor."

"We did," Emerson said, typing into one phone as he cradled another with his shoulder and chin, "but they split up to cover both sides."

"Who's down?"

"Sanderson."

"You put a rookie there on this!" Reyland yelled.

"No, you did, Reyland," Emerson said, glaring at him. "I told you she wasn't ready for our New York team, but she's your buddy the senator's niece!"

Reyland stood there infuriated. He looked back up at the screen. You could hear feet running somewhere in the distance, the sound of pounding.

"Fire! Fire! Fire!" someone yelled as an unseen door boomed open and closed followed by the bedeviled clown whistle again.

"Which one of you assholes did it?" Reyland yelled into the comm link on the desk speakerphone.

"What was that?" Ruiz yelled over the rotor thump.

"Who set the hotel on fire? Did I tell you to burn the place down?"

"It wasn't us. It was the target," Ruiz said over the rotor roar.

"Wheldon?"

"No, he's down," Ruiz said. "The other one. The guy. He lit the room up after we popped Wheldon. Then he dipped with the girl."

"What guy? There's a guy? Who?" Reyland screamed. "Where's the girl? Where's Everett?"

"She's with the guy who set the room on fire. They made it out onto 31st heading east."

"Arietta, what the hell is that drone for? Get me eyes on that street!"

"On it, on it," Arietta said.

The screen changed to show the intersection of 31st Street and Sixth Avenue. A man and a woman were rounding the corner turning left, running north up the west-side sidewalk of Sixth Avenue.

The camera zoomed in.

The woman had brown hair.

"Ruiz, get that bird over Sixth Avenue. We see them. They're heading north toward 32nd."

They watched as the couple ran diagonally through the intersection on 32nd Street into a little park.

Reyland slapped a palm down on a desk as they suddenly disappeared under some leafless trees.

"Where the hell did they go?"

"Shit," said Emerson, now standing by a laptop. "They went down some subway stairs into a station."

"No, wait. 32nd and Sixth. That's not the subway. That's the PATH train entrance, isn't it? The Jersey train?" Arietta said.

Emerson clicked at the keyboard.

"Double shit. It's both. There's a corridor that leads to the PATH train and another one a block long that leads to the subway."

"Where the hell is our team from the hotel? Get them over there!" Reyland yelled.

"Wait, wait. No, this is a good thing. We have this… I'm patching in… We have a link to the MTA CCTV system," Arietta said.

The big screen changed to show a tremendous grid of cameras, and Arietta brought up a screen of a platform with the commuter PATH train.

"I don't see them," he said.

"Gee, Arietta, I guess they're not headed out to the Jersey Shore in January. Go figure," Reyland said.

"It's them! Look! Number 23. I just saw them," Emerson said, pointing. "What's that? The corridor. Where's that?"

"It's the two-block underground corridor that runs toward the subway station at Macy's Herald Square," Arietta said.

"Get our team down into the subway station at 34th and Sixth now," Reyland said into the comm link.

"No, no! Tell them to stay on the road," Arietta said, watching the screen where now the man and woman were running past homeless people down a wide gray corridor.

As they disappeared out of the frame, he brought up the next camera and picked them up again.

"We have eyes on them now. They have cameras throughout the entire system. If they get on a train, we'll see them. The teams can follow from the surface."

Reyland rubbed at his chin as they followed the targets across the grid of screens. At the entrance of the subway, they watched as the man paid for a metro card at a machine.

They got a closer look at him for the first time. A stocky white guy, close-cropped sandy hair, about six foot or so, around forty but lean-faced and fit.

Reyland looked at the shoulders on him. Reyland had played Division One college ball, second-string left tackle at Notre Dame, and he thought the guy looked like a running back, a tough, sneaky white boy faster than he looked.

"Arietta, hit this fool with the facial recognition," he said.

A red square appeared around the man's profile. Reyland took in his lean face, his blue-gray eyes. His goatee was the color of the Carhartt jacket he was wearing. *Is he a hick or something? The reporter's friend?*

They waited. After a minute, the square turned purple.

"What happened? Where's his license?" Reyland said.

"Purple means the computer can't find it. Or he's not in the DMV system."

"It just works for the New York DMV system?"

"No, we're tapped into all of them. It's a national database."

"What do you mean? He doesn't have a frickin' driver's license?"

"Maybe he's not American? Or it could be a glitch. Like I said, we're still in the first stages of this thing."

"Is he using a credit card?" Reyland said.

"No, it was cash," Emerson said as the stocky guy swiped himself and the woman through the turnstile.

They watched them go down some steps to a platform. A train pulled in.

"Okay, Ruiz. Coordinate with the other teams," Emerson

called over the comm link. "They're getting on an uptown F. Next stop is 42nd. Bryant Park."

"Is there a camera on the train, too?" Reyland said.

"No," Arietta said, "but there's one in every station. We just need to keep tracking them. As soon as they get off, we'll be waiting."

53

Gannon got off the F train at 59th and Lex with the woman, and they went through the crowded station and down some dirty stairs to another platform and got a connecting uptown 4 train that had just pulled alongside the platform.

As they sat in the half-filled car, he took his first good look at the attractive young navy lieutenant. He saw there was a dazed, stalled-out look in her light brown eyes. She seemed to still be in a state of shock, but at least she was letting him lead her.

"Hey, how you doing?" Gannon said.

She blinked at him and took a breath and started coughing.

He patted her on the back.

"It's just the smoke. I know this is crazy, but stay with me. We're going to get through this. I promise. My name is Mike. What's yours?"

She looked up at him wide-eyed.

"Hey, come on. It's okay. Just talk to me. What's your name?" he said again.

"Ruby," she said, finally looking at him. "I'm Ruby."

He took her hand again and stood with her as the train screamed into the East 68th Street–Hunter College Station.

"Okay, Ruby," he said to her as they came out of the rattling doors. "Stay close. I know a place we'll be safe."

Up the stairs on Lexington the street was filled with moving cars and buses and there was a bunch of people milling around in front of one of the Hunter College buildings beside the subway.

They were stepping onto 68th Street's southeast corner's curb when the speeding SUV came at them out of the traffic on Lexington in a mad-dash diagonal. It was a black Cadillac Escalade with midnight tinted windows and there was a roar of horns as it jumped the curb twenty yards ahead of them and shrieked to a rubber-smoking skidding stop.

Gannon had just registered that its rear left passenger door was already open, when a slim man wearing black tactical clothes and a black balaclava popped out of it. Gannon watched as the man did a graceful crow hop onto the sidewalk and turned directly toward them, hunched over something in his hands.

It was a bullpup submachine gun, and as he leveled up with it to his shoulder to kill them, Gannon, already squared to target with the stainless-steel .45 up to his dominant right eye, shot him twice through the bridge of his nose just below his tactical goggles.

Gannon, moving at the waist to keep his center of mass, put two more in the driver's door glass and two more through the rear windshield.

The slim man Gannon had killed was down against the left rear tire when he closed the distance between them. Gannon dropped the .45 and snatched up his fallen snub-nosed machine gun by its smooth doughnut hole–like grip.

It sounded like a box of dynamite was going off in Gannon's

face as he crouched and fired the unsilenced machine gun full auto into the car. Casings pinged off the inside of the open back door as he raked it back and forth and back and forth.

In the spray of the bullets, he killed the already-wounded driver with a head shot and hit the balaclava-wearing passenger beside him with another.

The last of the balaclava-wearing men was in the back seat. His left hand held a semiauto while his right scrambled at the door latch beside him like a falling man at the edge of a cliff.

He lifted the pistol as he turned.

Gannon put a point-blank burst into the side of his head.

In the ringing silence, Gannon raised the rifle to his right and to his left toward the sidewalk and street. He peeked behind him quickly over each shoulder, checking his spots.

There was a wind chime sound as he dropped the emptied rifle into the gutter on top of the pile of spent brass.

He turned to see Ruby standing there in frozen shock. He took her hand again without speaking and led her back the way they had come. Most in the pedestrian crowd around had also frozen up, but cars and buses were flowing by on Lexington as if nothing had happened.

As they walked away, Gannon turned and saw the second man he had shot haltingly get out of the driver's seat. The whole front of him from head to crotch was completely splattered in blood. As Gannon watched, he sat down on the sidewalk casually with his hands behind him and his head tilted back. Like Lexington was a beach, and he suddenly wanted to catch some rays.

They made the corner of 68th and turned east. The only sound Gannon could hear in his ringing deafened ears was the thump of his heart. Everything felt numb and dull. Like he was underwater. They walked toward Third Avenue slowly. The woman's mouth moved. He tugged at her, nodding.

"Slowly," he said.

It was hard to talk because he could only barely hear himself.

"We need to go slowly," he said again.

They made it half the block. He wondered if he should turn around. He decided no. A quarter block left. Twenty feet. Ten.

Then they hit the Third Avenue corner and Gannon pulled Ruby to the right and yelled "Run!" as loud as he could.

They ran. Hand in hand at first, but then Ruby was getting it, running beside him on his left, matching him stride for stride. They made it to 67th and Gannon turned right again, running back up toward Lexington.

"No," he heard Ruby say as she tugged at him.

"It's okay," Gannon said, heading back toward Lexington. "This is the way. The only way. Trust me. It's okay. I promise."

54

A dark blue evacuation of fired-up cops was pouring out of the 19th Precinct when they arrived at it. Without pausing, Gannon maneuvered around them as he tugged at Ruby's hand, leading her straight in up the steps of the old ornate stone building.

In through the front door, a full-figured cop grabbed at Gannon as he was halfway through the worn vestibule. He was a puffy, pale uniformed sergeant with a pockmarked face. Gannon looked at the man's eyes through his thick glasses.

"Jimmy Farina," Gannon said, smiling widely. "You gotta be kidding me."

"Hey, Mickey. Kidding me? What the hell? Is that really you?" the cop said.

"Hey, hon," Gannon said to Ruby. "You know who this is? It's Jimmy Farina, an old boss from my days on the West Side."

Ruby stood wide-eyed and managed a smile.

"What the hell, Mick? You back now?" Farina said.

"Yeah, Sarge. I'm back. Not a moment too soon, it looks like. What the hell's going on here? You need any help? This a fire drill?"

"Yeah, I'll say. It's a shots-fired drill. Only it's not a drill. There just was a shooting at the college around the corner. Somebody with a damn machine gun, they said. I heard it myself there at the desk or I wouldn't even have believed it. Believe this shit? Probably some Columbine deal with these nutjob blue-hair college kids. It's just all-out pandemonium these days. ESU is on the way."

"Crazy, man. Wow. Maybe you should retire, too, huh? Before it's too late. Hey, is my boy Danny up there?" Gannon said, sliding past him.

"Yeah, Stick's up there minding the store," Farina said, looking at Ruby approvingly as Gannon pulled her with him.

"Doing well for yourself, huh, Mickey?" Farina said, giving him an A-OK sign with his fingers. "When you get back?"

"While ago," Gannon lied, hoping his voice didn't sound bizarre. "Been back for a bit."

"We should go out for a Guinness," Farina said.

"If you're buying. I'm a pensioner now, remember?" Gannon said, grinning like a fool.

"Mike? Is that you?" Stick said from his office doorway as Gannon finally got up the stairs and came through the detective room door. "What in the stone-cold hell are you doing here?"

Gannon brought Ruby past the empty cubicles into the office and sat her down on Stick's couch.

"And this is?" Stick said.

"Close the door, Stick," Gannon said, looking down at the floor, his mind racing.

"What?"

"Close the damn door, Stick," Gannon said, looking at him.

"What is it?" Stick said as he closed the door. "Which one

of you smells like a mattress fire? What the hell, Mick? What's going on?"

"We've got a bit of a situation," Gannon said.

55

"He's dead, boss," Ruiz said over the comm link.

"Daly is dead?" Reyland said, standing before the wall screen.

"Yes. And all of his New York squad guys, too. I just got off the bird in Central Park. I'm at the scene."

"Yeah, okay. We see you on the UAV," Reyland said as he scanned the live feed they had over Lexington Avenue.

"Actually, they're working on Janowski," Ruiz continued. "But it's no use. Three-quarters of his skull is gone. This guy blew everybody away. All pop tops, too. He must have had help, right? These men were no weekend warriors, Reyland. I was in Fallujah with Daly. He was one of the best I ever saw. What the hell is this? Did you see it?"

"No. That doesn't matter. Ignore Janowski. You need to find them."

"We have a problem," Arietta called out.

"What?" Reyland said.

"We just got the feed from the 19th Precinct security camera. The guy in the Carhartt went in there five minutes ago. He's in there right now with Everett."

"Whoa, whoa. What? The police precinct?" Reyland said.

"Yes. They're in the 19th Precinct right now," Arietta said. "On one of the upper floors. I'm not sure which one. Only the ground floor has cameras."

"What!" Emerson said. "The precinct? We're done! This guy who grabbed her must be a cop or something. That's it. We're cooked, Reyland. This is… This whole operation is… We're done!"

"Get a hold of yourself, Emerson," Reyland said as he pressed the comm link to Ruiz. "Our targets are around the corner in the 19th Precinct. We need you and your men to go in, Ruiz."

"Go in where?" Ruiz called back.

"The 19th Precinct."

"Go in? They're cops!" Ruiz said. "How can I go in?"

"I don't give a shit. It doesn't matter. Eliminate those targets. That's a direct order. You need to go in there and do it."

"But they're cops. My freaking dad was a cop," Ruiz said.

"You want to go to jail, Tommy?"

"You can't cover this," Ruiz said.

"I can cover anything. You think this is the first time I've done this? When the well is on fire, you have to use dynamite, Tommy. Now go in."

"How will you cover it?"

"That's my lookout. The entire building is empty. You have to go in right now."

"I can't believe this. You're actually crazy."

"Crazy like a fox, Ruiz. Go in. We're all in here, buddy. You, me and every last damn one of us. We're halfway through, and the other side is paradise. Or you might as well shoot yourself. The graveyard or paradise, Tommy. Which one?"

"Double, then. Double our fee. For me and all my men."

"Done. You're a millionaire now. Congrats. Now go in."

"Fine. Give me a second to think," Ruiz said.

"We're out of those, Ruiz. Get in there and kill them."

56

Stick sat at his desk and Ruby sat on the couch, but Gannon kept pacing.

It was blazingly bright and steamy hot in the old government building office, and as he paced, Gannon began to sweat. He wiped at his brow, wondering if he should take his coat off. But he didn't take it off. He didn't know what the hell to do.

As he paced, the police radio in the corner behind Stick's desk gave out a manic triple beep.

"Crowd control issue at location," cried a fired-up cop at the scene.

"Clear the air," said the female Hispanic dispatcher. "Sector units on the way."

There was a radio break and another cop said, "Where are those buses? We got likelies, four of 'em."

Gannon could still smell the cordite on his hands as he bit at a fingernail.

"En route, en route," said the dispatcher. "Less than a block. To clarify, are the shooting victims police? Over."

There was a beep followed by a screech of feedback.

"We're waiting on that, Central," said the cop.

Boy, are we ever, Gannon thought, wiping at his sweating face with his hand.

"They're feds," Stick said grimly as he got off his cell phone. "My guy on scene just pulled their IDs."

Gannon finally sat down on Stick's couch beside Ruby. He bent over and cupped his hands over his face for a moment then sat back, folding his arms.

"FBI?" Gannon said.

"Two were Department of Energy. One was DEA and one was ATF," Stick said with a hushed tone of awe.

Just as he said this, Gannon glanced over at Ruby on the couch as she started to double over with a greenish look on her face.

He lunged and grabbed Stick's wastepaper basket and whisked it under her just as she began to retch. He knelt down beside her, deftly keeping her hair out of the stream of it.

Can you blame her? Gannon thought, shaking his head.

He was feeling pretty damn sick about the situation himself.

"What the hell, Mick? Feds? Four feds? Four dead feds?" Stick said, folding his arms nervously.

"No," Gannon said, turning toward him. "Aren't you listening? They're not feds. Or they're dirty feds. Hell, screw it. I don't give a shit who they work for. These folks, whoever they are, just blew a reporter's fricking head off, an innocent American citizen's head off, back at that hotel.

"They shot the room to pieces, man. It was a miracle we got out. Then they drew down on me on the street not five minutes ago, Stick. No 'freeze.' No 'you're under arrest.' Just up comes an Escalade and out pops an assassin with a machine gun. I don't know about you, but for me, that's a lot of machine guns for one evening!"

Stick stared at him.

"You need to pick up on the theme here!" Gannon said. "These guys are trying to kill us."

"Four dead feds," Stick said quietly, shaking his head.

Gannon looked at him, looked through him, pacing now, trying to think.

How in the hell did they find us so fast? he wondered.

It was impossible. Pure dumb luck. Or had they tracked them on the subway somehow? That must have been it.

They can do that now? he thought. *Surveillance and artificial intelligence is that good now? To track someone in real time through Manhattan?*

Think about that later, Gannon thought. *Now matters. What does it mean for us now?*

He stopped pacing, his hands coming together as he closed his eyes.

It meant they knew they were in here.

He thought about Wheldon. The reporter's brains staining the bad carpet.

He turned and looked at the pebbled-glass office door.

They would come in, he knew.

It didn't matter that it was a precinct. All normal rules had been cast aside. The gates of hell had been unhinged over this.

They would actually come in.

A fire team was what? Four? There would be two of them. Eight!

He let out a breath.

Eight professionals. Eight elites with a whirlybird. Four would come from the top, four from the bottom. And they'd be in between, stuck in the middle to play the shit part in the shit sandwich.

He thought about the back way out, windows, but they could already be on them.

Then he hit on it. Pacing toward the door, he saw it across the bull pen, leaning up in a corner.

Plan C, he thought.

"Okay, listen up. I know what to do," Gannon said, throwing open the door.

57

"Hey, Sarge, these are the other members of my team," Ruiz said to a pudgy NYPD sergeant named Farina as Shepard and the rest of his men showed up in their tactical fatigues and backpacks.

From the corner of his eye, Ruiz watched Farina give Shepard a thumbs-up. He had already shown the cop his fed credentials that said he was a member of the US Marshals Service. He had given him the vague impression that the dead men in the truck were his colleagues and that the shooting might have been related to some fugitives they were in pursuit of.

Ruiz glanced out on the Lexington Avenue sidewalk behind them. There were four NYPD patrol cars and a fire truck around the shot-up SUV like a wagon train.

And more coming, Ruiz thought with a groan as he saw two more radio cars show up.

"You have a description of your perps yet so we can put out a BOLO?" Farina said.

"I'm still waiting to hear back from my boss," Ruiz lied. "Until then, I was wondering if we could set up a staging area inside the precinct house. Like right now, if that's possible."

"You got it. Of course. Follow me," the doughy cop said, guiding them through the lights and cops and lookie-loos already four deep on the sidewalk.

"Is there a back door to the precinct? The damn press is going to be all over this," Ruiz complained as they turned the corner onto 67th.

"No, but there's a garage just to the left of the front door with a rolling door. You can use it to get in and out without being seen. Will that work?" Farina said.

"Sounds perfect. Show me," Ruiz said, quickly picturing the garage from the blueprints of the precinct that Reyland had already sent him.

They walked east down 67th to the sound of the screaming ambulances. Farina led them down a little alley beside the precinct. He opened a call box and pressed a code. Ruiz kept his head down at the overhead camera. The garage door began to roll open silently.

Inside was a dim and tiny exhaust-reeking garage with three personal cars in it and a row of NYPD moped scooters. To the left of the scooters was a pile of garbage bags and an old gun locker with a peeling American flag sticker on it.

"So do I have this right?" Ruiz said, pointing at a door on the right as they walked in. "Through that door is the patrol supervisor's office and beyond that's the muster room? And the back stairs are in the hall beyond that, right?"

"Yeah, you're right. How'd you know?" Farina said.

Ruiz smiled as he raised his right arm up behind Farina as if he was about to give him a pat on the back.

Instead, he pressed his SIG Sauer P226's long squared-off suppressor to the base of Farina's skull and blew the back of his head off.

58

"How are we looking up top?" Ruiz called into the radio as two of his men dragged the cop's body out of sight between the parked cars.

"They're rappelling in as we speak," Reyland said.

"Okay, inserting now," Ruiz said as the four of them went in through the door behind the silenced H&K MP5 submachine guns they'd removed from their bags.

The dimly lit hallway inside was painted cement block. The four men moved down it in a silent flow, leapfrogging each other smoothly and quickly, keeping both ends of the hall covered at all times.

Ruiz hand signaled at a closed beige metal door on the left-hand side of the corridor and two of his men stopped and crouched along the side of it. Ruiz came forward, crouching low with Shepard behind him walking upright, his MP5 up over Ruiz's head covering their twelve o'clock.

Ruiz checked the door's knob. It was unlocked. He opened it.

Inside was an office space, chairs and desks and cubicles. Catty-cornered from the cubicles was another open doorway that he knew led into the muster room, and beyond that was the back stairs up to the second floor.

As Ruiz leaned in behind his SIG to check the corners, a uniformed female Hispanic cop walked in from the muster room doorway with a can of Diet Pepsi to her lips.

Ruiz didn't think she had even had a chance to notice him before Shepard shredded the can and her face with a tight controlled burst.

Ruiz breezed forward over the dead cop's feet, careful of the pool of soda and blood. He poked his head through the muster room doorway. There was a podium, a TV in the corner. A flyer tacked to a bulletin board beside the TV advertised an upcoming blood drive. He scanned the empty tables.

"Clear," he said.

They pressed forward through the empty muster room and pulled open a door in its corner into a back concrete stairwell. There was a low whistle from above and they filed upward and linked up with the top-down team already waiting on the next landing.

"In, in, in," Ruiz said, pulling open the detective room's side door.

Inside was a surprisingly beautiful, high-ceilinged room. Paneled in old dark oak, it seemed formal, like a library. It was filled with cubicles, all empty now. Along the back wall was a row of old-fashioned pebbled-glass–doored offices.

Ruiz hand signaled at the one farthest left.

It was the only one with a light on inside of it.

The commandos hurried in a silent column, going low past the desks. Two men flanked the lit office door as Ruiz and his backup man came forward again.

Ruiz put a couple of pounds of pressure on the short reset trigger of the SIG and turned the knob and pushed open the door.

"Oh, shit," he said, immediately letting off the trigger as he saw the bricks and rubble and dust on the carpet.

In the left-hand wall of the office, there was a hole. It was three feet high and three feet wide, and from it poured in cold air and the sound of loud sirens.

Before the hole on the dusty carpet were a couple of sledgehammers. Ruiz lifted one. *NYPD Anti-Crime* was written on the yellow handle in Sharpie.

Ruiz crouched and clicked on the flashlight on the bottom of his SIG's barrel and turkey peeked his head and shoulders out of the hole. He looked left and right. The hole led out onto a one person–wide breezeway that separated the precinct from its neighboring building to the west. The thin alley at its bottom was blocked off on the 67th Street side, but the other end of it led north into what looked like a backyard for the adjoining building.

"Bad news, boss," Ruiz said into the radio after he crawled back inside.

Shepard helped him easily up to his feet.

"They freaking mouse-holed us," he said.

"What?" Reyland said.

"They busted a hole in the outside wall of the building on the second floor. They went out of the building into an alley to the west. It looks like it might lead out onto Lexington."

"What are you waiting for? After them, Ruiz. We can still get these bastards," Reyland said.

"They've got eight, ten minutes on us," Ruiz said, looking at his watch. "It ain't gonna happen, Reyland. We lost this round. They're gone."

PART THREE

IT'S DEADER IN THE BAHAMAS

59

Around five in the morning, after their second truck stop somewhere in northern Virginia, it started snowing heavily.

Wired tight on panic and bad gas station coffee, Gannon, at the wheel, cracked the window and clicked the seat up straighter.

The very last thing they needed at this time, he thought, blinking in the cold bracing air, was to spin out or to hit something or to get stuck.

They'd left New York at a little after midnight over the Goethals Bridge in a Subaru Baja crossover pickup truck they borrowed from Stick's cousin out in Staten Island. They stayed on 278 until it ended in Elizabeth then drove backstreets through there and Plainfield until they got onto 78 West.

An hour later, they crossed the Jersey state line into Pennsylvania. Then just before they reached Allentown, religiously following the speed limit, they swung south on I-81.

He looked at Stick sleeping in the back. He felt terrible dragging him into this. *But what a friend, huh?* he thought, smiling, as he heard the big galoot start to snore.

He'd shown up at his office with the minions of hell at his back and his old crazy partner hadn't batted an eyelash, had he? Not only that, five seconds later he was actually swinging a sledgehammer, helping Gannon bust a hole through his own office wall.

Gannon's smile left as he blinked out at the rushing highway. He couldn't stop thinking about the four men he had killed in the Cadillac. He thought about their wives, their kids. The phone ringing to tell them Daddy wasn't coming home.

The men had probably been decent fellas, decent cops. The jackasses behind all this corruption had probably said he was a terrorist or something, lied to them.

Then he thought about Wheldon blown across the hotel carpet.

He wasn't going home either, was he? he thought. *What about his wife? What about his kids?*

What an unholy mess, he thought.

"Hey," Ruby said, suddenly sitting up in the passenger seat.

"Hey," Gannon said.

He turned the bad wipers up higher and glanced over at her. She seemed different now. Normal. Calm and alert.

Incredible what just a few hours of not being shot at could do for one's general health and demeanor, Gannon thought.

"You okay?" she said.

"Me?" Gannon said. "Never better. I thought at first that this government-trying-to-gun-you-down stuff wasn't really my cup of tea, but now I have to say, it's really getting my blood pumping."

"You, too, huh?" Ruby said with a small smile. "Even so, you look beat. Let me drive."

"No, I'm fine," Gannon said.

"C'mon. You need some sleep," she said.

"So do you," Gannon said. "I got this shift."

"No, for real, Mike. I've slept. It's your turn. Pull over, and we'll switch."

Gannon smiled at her.

"You're pretty stubborn, huh, Lieutenant. Are those navy orders?" he said.

"Yes," she said after a yawn. "Navy orders."

"In that case," Gannon said with a yawn of his own, "aye, aye, Captain. Next exit, I'll pull off, and we'll switch."

60

The snow was starting to turn to rain when Ruby got off the highway. It was just before the Tennessee border, and they took back roads west into hilly southern Kentucky, following the instructions Stick had typed into the Garmin GPS on the dash.

It was still raining at around noon when they finally found the address down a rolling hill in the middle of a tree-filled no-where. Ruby pulled over onto the shoulder before an old rusty mailbox. Gannon turned and shook Stick's leg in the back seat.

"Hey? This it?"

Stick blinked and looked around.

"This is it," he said with a yawn.

"And your uncle won't be home. You're sure?"

"Positive," Stick said. "The lucky son of a gun owns several beer distributors along the Jersey Shore. He's got hunting cabins all over the country."

"Any chance he'll be here?"

"No," Stick said. "He leaves for his elk-hunting place in northern Arizona day after Christmas."

"Okay. Here goes nothing," Ruby said as she pulled off the old road onto a muddy driveway.

The steep slope of the drive leveled off, and then about another half football field in off the road was a double-wide trailer beside a barn the color of driftwood.

Best thing Gannon could say about it straight off was that there wasn't another neighbor in sight.

Ruby parked behind the trailer, and they sat listening for a moment to the rain drumming atop the car.

"Looks deserted. Good," Ruby said, finally killing the engine.

The trailer was actually all right. It was furnished with Ikea stuff and had a pellet stove that warmed up the space quickly. Stick turned on the water and the propane tank beside the house that powered the water heater and the stove.

Gannon peeked out the living room blind as Ruby went into the back bedroom to take the first shower. There was an empty field across the narrow road, and in the distance stood a sole old leafless oak tree that was dark and ominous against the gray of the rainy sky.

Staring at it, Gannon tried to gauge his thoughts and feelings about all that had just transpired. What it meant. How he felt. What to do about any of it.

He stopped after half a minute. He'd have to try again later.

He blew on his cupped hands and rubbed them together and stamped his feet.

The only thing he could think about was how much he missed his son.

61

"What do you hunt down here?" he said to Stick, who was turning on the TV.

"Quail and turkey," Stick said, turning up the volume. "What in the—"

Gannon walked over. On the news channel, there was a helicopter shot of the black Cadillac Escalade he'd shot up, now sitting sideways on the Lexington Avenue sidewalk. It looked like the carcass of a large dead animal that had been brought down. There were half a dozen cop cars around it. A fire truck. Gannon felt like he was going to be sick.

FOUR FEDERAL OFFICERS GUNNED DOWN, it said on the screen crawl beneath.

"And in further developments," said some male talking head, "to those of you just tuning in, as if the shooting of four federal officers wasn't shocking enough, we have just learned that three officers of the nearby 19th Precinct, Sergeant James Farina,

Sergeant Carla Diaz and Detective Daniel Henrickson, seem to have gone missing during the shooting."

"What?" Stick cried.

"Investigators are looking into it, but there are some still unconfirmed rumors that the police department coworkers used the emergency to ransack the precinct's evidence locker of a drug cache and have fled to places unknown."

Stick started actually laughing.

"Me and Diaz and Farina just became the Jesse James gang or something?" he said, wide-eyed. "That's what they're trying to sell?"

"They're both dead, Stick," Gannon said.

Stick turned to him wordlessly.

"They shot them when they came in to get us, and then they took the bodies with them," Gannon said. "You can't think of these guys as just bad cops, Stick. This was a military operation with highly trained soldiers and helicopters. This was straight-up covert urban guerrilla warfare."

Stick was silent for a moment.

"We're like Fallujah now, Mick? Or Somalia? Except instead of crazy warlords, the FBI is gunning after the NYPD?"

"No, it's not the entire FBI. Just a rogue group within it. Hell, the guys I shot might not even be Americans. They've got multinational mercenary contracting companies now."

"Government special forces murder American citizens now," Stick said, nodding, absorbing this new reality. "Reporters and even cops. Then the press spins it. These damn feds. Top secret, my ass. Makes sense now why I quit the JTTF. Politicians and all that corporate cocktail party news network anchor reporter bullshit. Money, money, money. Pack of pencil-neck jackasses. I knew something wasn't right."

Gannon went into the kitchen. There was some instant pancake mix in a cupboard, and he poured it into a plastic mixing bowl with some water. He began beating it with a big fork he found in a drawer.

"This is some pretty unacceptable shit, Mick," Stick said, following him into the kitchen. "Farina was kind of a jerk, but he was our brother, man. And the Spanish kid had just started. I'm not sitting still for them getting whacked. I need to…I need to call people."

Gannon looked at his friend.

"No, Stick," Gannon said, shaking his head slowly. "They know from the precinct video they scrubbed that we were in your office, that you helped us and left with us. Your house phone, your cell phone, all of it is tapped now. You try to contact someone, hell, you put your battery back into your phone, they'll be here in an hour."

"What the hell are we supposed to do, then?"

"Nothing," Gannon said.

"Nothing?" said Stick.

"Not yet. We rest up for a while. Stay hunkered down. They'll be looking for a moving target," Gannon said.

62

When Reyland woke up at his house, it was eight in the evening. He went down into the empty kitchen and put on some coffee. A note on the granite kitchen island said that everybody was at Sadie's clarinet performance. His knuckles cracked as he balled the paper into his fist.

Two hours later, he had his driver let him off at the Hoover Building's 10th Street side.

"Evening, Deputy Assistant, or is it Director now?" Harry Naylor, the most veteran of the FBI security cops on the night shift, said quietly as he came into the lobby.

Reyland stopped and looked down at the mustached veteran's poker face. Like everyone else there at the puzzle palace that was FBI HQ, even the damn security guards were coy and cryptic masters of innuendo and rumor.

"When I become director, first order will be purging the

deadwood," Reyland said coldly as he passed the desk. "So believe me, Naylor, you'll be among the very first to know."

Off the elevator on seven, instead of making a left down the long corridor toward his office, Reyland immediately made a right.

He came around a deserted corner and key fobbed himself in through an unmarked gray door.

Five feet from the hall door inside stood a white steel box that almost looked like a small shipping container. There were thick beige-colored electronic cabinets attached to the front of it, and to the right of the cabinets was a small shiny silver metallic door.

The antiseptic white walls and fluorescent light inside the box gave it a look of a doctor's examination room. In its center was a rolling office chair surrounded by three computer terminals and two huge black flat screens.

The room inside a room was called a SCIF, short for Sensitive Compartmented Information Facility. Sound-baffled with electromagnetically sealed steel plate walls, it thwarted even the most sophisticated remote electronic eavesdropping methods.

He wouldn't have come in to the office at all except that he wanted to return a call from London. Technically, it had been a text message. One with three long-awaited, very intriguing words.

Very Good News, it said.

He closed the door and typed the required coding into one of the terminals. The closest of the two screens blinked on a moment later, and a short sixtysomething woman with overdone glamour-puss makeup and big owl-like spectacles was staring at him.

"Well, you're looking cheery, Robert," the woman said.

The woman's name was Brooke Wrenhall, and she was his contact at MI6. He had worked with Wrenhall several times over the last fifteen years and liked the feisty, extremely sharp, bitchy Brit.

"It's this wonderful lighting," Reyland said.

"Long day?" she said.

"Long career," Reyland said. "Just trying to keep it going. Getting harder and harder these days."

"Well, hopefully my tidings will help on that front."

"News?"

"The doctor picked up our package."

Reyland fell back into the office chair as if he'd been shot.

"No!" he yelled.

"Would I lie to you, Robert?" Brooke said, smiling.

"When did this happen?"

"Six hours ago."

"And everything is in there?"

"Yes," she said. "All of it. He took it back to his apartment. He stared at it for quite some time. There was some crying. When he put it away, he hid it in his closet in an old suitcase."

"So the wife doesn't know?" Reyland said, pumped.

"Presumably."

"That is very good news. He's committed. He's really going to do it."

"It certainly looks like it."

Reyland found himself suddenly smiling.

"So we're still on."

"Yes. Full speed ahead. We seem to have him on the hook now. Congratulations. I knew you'd be pleased. How long have you been planning this? A year?"

"And a half," Reyland said.

Reyland, still smiling, shook his head at the white walls as he pondered the ways of fickle fortune. Even after everything. Even after the disaster with the plane and Dunning's death, the last phase of the operation had just clicked into place.

They could still pull it off, Reyland thought. They really, really could. They just had to seal up everything.

"Okay. Very good. But don't pop the champagne yet, Brooke."

MICHAEL LEDWIDGE

"I know full well. We still have what? Six days?"

"Yes. We just need to keep everything under wraps for six more damn days," Reyland said.

"How's things on your end with the crash management?" Brooke said.

Reyland looked at her. She obviously hadn't looked at the news in a while.

"Still not one hundred percent, but we're getting a cover on it."

"I thought you said you had eyes on the issue," Brooke said, raising an eyebrow.

"We did but…"

Reyland thought of Mr. X factor, the way he took out his contractors. The fact that they had completely lost the trail on him and Everett.

"But what?" Brooke said.

"Don't worry about it, Brooke. Don't spoil my good mood. We'll sew everything up on this end. Especially now that the good doctor has shown his fresh new commitment to the cause."

"Shall I give word to our special friends of the latest happy developments?" Brooke said.

"No," Reyland said as he glanced at the text on his encrypted phone. "Please allow me, Brooke. I'm actually meeting with them in the morning."

63

Gannon didn't know what time it was when something woke him.

He was in the trailer's living room on an air mattress they'd found, and it squeaked as he sat up in the complete darkness.

"What is it?" Stick said from the couch.

"I don't know," Gannon said, standing.

He crossed past the kitchen into the hall. He knocked on the back bedroom door and waited a moment then opened it and turned on the light.

The bed was empty. The pillows and blanket were gone. He crossed past the bed and checked the bathroom. Ruby wasn't there either.

"What's up?" Stick said as he came back out into the hall.

"She's gone."

"Gone?"

Gannon lifted Stick's Glock off the kitchen table as he pushed out the door.

He'd been sleeping in his clothes, and he stepped down the stairs in his boots into the yard.

He scanned the cold, open, dark outside and glanced over at the truck. She wasn't in the cab. It was dead silent. There were no cars on the distant road. No lights anywhere.

"Please," he said.

He was quickly crossing the yard for the barn in the starlight when Ruby stood up from where she'd been sitting in the bed of the pickup.

"Oh, hey," she said.

"What the hell? Are you okay?" Gannon said, rushing over.

"I'm sorry. I'm fine. I didn't mean to wake you."

"What are you, um, doing?" Gannon said, slipping the Glock into his coat pocket as he arrived. He could see she was fully dressed in her hoodie and boots and had brought out her blanket and pillows.

"I woke up to get a glass of water, and I saw all the stars, so I came out to take a look."

"The stars?"

"Yeah," she said, smiling. "See for yourself. They're really incredible here."

The screen door creaked.

"Mike, what's up?" Stick called over.

"I'm sorry," Ruby said. "Now I've woken everybody up."

"Nothing. It's fine. False alarm," Gannon called back. "Ruby was just getting something from the truck. It's all good."

"I can go back to sleep?" Stick called.

"Yep," Gannon called back.

The screen door creaked again.

"I'm sorry," Ruby said again.

"Nothing to be sorry about. We were just a little worried for a second. So you're into astronomy, huh?"

Ruby nodded, looking up at the sky.

"From my father. He was a high school science teacher, but space was his passion. Every summer we'd camp at stargazing places all over Ohio. My little sister about died with boredom, but I actually started to get into it. It's all about getting away from light pollution from cities and highways. There's hardly any here. It's pretty perfect."

Gannon looked up at her, at the light in her eyes as she gazed up.

"Don't you need a telescope?" he said, watching her.

"Actually, no. I mean, it's good to have one, but you don't need one. To me, it's more exciting with the naked eye. More, I don't know, old-school."

She looked at him, almost blushing.

"I know what you must be thinking. 'The whole world is after us, and she's out gazing at the night sky. This chick has lost her marbles.'"

"If anyone has lost their marbles, it's me," Gannon said as he helped her down out of the truck bed. "I got myself into this by taking that money. What did you do? Just your job?"

"Not even," Ruby said as they walked in the cold. "They wouldn't even let me near the plane."

"Exactly," Gannon said. "You're on the run for the seditious crime of wanting to do your job."

Gannon looked up at the sky.

"You ever see them from way out in the ocean?" he said.

Ruby shook her head.

"Come on. You were in the navy, weren't you?"

"They started me in the Office of Naval Safety straightaway. I've never been assigned to a ship."

Gannon looked up.

"This is nothing," he said. "You should see them thirty, forty miles out in the Atlantic off Eleuthera."

"Yeah?"

Gannon nodded.

"It's like outer space. Tell you what. If you ever get down to the islands, I'll take you out. I'll teach you how to swordfish. You can give me an astronomy lesson."

He held the screen door for her.

"Are you putting me on?" she said.

"No," Gannon said. "I'm serious. Once we get this garbage sorted out, we'll go out on my boat. We'll have ourselves a whistle-blowers' night cruise."

Gannon watched Ruby's face brighten for a moment as she thought about it. Then her expression collapsed.

"You mean *if* we get this sorted out," she said quietly as they stepped out of the cold back into the warmth of the trailer.

64

It had started snowing when Reyland left the house at 10:00 a.m. that morning, and by the time he made it to Annapolis and finally pulled to a stop before Griffin Island's one-car bridge, a square of snow fell in one piece from the gatehouse's sliding window.

He gave his name to the guard. Then he looked over the water at the snow falling gently onto the misty trees.

He had grown up a navy brat in Annapolis nearby and always thought Griffin was more like a resort or a private country club with its own zip code than an actual town. Most of its small body of land was taken up by its world-renowned golf course, for one thing, and there were exactly zero businesses or stores. Even the island's narrow roads were like golf cart paths, and in the summer, there were more golf carts in the circular driveways of the mansions than cars.

When the booth's stick went up, he drove to the other side

of the causeway and made a left into a zillion-dollar neighbor-hood they called Cherry Hill Forest. Down on the other side of it was the island's East Shoreline Road, and he sat for a moment at the stop sign.

Across the road was the island's famous country-club boat-house and there was a huge peace sign lit up with Christmas lights hanging upon its clapboard side. In the pale yellow glow beneath it was a Crayola box–colored row of flipped-over canoes peeking out of the snow.

Reyland often fantasized about buying a Griffin Island bay-side vacation villa one day, and as he sat there, he closed his eyes, imagining it was summer. Breathing deeply, he thought of him and Danielle and the kids walking a canoe across the boathouse dock in life jackets as their goofball hound dog, Charlie, barked excitedly, trying to catch up.

He thought of three hundred–yard drives pin straight down the fairway, martinis at sunset, cookouts with fireworks. Tow-headed toddlers collecting fireflies in mason jars. In his mind, he saw himself at exclusive parties where all the wives were blonde and thin and pretty, and all the men were lean and tan and wore dinner jackets with Bermuda shorts.

After a few more deep breaths, he opened his eyes and looked at himself in the rearview mirror.

"Now go and get your future back, you son of a bitch," he said as he put the Audi back in Drive.

The driveway that Reyland pulled into two minutes later was the only one on the shore road with wrought iron perimeter fencing and a solid gate. There must have been a hidden camera somewhere because the gate opened inward as he slowed for the call box.

The gatehouse he'd been told to park at was a whimsical fieldstone-and-glass castle-like building with a pointy Roman-esque roof. Up the stairs on the cold, windy porch stood two large hard-faced security men in black overcoats who asked for his cell phone. There was another security team inside on the first floor who wanded him before he was guided to the stairs.

Up on the dimly lit second floor, it looked like an arcade at an amusement park. There were pool tables and poker tables and a foosball machine and a pop-a-shot basketball court. There was even one of those dance machine games with the floor squares that lit up.

Beyond it were the men he was there to explain himself to.

They didn't seem like they were in the mood for any boogying, Reyland thought, taking a deep breath as he stepped over.

65

By the huge water-view window, the three old men sat side by side silently at a poker table.

The man on the left side was wiry and buzz-cut and pointy chinned and had a professorial air about him. The one farthest right was quite fat and had tortoiseshell eyeglasses.

In between them, the eclectic owner of the bayside estate gave Reyland a pleasant nod, which Reyland immediately returned.

He was small and handsome and blue-eyed and had backward-swept steel gray hair and baby-soft skin so pale and white it looked powdered.

That the pointy-chinned man and the fat man were midlist Forbes 500 billionaires would have been quite impressive had it not been for the striking ghostly blue-eyed man sitting between them.

He was from one of those old European banking families

whose whispered-about wealth was so vast and unfathomable, it never showed up on any lists at all.

Without prompting, Reyland stood up as straight as his six-foot-six height would allow and delivered his full report to them. He left out nothing. He didn't try to minimize his role.

When he was done, there was no yelling or outrage from the three highly intelligent worldly men sitting at the table. What mattered blame at this point?

Reyland stood calmly in the silence, waiting for their reply. Like a baseball manager who had put in his best pitcher yet still lost the World Series, he stood by the logic of his decisions. Given another chance, he would have done it exactly the same again.

The fat man spoke first, and when he did, his Texan's voice was unexpectedly deep and gruff and buzzy with what linguists call vocal fry. It could have been the voice of a drill sergeant who smoked three packs a day.

"And is there any trace of them now?" he said.

Reyland was about to tell him the difficulty of the task, to tell him how many analysts they had at this moment sitting in front of computer screens, devising new algorithms and looking for anomalies and clusters in the data mine.

He was going to tell him how thorough a proctology exam they were giving to the life of Ruby Everett and the mysterious, now-missing NYPD detective Daniel Henrickson. How several of his staff would literally be living at the office until they were found.

Instead he said simply, "No."

The old men pondered that some more.

The pointy-chinned man spoke next with an East Coast lockjaw voice that was high and almost effeminate.

"Damage control aside for the moment. What is your recommendation for moving forward on Director Dunning's initial mission?" he said.

"Glad you asked me that, sir. London is a green light. I just got off the phone last night. Despite everything, we're still looking very good. Our asset is ready to operate as scheduled."

"So it's just a matter of discretion, then," the ghostly white blue-eyed man beside him said with a pleased surprise.

"Yes, sir," Reyland said. "We just need to keep it all under wraps for five more days."

The old man looked down at the table, his striking eyes half-hooded. There was a strangely amused look on his face, like he was about to tell the punch line of a funny joke. Reyland watched him. This mysterious man who collected CEOs and senators and Congress people like baseball cards.

When he suddenly smiled, it was like the whole dim room lit up. He flashed deep dimples, and his soft multibillion-dollar Dodger-blue eyes twinkled like the lights on the Chesapeake Bay Bridge out the window behind him.

"Then by all means I think you should continue, Robert," he said with his plum-in-the-mouth British accent. "Plug this potential leak. We'll handle the media. You leave that to us."

"Still with no parameters, correct?" Reyland said, staring at this famous secretive man who many said had economically devoured his first country, a small South American one, before he was thirty.

"Correct," the blue-eyed man said.

"With all available resources at my command?" Reyland said.

The elegant old man's amused, ever-playful smile didn't waver one iota.

"By any and all means necessary, Robert," he said with a slow wink. "How could we have it any other way?"

"Glad you asked me that, sir. London is a green light. I just got off the phone last night. Despite everything, we're still looking very good. Our asset is ready to operate as scheduled."

"So it's just a matter of discretion, then," the ghostly white blue-eyed man beside him said with a pleased surprise.

"Yes, sir," Reyland said. "We just need to keep it all under wraps for five more days."

The old man looked down at the table, his striking eyes half-hooded. There was a strangely amused look on his face, like he was about to tell the punch line of a funny joke. Reyland watched him. This mysterious man who collected CEOs and senators and Congress people like baseball cards.

When he suddenly smiled, it was like the whole dim room lit up. He flashed deep dimples, and his soft multibillion-dollar Dodger-blue eyes twinkled like the lights on the Chesapeake Bay Bridge out the window behind him.

"Then by all means I think you should continue, Robert," he said with his plum-in-the-mouth British accent. "Plug this potential leak. We'll handle the media. You leave that to us."

"Still with no parameters, correct?" Reyland said, staring at this famous secretive man who many said had economically devoured his first country, a small South American one, before he was thirty.

"Correct," the blue-eyed man said.

"With all available resources at my command?" Reyland said.

The elegant old man's amused, ever-playful smile didn't waver one iota.

"By any and all means necessary, Robert," he said with a slow wink. "How could we have it any other way?"

66

Happy to have the situation somewhat stabilized and still have his head attached to his shoulders, Reyland was turning from the table when the infinitely rich old blue-eyed Brit stood.

"Robert, wait. I'll walk you out," he said.

Oh, boy, Reyland thought. An audience with His Serene Eminence. *What now?* he thought as the rich man stepped over.

The old man put his arms behind his back in a formal, almost military posture as they walked slowly alongside the arcade games.

"Tell me, who is your contact on the London end? That Watkins fellow?" he said.

"No, Wrenhall," Reyland said. "Brooke Wrenhall."

"Ah, yes. Ms. Wrenhall. She is quite good. Sharp. Yes. Quite sharp. Her father worked for me once years ago. Or was it her grandfather?" the billionaire said, wrinkling his brow.

They continued walking.

"I'm sorry to further burden you, Robert, but I have a question concerning the director's plane."

"Of course," Reyland said, stooping to listen.

"I was told that this Mr. Biyombo individual brought a package with him out of the Congo. Is that true?"

"Yes," Reyland said, nodding. "He did."

"May I ask how you know this?"

"I was on the phone with Dunning before they took off," Reyland said. "Biyombo showed him the case. The director told me there was what appeared to be a very large amount of diamonds inside of it."

The rich man nodded.

"And your report said this case is still missing?"

"Yes. Along with the money. We're still looking. As I mentioned, we still have a team down in the islands working solely on that," Reyland said as they made the top of the stairs.

The ghostly blue-eyed man nodded again.

"Now, this is just an ancillary matter, Robert, but we believe Biyombo's diamonds were actually stolen from a convoy out of one of our mines on the Zaire border three years ago."

Reyland blinked as he thought of whom the rich man meant by the word *our*.

"If you come across these diamonds in your travels, Robert, I would be forever in your debt if you brought them directly to me."

Forever in debt to a man with an infinite amount of money, Reyland thought, looking into the icy blue of the man's eyes.

It was here, Reyland realized.

The opportunity that he had always dreamed of but was hesitant to ever actually expect, even to himself.

He would be a player. That was what he was being offered here. World-Class Player Status.

If he retrieved Biyombo's satchel, he would get his own golden passport into the sky city.

He thought about the boathouse again, about the fireflies.

"I'll make it a priority, sir," Reyland said with an impossible-to-hide smile as he started down the steps.

67

Gannon woke up at around five thirty in the double-wide's small bedroom. When he went into the living room, Stick and Ruby were sitting silently watching the news.

"Are we still the lead story?" Gannon said.

"Yes," Ruby said. "But at least they're not showing photos of us yet."

"Is there anything about Wheldon? About the fire at the hotel?" Gannon said.

"No," Ruby said. "Not a thing."

After the news was over, the only thing to eat was more pancakes, so they had them for dinner along with some bacon that Gannon defrosted from the otherwise empty freezer.

After they were done eating, they stared at each other in silence. Then it was Stick's turn to do some pacing. Ruby and Gannon sat at the small kitchen table, sipping instant coffee as they watched Stick walk the length of the small living room to the pellet stove and back.

"Hell, I need a drink. Is there anything to drink?" Stick said.

Gannon got up and looked in the pantry where he'd found the pancake mix.

"You're in luck. There's beer," Gannon said, kneeling down. "No, no. Wait. Sorry. False alarm. It's just that O'Doul's non-alcoholic stuff."

"Screw it. Bring it out," Stick said, making a gimme gesture with his big hand. "I'll take even a pretend beer at this point."

They watched him crack the bottle open and drink while he continued to pace.

"Okay, so there's obviously something there about the plane," Stick said. "Something about the director and the people there with him that is so unholy, there isn't anything they're not going to do to cover it up. So what the hell could it be?"

"Before he was shot, Wheldon was speculating it had something to do with the uncut diamonds," Gannon said. "He said maybe they were illegal blood diamonds from some war-torn African country and that the exposure of the FBI director on the plane with the diamonds would expose some kind of Iran Contra–type deal with African warlords."

"Maybe that's true," Ruby said. "The range on a G550 is transcontinental. They easily could have traveled from Africa to the East Coast of the US."

"Or maybe the dead guy in the hoodie was some kind of African terrorist or something?" Stick said. "And they were doing some kind of off-the-books deal with him? Sneaking him into another country or something?"

"Awful lot of maybes and somethings to go on there," said Gannon.

"You're right," Ruby said, letting out a breath. "We can't really say what it is."

"So what do we do?" Stick said.

"I think we need to do what Wheldon said before they shot him," Gannon said.

"Which is what?" Stick said.

"Get the tape out there," Gannon said. "We need to go back to my place and get the video. Get it out to the world. It's the one thing they don't want."

"That actually makes a lot of sense," Ruby said. "They're willing to kill us to cover it up, right? But if the truth gets out, it's out. The reason to kill us suddenly disappears."

"Plus, at the very least, we're going to need money and plenty of it to keep staying under the radar with these jacks hunting us," Gannon said.

"Just one little detail," Stick said. "How do you plan on getting us from here to the Bahamas with the FBI and probably every cop in the United States out looking for us?"

Gannon smiled as he thought of something.

"We'll take the back roads," he said.

68

They were just over the border of Kentucky the next morning when they saw the gas station.

They were on a two-lane strip of desolate Tennessee hill country road heading downward into a valley, and Gannon saw it ahead on his left off by itself in the middle of nowhere.

It was a blue-and-white Marathon station with a little mart attached to get doughnuts and Gatorade and lottery cards. Behind it was a tree-filled hill edged with a small cliff of striated brownish-gray rock.

"Guys, what do you think? Stop for gas?" Gannon said.

In the back seat, Stick lifted the binoculars they'd brought with them from the hunting trailer.

"Do it," he said. "There aren't any cameras that I can see."

It was cold when Gannon stepped out by pump number one. He looked up at the dawning overcast sky. The forecast called for rain, but snow made more sense. He stepped past the cigarette ads and the propane cage and opened the door.

There was a middle-aged couple inside, a heavyset lady with silvery blond hair and a skinny man with a mustache and glasses.

"Forty bucks on pump one, please," Gannon said, putting a couple of twenties on the counter.

He saw the cruiser straight off as he came back out the jingling door. It was a Tennessee state trooper Dodge Charger detailed in cream and black with a yellow stripe. Gannon had the pump clunked in and had just squeezed the handle as it pulled to a stop right behind them.

Just bad luck, Gannon thought, trying to calm his breathing. *Just full-out bad luck.*

The trooper who climbed out of it was pale and square-jawed and about thirty. He was medium-sized, five-nine or so, but bulked up wide with muscle from working out. Gannon, seeing the no-nonsense expression on his lean face beneath the green Smokey the Bear hat as well as the shine to his patent leather cop shoes, did what he could only do.

He smiled and nodded.

"Morning," he said.

The trooper looked at him, looked at Ruby, looked at Stick, and gave him a fake smile back.

"Taking a trip, huh," he said.

"Yeah, how'd you know?" Gannon said. Then he laughed. "Oh, right. The plates. Yeah, my old lady's idea. Got a vacation week off from work, and two nights ago, out of the blue, she says she needs to see Graceland. Bucket list thing."

"Happy wife, happy life," the trooper said, peering into the back. "Got a buddy with you?"

"Kinda," Gannon said.

They both looked out at the road as a rattling dump truck went by tugging a backhoe on a trailer.

"How's that?" the trooper said.

"That's her brother," Gannon said.

"In-laws," the trooper said, nodding knowingly as he stepped for the mart. "I get you there, partner."

Gannon heard the door jingle.

"Let's get going," Stick said, rolling down the window.

"Shit," Gannon said as he clicked the nozzle back into the pump.

"What is it?" Stick said.

"It's only thirty-four."

"What does that mean?"

"I got change coming."

"Screw it. Let's just go," Stick said.

"Relax," Gannon said, turning for the mart. "Take it easy."

The trooper was coming out with a coffee in one hand as he was going in. He gave him a look as Gannon held the door for him but said nothing as he passed.

"Looks like I overshot it a bit," he said to the heavyset lady behind the counter.

She smiled, opening the register.

Shit, Gannon thought as he looked out at the trooper where he was sitting in the cruiser typing at his terminal now.

69

"You know he's running the plate," Stick said as Gannon got back behind the wheel.

"I know, I know. Just take it easy."

"You keep saying that, but it's getting harder and harder," Stick said as they pulled out.

Gannon watched the trooper in the rearview as he slowly accelerated. He was on his radio. Then Gannon saw him move the cruiser just as they hit the bend in the descending road ahead.

"He's following us," Stick said, glancing back, "and he's on his radio now. They've got a BOLO on the truck. Has to be. What do we do?"

"Nothing," Gannon said. "Just hold on. Let's not get too hasty, okay?"

"But you know he's calling for backup."

Gannon looked ahead. Far below down the slope of the road

they were descending, there was a car. It was coming up, heading toward them at some speed.

"Dammit! It's another cruiser!" Stick called, pointing the field glasses over Gannon's shoulder. "I knew it."

Gannon looked ahead where some high voltage lines bisected the road at a high-to-low diagonal. He looked at the rusted red transmission towers over the trees on his right where the lines went down. They were a hundred yards from the utility cutout.

"Put on your seat belts! Now!" he called out.

"You have got to be shitting me," Stick said as Gannon wheeled to the right off the road.

There was the snap of fallen tree limbs then a crunch of flying gravel as they swooped down an embankment onto a tire-track dirt path. Thirty feet from where they caught the path, there was a fenced-in stand of electrical equipment at the base of one of the transmission pylons, and the back end of the Subaru clipped one of its corner poles smartly as they skimmed headlong past it.

Coming down the cutout was like riding a bucking bronco down a ski slope. Dirt showered off the hood as they seesawed into the hill face and crunched over tree stumps and slid over gravel.

After a few hundred terrifying more feet, they suddenly hit a flat of concrete that supported another of the electrical pylons. Then they were off-roading again, zigzagging left and right as they bounced up and down hard over the rough descending terrain.

Gannon managed to halt the truck with a high screech at the cement base of the next pylon, and he rolled down his window and looked back up the slope.

Not surprisingly, the cruiser hadn't followed them.

Of course not, Gannon thought. The guy was young, took care of himself. He didn't want to die just yet.

"Mike, there's an access road. See it?" Stick said, pointing another thirty feet below.

"Hallelujah," Ruby said when they were finally on asphalt again.

The access road ran alongside a river onto an actual road.

"We need to ditch the car," Gannon said as he gunned it past an old farmhouse. "Get a new one. They're going to have every cop in the state looking for us now."

They came to an intersection and hooked a right. They'd just crossed a bridge over the river when Ruby grabbed his arm.

"Wait, wait. Slow down."

"What's up?" Gannon said, easing off the accelerator.

"Turn left here. See?" she said, pointing at the road they were coming up on.

On the corner, there was a little green sign with an arrow on it.

Hollytree Airport, it said.

"Yeah?" Gannon said.

"Trust me," Ruby said.

70

The road curved up a wooded hill for about a mile and a half before they came into the small airport's parking lot. There were a half-dozen cars there that they sped past as Ruby guided them toward a utility road that ran parallel to the tarmac fence.

After twenty feet down the road, they came to the back of a long white metal hangar that fronted into the airport.

"Stop right here. Right here," Ruby said, pointing at a little set of stairs that led to a door at the hangar's end.

Ruby had her door open even before they stopped. She flew up the stairs and rattled at the little black box that hung from the door's knob.

"Good. See, it's just a key holder like real-estate agents use. I knew it. Is there a crowbar in the truck?"

Gannon took the Glock out of Stick's leather jacket pocket and stepped up the stairs and shot the lockbox with a sudden loud pop.

"That'll work, too, I guess," Ruby said as she grabbed the key from the grass and opened the door and clicked on the lights.

The hangar inside was pristine. On one wall hung a huge American flag, and under the fluorescent lights in its center gleamed a new-looking cream-and-white single-engine prop plane.

"What do you mean to do?" said Stick.

"What do you think?" Ruby answered. "We're flying the hell out of here."

"You can fly?"

"No, I just thought I'd suddenly give it a shot. How hard can it be?" Ruby said as she went to the plane and threw up the pilot-side batwing door.

"Of course I fly," she said as she climbed in. "Since I was in high school. You need a pilot's license to even join Naval Safety."

They stood watching as she checked the instrument panel and clicked some buttons.

"Gotta love rural airports," Ruby said, looking down at them. "The key's already in it."

"People just leave the damn keys in?" Stick said.

"Of course," Ruby said. "You know how much trouble you get in for stealing a plane?"

"What's the plan?" Gannon said.

"The power is good to go, and there's half a tank of gas. On a six-seater, that's a range of about five hundred miles. I get this Beechcraft up and run it dead open for fifteen or twenty minutes to the south. She'll go two hundred knots, and I'll keep it low, under the radar. By the time they figure it out, we'll be over the state line in Georgia."

"Where are you going to put it down?" Gannon said.

"On a rural road," Ruby said. "Or a field even. The tires looked pretty good."

"Then what? Hitchhike?" Stick said.

"We'll call a cab."

Gannon laughed.

"That's hilarious. But that just might work, sailor."

"Hurry now. Get the gate," Ruby said.

Gannon hit the button beside the roll-up gate and ran back as it started to rise.

Ruby turned over the engine and the propeller began to spin as Gannon and Stick climbed in.

The radio crackled on as they were outside on the taxi road about to get on the runway.

"This is tower. You are not authorized to take off. What the hell are you doing?"

"Tower, we have a sick child aboard. We need to take off now. Clear the air," Ruby said.

"You are not authorized!" cried the radio.

"We have no choice. Divert all aircraft. We're coming out," Ruby said and turned down the radio volume.

They hit the tarmac and turned and began to pick up speed.

"I can't believe we're actually doing this," Stick said over the rising roar of the engine.

"Yep," Gannon said as he crossed himself and began a quick "Our Father."

"I never should have let you into my office," Stick yelled as they suddenly left the ground. "I knew you were trouble, but I had no idea this chick was as crazy as you!"

71

In the gilded mirror, Reyland held his right hand over his chest like he was about to pledge allegiance.

Then he tilted up his chin and slowly drew the razor up his shaving-creamed throat.

As he clicked the steel against the rim of the full washbasin, they hit enough turbulence to make the water slosh.

As the rattling subsided, there was a change in light at the porthole window above the commode and Reyland stepped over and looked out.

The clouds they had been in had thinned out, and now seven miles down beneath the Gulfstream, he could see the bleached-salt white line of the North Florida coast.

The G550 they were on now belonged to the attorney general. Reyland had heard that the AG tried to block his use of it. Well, at least until he heard the nosebleed height from which the request had originated.

Reyland went back to the mirror and paused again with the razor as they hit some more bumpy air. He squinted at the back of Emerson's head where he was sitting with a PowerBook on the jump seat just outside the restroom's open door.

"Hey, you didn't tell the pilot I was shaving, did you, Emerson?" he said.

Emerson swiveled and smiled.

Reyland kicked the door shut and finally smiled himself.

Now that they actually had something to smile about.

They had finally found the mystery man.

His name was Gannon. Michael Gannon. He was a diving instructor who lived on Eleuthera Island in the Bahamas with a boat registered in the Bahamian database called the *Donegal Rambler.*

Even with all the technology at their disposal, it was sheer unadulterated shoe leather that had finally broken the logjam.

They had taken screenshots of their pesky unsub off the MTA closed-circuit system in New York City and had them sent to their team of agents still down in the islands.

Their agent on Eleuthera had just lost hope when a guy in a bar said he knew the man in their picture, had fished with him. The agent had asked him where they had fished. The man had said they had gone marlin fishing in the Atlantic falloff thirty miles out north of Little Abaco.

It was this Gannon who had found the money. Reyland was sure of it. Gannon had come across the plane and had taken the money. Since he was a diving instructor, he had probably even dived down for more loot and had seen the director dead in the plane.

Which was the reason why, like Everett, he had apparently come up to NYC to talk to that puke, Wheldon, to blow the whistle about it.

Oddly, Gannon was an Irish national. Or at least he had used an Irish passport when he flew into the States from Eleuthera Island. He had flown to Tampa and then to Phoenix, of all places, and then on to New York City.

But besides that, all they knew about Gannon apparently was his name, address and boat. He had no social network presence. No credit cards at any major banks.

They had even hacked the Irish government records to see if there was any clue to his origins, but no dice. Not only was the Irish database a primitive, disorganized nightmare, there were actually thirty-seven bog-trotting Irish Michael Gannons running about in the world.

No matter, Reyland thought. He and his team were now on the way to Eleuthera right now. When they got there, they would go to Gannon's house and hopefully find him there with his pants down. If not, they would tear his place apart and find out everything they could about him. Pick up his computers, any physical files he had.

Who knows? Reyland thought pleasantly. In their search, maybe they might even come up with the items the man had stolen.

Done shaving, Reyland let the warm water out and turned on the cold and splashed some on his face. When he glanced up, the electronic in-flight display board to the right of the mirror said that they would be arriving at Nassau in forty-seven minutes.

He patted at his face and neck with a fluffy cream-colored towel that smelled like a scented candle. As he did this, the ETA on the screen suddenly changed to forty-one minutes.

How do you like that? Reyland thought, smiling. They were making even better time now. Things were coming up rosy all fricking over.

72

Coming on 3:00 a.m., Sergeant Jeremy was out at the Coral Castle Resort in Charles Bay.

He was sitting in its lobby, and beyond the arched opening in front of him he could see the bartender turning off the lights of the straw hut bar beside the elaborately lit pool. To his left on the bench beside him sat a man. He was a large white man with a bad sunburn and a prodigious gut that protruded through the curtain-like gap of his unbuttoned Hawaiian shirt. The man's eyes were closed, and he was sweating profusely.

Sergeant Jeremy sat beside the big man patiently, listening to his breathing. He had caused quite a ruckus forty minutes before, and Sergeant Jeremy, always reluctant to make an arrest, was hoping that the drunken tourist was about to finally fall into a restful slumber. He was beginning to edge away when the big man snorted himself awake.

"Where is she? Where is she?" the man said with German or maybe South African–accented English. "Is she back?"

"Not yet, but I am sure you will see her soon," Sergeant Jeremy said with soft encouragement.

"Why aren't you taking me seriously?" the man said, punching on his own thigh. "She was kidnapped, I tell you. Kidnapped!"

"Yes, I know. I remember," Sergeant Jeremy said quietly.

Sergeant Jeremy nodded as the man mumbled to himself incoherently. He had been called to investigate such kidnappings before. It usually happened after the rum began to flow. Boyfriends and girlfriends and sometimes, as in this poor man's case, even spouses would disappear. But in almost every case, such disappearances were the result of the victim voluntarily heading into the bedroom of another inebriated guest.

"Then why aren't you doing anything? Shouldn't we fill out a report or something?" the large man cried.

"We were just about to, sir," Sergeant Jeremy said, lifting the clipboard in his lap.

He had taken out his pen and was about to click it when he finally heard the best possible resolution to the situation. Incredibly loud snoring. The man had slumped over with his sweating head against the palm pot beside him.

"Is he okay there for now?" Sergeant Jeremy asked, walking over to the desk clerk.

"Is he really asleep this time?" the clerk asked.

"Out for the count, I would say."

"Not so fast," the clerk said, tossing a chin.

Sergeant Jeremy turned to see a skinny middle-aged blonde woman come in off the beach. He thought there would be some fireworks as she started shaking at the large man. But he was wrong.

"Another kidnapping successfully solved," Sergeant Jeremy said with a click of his pen as the two tourists stumbled off down the corridor together, singing and laughing.

He was heading back up Sherman's Highway near Tarpum Head in his Jeep when he came up on his friend Michael Gannon's cul-de-sac turnoff.

He found himself putting on his clicker. There had been some break-ins in nearby Rock Sound and on White Road Beach to the south, and he thought he'd do a quick spin past.

He was approaching the second-to-last old bungalow when he saw the light in the window of Michael's house. It was blue and flickering, his friend watching TV perhaps.

Home early? Sergeant Jeremy thought, rolling up.

He had parked the car in front of the house and was coming up the path when the blue light suddenly shut off.

That was strange, he thought.

He stood there in the darkness for a moment waiting, listening. The clicking sound of some kind of bird in the distance had just started up when the door to the house opened silently. A man appeared in the threshold. A tall man. He was smiling serenely in the moonlight.

Michael's son?

Then Sergeant Jeremy saw the pale bald round head and a sudden sense of panic rattled through him.

"You," Sergeant Jeremy said in utter confusion.

"Yes, it's me, Sergeant. Funny meeting you here," said the FBI man with the wolf's eyes.

"I should say the same thing," Sergeant Jeremy said. "This is not your house!"

"And whose house might it be, Sergeant?" the FBI man said. "In fact, why don't you come in here, Sergeant, and talk to us. We're all friends, right? Colleagues, fellow law enforcement officials. Perhaps you could help us with the investigation we're conducting."

Sergeant Jeremy stiffened as something cold touched his neck at the back of his collar. A short muscular man in black tactical clothes and some kind of goggles over his eyes was standing there with a gun pressed to the back of his skull.

"After you, Papi," the soldier said.

The blow to his chest that came when he set foot into the house was like a sledgehammer. Sergeant Jeremy went back off his heels onto his ass with his breath gone. He actually skidded a little down the short corridor before he came to a stop against the wall.

It took him a second to process that the FBI man, Reyland, had kicked him. The huge bald man had just stomped him in the chest with the heel and sole of his big dress shoe.

"There you go. Have a seat, *mon*," the FBI man said. "You sit right back and get real comfy, you little lying sack of shit."

73

It was eight thirty in the morning, and out on the faded sunny South Florida concrete, the Beatles' iconic song "Day Tripper" died down from the speaker above to be replaced by some driving steel drum Bahamian dance music.

For the twentieth time.

Gannon sipped on the dregs of his iced coffee as a yellow forklift loaded with pallets rumbled by on the quay.

They were in Fort Lauderdale now at the busy Port Everglades Harbor. The terminal they were sitting outside of was for a US-to-Bahamas daytrip high-speed ferry service called Raytrippers.

Gannon's son, Declan, had taken it a few times because it was cheaper than flying and only a driver's license was required to get through customs if you told them you weren't staying overnight.

Gannon smiled as Ruby came out from the lounge inside and sat beside him.

Forty minutes after they had taken off she'd landed the plane as pretty as you please in a hayfield in a little town called Dalton, Georgia. Since then, they'd been heading stealthily south via local taxis.

"You must speak Bahamian by now. What do they keep saying?" said Ruby, who was dressed now in a maxi dress with a ridiculously garish sunset on it.

On their way south, they had stopped outside of Jacksonville and bought some beach stuff at a Dollar Store that didn't have a camera out in front of it. With Gannon's new madras shorts and a seagull T-shirt and floppy golf hat, they could have been a blue-collar couple doing a second honeymoon on the cheap.

"What do you mean?" Gannon said, thumbing his cheap sunglasses up the bridge of his nose. "What does who keep saying?"

"In the song," Ruby said, pointing at the speaker.

Gannon bopped his head to the steel drum rhythm, listening.

"Party in the backyard," he said with a grin. "I tink, mon."

Ruby smiled.

"Any word?" she said, checking her watch.

She was talking about Stick. He had headed down to Miami three hours before. In his younger days, Stick had worked on loan from the NYPD as an undercover with the Miami DEA, and he had gone down there to ask an old criminal informant for a favor.

"No, not yet," Gannon said, glancing at his burner phone, "but don't worry—he'll make it."

"You know," Ruby said, looking at him intently. "I was thinking about what you did back in New York."

"What do you mean?" Gannon said.

"How you got us out of the hotel, took down that agent and those other armed men. Opening the wall of the precinct? Not to mention your expert work with the wastepaper basket."

Gannon laughed.

"So what about it?"

"What was it that you actually did in the NYPD?" Ruby said.

As Gannon opened his mouth, a huge cruise ship from the nearby Princess terminal let off its departure air horn. Just as it stopped, Stick came out of the terminal door behind them. He looked even more ridiculously touristy than they did in his surfer jam shorts, golf visor and yellow T-shirt that said California Dreaming on it.

"So did you get it?" Gannon said.

"Did I get it?" Stick said, flicking their new fake Florida driver's licenses across the outdoor table's white metal top like a blackjack dealer.

Gannon thumbed the waxy paper and looked back at the Walgreens picture of himself that had been taken this morning. He nodded, impressed.

"These are good, Stick. They look real," he said.

"They are real, or so my guy claims," he said. "There's a guy in the DMV who he gets them from."

"Even the DMV is corrupt, huh," Ruby said. "Is nothing sacred?"

"How much? Five hundred apiece?" Gannon said.

"Six actually," Stick said with a nod.

"I'll pay you back when we get down to my house. Hope hundreds are okay," Gannon said.

"Sure," Stick said. "Hundreds are cool."

"Or diamonds. We could do diamonds," Gannon said.

"Diamonds? Hmm. I know the ladies like those things. Let me think about it," Stick said.

"Wait, Jessica Roberts?" Ruby said, annoyed as she squinted at her license.

"What do you want?" Stick said. "You kinda look like Julia Roberts to me, so I went with it."

"She was a movie star back in the olden days of the eighties," Gannon explained.

"Duh," Ruby said. "I'm thirty-five, Mike, not ten. *Steel Magnolias, Mystic Pizza.* I've heard of her. But Jessica? Ugh. Jessica?"

"Hey, you're lucky. Look at my new name," Gannon said, showing her his ID.

"Burt Clancy," Ruby said. "Stick, really? Burt? That's the worst name in the history of names."

Stick suppressed a grin.

"What are you talking about? Burt is a tough name. It's making a comeback," he said.

"Oh, sure. What's your new name?" Ruby said. "Let's see it."

He passed it over. She showed it to Gannon. He looked at it and laughed.

"Wow, you're an idiot," he said.

"Steven Van Damme?" she said.

"What?" Stick said with a smile. "I always wanted to have a real kick-ass name."

74

The high-speed ferry left Fort Lauderdale at nine on the button and landed at a marina dock near Princess Beach in Freeport on Grand Bahama at a little before noon.

It was an uneventful crossing except for some choppy water as they came through the Gulf Stream. The seesawing of the ferry had woken Stick from where they'd been napping in one of the inside lounges and sent him green-faced into the bathroom.

Standing in line at the deck rail to get off, Gannon searched around nervously until he turned and saw the *Donegal Rambler* waiting at the other end of the dock behind them. He waved back to Little Jorge standing in the stern.

"More boating now. Oh, and a smaller one now, too. Super," Stick said as they got off and headed down the dock toward the *Rambler*.

"All gassed up, stocked and ready to go, Captain Mike," Little

Jorge said as they stepped aboard. "You said we were in a hurry, so I grabbed you guys lunch. Should we just get going, then?"

"You took the words out of my mouth," Gannon said, untying the line and giving Little Jorge a high five.

Tourists were already being tugged around on banana boats out in front of the pink-and-white stucco hotels as the *Rambler* pulled out of the marina. When they'd cleared the bay, they went dead southeast with the throttle open.

They put Great Harbour Cay and the Berry Islands behind them and kept going out into the open water. It was a gorgeous day, temperature in the low 70s and hardly any wind.

At around five, Ruby came up into the flying bridge, where Gannon had just relieved Little Jorge. She had her hair pulled back and her sunglasses on and was smiling as the breeze ripped at her maxi dress.

"How's Stick doing?" he said.

"He's asleep."

Gannon laughed.

"Hey, good news," he said. "I saw the weather report. It's going to be a crystal clear night tonight."

"Oh, yeah?" Ruby said.

Gannon smiled.

"For our cruise, remember? You're not getting cold feet, are you?"

Ruby laughed. She looked out at the water through the rushing wind.

"What do you think is going to happen, Mike? I mean, this is a level of nuts never seen before. The FBI is making people disappear? Killing reporters and cops? That's hard to even say, let alone believe. I mean, is it even possible to straighten this out?"

Gannon looked at her, looked out at the water.

"Anything can be straightened out," he said.

"Do you really think so?"

"Anything," Gannon said.

"You're unbelievable," Ruby said.

"How so?"

"How the hell are you so confident?"

Gannon shrugged.

"I don't know. Good genes? A happy upbringing in the home?"

Ruby laughed.

"You know, I almost believe you."

"Believe what?"

"That you're not shitting bricks, too."

It was Gannon's turn to laugh. Then he pointed out through the breeze.

"Hey, look," he said.

There was an island, faint in the hazy blue up ahead.

"You see there? That's Pimlico Island. That's at the tip of Eleuthera," Gannon said.

"Home?" Ruby said, smiling.

"Yep," Gannon said, smiling back. "We're almost home."

75

Instead of going straight to his berth in Davis Head, Gannon had Little Jorge go a few miles farther south down the beach on the island's Caribbean side.

The dock they finally chugged in toward was very old and had several missing boards. It belonged to a place called the Ocean School that was just a two-and-a-half-mile walk to Gannon's house.

"Are you sure you want to go in alone?" Ruby said.

"Don't worry," he said, smiling. "You guys go back up with Little Jorge to Davis Head and get some dinner. I'll come up to get you in my truck after."

"No, really, Mike. Why don't I come with you? Hell, why don't we all just go?" Ruby said.

Gannon looked up at her from where he was throwing a couple of things into a knapsack. She'd gotten some sun on the crossing, her skin glowing. He remembered holding her hand as they ran through the cold dirty subway what seemed like a lifetime ago. And how cute she looked in the headset she'd put on in the prop plane.

Pretty Woman, he thought.

"No, Jessica," he said. "I got this."

"But," she said.

"No buts. You head to dinner. Naval orders," Gannon said.

"Wait," Ruby said. "I thought I gave those."

"Only in the US," Gannon said, holding up a finger. "We're in the Bahamas now. You heard Little Jorge, right? I'm the captain down here."

Gannon watched until they made the wide turn in the water before he came in off the beach toward a cluster of low one-story buildings. A gypsy cab came around a bend as he came out of the school's driveway onto Sherman Highway. It was dark enough now to notice the glow of its brake lights as it slowed. But Gannon waved it on, and its brake lights went off, and it kept going.

When he got to his cul-de-sac, the first thing Gannon did was to go off into the brush. He reached into his bag and stood scrutinizing his house and the other three of his neighbors' houses with binoculars.

Two of the bungalows belonged to American families that only sporadically came down and were often deserted. The last of his neighbors was a cranky retired Canadian doctor who was usually around, but he'd gone back to Toronto to take care of a sick relative two months before.

Gannon knew he was probably just being paranoid as he scanned the front and side of his house. He didn't think it was possible for them to catch up with him this quickly.

But then again, he hadn't known they could track people through the NYC subway in real time either.

He came farther down his street in the twilight and stopped beside one of the absentee neighbors' houses and stood looking at his place. At the dark windows. It was a very nice evening. There was a rose-gold quality to the evening light.

There were no vehicles except for his truck. Everything seemed in order.

"Okay," he said and took a breath and came out of the shadowed brush.

He closed the final couple of hundred feet and hurried across his front yard and keyed open his door. He stood for a moment, looking at the dark inside. He sniffed at the air.

Was there a hint of something? Cologne? Or was he just being paranoid?

He was still standing there, still wondering, when quick as a weasel, a man with a gun popped his head around the side of the house at the carport.

He was a heavily muscled black man in a blue Hawaiian shirt and silver mirrored aviator sunglasses. The gun looked like a .45. The squarish silencer on the business end of it was pointed directly at his face.

"Go on in, friend," the man said in his American voice.

He smiled, showing very white teeth, as he tilted his head and the gun at the door.

"I insist," he said.

76

Gannon stood there frozen in the evening twilight as the man in sunglasses stepped up onto his front yard path behind the gun. He was about six foot three, in his early thirties, trim-waisted as an athlete, moving easily.

Through the heavy thumps of his heart in his ears, Gannon turned and looked through the dim doorway.

How stupid could you be? he thought.

The guy stopped three feet away.

"What are you? Hard of hearing?"

Gannon looked at him.

Run? he thought with desperation. *Fight?*

Gannon looked back at his dark doorway. He definitely did not want to go in there.

Still not moving his feet, he glanced back at Sunglasses, his vision tunneling in on the steel of the .45 in his hand as the guy thumbed back the hammer with a loud click.

"You hear me now? Get in that house or I'll blow your brains out," he said.

He had thought he'd been prepared for something like this, but now that it was right here before him, moving too quickly for him to get a handle on it, he realized he had thought 100 percent absolutely wrong.

Gannon finally took a step forward toward the door. As he did it, he suddenly felt exhausted, his body heavy and slow and weak, as if he were slogging through wet mud.

No, it wasn't mud, he realized from a distant memory.

It was sand, he thought, as he stepped over his threshold into his house.

It was wet sand and then a voice from long ago violently yelled in his head, "Get in the game, puke! You even think about checking out, I will personally drown your damn scrawny ass in this surf!"

The memory evaporated with the heavy thunk of the door closing behind him.

77

There were two more men inside of his house sitting in his living room.

They were both lean and clean-cut and wearing business attire.

They actually looked the way FBI agents were supposed to look, Gannon thought. In their crisp khakis and polos and Top-Siders, they could have been a couple of finance guys down to the islands for a corporate conference.

The one sitting in his leather recliner was older and taller and completely bald. There was a crackle of plastic as he reached into the bag of shelled peanuts that was in his lap. He had stolen them from his cupboard, Gannon realized.

As Gannon watched, the man cracked one of the peanuts open and picked out the nut and let the cracked shells spill from his palm almost playfully to the floor. He must have been doing this for some time because the Spanish tile between his size-thirteen new boat shoes was completely littered with shells.

"Well, well, well. If it isn't Mystery Man," the bald agent said, cracking open another peanut and licking it out of his palm.

"Mike, I'm FBI deputy assistant director Reyland," the bald man said with a grin after he had chewed and swallowed. "And on the couch over there is FBI special agent Emerson."

Emerson gave him a wave from the couch. He was dark-haired and younger and metro preppy. There was an open Apple laptop on the couch beside him.

Gannon looked back at the bald man. Then he looked back at Sunglasses, at the large bore of his Smith & Wesson trained three feet from his face.

"You're not an easy man to catch up to," Reyland said. "And we'd love to ask you a few questions. How are you doing this fine evening?"

Gannon watched as Reyland slapped bits of peanut shell off the lap of his slacks. After he was done, he smiled broadly as he crossed his long legs and placed his big hands onto the ends of the chair's armrests. He settled back and raised his bald head high with a relaxed, ready-to-be-amused expression on his face. A king on a throne ready for the jester's performance.

"Cat got your tongue?" Emerson said.

"Can I help you?" Gannon finally said.

"Oh, you've helped enough, I think, haven't you, Mike?" Reyland said. "First by taking what didn't belong to you. Then by killing our friends. Or maybe we have the wrong house? Tell me, you weren't around Lexington Avenue this week, were you? With a gun in your hand? Killing four US federal law enforcement agents?"

Gannon looked down as a flash of the inside of the Escalade suddenly came to him. The reek of cordite and smoke and the three men shot to pieces with their blood splatter up on all the shattered windows.

He shook the memory away as he put a knuckle to his lip as if he were trying to remember.

"Around what time would this have been?" he said.

Reyland smiled.

"Oh, around seven Friday last."

"Oh, yeah, now that you mention it," Gannon said after a pause. "As a matter of fact, I was out on Lexington that night. But I didn't shoot any law enforcement people."

"Is that right?" Emerson said. "Are you sure?"

"Positive," Gannon said, looking at him. "That night I was only killing reporter-murdering scumbags."

Reyland smiled even wider. He had nice clean white teeth. Dimples.

"Funny," he said, swiveling to and fro in his chair. "Now for something not so funny. Agent Emerson, if you would do the honors."

"It would be my pleasure," Emerson said, smiling as he stood in his razor-creased khakis. He walked past the small kitchen into Gannon's back bedroom. A moment later when he came back out, he was dragging something heavy.

It was a man.

A short naked black man, and he was covered in blood.

78

Emerson dragged the little black man over among the cracked shells.

It took a full thirty seconds of looking at the swollen, broken face to verify it was Sergeant Jeremy.

The bald man laughed as he dumped out what was left of the peanuts over Sergeant Jeremy at his feet.

"You sons of bitches!" Gannon said, wild-eyed, stepping forward.

As he did this, Sunglasses clocked him hard with the gun in the temple. As Gannon put his hands to the spot, his right leg was kicked out from underneath him and he fell backward. He landed hard on his ass, banging the hell out of the back of his head against the tight hallway's Sheetrock wall on the way down.

Gannon's lower lip split as Sunglasses kneed him explosively in the face a few times. Then the barrel of the gun was jammed painfully in his ear.

"You have a choice here, Mike," Reyland said, standing as Emerson dragged Sergeant Jeremy back into the bedroom.

"An end-of-life decision actually," he said as he crunched over the shells.

He crouched down until they were eye level.

"We can either take you and your friend back into that bathtub of yours and get busy slowly lopping you into pieces small enough to wash down the drain. Or you can tell me where our property is."

Gannon stared down at the tile. A drop of blood from his split-open temple plopped down onto it. Then another drop from his lip followed it. One of his lower teeth was loose. He could actually move it with his tongue.

He looked up at Emerson as he returned from the bedroom alone.

Then he finally played the only card he had left.

"I have a video of the people on the plane," Gannon said, looking up into the bald man's gray eyes. "I had a GoPro camera when I dived down. It shows the FBI director, the black guy, and the other two white guys. It shows their faces. All close-ups. That's what you want, right? That's what all this is about?"

In the silence, Reyland peered at him poker-faced.

"And let me guess," said the younger agent, Emerson. "If you're not back somewhere by the right time, it gets released by a lawyer or some other bullshit?"

"No," Gannon said, shaking his head. "I didn't make any copies of it. The tape's still in the camera, and I can get it for you. Right now."

Reyland continued to peer at him.

"What about the missing items? Don't lie and say you don't know what I'm talking about. We found the empty case."

"It's there, too. I hid everything together."

"Who the hell are you, anyway?" Emerson said. "You're obviously NYPD or something. Except your fingerprints aren't in the NYPD database. You have no Social Security card, but you have an Irish passport? You don't even have any records here in the Bahamas except for your shitty boat."

"A New York cop? Me?" Gannon said. "Okay, fine. Guilty as charged. I was a cop. But I've been clean for a few years now. Don't ask me about the records. The Irish passport thing was because my old man was from Donegal. I registered for dual citizenship because I didn't want to pay taxes back to the States. I'm just a retired cop who happened to see a plane go down. I want to work with you here, okay?"

Gannon turned to Reyland.

"Listen, I have what you want. I'm just going to need my diving stuff. I hid the video nearby underwater in a blue hole."

"You hid the video in a what?" Emerson said.

"It's an underwater cave," Gannon said. "They call them blue holes. It's about half an hour south from here."

"Well, Mike, I'm glad you're cooperating," Reyland said, putting an arm over his shoulder. "I'm on a pretty tight sched-ule, and I'm overjoyed at least that you're not being a deaf-mute pain in the ass like your stupid stubborn old friend back there."

"Let me just go get it," Gannon said.

"A man of action, Mike. I like that," Reyland said. "But do me a favor and go to the front door, would you?"

Sunglasses opened the door for him. The barrel of the .45 stayed rammed in his ear as he pulled him up to his feet.

On the other side of his lawn, a sky blue painters' van with ladders on its roof was pulling up at his curb. There was a short, stocky Spanish guy in the front passenger seat, and there was an extremely jacked black-bearded guy with a lot of tats be-hind its wheel.

The Spanish guy got out and opened the van's side door.

Inside, Ruby and Stick and Little Jorge were all down on the floor next to each other. Their hands and feet were secured with zip ties, and they had duct tape covering their mouths.

"Please," Gannon said to Reyland as his front door was slammed shut. "I'll get you everything you want. You can't hurt them. They have nothing to do with this."

"First he's a wise guy. Now it looks like Mike, the cop, here wants to make a deal all of a sudden," Reyland said as they all laughed.

"Why the hell are you doing this?" Gannon said, looking at him. "What the hell is this even for?"

Emerson stepped over and put a hand on Gannon's shoulder again and leaned in. Fatherly. The way a coach would in a close basketball game.

"We couldn't even tell you if we wanted to," he whispered in Gannon's ear. "It's a matter of national security, Mike. Strictly need-to-know."

79

When they went outside into his warm backyard, the sun was completely down, and it was raining slightly. With the help of the mercenaries forming an assembly line over the scrub grass from his storage shed to the carport, it took almost no time at all to load up his truck with the Gator and the diving equipment.

Gannon watched as they clunked several more tanks than necessary into the truck's bed.

"You don't need to do that. Two tanks are more than enough," Gannon said.

"Good one," the short, cocky Spanish thug from the van said. "You think you're going anywhere by yourself, think again."

Gannon looked at him. Like the rest of them, he was an American. He reminded him of a guy he once knew, a little all-state wrestler at his high school in the Bronx. What had they called him again? El Mighty Mouse, Gannon remembered.

Sunglasses zipped Gannon's hands behind him hard and tight

with some plastic ties and put him into his pickup's crew cab. Gannon watched as he went over to the van with Blackbeard. A moment later, El Mighty Mouse got in behind his truck's wheel with Agent Emerson riding shotgun.

"Pardon me for stating the obvious," El Mighty Mouse said as he sorted through Gannon's key chain, "but your truck here's a real genuine piece of shit."

"Well, now we know why he took the money," Emerson said as he rolled down the window.

Gannon stared at the blue van with Ruby and Stick and Little Jorge in it. After a minute, the big bald son of a bitch, Reyland, came out of his bungalow's front door.

At least they were getting away from the house, Gannon thought. He wondered how long they'd had Sergeant Jeremy for. Over a day at least. His wife, Emmaline, had to be crazed. He was badly beaten, but he was a tough old codger. Maybe someone would come by looking for him.

Reyland walked over to the truck.

"Ruiz, if you would," he said, gesturing toward the house.

Ruiz grinned back at Gannon before he climbed out and walked across the lawn.

"What the hell is he doing?" Gannon said frantically as El Mighty Mouse went in through the open front door. "What's he doing in there?"

The FBI men said nothing. They all stared at the house.

No, Gannon thought, biting his lip. There was no way.

Gannon reared back in his seat as if he'd been Tasered as the two shots boomed.

As El Mighty Mouse walked out of the house whistling, Gannon's gaze slid down onto the inside of his truck floor. There was an empty Gatorade bottle there. It was next to an old sky blue kid's flipper from when Declan was young.

He felt dizzy as El Mighty Mouse, still whistling, climbed back into the truck and turned over the engine.

The sergeant had five kids, Gannon thought. Twenty-something grandkids.

As the engine revved and they began to pull out, Gannon remembered Sergeant Jeremy's invitation to his sermon.

He closed his eyes.

There would be only one way out of this now.

80

Two hours later it was full dark, and they were all back behind the pine woods on the rough rock shelf above the blue hole.

Along the ridge of the water hole, the mercenaries made an actual campfire, and there were chairs and a folding table with coffee and radios on it. Behind the table was Gannon's Gator as well as another 4x4 quad they had in the back of the van.

It looked almost like they were on safari or something.

They had done a better job of setting up shop than he and the Aussie geology professor had done, Gannon thought as he sat there. And they had been there for over two weeks.

Beside Gannon sitting on the uncomfortable rock were Ruby and Stick and Little Jorge. Reyland was seated to their right about five feet away on one of the camp chairs.

As they sat silently in the firelight, Gannon busied himself by vividly wondering how the skin of Reyland's neck would feel in the palms of his bound hands.

He was still quietly staring and imagining when there was a sudden loud splash from the water below.

"He's right. It's like a damn maze under there, boss," Blackbeard suddenly called up from the hole's pond-like surface. "There are tunnels at every damn turn. We could be here for months. Shit, years!"

Reyland turned in the campfire's light.

"You sneaky little prick," he said, flinging the dregs of his coffee thermos at Gannon across the firelight.

"You're wasting your time," Gannon said as he chinned coffee off his face onto his shirt. "Just send me down already. I know exactly where it is."

"I think this cop is playing games, boss," he heard Blackbeard call up from the water hole. "There's so much silt in the water you can hardly see even with a flashlight. I think he's lying. I don't think there's shit down there."

Gannon took a relieved breath as he heard this. Twenty minutes before as the mercenary suited up and went under alone, Gannon had started worrying that maybe the son of a bitch might actually come across the bag by sheer luck.

Guess not, dumbass, he thought.

"You hearing me, boss?" Blackbeard called up.

"Shut up," Reyland said, staring at Gannon.

"I know you have a map. Where is it?" he said.

"I already told you. I had a map, but I burned it after I hid everything," Gannon explained. Which was actually true.

Reyland wrinkled his large brow as he leaned back in the folding camp chair, thinking.

In the silence, the only sound was Emerson sitting at another chair behind Reyland, typing at his computer.

Gannon looked across the limestone rim of the hole to where Sunglasses and El Mighty Mouse stood strapping what looked like fully automatic M4 military rifles. They carried them with a casual ease up before them in the position known as high ready. Butt tight to shoulder, elbows in, trigger finger against the receiver.

Textbook, Gannon thought, watching them. Professional.

"What are you looking at?" El Mighty Mouse said to him as Reyland finally nodded.

"Boys, new plan," Reyland said, pointing at Ruby. "Take the woman and take her clothes off and tie her to that palm tree there."

"Wait for me, fellas," Blackbeard yelled from the water. "Toss me another rope. C'mon. You can't start the fun without me."

"If you touch her," Gannon said, calmly shaking his head, "if you touch any of us, you never get it back."

"Who are you kidding?" said Sunglasses. "Your girlfriend will be squealing so loud, you'll tell us the moon is made of queso dip to make it stop."

"The only thing you'll get out of hurting me or my friends," Gannon said, squinting at Reyland, "will be the joy of me making sure you never find what you're looking for. Ever."

"Oh, listen to this, boys. Supercop here is going to stand up to torture. We've got a tough guy here among us," Sunglasses announced.

Gannon's smile was almost wistful in the firelight.

"I'm not that tough," he said, staring at the water.

Gannon's smile evaporated as he stared at the man level in his aviator sunglasses.

"I'm just tougher than you," he said.

"Sit your silly ass down," El Mighty Mouse said to the mercenary as he started to come around the rim of the hole at Gannon.

Gannon turned to Reyland.

"I said I would get what you need. Untie me, and I'll go get it."

"Maybe this information is time sensitive," Reyland said. "Maybe I don't care as long as it stays buried."

"And all those diamonds?" Gannon said, staring at him. "Are they time sensitive, too?"

"Diamonds? What diamonds?" El Mighty Mouse said.

Gannon looked over at him and then back at Reyland and smiled.

"You didn't tell him?" Gannon said. "Oh, wow. You didn't, did you? He doesn't know. And here I thought all you guys were friends."

"What diamonds?" El Mighty Mouse said again.

"I mean, the money is nothing," Gannon continued. "Two point eight million. What's that? Chump change. The stones down in that cave are worth ten, twenty—who knows, maybe thirty—times that."

El Mighty Mouse looked at Gannon, then back at Reyland.

"Is that true?" he said.

"No. I don't know. Maybe," Reyland said, putting up his hands. "You think they tell me everything, Tommy? Was I on the damn plane?"

"It's true," Gannon said. "There's a fortune down there."

Gannon strained to hide his elation as El Mighty Mouse walked over and knelt. There was a quick metallic snick of a knife and then the zip ties were cut from his wrists.

"You win," he said to Gannon. "We won't touch the girl. Put your shit on. You're going down with our boys to find it."

81

Blackbeard stroked across the surface of the blue hole as Gannon came down the rope, lugging his tanks and vest. Gannon looked at his tattoos. There were plenty to look at. In fact, from his bull neck on down, there seemed to be virtually no uninked skin at all.

He tensed at the playful expression on the mercenary's face as he arrived.

"Hey, boss," the huge killer said, smiling widely.

"Hey," Gannon said.

"C'mere. Let me show you something," Blackbeard said, swimming up close.

As Gannon watched, the commando grabbed his rope. As he did this, he drew from somewhere a machete-sized black knife. It had evil high-tech lines and a silvery razor-sharp scimitar-like edge that glittered in the firelight as he laid it none too gently up under Gannon's jaw.

"Hey, it's cool, man," Gannon said, trying to hold the rope and his heavy gear and stay very still all at the same time.

"I don't give two shits about recovering anything or whatever they said up there," he said, staring in Gannon's eyes. "You mess with me when we go down, you're going to be the world's first recipient of underwater open-heart surgery."

"No problem," Gannon said, swallowing carefully. "Gotcha, man."

As the blade was withdrawn, there was a tremendous splash. When Gannon turned, he saw Sunglasses was there in the water behind them.

Gannon winced again as the man smiled at him. He was without his sunglasses now, and where his left eye should have been was a hole you could have putted a golf ball into.

Where did Reyland get these people? Gannon thought as he began to strap up.

Three quick minutes later, Gannon adjusted his mask, popped the regulator's gummy rubber piece into his mouth and let go of the rope. He went down first with Blackbeard following almost at the end of his flippers and Sunglasses close behind him.

He had been walking it all through in his mind, so as they got to the floor of the blue hole's bowl, he softly tapped the BCD valve to get the horizontal perfect and went easily and immediately into the corridor-like passageway to the east.

He turned around for the first time when he got to the limestone stairwell with no stairs about a minute later.

Shit, they were actually good divers, Gannon thought. Still Blackbeard was right behind him, shining his light in his face, and his buddy Sunglasses was close behind him.

It didn't matter, Gannon thought as he turned and began to descend lower and lower into the darkness.

There was no other choice. No other play.

He breathed in deeply through the hissing regulator and

slowly let the air bubbles flow out behind him. He closed his eyes and listened to the silence. After a moment, he began to hear his heartbeat pulse faintly against his eardrums.

He would just have to get everything done in the eyeblink of time that he would have.

82

"How long has it been now, Emerson?" Reyland called into the radio.

"Twelve minutes," Emerson called back over the Motorola.

Ruby glanced over at Reyland.

Emerson had just left on the Gator quad a minute after they had gone under. Ruby had overheard him say he was having trouble getting a cell signal for the laptop and wanted to try to get better service out closer to the road.

Ruby looked back across the depression at Ruiz standing there with his rifle. As they sat there, from way up the beach or perhaps from a boat moored out at sea, there was the faint sound of music. It was a slow mariachi song, some sad guitars and lamenting trumpets. Then just as suddenly, it cut off.

"How long can the tanks go for?" Reyland called into the radio after another minute.

"I don't know," Emerson called back out of the radio. "Doesn't Ruiz know this shit?"

"Don't ask me," Ruiz said to Reyland. "I was army, man. Delta. Shepard is the one who was in the Marine Raiders. I can hardly even swim."

Ruby looked at Stick, who looked at Little Jorge.

"Yeah, right," called Ruiz, looking over at them. "Like I can't see you stupid fools eyeballing each other. You want to get a good look at your bone marrow in this romantic firelight, please, by all means, try something funny."

Ruby looked up at the sky. She suddenly remembered what Gannon had said about taking her out on his boat.

She looked down at the black water where Gannon had gone.

There were no stars out tonight after all.

83

The blue hole's corridor-like passage began to close in narrower and narrower. As Gannon got to the extremely tight pipelike end of it, he suddenly put on the jets and swam hard into the tiny entrance of the cathedral.

He felt his right shoulder slice open on a sharp rock as he squeezed through the pipe, but that didn't matter. He ripped himself inside into the huge space, swam straight in for ten feet, dropped his light and left it there on the chamber's floor. Then he turned and swam upward and back over the opening where he had just entered.

Gannon floated there, probing with his hands. There was nothing and still nothing, and he almost went into full out-of-body panic mode, trying to remember where he put it, thinking maybe someone else had found it.

Then his hand found the old duffel fishing rod bag.

Gannon's heart rate and breathing came faster and faster as he pulled the bag to him and unzipped it.

The yard-long piece of metal he pulled out of it looked like a spear gun except instead of a spike at the end of it, there was a short squat length of steel tubing that almost looked like the coupling for a water hose.

The device was called a powerhead, and it was a one-shot underwater firearm that was triggered by making jabbing contact with something.

Due to the retarding density of water, a bullet shot from a regular gun at a distance under water was virtually harmless. But a powerhead set off by spring-loaded direct contact ripped into a target no differently than any other firearm round fired into something from point-blank range.

Already loaded with a waterproofed shotgun shell of double-aught buckshot, the powerhead Gannon pulled from his bag was the kind that spear fishermen used as a backup to protect themselves from sharks.

Gannon pulled out its safety pin and placed its shaft between his teeth like a pirate's knife and took the second powerhead from the bag.

He'd just pulled the second one's pin and was turning down toward the entrance of the cathedral double-fisted when Blackbeard's head emerged into the chamber through the opening just below him.

Floating unseen in the dark two feet above, Gannon waited until he saw the commando's tattooed bodybuilder shoulders.

Then Gannon swung the powerhead down at the base of the big son of a bitch's unprotected skull with every single solitary fiber of fear and fury and life force he possessed.

84

Everyone turned to Reyland's radio as it suddenly began to sputter out static. There were several frantic clicks followed by a short loud beep.

"Emerson? What is it?" Reyland called into the Motorola.

"Holy shit! Reyland!" Emerson called out in a loud, suddenly very clear panicked voice.

"What!" Reyland said.

"The email I was waiting for," he yelled. "Holy shit! I knew it!"

"What?" Reyland said.

"You have got to be kidding me!" Emerson yelled.

"WHAT!" Reyland screamed back into his handheld.

"This guy, Gannon. The report just came in on him. I had Rayne cross-reference his fingerprints with the covert database, and it popped. It popped. We got a hit! You're not going to believe this."

"What are you trying to say?" Reyland called on the radio.

"Reyland, stop interrupting him!" Ruiz yelled from across the hole, sounding suddenly nervous. "How many times I gotta tell you? Every time two people key a mic at the same time, it kills the signal. Keep the line open!"

"Come in, Emerson. Over," Reyland said into the radio.

There was another crackle and then Emerson said clearly:

"I have the report on Gannon. Listen, he was NYPD, but before that, he was DEVGRU, Reyland. Top echelon. Task Force Blue."

Ruby's mouth dropped open as she sat there.

Being navy, she knew that DEVGRU was short for the Naval Special Warfare Development Group.

The special operations organization previously known as SEAL Team Six.

She thought about Gannon. His diving skills. The way he had handled the SWAT team in New York. His preternatural calm.

Gannon was a SEAL! she thought, wide-eyed.

"He's a SEAL?" Reyland said.

"Yes. Listen to this record. Navy SEAL Buds training, 1995, at age twenty-one one of the youngest ever to go through. SEAL Special Sniper School, San Diego, California. SEAL Covert No Contact Urban Environment Recon Course at Fort Gordon in Georgia."

Ruby beamed at the growing dread on Reyland's face.

"He's also done covert ops, boss. Ninety-six, he was Special Actions Division in Africa. In ninety-eight, he was South America with the same group. In twenty-oh-one, he was deployed to Afghanistan with the CIA first expeditionary force in search of Osama bin Laden."

"Shit, shit, shit!" Ruiz said.

"After that he switched to the DIA. Iraq and Afghanistan ops. Year after year after year. Eight tours, Reyland. Eight! This guy's killed more people than fentanyl. He must have joined the NYPD after cycling out of the SEALs."

Ruiz looked down at the water in panic.

"I knew it," he said. "This guy is a seasoned hunter-killer recon cowboy, and my guys don't know!"

"Emerson, listen to me. Are you sure about this? Are you sure?" Reyland said into the radio as he sat up straight.

They all listened. There was the scratch of empty signal. The sound of the wind.

"Emerson, come in. Over," Reyland said.

Reyland crackled the thumb piece again but there was just more fuzz.

"Emerson, come in. Over," Reyland said again.

They listened, but there was still nothing but the sound of crickets from the darkness and the soft rustle of wind in the fronds of the palms.

85

Across the rim of the depression, Ruiz suddenly crouched and backed away from the firelight. His M4 glistened as he shifted it up to his shoulder, pointing it up the path Emerson had gone.

"Reyland, listen to me," he called across the sinkhole. "Where the hell is the other gun? The one with the FLIR heat scope?"

"It's in the Gator. Emerson has it," Reyland said.

Reyland lifted the radio and keyed it again.

"Emerson. Emerson, come in. Over," he said.

"Emerson is dead," Ruiz said, not taking his eyes off the trail.

"What the hell are you talking about?" Reyland said.

"I don't know how, but this script has shifted," said Ruiz. "This SEAL has pulled a fast one on us. We need to get out of here and I mean now, Reyland. Get on that quad and turn it over and drive it over to me here. Do it now."

"You're crazy," Reyland said. "Emerson's battery died or something. This guy's still under the—"

The radio dropped from Reyland's hand as a sharp crack of scratchy signal feedback suddenly sounded out of it.

"Hello, Reyland," said a new voice from its speaker where it lay between his feet.

Ruby looked up at the dark sky, smiling as she felt her heart soar. It was impossible. But yet there it was.

It was Gannon's voice.

"Reyland. Come in, Reyland," Gannon said with a sharp whistle. "Come in, Assistant Special Deputy Agent Reyland, you bald ugly bastard. What? You don't want to talk to me now?"

Reyland stood up out of the camp chair slowly.

"No sudden movements, asshole," Gannon said from the dropped radio. "I have a bead on you right now with this rifle's beautiful FLIR scope. What did you think? I'd hide everything somewhere where there was no back door? Welcome to my house, shit for brains.

"You have a choice here, Reyland. You lie the hell on the ground, you get to live. You don't, I'm going to blow that big ugly Charlie Brown head of yours clean off your neck. Tell El Mighty Mouse same goes for him. Tell Short Shit to lay down his rifle or I will grease his spunky little ass."

There was a scuffling sound, and when Ruby looked up, Ruiz was running full sprint along the rim of the depression.

The rifle crack that came from the trees behind them a moment later seemed inconsequential, a car door closing. Ruiz screamed out mournfully as he went sprawling across the rough limestone face-first.

When he slowly regained his feet, he was clutching at his lower back with one hand like an old man in an aspirin commercial. Using his rifle like a kind of crutch, he began moving again much slower now, his feet shuffling, kicking up rocky dirt along the blue hole's rim.

The next shots from the trees came in a louder cluster. A kla

kla kla–ing burst of fire that made Ruiz's baggy yellow guaya-
bera shirt billow outward as he stopped dead in his tracks.

When he turned slowly, you could see the dark blood splatter like huge ink stains all down the front of the shirt. He was
attempting to lift his rifle to his shoulder when there was another shot that took him through the hollow of his throat just
above the breastbone.

Then Ruiz teetered over headfirst into the depression and
fell from sight.

His heavy little body had just hit the water with a cannonball-
like splash when Ruby was suddenly yanked to her feet.

Gripping at her bound hands and the back of her hair, Reyland ducked in behind her. He swung her hard between him
and where Gannon's fire was coming from.

"You keep backing away with me," Reyland said in her ear as
he began to pull her backward past the campfire, "or, by God,
I will snap your neck clean in two."

"Let her go, you son of a bitch," Gannon called from the radio
as Reyland shoved her to the right beside some palm trees where
the other 4x4 quad was parked.

As she tried to pull away, Reyland swung her hard by her
arms off her feet. The air was knocked out of her as she landed
stomach first into the metal side of the quad.

She was still gasping to catch her breath, still in a daze, when
Reyland kicked her away from the vehicle and leaped on top
of it.

Reyland got the four-wheeler started. As he revved the throttle, the palm tree trunk just beside the left side of his face exploded.

But Gannon's shot had just missed him, and Ruby screamed as
Reyland crouched his pale bald head down between the handlebars and tore off into the woods, the engine wailing.

86

Shirtless and soaking wet, Gannon ran top speed out of the shadows into the firelight beside the blue hole, carrying the M4 carbine he'd taken off Emerson.

He peeked over the rim of the depression and saw Ruiz floating facedown there in the water. Then Ruiz's head blew apart as he clacked another tight burst of 5.56 NATO rounds through the back of it.

Gannon squinted down at the cocky little prick who had killed Sergeant Jeremy.

He only wished he could bring Ruiz back to life. So he could kill him all over again.

"Mike! Over here," Little Jorge called.

Over the rim of rock, Stick was laid out on the stone on his side with Little Jorge kneeling beside him.

"Everybody okay?" Gannon said as he arrived and began slicing off zip ties with Blackbeard's knife.

"Yes," Stick said, smiling, "thanks to you. I never doubted you for a second, brother."

"Really? Then why did you keep saying 'we're dead, we're dead,' over and over again?" Little Jorge said, giggling, hugging Gannon after he helped him up.

Gannon ran over to where Ruby lay on the ground.

"You okay?" he said, kneeling down.

When he sliced off her zip ties, Ruby doubled over, clutching her stomach.

"Hey, are you hurt?" Gannon said, pulling at her baggy dress. "Let me see. Maybe you broke a rib or something."

"No, no. It's okay," Ruby said, immediately shoving him away. "It's better now. Much better. I'm fine now. Perfect, in fact."

"Suit yourself," Gannon said with a wink as he pulled her to her feet.

He led Ruby back to the others and crossed over to the other side of the campfire and started dumping out bags the mercenaries had left. In the second one, he found his truck keys. In the third one, two full magazines fell out and bounced off the rock.

"Little Jorge, listen," Gannon said as he tucked a magazine into the back pocket of his wet madras shorts. "You get everybody back to the Gator and go straight to your place. I'll meet you guys there."

"Where the hell are you going?" Stick said.

Gannon listened to the rip of the quad's engine getting fainter and fainter in the southern distance. He raised the M4, punched out the half-shot magazine, inserted a fresh one and ran the smooth-oiled action with a loud snick.

"To end this bullshit once and for all," he yelled as he began to run.

PART FOUR

THE ONE THAT GOT AWAY

87

It took Gannon under a minute to run back down the forest trail. His Sierra was parked there on the dirt road they drove in on, and he turned it over with a roar and laid the rifle down into the passenger-side foot well and opened the crew cab door.

When he came around to the tailgate, he saw Emerson on the other side of the dirt road. He was unmoved from the spot in the grass beside the Gator where Gannon had sneaked up behind him and choked him out.

He saw he was semiawake now, groggily staring at him from above the wraps of duct tape he'd tied him with.

"On your feet, you damn weasel," Gannon said, grabbing him by his hair. "We're going for a ride to find your boss."

A ragged column of trailing dust rose behind the speeding truck as Gannon hauled it up the dirt drive. When they hit Sherman's Highway, he was doing close to eighty, and the Sierra's spinning back tires gave out a long, high scary bark off the asphalt as the rear end fishtailed.

He went flat-out south as fast as he could for another mile. Then he let off the throbbing engine and rolled all the windows down, listening.

When the ripping sound of the quad came ahead through the trees on his right, he quickly pictured the terrain in his head.

Reyland was along the water now on the Bahama Banks–side beach. South of him where he was headed was Lighthouse Point, where the island ended.

The truck's V-8 throbbed to life again as Gannon buried the accelerator.

"I got you now, you son of a bitch," he said.

A quarter mile to the south the road began to dogleg to the left. When he saw the palm trees on the far side of it, he realized they actually rimmed the beach Reyland was currently driving on.

Gannon reached over and grabbed his seat belt.

"Bump!" he called back to Emerson as the Sierra bucked up off the road and plowed through the brush.

The speeding pickup just fit between two palm trees and then there was a crunching sound as it bottomed out on some jutting rocks. Beyond the rocks there was a descending sand dune, and Gannon felt his stomach drop as the truck's front end got sudden air.

He was rocketing down the curve of the dune, frantically pumping the brakes, when Reyland blew past at incredible speed from left to right across the beach right in front of him.

Gannon spun the wheel and locked his eyes on the quad's cherry-red running light and gunned it down the beach. He was reaching over to grab the rifle a split second later when the quad suddenly zoomed out of his headlights to the left.

"No!" Gannon screamed as he watched the red light disappear from the beach up a dune of sand that sloped up toward the ridge on their left.

He was halfway up the slope after it a moment later when the truck's tires began to slip.

"No!" he screamed again as the rear end swung back and forth in the loose sand as he revved it.

But it was no use.

Gannon slammed the stuck truck in Park and grabbed the rifle and bailed out the driver's door. He sprinted up the dune between the quad's tire tracks past the island's abandoned old gray concrete lighthouse and then came running down the ridge's other side.

He'd just made the flat sand of the Atlantic-side beach when he saw a spot of red to the north.

He halted and brought the infrared scope of the rifle up to his eye.

The quad had stopped. He could see Reyland's heat signature light up white against the dark as he stood beside it. He seemed to be talking on his phone.

Gannon blinked in the scope, gauging the distance. Four hundred yards, he thought. Four-fifty, tops.

Gannon hurried to his left. He braced himself in against the rough trunk of a jutting palm tree trunk and clicked the scope's range selector to four hundred and tucked the butt of the rifle tight into his shoulder.

He'd steadied the cross of the scope's reticle on Reyland's brainpan and had just begun pulling the trigger when he heard the chopping rumble behind him.

Gannon let off the trigger and turned with a mind-boggled expression on his face.

Back over the lighthouse ridge he'd just come down was the unmistakable metallic churning sound of a helicopter flying low.

A *bup-bup-bup-bup-bup-bup* sound of gunfire started up a split second later.

Gannon's eyes almost bulged out of his head.

The six-round burst was followed by another.

Bup-bup-bup-bup-bup-bup.

It was the rattle of a chain-fed machine gun.

"No," he whispered.

It was a gunship, Gannon realized.

A helicopter gunship had arrived now, and it was shooting up his truck.

88

Gannon immediately strapped the M4 on his back and began scrambling up the rock and through the heavier vegetation of the ridge beside him as fast as he could. He was halfway up the promontory when the helicopter roared in over the tree line twenty feet to his right.

It was a gunship all right, Gannon saw as he pressed himself dead still against the shadowed rock with his breath taken. It was a large Bell helicopter like a news chopper, and there was the long black barrel of an M240 bristling sideways out the side of its open sliding door.

As it crested the slope toward the Atlantic-side beach, a blinding white spotlight shot out of the far side of it. The light was probing at the silver palm he'd just been hiding behind when Gannon finally reached the top brow of the ridge.

He was on his hands and knees tucking in under a rock overhang he'd found in the promontory about three minutes later when he heard the helicopter come back over to the Bahama Banks side again.

He crawled out from under the rock and stood and listened to it getting fainter and fainter. After thirty seconds, he saw its lights heading way to the north and west out over the water.

He was terrified that it might head back to attack Ruby and the others, but he realized that Reyland was evac-ing off the island.

Heading where? he thought, tracking the aircraft as it went west. To Nassau? Where else? Had to be.

He hurried quickly south to where he had left the truck.

He shook his head in wonder as he climbed up the sand toward it a minute and a half later. He'd been right. All the windows were shot to shit and the hood and bed had been Swiss cheesed.

But for all that, its engine that he'd left running was miraculously still chugging.

"And they called you a piece of shit," Gannon said as he climbed in over the broken glass and clicked on the dome light.

There was a sound of ragged breathing behind him. He winced as he glanced back into the crew cab thinking surely Emerson must have been turned into a bunch of bloody rags.

But no. Emerson, wide-eyed and very much alive, sat on the floor of the crew cab staring back at him.

He leaned in closer and looked him over. There was blood on the right leg of his khakis. He took out Blackbeard's knife and slit open the pant leg and looked at the gunshot wound.

Emerson had been shot through his right thigh. Gannon turned him to the side. The exit wound was nasty.

But at least it was off center on the outside of the leg. It didn't look like the bullet had hit any bone or arteries.

He slipped Emerson's belt from his khakis. He cried out as Gannon tightened it into a tourniquet above his thigh.

He rolled him back over and checked his pulse.

He was in a bit of shock, but what do you know, Gannon thought with a shake of his head as he clicked off the dome light.

Like the truck, Emerson was still kicking, too.

Gannon brushed the glass off the seat and sat and put the truck into Reverse. When he let off the brake, gravity began immediately rolling them back down the hill of sand.

After he got the truck turned around, he had to stick his head out the door window to see past the shattered glass.

After a moment over the hiss of the radiator, he heard Emerson begin to cry softly behind him.

"I know, right?" Gannon said. "Shoot up a fine vehicle like this. How could they? Make a grown man cry."

89

"Emerson, enough already. Wake up," Gannon said, softly slapping the young agent on the cheek.

"What's going on? What the hell?" Emerson said weakly from where he sat taped to a kitchen chair.

Gannon watched the young agent's eyelids flutter open. Then Gannon smiled as he watched them shoot wide as he took a good look around at the windowless rusty Quonset hut they were now in.

It was three hours later, coming on midnight, and they were in the northernmost opposite end of the island in an area known as Lower Bogue. They were behind the razor-wired fence of a business called Island Safe Storage that belonged to an associate of Little Jorge.

Gannon gave Little Jorge and Stick and Ruby a thumbs-up through the glass of the office behind them. They were drinking soda and eating pizza as they went through the money and diamonds they'd already taken from the recovered sea bag.

Gannon loudly dragged an old kitchen chair over the battered concrete floor and sat before the one Emerson was now duct-taped to.

"I know you're still a little groggy from the painkillers, but it's time we started talking, Emerson. Bad news. Turns out, you're not doing so hot."

Emerson moaned as he looked down at himself where he sat shirtless and in his underwear. There were bloody bandages all over him, at his shoulder, at his crotch, at his right thigh where the tourniquet was still cinched.

"What is this? What's going on?" he cried as he shook in the chair. "Untie my hands. Untie my hands."

Gannon leaned forward and lifted one of the incredibly bloody bandages off Emerson's abdomen.

"Emerson, stop. Get a grip," Gannon said, showing him the bloody rag. "Your stupid friends shot you in the truck back at the beach, remember? One of the bullets came in through your shoulder here, see, and went down your torso doing who knows what to you before it came out here next to your hip."

"Nooo!"

"It's true. I'm worried about you. Your lungs, your major arteries. You were shot with a 7.76. That's a very large fast-moving piece of lead, son. Do you feel hot? Like you have a fever? You're in incredibly serious need of medical attention."

"Then get me to a doctor!" Emerson cried.

"I want to, bro. I really do. And I will," Gannon said as he placed the bloody rag back onto Emerson's stomach.

"But I need to find out what in the living hell is going on first. What the hell is going on?"

Emerson looked at Gannon in complete horror. He looked down at his shirtless self, at all the blood and rags.

"This can't be happening," he said.

Gannon folded his hands in his lap as he sat there. He crossed his legs as he calmly bit at a thumbnail.

"You're wasting time, Emerson. Precious seconds. But hey, it's your life. Not mine. I didn't get shot. My heart and arteries and internal organs are intact and working fine."

Emerson took a deep breath and held it. Then he let it out in a loud rush. His eyes were huge as he stared at Gannon.

"It's about Messerly," he said.

"Messerly?"

"Yes, Messerly. The NSA defector at the embassy in London. The entire operation. It's all about him."

"Oh, that Messerly," Gannon said. "Assange 2.0. How is it about him?"

"He's about to release a trove of classified emails that will rip the roof off the Western global intelligence apparatus. It reveals all of our black ops, our black sites. It also reveals some very questionable Bitcoin financial transactions between some very nasty people around the globe and members of US and British intelligence. Many people, especially a lot of higher-ups in the NSA and CIA and FBI, will go to jail for treason if it comes out," Emerson said.

"I see," Gannon said. "You guys are fighting to stay out of jail. I can buy that. That actually makes some sense considering your recent behavior. But what the hell does Messerly have to do with the FBI director's plane?"

"Our mission was to stop Messerly from releasing the information. But he and the information he has are secured behind the walls of the Chilean embassy in London, where he was granted asylum. Since then, we've been scouring the Chilean embassy staff for a turncoat. Someone with enough bad habits to be blackmailed or possibly bribed."

"Cut to the chase, Emerson. Clock's ticking, remember?" Gannon said.

He took a deep breath.

"But the problem is that Messerly is very well protected even in the embassy itself. A guard is staffed 24/7 outside his room, and only a handful of people are actually allowed to come into his tiny windowless third-floor suite. That's why we finally homed in on the embassy doctor, Raphael Santos, who has routine access to Messerly. We looked for a way to blackmail him into knocking out Messerly and retrieving his data, but it turned out that we were digging a dry hole."

Emerson took another deep breath.

"So that's why we kidnapped the doctor's kid," he said.

90

"You kidnapped his kid! *His kid?*"

Emerson blinked at him.

"Isn't the FBI supposed to solve kidnappings?" Gannon said. "Now you commit them?"

"His name was Scott. He was a college kid. He went to Cambridge. He was nerdy but real smart and caring and socially aware. We learned that he had an internship with the French refugee relief group, Cesse de Pleurer, that was going into eastern Gabon for the summer. The CIA had contacts in the rebel groups just across the border in the Congo. So we hired one of the Congolese warlords down there to grab him."

Gannon shook his head, dumbfounded.

"So the young guy with the headphones on the plane was the embassy doctor's son? That was Scott Santos?"

"Yes," Emerson said.

"And the dead black man was your African warlord?" Gannon said. "He was the kidnapper you hired?"

Emerson nodded.

"Yes. His name was Biyombo. Terrence Biyombo. After he grabbed Scott, he read from the script we gave him. At first, he asked the doctor for money like in a regular kidnapping. But after three million dollars was delivered, he called Santos back and told him that he had learned who the doctor was and where he worked and the Russians he bought his weapons from now wanted something else."

"Messerly's data," Gannon said.

"Yes," Emerson said. "Messerly's data."

"Why was the FBI director involved?" Gannon said.

Emerson looked up at the rusted ceiling.

"For a bunch of reasons. Dunning was neck deep in Messerly's data, for one. Also, Dunning worked with MI6 during the tail end of the Cold War, and we needed him to smooth things over with the British intel people in London who were helping us in the operation.

"But most of all, we needed his radar-jamming G550 to smuggle Scott and Biyombo out of the Congo. The area where Biyombo was holding Scott was in a war zone, and it was becoming increasingly unstable. So Dunning agreed to stop there covertly in the jungle on his way to an Interpol conference in Milan."

"That's where they were headed when the plane malfunctioned? To Italy?" Gannon said.

"Yes. The cabin pressure failure problem must have happened as soon as they got to altitude. The plane was supposed to make a turn to the north, but it never did. It kept going west out over the Atlantic."

"Until it ran out of gas," Gannon said.

"We had no idea where it was until it crashed," Emerson said. "We couldn't track it because the radar-jamming device was on."

"Who was the other guy on the plane? The other stocky white guy?"

"His name was Oliver Buchanan. He was an undercover MI6 agent working with us. He was posing as a hostage negotiator working with the doctor's family for Scott's release."

"Wow, quite an elaborate production," Gannon said. "A cast of thousands."

"Are you familiar with the term *parallel construction*?" Emerson said. "It's standard operational procedure in a case like this. We needed to put the doctor in a moving box, cover every angle."

"You certainly seemed to have accomplished that," Gannon said. "You must have had him coming and going."

"Yes. Please, now you know everything. I've told you everything. Get me to a hospital now. Please, I'm begging you," Emerson said.

Gannon stood and started pacing back and forth behind Emerson.

"Not so fast. I don't think you're telling me everything," Gannon said.

He walked over to a computer on a desk in the corner. He shook the mouse, brought up Google, typed into the search bar and hit Enter.

"I knew it," Gannon said, looking up from the screen. "It says here Messerly's big info drop is in two days' time. This operation is still on as we speak, isn't it? Dr. Santos is still about to take out Messerly for you. He still thinks he can save his son."

"I don't know," Emerson said.

"You don't know? Okay, fine," Gannon said as he came over and started peeling off Emerson's bloody rags. "Are you familiar with the term *bleeding out*?"

"Stop!" Emerson screamed. "Okay, okay! Yes, you're right. The doctor is still in the dark. He picked up a package in London we sent him three days ago. It contains sedatives and a drone he's to use to get all the data out of the embassy for us. That's why the diver was renditioned and the reporter killed. All the potential leaks needed to be plugged in order to keep the doctor in the dark."

"Because if Messerly delivers the truth," Gannon finished for him, "then all you corrupt rotten filthy pieces of money-grubbing shit go to jail."

"Yes," Emerson said. "That's really it. That's all of it. Now please just drop me off at a hospital. I don't care if I go to jail. I'm twenty-nine, man. I just don't want to die!"

"Relax, bro. You'll be fine," Gannon said.

"But the internal bleeding!"

"There isn't any," Gannon said. "You were only shot in the leg. It's a through-and-through. I just covered you in some of your own blood. You think you guys are the only ones who can make shit up?"

"You son of a bitch!" Emerson said.

Gannon nodded.

"You better believe it," he said. "I'm about as nasty a son of a bitch the friendly neighborhood psychopaths of the Naval Special Warfare Command and Joint Special Operations Command and the theater of combat ever created."

Gannon shook his head as he laughed.

"And what do you know? You and your genius boss just pulled me out of retirement," he said.

91

The most important briefing in Reyland's life took place at eleven thirty in the morning off-site in a ruddy brick antique furniture warehouse in the Camden section of London.

Reyland rolled into its rainy cobblestone courtyard with his new team in two Range Rovers at eleven fifteen. There were eight men in his new British operational detail. He thought they looked much like his old American team only they were paler and better dressed.

He left his new men on the ground floor and came up the warehouse's creaking stairs alone. Coming along the grim and grubby walls, Reyland thought the massive furniture-filled space looked old enough to have stored the tea bags that started the Revolutionary War.

He took a breath and sneezed. It even smelled old. There had been a consignment shop just down the road from where they'd summer sometimes with his grandparents in the rural hick kingdom of southeast Indiana, and it smelled like that. Like old church ladies' coats that had been sitting up in a hot, dusty attic.

Reyland was standing by the window when his MI6 counterpart arrived with her people at twenty past. Reyland smiled as he watched her clop over between the old sideboards and rolled-up rugs in her ridiculous heels. Brooke Wrenhall was shorter in person than she had seemed in the SCIF screen, and her makeup was even more garish.

For a moment, they watched the rain pissing into the green water of the Regent's Canal outside the dusty old arched window.

"Ah, another sunny day in London," Reyland said.

Wrenhall took a fat file folder out of her bag and slapped it onto the top of a tarp-covered desk they were standing beside.

Reyland didn't even have to look at the title beneath the national security designation to know it was Michael Gannon's covert military records file. He had just read some of it himself on the plane. He'd actually asked the Pentagon for a completely unredacted version and had straight up been denied. There was no love lost between them and the DIA.

"Doing a little light reading?" Reyland said.

"I just got off the phone with a friend of mine in California about this Gannon. This Michael Gannon," Wrenhall said.

Reyland lifted his chin.

"Interesting conversation, was it? How's the weather out there?"

"Do you know Bill McKendry?"

"The recently retired head of JSOC? I've met the admiral," Reyland said, nodding.

Wrenhall patted the fat file folder.

"Bill says this Michael Gannon was a legend among legends in the SEAL community and was nice enough to send me some of his records. He's been through the CIA's Farm, did you know that? He has tradecraft."

"I vaguely remember hearing that."

"What's especially interesting for me personally, Robert, is the title of the special forces program he helped start at Fort Gordon in Georgia. The Covert No Contact Urban Environment Recon Course. He virtually wrote the textbook on infiltrating, hiding and surviving in a city. And what do you know? Here we are in a city. My city."

"Stop being paranoid," Reyland said.

"And," Brooke said, ignoring him, "some of these covert military ops in which he was involved are quite familiar to me. They were SEAL-SAS joint operations, which means it's probable that Gannon might have actual contacts here in the UK."

"We'll find him," Reyland said. "Santos is in a box. NSA is in complete control of his communications now. There's no way to make contact with Santos by phone or text or fricking carrier pigeon."

"How much time do we have on that end?" Wrenhall said.

Reyland looked at his phone.

"We have T-minus eleven hours and eight minutes."

"You knew this Gannon was involved. His background, his training, and yet you failed to mention it?"

"I found out five seconds ago, Brooke. I had no idea," Reyland said.

"You know what McKendry said about this? Do you know what he said when I suggested Gannon might be at loggerheads to our operation? He said, and I quote—"

"Brooke," Reyland said.

"And I quote," Brooke repeated. "'You folks just opened yourselves up a box of hell.' End quote."

"A box of hell?" Reyland said, wincing.

"That's what the man said," Brooke said.

"Even so, Brooke, what should we do? Abort? And what then? Shoot ourselves? We're in this completely, and there's only one way out. We either pull this off or…" He trailed off.

Out on the water, a low canal boat went by, the wood roof glossy like the lid of a coffin.

He tapped at the glass.

"Or that, Brooke, that right there. Only over a waterfall and on fire."

She looked with him out at the coffin-like boat and took a deep breath.

"You're right, Robert," she finally said. "Of course. Tell me what you need."

92

"Taxi, sir?"

Rolling his carry-on into the drizzle out the front doors of Heathrow, Gannon shook his head.

"No, thank you. I'm waiting on a ride," he said.

Twenty-four hours before, Little Jorge had smuggled Gannon into the Dominican Republic near the port of Bajos de Haina just west of Santo Domingo.

The Dominican Republic was the center hub of Caribbean drug smuggling, and with a little help from some friends, Little Jorge was able to get Gannon everything he needed in quick order.

They had found a very accommodating Venezuelan bank to open up a two-hundred-fifty-thousand-dollar account in cash, and Gannon had put the rest of the money along with the diamonds in a safety-deposit box in a large Canadian bank across the street.

The stolen Canadian passport Little Jorge had scored for him six hours later had cost five grand, and Gannon had flown first-class out of Puerto Plata on an overnight Eurowings flight.

Stick and Ruby had wanted to come, but they could score only the one passport, and there was no more time.

Being an international fugitive wasn't that difficult, Gannon thought, as he removed his burner phone from the pocket of his new raincoat.

All you needed were extremely heavy-duty criminal smuggling contacts and an unlimited amount of money.

"Yes, hello?" a voice said when the phone picked up. It was a little boy's voice in an almost whisper.

"Hi. Is Callum there?" Gannon said.

"Yes, but Daddy can't talk to you. He's driving."

"Oh, okay. My name is Mike, and I'm a friend of your dad. Could you tell him I'm outside of the airport?"

"Daddy says don't worry—we're on our way. We'll be five minutes."

"Thank you," Gannon said, smiling as he hung up.

It was more like three minutes when the beat-up white Volkswagen Golf pulled out of the busy traffic to a stop in front of him.

"Mickey! Screw me sideways! Mickey! How ya been?" his tall lanky old buddy Callum said, wrapping him in a bear hug as he leaped out.

He'd lost most of his sandy hair, Gannon could see. He was also thinner than he remembered him and was wearing glasses. He almost looked like a professor now.

Gannon remembered where they'd met. Some shithole outside Kirkuk where Callum and his SAS guys got cut to ribbons trying to free some brain-dead Brit tree huggers who got kidnapped by al Qaeda. Callum had been shot five times, and the bad guys were pulling him into the back of a technical when Gannon and his boys had shown up.

"I'm really sorry to bother you, man," Gannon said, frowning at him. "I didn't know who else to call."

"Sorry? Get stuffed. Here, give me that," Callum said, grabbing his carry-on and going to the trunk.

There was a strawberry blond–haired kid of four or five in the back seat playing a game on an iPhone.

"Are you an American?" the boy said as Gannon put on his seat belt.

"Yes. Born and raised."

"Did you know Daddy when he was a soldier?"

"Yes, I did," Gannon said. "That's when we met."

"Were you there when he got his scar?"

"Just after, son," Gannon said, smiling.

"He's the one who gave me the ride in the dune buggy," Callum said, slamming the driver's door.

"Oh, with the camels! When you saw the camels, Daddy!" the freckle-faced boy said, his eyes as big as saucers.

"Yes. Now play your game with the headphones," Callum said.

"But—"

"Play!" Callum yelled.

"I wish I had a dune buggy," the little boy mumbled to himself as he pulled on a pair of headphones.

Gannon laughed as he looked out at the traffic.

"I forgot about those camels," he said as they pulled out.

"I didn't," Callum said, smiling, as he pushed his glasses up his nose with a thumb. "Nor the ride."

93

The farm was in Wycomb in the Midlands about an hour west of London.

Callum listened patiently, and when Gannon was done, he put down his tea mug with a clack on the kitchen counter. He folded his arms.

"Lying about the dead FBI director. They're all mad now. Just mad. They'll do and say bloody anything. And even the press doesn't care? I knew it was heading this way. I worked for a contract company for over ten years, but it just got to be too much. Just bedlam on every level. Anyway, ready to see the stuff?"

They went out the front door of the damp little stucco house and walked along a field with two fat red cows in it toward a concrete barnlike building. As they came around its corner, Callum's son was kicking a muddy soccer ball off the side of it.

Inside, there were milking stalls and an office with a window. Callum led them into the office and clicked on the light and closed the door. He opened a large steel locker in the corner.

"I think I was able to get everything you asked for."

Gannon looked at the night vision goggles. The two Heckler & Koch MP5 submachine guns.

The oiled black pistol he lifted looked almost like a Colt M1911 .45 automatic but the barrel was too small.

"MAB?" Gannon said, squinting at the markings.

"Yes, it's a French company. Fifteen in the mag and one in the pipe. A *pistolet automatique très bon*."

"What is it? A thirty-eight?" Gannon said.

"Nine millimeter," Callum said.

"Ah, of course, the metric system," Gannon said. "And that was the box truck we passed on the way in?"

"Yep. Rented on the sly just like you requested. So it's all good, yes?" Callum asked.

"Yes, it's good, Callum," Gannon said with a nod. "Very, very good."

Callum went to the computer on his desk and clicked at the keys.

"Screw me, you're right. Here it is in the *Daily Mail*," he said. "'Messerly announces newest leak is a major one. Tomorrow night, the people of the Western world will learn what their governments are supposedly doing in their name.' End quote. Listen. They're speculating there's evidence of illegal arms trading, drug smuggling, satanic shite, pedophilia, you name it. And that many brand-name multinational corporations might be involved. A bunch of major banks."

"I told you Messerly's about to blow the sewer wall," Gannon said. "And fifty years of the rankest filth and corruption the world has ever seen is going to come a' flooding down Fifth Avenue and Downing Street and the Champs-Élysées."

"And you're saying your FBI friend, Reyland, is going to try to grab Messerly's data tonight to prevent it from coming out?" Callum said.

"Yes," Gannon said. "That's why I'm here."

"You're going to stop him from stealing it."

"Yes."

"How?"

"I'm not exactly sure," Gannon said. "I haven't thought that far ahead. But I'll think of something."

"But why?"

Gannon thought of Sergeant Jeremy. His starched shirts. His kindness. What he had done for him.

Hair actually stood up on the back of his neck as he suddenly remembered the title of the sermon the good sergeant had never gotten to deliver.

God Has a Mission for You.

"Because I have to," Gannon said.

"But you have that bag of money," Callum said. "Why not take off? Why not go fishing forever?"

Gannon laughed. Ruby had said almost the same exact thing to him at the airport in the Dominican.

Before she had unexpectedly kissed him goodbye.

He gave Callum the same answer.

"But I am going fishing," Gannon finally said with a smile.

He thought of Reyland.

"Tonight, I go for Moby Dick," he said.

94

Two hours later, at ten o'clock, everything was ready.

Reyland, with all his notes memorized, turned from the window at his agents and analysts. He smiled at the buzz in the air, smiled at his security men standing at the back of the room with their blunt, hard faces.

All the king's horses and all the king's men, he thought.

There was a blown-up map of the city of London on the whiteboard behind him, and in front of him on the conference table was a 3-D cardboard mock-up of two buildings, one marked EMBASSY and one marked WORK SITE.

Reyland took out a pair of reading glasses and a laser pointer as he cleared his throat.

"Ladies and gentlemen, this," he said, waving the laser pointer across the shorter side of the box marked EMBASSY, "is Upper Belgrave Street.

"This," he said, pointing the laser between the boxes to its shorter side, "is Wilton.

"Our setup is at this work site here across Wilton, which we will infiltrate from Wilton Mews here to the north. Our agent in the embassy will open a window here on the Wilton side of the embassy in the back. Once the exchange from the window to across the street to the work site is complete, we will exit here down the work site scaffolding on Upper Belgrave into a waiting vehicle here. Once in the car, we will go in a protective convoy back here in the route that you've all been given. So far so good?"

He looked at the faces. Everyone was nodding.

"Any questions?"

"What about the foreign service security at all the embassies on Upper Belgrave? What if we're spotted?" asked an agent.

"You don't have to worry about that. We will be jamming all communications," Reyland said.

"In addition, all pertinent staff at surrounding allied embassies have been briefed. The whole area will be on stand-down," Wrenhall added.

"What if there is resistance from the Chilean embassy security or another intel force? Do we have permission to engage?" said another ops agent.

"The sensitivity of this operation could not be greater," Reyland said. "With that said, the acquisition and protection of this asset supersedes everything, and I mean everything."

"Engage anything that jeopardizes the mission?" said the security man.

"Yes, treat Upper Belgrave as a battlefield. Engage and remove all threats," Reyland said.

"Robert, if I could?" Brooke Wrenhall said, standing from the table.

"By all means," Reyland said.

"As you all know, this operation is in no way, shape or form authorized by any local police, so use the highest levels of stealth and aversion at all times," Wrenhall said.

"But remember," she said. "There aren't any words to explain exactly how important this mission is. I've been working in intelligence circles for almost forty years, and what we are seeking to recover is the most important piece of actionable intel I've ever come across.

"This mission is tide turning, ladies and gentlemen. History making. Or breaking. We all know our jobs. Let's do them."

95

Belgravia in London was a neighborhood that seemed to consist solely of large white bank-like buildings.

From the box truck's front passenger seat, Gannon looked out at the perfect columns and pristine arches, the stone balconies, the high dark windows.

"Ritzy," Gannon said as he went around a double-parked Rolls-Royce.

The Chilean embassy at 14 Upper Belgrave was on the northeast corner of Wilton. As he passed it, Gannon surveyed its security cameras, its twelve-foot-high thick wrought iron gate. The heavy black metal door behind the gate was as featureless and formidable as a bank safe's.

No wonder the intel services had gotten so desperate, Gannon thought. No one was getting in there without a wrecking ball or a five-hundred-pound bomb.

He passed the embassy and made a right onto a tree-flanked

road then another onto Belgrave Place, and then twenty feet up past a road called Eaton Square he pulled over.

Gannon got out and went to the back of the box truck that now had telephone company markings along its side. He popped the doors and put on a hard hat and orange traffic vest. There was a telephone company manhole just in off the corner, and he took out some traffic cones from the back of the truck and placed them around it. Then he lifted a crowbar off the floor of the truck and bent and popped the manhole.

After he dragged the lid aside, Gannon stood on the street glancing nonchalantly at the passing traffic. Then he went down into the hole with a flashlight and a pair of bolt cutters.

There were four old lead-covered phone cables and five fiber-optic cables leading into the block of buildings he was parked in front of, and it took him less than two minutes to cut every single one of them.

When he was done, he climbed out of the hole and slipped on a large backpack from the rear of the truck and lifted the crowbar. There was a work site there at the first building of the block he'd just blacked out, and he ripped open its plywood door at the hinges.

Inside was a completely gutted hollowed-out building with just a staircase left. There was no alarm clang even after a full minute, and he closed the plywood door and quickly went up.

It was three flights to its roof, and he came out a little attic-like door and stood up on the tar paper roof in the cool air looking north over the chimney caps. From Eaton Square to Upper Belgrave were fourteen separate town houses that butted up against each other so tightly they looked like the same building.

Gannon hefted his bag and walked north to the first terra-cotta roof edge and quietly stepped over it and kept going.

Two minutes later, he stood near the northern edge of the last building overlooking Upper Belgrave directly across from the embassy. There was a large air-conditioning unit there about the size of a minivan and he pulled himself on top of it and un-strapped the knapsack.

Of all people, Gannon knew exactly how ballsy it was to just walk into the middle of an intel op.

But also of all people, he knew what such an op was like from the inside.

He'd been on manhunts before. All eyeballs involved were now Krazy Glued on Messerly and the embassy and whatever the hell was going on in there. The last thing any of them would be thinking about was someone coming up on their six.

He zipped open the pack and opened the first flap and began laying everything out on the metal roof of the A/C unit.

The barrel of the sniper rifle came first. Then the bolt. Then the suppressor. The lower part of the rifle was under the second flap and he lifted it out and extended its bipod. He turned on the FLIR scope that was already attached and then slapped in the magazine of ten .338 Lapua Magnum rounds and slipped in the bolt with a click.

He played with the FLIR scope's settings until the contrast was just right, and then settled in flat on his belly.

It took only five minutes before he saw one of the white panel-like coverings on the third floor of the construction site across from the embassy on Wilton Street open up.

Someone appeared in the gap. Someone with binoculars, pointing at the embassy.

Gannon checked his watch and smiled.

"Thar she blows," he said.

He'd guessed right. Small smartphone-powered drones had limited ranges. He'd studied the map around the embassy. The work site was the only logical place for Reyland to wait to receive it.

As he focused in the FLIR's zoom, he saw that the figure in the work site flap wasn't Reyland but a woman.

But that didn't matter, Gannon knew. Reyland was up there.

He'd known men like Reyland. Psychopaths. He'd met his share of them.

Reyland wouldn't miss being front row center for the grand finale of his sick little play for all the world, Gannon knew.

Gannon tilted the rifle right and eyed the embassy.

"Shit!" he suddenly said.

His plan was to shoot the drone as it came out of one of the windows and knock it down safely behind the embassy gates.

But as he lay there, he realized a problem he hadn't anticipated.

There was a damn Chilean flag flapping on a pole at the top corner of the Wilton side of the embassy.

If the drone came out from one of the back windows on the other side of the flag down Wilton, he wouldn't be able to see it until it was too late. At best, he'd only be able to knock the drone down into the middle of Wilton Street, where the bastards could still retrieve it.

"Shit!" he said again, taking his eye off the scope.

What the hell was he going to do?

He was thinking of maybe laying fire on the embassy itself, shattering some windows to raise the alarm, when out of the corner of his eye he caught movement, and he turned.

A piece of scaffolding sheet on the Upper Belgrave side of the work site where Reyland and his team were now hiding was wafting back and forth in the breeze.

"Screw it," Gannon said to himself as he suddenly leaped up.

He left the sniper rifle where it was and started running with everything he had back across the rooftops the way he'd come in.

96

Up on the third floor of the construction site, Reyland squatted by a concrete mixing tray as a muscular female MI6 agent slit open another piece of the white plastic construction scaffold wrapping.

She turned and handed him the binoculars.

From where Reyland peeked out, it was a level clear lane straight across Wilton to the embassy's rear stairwell window where Dr. Santos would make the drop.

Reyland checked his watch. It was 11:25 a.m. Any minute now.

He looked at the dark window of the embassy, thinking about the doctor. What he had to be going through. The despair of betraying his patient and possibly going to jail warring with the hope of getting his son back.

Yes, that one hope, that tiny beam of light, was guiding him toward Messerly's room at this very moment.

Reyland's phone vibrated. He looked down.

It was an empty text from the good doctor. The signal.

He was by the window now.

"Keep your eyes peeled. It's on," Reyland said to the agent beside him.

In the end, it was almost ridiculous how easy it was. There was a sound of a window opening across the street, and then out of the window came a quad drone the size of a radio-controlled plane.

Then Reyland heard the embassy window shut as the agent leaned out of the panel slit.

"Gotcha," she said.

"Are they there? Are they there?" Reyland said, and then his eyes lit up as the female agent dropped the thumb drives into his palm.

He gazed on them, three little smooth white slabs of plastic each no bigger than a gum eraser, *Toshiba* written on their sides.

Over this? he thought, shaking his head.

A year's work. Millions spent. Lives lost. Over a gram of plastic and silicone?

"Time to go," he said.

The line of his British security commando men waved Reyland west over the construction site roof like coaches at an obstacle course. He passed some aluminum framing beams, a pile of steel rods, a rolled-up hose. There was a stepladder that went up over the roof wall to the scaffolding on the Upper Belgrave side of the building, and Reyland went over it and started down the nine-story scaffold's steps.

They were coming down the seventh-story flight of stairs when Reyland heard it. There was the high scream of a car engine on Upper Belgrave, and all five of them stopped on the stairs and went over to the street-side railing.

At first Reyland couldn't see because of the plastic sheeting, but then he pulled at the plastic until he got it to part like a curtain.

Then he turned to the right.

Down Upper Belgrave came a huge white work truck flying like a runaway train.

It was a phone truck, Reyland could see, as it jumped the curb onto their block and came roaring up the sidewalk directly at them.

"Back! Back! Back!" Reyland cried.

Then the truck smashed somewhere down below into the scaffolding they were standing on, and Reyland yelled as he felt the stairs jolt and heave beneath his backpedaling feet.

97

The fifteen-thousand-pound truck's speedometer was hovering around the eighty mark when Gannon plowed it into the base of the scaffolding.

The rapid-fire bongs of the ripped-free galvanized steel pipes blasting off the speeding hood and grille sounded almost festive, like wedding bells.

He ducked down as one of the pipes jumped up sideways and shattered the windshield. Another pole came into the cab itself a split second later like a spear where his head had just been.

Gannon kept his foot pressed down on the accelerator in the fantastic gonging as support pipe after support pipe after support pipe popped free.

The runaway truck had just torn loose the last of the supports at the end of the block when one of its front tires exploded like a bomb blast. Gannon closed his eyes as he felt the truck wobble crazily toward the right. It was actually on two wheels when it came off the sidewalk into the street again. Gannon hugged the steering wheel to brace himself as it toppled over completely on its right side and went skidding through the intersection in an incredible screech of metal and clanging support pipes and spitting sparks.

Reyland and the rest of his team were still scrambling up the stairs between the sixth and seventh floors of the scaffold when the heavy ninth-story transom of the compromised structure suddenly ruptured.

They were still running as the ninth floor pancaked into the eighth floor and the eighth floor into the seventh, and then the heavy wooden seventh floor slammed down onto them like a giant textbook onto the heads of a half-dozen scurrying ants.

The entire superstructure of the scaffolding ripped completely free from the building a split second later and tipped over into the street.

The screams of the dying and the mangled among Reyland's party were lost in the banging as pipe upon pipe rained down mercilessly onto the sidewalk and asphalt seventy feet below.

Along with the pipes, lethal arrows of rebar, pallets of bricks, and boards flew down by the dozens. A falling construction dumpster went through the roof of a street-parked Mercedes like a knife through warm butter as half a dozen fifty-pound bags of concrete shattered off Upper Belgrave street all around in reverberating, bursting clouds of gray dust.

The critically collapsed scaffolding was still clanging and splintering and exploding into the narrow street even as Gannon pulled himself up out of the knocked-over truck's passenger-side window.

He hopped down into the street over the hood of the cab and looked around and saw that he had come to a stop in the street almost directly in front of the Chilean embassy's wrought iron gate. As he leaped down off the toppled truck, he saw the embassy front door open and some confused-looking men emerge from it.

"What happened? Are you okay?" one of them yelled as Gannon headed into the cloud of silvery dust that now almost completely obscured Upper Belgrave on the other side of Wilton Street.

The first human he came across in the thick mist was one of Reyland's commandos. He was on one knee, coughing. Gannon saw the machine gun on a strap at his back and lifted a broken two-by-four up off the asphalt as he came in behind him, brought it down with a bonk over the guy's head and took his gun.

A moment later, there was the rev of an engine through the dust, and Gannon walked toward it.

"Hey, hey, hey! Over here, Reyland!" called out a man's voice with a British accent. "Where are you? Where is everyone? What bloody happened?"

As Gannon got closer, he could see the man, some stick figure–skinny English guy. He was standing beside the open door of an idling black Range Rover.

Gannon put the bead of the Heckler & Koch between the guy's suddenly hugely wide eyes as he approached.

"Get away from the car!" Gannon yelled then let off a clacking burst at the guy's feet to give him some incentive.

Gannon found Reyland thirty seconds later ten feet from the Range Rover.

He was under a sheet of plywood between a couple of parked cars, and as he stood over him, the FBI agent moaned sorrowfully.

Then Gannon saw why.

There was a pole sticking out of him. It was a piece of galvanized steel pipe about three feet long and it was jutting from his torso just below his chest. It had sliced cleanly through his windbreaker, which was now completely drenched in blood.

Ouch, Gannon thought when he saw the rest of the galvanized pipe sticking out of Reyland's back. The pipe he was skewered with was actually leaning sideways against one of the parked cars, and it was kind of propping him up in a seated position as he sat there in the gutter.

"I'm hurt. What is this? What happened? I'm stuck. Why am I stuck?" Reyland suddenly said.

It was a miracle that Reyland was still alive, let alone conscious, Gannon thought as he shook his head.

Gannon knelt and patted and then reached into Reyland's bloody windbreaker pocket and removed the three thumb drives there.

He pursed his lips as he thought of what to do with them.

"What are you doing?" Reyland said as Gannon pulled off one of Reyland's boots.

"It's okay. Everything's okay, big man. You just sit tight," Gannon said as he peeled off Reyland's sock and put the thumb drives into it and tied the sock up into a ball.

He was going to throw it back over the Chilean embassy fence. But as he jogged back across Wilton, he actually encountered one of the burly guards he had seen by the door. He was now standing out on the sidewalk on the corner.

"Here," Gannon said as he untied the sock and poured the thumb drives into the startled guard's hand.

"These belong to your guest," he said. "Dr. Santos dropped them out the window. You should probably talk to him about that. Also, you should probably check on Mr. Messerly."

"And you are?" the guard said with a Spanish accent.

"No one at all," Gannon said as he started running back toward the destruction.

"Help," Reyland said as Gannon got back to the idling Range Rover.

Gannon stopped and looked down at the deputy assistant director as he began making loud huffing and puffing sounds.

"There's something stuck in me. Pleeeeeease! I can feel it," Reyland said. "It's between my ribs! It's stuck. Stuck."

Gannon peered at the shaft of blood-slicked metal sticking out of Reyland's guts and suddenly smiled as he thought of what he had told his buddy Callum about going whale fishing.

How do you like that, he thought.

It looked just like a harpoon.

"You must help me," Reyland said. "I have a family. My wife. I'll give you anything."

In the distance, Gannon could hear the first sirens approaching. He thought they would have that weak *weee aw, weee aw* Euro sound from the movies, but they sounded just like American ones.

"Sounds like you need a doctor, Reyland," Gannon said as he got behind the Rover's wheel. "Maybe Dr. Santos over at the embassy could help you out."

Gannon slammed the door and zipped down the British luxury car's window.

"But on second thought, probably not," Gannon said as he slammed the gas into the floor.

EPILOGUE

When Gannon finally appeared out of the sliders onto the upper terrace, he was wearing a new pair of cargo shorts and a black T-shirt with a neon blue barracuda on it that he had bought at the airport.

It was coming on seven in the evening, and he was back in the Dominican Republic now at a gated vacation villa in the La Costa Brava neighborhood of Santo Domingo up in the hills high above the bay.

He walked to the rail and looked out on the sea, then down at the lower terrace where Little Jorge and Stick were laughing and drinking beer. They were grilling steaks beside the infinity pool with some reggae music bopping out of a speaker beside the grill.

"There you are," Ruby said, coming out onto the deck behind him.

"How do I look?" she said, showing him her new long-sleeved T-shirt and capri pants.

"Are these sneakers okay for a boat?" she said, showing off her pink Converse low tops. "I never went deep-sea fishing at night. Or actually during the day either, to be honest."

"You look marvelous, Lieutenant," Gannon said. "Especially the sneakers."

"How's your son? You called him, right?"

"He's doing fine," Gannon said. "The Brewers turned him down, but he got another tryout with the Mets in Port St. Lucie. Fingers crossed."

"That's awesome," Ruby said, holding up her crossed fingers on both hands. "The Messerly information drop just happened, by the way."

"He's back on his feet?" Gannon said.

"Uh-huh. It happened half an hour ago. The internet is going insane. It's all unredacted. Thousands and thousands of pages. Emails. Videos. Swiss bank account numbers. These intel people must be beside themselves."

"Intel people?" Gannon said. "Global mafia, you mean. Enough of those fools. Time to head to the dock. You ready?"

"As ready as I'll ever be," Ruby said.

"Good," Gannon said, walking over to the steel bucket by the door he'd already filled with ice and beer. "Grab the other end of this, would you?"

"Come on, guys. Time to catch us some fish," Gannon said excitedly as they came out on the lower deck by the pool.

"Actually, Mick, we're calling a mutiny," Stick said. "After a few more cervezas, me and little Jorge here are heading down to a club nearby. He's going to introduce me to some *las chicas bonitas* he knows."

"*Las* what?" Gannon cried. "The blues are biting, Stick. The blues! And Little Jorge. How could you? You're going to let me and Ruby here go out on that fine vessel we rented without a first mate?"

They heard the honk of their taxi sound as Little Jorge sat there giggling.

"It's okay, Mike," Ruby said. "I think we'll be okay by ourselves."

"Just you and me?" Gannon said, squinting at her.

Ruby looked up at the stars that were just now starting to show themselves in the darkening sky.

"Just you and me," Ruby finally said with a nod. "I think we'll be just fine."

★ ★ ★ ★ ★

CONJURE
WOMEN

RANDOM HOUSE

NEW YORK

CONJURE
WOMEN

A Novel

AFIA ATAKORA

Copyright © 2020 by Afia Atakora

All rights reserved.

Published in the United States by Random House, an imprint and division of Penguin Random House LLC, New York.

RANDOM HOUSE and the HOUSE colophon are registered trademarks of Penguin Random House LLC.

LIBRARY OF CONGRESS CATALOGING-IN-PUBLICATION DATA
Names: Atakora, Afia, author.
Title: Conjure women: a novel / Afia Atakora.
Description: First edition. | New York: Random House, 2020.
Identifiers: LCCN 2019015814 | ISBN 9780525511489 |
ISBN 9780525511496 (ebook)
Subjects: LCSH: African Americans—Fiction. | Plantation life—Southern States—Fiction. | Race relations—Southern States—Fiction. |
GSAFD: Historical fiction.
Classification: LCC PS3601.T35 C66 2020 | DDC 813/.6—dc23
LC record available at https://lccn.loc.gov/2019015814

Printed in the United States of America on acid-free paper

randomhousebooks.com

2 4 6 8 9 7 5 3 1

FIRST EDITION

Title-page and part-title images: © iStockphoto.com

Book design by Dana Leigh Blanchette

For Mum,
the first storyteller I ever knew

PART ONE

FREEDOMTIME

===

1867

The black baby's crying wormed and bloomed. It woke Rue by halves from her sleep so that through the first few strains of the sound she could not be sure when or where she was, but soon the feeble cry strengthened, like a desperate knocking at her front door, and she came all the way awake, and knew that she was needed, again.

She unwound herself from her thin linen sheet. If there were dreams, she'd lost them now that she'd stood up. There was only the crying, not so loud as it was strange, unsettling. She smoothed her nightmare hair and made ready her face. Stepped out from her cabin, barefooted.

At the center of the town, between the gathering of low cabins that sat close and humble, Rue could make out the collection of folks, like herself, who'd been drawn from their sleep by the haunting cry. Anxious, bedraggled, they emerged to suppose at that unearthly sound. It was a moonless night, the clouds colluding to block out the stars, and the crowd knitted itself tightly in a weave of black whisperings.

"You hearin' that, Miss Rue?" one of them said when she approached.

What little light there was streamed down from behind the crowd, hiding them, illuminating Rue. She couldn't make out their faces for the darkness but replied just the same. "Can't help but hearin'. That some poor sufferin' somethin'?"

As she walked, already she was holding herself straighter, prouder. It's what they were expecting. No matter how weary she was feeling on the inside, she knew she had to walk easy, like she were floating, same as her mama used to do. Rue's magic ought to be absolute, she knew, not come to them sleepwalking and unsure, or it wasn't magic at all.

"Never heard nothin' come close to that cry."

"Ain't no creature."

"That's one a' Jonah's li'l 'uns."

Rue knew they suspected already what child it was. That wrong child, born backward in a caul, a bath of black.

Jonah himself was opening the front door of his cabin and stepping out of it, and Rue did hope that Jonah, calm and right-headed, had come to silence the rumors on his child. But there was no denying that beyond him was the origin of the crying. Even his tower-tall presence in the doorway couldn't block out the menacing sound.

"Miss Rue," he called, and his voice was thin like river silt. "You there, Miss Rue?"

Rue did ache for Jonah's predicament. She answered, "I'm here."

"Sarah's thinkin' the baby's took sick. She's wantin' you to look him over."

Rue stepped forward, took her time going up the few sunken-down steps to the little porch. She could feel all them eyes clinging to her back like hooks. At the top step Jonah, dark-skinned and strong and sure, reached down for her and took her elbow in his hand, guiding her. His callused palms were hard against her bared skin, rough the way only a man's hand had cause to be, and as he moved her through the door, he gave the point of her elbow a slow rub, a caress away from their fastened eyes.

"Thank you, Miss Rue," he said and showed her in.

The home was made up of two rooms, more than most folks could boast, though the thatch roof wept from some long-ago storm. Rue followed Jonah to the front room's far corner where Sarah was knee bent, washing the children.

The tub was large enough to fit all three of Sarah and Jonah's little ones, but their elder boy and girl stood outside of it, naked but dry, waiting to be washed. Their faces were damp and ruddy beneath their high-yellow skin, like they'd been crying but had exhausted that sorrow, left it to the baby to do the weeping for them.

Inside the tub the baby was on his back looking like a white island. The steam rose up from his skin in waves. He was crying, Lord, was he crying. Rue heard in it a lost cry, and it was a call she felt compelled to answer, if not with comfort then with a mournful cry of her own. In the water beside the baby a chipped cup bobbed along the ripples created by his movements. It hit the walls of the tub out of time with the high, piercing whine that had snaked its way into Rue's dreaming.

When she leaned forward, the baby stilled his squall. He opened his eyes as if to look upon her, revealed the oil-slick black irises that had heralded his strangeness, that had prompted the name Rue had given him at his birth: Black-Eyed Bean.

Rue said to Sarah of the baby's eyes, "They ain't changed." She spoke it low enough to be out of Jonah's hearing.

"No, they ain't," Sarah said, in just the same whisper. "He ain't changed."

———

There was no magic in birthing. No conjure, neither. The birth of Black-Eyed Bean had occurred one year back. Had begun no different than any other birth that Rue had known, and she had known many.

Rue just walked the women. That was it. All it took in the birthing room was good sense, the good sense that a thing hanging ought to fall, the way swollen apples brought their branches low before the apples plopped down to the ground. Shouldn't it be the same with a baby? Let them hang low in the mama when it was time to fall, the mama being the branch near snapping.

Since the end of slaverytime, Rue had birthed every last child in that town. She knew their mamas and their daddies, too, for she was allowed into sickbeds for healing and into birthing beds alike, privy to the intimate corners of joy and suffering, and through that incidental intimacy she had come to know every whisper that was born from every lip, passed on to every ear. She knew what folks said about each other, and Lord, she knew what they said about her.

What folks said about Sarah, Jonah's wife, Bean's mama, was that she was beautiful, and it was so. She was a fiery woman, petite as an ember but just as dangerous, with skin light as wheat. Sarah was one of those who had sung when she walked the birth walk, had done so the two births before this, sung and moaned and sung right up to the moment that her bigger than big babies came on out to the world. Sarah had sung while she was heavy with Bean, a sonorous song with no words but so much soul. Her one hand gripped on too tight to Rue's while the other hand beat out the tune she was singing against her sweat-slicked thigh. It was when Sarah's squeezing got too tight, the veins standing up like blue rivers in her high-yellow hand, that Rue started her usual worrying.

⚔

Truth was Rue didn't want nothing to do with any of that mess, the moan-singing mamas or the anxious daddies—when there were daddies—wringing their hats and their hands outside the door, or the wet and wailing babies, or, worst of all, the babies that came into the world just quiet, gone already before they ever lived, just lost promises with arms and legs and eyes for nothing. Why would she want to meddle in all of that?

As she laid Sarah down Rue had begun to think of how it all could go wrong, and if it did, what was she to do? Because just as easy as folks' praise came, it could turn to hating. Magic and faith were fickle. Life and living were fickle. And didn't Rue know that as well as anyone?

Still, when the time came for bearing down—the women praying with their cussing and cussing with their praying—it was in the way they looked up at her, weepy eyes filled with worship, that kept her door open. Like apples, babies came in seasons, and Rue would always tell herself in the lull, *Not next year. Next year I be done.*

Bean had been born in one such lull, Sarah being the fertile kind. The "Her man gotta do no more than look at her" kind, like Rue's mama used to say of the women who could show up twice in a year with their bellies making tents of their dresses.

It was easy going year after year with Sarah. She was still young, twenty-and-some, and already she'd made two babies who had been born after no more than the usual struggle. Still she stayed smooth and sweet, and her breasts remained like two fat fruits just shy of ripe.

"He's a'comin'," Rue had said, laying her open palm on Sarah's restless belly. How Rue knew even before the crown of him started pushing through that Bean would be a boy she could not account for, not in words. There was just her knowing.

Rue had rolled her rough-hewn sleeves on up—just about everything she wore and ate and owned was a gift from those mamas who had no other way to pay—and she had knelt the way she had knelt near a hundred times now, though her knees did ache for it despite her youth. Rue was nearabouts twenty also if her old master's accounting was to be believed, not much younger than Sarah, though every day Rue felt more worn, like she were living out each one of her years double, aging out of time.

They'd grown up together, true, through slaverytime, wartime, freedomtime, but Sarah had kept herself young, and even here, at her most vulnerable hour, the sweat sitting on her skin had the audacity to glisten. In every way they were opposites—that was clear enough as Rue laid her thick dark fingers on Sarah's thin thighs and parted them.

"Lord. Miss Rue." Sarah sighed, praying to them both.

Rue had to love and hate equally being called *Miss*. She was every time reminded that she'd earned the title—and the respect of it—only after her own mama's dying.

Rue's mama, called Miss May Belle, had gotten the kind of sickness that could not be seen and for that reason could not be cured. Its origins were in heartache for her man, Rue's daddy, who some said ran himself crazy for lust of a white woman.

Well, let folks have their stories. The only truth was he'd been hanged, strung from a tree just outside the town, his dangling toes making circles in the dirt as his body spun on the rope. And Rue had hardly known him.

She'd been under Miss May Belle's tutelage the whole of her life. From her Rue had learned one true thing, that all birthing was performance. Mamas were made to believe that a bit of pepper by their bed would ward off evil spirits, but it was only meant to cause them to sneeze if what was required was a good last push to get the baby out. Rue learned to tell women to blow into a bottle or to chew on some chicory or to squat over a pot of boiling water to make their babies strong, to make the birthing easy, to protect them in that most crucial hour.

Bean's mama was easy. Birthing came as natural to Sarah as it did to animals who need only to pause and squat and be off again.

Rue knew that she ought to be glad of that, but she wasn't. Sarah was silk, free to slip from one type of wanting to another. Rue was rough, coarse linen, starched in her life. Freedom had come after the war for all black folks. All excepting Rue, she felt, for she was born to healing and stuck to it for life. And stuck to this place. Her own doing that, a secret curse of her own making.

"Lord Jesus," Sarah had crooned as she'd labored. She'd gripped the bedsheets near to ripping. "Get me through this 'un. I swear, Miss Rue, this here's my last."

Rue knew sure as she knew the sun would rise that Sarah would come up pregnant again soon enough. Weren't men drawn to her like flies to shit?

And it was on that thought, potent as a curse, that she realized something between Sarah's legs was going wrong.

Rue nearly drew away in shock. A black mass came out, all in a forceful gush. The coal-dark sack squirmed in Rue's hands. The blood that surrounded it was a red made more ominous by the darkness it covered. Through that black sheath Rue could make out the small surprise of a pale face, the mouth working sound-lessly, nothing like suckling but more like an old man chewing on the words of a curse.

It wasn't unusual for babies to come still wearing the veil. "It means good luck," Rue would be quick to tell the mamas when they saw the extra skin wrapped around their baby's heads, looking as final as a shroud. In a moment she could wipe it away, and the healthy wail would fight back the unsaid fright in the mama's eyes that from her womb had come something unexpected, something unnatural.

Bean made Rue's heart jump in absolute horror of him. She felt then that she knew him for what he was, a secret retribution for a long-ago crime, the punishment she had been dreading.

He was fighting, his arms moving inside that black wrapping like he was swimming, or more like drowning. She had never seen a baby so fully encased in the caul.

Rue forced herself to draw up the scissors she'd heated in preparation to cut the cord; she held them near the baby's mouth. Sarah had not moved at all from her position braced against the sheets.

"He come dead?" Sarah said, straining to hear the telltale cry.

Rue might've said yes. The black thing curling and quivering in her palms stayed gasping. It could not break through the veil without her intervention. She might've left it to struggle or smother in its own black sheet.

"Oh, Miss Rue," Sarah started moaning, squinting her eyes hard to get a look at the bundle. "Don't say he dead."

A snip. That's all it took, and Rue did it. A snip beneath the little nose and then slowly, like peeling back the skin of a strange fruit, she shucked Bean of his dark veil and revealed him to the world. He began, finally, to cry.

"He alright," Rue heard herself saying. But was he? Was she?

Divested now of the veil that was like his second skin, his true coloring showed, lighter even than his mama was. There was no warmth to the color, only a pallid white. The baby's skin was peculiar dry too, near scaled, dry as though no loving had ever touched him. Rue had the urge to do more than rub him the way she did to warm life into all the new babies. She had, instead, the urge to scrub the strange skin clean off.

The eyes were the next shock, for when they blinked open they were full black, edged thinly in egg-boil white. The baby's eyes were the same glossy black as the veil-like husk that had held him.

He rolled them slow and looked up at Rue as if he could see clearly through to every thought she had in her head.

When she'd sucked the blood from his nose and had him clean as she could get him she tied off the cord. Her practiced hands shook with the force of her nerves as she hurried to lay this strange baby by his mama's side and wipe off the stain he'd left on her hands.

Sarah looked at the child. She did not move to give him her breast. Instead she pulled the dirtied sheets around herself, and when Rue came to press on the stretched skin of her belly to check that nothing had been left in the womb, Sarah would not let her near. She wanted only to stare at her baby, not with that new-mama affection but in the very same way you'd stare at a snake you'd woken up to find coiled beside you in your bed.

"He's a big 'un," Rue said, to say something.

"Them eyes?"

"Like little black-eyed beans, ain't they?" Rue said. She wished she could snap back those words soon as they left her lips. She should have pretended that everything was as it ought to be. Her mama, Miss May Belle, had she been living, might have had the words of reassurance, might have made the baby a miracle, for she had that way about her that Rue had never learned or inherited.

Sarah still would not take the baby up. His crying grew more shrill in the silence, like an accusation, and Rue felt she had to go on talking.

"Folks says babies born under the veil got the gift a' the Sight," Rue said. It was meant to be a comfort. It came out sounding grim as a burden. Rue found that she pitied that babe if it were true, for here he was not a clock's tick old and already he had to bear the whole knowledge of the world.

Rue had stripped the sheets, stepped out of the cabin without saying any more. There was Jonah, the daddy, waiting. He'd been keeping himself busy chopping more firewood than the hot summer day rightly called for, and when he saw Rue step out, he stopped mid-swing and smiled.

She studied him, taking in his sun-darkened skin and his eyes that were the same easy brown as the bark he was cutting. He bore no resemblance to his son. His son bore no resemblance to any living thing she had ever seen.

When Rue stepped forward, the bloodied birthing sheets bundled in her arms, Jonah looked up at her with trepidation. He could not lend voice to the question that needed asking.

Rue spoke to spare him the effort: "You got yo'self a thrivin' baby boy."

His sweat-shining face broke out into a grin and before he could ask her anything more, she handed him the bundle of sheets that contained the damning black caul, bloody and shapeless, in its center. She knew even if he got a look at it, he wouldn't understand it. Men could not make sense of women's work.

"What do I do with all a' this?"

"Burn it," she said, telling him what he was needing to hear. "Burn it for luck."

SLAVERYTIME

===

1854

Miss May Belle had used to turn coin on hoodooing. As a slave woman she'd made her name and her money by crafting curses. More profit to be made in curses than in her work mixing healing tinctures. More praise to be found in revenge than in birthing babies.

In slaverytime a white overseer had his whip and a white patrolman had his hounds and a white speculator had his auction block and your white master had your name on a deed of sale somewhere in his House, or so he claimed. But those things were afflictions for the battered-burnt-bruised body only. Curses were for the sin-sick soul and made most terrifying because of it.

"Hoodoo," Miss May Belle used to say, "is black folks' currency."

She had admitted only once, to Rue, in confidence: "The thing about curses is that you can know who you've wronged the most by who you fear has the notion to curse you."

Black neighbors would whisper against black neighbors, sure, but by and by a white man would come from afar having heard of Miss May Belle's conjure, asking for cure of some affliction set upon him by an insolent slave, or even by his own white wife.

Other slavefolk got hired out for their washing, for their carpenter-
ing, for their fine greasy cooking. Miss May Belle was hired for her
hoodooing.

So it was that Big Sylvia, the cook of the plantation House,
came to the slave cabin where Miss May Belle and her daughter
lived alone, to ask after a curse.

Rue saw her coming from afar. The diminutive house slave had
a crooked walk on bowed little legs, and Rue stood tiptoed in the
cabin's one window, watched as the cook came down the dust road
at dusk, determination in her little steps but a look like fear on her
face, as she headed to the healing woman's house. Beyond Big
Sylvia, Rue could see from where she'd come. Marse Charles's
white-pillared House blazed big and hazy opposite the setting sun.

"Come away from there, Rue-baby," Miss May Belle said, and
Rue obeyed her mama. "Cook's comin' to ask after hoodoo. Now,
you know that ain't nothin' that a child needs to hear 'bout."

How Miss May Belle knew before Big Sylvia's knock what the
matter was Rue could not rightly say. But she tucked herself in
the corner of their one-room cabin, balled herself small between
the stove and the bedpost, and pretended at not listening.

Miss May Belle creaked the door open, allowed their visitor in.

"I ain't been workin' in the kitchen for some months now," Big
Sylvia complained. She sat across the supper table from Miss May
Belle and held out her right hand. It was bundled up covering a
deep cut that some weeks back had near took away her fingers.

Rue's mama undid the bandages, revealed the hideous slash
from finger to wrist. It was deep, angry, and oozing. Big Sylvia's
dark skin and eyes were shining with a fever she couldn't kick. "It
won't never heal 'cause somebody's put a fix on me."

"Who you think done it?"

"Who else? That woman. Airey. She the one that's took up

cookin' in my place. She's been schemin' after it for years tryna get herself a place in the House."

Fact was that Airey's mama had been the cook when Marse Charles had been a child, back when the plantation had been all but a few rows of hopeful seedlings. By all accounts Airey's mama hadn't been all that good of a cook neither, but there was no taking a white man from his auntie nostalgia. Airey had believed that because of her mama she was owed the kitchen, with a lineage as good as a lordship, but Big Sylvia had been bought special with commendations for her cooking. Airey had taken after her field-hand daddy instead, a sharp beauty but mule-strong, bred with hands for picking.

"Now I'm left to do the washin', even now I'm one-handed, mind," Big Sylvia said, "and Airey, she at the oven, got Marse Charles smackin' his lips after every meal, thinkin' he gon' get rid a' poor ol' Sylvia, maybe sell me next time the prospector come 'round, keep Airey on."

Miss May Belle tutted. She shut her eyes as if consorting with herself, let Big Sylvia stand there panting for a long while, working herself up into a deeper fury the more she thought on the unfairness.

"You best be sure now," Miss May Belle finally said. She rebandaged Big Sylvia's hand good and tight.

Big Sylvia nodded in earnest. "It was her face I saw when my hand slipped and the knife cut me. Yes, I saw her face plain. She tol' me I was to die. Now I see her in my sleep every night. She set by the foot of my bed with the devil on her left side stabbin' at my hand."

To undo Airey's magicking Rue's mama advised that Big Sylvia circle her own bed with a sprinkle of salt, nightly. This Big Sylvia swore to do.

"But, Miss May Belle, how am I to get my place back?"

"You'll needa take somethin' a' hers. A piece a' her hair like. When you fetch it, come back to me on Friday."

Big Sylvia repeated her thanks over and over. Her rewrapped hand was thick and clumsy with the new bandaging, and she struggled at the pocket of her apron 'til she produced a silver dollar with the promise of more coin to be had come Friday.

"I'd bring you them good ashcakes a' mine too, but I can't cook nothin'."

Rue watched her mama slip the coin easy into her own pocket.

"We'll see to it that you back in yo' rightful place, by the Lord's grace," Miss May Belle promised.

Rue knew that her mama, thin as she was, did have a love for Sylvia's ashcakes.

On Sunday her mama picked nits from her daddy's hair and Rue pretended to be asleep. Half days were for praying and for visiting, the one day that Miss May Belle saw her man. He journeyed from the neighboring plantation, a trip that took him 'til nightfall, and Rue would struggle to stay awake to see her daddy arrive in the doorway and greet her mama. From the bed, Rue strained to watch them, but she could see only their shadows twist and join, stretched out black and big on the dirt floor.

Rue fought off sleep but she did every now and again succumb, and their hushed, soothing voices—her daddy's as hard as timber, her mama's as soft as pulp—were sometimes things of her dreams. Her daddy sat on the floor between her mama's bare thighs, his head pushing up her dress, his lips kissing healed-up grazes on her kneecaps, and her mama sat in the chair above, cussing softly at tangles.

When next Rue jerked herself awake, her daddy had the doll baby in his hand. He was turning it around in his thick fingers. He was displeased; she could tell by the lines etching themselves deep in his forehead.

"It look like her," he conceded.

Indeed, the doll baby Miss May Belle had made of blackened oilcloth and stuffed with straw, though crude, resembled Airey completely. She'd embroidered a face even, wide-set eyes and a line of red stitching for Airey's thin, proud mouth. The doll wore spare calico and the type of red kerchief Airey often favored. But the most prominent detail was the mismatched black paint of the legs where Airey was known to have a pattern of birthmarks that freckled in circles black and white up to her thighs, varying smatterings where her skin lacked color, where she seemed almost to be white in unplanned for places great and small. The real live Airey kept the marks hid the great majority of the time, but everybody knew her to be proud on them; she'd hike up her skirt and show them off sometimes in the swirl of her dancing. They were there on the doll hid beneath the blue calico rag dress, beneath the white napkin, an approximation of the kitchen apron Big Sylvia coveted. Miss May Belle had made that miniature live.

"It's a sinful thing to be messin' with," Rue's daddy warned.

Rue watched her mama pause in her brushing. She kissed the very top of her man's head, left her lips there when she answered. "I won't hurt her none."

Rue's daddy set the doll down on the floor gentle, like he feared it might start living.

"What is it you mean to buy with all them silver coins?" she heard him ask.

Rue, dozing, might have dreamed the answer her mama gave her daddy: "You."

Friday came, wicked with rain, and Rue, sent to beg a needle off the seamstress, came back to the cabin wet and cold to find her mama and Big Sylvia, heads bent and conspiring. Beneath the doll's red kerchief Miss May Belle worked in quick, neat stitches to sew down the tuft of thick black hair Big Sylvia had stolen from Airey's comb.

"Didn't hardly think you'd get it," Miss May Belle said of the hair.

"Weren't easy. Had to wait 'til Sunday, 'til she'd gone visitin' that Charlie."

"They still courtin'?" Miss May Belle asked, though she surely knew—didn't she know everything?

"They fixin' to get proper married, iff'n Marse Charles will 'llow for it. And he surely will as he's like to get from 'em good strong babies."

Miss May Belle said nothing. Moved or not by talk of sweethearts, she waited patient as Big Sylvia drew two more silver coins from out of her apron pocket. Only then did Miss May Belle hand her the doll.

Big Sylvia's eyes near gleamed. "What do I do?"

"Scratch off a li'l a' the black paint from the arms of the doll baby every mornin'. Not too much now, but slowly, and by and by you'll get what you're wantin'."

Rue wished for her own magic and, failing that, wished for coin. She had no use for money, had no sense of what she might or might not buy, but she wanted to feel them, as though the action of slipping her hands across the cool, rare bits of silver, carved with regal fine-boned faces, could elicit a kind of magic in and of itself.

She had been spellbound, at that small age, by the curious mystery of white faces. She saw so few, save the master and his sons, more rarely his wife. Rue was acquainted with only one white face in particular—Varina, Marse Charles's red-haired, freckle-spotted daughter.

They were both of them six years old, of an age because the master made it so. Varina's birth was the only clear bright star around which the younger slave children might revolve—you were born after or before the master's daughter, thereabouts. Rue could hitch her birth in the same season as Varina's and so they oft played together, kicking up dust in that one precious hour of their mutual freedom, between dusk and candlelight. Varina wasn't allowed to play at any other time, for the Missus was afeared that her daughter would catch color, spoil away her milk-skim skin.

Rue spent her own days in running favors, not much use in the field or the House and not yet as knowledged as her mama would someday make her. The best use for Rue then was to dash about with a basket, a bucket, or a broom, getting switched on her behind by older folks who complained she was too slow no matter how fast she ran. She was often underfoot. She was often forgotten.

Rue would sometimes look up at the House and spy Varina at the third-story nursery window, knew her for a white figure behind a whiter curtain, looking down. Did she appear wistful? Rue could not truly tell, not from that distance, not with only her hand over her eyes to shade out the midday sun. But it was as though Varina was looking out at her as well, with a sort of wanting, and Rue got to figuring if she ever had magic or money, either, she'd make it so the two of them could play and laugh together in the full sunlight as much as they could stand.

It seemed to Rue that Miss May Belle never had to fetch her coins but could will them into existence, suddenly flipping a flash of silver between her fingers in trade for something or other she was wanting. But where the source was was anybody's imagining.

Rue watched as her mama slipped her daddy one such coin of a Sunday. She slid it clear across the table over knot holes and scratches and set it in front of her man, who did not take it.

"Nah," he said.

Miss May Belle was sore. "Why?"

"That's conjure money."

"Money is money is money," she said and he said nothing and the coin gleamed between them.

"Or is it 'cause it's woman's money?" Miss May Belle took it back and Rue tried to watch where it went but missed that too, an illusionist's trick between her mama's delicate fingers.

Rue looked and looked but she did not find the coins, not in the way she thought she would at least. One day, after the birth of the Airey doll baby that Big Sylvia had bought, Airey herself came to Miss May Belle to ask after a bit of hoodooing. She came upon them at the river where the water was swelled from a season turned rainy before its time.

Rue's mama said, "I been expecting you to come on round."

Miss May Belle was not the type interested in making enemies. That was the reason she only advised on how to make a trick, but she never did dispel it with her own two hands. She oft said, *The hunter in settin' his own trap'll sometimes spring it on himself,* which was true, of course—they were forever bandaging up men fool enough to go catching rabbits in the dark of night.

Rue looked over their visitor. Airey was truly pretty, made all of thick bones and fine features, such an amalgamation of two kinds of beauty that she could be admired from one direction and feared from another. But now in person it was clear to see just what Miss May Belle's magicking had done: The spangled pattern of white skin that had once been on her legs alone had begun to spread up her arms and to the sides of her neck and along her jaw and nose; a round white swathe sickled around her eye.

If Miss May Belle was shocked by what she'd wrought, she didn't show it, and Airey for her part didn't look vengeful. She came to sit by them at the river's edge, and the reflection of her skin shimmering in the water seemed to make her look like the night sky dotted with stars, beautiful.

"I ill-wished Big Sylvia. I wanted her place in the kitchen," Airey began. "I been up all night with the regret. I had the notion that life would be easier for me in the House, but it ain't easier. No, life just ain't easy nowhere. That's why I come to see you."

Miss May Belle shook her head. "No more conjure," she said. "Y'all settle things between yo'selves. I'll tell Big Sylvia to be rid of the doll and she'll do it if I tell her to."

"Big Sylvia will get her place back I reckon." Airey held up her hands, and Rue saw that the affliction had taken over her wrists and her knuckles. The thumb of one finger looked as though the black had been sucked clean off the skin. "Missus won't let me cook her food no longer, won't let me touch it, thinkin' this is a sign of some cursedness. Marse Charles'll listen to her, just to quit her from her naggin'. He's like to sell me away the next time he's able."

"You wantin' a charm to prevent it?" Miss May Belle asked.

"No'm. I'm wanting a charm to help me run away."

Miss May Belle looked to Rue beside her and Rue knew the look, the get-gone look. This she was good at, becoming invisible on her mama's whim. She strode over to where the river started thinning toward the creek and let her mama think that she wasn't listening.

"I can't make you no promises," Miss May Belle said.

"You made this," Airey accused. She held out her arms.

Said Miss May Belle, quietly, "I don't know that I did."

Rue tried to look busy as the women kept on, talking in hushes. They were similar, Rue came to notice, both soft enough to be shaped by life and hardened by it too. She wanted to learn that type of woman magic also, thought she'd find it in the words they traded if she could only pick up on the strands, the half-speak adults often took up when they were aware of a child listening in on them.

"I can't risk it," Miss May Belle was saying. "Iff'n you do get away, but they catch on to it that it was me that helped you . . ." It was a sentiment not worth finishing.

"Figured you say that, but if you got some charm some somethin', I can pay you for it."

"I'll give you this for free: Stick to the river," Miss May Belle said. "And don't you never look back for nothin'."

"I won't."

"Not even for yo' man? That Charlie?"

"He ain't comin' with me. He think he owe somethin' to these people. And I"—Airey kicked up water with her toes—"I can't be slowed down by nothing. They got all sorts of ways to weigh you down, don't they?"

Rue felt their eyes on her. She pricked up like a rabbit might at some slight, shifting noise, and saw Airey and her mama considering her with their hard, grave expressions, the far-off thinking look of grown folks.

Miss May Belle finally spoke. "You'll wanna rub oak gum on the soles a' yo' feet. Keep to the river, like I say. That'll throw the scent a' the hounds they gon' send. That's all I can give to you 'sides what you already know. An' if you can help it, don't let nothin' or nobody slow you down."

Airey agreed and left then to prepare for it, whatever preparing to leave your life meant. Rue watched her walking away. She was visible for a great distance, her proud back, her speckled legs bared.

By next morning Airey was gone. By late afternoon she was brought back.

They drug her by her arms through the whole of the plantation, her legs kicking, her body twisting and turning over grass and rocks and dirt in a never-ending dust-billowing futility.

The white men she hung between were catchers by trade. Marse Charles paid them handsomely, it was said, heaping handfuls of silver dollars, for the pleasure of having his favorite cook returned to him in a bruised pile. They left her tied up to a horse post out front of the House. Even tied down, Airey bucked and pulled at her bonds, and all the passing black folks watched her do it, watched her scream and piss herself and work one wrist free just far enough to yank at her own thick black hair. They weren't none of them allowed to go near, except at last for Charlie.

Marse Charles gave Charlie Blacksmith the honor of whipping his would-have-been wife, because Marse Charles himself could not be bothered to come out of the House, particularly as the clouds grew dark and it began to rain. He handed Charlie Blacksmith a whip, told him to use all the strength he'd use to forge a horse's shoe, and Marse Charles swore he would know it if he didn't. He'd be checking and expected to see ten good lash marks, drawn blood on Airey's bare back.

Assembled, bade to watch, all the slaves in the plantation came and stood in the yard of the House even as a driving rain fell and slicked down their hair and darkened their clothes and made everything cling.

Marse Charles was somewhere up above and Rue strained to make him out in the windows, not sure what to look for besides a hint of the shape of his darkness behind the billowing white curtains of his daughter's nursery. Or was it Varina herself that Rue spied, looking down on them? Rue searched so hard that after a while she made herself see shadows where there were none.

Whether he was watching or not, Marse Charles surely heard it when the first lick lay into Airey's back; it was that loud.

She hid her breasts the best she could with her arms wrapped around the post she'd been tied to, pushed them up against the raw, splintered wood. She shook with fear as the rain bounced off her, waiting for the fall of a hit she could not see coming, and her heaving panicked lungs rounded out her back just as the whip came down and split clean the skin. Charlie reared his arm just so far back that it looked like there was more force in the action, and the whip whistled through the air and another thwack landed squarely on her spine. Airey hollered and hissed and choked on her sorrow, gurgling out a bit of red-tinged spit. She'd bit her tongue.

"Boy," came Marse Charles up from the window on high. His voice boomed even over the rain, and Rue would have sworn that everybody assembled shook. Up above, Marse Charles was framed in an open second-story window, his arms braced against the sill, the tips of his curly dark brown hair catching the wet. He didn't have to say any more. Charlie brought down the whip harder the next time. Harder still the next.

Rue had to shut her eyes. But there was no blocking that high, fine whistle through the air or the sound of Airey's resistance, quieted from screams now to gut-deep moans then to a silence that seemed altogether worse.

When he was done, Charlie threw down the whip, his one act of defiance, let it sink in a puddle. There they were, the ten strips of open flesh wrought neatly in Airey's back like the lines of crude accounting marks. Already the force of the rain was thinning out the intensity of the blood, and Rue found herself worrying, as the crowd began to murmur and break apart, that if Marse Charles didn't hurry down, he might not see the blood he was after as proof. They might, she feared, have to do it all over again.

———

Spring came on, like it did, and Rue and her mama stayed busy for seven straight days serving bitters to the slave folks Marse Charles sent through their cabin—a spoonful for each was meant to set his field hands ready for the coming heavy season. By the sixth day Rue was more than tired of looking into the pink expectant quiver of other folks' mouths, of observing their outstretched tongues and the dangling fleshy marble at the back of their throats. Her mama relegated her to filling up the waiting wood spoons, a dull task.

Rue looked up and there was Airey, strange to behold in the sunlight, nothing to her but deep pockets between her bones. Sunken—shoulders and chest and all around her eyes. Her voice came out gritty.

"Thank you," she said, "Miss May Belle."

Rue handed her mama a spoon, and her mama began to hold out the mixture to Airey's small beak of a mouth, the edges of which were white and dry. At the last minute Miss May Belle pulled the spoon away. The pour puddled down to the floor, wasted.

"Rue-baby," Miss May Belle said. She didn't take her eyes from Airey. "Fetch me a cup instead."

Rue had to dig to come up with a small cup of tinned iron; she handed it to her mama, who filled it high with the bitters. Airey drank it all down at once.

"Meet me Friday night," Miss May Belle said, in a voice hushed and hurried. "If you still wantin' what you wantin'."

Airey nodded once. She gave her cup back to Rue and moved on down the line, her face betraying nothing, no elation and no fear.

The fact was if there was magic—and Rue, as a child, believed earnestly that there was—her mama had not taught it to her, had not wanted to.

On Friday night, Rue lay in their bed with her eyes closed, listened to her mama move about their small cabin. Miss May Belle took her time leaving, as if she sensed that the moment was not quite right or else sensed, in the knowing way of mothers, that her daughter lay tense and restless beneath the thin sheet ready to follow her into the night. They waited each other out.

Rue dozed and found herself dreaming. She was in Marse Charles's House, which could not be so, she was hardly ever allowed in there, yet there she was in a room so white it was as though the very air was ash water, the world all bleached through as though by lye. In the center of the white room was Varina, the master's daughter, waiting on Rue like a prize.

In the dream, Rue took Varina's hand, led her away, took her down the stairs from the nursery and through the House kitchen and there was Big Sylvia, removing ashcakes from her stove. The cook set them by the window to cool. Wriggling free of Rue's hold, Varina aimed to pluck one of them ashcakes from the pile. Rue hissed after Varina, but the cook seemed not to see the little girls. Instead Big Sylvia opened up the fire-spitting mouth of her stove, and now she drew from her pocket the little doll Miss May Belle had made of Airey. Easy as that she tossed it into the waiting fire. The doll made of straw and hair caught instantly in the flames, and Rue woke. She sat up from sleep sweating like she'd been in the oven herself.

The cabin was still. Miss May Belle was gone.

Outside the night was allover chill, the road through the slave quarter empty of souls. Rue steeled her shivering little body and walked through the blue midnight, picking her way to the river by way of recollection rather than by sight.

She found them a ways down the rushing river. Airey had her feet ankle deep in the water, and Miss May Belle had her arm in the knot of a tree. When she pulled her arm slowly out, the silver dollars in her hand glimmered in the moonlight. Miss May Belle had crossed to the river, was speaking in urgent whispers to Airey with all those coins offered in her outstretched hands. But Airey didn't move to take them, and Rue soon saw why. Miss May Belle, one by one, began to drop her silver dollars into the stream at Airey's feet. As she watched them go, Rue had half a mind to jump in after them. They made tinkling little splashes as they hit the surface and sparkled and spun, and then disappeared.

"Travel by night. Follow the shine of 'em coins on the river surface," Miss May Belle told Airey. Suddenly Rue could hear her mama's voice impossibly clear, like it boomed from the river itself. "That shine'll take you where you goin'. All the way to the North."

They embraced there, one woman in the river and one woman out, and Airey who had become so thin looked frail in Rue's mama's arms, she seemed liable to disappear. But when Airey pulled away, her arms flew out with fearsome strength. As Rue watched, Airey seemed to dance, her bones twisting, reshaping beneath her skin; her pouting lips grew sharp and pointed and hardened and, by and by, her back arched and her frame narrowed, and Rue watched as Airey at last sprouted big, thick black wings.

Rue was still breathless in her bed when her mama returned some time later to the cabin. Miss May Belle crawled in quietly beside her, her body radiating warmth like a furnace. Now Rue was sleepless. She lay still the whole night trying to make sense of what she thought she'd seen. A woman become a bird. There was no sense to be made of it. It had to be dreaming.

The very first moment of sunup, Rue stole away, took herself to the river to see if she could make out any bits of silver in its bed. But the stream was calm and quiet, undisturbed, reflecting the

FREEDOMTIME

—

Black-Eyed Bean was one year old the night his eerie crying woke the townsfolk, roused them to stir from their beds and whisper their growing suspicions about him aloud in the street. Staring down at the odd little child, Rue was just as staggered by his eyes as she always was, as the folks out there were.

"The water." Beside the bathtub, Sarah spoke it low. "He got a fear a' it."

In the tub Bean thrashed as he'd thrashed beneath the black veil he'd been born in. Now his pumping little legs and arms managed to push round in a swirl the water that surrounded him as he howled.

"He ain't normal," Sarah muttered. "Screamin' like he's bein' killed soon as I lay him down to bath."

Jonah spoke up. "Miss Rue, ain't the water too hot? I keep sayin'. That water be too hot."

"Hush," Sarah said back. "I gotta wash him, don't I?"

Sarah was a sight, her hair in unkempt kinks beneath a roughly cut kerchief. The loose ends of the cotton were streamed through her orange curls like a shredded spider's web. She looked up when

Rue stepped forward. Her eyes said something to Rue her mouth couldn't shape.

Rue knew Sarah was waiting for her to get down on her knees beside her and tend to Bean. But Rue couldn't seem to bring herself to it. She felt all at once afraid that if she picked up Bean she'd be accepting some responsibility for him, when all she wanted was to get away from him and his eerie black eyes.

Rue knelt. She dipped her hand into the farthest corner of the tub, keeping clear of where she might touch Bean or the irregular pattern on his skin. "Wet a bit a' cloth, wipe him down good 'til he grow older, 'til he get accustomed to bein' put in the deeper water."

Was it true what folks had been whispering—could Bean be something sinister amongst them, something dark come again? Rue pulled her hand away.

"It's mighty strange," Jonah said. He crossed the room in long strides to help Sarah to her feet, and even when she was steadied he remained, Rue saw, his big hand gentle on the curve of Sarah's hip.

"I done him same as the others," Sarah spoke up. "The other children ain't never cried like that. They ain't never had such a fear of water as this." She shuddered. "Such a cry."

Rue looked at those others, Sarah's daughter and son. Like their brother, Bean, there wasn't much to be found of Jonah in them. They shared their mama's coloring, the orange-brown coils of her thick hair, and the fleshy fullness of her lips, the top slightly plumper than the bottom in them both. *My babies,* Rue's mama would have called them. She'd called all the children hers. Rue couldn't see them that way. When they were born, she handed the babies over to their mamas and she handed them over quick. Rue wanted no babies.

Sarah picked up Bean from the tub with a splash of bathwater.

Curled up against his mama's chest, perhaps soothed by having his head near her beating heart, Bean quieted.

"He's surely different. But we all come different," Rue said. "Ain't no accountin' for why we is the way we is."

"That's for God to know," Jonah supplied, but Sarah wore a scowl, like Rue ought to know as well as God did what the matter was with Bean. The skin of his legs bore the faint blue interlocking pattern that was like the scales on the back of a creeping serpent, and from his warm, wet body, steam still rose in coils.

"Awful sorry to call for you in the middle a' the night, Miss Rue," Jonah said.

But it had been Bean that had called for her. Hadn't she been pulled here by his strange cry?

Rue made her goodbyes, walked herself to the door. Stepping out, she fixed her face purposeful-like, ready to meet the waiting crowd, but there was no crowd now, only the dusty road and the moon that had found its way to shining. She felt unsettled in the bottom of her stomach where there began to be a small ache: fear.

She'd already started back for her own cabin when a hard grasp on her shoulder made her spin, but it was only Sarah waiting behind her, her arms free of children, her head now bare.

"Miss Rue, I got somethin' to ask a' you," Sarah said.

She looked unearthly tired. The front of her thin linen nightdress was dark with wet from where she'd held Bean firm to her chest. Through the damp spot, Rue could make out the shadows of Sarah's heavy breasts, still weighted, a year out, with milk.

"Only I was wonderin'," Sarah spoke soft. "If you had somethin' I could use. To keep myself, I mean, to keep from havin' anotha conception. Secret-like."

Rue knew secrets. She knew many a secret stretched out amongst the folks of that little town, some shameful, some devastating, some just too sad to shape into words. Rue kept them all and kept them well and so folks kept giving them to her, their secrets. And never mind that she knew she had some of her own to keep.

"You come and see me tomorrow mornin'," Rue said, "and I'll have what you needin' at hand."

Sarah nodded and turned back to her door, in no hurry to return, it seemed, to what waited for her there. Rue watched her go, watched her slip into her home, haint-silent, like a ghost, and Rue could have gone on and done the same, but there was no man waiting on her and no crying child, or two, or three. So instead, by instinct, she turned the other way, the way of the wilderness, and started walking.

Rue knew that wide road made of dust better than any road in the world. She had walked it so many times she half-expected to see her own footsteps coming and going as she passed, from the slave quarters that were now their cabins, to the field that was now scorched land, to Marse Charles's grand old plantation House, which was now in the final stage of its ruination, and yonder, to the old white church.

The pillar was how she knew she'd reached what was left of the House. Part of the column still stood, as it had stood with its twin years ago, in a stately portico announcing the door to Marse Charles's mighty entranceway. Despite the ash, the pillar was nearly still white, and Rue stopped there as though knocking at the door of an old friend.

The foundation of the House remained enough to mark the ghost of the burned-down rooms and little more. In the very center of the entryway the old staircase made its way up five noble steps toward the sky, then dropped off in a crumble. Rue could, and did, walk straight through the ruin of the House. Her destination was not the House after all but the woods just beyond it.

Trees remember, Rue's mama would say, and so it was. The trees behind the House remembered the war and its bitter end, that southward march of the Yankee soldiers and the destruction that was part of their style of victory.

Folks didn't like to come out this far, not anymore. Cursed, they called it. Word was that Miss May Belle had hoodooed the whole of those woods, laid a curse with the strength of her love for her man and her sorrow at his dying, hanged from these very trees. For wasn't it in those same woods that they'd hanged Miss May Belle's man, lynched him and left him to swing? Miss May Belle's grief had risen there like a flood. Ever since, their used-to-be plantation had existed in isolation, like something locked away and forgotten by time. Nobody came into their town unmolested, folks said, and nobody came out.

If you went looting, you were like to disturb the dead, wake the ghost of Marse Charles, or worse, call up the jealous ghost of Varina, his one redheaded daughter and Rue's old playmate. Beautiful and scorned, they said of Varina, and robbed of her prime, she made a vengeful haint. Rue alone was not afeard—not of Varina, not of her spirit neither.

All that remained was dead earth, then dirt, then wild grass, peeking up from the ground in knots, and it was from this earth that Rue found her plunder, the herbs she used for healing.

She sat down heavy amongst the weeds as though she were one herself. She felt awful weary, but there was solace in the mud, in the dew, in the aroma the earth made when it sighed. Rue made a bowl of her skirt and let the plants she picked puddle in her lap: feverfew for tired blood, stems and leaves and seed of boneset, longwood chips to be mixed with brandy, berries of pokeweed to soothe breasts grown sore and stretched, and the head of a daisy, which she simply found pretty and stuck, on a whim, into the coils of her hair.

There was a clearing where the grass didn't grow, and just past that was the only thing that stood tall in that Eden, save for the trees: a shed that had somehow kept all its four walls and the idea of a roof.

There, sat up with her back against the trunk of a tree, Rue stopped to think about Jonah, particularly his passing touch on her arm. She tried, with some difficulty, to remember the feeling of his fingers when he'd guided her into his house.

They had been rough when they'd closed on her elbow, as rough as the bark of a tree, and Rue loved his callouses, knew they were thick and well-earned. He'd go find work, when he could, on distant coastal islands, unloading at the docks, or handfishing in rivers. He'd be gone for long stretches of months when it was the season for it, and Rue longed after him when he was away, tried to imagine him there, on the banks of some other river, some river she could not know.

Maybe Rue could feel sorry for Jonah, this man with the calloused hands, or maybe she could feel what Sarah felt when he finally came home, for his woman must have felt some relief, and surely some desire. And thinking this, Rue ran her own hand up along the inside of her thigh. Her fingertips were rough from her work, certainly, but not quite so rough as a man's. There was a swell in her of sharper loneliness, but also of satisfaction, because wasn't she in her place, her conquered ground? And as she moved inside herself, all her roots and flowers scattered and fell, for a moment forgotten and reunited with the earth.

SLAVERYTIME

===

Folks said Rue's mama knew everything the foxes knew. Weren't they her eyes in the woods? Her familiars. How else to explain the uncanny way she figured out everything and everybody's business all about the plantation?

The feral foxes owed their life to Miss May Belle as if she was their own mama, for word was they were not foxes at all but the departed souls of used-to-be human beings, and Miss May Belle had given the dead a kind of immortality by hiding them at the edge of Marse Charles's land. In return they were her sharp eyes, her keen ears. Her survival.

Rue could not have said one way or another how far reaching Miss May Belle's hoodoo reigned. To Rue her mama was always a mystery; in all things great and small, she showed her magic as mamas do, with their knowing. Miss May Belle had a way of anticipating what trouble Rue would find herself in before Rue had even devised the trouble itself.

Trouble usually meant Varina, who often rebelled against her white girlhood and needed always an accomplice to witness her rebellion. That long last summer before the war came upon them,

while the white adults fretted and the black adults labored, Varina
ran half wild and took Rue running with her.

One particular high noon, they would make their way, without
even having to agree upon it aloud, to their usual place by the
creek. They ran despite the weight of the heat, trying to catch the
wind with their speed; and running behind her on the narrow
path, Rue had the pleasure of watching a number of Varina's ribbons come streaming off her curls and getting tangled up in high
branches.

Varina reached the shed first and declared herself the winner in
a race Rue hadn't known they were having. Then Varina, her
cheeks still spotted pink, lay herself down on the grass and in one
inelegant swoop divested herself of her calico dress and tugged her
lace bloomers down to her ankles so that she sat in only her frilled
white chemise, bare-bottomed and unashamed.

She said, "This time you can be Miss May Belle."

They had many fights about this very thing, who got to be the
mama and who got to be the healing woman, so that most of their
games ended in tears, and for a moment Rue hesitated, wondering
what Varina was wanting from her to be so suddenly kind, allowing her to be Miss May Belle.

Before her mind could change, Rue put her hands on Varina's
pale legs, examining as she had watched her mama examine, gently parting the skin between Varina's legs, which at first was
smooth but prickled up to gooseflesh at her touch. Varina leaned
back on her elbows and watched Rue as she did this, not closing
her eyes as Rue sometimes did when she was pretending to be the
mama. Instead Varina was following Rue's every movement with
those blue eyes, which had turned a dull, still-water color in the
shade.

"It ain't time yet," Rue said and took her fingers away.

"It is time," Varina spread her legs wider, which was not how the game was meant to be played. The mama was meant to just lie there and wait.

Rue thought about arguing this; she was the one who had taught Varina the game and so best knew the rules. She was the one whose mama was magic.

"It's time," Rue agreed instead, placing both of her hands on Varina's mound, drawing her open with her thumbs.

"It's a big 'un," Rue proclaimed, imagining a baby with black skin and red, red hair.

"I'm so very happy," said Varina.

"What you gon' name him?"

"It ain't a him." When Varina was the mama all of her babies were girls, and Rue had explained again and again that it was not the mama that got to pick.

"It's a boy," Rue insisted.

Varina growled, or so Rue thought, the sound seemed so loud in her ear. Then she heard grass and twigs crunching underfoot and she pulled away as quick as she could, certain Varina's nurse had come over from the House and was about to catch them at something she would not like to see.

Varina crawled on hands and knees through the grass to reach out for her discarded dress, and so when the fox appeared she froze like that, her hand partway out in front of her as though she might ward him off.

The fox would be the silver of ash forever in Rue's memory, though looking back she figured it had to have been gray. It came all the way out to them, straight into the clearing as though to get a better look at the little girls, one black, one white, playing together in the high grass. Rue could not find her voice to scream, but she didn't need it. The fox stopped only to cock its head at them, then it turned its bushy tail and bounded away into the thick dark of the woods.

———

Miss May Belle must've gotten her whispers from a fox because come Saturday she beat Rue with the branch of a birch tree.

What Rue remembered more than the pain of the beating was the pain afterward when her mama left her to cry in the dirt of their floor and the pain the next day when they stood in the upper gallery of the church during the service.

The Protestant minister was a white man that Rue had never seen before and could not see now from where she stood amongst the other slaves on the second-story platform in the very back of the church. Rue's view instead was of backs of knees, hems of skirts, peaks of legs stockinged despite the heat to hide fatty veins. Through the gaps of the wooden slats the white folks below were a blur of somber colors made blurrier by the sweat that dripped down Rue's forehead and stung at her already teary eyes, and every time any of the tightly packed black folks around her moved or sighed, itched or coughed, the wooden gallery would moan like it was about to give up.

Any other time to be brought to church would have felt like a treat, to feel the close press of those in the quarter that only ever thought of her as Miss May Belle's girl and to feel like one of them.

She dared to look up every now and then and caught sight of her mama looking tired, restless; she was not listening to that fly-buzz sermon. A sheen of sweat was in the bow of her upper lip, and beneath her one eye was a heavy purple bruise that spread down her cheek and sunk to yellow like the sky of a sunset. Someone had hit Miss May Belle and so Miss May Belle had hit her. That's all Rue believed to be true, but she couldn't think on the meaning of all that.

After the sermon they had to wait for the white folks to leave the church in a slow, repentant tide before it was proper for them to descend from the upper gallery one by one on the narrow stair. Rue and her mama were the last ones down. Miss May Belle pulled her along behind her, her hand holding on so firm that Rue could feel her mama's fingers on the shifting bones of her wrists. That shackling squeeze was as good a way as any for Rue to know that she was still in trouble, though for what she could not figure. Out through the double doors of the dim church they went, where, for a moment, Rue was so dazzled by the sudden bright afternoon that she could sense nothing but the heft of the heat and the sweetness of a voice that was singing.

It was Sarah that was singing. She stood in the very center of everyone, a matchstick of a little girl, small but made large by her inhibition, all eyes on her. The crowd hummed low in their throats for her but Rue could tell Sarah didn't need them, she could have found the tune herself. She was the tune.

"Thank ya', Marse Jesus," Sarah would sing and the crowd would mumble their encouragement, "Yessuh, thank 'im, Lord Jesus."

Rue's mama pulled her away with two hands heavy on her shoulder that set the rawness of her back to screaming.

Miss May Belle turned her around, and when she did Rue saw that her mama's hands were stained bright red.

"You bleedin', Mama," Rue said but her voice was empty of panic. It seemed to come from far away.

"Fool child, you the one bleedin'," Rue's mama said.

She could see Varina coming down from the House to meet them, and in her hands she held new, gleaming marbles. They looked cool, like ice, and Rue longed to touch them, but her mama was pulling her away.

"I wanna play with Miss Varina," Rue heard herself saying over and over. She was crying in her mama's arms, beating at her, kicking at her, sobbing. "I wanna play with Miss Varina."

Rue cried until she couldn't cry anymore and then she slept.

———

For a while she kept her eyes closed, just to feel. She was awake but not ready to wake up, and the pressure of her mama's hands on her bare back was a wonderful pleasure after all the pain that seemed to have been centered there. The herbs Miss May Belle used were sweet but strong and when she lay them, warm and wet, on the vertical cuts on Rue's back, what ought to have stung felt soothing, the reverse of a lashing.

Rue might have dozed back into sleep. She was thinking of a game of marbles that she was winning when she heard the rumble of her daddy's voice.

"What's all this now?"

Rue felt her mama pull away from her as a vanishing of her warmth. She peeked open one eye. Her father stood in the doorway of the cabin. He held a pass in his hand that was becoming crumpled in the fist he was steadily making. Rue's mama took the paper from him, set it down on a chair. She reached up to kiss him, and he let her for a while before he pushed her firmly away.

He touched the swelling colors on her face. "Who done this?"

Rue's mama touched the scar that showed beneath his collar and wrapped around to the front of his neck. "Who done this?" she said. She touched a scar that worked its way up behind his ear. "Who done this?"

He pushed away her hands.

Rue's mama said, "I caught Missus in a mood and with her ring on, is all. She remindin' me of my place."

"She puttin' you back in yo' place is what she doin'. She fear you know too much."

Rue's mama smiled, her swollen face stretched to a new pattern. "I do know too much."

Her daddy shook his head. "And the girl?"

Here Rue's mama was quiet for a long while. "I did it myself. I'd sooner I do it myself than let anyone else do it. But I gotta make a show of it, don't I, so they know I'm raisin' her up right. It's gotta show."

"Why?"

"She's gettin' to like that Miss Varina too well."

Rue's daddy sat heavy on the end of the bed, and as Rue dipped toward him she closed her eyes down to the tiniest crack. He put his head in his hands, rubbed his fingers along the sharp edges of his hair. They made the sound Rue knew cats' fur made rubbed wrong.

"We some kind of family, ain't we," he said softly. Rue could feel him looking at her, though she'd shut her eyes at the first shocking vibration of his voice. "I guess she mine."

"Ain't no question."

"We got the same birthmark now," he said, touching Rue's back, and Rue near jumped out of herself when she felt his fingers just above the highest of her wounds. But like her mama's healing, his hands didn't hurt her. They were hard but kind, rough but warm.

"Don't you worry, baby girl." He was speaking to her in near a whisper. "I know better'n anybody. These'll harden so's the next time and the next time they beat you it won't hurt quite so bad."

Rue didn't want there to be a next time, but she felt something in his words and in his touch as though he was putting a kinship into her wounds, and a promise.

FREEDOMTIME

==

There was still the heat of the prior night's impulsiveness coursing through her when Rue forced herself to rise from her bed. Unrest thrummed in her body like drink, and she felt she could still hear the echo of Bean's crying.

She plucked the daisy from her hair, put on her sun hat, gathered a few necessities in a basket, and went calling on Ma Doe.

The day was cool as the night had been cool, and Rue had to keep one hand on the straw brim of her hat so as not to be caught unawares by the sudden whistles of wind. At first, she was not much disturbed when she encountered no one on her walk. It was midday. The men would be out in the fields; the women would be just now preparing their families' suppers.

The old slave quarters had been plotted, boldly, in the shape of a crucifix. Rue's cabin sat at the lowermost point of that cross and so she walked the whole of the empty dirt path, past all the quiet homes. Suddenly, she was struck with the absence of everyone, a swelling goneness.

Ma Doe was there when Rue stomped up to her door, and at her feet were two small children, just past toddling age.

"Afternoon, Miss Rue," Ma Doe said.

Rue drew off her hat and looked around. Long as Rue had known her, Ma Doe's slow gait was trailed by nine or ten children, all of them pickaninnies. In the height of slaverytime Ma Doe had brought up the master's four children too, Marse Charles's three sons and Varina. In rearing them, Ma Doe was known to be twice as fierce as any white governess. Since then she'd become something of a teacher, made a kind of freedfolk school right there in her home where the children scratched their letters into the dirt. Rue knew them to be letters but what they meant she could not say.

"Where's everybody got to?"

"That how you ought to greet me?" Ma Doe said. Rue shushed the woman by kissing her on her leathery cheek.

"What have you got for me, baby?" She locked eyes onto the basket Rue had tucked under her arm.

Rue had known that the charm she'd brought would offer luck, of a kind. It was a packet of leather tied to the end of a coarse string, and it gave off an awful stink as Rue snaked it from her basket. In the crude pouch she had stuffed asafetida powder, as much as she could manage while holding her breath. Ma Doe had been in the habit of wearing such charms all her life, believing that they could ward off all manner of illness and evilness, and she believed her old age to be testament to that fact, though Rue had her doubts.

She tied the charm onto Ma Doe, who bowed her head to let her do it. The rope disappeared into the rolls of Ma Doe's neck. She tucked the pouch down her shirtfront and it was almost as if she weren't wearing it at all, save the smell.

"Now. You're wonderin' where everyone's taken themselves," Ma Doe said. "They all of 'em hotfooted it out a' here as soon as they caught wind a' the news. I expect they're havin' a fine time down there by the river. For Bruh Abel has come."

Rue startled at the name. She tried not to let her upset show but there was no hiding the quiver of discomfiture that ran quick up her spine like wind up a shivering tree limb.

Bruh Abel. She ought to have foreseen it. It was the season for him after all. He came to preach and to perform miracles. And he came to spread lies, or so Rue believed. How else to make sense of such a rootless man? He traveled everywhere with a Bible in his hand and a too-wide grin on his face. He seemed to want nothing. In Rue's mind folks who didn't say plainly what they wanted harbored the most pernicious type of wanting.

She might have accused him of it if she weren't so guilty of the same. Wasn't last night in the woods evidence of her own reckless wanting?

"D'you plan to go hear him preachin', Miss Rue?" She heard the wistfulness in Ma Doe's voice, like the old woman wished that she could still walk well enough to go with the others to the riverside and see the preacher man too.

Rue closed the top of her basket sharply. "No'm, I'm mighty busy today as it happens."

In truth, she was not busy.

Ma Doe said, "Maybe just as well you stay clear of Bruh Abel."

Rue flushed hot. "Why you say that, Ma?"

Ma Doe shrugged, busied herself observing the letters of her two youngest students, nodding encouragement as they struggled to make meaning out of dirt. Rue doubted the old woman could hardly see anymore with her overcast eyes. But who knew what Ma Doe observed keenly that others could not?

"I only mean that Bruh Abel's so much like your mama was. He's got a nose for secrets," Ma Doe said. "Mind he doesn't catch wind a' yours."

Rue could smell the charm she'd made. A damning stink, it was.

———

Rue hid herself in the thick of the woods. She simply wanted to know how Bruh Abel did it, how he worked his magic on her people. That was the reason why she was coming round the river from the woods where she could hide in the green and watch him, unobserved.

She feared that once again Bruh Abel had shown up to shake up folks' faith. It would be a fool thing to make an enemy of him. Ma Doe's warning against Bruh Abel's keen sense for secrets clanged in Rue's head. The old woman knew her words, knew to wield them expertly. And these words she had meant to singe in Rue's mind as a brand: "He's got a nose for secrets. Mind he doesn't catch wind a' yours."

But Rue just had to know what sort of healing Bruh Abel had brought with him, what he meant to do to settle folks' fear and gossip about Bean and the clamor of unease and superstition that Bean's strange eyes and cry had raised within the townspeople. The years had passed in peace since the end of the war, yet all of them suspected that peace could not last. They'd listened to cannon fire for so long that the quiet made them anxious, waiting for worse to come. Then a seemingly accursed baby had been born amongst them, suddenly, like a lobbed shell. They had been waiting on reprisal, reprisal for freedom, for the joy of being free, and when that reprisal wasn't fast coming, they'd settled on the notion that that punishment was finally come in the black eyes of a wrong-looking child. Truth was Rue had a share in their suspicions. She had shied away from Bean as they all had. Worse, she'd taken his wrongness as an omen against her and her past sins.

Rue figured it was no coincidence that Bruh Abel had shown up the day after Bean's horrid wailing. Why else had Sarah chosen that night of all nights to try to bathe her youngest child in hot water? Bruh Abel would soon come upon his seasonal visit and set his sights on Bean. He would find the evil in Bean and cure it. Rue felt she could not allow him to be the one to do so.

She came to rest at the seam of the woods and leaned the whole of herself up against the trunk of a tree, peered just around the edge so she could see them all there at the river, but they could not see her.

She hardly needed to hide, for they watched Bruh Abel as though he was the only thing worth seeing, that assembled crowd of poor black folks.

Bruh Abel was a fine-looking man in that same over-big suit, and he carried a Bible though he wasn't ever seen to read from it—likely he couldn't read at all. He didn't need to look at the Bible to do his preaching.

He could pass, that's what folks whispered about him soon as he appeared each year, as if in the time since they'd last seen him he'd grown more fair. He could quite easily pass for white with that light skin and the brown in his slicked hair showing golden in the sun, but sure enough he was colored and he did have a gift for speaking, for lighting up the dullness that had some time ago settled over that town like the dust of the Northern soldiers' retreat.

Bruh Abel spoke with the lilting tongue of some other county, it was there in the spin of his *r*'s and the caper of his *s*'s, a twang like the beginning of a good song. His talk was sweet to listen to and he did talk, not from a pulpit, not even from one place on the sandy edge of the river. Instead he walked back and forth through the crowd. Rue saw the way everybody trained their eyes on him. He'd sometimes walk straight into the river as though he thought he'd float right on top, and he didn't seem one bit bothered by the water that lapped at his ankles.

"Do y'all wanna hear what the Lord say?"

They did.

"He say this: 'It shall be on the last days that I will pour forth my spirit upon all flesh and yo' sons and yo' daughters shall prophesy.'"

Bruh Abel put his hands to his head, shut tight his eyes. "And yo' young men shall see visions. And yo' old men shall dream dreams."

He snapped open his eyes. He looked straight at Rue. Shocked, she didn't move, only dug her fingers deep into the unyielding bark of the tree, went allover still, except for the twist in her stomach, the unrest of her beating heart.

He was not looking at her after all, she realized; he was reading his scripture in the sky.

"'Even on my bondslaves,' the Lord say, 'I shall pour forth my spirit. And *they* shall prophesy.'"

Bruh Abel walked through the crowd, searching for something. Rue searched with him, trying to see what he saw. There was Sarah standing off to one side, with her three children, Bean sitting on the swell of her bent hip. Rue imagined his sharp black eyes taking in the proceedings. Jonah, Rue noticed, was not with them. Bruh Abel's gaze seemed to linger on the family, on Bean especially, and Rue swore she'd holler, put voice to her panic, if the preacher man so much as picked Bean from his mama's embrace.

But Bruh Abel in an eyeblink passed the baby by. He came instead to Ol' Joel, a man who had always been old in all of Rue's memory. Time had made him stooped, as though he were perpetually bent over in the field. He still worked the land but walked everywhere with the aid of a cane, a fine lacquered wood one that had been given to him by Marse Charles, their former master. Bruh Abel stopped before him.

"You tired, Bruh Joel?" he asked him in the soft, sympathetic cadence of an old friend.

"These ol' bones ain't ne'er too tired to hear 'bout the Lord."

Bruh Abel grinned. "Will you pray with me?"

They prayed with their heads together, too quiet for Rue to hear from that distance. She watched as Bruh Abel placed his hands along the old man's back, Joel's crooked spine showing through the thin cotton of his shirt, and when they parted Ol' Joel had tears wetting the creases of his weathered face. He stood at least an inch taller, and with a flourish of strength befitting a man a quarter of his age, he tossed the cane into the river, where it hit the surface and then sank with nary a splash.

Bruh Abel next drew a young girl from the midst of the crowd. She was a wispy thing, maybe fifteen, that Rue had spoken to but once when she'd asked, quite earnestly, poor fool, if there mightn't be something she could take to stop her monthly courses for a turn or two. Now Bruh Abel was leading her into the deepest part of the river.

Rue knew that Bruh Abel had already baptized a number of people in the town, particularly the young women, but she had never seen it done. She watched now and it seemed almost loving, the way he tipped that young girl back. He controlled her fall with one hand on her shoulder, the other spread on her back, and he held her there, as strong as a pillar with the river rushing around his waist. Rue wondered what it must feel like, Lord, to be held down by that man's hand.

He kept her there so long, fully immersed in the name of the Father, the Son, and the Holy Ghost, and finally, when he allowed it, she came up gasping and saved, her hair matted to her forehead, her white dress clinging clear to her little bud-hard chest. He had his arm firmly around her as he helped her step high over rocks and branches. They made their way back to the shore.

Rue wanted to know what he would do next. It seemed impossible that he could perform anymore, dripping as he was, but he shook his hands dry and took up the Bible he'd bade someone hold, and he flipped it open, letting it fall to its natural, spine-worn center.

But the Bible's pages started fluttering in a sudden wind that grew into a gust and before she could reach up and stop it, Rue felt her hat fly straight off her head. It floated down from the woods, clear past the crowd, headed for the river or for Bruh Abel, she could not know, she did not stop to see it land. Rue turned and ran.

SURRENDER

===

1865

It had been in the high heat of June, two years back, that black folks had been freed. When the last of the war's rebel fires petered toward Surrender, gossip of that lofty Proclamation had finally come to their isolated corner of torn-up country, the weight of it all winnowed down so that they hardly knew what any of it meant, what good it might do them. Freedom seemed to them to be as useless as the currency of a nation that didn't exist anymore.

Then Bruh Abel had come amongst them for the first time. He appeared one hot day late that June, gusted in as unexpected as cool air off the distant ocean. He'd arrived only days after they'd been told that they, slave folks all of their lives, were free. That nonsense word. He had come and defined it for them, came into their square and showed them just how free could saunter into town and say the most dangerous, daring things.

"This is to be our prosperity," Bruh Abel predicted. "This will be the Promised Time for black folks."

Lofty prophecies. They were wanting to believe him. Couldn't quite yet. Not without proof.

The first time Rue had heard tell of him she was eighteen or so. She had not yet become Miss Rue but was soon enough to be, for her mama, Miss May Belle, had not stirred from her self-made mourning after the death of her man.

It was Sarah who had stood outside of Miss May Belle's cabin door that day, waiting on Rue to come home. Sarah, eighteen too, and pregnant then with her very first child, wide with it, though dignified. With her hands cocked in the small of her back, arms akimbo, stomach jutting, she said, "The preacher man is in there with yo' mama."

"Who?"

There the preacher was, kneeling at Miss May Belle's bedside, a broad-shouldered man, stranger to Rue. His good brown suit was surely borrowed, stolen, or gifted from a white man, and either way Rue didn't trust him on sight. There was something about his goose-greased hair, slicked down to beat back his curls. One stiff brown lock swung free as he bowed his head to whisper some private something in Miss May Belle's ear. Whatever he'd said, it had her lifting her bed-bound head for the first time in a long while. Miss May Belle laughed in that big-mouthed, full-toothed way that recalled the old days so much that Rue ached with envy over their closeness. She stopped in the doorway not knowing what to make of her mama's happiness, but distrustful of it.

"Come on, Rue-baby," her mama croaked. Miss May Belle had been thrifty by then with her words, mean even, saving her speech-making for phrases she deemed of the highest importance. "Come on and meet this Bruh Abel."

Bruh Abel said he was a traveling preacher. Way he told it, he'd got religion from a white master who'd set young Abel and all the other souls he owned to freedom just before the war.

Even back then, Rue had spat at the idea of a story that saccharine being true, but there was no denying that Bruh Abel's presence seemed to soothe Miss May Belle's sadness—a thing that Rue had never been able to do, no matter how badly she wanted to save her mama, not with all the roots and herbs and tinctures in creation.

By that same evening it had been on everybody's lips that the preacher man had laid hands on Miss May Belle, given her a sip of good holy water. Folks said that she had sat up then and spoken clear from her mad stupor for the first time in weeks. They said that this newcomer must be a real man a' Jesus if he could so ease Miss May Belle's pain, a woman who'd eased the pain of so many.

Rue sat with her mama that night, watched her sleeping. Outside she heard them all begin to hum a song of Bruh Abel's. *Lord laid his hands on me.* By the tilt of their voices they were going toward the river, carrying him away amongst them in a swollen tide of worship.

When their voices grew dim and distant enough, Rue had gotten up her courage and stolen through the night. She'd made her way to where Bruh Abel's scrawny mule was hitched up and asleep, left alone to guard a saddlebag filled with the preacher man's belongings.

Suspect, she rooted through his trinkets. There was a knife atop a folded piece of paper, which, held up to Rue's candlelight, bore long-scrawled blue letters through the thin skin of a badly wrinkled envelope. There was too a pockmarked brass harmonica and a fat button trailing string, but there, beneath that clutter, were three small vials, the exact thing she'd been after. They were markless bottles with cork heads that trapped in them clear liquid. As she wrapped her fingers around them they rolled and clinked together ominously like glasses for a toast. She took one out and put it to her eye to see what it held, and with that done and yielding nothing, she pulled up the stopper and put the liquid to her tongue. It was a mad thing to do. She was killing herself if it was poison that this strange man carried. Still, she did the same with every one of those little bottles, licked the tip of the cork, sipped up the residue on every single one of them, and came quick to realize they held nothing more than a bit of whiskey watered down.

She'd known him for what he was then. His was a clear-water cure sweetened with nothing more than clever words, a con man's type of conjure.

Did Bruh Abel know she'd done all that? There was something in the way he looked at her all the times he came back after, season after season. Like he was itching to accuse her if only he could figure just what she was guilty of. They were suspect of each other, she and him, from the very start of their acquaintance, and the askance Bruh Abel sent her way only got weightier after Miss May Belle passed. Rue had not been near to comfort her mama when she finally went to her rest—but Bruh Abel had been. They said he'd been right beside Miss May Belle, praying and holding her hand.

Miss May Belle's final curse would go on and outlive her. It was said that she laid it in her grief after her man had been strung up, lynched for lusting after a white woman, or so the story went. Miss May Belle cast her agony over the whole of Marse Charles's burnt-down plantation, folks said, and over the wilderness just beyond.

After the war came Surrender and in that time of flux, of fortune and misfortune, of raised white flags and dead white folks, Miss May Belle had believed, or so it was told, that the only way to keep their isolated plantation and the colored people in it free was to keep them chained up, to make for them a master out of the invisible white of the river fog.

This master was not a fat-bellied cotton king in a big white House—was not, as it was told, a master at all but was in fact a conjure come to form as a haint. A ghost was said to weave in and out of the woods surrounding their town on gray nights, was said to wail and to howl, to rule the packs of rabid foxes that overran the unkempt wilderness. The haint she'd made, they believed, lamented the lost war and the Lost Cause. Was said to be so greedy over the land as to keep away all the other whites who might covet their little lost country.

But nothing comes free. It was a tale oft told that Miss May Belle had made her curse like as if she was sat at a blacksmith's wheel, so expert had she honed her hoodooing, as though to make a double-edge sword, for hadn't all their white folks died as she had foretold? Dead but not gone. Three years after the war, still among them, their white masters were ruling over them as ghosts. Haints in the woods. Haunting.

After Miss May Belle died, they said the river swelled up fit to weep for her. It occluded the roads and the old byways; it ruined the roots of the trees. Living water, it swallowed up the old, proud stalks of cotton, and still the river rose. And Miss Rue, the only one left to sustain her mama's curse, found herself afeared of what the river water might dredge up, secret things better left hidden that haunted her, a curse that might rise to the surface.

In that same season of Rue's fear, Black-Eyed Bean was born, as though he were the new leaving of an old black tide.

FREEDOMTIME

==

One night, just after Bruh Abel's arrival, the plantation's old corpse bell snuck its way into Rue's dreaming. She was shocked awake, halfway out of bed and partways dressed when she put it together that what she heard was the ringing of that church bell that had no earthly business being rung.

The evening was a perfect mirror of the night that Bean had cried and unsettled the whole of the town. Rue could see it on folks' faces that they were thinking the same. They stood in the road, hesitated on their porch steps.

The bell stilled to silence, and there was Sarah with proof that Bean was not the cause of the disturbance, for she had come amongst the crowd with the baby asleep and silent on her shoulder.

And there was Bruh Abel too, pristine in his good pressed suit.

"What's the cause a' all that commotion?" he said.

Didn't the man ever sleep? For he looked always ready to come amongst them. Rue squinted to see which house he had come from, where he had been fed and bedded for the night. There was always some or another of the womenfolk after having him stay with her family, taste this and that bit of cooking.

"The bell," folks were telling him now. "Ain't heard it ring in an age."

It had rung harshly only once and then again weakly like some-body, or something, had only the strength or the daring to ring it but the one time and no strength to stop the clapper from coming round the second time and giving out one more hollow knell.

Bruh Abel looked at Rue. His expression was one of benevolent amusement, like he'd figured out the lesson but was ready to let them struggle over learning it.

"What y'all think that clanging was, Sister Rue? You know this here town better'n I."

Rue kept her face hard. "There's an old fall-down church way out what used to belong to our marse."

"Is that right?" Bruh Abel said. "Maybe I oughta take up preachin' there?"

"You wouldn't want to," Rue said in a rush. "The ol' church just about come to its collapse durin' the war. More like than not that sound we heard was the old bell fallin' over, breathin' its last."

"Just as well," Bruh Abel said. Did he wink or was it a sparkle of starlight? "Me myself, I prefer to pray with nothin' but sky between me and the Almighty."

He shepherded the townsfolk over to their homes, easing their worries. Rue didn't follow after but kept her sights on the east ho-rizon where she knew the white church stood just as strong and sure as it ever had. She feared the ringing would sound again. But all was as silent as silent got.

When all the good folks of the world were sleeping, Rue crept out of her cabin. She had not been out in the woods for some days. She'd stayed away too long. Now she felt she'd grown arrogant in things kept hidden, grown too proud and sure. Bruh Abel's com-ing had stoked a fear in her. Ma Doe's warning about secrets clanged. She had let him catch wind a' her alright. But she wouldn't allow him to discover the precious thing she kept hid.

She had feared she'd become lax on her sojourns, forgot to make certain that no one saw her coming and no one saw her going when she made these clandestine trips of miles to the old white folks' church with a brimming basket of secret provisions in tow.

In slaverytime, the black folks had been taken to that church like a marching army, driven there by their Missus especially, who seemed to think on it as her Lord-ordained duty to save her black folks' souls on the one day a week her husband wasn't breaking their bodies.

There was a rectory there meant to house a minister Marse Charles had never been able to entice to stay, no sir, not out there in the heat and the solitude of their vast land, not amongst his slaves, who outnumbered his white family something like one hundred to one. Marse Charles had ousted all his white neighbors over time, bought up their land, and made himself an island in the center of a wilderness sea so impenetrable few would brave it, even, or especially, a man of God. Marse Charles hadn't cared much for religion anyhow except to pay a minister every now and then to make the trip out of a Sunday to say, "Slaves, obey your earthly masters with fear and trembling," and then be gone again. Eventually, the South had fallen in surrender and all those white folks were busied with a different manner of praying.

Now Rue's lone penance was an irregular one, and it had naught to do with God. But times like these when the townsfolk got to gossiping, when an unrest settled around Rue skin-close as clinging vine, she had to go and look at the church, even if she couldn't always bring herself to go all the way inside. It was enough to know that the woods and the church were undisturbed, the double doors still shut like she'd left them last. Rue would set down the burden of her basket, stand on the steps, and breathe in the still of the wood and know that all was calm and right, and then she would journey back to the town.

It was Ol' Joel who caught Rue this night as she made her way back home. He grabbed her at the last half mile where the trees grouped so thick that even the river lost its way. He seized her by the arm and squeezed, his grip surprisingly sure. He squinted at her as the crickets chirped their alarm. There was a sour smell about him stronger than his usual rotgut stink.

She took in his shriveled frame, the way his body seemed to tremor with impatience beneath his nightclothes, a thin shirt with the buttons mismatched in their holes. And he was leaning again, on that old lacquer cane. Had the river brought it back? Spat it up like something distasteful? Or had the whole scene been bunkum, with Bruh Abel brandishing a smartly painted stick?

Rue loosed herself from Ol' Joel's hold.

"Miss May Belle, where you think you comin' from at this hour?"

"It's Rue," she corrected.

Ol' Joel waved that fact away. "You best stay clear a' patrolmen. It's after curfew."

"No, suh." Rue spoke in slow, gentle rolls like she was calming a spooked horse. "Ain't no curfew no more. Remember? Ain't no slavery no more. War's been over and we been freed."

Ol' Joel scratched at his hair, a meager snowcap that looked alarmingly bright next to his blue-black skin. He was old, folks said, so old he dreamed of Africa, woke some nights and thought that he was there again. Was this one of them nights? Rue took him by the elbow and tried to guide him home with her. In the morning he'd be back to himself, sharp-minded as a laid trap and just as likely to bite. But the sun would dip low again and so would his senses. It was a madness that reminded Rue so much of her mama's final demise that she could hardly wait to be away from him.

"I know what you been doin', May Belle. Don't you deny it."

Rue patted his elbow and sighed. "Been doin'?"

"I seen you with her."

"With who?"

"That haint in the woods."

Rue halted at the gravel road, stopped at the head of the cross that started the old slave quarters that were slave quarters no more. She could turn around now. No one would have seen her with him. She could lead the old fool back into the tangle of woods. Turn him round 'til he worked himself lost. She could make the trees swallow him up if she needed to.

"Ain't no haint in no woods," Rue spat.

"I seen you with her." Ol' Joel tried to free his arm from the crook of her elbow. She wouldn't let him. She had a hold of him and he was curling in on himself, his lips flapping, his voice rising near to a holler. "I seen you walkin' through the trees with her, visiting her, whispering with her. I seen you summoning her. The haint. The ghost."

"Stop that. You ain't talkin' sense." Or he was talking too much sense for her to stomach.

"You a witch, same like yo' mama was," he said, and Rue did not know if he was accusing her mama or her grandmama. He'd got his generations, his healing women, all tangled.

"Y'all alright? I heard hollerin'."

Rue was more relieved to see Jonah then than she could say. He came up the path to them quickly, threw her a knowing look as he steadied Ol' Joel. Jonah's broad, sure frame towered over Rue and the sunken old man both.

"Marse Charles'll hear of it," Ol' Joel kept on. "Just you wait, now, Marse Charles'll see to ya."

Rue looked to Jonah but it seemed neither of them would correct Ol' Joel, would tell him that Marse Charles was long dead. If Ol' Joel could not recollect his own liberation then he was locked in a different kind of hell from which there was no emancipation. Rue would pity him if he hadn't made her so afraid with his accusations.

"I'll take him home, Miss Rue," Jonah said. "Thank you fo' findin' him."

Rue nodded, tried to come up with more, some easy explanation should Jonah ask just how Rue had found him so far from her own home, so very late at night. But Jonah was preoccupied with the care of Ol' Joel, who struggled against him too—whose hoarse voice took up a cry again: "She turnt yo' baby evil, Jonah. He a devil, ain't no flesh a' yours. She made him in the woods from river water, from clay. I seen her."

Bean. He was speaking on Bean.

"I seen her."

But Jonah shushed him, led him away, and still the old man raved 'til he got so far out of earshot that Rue couldn't make out what he was muttering, couldn't account for which things were lies and which things were truths so that all of it began to feel, not like words, but like a danger rising up all around her.

SLAVERYTIME

===

May 1861

Miss May Belle says: Marse Charles comes to me talking about War.

He don't knock. He walks straight into my cabin in the very middle of the day, something he ain't ever hardly do no more. I'm warned of his coming before I even see him 'cause outside the slave quarter goes allover hush except for the trumpeted-up sounds of slaves attending to hard work. The repeated greeting comes out like blackstrap molasses, bitter as it is sweet, "Good afternoon, Marse Charles," and it ripples all the way to my doorstep. But the wave of fawning gives me time to sugar up my countenance so I'm smiling like I ain't got a thing to hide when my marse comes charging into my cabin.

He sits hisself right down in the center of my bed, says, "It's to be war, May Belle. Do you know what that means?"

I ain't say nothing, ain't know what to say. I'm sweating. It's one of them blazes-hot days that drag long, never-ending, what with tending to my work round the plantation. The sick and the soul tired, the overworked and the underfed. *War*, my marse is saying, and nervous sweat drips down my spine like lazy sap off a sycamore. Is he asking if I know the meaning of the word?

"Where's that girl a' yours?" Marse Charles looks round my little home like the cramp of it displeases him. I smile so that he
keeps his eyes on me instead of picking out anything that might be
amiss. But I don't like him asking after Rue and I know I can't
answer the truth, which is that my Rue's like as not off mischiefing
with Varina, his white daughter.

"Rue ain't here, suh," I tell him. "I sent her to look over Homer."

"Who?"

"Field hand what fell over in the heat yesterday."

"He malingerin'?"

"No, suh," I say. "Homer done fell over onto his threshin' knife."

Marse Charles grunts. "You teachin' yo' girl yo' knowledge?"

"Sure am," I say, and that much is the truth. Ain't that the deal
I have with my marse? He keeps my child in his ownership and I
make her worth the owning. Marse Charles has far sights. Already
he's thinking when I'm dead and gone he'd like to have another
healing woman trained up. I can't fault him that, or fault Rue neither. Ain't every woman's daughter made from the death of the
mama, somehow or another?

"War," Marse Charles mutters.

So we back on that? I shift from foot to foot impatient to have
him outta here but not fool enough to let him know it. I do not
wish Rue to be witness to this visit. My child may be knowledged
in healing, but she don't know nothing of the ills of the world, and
I intend to keep it that way long as I'm alive and able.

Marse Charles unbuttons his shirtsleeves at the wrists, rolls the
cuffs up; he's mad enough to near rip the good fabric.

"This bastard Lincoln, he's took the reins and now he's smartin'
at the loss of us Southern states," he says. "As well he might, seein'
as we make all a' America's worth on our goddamned backs. Now
we Southerners are seein' our own way, son of a bitch won't let us
go free."

Marse Charles leans his big body back. My thin mattress in its creaky wood frame shifts noisily beneath him. He works at the worn leather of his belt, struggles to reach the buckle under the paunch of his belly. When we was both of us young and his stake was new, Marse Charles was lean, strong. Ambitious. Now he's the most prosperous landowner for miles and miles. His fields spread; his body do too.

"It's an ungodly business, Belle. I've just had a letter from an associate who witnessed the siege. He's thinkin' on sellin' his slaves all away. Better that, he's sayin', than the Northern hounds descendin' to take his property away by brute force. Cussed coward." Marse Charles punches his meaty fist into his empty hand. "I sure ain't of the same mind."

I'm glad to hear it. Every soul sold away feels to me like flayed skin ripped off the flesh. I keep my face peaceable.

"But if it is to be war," Marse Charles goes on, "changes gotta be made round here."

"How you mean, suh?" I don't much care at all about his gossip of war. Ain't I fighting little battles every day just keepin' his slaves alive on his behalf?

But I gotta keep talking. Keep his attention on me and no place else.

"You let me know who ain't pullin' his weight, May Belle. If there's a hunkerin' down to be done, that'll be where I start sellin', you hear?"

"Yes, suh," I say. It's a sick power, but it's a power, ain't it? Who stays? Who goes? Keep his eyes on me.

Now that Marse Charles has mastered his belt buckle, he shucks off his pants. Leaves them to fall in the shape of him on my floor.

"Come here, May Belle," he say.

I kneel between his legs, keep my eyes on him, only on him. Can he tell I'm afraid? Scent my fear?

He partway lowers his drawers, just enough so that they choke at his thighs, and I can't say if the flush that flames his cheek is from bashfulness or exertion. Or shame.

Two weeks back a canker bloomed up like fire, red and angry, on the tip of his prick. Now it's given over to a blotchy red rash, like I told him it would. Marse Charles come to me too late with the symptoms of this sickness to nip it early. He delayed over the choice: me or the white doctor a county over. But the white doctor's a relation of Missus's. And Marse Charles told me that he could not live with the guilt if his wife was to hear of his ailment. More like, he can't live with her exiling him from her bed once and for all.

"The rash is clearin' up some," I tell him, and it is too. It ain't too proud to say the truth. I do good work.

"I've heard passin' talk 'bout the mercury cure," Marse Charles says. "Men say after a few rounds, this dang sickness gets all the way cleared."

I suck wind through my teeth. "Sure, suh. Can't be sick if the cure done killed you."

He chuckles, rubs my head like I'm his best dog. I help to get him back into his pants so he don't go bending over. Eyes on me. Only on me.

"You stay takin' the rabbit root," I tell him. I've got his cure ground down to a fine powder and always at the ready, thank the Lord, so it's enough to give him a pouch with one hand and guide him out the door with the other.

"Y'all will keep all I've said to yo'self, Belle?" He says it to me sweetly, as if I'm a good friend doing him an easy favor, instead of a bit of good property without even the right to say no when it comes to touching his pockmarked pricker.

"'Course I'll keep it hush," I say, and it's a lie. There's a number of his favorite house girls that I've already warned after. Little use a warning is. I keep the rabbit root at the ready for them also.

But it ain't his sores he's speaking on.

"No sense worryin' the lot of 'em with talk a' battles and warrin'." Marse Charles inclines his head in the general direction of his fields, like to encompass the whole of his three-hundred-odd slaves. "They'll be afeared over nothin', get wrong ideas in their heads. They can't understand, they're like children. Not you though, Belle," he says fondly. "You about the smartest nigra I ever did meet."

He bangs out of my cabin, satisfied. I stand alone, shaking for long minutes, 'til I'm sure he ain't comin' back.

"He gone," I say at the bed. "You can come on out now."

My man slides his body out from beneath the wooden bed frame in slow inches 'til he's all the way clear. I try to help him up, but he refuses my hand. It's afternoon and he's meant to be in his own marse's field, working to death and whistling with the glee of it. And I've kept him too long already. But at least I kept him safe.

"You hear what my marse say?" I try to put some cheer to it. "War. The Northern hounds is comin' for the Southern foxes."

My man shrugs off dirt and dust, says, "Iff'n the hounds do come, May, you best be sure you ain't turnt to a fox yo'self by then."

"What's that s'posed to mean?" I bark. But I know exactly what he means. He's told me and told me, my man has, that he won't abide my spying on Marse Charles's behalf. But how else am I to keep the things I love protected? I reach out to kiss him, but he slams out the door too, albeit a sight quieter than Marse Charles just done.

Now I'm truly alone, but I don't suffer for it. My Rue-baby'll be back any minute now. Safe. Near me another day. Marse Charles won't cross me. And that makes anything I see or say or sell well worth the loss.

You can lose a hundred battles, 'long as you stay winning the war.

FREEDOMTIME

Rue saw Bruh Abel for what he was, a thief in the night. The thing he meant to use to snare folks was Black-Eyed Bean, the child that many had begun to whisper was the herald of some dark despair. Bruh Abel promised to baptize Bean before everybody and in the eyes of the Lord. To save him. A spectacle.

The baptism would mark the culmination of Bruh Abel's seasonal appearance in the town, and amongst folks it held a rising anticipation like the peak festivity of a fervent holiday. It was all anybody wanted to talk about. The baptism of Black-Eyed Bean. The day he would be washed clean. Saved.

Throughout the former slave quarters, Rue saw the baptism clothes folks planned to wear hung like white flags of surrender, flapping from washing lines, billowing in the wind so that from afar it seemed as though souls hung in them, too, writhing. Rue had never quite understood it, the airing of one's belongings on lines for everybody to see. Neither had her mama. When Miss May Belle was living, she'd hung their clothes indoors, never mind that it took longer for their clothing to dry in the close warmth of their cabin. Just one more intimacy they kept close.

But the white clothes did make a lovely sight from afar, Rue had to admit, strewn like decorations from house to house, all through the old quarter.

Rue troubled on the problem of Bean alone and came over and over again to the same dissatisfying conclusion: Miss May Belle would've known what to do about Bean. Rue herself did not.

Dinah, a slight mulatto woman who was known to mend clothes, ran to catch up with Rue. As much as she was pretty, she was talented, and Rue liked her fine for this, thought on her something like a friend, if she were to allow herself to indulge in friendships.

"Y'alright, Dinah?"

Dinah's tiredness showed in the squint to her light-colored eyes. She'd wrapped her little baby to her back to make her arms free, a little girl whose name Rue couldn't quite recollect.

"She's caught a chill, I'm thinkin'." Dinah tilted her back and arched up her behind so Rue could look at the child up close.

Rue tucked the wayward arm of the sleeping baby into the fabric belted at the small of Dinah's back. Without waking, the baby girl sucked appreciatively at her thumb. Her skin was warm but not alarmingly so.

"She'll come right," Rue said, and Dinah beamed, took her word on it that easy. "Feverfew. I'll bring some over to y'all presently."

"Y'all goin' to see Bean be washed?" Dinah asked.

Rue shrugged like she'd shrugged every time somebody had asked after Bean. "Surely," she said, "this town got more pressin' matters than the baptism of one li'l boy."

The room they'd put the struggling baby Si's crib in might as well've been in the ground already, so dark was it and so chill. It was an old mud-made room that had belonged to Marse Charles's kitchen, meant for storing things that couldn't last long in heat, and the clay walls made the outside world's sounds come together muffled and wrong. It was a rough quarantine but a necessary one, she'd thought, to keep little Si from suffering the heavy air of the late summer heat, to keep him away from his brothers and sisters. Si was only three days old; still his heartbeat had that telltale tripping of a drumbeat out of time. Rue had heard its like before; she knew well what it meant. Stillborn babies happened more than she liked to think on, but the ones born alive who did not thrive were a more weighty kind of tragedy. It was the waiting for the next breath and the next and the last. It made her sick and sleepless every time, that helpless waiting.

Rue jumped as Si's daddy came into the room. The sound of his steps had been swallowed up by the clay floor and her own overthinking. And now he stood close behind her. She felt him, watching her watching his son.

"It's a hard thing, Miss Rue."

"It is." What else was there to give than that?

"Heard other babies round here been fallin' sick also," Si's daddy said. The words sounded ominous and cruel and he'd meant for them to, laid out in the room, a threat against her healing power, and an implication.

His voice seemed too harsh to Rue, what with his sickly boy near. She didn't much like the man. He was one of those come lately after the war from yonder knows where, dragging along his freedom in search of some woman he'd been separated from years back. Well, he'd found her, Si's mama, and gave her four other healthy babies before this weak, wanting child had come. Now he stood with his whole weight blocking the doorway, and he seemed more put out than grieving. He seemed to be watching Rue, or so she thought. He was baiting her like she were an unruly creature. He said, "All these babies fallin' ill. What you make of that, huh, Miss Rue? Is there a sickness come onto us?"

"Nothin' of it to make," Rue said. "Cooler seasons coming on is all."

"Heard newborn children ain't hardly thrivin' this whole year. Not since you birthed that Bean."

Suddenly Rue was full aware of just how large Si's daddy was in the doorway, overflowing the close room with accusations against her, against Bean. She came aware of how fully Si's daddy blocked her one escape from the room, standing squarely in the outside light.

She thought on Ol' Joel's wild accusation declaring that she herself had made Bean as a haint and a blight against them. Ol' Joel had found willing ears for his conspiracy, and who better to fill up with lies than a daddy made empty by the shame of his weak son.

"And this one here, he won't latch on the teat." Si's daddy had clearly decided Rue was guilty of every one of those wicked rumors.

"He needs rest," she managed.

Si's daddy shook his head. "We mean to see him baptized by Bruh Abel."

Si gave off a cough then. Rue leaned over the child, cooing nonsense words as much to quiet him as to get out from under his daddy's stare. The baby struggled to open his eyes, gave up on it, returned to uneasy sleep.

"I don't think it's wise to put him to the water," Rue made herself say.

"Weren't askin' you if it were wise."

Rue pulled back from the crib like it'd burnt her. No one had ever before turned away her healing.

Si's daddy kept watching her and did not stop watching her as she moved around him toward the door.

"Keep him restin'," she said. "It's good to speak to him. Even a voice can soothe. I'll be back in the evenin' time." She couldn't keep away, not with a sickly child involved, and she hoped that later it would be the mama she'd find tending the boy—someone softer, sympathetic. Women tended to look more kindly on her, Rue knew. They understood the necessity of her work better than the daddies did.

She'd hoped to return to her own cabin and collect her troubled thoughts, but there, just past the doorway, was Bruh Abel. The good book was gripped in his right hand, like at any moment he'd be called to fight something off with its heavy binding, its flock of pages.

He smiled when she neared. Did he smile that bright trickster smile for everybody? Why was it that no one else seemed able to figure him for what he was?

"Sister Rue," he said. She balked. She was nobody's sister, and if she had a quicker wit or a whittled tongue she would have said so.

"Miss Rue," she corrected.

He barreled on forward like she hadn't spoke, said, "I was hopin' I'd cross yo' way."

Rue was aware that from a distance folks were watching them. She didn't have to turn this time to sense Si's daddy's approach from behind. He didn't bother to invent a pretense to look on this moment—when the healing woman and the preacher man were stood toe to toe.

Rue had to make herself speak up. "If it's about li'l Si, I tol' his daddy already. Y'all will only make him weaker if you take him to the water."

Bruh Abel's smile widened. His face was near pretty, up close, she had to admit. He had a spray of freckles on his nose from the sun, and even the way he looked down on her had an air of respectability for all that it made Rue wary. She squared her shoulders. He was a foot taller than her, easy, but not so broad as Si's daddy, and even if he was laughing at her she felt she'd sparked something in him that wasn't all the way saintly.

"Now, you may know better than I, Miss Rue. After all, the gift of healin' was put in yo' hands." If Bruh Abel was bothered by the gathering audience he didn't show it. He kept his focus on Rue. "But I'm only lookin' to ease the way for our li'l Si should the Lord see right to recall him to heaven."

"Our Si?" She was surprised by the bitter flavor of her own venom. "It's my thinkin' that our Si ought to have the easiest path to heaven, seein' as he's nary a week old. Baptism? Ain't no sense in it."

"Ain't no sense in salvation?"

Rue managed to still her tongue before she said more. Here she was, handing him the rope to hang her, with everybody looking on. She took a step back. "I only mean that I hope to give Si every chance at seein' another day, good Lord willin'."

Seemed Bruh Abel could use patience like a weapon. He paused to mull over what she'd said in what looked like pious consideration.

He spoke at last. "Lord willin' an' if the creek don't rise, we'll all see another day, Miss Rue."

She shook at the old nonsense saying, took it as her leave to go. It had been a favorite of Miss May Belle's when she'd been alive, and Bruh Abel surely knew it. The two had talked together, right up 'til the very end.

"Oh, Miss Rue," Bruh Abel called after her. His voice was teasing, lilting. "I ain't even get round to sayin' why I'd been lookin' to speak with you."

She'd made a mistake by walking away from him; now he had to yell to her to carry across the distance. Surely everybody for miles was listening. She turned to him, and her face felt hot.

"Only I was wantin' to ask you formally to come down from outta the woods and join our worship, Sister Rue."

So he had seen her that day at the riverbank. And he'd waited 'til now to slip the knot. She walked on, feeling dismissed and not liking it the least bit, not with all those folks watching and counting it as a retreat.

Rue returned that night to see Si as she promised she would, found his mama and daddy both in the chill room hovering over their sleeping baby like new parents over any ordinary newborn. But in his crib Si was still, his face almost waxen in its serenity.

"How he doin'?" Rue stepped forward but their eyes on her felt as cool as the room did.

"He'll be baptized, and in the care a' Jesus, soon enough." That was the mama, voice hitching. She was slight and soft-spoken, barely old enough to be called a woman, let alone a mama. She moved toward Rue, as if to block her from Si, and the light made visible a bruise at her jaw so garish Rue let out a hiss. Purple as bloomed larkspur the bruise ran down her neck, perfect in the shape of a handprint.

"What happened?" Rue asked, though wasn't it clear? Si's mama said nothing, and behind her her man towered. He picked up his dying son. Si was so little he took up not much more than the wide stretch of his daddy's open palm.

"We mean to have the boy baptized," Si's daddy said.

Rue appealed to the mama. "I come to tell you again that you ought not to."

"Ain't it the Lord's plan?" The bruise stretched with her speaking. Rue tried to catch her eye, to will some honesty between them, but the mama didn't want to receive it. Rue pushed round her to look over Si.

She meant only to feel the baby's forehead for fever, but Si's daddy caught her by her outstretched wrist. He squeezed that wrist so hard Rue felt the burn of her skin splitting.

"Woman," the daddy spat the word as a curse. "We don't want none a yo' devilment near our boy," and threw Rue toward the door by her arm.

She caught herself, only just, on the edge of the crib with the same outstretched arm he'd mangled. There was a loud pop in her wrist, not so much heard as felt, and Rue curled around the throbbing pain. It shot through her arm like a lightning bolt and stayed throbbing, but she held her face and looked to Si's mama.

Rue spoke with her jaw clenched like to crack her teeth. "Si needs lookin' after."

"Not by you," the mama said in her soft nothing voice.

Rue turned her back on them, on Si, stumbled for the door, and as she fled, she thought she heard, though she could not be certain, Si's daddy hock and spit in the path of her retreat, that old true method for dispelling a witch.

Rue put her broken wrist in the river and howled. The water was inky and cold and it eased the damaged limb as much as it pained her. Like a whetstone, the rushing current honed her senses to a wicked sharpness. She might have done better to go on home, to calm the swelling with a poultice of comfrey and to soothe her upset with a draught of brandy.

Instead, at the riverside Rue set her wrist with one slow, agonizing twist, tasted blood in her mouth but kept her eyes on her destination. In the distance over the treetops she could just see the bell tower of the old white church.

"It's Rue," her voice echoed. "You listenin'?"

She did not make her entrance quiet. What was there to fear? She walked down the center aisle, knowing she had an audience even if she couldn't make out any movement in the shadowed corners of the church's vaulted second story.

"That was a fool trick you done with the bell," Rue called up to the haint. But she felt a certain guilt as well, as good as if she'd rung the bell her own damn self. Because she'd stayed away too long. Let this whole fool thing go on too long. But she had to go on with it, particularly now with Bean's eyes on the back of her mind.

So Rue thought on what her mama might have done. What a haint might do. She cradled her aching wrist near her body, spun to see all the shadowed corners of the old church at once.

"I need you to go out there."

That night everybody in the town said they heard it clear, the screaming in the woods. It was a sharp, suffering scream, high-pitched and awful, roiling louder and then cut off abruptly. In the morning they saw what it had done. Strewn out on the muddied ground were all their baptismal whites in piles on the ground, muddied and ruined.

Already by midafternoon folks had built stories on top of other stories about the haint, so that in a matter of hours it was no longer a faceless spirit but one jealous of their glory, come to tear down the marks of their freedom-worship.

When anybody asked her straight out what it might have been that night in the woods, Rue put it to foxes. Their wilderness had a long history of foxes who were vicious, fearless, who came into town looking to tear up chicken pens and rabbit holes, just because they could. Foxes had that sort of cry that sounded like a woman in terror and, heard in echo, it could come out all wrong. But when folks started saying for themselves it was the haint, the drifting ghost some had half-seen in the woods, Rue did not immediately dispel them of the notion. A haint was an affliction she could deal with, or appear to leastwise. Something she could care to that Bruh Abel and his Bible could not.

Rue again met the preacher man in the square. This time he was on hands and knees alongside his flock, helping to pick up the ripped-down white clothing. She joined him in his stooping, though it vexed her to do so. Better, she figured, to seem to be just another knee-bent sinner in his estimation. Together they shook out a dusty bed cloth, held out opposite ends, and met at corners to fold it and fold it again. Bruh Abel set the neatly folded sheet down at the bottom step of somebody's porch, then took a hand-kerchief to his forehead like he'd done a whole day's labor.

"Thank you, Sister Rue." His eyes flashed warily at her bound-up wrist. She'd fashioned a splint of tree limbs and twine, the loose ends of which rattled when she moved. "I can't seem to disabuse yo' people of their backwards superstitions. Tell me, why is that?"

Rue shrugged. "You newly come to these parts. We got a long history that ain't easily laid to rest."

"Even so," Bruh Abel said, "the baptism of the baby Si will renew their faith."

Rue frowned. It was not altogether what she had expected to hear. "You mean to go on with it after all this carryin' on?" She gestured round the square where even now folks were discovering their washing in far-flung places. The white clothes had settled everywhere like an early frost foretelling winter.

Bruh Abel stood, brought himself up to his full height. Rue took a step back and cussed herself for it. Her wrist throbbed and maybe Bruh Abel sensed that, as any animal might sense another's weak spot and prey upon it. He took her bandaged hand and held it gently between his larger, lighter two hands, as though he meant to pray the break away.

"Tomorrow mornin' will see Si baptized," Bruh Abel promised her.

"It ain't right," Rue said.

"It's what the folks are needin'." He turned over her hand, gently. "You can't change faith, Sister Rue. And a haint can't neither."

In the end, neither Rue nor Bruh Abel was proved right. Si died that night. His body met the grave unwashed, unbaptized. Unsaved.

SLAVERYTIME

===

How long could a white girl keep sucking at her thumb? It was the year that Little Miss Varina would turn seven years old, and everywhere through the quarter the slaves gossiped on her outside of their master's hearing. They had it in whispers she still behaved like a small child with a small child's desperate habits. Yeah, they'd laughed about her, wondered at what it was that had made her so strange, and they came down on the fact that it had to be because her mama, the Missus, didn't ever love her, not even for a minute.

"You don't love on a baby enough they come up wrongly," Miss May Belle told folks who'd asked for her wisdom on the matter. "It's the same as lettin' 'em to starve."

They'd been corn shucking and they'd been singing. Seemed that they were surrounded on all sides by pale yellow kernels and the fresh green shed skin of corn that'd already been shucked and the darker green husks of those still wanting shucking. Everywhere were the white silky strings, which had gone all up in their hair, rendered them cobwebby and wild. Rue sat near her mama's feet, letting Miss May Belle drop husks into her lap.

Up above, Miss May Belle sat on a stool someone had brought

out. She was winding her toes around the legs of the stool, and Rue knew she was anxious about something, though her mouth smiled as she gossiped and her fingers flew as she tugged and plucked.

The mismatching collection of benches and stools and house chairs dragged outside made the square in the quarter look like a parlor room had bloomed from the center of the earth. The corn they worked was piled high, a proud mountain of bounty. Above, the sun was dipping down in the sky, shining its last rays on them sweetly, and Marse Charles had seen fit to give them a few jugs of whiskey, which they were allowed to pass amongst themselves as long as their hands didn't stop moving longer than it took to sip. The world had gone all golden, and their tongues were loosed.

"Don't think that Missus picked up that child but the one time," Fannie the housemaid was saying with a glob of tobacco thickening her lip.

"And when was that?"

"To hand her over to Ma Doe, 'course."

Ma Doe for her part huffed and said no more. Her arthritic fingers worked slow at peeling back the corn skin, and every now and then she'd set her work down and sigh. Those times Rue would see Miss May Belle reach out to the woman and rub at her fingers and then Ma Doe would begin again.

It was well known that Ma Doe had seen to the rearing of all of Marse Charles's children, his three sons and his one daughter. To Rue, Marse Charles's eldest were as solid as suggestions. The three boys had come to him by his first wife, a woman Rue had never known alive, though she'd heard of her from her own mama, who looked on the dead woman with a sort of reverent respect.

"She had too much beauty, that 'un," Miss May Belle would sometimes say, and the saying of it would come out of nowhere, as though Mistress Violet, for that had been the first wife's name, had just then left the room, her ever-present scent of peppermint oil left to linger.

"Was my mama what commended it to her, that oil she got to love so well," Miss May Belle would say, proud. "And she knew there was stock in it. Mistress Vi, she believed."

Mistress Violet in stories was pale, thin, her wrist and temples always wet with the anointing of oil. But the sons she made in quick succession were strong and overconfident in their own strength. The coming war would take them quickly in the order Mistress Violet had brought them into the world. But that was not to be for a while yet.

"You think he'll send Varina away? Make a belle a' her?" asked Big Sylvia, who had little patience for Miss Varina. The girl was forever in her kitchen stealing away with the ashcakes left cooling on the windowsill.

"Varina's not going anywhere for a long while," Ma Doe said. She divested a thick piece of corn of its covering in one irate tug. "Ain't that so, Miss May Belle?"

Rue's mama had that far-off thoughtful look on her face. She was looking into the woods, which just then echoed with a chittering of unseen animals. That wilderness seemed louder even than their singing, than the soulful plunking that came from across the high piles of corn where one of the drunker hands was entertaining himself by picking at a fiddle.

The high, woman-like scream of a fox cut through the newly fallen night, and one of the house girls leaned in and hiccupped and said gaily, "Now, Miss May Belle, ain't that yo' babies callin' to ya?"

The other women laughed but Ma Doe didn't and Miss May Belle didn't. Sitting skin close to her mama's leg, Rue felt her mama go rigid like she was holding on to something tightly.

Playing along, Miss May Belle said, "I'll see to 'em presently," but there wasn't any playfulness in her voice despite the good, hard work of the night, despite the harvest, green and yellow and white all around them.

Rue came home alone one afternoon to find their cabin door was slight-ways open. It didn't lock like the doors in Marse Charles's House did, with their heavy brass knobs and heavy brass keys, but it was a rule between Rue and her mama that their front door be kept firmly closed whether they were in or out. Miss May Belle said it was to ward off creatures, spirits, and bad air.

Could a creature have gotten in now? A spirit? A type of badness? Rue knew she'd closed the door firmly when she'd gone out. She always did everything her mama said to; her voice was always in her ear.

"You want me weepin'?" her mama would always say when Rue put herself into some childish danger, went picking flowers too close to where the patrolmen snatched up runaways, or climbed up a tree she couldn't climb down from, or waded into the river past where her toes could feel the bank. Never you mind the pain of death or injury; the worst pain was to make your mama cry.

Rue pushed open the door of the cabin anyway, thinking herself brave. She still jumped when she saw Varina. The white girl was sitting up on their dinner table, her dress spread out around her like a tablecloth, her legs back and forth dangling, her thumb, as always, in her mouth.

"What you doin' here?" Rue asked. She knew she wasn't meant to speak to Varina that way—was meant to call her Miss Varina, give her all the respect a white girl was deserving of. "And why you all pink?"

Varina's face up close was mottled with blushing. Snot glowed from the hollow beneath her left nostril, and before she answered

Rue, she took the time to rub furiously at her puffy eyes with both fists.

"Mother slapped me for sucking my thumb. She said she 'shamed of me."

It was unlike Varina's mama to say anything to her, kind, cruel, or otherwise, but it was well known to everybody—to the black folks at least—that the master's second wife was not much proud of what she'd produced, her one child, his only daughter. And Lord that red, red hair.

"I'm lookin' for the healing woman. May Belle," Varina said.

"That's my mama. What you want with her?"

"I want to be cured."

Rue crawled up onto the table beside Varina before she could think better of it. She half-expected that the master's daughter might push her away, but instead Varina made room for Rue on the table's surface, scuttling unladylike, baring white frilled bloomers that Rue decided were the prettiest things she had ever seen.

Varina wiped up snot with her forearm. "Will she help me, you think?"

"She surely will," Rue said.

Up close Varina had only her daddy's face and none of her mama's. Marse Charles's severity, his thin pink lips, the small ears with the heavy loose lobes and hair in dark, curling barbs. But where had that red color sprouted from? It came up from her head in corkscrews.

Rue let Varina rest her head on her shoulder. After a while she looped her arm around her waist, and that seemed to quiet Varina's sniffles. Miss May Belle would have words here, but Rue had none except "Mama will know what to do."

When Miss May Belle came in, she did not look surprised at all to see the two girls on her supper table. She only looked weary and stopped to pull off her hat. "Afternoon, Miss Varina," she murmured.

Miss May Belle set down her basket, sat on the bed for a spell, and gave her left arch a forceful rub like she could squeeze out her foot pains. Only then did she say, "A'ight, what's the trouble?" as if trouble was a constant, and not particularly urgent, part of every day.

The question set Varina off weeping again. She told it between hiccups, that her mama had come into the nursery and seen her at her studies. Varina was tasked with copying a page of the Bible as a means to perfect her crooked script. She did so every noontime, for she wasn't allowed to go out when the sun was high and like to spoil her skin with freckles.

"I was making the most lovely V's," Varina said, and she did one there in the air to show them, her wrist flicking about the invisible flourishes. There weren't, she despaired, enough letter V's in the Bible.

Ma Doe had stepped out to see Big Sylvia down in the kitchen about their luncheon and Varina had been there alone thinking very hard on her lessons and her piety, she swore. Well, everybody knew when Miss Varina got to thinking hard she was liable to suck her thumb with a distinct abandon, and that is when her mama had come in and seen what she was about.

"She smacked my hand from my mouth. She called me dirty as a nigra and sent me out the House saying I belonged out in the slave quarter. So," Varina sobbed, "here I am."

"Oh, Jesus," said Miss May Belle, and that made Varina cry harder. "S'alright now, Miss Varina. But we just gotta try to heal you off the habit."

Varina looked at her thumb. Rue looked down at her own thumbs, trying to figure what the pleasure in sucking them might be. Her hands were work-worn, the nail cut down to the quick. Rue's hands were too busy to spend time in her mouth. Now that, she thought, was where Varina's trouble was.

"What if I tell you a story to ease yo' mind from it?" Miss May Belle said.

Varina sniffled. "Yes, please."

"Now, lessee," Miss May Belle began from her seat on the bed.

It went like this, that Bruh Rabbit was going all throughout the wilderness, bragging on himself, saying how smart he was, smarter than any animal in the wood.

Well, Bruh Fox, who had declared himself the master of that wilderness, did not like hearing Bruh Rabbit's claims, and he set out to prove Bruh Rabbit wasn't so smart after all.

"'Good gracious. Who he think he is anyhow?'" Miss May Belle mimicked Bruh Fox and the girls laughed. She was a good mimic, gave the fox the type of high-minded tongue of a fine, white gentleman. Bruh Fox's companion, the Snake, she made slither out his words like any upstart overseer.

Bruh Fox, just to put Bruh Rabbit in his right place, set him a task, gave him a haversack and told him to bring him something back in it.

"Somethin' like what?" Varina asked gamely.

Miss May Belle wagged her finger. Bruh Fox wasn't about to tell Bruh Rabbit what he ought to bring. If Bruh Rabbit was so smart he'd surely figure it out. But Bruh Rabbit stayed puzzled. He got to talking to the birds—maybe they had an idea how to oblige Bruh Fox? They just shrugged their feathered shoulders.

"By and by, an idea come into Bruh Rabbit's head. He asked them birds if he might beg a feather off a' each a' them."

From beneath their bed Miss May Belle began to pull up lengths of fabric scrap cut to long, spooling ribbons of the type she'd use to tie up newborn baby cords.

"Bruh Rabbit stuck all 'em feathers to himself and soon he had, there gathered, enough feathers to fly over to the Big House where Bruh Fox lived."

Miss May Belle tied neat fast knots of ribbon all the way up Varina's arms, a prism's worth of color, and bade her flap her new wings. Varina did so, stuck her arms out stiff and let her ribbons stream with her flapping. Rue, beside her, had no ribbons. She felt earthbound and ordinary.

In the story, Bruh Rabbit perched himself on a tree outside of Bruh Fox's house. There he spied Bruh Fox chatting with his old friend Snake.

"What kind a' bird is that?" Bruh Fox asked, squinting at the creature dressed in the strange mix of colors, like nothing he'd ever encountered. Snake could not say, and suggested that they might go down and ask Bruh Rabbit, since it was true he was mighty clever.

"Y'all won't find him," Bruh Fox declared. "I sent him on a task he won't figure. He don't know that he's 'posed to fetch me the Moon, and the Sun, and the Darkness."

"Once he overheard that, Bruh Rabbit flew away," Miss May Belle said. One by one she untied the ribbons from Varina's arms. Before Varina could complain, she left two ribbons behind, one on either arm, red strings knotted around the hitch of Varina's elbows.

Meanwhile, Bruh Rabbit went around creation. He snatched the Sun from the east and the Moon from the west. He snatched the Darkness out of night itself. He put them in the sack and lugged them up to Bruh Fox's Big House, where all the animals were gathered, waiting.

"'Lessee how you done, Bruh Rabbit,'" Miss May Belle quipped as Bruh Fox. Enthralled, Varina went to raise her thumb to her mouth, but the ribbons hitched around her elbows made the movement clumsy. She put her hand down, leaned closer instead, better to hear the end of the tale.

First Bruh Rabbit brought out the Darkness. The assembled creatures screamed and shivered in the total dark. Then Bruh Rabbit brought out the Moon, and they were calmed by the low light. Lastly Bruh Rabbit tugged the Sun out from his sack, but it was so brilliant and bright that it burned at the animals' eyes.

"And that," Miss May Belle finished, "is how Bruh Rabbit brung a sometimes blindness into the world. Because he may be smart. But ain't no one smarter than God. And sooner or later they gon' learn it."

PART TWO

FREEDOMTIME

==

1868

The men began to spit wherever Rue walked. They did not do it in her sight. They were not so bold as that. Not yet. But they saved up their spittle behind their lips like cud, spittle being the best defense to ward off what they'd decided must be the cursing of a witch.

Rue felt it, and she felt the men watching her as she walked through the center square of the cabins. They still nodded greetings, tipped their hats. But when Rue went round the corner she knew that behind her back they were hocking up their hate, swirling it in their mouths. Spitting that hate in the path she'd just walked through like she'd left a bad taste on their tongue they could not wait to be rid of.

Rue had thought of running away long before the spit began to fly. In the years after Miss May Belle's passing, the urge would sometimes come upon Rue in the middle of some effort. Say she had to reach up on a high shelf for a vial of medicine, say she was walking clear across the town on a rain-blustering day. Now, after baby Si's passing, all the mamas were watching her like she had the dust of his death caught under her fingernails. And all the while, Bean, the strange child, thrived.

After they'd laid Si to rest, Rue resolved to work harder. She paid no mind to the spittle or the suspicion that trailed her like runoff of some venomous sea. She looked in on the sick folks and the elderly and the new mamas like she was dim to their whispers and accusing stares. There were things she'd been neglecting. Things that wanted seeing to. It was the opposite of running. A digging in.

She was isolated, estranged, but hadn't she always been? Perhaps from the very moment she'd been born, if memory could take her back that far, for from the start Rue had ever been Miss May Belle's daughter, her destiny marked because of it.

Rue knew there was only one other baby born as she had been with distrust heaped upon him, as soon as he blinked open his bean-black eyes. The more alone the townsfolk made her feel, the more she felt a pull toward Bean. The more she felt for him, the more she feared for him.

Folks did not like what they could not put an explanation to. All she could think, over and over, was that she had not been able to save Si from the affliction he was born with. She would not let Bean fall too, to add to that number of perished children whose births had not saved them from death. Her fear of the dead clawed at her, buried secrets that might surface from her dreams into the waking world. Didn't everything over and over surface and come again?

And so, one cool evening, Rue came into Bean's family's cabin, unannounced. She had been looking for Sarah, had gathered up all her courage to ask after Bean. The grim fact was that where Rue's name was whispered, Bean's was often liable to follow. They could hurt Rue with their tongue wagging and their cussing, but Bean was just a baby still, and it made Rue's freshly healed wrist ache anew to think what way they might devise to hurt a child like Bean if words were not enough.

Rue was looking for Bean's mama but she found his daddy instead, and she paused on the threshold unsure if she ought to turn and go before Jonah saw her. She couldn't help watching him, unobserved, a part of her thrilled. Jonah was head bent at the family supper table shifting grain into a haversack, a strangely womanly task that endeared him to her, for he seemed to be practiced in it. She watched as he took a well-measured cupful from the larger barrel and transferred it to the sack, keeping a count of what he was about with a silent movement of his lips.

Behind him a suppertime fire was burning itself down. There was Bean on the floor, braced on his hands and knees, his black eyes staring into the fireplace, unblinking. He was still and silent, focused wholly on the dying flame.

"C'mon in, Miss Rue," Jonah startled Rue by saying. She hadn't thought he'd noticed her there half in his doorway.

"Night's unseasonably cool, ain't it?" he said. "Come in an' warm yo'self."

She knelt beside Bean, who looked up at her. She sat herself down heedless of the ash near the stove and pulled Bean into the cradle of her lap. He was small for his age, and she could feel his little jutting ribs beneath his shirt. He did not start up his crying, even as Rue held him at his wriggling waist, but seemed content to be held by her.

"He likes to sit there 'cause it's warm," said Jonah. "He won't go near the fire."

"How you know?"

"Sarah teaches 'em young how to stay outta the flame. She make sure they know well enough that it hurts."

Rue did not make it her place to tell folks how to rear their children. But she did wonder what Jonah, placid as he was, thought of Sarah and her ways. They were both of them orphans—Sarah after her mama's passing, Jonah sold to Marse Charles in an ill-assorted lot of slaves. They had chosen each other, Sarah and Jonah had. After Marse Charles, after the war, after freedom, they had chosen each other in that hazy time when everybody was pure drunk on choosing. Made a home in this cabin, and a baby, and another, and then this third child that wriggled now warm in Rue's lap, still mesmerized by the fire and sucking at his thumb. The low flames were reflected in the flat black of Bean's eyes, and Rue felt Jonah as a safe presence behind her.

Her skin just about buzzed when Jonah leaned in toward her, though he hadn't touched her. He said, "You here after Sarah, I expect? Women's work?"

Rue had near forgot why she'd come. It was comfortable by the fire and in Jonah's company. Bean eased himself into her arms, dozing.

"Yes, I'm lookin' to speak with Sarah. She here?"

"She down at the river. Bruh Abel got most of the womenfolk out there prayin', showin' they thankful as we got such a good harvest this year."

It had in fact been a miraculous harvest, and Bruh Abel had appeared right in the heart of it. Rue wondered if that was no simple coincidence but a type of divining. Had the preacher known that it would be the best moment to descend upon them, what with full stores and satisfied bodies?

"You eat yet?" Jonah shifted the full sack of grain from the table to the ground, proceeded to fill another.

Rue had not. She often found her meals here and there, a collection of benevolences from the mamas that she looked after, as were her clothing and her other little comforts, and a fair stack of coins that she hid in a distant knothole as Miss May Belle had done. Just in case. But there was no denying that lately Rue had found those favors harder to come by.

Rue grinned up at Jonah's work. "You look like you fixin' to cook a feast."

"No, ma'am, I'm tithin'," he said.

"Tithin'? To that preacher man?"

Jonah nodded. He did not look up from the careful transfer of the next cupful. They had not fed her like this. Never tithed to her, nor had she expected it.

Rue set Bean down, back farther from the fire than he had been, and she stood, the better to look at the grain Jonah was giving to Bruh Abel as it moved from the depleted barrel to the fat haversack. They had used to give Marse Charles a portion of what they'd been allowed to grow for themselves in the piteous gardens in front of the slave cabins. Those growings made up their only food aside from the slave portions. Jonah's tithing now made Rue envious. It smacked to her of that time before the war that she had thought was safely in their past. But here it was again, taking on another type of robbery: no Big House, but now a fair-skinned black man who'd set himself up above them on little more than his talent for telling tales down by the riverbank.

"Bruh Abel ain't ask for it, mind," Jonah was saying, perhaps guessing at Rue's unease, hedging it like a wildfire before it could get blazing. "Folks spoke on it and decided amongst themselves that they ought to offer him somethin' regular-like. In hopes that he might deign to stay on out here, where he's needed, rather than move on to some big city."

"Where he's needed?" Rue felt she'd be wiser to hold her tongue. She did not like to show to Jonah especially that bitter side of herself that felt so quick to turn to distrust and envy. But she could not overlook those nettles of fear, the clinging notion that something dark was rising up higher and higher against her. Turning her over like loose sand in this town where she had thought she could stand forever sure-footed, respected.

Jonah spoke on the many wonders that had come to pass now that the town was turning more solidly toward its own faith, not the one pressed into their backs by Marse. The good crops and fair weather, the wind blowing and the moonglow shining and the sun rising and setting as it was supposed to, seemed all of it was down to the faith they'd found. The faith Bruh Abel was guiding them in.

"And Bean," Jonah added.

"What about him?"

"He ain't made that awful cry, not one night since Bruh Abel come and start prayin' over him. Seems to me we can't go on like we have been," Jonah said. He'd set down the measuring cup, came toward her empty-handed. "We was froze up. All of us been waitin' on the future to reveal itself. Waitin' on what freedom means. Bruh Abel say we don't gotta wait no more. We can just go 'head and put aside the old ways."

Rue felt it in her bones: She was the old ways to which Jonah was referring. Her and her mama and her grandmama. Made for a world that wasn't anymore, that had been shook off like fetters. But Rue was still bound, to this place, to these ways.

"What if it's nonsense?" Rue said. "What if it's all empty air what Bruh Abel speaks on and seems to do?"

Jonah shrugged. "Seems to me if faith was tangible it wouldn't be faith, would it?" He surprised Rue, reached out and touched her cheek like he was soaking up a tear that wasn't there. His touch was so gentle it startled her.

"What he makes folks feel is real, ain't it? You'd know that, if you went to pray with us."

Rue turned her head away from Jonah's palm, buried her face

in Bean's soft brown hair so she wouldn't have to look at Jonah and show him her hurt, or her wanting.

"'Llow me to fix you supper," he said.

Jonah served up dried fish stew on a tin plate. The food was still warm from when Sarah had made it earlier. Rue wondered if Jonah had caught the fish himself out there on one of his working trips on the docks of white men's boats, reeling in catches for them. Rue liked to think that he had. She motioned for him to eat along with her, both of them head bent over the steaming plate.

Bean grew restless in Rue's lap, leaned across the table, curious of the food. She pulled him close to her chest, fed him fingerfuls of corn mush off her plate. Bean gnawed at her fingers, sweet as any teething child. Why were folks so quick to heap their fear and foreboding upon him?

"I'd like to see after him, your Bean," she said, "to make sure he come up right." She did not know why she said it, only that she felt worry for the boy as much as she felt a kinship for him. It seemed right to promise it there in the quiet still of Jonah's home, her belly filling up warm with his easy kindness. What else could she give Jonah but that? Women's work, he'd called it. Rue wanted to prove herself worth much more.

She could smell Jonah this close. Scented of malt and of hay. He laid a hand atop hers, seemed to study her awhile. He nodded, maybe in acceptance of what she'd offered, but when he finally spoke he said, "Bean's to be baptized soon. Bruh Abel promised."

She thought again of the weak baby Si who had lived and died before Bruh Abel could make a spectacle of him. She had to wonder, if Si had lived would Bean now be saved from all this high-mindedness? Wasn't he just a child? He felt like one. Safe in her arms, he was banging at the supper table, amusing himself like any baby would with the discovery of his growing strength. But his arms did bare that strange hexagonal pattern, like the surface of a bee's hive, and that skin all over was sickly pale. And the eyes. Rue looked from Bean to Jonah.

Jonah spoke softly, so soft Rue had to lean in to hear. He said, "I want Bean to be saved."

"Yes." Rue was watching Jonah's lips. "So do I."

The sound of the front door hitting the clapboard startled them apart. Three sharp footfalls and there was Sarah in the doorway. Long and thin, willow reed in coloring and in ease, Sarah seemed to mold herself to the doorjamb. She looked at Rue and Jonah and Bean through slant eyes, like there was something about them to see if only she could squint harder.

Rue stood from the table, jarring Bean suddenly. He let out a low of displeasure. She clutched him closer, like a thief hiding behind the very thing they meant to steal.

"Sarah. We was waitin' on you," Jonah said. "Rue wished to speak to you on some matter."

"Evenin', Sarah."

"Miss Rue." Perhaps the address galled Sarah, for she said it in a bite. After all, they were near the same age and yet so different.

"I'll let you two get on." Jonah took Bean from Rue's hands, but Bean struggled to stay with her. He cried out to her like to break her heart. Jonah took him into the next room, deeper into the dark of the house.

"If we talkin' let's do it outside," Sarah said. "It's too hot in here."

Rue followed Sarah out onto the narrow porch. They both leaned on the slanted railing, uncomfortably close in the thin space. It was too dark to make out Sarah's expression but there was the quirking open of her mouth, the baring of teeth as she said, "Hope my cookin' was to yo' likin', Miss Rue."

"Yes," Rue said baldly. "It was. But that wasn't why I come callin'."

Rue shuffled in her pockets, her hand grasping around a vial. It was warmed from where it had stayed pressed against her body and Bean's. She pulled it out and showed it to Sarah, who made no motion to grab for it.

"Some time ago you asked me after a protection for yo'self. You said you did not wish to have more babies. I ain't want you to think I had forgot. Or maybe, it was more you didn't feel quite comfortable askin' again."

It was a delicate business, Rue knew. It was a secret thing that Rue and before her Miss May Belle would spirit to women who could only hint at wanting it, fearful of either their man's hearing or their master's. Sarah, brave as she was, had said the words in a stutter after Bean, who she had devised to keep hid, caught the town's tainted attention. But she never had come back for the cure. Now Rue turned the vial in her hands so it glistened in a twinge of moonglow.

"I ain't want it no more," said Sarah.

"No?"

"No."

The bottom of Sarah's dress, Rue noticed, was shadowed in wet, damp all the way up her legs from kneeling at the river. Bean wasn't yet two and Sarah had regained her thin frame, her small sharp breasts, her sweet girlish shape, like Bean had never been part of her body at all. Rue found she hated her for that, the way she'd shrugged Bean off.

"I don't wish to stop havin' babies." Sarah sounded sure of herself. "It ain't a godly thing to do."

"Who tol' you that?" But Rue knew who.

"Please," Sarah said, turning her back toward Rue, retreating to her cabin. "Don't worry after me or my family no more."

SLAVERYTIME

===

"The water ain't worth more than the bucket."

If it were a song, her mama would have sung it as gospel 'til her throat ran hoarse, and after her mama was dead and gone, Rue had a habit of saying it to herself, below her breath, as a kind of prayer.

Miss May Belle had spoken many things before she passed on and most of them Rue had let the years take away, had let erode on purpose, but there were some she held on to fast and kept whole.

"Scrub," Rue's mama had said, so that the whole of Rue's first memory of Miss May Belle was the smell of lye soap and the sensation of her skin prickling as the water dripped down her elbows.

"You clean?" her mama would always ask.

"Yes'm."

"What you do next?"

"Don't touch nothin'."

"That's right, don't touch nothin'."

For sure it seemed always to be in the middle of the night, what her mama called the witch's hour, that they'd find themselves yanked from floating dreams and the freedom of sleep, to stumble half-blind to some woman's bedside with her particular howling filling up the whole of the plantation, and Rue, herself half-asleep and waiting with her little sleeves rolled up her little arms and her arms held out in front of her, wet but drying, and her jaw clenching with the urge to catch a yawn in her palm but with the instructions *Don't touch nothin'* steadily knocking around in her head as good as law, 'cause if she touched something the baby might die.

"Thank the Lord, you come just in time, Miss May Belle," the man might say when they'd first arrive. His face would be twitching restless with the desire to look brave. It seemed to Rue that the men were always trying to look brave when really what they wanted was to leave Miss May Belle to it.

Rue's mama kept her dark face hard and neutral, for she believed excitement or fear, love or loathing, could spread through the touch with the ease of pestilence, and the last thing you wanted was an excited mama too near her time. Miss May Belle was known to look bored, as if the making of life, the creation of a whole person, was simple and ordinary, and to her it was.

"Brought my own baby out on my lonesome," she liked to tell folks.

Miss May Belle was something else, a soul come again, people said, born and born, with the knowledge of some other place.

And if Miss May Belle insisted on a thing, she'd have it, as good as willing it into existence. She found fire to warm up babies born too soon, and old sheets to keep down the dust from the floors, and soap, soap in frothing handfuls, and because she kept their property from dying, white folks let her have it. They let her have her own way, and the other black folks looked on in just as much awe as envy at how she lived like a white woman amongst them.

She'd show up moments before a miracle, wash up, flick her wet hands, first the left then the right, always the left then the right, and the excess water would arc off her and sparkle by the light of the candle she alone was allowed to have, and that meant it was time to settle in.

"Oh, we got a while yet," she'd say, and she'd shoo the man off with the reasoning that men were bad luck around birthing. Truth was they just ran her nerves.

"Now, who you think help Eve push out Cain and Abel?" Miss May Belle was heard to say, loud and often. "Surely wasn't no Adam."

And folks got to saying that Miss May Belle hated men though that was not true—"I wouldn't have no work if there weren't men to keep women bothered"—because by and by she did let herself get bothered by a man, and that man was Rue's daddy.

Rue couldn't know if what all she knew of her daddy was from real knowing or if it was from hearing the same story over and over 'til the story became as good or better than remembering.

What she did know was this: what the network of raised scars looked like on the bare skin of his back, the puckered flesh ridged in ruined pink, and how the pattern of the long, thick lines had always made her think of the pattern in the palm of a hand. How the line that was the longest wormed its way from the bowl of his neck and traveled around to his back and down his spine. The ugliness of it never scared her before she understood that they were the lines from a long history of whippings and how that was what she could make out the most in the moonlight on those nights when he'd crawl up the bed on hands and knees, like some pleading nighttime creature, to bother Rue's mama.

"I didn't have any wanting for him at the start," Miss May Belle would say. But in Rue's memory her mama always seemed to want him as if she was half a woman without him, would wait and wait for Sundays when visiting was allowed with the kind of shrugged-off longing kept by someone who near believed Sunday wouldn't be coming that week.

And in those Sunday nights Miss May Belle showed her wanting. Rue would wake to her little breath-catching sounds, like the reverse of weeping. Rue's daddy crouched down over Rue's mama, and on the fullest of full moon nights Rue could see the arc of her against him as if she were floating up off the bed into his body, and Rue could see the tense fist of his left hand baring all his weight against the mattress and the softness of his right hand as it went off by itself and burrowed in the cotton of Rue's mama's hair, or drifted down her cheek to rest a thumb in the dimple of her lip, or disappeared completely downward to fill up the little space left between them. And Rue could see the muscles shifting beneath the damaged skin of his back, like clouds stirring in the night sky, until she lost herself in sleep again.

When Rue's daddy died, Rue's mama died, though his death was a grim and sudden surprise and hers was a slow consumption by way of vengeance, spread out one long year after her man's death, easy as decaying.

"You clean?" Rue's mama was forever asking.

"Yes'm," Rue would say and shake dry her left hand and then the right.

When Rue's daddy died Miss May Belle stopped wanting to touch the mamas, maybe suspicious of the warmth of their flesh or the roundness of their baby joy. Whichever it was, she certainly had a distrust for them, which started up one day from a bad taste she found in her mouth.

"A curse been put onto me," Rue's mama said and she spat on the dusty ground, not even caring they were right outside of Marse Charles's House. Rue looked down at the pink tinge to the white foam of her mama's spittle and wondered if it were so.

In the cabin they shared alone, a privilege to be sure, Rue's mama began hanging fruit from the wood beams of the ceiling, any fruit she could get hands on, mainly apples, cut in half, their black seeds gleaming like eyes in their white flesh. Even mealy, even molded, they spun in lazy circles and drew lazy flies. And Rue could not know if her mama had run to her madness or if she was warding off something she didn't want to name. The redder Miss May Belle's spit got, the more fruit she'd find to let swing.

If her mama was mad then Rue was mad too, at least in the eyes of other slavefolk. The rotting fruit smell clung to them both, trailing them, persistent as haints. It was beneath her mama's fingernails, which she had let grow long as creature claws, for she would not cut them, afeared that somebody would gather up the nail clippings to use against her in conjure. Rue, herself, washed and washed, trying to get the smell out from under her own skin. Now they'd kneel down at the birthings together, but it was Rue who touched the mamas, who tugged the babies into being. Her mama's guidance was as good as if Miss May Belle had her hand atop Rue's, as if their touch was one touch.

There came a day that Miss May Belle and Rue returned from a birthing of twins, an all-night and all-day affair, as if the twins had not wanted to come on out to the world but had preferred to stay curled together with just themselves for company. Rue and her mama returned to find that all the fruit in their cabin had dropped to the ground, lay in blackened, defeated piles, on the chairs, on the stove pot, in the rut of the bed, and the once-languid flies had lifted and made a frenzy in the air like they'd lost their sense of meaning. But Miss May Belle didn't weep like a more earthly woman might. She walked around stooping, collecting the bits of skin and pulp and seed that near turned to nothing at her touch, and it was because of this quiet triumph against ruin that

Rue couldn't bring herself to say, and never would, that she had been the one to pull the fruit down in a sudden fit of rage against her mama's rising madness. Hoodoo would not bring Miss May Belle's strength back, nor her man back. But neither would Rue's bitterness.

Miss May Belle pounded what was left of the fruit. She sat up in bed, for six days and six nights, from can-see to can't-see, a crude mortar in one hand, a rock for a pestle in the other. It was on the seventh day, when she'd become like a ghost in her own imprint in the mattress made of straw and pine tags, that they were told they were free.

Rue carried the message on to her mama, the words sitting like tar on her tongue, for it was something they'd so long wanted and now had but couldn't figure the use of.

"Free." Rue's mama said the word and then lay back down in her own hollowed-out shape in the bed. She let the mortar fall sideways and moved only to give herself room to spit a glob of red onto the blackened pile of mashed fruit, done with it at last. And Rue knew at least some part of Miss May Belle's sickness was healed, though it felt like a cure come too late to save her.

Even when Miss May Belle stopped going out, the women stayed coming to her. It was the end of secession, the end of the war and the beginning of that thing, freedom, that idea that had been bandied about for four long years and more, lobbed like cannonballs by the North into fine Southern houses. The smoke cleared and freedom stood. But freedom hadn't changed things much, not in their isolated country, down in the quarter, where women still had the same aches and pains, the same swelling and suffering, the same look of pure dumb wonder when Miss May Belle let them put their newborn to the safety of their chest. Maybe now they needed her even more because freedom was a word with weights. It meant deciding—to stay or to go. To have or not to have. It was a heady change—becoming the master of one's own self.

"Not all women is intended for mamas," Rue's mama liked to say, lying on her back in bed looking up like she was looking for stars on the inside of her eyelids.

Even with her eyes shut Miss May Belle could direct Rue to this or that sachet or herb or salve, and it didn't take long 'til Rue knew what to fetch her before she even asked it. And then she knew what to fetch before the women finished describing what it was that they were needing. Soon enough Rue could just tell by looking at the expressions on some of the women's faces that they had come for that particular type of magic that Rue's mama kept hid.

The water Miss May Belle gave them was so clear it felt harmless enough, though what it tasted like Rue could not say. She only knew from watching what they experienced, and it looked to her no worse than the agonies of birth, only what they were pushing out was nothing but blood, not much heavier than what came month to month. Still, sometimes they'd cry and cry and always it amazed Rue, and still did, how hard it was to keep a baby and how hard it was to be rid of one.

"You clean?"

"Yes, Mama," Rue'd say, only sometimes they weren't doing anything at all; sometimes they were doing little more than sitting around staring at each other on a Sunday, the day of rest, waiting for the next time they were needed, because they were bound up together by blood but also by the way folks had of keeping their distance. Inside of her on-and-on sleep, Rue's mama was beginning to get muddled; for her the present was the past come again.

They could just about hear the singing from outside if they felt like reaching out their ears to where the whole of the town was gathered in the church down the way, singing up to the Lord, thanking him for the day he'd made. And to Rue the sound of their voices was so absolutely lovely, like a thing she could hold in her hands, like a faith she could touch.

"Don't touch nothin'," her mama would say. A bad touch was all it took. A bad touch could kill.

The first time Rue pulled a dead baby from its mama, she felt that she had killed it herself. It was a baby boy, or would have been, sweet and black and small, a perfect fit for Rue's two cupped hands. He was still caught up in the cord he'd come out with, a constricting braid of blue and red, that wrapped too tight around his neck.

It had been a rough time from the very start. The mama was mostly a child herself with her eyes turning big and red and watery as the heat of her flesh rose. Her husband was an old man—his eyes were filmy and white—and he'd taken the young girl up because she had no people left of her own and he'd molded her into a wife.

There'd been a choice.

"Freedom," as Rue's mama liked to say, "be all about choices."

And so Rue had put the question to the man: his little woman's life or his little child's.

"Well now, Miss Rue," he said, his white eyes roving around lost and looking for somewhere to settle. "You know better than I do."

But how could she?

"The water ain't worth more than the bucket," Miss May Belle had said, not aloud in that moment, but loud in Rue's memory, as she'd said it so many times before.

No, Rue's mama was at that moment in her bed, in the cabin she'd had built especially for her, far away from everybody else, for a healing woman had to live her life separate and die that way also. There Miss May Belle lay with the spit frothing red at her lips, the black cotton hair her man had loved so much in tangles, and the things she said choked by nonsense so that her very last words received and relayed by a lone traveling preacher had meant nothing. Rue had had to replace them in her memory with better words, with ones she wanted to keep: The water ain't worth more than the bucket.

Rue sent the old man away from the birthing—men, after all, were bad luck—and alone she spoke in a soft voice to the young mama, trying to give her comfort. For childbed fever there was black snakeroot, for grief, a few soft-spoken words.

"You gon' be alright," Rue told the young woman. "You gon' live to love lots more babies."

Miss Rue chose the bucket then as she would over and over and over again. She let the water slip right through her fingers.

FREEDOMTIME

===

More and more children were falling sick. There was no denying
it or ignoring it or quieting it neither. It was most apparent in Ma
Doe's schoolroom, where every other seat sat empty, words not
written, lessons not learned. The illness had come on sudden and
at a speed that shook Rue, core-deep. Out loud she blamed it on
the cool weather, on those childhood ailments that came and
went. But this sickness was clinging on in a way that worried her.
Maybe Rue was glad then of the draw of Bruh Abel. At least it took
folks' minds away from their suspicions about her. Still, the illness
was unnatural, they were saying, an ill punishment brought on by
the few sinners left in their midst. For Bruh Abel had baptized just
about every willing sinner he could find, excepting Bean. And
Rue.

And *that* woman. That woman—her name was Opal, and everybody knew her, biblically, as Rue's mama would have said.
She'd lived on the only other plantation neighbor to theirs, the
smaller settlement where Rue's daddy had lived. It was owned by
Marse John, a piteous white man always in Marse Charles's shadow
and in his debt. Opal had been Marse John's favorite right up 'til

the day he died, *the damned apple*, Marse John had used to say, *of his goddamned eye.*

The rumor of it was that her master had died in bed with her, in fact, deep inside of her, his foul mouth running the whole time, until it wasn't.

"Goddammit goddammit goddammit god—" Those had been his last words if the things folks said could be believed, which in Rue's estimation, they usually couldn't.

Whatever the truth was, Opal had rolled right out from under him and made a life for herself the only way she could after that, which was by offering what she had to offer, on roadsides, in out-houses, more than once in the chicken coop, and Rue had had to treat the cuts from the chicken wire that made dizzy patterns on Opal's back. And Opal seemed alright with it, sure enough, there wasn't a bit of shame on her, *not enough shame to sew a stitch*, was how Miss May Belle might have said it, and Rue liked that about Opal, the way she owned her place and lived it, whisperings be damned. 'Til Bruh Abel set on her.

When Bruh Abel came into town he took up quarters where he could, expecting a bed and finding a different one weekly or even nightly in the houses of the most devout. Opal kept him for three days, and on the third day she shrugged off her wickedness and was reborn.

"I'm just tired," Opal had said and maybe that wouldn't have been enough repentance for most preachers for a lifetime of wild lusting, but it was enough for Bruh Abel.

He did it in the square, in the center of the cross that was their town. Someone had brought out a stool, so Opal sat with her feet hovering over the bucket, her toes twitching above the water in spasms of virgin hesitation.

"Like this?" she asked, but already Bruh Abel was rolling up his sleeves.

Rue wouldn't have watched except that she was already at Ma Doe's, bringing a new pouch of herbs to wrap around the superstitious old woman's neck.

"All of this carryin' on. I liked the old prayin'," Ma Doe had said. "'Twas quiet."

But same as everyone Ma Doe went out to her porch to have a look at Bruh Abel, whose preaching she didn't often get to witness, the river being too far for her rheumatic knees to take her. Today Bruh Abel had brought the river to them, by the sloshing bucketful, and had placed it at Opal's feet.

Easing herself down into her rocking chair, Ma Doe nodded appreciatively. "He is fine lookin'," she said to Rue. "Who on earth wants an ugly preacher?"

This day Bruh Abel's expression was closed off and serious as though there was great focus required in washing a whore's feet. Opal had her skirt tucked up beneath her knees. Bruh Abel knelt before her and took both of her arches in his two hands and lowered her feet into the bucket. He had a small chipped cup that he dipped into the water between her legs, and he drew up a cupful and poured it onto one foot. Bruh Abel switched to the other foot, again pouring a stream of water as he held on to her heel, leaned forward, and placed a kiss between her biggest toe and its smaller partner. He held his lips there for a long reverent while.

Ma Doe drew Rue into her empty cabin with no more than a sly cant of her head.

No children in there. Rue flinched away her foreboding.

"I've had news from up north," Ma Doe said.

She settled herself down behind the desk that had used to belong to Marse Charles. They'd only just rescued it from the fire that had destroyed the House. Now it dominated Ma Doe's schoolroom, a burnt-out treasure chest that held their secrets. Ma Doe's arthritic fingers turned the brass key and from one locked drawer she pulled out a letter, still in its envelope, and held it up to Rue. "Do you know what it says?"

No, Rue did not know, not by reading, but she recognized the big scrawling letter V that named the intended recipient of the correspondence, Varina, and from that she could easily imagine the rest. Ma Doe had read to her every one of those Northern letters which so rarely said anything new.

"The lady writes to her dear niece with concern for her niece's health," Ma Doe read. "Asks Varina, once again, to join the family in Boston. Says Christmastime is a most lovely occasion for the blessed reunion of estranged relations."

Rue tutted, "Ain't any time a lovely occasion for the reunion of relations?"

Ma Doe ignored her, went on, unspooling the letter to reveal its second page. "The lady asks that her beloved niece think again on the proposition of finally selling her stakes of this ruined Southern land altogether. She writes that she understands the reluctance to give up one's childhood home and its fond memories, but mightn't Varina, her dear niece and the last of her brother's living children, come up to Boston to live permanently where she will be lovingly received?"

Ma Doe set the letter down on the top of the blackened desk. The fat, looping words of the letter written by Marse Charles's sister meant nothing to Rue, never had, not in their individual meaning, nor in each single character crowded on the page. But the piling-up pieces of paper, which Ma Doe had hoarded in the desk these three years—which formed an organized stack in that selfsame desk—the mere existence of those letters meant everything to Rue, for they meant that their secret conjure held, hers and Ma Doe's. The aunt did not suspect the hoax.

It was necessary that somebody out there where it mattered in the white world of records believed that the blacks of Marse Charles's former land were still owned—yet in the new way they were now meant to be owned, as devoted sharecroppers working the land for love of their stalwart white mistress, Miss Varina.

"What you gon' write back?" Rue asked.

Ma Doe worried the string of the good-luck charm around her neck. Said nothing.

"You gotta write back, Ma." They'd had this conversation before. Likely would have it again. It wearied Rue's soul but not her resolve. That correspondence, those bits of paper and their pen marks, they were more powerful a protection of the town's isolated existence than any curse that Miss May Belle had ever laid. Rue was proud on that fact, for it was an act of power better than conjure, the only real shield over their people being discovered by the type of whites who did not think much of government-given freedom.

" 'Thank you kindly, Aunt,' " Ma Doe said. Her wrinkled hand shook only slightly as she mimicked deft pen strokes in the air. "We'll say, 'Your concern as always is a great comfort to me. But I am most happy here and intend to stay on as long as I am able.' "

" 'God willin',' " Rue added.

Over some eighteen months of deception, Rue and Ma Doe had sent such fantastic tales up north they had a quilt's worth of stories about Miss Varina. To respond to the Northern relation, they'd given Varina Christian faith and a penchant for acts of charity. They'd given her a keen knowledge of the harvests on her profitable property. They'd invented for her good white neighbors and the earnest interest of a fitting suitor, a kindly widower who was winningly cautious in his courtship, and finally a husband so that Varina's aunt might believe there was a good Christian man to manage Miss Varina's property and her prosperity. This loving Northern auntie had not once met the Southern relation she wrote to, didn't know the willful child or the sick woman Varina had grown up to become. It was easy for Rue to dictate a Varina of invention and easier still for Ma Doe to sign Varina's name. After all, Varina had learned her penmanship by tracing her black nurse's hand.

"Are we wrong for carryin' on this deception, Miss Rue?" Ma Doe asked. She was looking out the window, watching the folks out there enraptured in their praying. The sunlight played tricks on her face, showed wrinkles like valleys.

Rue figured Ma Doe was not looking for her to answer. Wrong or right was of little use to Rue now. Better she stay keen to the greater danger she sensed building in the air about her. Rue was troubled over the babies and the young children who were falling sick with winter's maladies much too early this year. She troubled over the ire with which her name was spoken in the town. She troubled most especially over Bean, who so far had escaped the illness that had laid low the other children. She knew the strange little boy was soon to be Bruh Abel's next target. Rue was surrounded on all sides by more immediate fears and so she could only leave it down to trust that Ma Doe would go on writing the letters they agreed to, send each letter off by way of one of her students—one of the ones too slow to read it and make meaning of what the schoolteacher and the healing woman were keeping hidden between them.

Rue drew a newly made hoodoo charm from her pocket. Its wretched stink of crushed carrion flowers and asafetida powder was enough to ease the worry lines from Ma Doe's forehead. Rue untied the string of the worn-out good-luck charm Ma Doe had been wearing and replaced it with the new one. Knotting the string at the back of the ancient woman's neck, she came around her and settled the low-hanging pouch, making sure to tuck it neatly in the collar of Ma Doe's dress.

There, no one would see the conjure trinket Ma Doe kept near her heart, nor the thick strand of Varina's curly red hair that Rue had worked artfully into the knot—a lock that held their tenuous magic all together.

The townsfolk hesitated to hang out their white baptismal clothing again, even as the promised Sunday of Bean's baptism drew nearer. They reckoned that to do so would be to tempt the return of the haint that had come to tear down their faith before, along with their white washing on the occasion of Si's death. Yet they were afraid of Bean and demanded to see him saved, for their own sake.

"It'll be alright," Rue told them, and it would.

Rue took the climb to her mama's grave on the hilltop cemetery slowly. She felt she was dragging along all her fear behind her like a yolk. Fear for the sick children, fear of Bruh Abel, fear for Bean.

Folks believed they'd found in Bean the evil that needed washing away: Bean, a baby boy born with hideous black eyes like he'd come up from a coffin, rather than from a womb. Now they demanded to flush the evil out, through baptism.

As she walked, Rue came upon the newest graves first, closest to the town by planning. The white family's graves were as large as monuments—cherubs and weeping women and ornate crosses all.

When she and Varina were children they'd often played in the solitude of this cemetery. Varina had read aloud the headstones on one such visit. They had loved always to play the type of games that contained secrets, Rue and Varina had, loved even more the forbidden thing that was their friendship.

Beyond the white graves, where the former slaves were laid to rest, there were no headstones. There were, instead, bits of wood and pretty glass and here and there a natural stone, renewed each season like a clearing of harvest and a sowing of new seeds.

After Surrender, after the war and the fire that ate up the House, after the Northern army had marched through, plundered what they liked, and moved on to the next place they could pick at as any scavenger would, after all of that and after freedom, the black folks had made their way up onto this hill and begun calling out the names of their lost dead, names for bodies they couldn't bring home or bury.

Ma Doe, ancient as she was, learned her letters in a time when there weren't yet laws against slave-learning, and when the laws did come it was too late; they could not take the knowing away from her. On the plantation there were a few other former slaves who had also learned their writing and reading, in secret, all of them having done so despite threat of death or worse if they were caught at knowing. But just like that, the threat was lifted, knowledge emancipated. And so in the graveyard Ma Doe and the other learned black folks etched into crude planks the names of the lost dead. Everybody had promised that if by some miracle lost bodies came walking back from the far-off places they'd been sold to, then they'd pluck the crosses right up, but few of the lost had ever returned.

Folks had made a grave for Varina, after she'd been burnt up in the fire that took the House. Even though their young Missus was not their black kin she was still *theirs*, and lost, and they figured she needed remembering also. Remembering for good or remembering for ill—well, that was a private matter.

Rue touched the crooked cross she knew spelled out Varina's name, touched the first letter, which Rue knew was called V only because Varina had taught her that letter over and over in their girlhood.

In front of the little cross Rue bent her head and mumbled words like prayer, and anybody that might've spied her at it would think she was caught up in sorrow.

Rue moved on to sit at her mama's grave. Miss May Belle's body had been laid down in a most mighty plot, because Miss May Belle had dictated what it ought to look like. The planning of it was the only thing that had made her smile from deep inside the swamp of her sickbed. She'd chosen for herself pot marigolds in the yellow and orange of a slow-burning fire, and now, two years since she'd been gone, the things grew wild, threatened to spill over onto other graves, eat up the white folks' monolith headstones. For certain she'd meant it that way, and it fell to Rue to beat the plants back.

Rue pulled up an armful of her mama's weeds before they could come to seed. She swam in the musky scent. Whatever else her mama had intended, the marigold plant made for a fine base for a number of tinctures, a thousand kinds of healing. Might they be the first ingredient in a cure to heal the town's sick children?

It was only on her way out that Rue allowed herself to look at the newest grave, freshly dug, a small plot suited for an infant child: Baby Si.

Though she knew who was laid in that child grave, strangely she thought first of Bean and shivered. But that was wrong, and foolish besides; this grave was not his. She would not believe that Bean was some omen, nor some dead child come again. Rue was determined not to believe it. How else to go on and convince the town of the same, before their hate of Bean turned to some desperate, dangerous action against him?

Rue finally drew the strength to go back into the town proper, and even there she slowed to force a smile and talk a little with folks. Yet now they hurried past her, as though afraid to linger in her company, and the little children she came upon at the road-side declined the posy of marigold she offered them like she held out a bloom of poison.

Bruh Abel passed her, aloud wished her blessings, and whispered in her ear. "Soothe them away from this foolishness about the haint. They'll listen to you, Sister Rue. In matters of superstition," the preacher man said, "yours is the voice they hear."

Rue soothed them by bidding them to take a broom about with them to sweep away footsteps they left in their wake, so that the haint could not follow them home.

"You can be known by a footprint as sure as a face," she told Dinah, who began to sweep her pathway in earnest, her baby on her back. Dinah had got to feeling particularly fixed upon, seeing as she'd seamstressed so many of those fine white clothes that had been torn down.

"Will that haint try an' take out my eyes, Miss Rue?" Dinah asked as she moved the dust in swirls behind her. On her back her baby still looked sickly. Looked worse. "I can't see my stitches. My eyes, they burn in my head."

"How long this been going on?"

"Well, now. Started up round the time folks started wanting to see Bean washed."

"Boil some mullein leaves in whiskey," Rue said, unsettled. "And rub it on the back a' yo' neck and the soles a' yo' feet, and any spirit will lose the scent a' you. Do it every morning, every night. Do it three mornings, three nights."

Dinah said that she would, and she would too, Rue reckoned. The cure would do nothing for a haunting, but it would keep Dinah off her sewing for a time and the smell of the leaves might cut through her baby's sniffling.

———

Sometimes Rue dreamed of Miss May Belle, and she dreamed of her on that next night before she got herself out of bed at the hour of the midnight moon.

Rue had nightmared a memory: Miss May Belle standing before her with a bloodied sheet bundled in her arms.

"Mama? Is it Varina?" Rue asked her dream-mama. "Is she alright?"

Miss May Belle wouldn't answer, only held out the black bundle.

"The shame," her mama called it. She said, "Bury the shame in the river and let us be rid a' it."

But there was no sure way to be rid of shame, no conjure to be rid of guilt. Even if the bundle never rose again it still flooded around Rue, the shame did. It rose in the mind, in her dreams and then in her waking, and in the face of every slowly sickening child she could not save.

She woke feeling as though Miss May Belle were truly there, standing over her. There was nothing for it but to get up and out of the cabin. She gulped the cool night air to clear her nightmare, like clarity was breath. She had to think. She had to act to save herself.

While others slept Rue walked a long lone circle round the plantation to weave a protection spell. A sprinkling of black pepper here and there on the long, sweeping trails folks had left with their brooms to dispel the hungry foxes that were said to be Miss May Belle's familiars—her eyes where her eyes could not see. Rue did not wish to be seen.

Then Rue went way out past the burnt-up edges of the plantation where most folks were afeared to go, on to the old church, a basket filled with fruit and biscuits and a bloom of fiery marigolds tucked under her arm.

The double doors of the church were shut against the night, but there was a slight, silent rocking up there at the top of the small bell tower. Its rope swung with a motion more forceful than could be accounted for by the wind alone. At the doorstep she laid down the basket and left, returned to her cabin, careful to see that she had not been followed or observed. There she waited, sleepless, for morning.

It was the day that Bean was to be baptized and so folks hardly paid much mind to the other news: Dinah's baby girl had died in the night.

"I called for you," Dinah said when Rue came to confirm what was already cold and clear. The little baby's body was wrapped up in the fine linen Dinah had seamstressed herself. "You wasn't home."

Rue had missed the knock at her door. It had come when she'd been out, tending to haints, and in that little time Dinah's baby had sickened and died.

In folks' fervent enthusiasm for Bruh Abel they did not pay much mind to one more quiet tragedy that had moved through the town while they slept. But Rue was altogether haunted by this new-come illness, by its stealth and its power.

Bean was to be washed in the eyes of the Lord at midday.

The townsfolk passed by Rue's cabin on the way to the river, and inside Rue pretended at grinding pokeweed berries for longer than was needed. She burst the black skin of the berries in her agitation, freed the red juice and still continued to pound and pound. Errant flecks of red stained the front of her dress and still she pounded as though she could work herself to the kind of exhaustion they'd all felt in slavery times, a complete utter exhaustion too great to leave room for rage. She felt rage at herself for allowing Bean to dredge up that old secret shame inside of her. The past was made up of bloody losses she could not change, while here, now, real living babies might suffer and die.

Yet Rue's rage grew, not only at herself but also at Bruh Abel and his false spectacle 'til finally she marched on out to the bright morning. Still she took the long way round, came upon them at the river from the height of the trees.

They were all in white. Bean, Jonah, and Sarah with their elder boy and their only girl. Someone had made them all little white caps that gave them the closest approximation they had ever had to a unified family resemblance. Bruh Abel, for his part, was not in his usual suit but was instead dressed in white too, in a robe that showed his audacity as the length of it caught and rippled on the water's surface.

Rue took careful steps on the slope that led down to the river-bank, and many times her feet failed to find a grasp on the shifting silt and rock, but she didn't look down; she kept her eyes on the curious scene, on Bruh Abel, who was leading the family one by one into the river. She kept right on watching them as she reached the edge of the crowd, where a few people murmured or nodded to her, said in greeting, "Miss Rue." They couldn't hardly pull themselves away from the show to look at her; they were transfixed, all of them, and singing.

Rue did not know the words to their song. She could not join them but she could listen, and she picked out the words on which their voices lingered: *Jesus* and *Jordan* and *river*. The refrain was something heavy with wanting, and she liked the part they kept repeating about going home, going on home.

Out in the water they had formed a snaking chain, Bruh Abel at its head, then came Sarah holding Bean, then the boy and the girl and last Jonah. He made them form a half circle, so that the two older children stood in the shallowest part of the river where the water lapped up against their chests, and Jonah and Sarah beside them looked as small as the children because of the way the bank dipped down. Bruh Abel stood just beyond them and took Bean from Sarah's arms.

Bean was in Bruh Abel's hands when the first splash of water reared up against his skin and there it was, his horrid cry. It pierced their ears as Bruh Abel tried to cross the boy's pale arms against his chest. Everyone hushed their singing, waited for Bruh Abel to set things right, to stop the awful child with his awful crying. If only he could catch Bean's flailing fists, could halt that otherworldly wailing.

Bean's family stood in the water beside him and seemed shamed, like they wanted to look away but couldn't. You could not draw away from such painful screaming.

Rue didn't know she was moving. It was not until she felt the shock of cold water at her thighs—each step was a struggle of pride, a struggle just to push her legs against the water. Her last thought before she reached for Bean was that there could be no worse death than this, being pulled down by a river. But that was a pure fool thought as well, because there were so many worse ways to die—hadn't she seen some of them?

Her foot hit a loose stone that spun and bobbed away from the riverbed and she was falling sideways. Rue saw Jonah's shocked face first and then Sarah's blank one, then she saw nothing but the expanse of the river's underside, which was black and black. There was no bottom and no top to swim to, and all the while she heard Bean's crying and yearned to comfort him the way she yearned after air.

Bruh Abel caught her and pulled her up and set her on her feet again with one hand, Bean clutched in the other. Water ran down her face into her mouth. Jonah and Sarah had not moved to help her. Already Bruh Abel was placing Bean into Rue's arms. The baby reached out to her. His crying stopped and she held him tight.

Around her Rue heard voices begin to pray. *Lord trouble the water.*

In her arms Bean had quieted. She didn't know what it was about her that soothed him, and he her. Maybe it was that he remembered her, the first person that had held him. Or maybe it was that he remembered her, from before even that.

Rue felt Bruh Abel's hand squeeze the nape of her neck, felt his other hand rest on her waist a moment before he tipped her backward.

When she felt the water again it was a shock, like she was falling in a dream when she hadn't yet figured out that she was sleeping. She held fast to Bean. His head on her breasts positioned him just high enough that he was not all the way submerged beneath the water. He was halfway in; she was the one who was submerged, who was drowning. She was the island he clung to.

Bruh Abel put his hand on her stomach, his thumb in the dent of her navel, and he kept her down, pushed her down even as she struggled to rise. She saw the flush of bubbles leave her nostrils and rush to the surface. Held just above the water, Bean was a weight on her chest and there was Bruh Abel's hand below her belly, pushing down into a place she'd never felt any hand pushing but her own.

Then that cold upward rush and Rue knew she was standing again only because she heard his voice, hard and brassy, confident: "As Jesus died and was reborn, so Rue and Bean, you have both died and been reborn."

Surely, they had died. With Bean in her arms Rue was shivering cold like they were still down there, stuck together in the watery grave of their shared baptism waiting to rise, waiting on a rebirth she did not believe in.

———

It was just after Bruh Abel left town that the sickness began to pull down more children. It had taken away Dinah's baby girl, but soon enough death rode boldly through the town, made itself well known in every home. The men plowed graves and laid the lost children in them, and Rue stood behind in the furrowed field, unable to offer any help or any explanation. Faced with the blooming grief of the mamas and daddies, she did not know what to think, nor what to do.

When Bruh Abel had been in town they'd all still been hopeful, basking in their fall of plenty. But as he did every year, Bruh Abel followed the warmth, descending south. The season turned quick to winter. An unusual cold glazed the grass in rare stiff white as more of the children began to burn with fever, to writhe in their beds, to moan and cry out and fight, and then to die.

Dinah's girl might have been the first, but gradually it took hold from all directions and before long there was at least one suffering child in each home with children. For the first three nights of the thick of it Rue did not sleep but drifted from door to door facing folks who wanted healing but didn't trust her to deliver it. Rue did not trust herself. *What would Miss May Belle have done?* they started asking, and she didn't have an answer there either. Folks blamed Bean and Rue. She knew that all round town they told and retold the story of Bean's baptism so that it had become more legend than memory in the retelling.

One truth was repeated over and over: Bean had not been fully submerged, nor fully baptized. For Miss Rue, the witch, had held Bean half aloft.

Rue did not have an answer for all the illness, but she did have a rule, one she had not learned from her mama, but one she'd come, in that grim time, to form for herself. That rule was to wait. It was only the difference of a moment, a hair's breadth of time between when the knowledge of a death came to her and when the grave words came out. But there was power in that moment of stillness, power in waiting before telling a mama her baby was dead, and Rue held tight to that power.

She told herself it was a kindness, the waiting, because a mama might know it already, holding her baby as a stiffened bit of flesh in their arms. Only moments ago, that same baby would have been writhing fever-hot. Now they were still.

The desperate mama had to know it, but 'til Rue said it, it was as if they could convince themselves it wasn't so, as if Rue might have a cure-all with which to raise the dead. She did not. What she did have was the power of pronouncement, the power to delay absolute sorrow for a few long, weighty seconds.

Dinah's girl and Beulah's boy were the first of them to die, though after those deaths many turned to saying it had all begun even before, when Bean's cry had yielded Si's death all them months back. Si had never been baptized and now look here, all these little children, dying, before they could properly get saved. Rue told them it was only a grim coincidence. After all, the sickness had taken Beulah's boy suddenly, in the space of a single evening.

"He was playin' just this morning," Beulah had said the night she'd roused Rue from her cabin to come have a look at her sick little child. When the fever started rising, Beulah had braided her son's Red Indian hair into a silken rope, perhaps to keep him cool. It lay beside him on the bed, that braid, and it was intricate and lovely, made of four wound strands that snaked in and out of each other, that held without the aid of a ribbon or a pin. Rue counted the knots with her eyes while she waited.

"I'm sorry," she said and she was, but more so, she was frightened.

———

Li'l Sylvia had five children and each of them caught the sickness, and each of them died of it, one by one. She took to her kitchen in her inconsolable grief, cooked ashcake after ashcake, good as her mama Big Sylvia used to make for the master in slaverytime. Li'l Sylvia set all of them ashcakes down on her supper table, a place laid out for each of her little ones, and waited and waited like she hoped they'd come back from the grave with a hunger.

Three of Ma Doe's orphans came down with it next. Two lived, one died, and though the one who died had no people alive to mourn him, the whole town took up the job of steady grieving. The sorrow was in everything they did, the sorrow and the fear.

When it got to be at its worst, Rue heard, though no one would tell her straight, that they had sent Charlie Blacksmith to get the white doctor down the way. Down the way was a journey of two days' walking, less if Charlie could beg a ride along the big road someplace, and at the end lived the Quaker doctor who was known to show a kindness to black folks provided they could pay. They'd sent Charlie with a purse of money, an appropriately enticing offering, and they had set aside another amount waiting for the doctor to arrive, which he never did. When it had gone a week with no sign of Charlie Blacksmith, Rue knew that they had all given up, though they hadn't said so. She could see it in the slack set to their faces that they had come to believe that what they were needing was not a healing woman, or a white doctor, after all, but a preacher man.

Ol' Joel was the first of the old folks to get it and to die of it. He went to bed in the afternoon and didn't get up after. Rue knew it was the same sickness. Folks said he'd been complaining all day of the heat though the day was mighty cold. The townsfolk sent Rue after him and she found him that evening, cocooned in his sheets like he was a body already bound for the coffin maker. When Rue neared his bedside he began thrashing, fighting like he had as a boy when the slavers had plucked him out of the jungle in Africa.

"There's a witch," the old man insisted. "She setting on my chest."

"Hush now," Rue said, glad no one else was there to hear. To accuse.

She was afraid to leave him lest somebody else were to take up the vigil and hear the madness that was frothing up like the spittle in the corners of his toothless mouth.

"Witch done made that boy-child outta river clay," Ol' Joel railed.

Bean. Rue wouldn't say his name, like to bring mention of him into this sick room was to curse him. But it was on her tongue. She knew he was the boy-child Ol' Joel was speaking on.

"Witch gave him air from her own mouth an' fire from her own belly. Marse Charles'll know of it."

Or was he speaking on the hidden shame? How could he know?

Rue stood up so fast the chair she'd perched in crashed to the ground.

"Marse Charles ain't know nothin' but what the inside of a grave look like," she said. "And you gon' know the same, soon enough."

Ol' Joel's cheeks went hollow as he gasped out his shock, like the sunken-down face of a skull. Rue stepped back from his bedside and righted the chair and tried to right her breathing but there was nothing for it.

"I ain't mean to say that," Rue said. "I'm sorry."

Ol' Joel's expression turned gleeful. He clapped his hands together like a child at play, spoke singsong as he made mud pies in the air. "I know about Bean."

"Hush," Rue said. If she could only soothe him. Get him to rest.

"Miss May Belle tol' it to me."

But Miss May Belle had not lived long enough to see Bean born. "Tol' you what?"

"She say Bean's eyes is the hole you dug to bury the baby in."

Rue had never left a dying man or woman or child, not ever, not even when she herself was a child, kneeling beside deathbeds. She'd listened to every rasp and rattle and final godforsaken wheeze. But she could not listen to this. She fled.

Come the morning, Ol' Joel was dead. She returned to his bedside at sun-up to find him still, silenced. Rue took up the chair she'd toppled over when she'd run. She sat herself down and let folks think she'd been sitting there all night.

Then Bean's brother and sister both caught the sickness. The skin of their high-yellow cheeks became dotted with twin flushes of red.

Rue, afraid for Bean, afraid for them all, was sleepless. She spent most of her evenings visiting the sick—children and the elderly came down with it the quickest and fared the worst—and even when she was not needed she'd wake suddenly in the middle of the night, imagining that somebody had been pounding at her door, though nobody had.

Sarah had the same harried look as all the mamas in the town, a kind of sickness in itself, that worry, but at the mention of Bean a line creased deeply between her brows.

"Bean, he's the onlyest one the sickness ain't touched," she said. And the suspicion was there in her voice. "These 'uns need you, now."

Rue looked over the brother and sister who lay together in the same bed, fighting against each other in helpless writhes against the heat, but at least they were fighting. The boy's ways for breathing seemed clear but the girl's nose was blocked up; it dripped in a sad puddle onto her upper lip.

Rue drew out her pipette. It was only a bit of tin that she'd found and rolled and smoothed so it had no rough edges, and ever so gently she placed it into the girl's one nostril and then the other, drawing the plugged-up business out of her with a careful inhale. The trick was to get it just far enough up the pipe to give the child ease of breath but not to draw so far as to have the snot end in her own mouth. It had happened once or twice, the sickness sitting thick on Rue's tongue. It had so worried her each time that she'd taken to her roots and plants 'til she was dizzy with it, unsure if she was suffering more from the sickness or the cure.

The trick with the pipette was more a balm for the mamas' nerves. They were given to panic when their babies gulped open-mouthed for air. The only cure she knew of was time. Either the babies would die or they wouldn't, but that's not what anybody wanted to hear, and so Rue knew better than to say so.

Rue insisted on looking over Bean before she left. She found him with Jonah behind the house. He was at the age of walking now, and he stood wobbly and watched with those wide black eyes of his as his daddy worked. Jonah was carving up the carcass of a wild pig for their supper. He had it hoisted up on a wood frame, swinging by its neck, tongue out and listless.

She observed them for a while, daddy and son, recollecting two years back. After Bean's birth she had spied Jonah cutting fire-wood, wet with sweat as he was now. Then she had shoved into Jonah's arms the black caul from which Bean had slithered and told Jonah to burn the sheets. For luck, she'd said. Now the whole of the town stunk of burning sheets, and behind each house great plumes of dark smoke would rise like a silent signal for a grief that had gotten so bad that they no longer had the words for it. The thinking was to get rid of the sheets as marks of their dead, but the sickness, Rue feared, was well beyond being burnt up.

Jonah put a long, neat slit down the belly of the barrow hog he'd strung up. He began to peel back the skin, buried his hands deep into its belly to tug away its innards.

"It's a bad year, sho' 'nuff." He spoke round a grunt of effort. The pig's intestines slopped downward. "Folks is down on they knees, prayin'. We needin' you to help us, Miss Rue."

Bean reached for her. "Up," he was saying. "Up, up." He raised his arms in that easy gesture of children, and Rue wanted to hold him as much as he wanted to be held. When she hefted him up, he was a nice weight in her arms, and that close he smelled sweet to her, healthy, even over the sickly smell of the hog Jonah was butchering.

"I can't answer all a' them prayers," Rue said.

"'Course not," Jonah said.

Rue wanted to thank him for that, his comforting lie. She knew what folks were saying. They'd lost faith in her, even feared her, some of them. She juggled Bean in her arms and reached out, touched the swell of Jonah's upper arm, the only place the pig blood hadn't reached. It was supposed to be a loving gesture, but she pulled sharply away before she could give it. She hardly had to get near him to realize: His skin was near to burning.

It would pass in him, wouldn't it? It had to, a man so strong and grown. Even if he had the sickness it would not ravage him like it might his children, but something about the power of it, to weaken even Jonah, made Rue feel weak herself. She told Jonah he better lay himself down for a rest, and she pulled Bean tight into her arms and hid her face in the softness of his baby hairs to rest there awhile herself.

———

Beulah, who had been among the first to lose her baby, was the worst.

"He gone," Rue told her. The woman had begun to wail as if the scream had been building and building in her, saved 'til just this moment.

Beulah collapsed like her legs were of no use and Rue went down with her as an instinct, afraid she'd smack her head against the ground. Beulah did the opposite. She reared her head back as she screamed those two words: *Your fault.* She smashed forward, catching the edge of Rue's jaw. Rue felt her mouth filling up with a rush of blood—she didn't have a second to worry or to spit—because Beulah was hitting her with her fists now, punching at her shoulders in time with the repeated hollow syllables of her son's name. She was saying it over and over, and saying, "You done this! You and that Bean. This y'all curse."

Beulah's man came out of nowhere to pull Beulah away. He did it easily, put his arms around her waist and picked her up like she was a child, and she weakened and wept against him, the whole shape of her fitting to his chest.

Rue heard it all over then in every corner of the used-to-be plantation, what folks were saying. They wanted help. But not from her. *Bruh Abel. Send someone to find him, to fetch him. Give him word. Bring him to pray over us. For Bruh Abel is,* they were saying, *the only hope we got* as more children sickened daily. It seemed to be passing through all of them in no sort of order, only weakening some, but snatching away others. It was Ma Doe's health that Rue feared after especially, though to say so was an ugly thing. If Ma Doe died all those orphans would be orphaned again, but most importantly, if Ma Doe died the spell of protection Rue had created with her over the town would be broken. Without Ma there was nobody Rue trusted with the secret, nobody to send correspon-dence north, nobody to pose as their white mistress behind the looping lines of oak gall ink. And if there were no letters to the Northern auntie it would only be a matter of time before some white official came along wondering after their white mistress and her untouched acres. Freedom wasn't free.

On this day Ma Doe was teaching in the usual way. She held up letters that she'd written big and bold, each one existing solitary on either side of thirteen sheets of yellowy paper. She made the sounds and the children made them back, a call and response that Rue found soothing. Sometimes she mouthed the sounds with them, though she did not add her voice to theirs. From Ma Doe's side she looked them over, the children, checking for sweat sitting on the skin of the darker ones, red blooming on the cheeks of the lighter, or for a pair of shiny, unfocused eyes struggling to make sense of their mud-made letters.

Rue hoped each day would be the day when they'd finally be free of the spreading fever. Winter would soon be giving way to spring, and everything, as her mama would have said, good or bad, had an end.

When Rue arrived this morning, Ma Doe dismissed the chil-dren in a hurry. The younger ones were pardoned to go play then return for a lesson in figures; the older went off for the work wait-ing on them at the side of their mamas and daddies. Rue found herself sorrowing after it, those blind simple days when she herself had been a child.

"How you doin', Ma Doe?" she asked. She took Ma Doe's hand in hers in greeting, believing that whatever the old woman said, she'd find the true answer in the heat of her palm. The skin was warm but dry, and Rue held on long to a callous that rose up when Ma Doe had been writing.

"Well, you know what folks are sayin'," Ma Doe said. She culled gossip from her children who were in the habit of repeating, with some authority, the things their daddies and mamas said in private. "They're all of 'em mistrustful of you and your Bean."

Now when had Bean become hers? Ma Doe was slowly retracting her one hand from between Rue's two.

"And what they sayin'?"

"He isn't sick. He hasn't been sick. So people are thinkin' he isn't goin' to be sick. Of all the children, seems he's the only one that's kept his health."

Rue frowned. "Say it plain, Ma."

"Some folks think you're the one keepin' him healthy. And some folks think you pullin' vitality from the other little ones to do it. Usin' that contraption you've got."

"Contraption?" Rue stumbled on the word.

"Your tool for suckin'. It isn't natural. Like root magic, they're sayin'. Like witchcraft."

"Where this come from?" But Rue, as soon as she asked it, knew where it had come from. It was inevitable, like birth and death and birth, like smoke rising toward the sky, it was just the way things went. Folks were scared. They needed their finger-pointing for succor.

"They talk of little Si," Ma Doe continued. Rue thought on Si often, thought on how he'd lived three days and died before they could put him to the water. They'd wanted him baptized but she'd wanted him to live.

"Folks say you went to see him and tracked graveyard dirt by his sleeping face. They don't want you near their children, Miss Rue," Ma Doe said. Her voice held that steely finality she used to end her lessons. "They've asked me to not allow you in here any longer whilst the children are near."

"You tol' 'em I could help their babies, ain't you?" Her voice was rising. "You tol' em that ain't none a' that foolishness is true?"

Ma Doe shrugged. "I felt I hadn't the right to tell them any-thin'." She touched a hand to the pouch of asafetida that she wore just under her collar, perhaps without even realizing. "I find in my old age I haven't got any more strength for lyin'."

Rue felt something awful building up inside of her chest, some-thing like a sob. "It ain't a lie."

Ma Doe's nimble fingers were unsteady as she pulled a key from a chain of many at her waist. She put it to the desk drawer, turned the key in the lock with a sharp *clink* that sounded loud in the empty schoolroom, like bullet to chamber. "I haven't yet sent a reply to our Northern relation. I don't know that I will."

"Why not?"

"Nigh on two years we've been tellin' lies about Miss Varina. One lie to the auntie, another to the townspeople. Our own peo-ple." Ma Doe bowed her head as if it was too heavy suddenly for her to hold on her neck.

"Ain't nobody the wiser," Rue said.

"Don't you sometimes think, Miss Rue, that the Lord has been takin' his good time to punish us? That the best contrived punish-ment is the one that you near forgot you deserved?"

"This ain't to do with us, Ma, or with Varina neither," Rue said, and she gestured at the empty air like their haint was right there with them. "It's a simple sickness. It'll pass. You best send that let-ter."

Ma Doe relented. But Rue couldn't help it: She thought of Bean and the day he was born, the moment she first saw him swathed in a caul as black as a blood-soaked blanket, like some-thing she'd seen before. Another ill omen. A wrong come again. Rue knew why she had thought about killing Bean in that mo-ment. But she had not. The past was the past.

Now she wanted Bean to live. Jonah already seemed stronger than he had on the night she'd touched his skin. Sarah had complained of a sudden bout of sweating, but there was little that could put her down, and anyway the sickness seemed to flutter more easily past grown folks and instead settled its grip on children.

But soon there was only Bean, untouched.

That night Rue didn't sleep. She felt she ought to be crying. But she could not make tears or didn't trust herself to. At any moment she feared she'd have to get up and answer another accusation. The pounding of death again at her door.

The longer the night stretched the longer her fear did. She thought on Bean, on the sideways glances folks would give him when they saw him playing in Sarah's yard. He played alone. Rolling a ball or a hoop from one end of the narrow garden to the other, then rolling it back again in the same little rut. He'd always been a solitary sort of child, but now the other mamas wouldn't let their babies play anywhere near him. Like he was the pestilence himself. It ought to have been the other way around. Their children carried the sickness; he thrived. And because he did thrive and showed no signs of sickening, Rue figured they were both of them in an even worse kind of danger.

Rue tried to clear her head, to think on how to avert their envy of Bean's vitality, all their loathing after his very life. She couldn't count on Sarah to protect Bean, even if he was her child. She had two other children to worry about after all. Would Sarah sacrifice the one to shield the two? Rue didn't know. She was not a mama herself.

What she was was a healing woman, and she found herself thinking on how to heal Bean from an affliction he did not have.

What would Miss May Belle do? It was a question that had been posed to Rue throughout the town as though they half-expected her to go on to the cemetery, to pull up her dead mama's body and ask her for a cure.

Rue paced the little length of the cabin. The room had seemed so much bigger when she was a child. She'd lived there all her life with her mama, but now, empty, it felt more like a cage than it had ever done. In her pacing she felt like Miss May Belle was there, sitting on the end of her bed like she'd just come in from a long day of hoodooing and healing to toss her basket down and throw off her hat and to look at her child with that certain furrowing of the lines of her forehead like she couldn't remember why she'd allowed herself a daughter in the first place if that daughter was going to go ahead and be so foolish.

"Rue-baby," Miss May Belle would've said, "there ain't no easier lie to tell folks than the one they wanna believe."

Miss May Belle had always spoke in loops and swirls that may as well've been written down for all the use Rue could find in interpreting them. But this bit of recollected wisdom Rue let latch on and suck at her 'til it became fully grown. Soon she had an idea.

SLAVERYTIME

===

1855

Miss May Belle had made another doll baby. Rue had found it hid amongst her mama's healing things and knew right away that it did not belong there standing behind the tinctures. Surely, the doll baby was meant for Rue, was to be a gift for her seventh birthday, the first birthday gift she was ever going to get. It looked like Rue. Had her flat nose and dark skin. It had her hair done up in black corkscrews, a bramble that stood up straight no matter how it was brushed. The doll baby had Rue's thick red lips, painted in a bow, and black beads sewn on for glistening walnut eyes. It wore a green dress, which was the color Rue most preferred because it reminded her of the woods, flush in springtime.

Miss May Belle had her ways. Healing herbs were in one place and cursing roots in another, and not a thing was ever mislaid or misplaced. Lord forbid she ever get the two things mixed up.

Rue found the doll baby half-made. Its fabric face was unstuffed, its sack arms dangled with unfinished thread. Beneath its green skirt the black body dropped off, all hollow inside as a tree trunk.

Rue was not supposed to be looking where she was looking. She was not allowed to get at Miss May Belle's medicinals when her mama wasn't at home to advise at them—and even then her mama hovered. But Rue liked to look on the liquid cures and poultices of dried herbs that sat up there on the high shelf. She wanted to ruminate on their ingredients, to memorize the plants from which they took their origin. Better than magic, that.

The doll was sat on the back of a high shelf in their cabin, behind a jar full of jimson weed tea, a place that a doll did not belong—and a thing in a place where it did not belong was oft there for secret reasons, Rue knew.

Rue figured she was about to turn seven years old that spring because Varina was about to turn seven. At about-to-be seven years old Rue's favorite thing was secrets, and she had become quite good at gathering them, the way she was good at gathering leaves and seeds and flower heads; *my li'l rabbit,* her mama called her.

With both seeds and secrets the approach was quite the same—go where other folks don't. The path between the House and the slave quarter, for instance, was over-trod, with the coming and going of hurrying black folks who woke at cock's crow and were off, to serve Marse Charles in his home or in his field depending on his pleasure. Rue found the best plants for her mama in far-off places, less traveled. At the wide part of the river or in a thicket beyond the hen house, or down at the edge of Marse Charles's land, the very edge of creation as far as she knew it—that was where the best wildflowers grew.

Secrets were the same. Rue heard them in isolated corners, and because she was slight and dark and quiet and because she was often dismissed as the strange healing woman's shy daughter, she could go where others could not and hide in sight of folks and not be seen at all.

At first, Rue gave Miss May Belle all her gathered secrets, same as any yielded crop. Say that Rue crept by the outhouse, overheard the house girls talking that Marse Charles had made a visit to their rooms, *chose a mulatta like he choosin' a horse from his stables for a day's ride out.* Rue might not know the meaning of the secrets, but she could repeat them fine enough, pass them on to her mama, and sure enough Miss May Belle would slip a cure to the mulatta in passing—a pouch cupped in a handshake—that would set the girl to rights before she would ever have to utter her shame.

Rue heard the secrets of white folks too, and that's how she first heard tell of the war, from Missus and a visitor of hers, a translucent pale woman in a big blue hat that highlighted the frosty color of her eyes and the veins beneath her pale skin. Rue had had the misfortune of walking past when the visitor had come calling. Perhaps Rue hadn't looked busy enough, being on her way to bring water to the hands in the field. Missus had bidden Rue to put down her bucket, picked her out to come and fan them with a fat palmetto leaf while Missus and the visitor took iced tea on the veranda. In sight of her guest, Missus rubbed Rue's head adoringly as a beloved pet, "for luck," she said and chuckled.

Rue spent hours there working the fan, listening to the women jaw on and on. The ice cubes in their glasses glinted like diamonds before they dissipated into filmy sugar water with the midday heat, and not a drop of it for Rue the whole long afternoon. The white women started to swim in her vision, hazy, and still she fanned.

"They talked and talked and talked like I was deaf and dumb besides," Rue complained to her mama that night. Her arms still ached, felt to her like they were still in motion, up, down, up, down to the rhythm of the white women's chatter.

Miss May Belle shrugged. She had her own hurts from a long day and evening and night of seeing to the hurts of others.

At the supper table, Miss May Belle shut her eyes. She did this sometimes, like to shut out the world, the eyeballs spinning clear beneath the lids like she was searching. Folks saw it and thought it was how Miss May Belle got her knowledge on what hoodoo to wield or what salve to soothe a pain with, but Rue knew the secret of it. It was her mama's way of snatching at a little bit of quiet, and Rue knew better than to talk when Miss May Belle was about her eye-shutting.

Unobserved, Rue let her sights drift up to the shelf where she knew the doll baby was hidden, wondered when her mama might give it to her. Perhaps her birthday, though she didn't know quite when that was. Varina got presents for her birthdays, pretty wrapped packages done up with bows. Rue wasn't for all of that wrapper fuss, but she wouldn't have minded just the present-getting. Maybe this year.

"What else did Missus have to say?" Miss May Belle had come back to herself.

Rue picked up the story of that afternoon's secret-getting. She told her mama all about the white women's terror, which was that their sons, their husbands, their menfolk all, would stomp off to war to defend King Cotton.

"Who's that, Mama?" Rue envisioned a white-haired master with a crown of thorny cotton bolls. Miss May Belle waved Rue's tale on.

Rue told of how the women spoke on the impetuous nature of men, always hungry after bloodshed to prove themselves. Miss May Belle grunted her agreement. Rue told her of how the women feared they'd be left alone if their men up and left—how they feared it and longed for it. They spoke on how the plight of the darkies shadowed all other concerns. *What of temperance? What of suffrage?* Rue worked the fan over the white woman words.

"They said if all the males is gone it ain't safe for the children, what with all the niggers growing bold with all of Lincoln's ideas," Rue repeated, proud she'd remembered the way the blue-veined lady had put it.

Rue soon came to the part of the telling that she deemed most important. "Mama," she said. "Missus say she thinkin' on sendin'

Varina away to Northern relations for what she call 'refinement.' Said if the world's goin' overall upside down she want her daughter to come out on top."

Rue told the secret to Miss May Belle and next morning Miss May Belle told the secret to Ma Doe who, once she heard of Varina's leaving, turned gray as a dropped stone.

"It ain't happenin' yet," Miss May Belle said. "You know Missus ain't got no say in it. She just like to think she do."

Ma Doe's face wrinkled down to a frown even as she set out one of Varina's cranberry red dresses for washing. You would've thought the little white girl was in it, the way the old woman laid it down lovingly, smoothing all the frilly edges.

"I don't wish to see her go," Ma Doe said.

On her knees at the wash basin Miss May Belle laughed in a way that Rue, listening from behind the washboard, thought sounded almost cruel. "Don't you got better things to wish after than one li'l white girl's comfort?"

Ma Doe didn't answer, only picked up the dress and shook it and laid it down again as if this time she might lay it neater.

"What you askin' for, Ma?" Miss May Belle said, gentler, though Ma Doe was not her mama any more than she was anyone else's. All of Ma Doe's sons had been sold away young, but that was the type of secret that everybody knew but didn't ever speak on. "You wantin' me to fix it so she stay?"

"No!" Ma Doe seemed to startle even herself with her vehemence. "No, none of your root work, Miss May Belle, none of your trinkets or devilment. I don't want any of that superstitious nonsense near Varina."

Miss May Belle met eyes with Ma Doe over the washboard. "I hear you, Ma," she said, and a solemn look passed between them, an agreement, fast as a whipcrack. Rue saw the truth and then it was gone again and they were just two slave women busy at the washing.

"You know I don't care one wit for conjuration," Ma Doe said even as she worried at the string of the new asafetida pouch Miss May Belle had only just gifted her that morning. She had it tucked under her stiff collar where it was hidden. It was well known that Missus expressly forbade any sign of hoodooing in the House.

"Why don't you just go 'head and speak to Marse Charles if it bother you so. Tell him you'll see to Varina's 'refining' just fine. He soft on you," Miss May Belle tutted to her. "He still think he in the nursery nuzzling at yo' teat."

Ma Doe swatted at Miss May Belle's upraised behind, same as she would any of her misbehaving children.

"Ain't nothin' to be promised for those boys, though," Miss May Belle said, serious all of a sudden. "But maybe if you do speak to Marse Charles about 'em?"

Ma Doe was quiet as she tied up all those little white ribbons on Varina's dress. For a while the music of Rue scrubbing a shirt along the boards was the only sound amongst the three of them. Her knuckles rapped rhythmically on the wood of the washboard as the water sloshed.

Finally, Ma Doe spoke slow, like the words were being pulled up from inside her body. Said, "Last time I spoke out of turn to Marse Charles on the rearing of his sons he drove a fountain pen through my palm."

Rue stopped scrubbing.

"You ain't never tell me that," Miss May Belle said.

Ma Doe sighed down at the red dress, worshipfully. "You can't know everything, May Belle," she said.

What Miss May Belle couldn't know she sent Rue to hear and see and gather, up through the winding back hallways of the Big

House. She sent Rue to the nursery to gather up a lock of Varina's red hair in Ma Doe's stead.

Miss May Belle, for all of Rue's life, had been banned from venturing into the House—ever since the birth of Varina, in fact, as though the disappointment of Missus's worm pink daughter wriggling out of her instead of a son of a type her predecessor had produced for Marse Charles had solidified Missus's distaste for all black healing. Indeed, Miss May Belle might've saved Missus's life during Varina's breached birth by tending to the emergency before the white doctor could even arrive, but the healing woman hadn't helped her where it counted—raising Missus's esteem in her husband's eyes required a son.

Folks said Missus was barren after the birth of her daughter and because of it had told Marse Charles that it was ungodly to take pleasure in her. It was a nasty secret, Miss May Belle said, and one Rue ought not repeat unless she wanted her skin whipped clean off her back. But the ugly bit of gossip was likely the truth, or close to it, and everybody knew Marse Charles took his fancies elsewhere.

Rue troubled her way in through the back door of the House, simply waited on it to swing open when the cook, Big Sylvia, bustled out of the kitchen heading to the storeroom set out in the yard. Rue slipped in the gap just as the door creaked shut and thankfully found the kitchen empty. It was easy then to steal up the service stairs.

Now Varina would be in the ladies' parlor, Rue knew, all the way on the opposite side of the vast House, in the middle of one of her daily lessons in needlework with Missus. The lessons always left Varina pinpricked and ornery even when she was finally set free to play with Rue and the slave children in the cool of the evening. Despite the good distance of a whole grand wing stretched between them, Rue still chilled at entering the nursery without permission. But she'd promised Miss May Belle that lock of red hair and there was no better place to snatch it but from one of the bone brushes Ma Doe used to rake at Varina's thick fall of curls.

Cursing, conjuring, Miss May Belle claimed, was easy enough done with any old bit of bodily property—a toenail, or a loosed tooth. Urine or blood or even tears. But a conjure that was meant to bind was something else, much like a love spell, Rue's mama had explained. It called for the deeper essence of the person the fix was to be put upon, and hair was most preferred. Hair tells, Miss May Belle often said, hair tells health and hereditary both. You and the roots of you.

The nursery was done up in white frilly lace that had aged to yellow in places over time. Rue knew it had been Varina's half brothers' nursery once and Marse Charles's before that. Varina often complained of the drab white and the stale air and the fact that the baseboards were all carved up, pockmarked in places where her half brothers had etched their initials, claiming everything long before Varina was even born.

The only thing not white was the crib, which was a solid red oak. Varina had outgrown it long ago in favor of the wide white canopied bed across the room, but the crib was still there and in it sat Varina's collection of blond-haired china dolls, which seemed to wink at Rue when she rounded the corner and came face-to-face with them.

There were a dozen at least, sat in the crib, arranged in a row like an audience, and Rue nearly fled from the room altogether when she met their glazed porcelain eyes gazing out at her from between the bars of the crib.

Shook up by the dolls, Rue crept past them quick as she could. The floorboards creaked wickedly with her every step. Across the room she could make out what she was after: All the combs and pins and brushes were laid out neatly in a row on the vanity, doubled in the mirror. Rue made her footfalls high and careful, tested each floorboard before she came to rest on it. Marooned halfway across the room on an especially whining plank, Rue leaned forward, reached out her arm. She snatched up the first comb she could lay hands on, plucked a clump of orange hair, and quickly replaced the comb next to the others. Now that she had the tuft of hair, she didn't know quite where to put it. She could hardly walk out of the house with a handful of Varina's hair. Rue settled on stuffing it into the lining of her dress and turned herself around, traced her laborious route back to the door.

She stopped again at the dolls, like to see if they had observed what she'd done. They hadn't moved from their faithful vigil, staring blind and straight out at the dust motes Rue'd unsettled.

"You're not so pretty," Rue whispered at them. "My mama's gon' make me a doll baby. One that smiles. Black. Sweet as can be."

Rue dared to reach her arm out to touch one and found it cold, as far from a baby as a rock at the river's edge was. None of them looked like Rue but none of them looked much like Varina neither, with their impossibly white skin and painted-on pink cheeks. The bodies of the dolls jutted out at hard edges beneath a rainbow parade of pretty dresses made of nicer fabrics than any Rue had ever owned. Rue's first thought was to grab the nearest doll and shuck off the dress to see if the white shining skin continued downward, smooth as a dinner plate.

"Are you meant to be here?"

Rue spun at the voice. It was a white boy, almost a man, behind her, one of Marse Charles's sons. Rue looked down before she could see which. She knew she was not ever allowed to meet their eyes.

He came into the nursery from the hall. Rue watched his black boots stomp up to her. He made the floorboards moan as loud as he wanted, didn't care. About him she could smell a heavy stink she knew to be liquor coming up out of his sweat. It was like a cloud he carried. He kneeled before Rue. Grabbed her chin in his rough, dry hand and pulled her face near to his. There was no-where else to look then.

Rue recognized it was Marse Peter who held her only because he was the youngest of the three brothers. He tilted back Rue's head roughly, and for a terrible moment they breathed the same air. She tried to figure what he was after by the tick in his jaw, the pulse of a vein in his temple. He had Varina's tight lips and round blue eyes. But his hair was a murky brown, and above his lip an equally dark mustache was pushing its way through. It looked like a smudge of dirt on his mouth.

He squeezed her jaw. "What you about, huh? Answer me, girl."

"Miss Varina sent me, suh," Rue stuttered out. Her mouth was near clinched shut in his grip. He shoved her off, and her teeth clicked together so hard she feared they'd shatter.

"I don't think you're tellin' me the truth," he said. "I think you're up here stealin' my sister's belongin's."

Rue cringed away and feared she would be hit for it. "No."

"No? I saw you. At my baby sister's hair things first and then at the dolls. Shall I tell my father that he's got a li'l thief in his house?"

"No, suh, no."

"Perhaps if you ask me kindly I'll keep it from Father. Rather I see to the punishment myself?"

Marse Peter grabbed the pull of her apron strings. The knot came undone easy, fell away to swing at Rue's bare legs.

There was a high-sharp giggle at the doorway, no humor in it.

"There you are, Rue." Varina bounded into the nursery, skip-ping, laughing again that high false laugh. Her face was overbright and flushed, her curls undone in the heat.

Marse Peter slid his eyes to his half sister, just rolled them like marbles in his head without even turning his neck.

Rue tried to catch Varina's gaze and plead, but Varina was grinning gap-toothed at her brother.

"We was playin' hide-and-go-seek, weren't we, Rue?"

They were doing no such thing. Rue didn't know whether Varina wanted her to speak the lie or if she'd be punished for it.

"Peter, do you want to join our game?"

Marse Peter spat. Right there on the nursery floor, a gleaming glob flecked black with old tobacco tar. "Shit no, I don't. That's children's stuff."

"I'll tell Daddy you were cussin'."

Marse Peter whirled on Varina. He grabbed his half sister's wrist as she let out a cry, seemed to crumple to her knees in pain.

"Peter, you're hurtin' me!"

"Aw, hell," he said. But he let her go.

He thrust his hands deep into his pocket and turned his back on them. He began to whistle, a jaunty manic tune, and he kept on whistling walking out of the nursery. They heard him descend the main staircase in great thudding stomps, whistling the whole while, so that they weren't sure he was gone 'til they couldn't hear him any longer. Only then did Varina rise from the floor.

"Y'alright, Miss Varina?" Rue's voice shook. "Let me look on yo' wrist."

"Oh, it don't hurt none," Varina said, waving the arm that Marse Peter had grasped. The expression of screwed-up pain she'd shown her brother was gone. She had a big pleased grin on her face. She'd played him like a song and now she looked about her room with her hands fisted on her hips, like she was figuring what she could conquer next. "Rue, shall we play a game?"

———

Rue kept it a secret. She couldn't say why precisely, only that she felt ashamed of the way Marse Peter had leered at her, of the way she'd stuttered, of how her apron had come untied like it meant to betray her too. She kept the secret even from her mama—whereas before she had told her everything—because Miss May Belle didn't lately listen well to her daughter's hurts.

"Ain't we all of us hurtin'?" she'd say, if Rue uttered any complaints.

Miss May Belle was making a doll baby at the supper table. A white one, with a face made from an old handkerchief, blue corn seeds for eyes, lips painted on red, thin as a wound. The hair was of straw, stewed to bright orange in calendula and carrot juice, save for a sprig of Varina's real hair in the very center. The twisting real strand was hid in plain sight, where you'd have to know to look for it to find it. That secret lock was where the magic lived that bound up Varina's fate to her home.

The doll baby was Varina all over, right down to the cranberry red dress, a scrap of fabric cut from a dress she'd fast outgrown.

"Why couldn't Ma Doe just've asked after the conjure straight?" Rue wanted to know. It hurt her somehow to see her mama put so much love and care into a thing that was not for Rue herself.

"She know the cost's too high for her, if she had a hand in it," said Miss May Belle. She didn't raise her head from her sewing to say it.

Seemed to cost Miss May Belle nothing to sit there and sew, humming to herself a little. Seemed it had cost Rue too high to do what Ma Doe wouldn't, to snatch Varina's hair for the conjure. But Rue thought on Airey, and the way she'd been whipped raw in the yard of the House at Marse Charles's whim. Was that the cost? Rue couldn't imagine Ma Doe treated that way. Ma Doe was everybody's mama, white folks' too, even if she was colored, and who could dare hurt their own mama?

"You thinkin' too hard, Rue-baby, I can see it." Miss May Belle clicked her tongue. "Lord, you just like yo daddy, ain't you? Come on over here."

Rue crossed the cabin to sit on the floor at her mama's feet. She was about-to-be seven—she was no baby, and Miss May Belle was never oversentimental, said she didn't have the time for petting. It was rare and wonderful for Rue to rest her head in her mama's lap, to feel her mama's long, thin fingers drift lovingly through the tangles of her tight head hair.

"Mama?"

"Yes, Rue-baby?"

Rue wanted then to tell her more than anything, about the hunger she'd seen in Marse Peter's eyes that had made her stomach curdle. But she didn't know quite how to begin it, and perhaps it was as Ma Doe had said. Miss May Belle didn't know everything, or need to neither.

"Nothin'," Rue said.

She let her mama's threading fingers on her scalp lull her into an almost sleep and she did not wake, even when she felt one sharp twang at the very center of her head.

Varina ripped through paper, through ribbon and lace. The box opened up, and from its innards she drew out a little model carriage pulled by a little white horse.

"How lovely," Varina cooed from up above. The rocking chair she sat in creaked with her delight.

Curled up at Varina's feet with the other black children, Rue bit back a yawn. It had been a treat at first, to be picked with Sarah and Beulah and Li'l Sylvia to make an oohing-and-aahing audience as Varina opened her birthday presents. But now the floor of the veranda was littered with ribbons and bows, with shreds of paper, with piles of toys and books, knitting needles and sewing sets, dresses and hats and hairpins, and Varina placed the pale horse burdened with its white carriage on the very top of that mess of gifts where it threatened to fall over but did not. Rue oohed and aahed with the rest of them.

"I painted it myself," Marse Peter boasted. He leaned on one white pillar of the veranda, watching at a distance, smoking from his daddy's pipe.

"Why, thank you, Peter," Varina said, but she was already on to the next gift. A simple box of brown paper and twine. "No name on it. Now who could this be from?"

Varina didn't wait on an answer but began working furiously at the knot of the twine. Rue peeked behind her to look at the white family. It was rare to see them all assembled, Marse Charles and his three sons, the elder two dressed in new, stiff military uniforms, and Missus there too, complaining of the early spring heat in little mumbles that no one was paying any mind.

Rue couldn't know it then, but it would be the last time she would see them all gathered, the last time she'd see the elder two sons at all. They'd joined up, to defend King Cotton and the honor of their womenfolk, showing allegiance to the very cause their step-mama was afeared of, to be called Rebels and worse. Marse Peter would follow not too far behind his brothers. He'd live two more years, dead before he was eighteen—or presumed so leastwise—on a battlefield, in the midst of a Northern ice storm. Varina would read aloud the letter that made it so, with her remaining slaves gathered around her, just like this, like children primed for a bedtime story, Rue amongst them, and Varina would not even weep on the words that presumed her last living brother gone to meet his maker. She had never liked him much and anyway with the last of her daddy's sons dead she would finally be the sole mistress of her daddy's land, which would soon be only vast ashes.

Varina would never leave that place and Rue wouldn't neither—
but they couldn't know that then, couldn't know how well Miss
May Belle's conjure would take. Today Rue was seven years old
because Varina was, and even that she couldn't know for sure.

"How lovely!" Varina said. She'd managed to work the box of
her last gift open and she'd pulled out the prize. Rue turned back
around to see it emerge, though she knew already that it would be
the little redheaded doll baby her mama had fixed to conjure for
Ma Doe to keep Varina tied to the land. Perched in her lap it really
was a perfect double of Varina. And Rue knew the girl would love
it for that.

"Well, ain't this darlin'," Varina said, inspecting the doll.

"Isn't it darling," Missus corrected.

Varina ignored her mama. Instead she turned the doll over and
lifted up its skirts, and for a moment, stunned, Rue thought she
meant to strip the baby nude right there, before her brothers and
her daddy.

But Varina flipped the doll baby on its head and pulled down
the bright red dress over the white face. Sewn on the opposite side
was another dress, a bold green one, as bright as the trees in springtime, and there where the white doll's legs ought to have been was
another head, this one black with fat red lips and brown eyes and
hair wild like bramble.

"It's a topsy-turvy doll! How clever!" Varina said. She hugged
the black side close. "Look! A li'l nigra."

Rue ached in secret where only she could know. Was this the
gift that Miss May Belle had all along meant for Rue to receive?
Not a present but an emptiness where a present might be? Rue at
seven realized then what she ought to have known all along—that
she, and even her own doll baby, a thing made in her own image,
would belong always to Miss Varina.

FREEDOMTIME

===

What would Miss May Belle have done? Rue had only the memory of her dead mama to put the question to. But the dead did sometimes answer, in their way, and Miss May Belle answered Rue now with a way to save Bean.

All at once that mind-apparition of Miss May Belle turned back to the empty dust-dark corners of the one-room cabin, and Rue might have felt lonely if not for the fact that she knew the spirit of her mama was upon her, that spirit being conjure.

She left her cabin almost in a run, her skirts fisted up in sweating palms so she could hit a full fast stride. If she was going to do it, if she was going to find the cure for Bean's vitality, she'd have to do it quick.

The skeleton of the House loomed, the black remains of Marse Charles's mansion, its charred stairs leading nowhere. Rue rubbed her hand against the white pillar at the entryway as she always did when she passed, but she couldn't stop there. She made her way into the clearing beyond. She knew at once which plant she needed but it was a struggle to find it in the little moonlight, and it had to be right.

It was a pattern to the leaf—Rue knew to look for black backward raindrops, and, true, she'd need only the barest hint of it, a
handful, no more, crushed down into a dust, into a powder; it
would be so easy to go into Sarah's house and put it on the tip of
Bean's tongue. He trusted her now. If she timed it rightly the swirls
of red would rise up on his pale skin as brightly as it had risen in
his sister and brother, and a fever was bound to take hold. If taken
by mouth, there might be vomiting, a flux—not quite the symptoms the other children had, though it would not be so different as
to raise doubt, and it was all good toward the growing curse and
toward the show. If Rue timed it rightly and gave Bean just enough,
the sickness would overtake him in the evening, so that Sarah
would have to knock at her door, would have to ask for her help
plainly where everyone could see, and by the morning the artificial sickness would pass, as though Rue had healed him, and likewise the pestilence of suspicion would pass, and pass by Bean and
Rue with it.

But with her face so close to the ground that the grass tickled
her ears she felt suddenly ashamed. Maybe she was ill herself to
dream such a wild thing. Was this the madness of fear, or a fever
coming on? Or worse, was this the way her mama had felt in that
final year of her hate-filled grief, hanging fruit that spun from the
eaves? Rue sat upright to catch her breath, to feel the cool earth
against her hands, which she had planted firm against the ground.
She was not Miss May Belle. She did not rush headfirst into madness, sorrow, or wanting. She did not spit curses. She had to think.
She waited.

The woods were almost quiet as she listened to the beating of
her own heart and tried to breathe away that coil of fear. In the
distance she saw the trees and heard something give a mournful
hoot from high amongst the leaves but that something did not

show itself. The creek beat quiet against the pebbles of the bank, rushing down a ways to the place it opened to the river and then, she supposed, somewhere beyond that, to the sea.

She stood and approached the cabin by the creek. Heard from within it the telltale sounds of a scurrying animal. A fox?

The door to the shed almost didn't move. The bottoms of the wood had burrowed themselves deep in the mud, and Rue put all her strength into one forceful tug.

Inside she found him, not a fox but a man. She near toppled over at the sight of him. He lay on his back fully on the ground, his legs splayed unnaturally, his fingers laced over his chest in the way she'd lately been arranging the dead. She would have thought him dead if not for the slight rising and falling of those pale fingers with his chest, and then he confirmed himself alive by giving off a grunt of a snore.

He was white. Had to be—the pale hands, the ease with which he slept out in the open. And what she could make out of his face in the shadow was the sandy color of wheat. She had not seen a white man in years. Not since the war, at its fiery end. If she stepped away slowly she would not wake him, but already her hand on the door was rattling with fear and if she had to walk backward the way she had come, she was certain she would fall.

Then Rue saw that his face was not his face but was a hat made of straw, one she'd lost, she realized, some months back. The clothes he wore were in the shape of a crumpled suit separated from its jacket. Then a flood of knowing came on to her so fiercely that she cried out. It was Bruh Abel. Come back.

His whole body jerked at the sound as though his sleeping had been only surface deep and he sat up without pulling away the hat, which tumbled into his lap. Bruh Abel's gray eyes quirked into a squint and he looked right at Rue in bafflement.

Was he ill? He had that glassy gaze in the brief blinking open of his eyes that she had seen over and over in the town. He leaned all the way forward, his head rolling in a tilt on his chest.

Rue crept closer. After some unsureness she picked a safe place on the inside of his wrist. His body felt warm beneath her hand and there was a slickness to his skin made of clammy sweat.

"Rue," he said in a husky hiccup and she knew then, from the smell that wafted out with her name, that he was not sick. He was drunk. She dropped his hand.

She didn't like the strength of the liquor smell that was suddenly all around her. It smelled to her of danger.

He said, "Don't go, Rue." It was the lack of "Sister" before it that made her stop a moment, one leg over him, the other still trapped against the shed wall.

"If ya go I might die."

Rue had heard of a man that had died that way, a white man who had drunk himself quite on purpose to his death when the Yankees took his little mulatto children away to freedom.

"Gimme a cure," Bruh Abel said and stuck his arms straight up. Rue feared he was grabbing at her, but as she stumbled back she saw he was not grabbing but pointing, pointing upward with both hands at a bottle that sat above them on the curve of a collapsing shelf.

"Oh, you don't need no more of that damned mess," Rue said and surprised herself. She sounded like her mama. "What's the matter with you? All them folks in town is waitin' on you and this is what you doin'?"

Bruh Abel swatted at her. He rolled over on his side, showed his back to her now. She grabbed his shoulder and rolled him back over, so he could be looking at her for what she had to say to him.

"You a shame," Rue said. "They need you."

She was upset with herself most of all because in that first moment when she had seen him and when she had recognized him, she had felt relief. A hope down in the warm of her belly. She could hear the voices of the townsfolk in the back of her head. *Bruh Abel has come. Bruh Abel will know what to do.*

But now, that hope had dispersed in her like so much smoke. He didn't know any more than she did. He wasn't a savior any more than she was. He was just a man, fallible as she was. More so.

Bruh Abel took her hand, squeezed it weakly the way any invalid might. He was lucky he hadn't froze to death, sleeping in this fall-down shed, gaps in the wood and sharp cutting drafts, and she found she wasn't mad enough to wish that he *had* froze.

"That's exactly what I'm afeared of. They need me." His words scuttled around on a slur but he seemed to want to make himself understood. "This winter I was down almost to the gulf, got me a good setup down there, ministerin' to dockmen and to the women that work the wharfs when the sailors come in. They got them a lot of sins, them women, and they cook mighty good too. I'm thinkin' to myself I could stay down there the whole length of the winter season. Maybe into spring too. But one fine day a rider comes up say he's been lookin' for me all over. Red-haired mulatto?"

"That'd be Red Jack."

Bruh Abel grunted, went on. "Red Jack say that he's ridden down the whole length of the coast lookin' for me. There's a terrible sickness, the Ravagin' he call it, in one of the out-of-the-way towns in which I sometimes stop. He say, 'We need you,' and I say, 'I shall pray for you,' and he say, 'Come on back to town with me,' and I say 'No.'"

"They believe in you," she said. But then, they had used to believe in her and look all the good that had done them, or her, or anybody.

"Yo' Red Jack took himself away and I stayed down there in the gulf. But I found that it didn't sit right with my soul, thinkin' on all 'em children, children I baptized. Just dead.

"I gathered my courage and I wound my way back up here and it wasn't 'til I was half a day's walk away that I realized I come empty-handed. I ain't got nothin to give y'all. They need me? I can't save nobody." He stopped himself with a hiccup. "Thought I'd buy myself some thinkin' time when I bought myself some whiskey at a stand along the road. But it ain't make the thinkin' any easier."

Rue stood up. "It seldom does."

She stepped over his body, clutching her dress tight to her legs for the long leap over his torso so he couldn't see up her skirt. He was only a man, after all.

"Why'd you tell me all that?" Rue half-expected him not to answer, expected he'd fallen back into the pit of his drunken sleep.

"You understand." He slurred. "Don't ya, *Miss* Rue?"

She did understand. What it meant to be praised and praised and then suddenly tumble from grace. It was a long, lonesome way down.

Rue left him lying there, and he let her go this time with only a mewl of regret. She didn't go far. What she could assemble would be crude, only the plants that thrived in the wet that could live in the ever-present shade cast by the shed. But they were there to be found and she picked them.

Back in the shed Bruh Abel's gaze followed her as she moved about. Rue stood on the tips of her toes to examine the shelves that hung by halves on the wall. Feeling in the darkness, Rue found his Bible and beside it the bottle of liquor with nothing but a puddle left at the bottom. She pulled it down. It would have to do.

"You lookin' like Miss May Belle," Bruh Abel said. "I used to pray with her, you know, before she passed."

Rue knelt on the ground. "She was foolish for believin' in you too."

She bashed the bottom of the bottle against the thistle she had collected. The poison she'd gathered for Bean was still in her basket, waiting. She thought about it and beat harder. She kept bashing 'til the job was done.

"Hey now, with that racket."

"See these here thorns?" she held up the battered stems to him. "They set out to prick you. Y'all can swallow 'em whole if you like, and bleed. Or y'all can do it my way. I'm curin' you like you was askin'. Unless you was hopin' to wake up with the devil on yo' back in the mornin'."

Bruh Abel smirked. "And look, here I ain't got nothin' to pay you with."

Rue said, "Don't come into town tomorrow."

He looked away, perhaps ashamed as he should be. He swirled the handful of seeds she had given him. They were smooth and as black as Bean's eyes, and free of nettles.

"But iff'n you do come," Rue went on, "then come as their preacher man. Don't show them yo' doubt or yo' fear neither; they got enough a' their own. You can't save them babies what's meant to die. And I can't neither."

Rue thought of her mama, saw her there, same as she had in the shadows of the cabin. Bruh Abel's kind of faith hadn't kept Miss May Belle from dying any more than Rue's healing had. But it had made the difference in her last few hours that he'd sat at her bedside. He had made her dying easier. Rue had never thanked him for that.

"If you gon' be a liar, Bruh Abel," Rue said, "then be a useful one."

When Rue walked back home she was looking for the sunrise but there was none to be had, only the gradual receding of the black night in favor of the hard glow of day. The morning was gray all over with a fog that came up heavy from the river and hung low, made it hard to see anything clearly through the thick of the woods and made her think of Bruh Abel's eyes, that same kind of unknowable gray.

She was nearly halfway up her own porch when she saw the billow of smoke, moving only the way smoke can move, distinguishing itself from the sedentary thick of the fog to say *Someone has died here.*

It came from the house nearest to hers where a family of three was living, a mama and her two boys, the daddy long ago gone, took up his freedom and left with it. Had one of them boys died? Rue changed course. In the pocket of her dress she held her pipette and she pulled it out, something like a talisman, hoping there was a child left alive that might need her. But when she came upon the house, there, blocking her way, were Red Jack and Jonah and Si's daddy and Beulah's man, their arms full of kindling to stoke the fire of the sickbed sheets.

"Both boys?" Rue asked it to Jonah but he didn't answer.

"The eldest passed," said Red Jack. "The younger one's caught it. He sweatin' fierce."

Rue meant to pass them, but they did not move for her. Those four men held bundles of wood in their arms and their eyes moved near as one to look her up and down. She'd forgotten where she'd come from and how she must look, her skin flush, her dress dotted with nighttime mud and stains of grass. Madness, that's what they were seeing. Her gone mad. The witch they had been whispering after.

Rue tried to smile at Jonah but he wouldn't let her. His face was set.

He asked, "Where you come from?"

Rue didn't know what to say. "I was out there," she answered as if she'd descended with the fog.

Behind Jonah, Beulah's man made a noise of disgust in his

throat, shared a glance with Si's daddy, who nodded at some unsaid thing. Rue wanted to smack the cradled wood from out of their hands. "It's true then," Si's daddy muttered.

"What's true?"

But they would not say more.

"Jonah. What's true?" Rue stepped forward that she might speak to only him but in the same moment he backed away, evading, as if to be touched by her was to know some plague.

"What Ol' Joel said before he passed." Jonah hesitated. "That you out conjurin' with somebody in them woods."

"You know ain't none of it true," Rue said. But she herself did not know it to be fully a lie. "Let me by now, let me see to the sick child."

Before her the four men were a barricade, and at any moment they could turn against her. In her eyes the sticks they bore were no longer kindling but menacing switches. She felt herself shrinking.

"Please let me by."

"We takin' care of him. He'll survive it," Red Jack said with finality. He stuck a bit of tobacco in his mouth, gnashed at it with a purpose.

Rue took a step back.

"Go on then," she said. "Don't waste yo' precious time threatenin' me. Go see to the sick boy."

They went. They moved toward the cabin that plumed still more black smoke. She knew that they thought they could do what she could not, those men with bundles of sticks cradled in their arms thinking the work of carrying kindling was as precious as carrying a newborn.

"Jonah, wait," she said. She feared he would ignore her.

Yet, he stopped on the porch and waved the others on into the cabin before he turned back toward her. His expression seemed as shut to her as a locked door.

"Jonah, what's happened?" She meant to ask *What's changed?* but couldn't. It cut too close to what she was feeling. "Is somethin' the matter with yo' li'l 'uns? Is Bean took sick?"

It was the wrong thing to ask. "Why you worryin' so much after Bean?"

"I tol' you I'd take care of him," Rue said and tried not to think of her deception, or her plan of false poison, lest it show on her face.

"Folks keep tryna tell me you workin' devilment." He looked about like he feared he would be heard. Or worse, like he feared he would be seen with her. "They wanna run you outta town. They say Bean's the only one that ain't took sick. That it must be your doin'. If you don't loose yo' hold over Bean they plan to leave him out in the woods for the foxes to eat."

To hear it said pained her, but she'd known all along that that's what this all was tipping toward. Ma Doe had warned her of it; even Bruh Abel in his way had suggested trouble would come from Bean. And to Bean also.

"Bean's just a child," Rue spat. "Yo' child."

Jonah flinched. She'd struck where she'd meant to.

He led her away from the main road, closer to the edge of the woods where no one was likely to pass and hear them.

"Sarah say he was born dead but that you brung him back from the dead. Is that true, Miss Rue?"

"He was born different," she said slowly, as if she were trying to remember. But of course she had never stopped fearing that exact thing, that Bean was a curse come back from the past, to be visited upon her alone. A shame she could not escape.

Rue said, "Bean was born with a caul. A veil like. Heard tell it's lucky, means he got the Sight."

"Sarah say you jealous a' her," Jonah went on. "That you made Bean as a curse on her. That you was gon' give her a poison to stop havin' more babies."

Rue felt horror stab through her, sharp as a dagger.

"Sarah say maybe you put somethin' evil in Bean when he was born. That you hid evidence of it. Somethin' sinister."

"I didn't."

Jonah looked ill. "I burnt them sheets he was born in like you said. Was it conjure, Miss Rue, what you tol' me to do?"

"No, no. It was only what Miss May Belle used to do."

"Folks seen you go out into the woods at night. They say you go to practice yo' witchery." Jonah was looking at her like he was afraid of her. She could not bear it.

"What about that night I saw you with Ol' Joel?" Jonah said. "Did he have it figured? Is that why he died?

"Where'd you go last night, Miss Rue?" He asked it like he was desperate for her to come up with a good lie, an explanation that would make the danger pass. But she didn't have one ready. Her head was full of secrets. Her basket was full of poison.

"Folks say you nigh on twenty but you won't take no man. Is it true you got a lover in the woods?" Jonah asked it like it was the worst of her sins. "That you conceived Bean there to lay in Sarah's stomach? Is that the truth of his black eyes? Why he don't cry when you hold him?"

By now Jonah's chest was heaving with the tumble of accusations, more passion than Rue had ever seen from him in all the years she'd known him, and suddenly she resented it, her anger coming on her like a hot brand, the realization that'd he'd never looked on her 'til now and that this was how it was going to be.

" 'Folks say,' " she mimicked. "What do you say, Jonah? You believe it? If I am a witch maybe you ought not to cross me."

Jonah took a reeling step back, good as if she'd slapped him. "I don't want no harm to come to the children."

"Neither do I," said Miss Rue. "You go on and tell folks I never did none of those things they say. I ain't much more than a woman that knows some things, things anybody could know if they wanted to. Ain't no devil in the woods, Jonah. Ain't no lover."

When Bruh Abel came amongst them, she heard it: the simple commotion of him, that thing she'd told him to stir up. Hope. By the way folks were carrying on, you would have thought Jesus had finally come, that or the white doctor with his shining black bag of medicine vials, but it was just Bruh Abel and his prayers, as though hope was better than healing. They were all of them out of their houses—the healthy, the living, the left behind—and then they were praying and then they were singing something mournful.

She tried to picture Bruh Abel coming out from the accursed woods, his timing perfect. They could have no sense of how he'd spent his night, or his months away from the town. He existed to them only when he came down from the trees, as seasonal as falling fruit. But she knew.

Rue was bent at the table with pestle, with mortar, grinding down the green leaves with their little black raindrop pattern, a sign she'd learned to avoid, a sign for poison. She ground the leaves down as fine as she could and finer still and swore to herself it was the right thing to do to save Bean and herself. Never mind the right thing to do, it was the only thing, and that mattered more. She would make him sick for a short time. A spell.

PART THREE

THE RAVAGING

===

Folks would not trust the healing woman to heal. All her days, Rue had been a healing woman, and that meant waiting her whole life on sickness. On some calamity to befall others so that she could come in and stop it. But for all the calamity amongst the children, Black-Eyed Bean had shown no signs of sickening.

Rue could not wait any longer for Bean to prove that he was an ordinary boy capable of ordinary illness. It might never happen. All the while other children would fall sick around them, fall sicker, die.

Rue was resolved to go on with her scheme. She had set aside her hesitation over serving Bean a treatment of poison. No power in hesitation—Miss May Belle had taught Rue that in her every action.

Rue commenced to cook the sickness up in her kitchen. She had no food to prepare there anyhow. The goodwill of the towns-folk had fed her before but that goodwill was gone, dwindling with every child she hadn't saved, with every whisper made against her that the pestilence that had befallen their babies was because of her and Bean.

Stooped at her fireplace, Rue tended to a swinging pot filled with the black dotted leaves she'd gathered and their rolling seeds. Poison. She refused to call it otherwise. She had to have a clear mind on what she was doing, on why she was doing it. No sugar, no dose of molasses syrup to ease the going. Poison, plain, simple. If Bean showed the same sickness as the other children for a spell—and Rue could make it so—then no one could think him special. Nobody could think him favored as some witch's creation, or by some conjure of protection that she had given him, nor could they go on believing that he was leeching away the vitality of the other children for his own benefit.

She'd fallen asleep with Jonah's threats inside her head and she woke that morning terrified. At her front door there came a scratching.

They come to burn me up, Rue feared.

She pulled the pot from where it hung; the metal handle burned her skin. Still she clutched tight to it. They couldn't find her out. She had to get rid of the poison before she was caught at doing precisely what they'd accused her of all along. Cooking up sickness. They'd kill her for it.

Rue tossed the simmering poison to the ground, stashed the heated pot amongst cool ones on a high shelf just as Bruh Abel barreled through, rocked the door on its hinges. He held in his arms bundles of vegetables. He wasn't in his suit but a pair of overalls too large and clean for working in, the shirt too small. Looking at her from the doorway he sucked wind through his teeth the way her mama might've if she weren't so long ago dead, so long past drawing breath, angry or otherwise.

No time to hesitate. Rue ground away her secret, crushed the leaves away with her boot heel.

"Why you here?"

"Christian charity," he said.

He set down the food on the table, and the spread rolled out wide enough to make Rue's stomach growl. She didn't move out from her corner, hid her burnt hand behind her back.

"Unless, you already got supper goin'." He glanced at her spitting fire and above it the empty place her cooking pot was meant to hang.

"No," she said too loud.

"Figured that." Bruh Abel looked down like he was embarrassed, or pretending to be leastwise. "Folks loaded me up with all they had when they saw me. In thanks for my comin' and all. You was right. It brightened 'em to see me come."

"I knew it would." She wasn't going to let herself get jealous for it, not now. She realized that Bruh Abel had the power to ease the suspicion amongst the townspeople. But he could just as easily stoke it if he had a mind to.

It came to Rue then that folks all had been waiting on his healing, same as they had once waited on her, and on Miss May Belle before her. Likewise they would wait on his assessment of the state of things. If he pronounced she was accursed, then she was accursed and Bean along with her. What would it take, she wondered, for him to pronounce them otherwise?

Rue crossed the room, blowing at her burnt hand. She tried to lead Bruh Abel to the door, but he stood still in the middle of her home.

"It was good a' you to come," she finally said.

"I ain't leavin'," he said. "I'm stayin' here."

"What you mean you stayin'?"

"You one a' my flock now," he told her. "I stay amongst my own and administer after they needs. There's somethin' asunder in yo' home, Miss Rue. Right here is where I'm needed. So right here is where I'm stayin'."

The air all around them smelled sweet with the poison she'd been cooking. No way he couldn't smell it.

"I'm to watch," Bruh Abel said, walking the length of her supper table. He began sorting through the food, busying his hands on leeks and squashes and sweet potatoes. "Three days. On the third day I ought to know the truth a' the matter."

"So you set yo'self up as the judge and the jury a' my trial?" And the executioner, Rue thought, and she clipped her mouth shut, suddenly afraid. "Is that why you come?"

"If I ain't come, they aimed to run you off, or worse." Bruh Abel's expression was more honest than she'd ever seen it. "They tol' me to come to you, the townsfolk did. They begged it. Do you know what they sayin' 'bout you, Miss Rue?"

She hadn't for one moment stopped thinking on Jonah's accusations. Knowing him like she did she didn't doubt that Jonah had softened the threat, only repeated half the hateful accusations he'd heard, too cowardly or too cautious to give voice to the worst of it.

"I ain't come to hurt you," Bruh Abel said. "I mean only to bring reason to the matter. I come to settle things before it's all gone too far. They all of 'em convinced that Bean's yo familiar. That he's workin' as yo' spirit to steal life from the li'l 'uns. They say it must be that Bean come from the Devil. What kinda preacher would I be if I ain't confront the Devil?"

"You ain't no real kinda preacher."

Rue's venom seemed to surprise him. Well, she had surprised her own self. She sat down heavy on her bed, her face hid in her hands, her poison crushed up in the dirt under her feet.

"Last night you saw my weakness for drink, it's true," Bruh Abel said after a time. "Just 'cause I'm a preacher man don't mean I can't sometimes lose faith. Just 'cause you a healin' woman don't mean you can't sometimes fall ill."

He came round the table to her and Rue did not back down. He laid his hand on her head like he was feeling for fever.

"Are you sufferin' some sickness, Miss Rue? I mean to find it and flush it out."

They passed the evening and late into the night like two strangers, man and woman in too small of a home.

Despite his swagger before a crowd, Bruh Abel was not altogether comfortable in the presence of one person, that one person being Rue, who was watching him from the corner of her home, distrustful.

Seemed Bruh Abel didn't want to be hated. He kept trying to talk at her. All the while her mind stayed hopping about, figuring at some way out. She'd play along at sweetness if she had to. For Bean's sake. And her own.

It brought Rue to mind of slaverytime when Marse Charles had took it upon himself to pick a man slave and woman slave to couple together for no other reason than that he liked the look of them and figured them for good stock. Sometimes they wouldn't hardly have the hour to get acquainted before Miss May Belle was sent in to scent the sheets, check between the woman slave's legs for blood if she were a virgin, leastwise for slick if she was not. As a child Rue had always figured if she were to ever get a man, that would be how it went. Hadn't that been how her mama had got her daddy after all, that first time? And Rue had followed some nine months after, just a tick mark on Marse Charles's accounting book.

Freedom turned everything all over. Now a man was something you took because you wanted him. A baby something you might have for the sake of loving it.

Maybe Rue had let some of her confusion snake onto her face because Bruh Abel asked, "What you thinkin' on?"

Rue could not say what she was thinkin', which was how to be rid a' you, so she answered instead "Bean."

Bruh Abel perked up. "You layin' some kinda conjure? Is that how it works? By thinkin' on him?"

She cussed. "I'm worryin' 'bout him."

Bruh Abel settled himself down. "I heard you the one that named him."

Rue shrugged. "I ain't mean to. Just somethin' I said, and Sarah repeated it to Jonah maybe and Jonah repeated it to somebody and it just got goin' like that and there he was, Black-Eyed Bean."

"Black-eyed peas what my mama called 'em where she from. Ain't that somethin'?"

Rue had not altogether thought that Bruh Abel had a mama. Thought maybe he sprung up like some weed of his own volition.

"We come from the same people," he went on, "but we come up with all different ways a' sayin' the same thing."

He said it like they were sharing a joke. It lighted the dimple on his cheek. Rue shrugged, decided it was better to not look at him at all if he was going to try to be friendly. She suspected his friendliness for a trap.

Having him there in her cabin reminded Rue of the first time she'd seen him at the side of Miss May Belle's bed, ministering.

He'd been there when Rue had not been. How much did he know of Miss May Belle? Of the townsfolk? Of Rue herself? Were there secrets Rue's mama might have told him? Confessions of her deathbed? Fact was at her end Miss May Belle had trusted in him, and in his vials of holy water. He had that way about him, to get everybody's trust. Whether he served poison or snake oil or whiskey water, why was it that they all of them were so ready to drink it up?

"You gon' save Bean, won't you?" It was the first thing she'd said without his prompting, and it got his attention right off.

He looked at her, somber. "I meant what I said. No harm is to come to him."

"Then do somethin'."

"That's my intention. I'll save yo' soul and I'll save him, also."

Rue meant to save herself and might have said as much. But an idea flitted through her head, small at first, on moth wings, then larger still.

"Minister to Bean, Bruh Abel," she said, "same as you did my mama. I ain't never rightly thanked you for that. But when you came to her, folks saw that she was healed."

Bruh Abel nodded like it was all his idea. "I mean to do the very same."

Rue smiled at him and her smile was all poison.

The second day he made a soup, he told her a tale, and Rue devised a way to get herself out.

She set down a bottle of good strong brandy on the table between them, the kind she saved for sicknesses, and she put beside it a crystal glass, a pretty one, one she'd saved from her white folks' house before the fire.

Didn't matter, she knew, if a fish saw the hook so long as the bait was something they couldn't help but hunger after.

"Go 'head, Bruh Abel."

Rue tried to make herself sweet, the least like a witch that she could be, and she filled the glass up high and set it before him glinting amber in the firelight. She knew men had a myriad of weaknesses, but she only trusted herself to seduce him with the one.

He pushed the glass over to her. "For you, Rue."

Then he took up the bottle itself, winked at her, and drank from it straight. Bottle in hand, he went on cooking.

Bruh Abel cooked with the same flare with which he preached. He alternated between a whistle and a hum as he chopped up vegetables at her small table, made a broth in her only pot, rolled dough in the bowl she usually used to make a draught for colic.

Sitting on the sharp edge of her bed, Rue watched him, sipped at the glass she'd poured. She aimed to keep her wits about her as his slipped from him. Then when he was fast asleep she could steal into the woods. Fetch more poison leaves for Bean. Finish finally the idea she'd started.

Bruh Abel came over to her with the soup and coaxed her to taste his concoction, proffering an outstretched spoonful. She looked into his heavy-lidded eyes and smiled, took the spoon for herself, and tasted. It was hot, it was good.

"Where'd you learn all that?"

"From Queenie, where else? My mama."

He told Rue about Queenie in a heavy slur. He called her Queenie 'cause everybody called her Queenie and everybody called her Queenie, he supposed, because she was the queen of her kitchen. Her master was a sea captain, though Bruh Abel in his overflowing enthusiasm made him sound something more like a pirate—thickly bearded, full gray eyes—and that sea captain had loved Queenie so much he'd had her likeness etched into the figurehead of his boat, down to every last quirk and birthmark. He'd made her a mermaid. The snaking curve of her back jutted her out over the sea, and the sea captain even had them sculpt in the two dimples on her back where her ass spread wide and became the scaled pattern of the bow. That ten-foot Queenie was made all of mahogany picked for its perfect match, the exact color of her skin.

"He weren't a superstitious man and he'dda had her on the ship with him if he could, but his men weren't gonna have none of that," Bruh Abel told Rue in a hiccup. "Women on ships is sour luck."

Rue had to wonder why the wood figure of a woman on a ship was good when a real, flesh woman on a ship was bad but she didn't ask, just watched Bruh Abel tip back the bottle.

Queenie lived on the quay, Bruh Abel explained as he ladled out a bowl of soup, in a sea-battered cottage with her baker's dozen of children, who had a way of being born nine months or thereabouts after the captain's ship left her port. Bruh Abel had been the youngest of those and the petted favorite. Her boys she offered to the sea, her girls to other folks' kitchens, but Bruh Abel, being her littlest, she kept close. He'd learned her cooking looking up from under her skirts.

Bruh Abel made his way to where Rue sat on the edge of the bed. He tasted his soup, made a noise of satisfaction, and tasted it again. He sat himself down on the bed too, his legs tangled in her sheet. Rue had to push up against the headboard to give his tall angular body room.

"The sea captain loved her and her way with food so much he done declared that when he died he'd free her and all us li'l 'uns with her. He died inside a year a' writing the words. Folks says she killed him on purpose."

Rue frowned. "Did she?"

Bruh Abel laughed so hard he spit out some of his soup. "Nah, just he loved her cookin' so much he got to weighin' half a ton and died from the strain of it."

He handed her the bowl and Rue ate from it, sharply hungry and hungrier still with each bite. The salty broth floated with greens and sweet potatoes that must have come from Ma Doe's garden, and a dark meat so smooth she could swallow it whole.

"Don't you want any?" she asked him.

"Nah," he said, smiling dreamily, "I got all I need right here." He patted the brown bottle like a lover. Rue felt almost sorry for him.

Bruh Abel didn't stir from where she'd left him, blanketless on her bed. She'd watched him sleeping for a while, perhaps longer than she should have, listening to his easy snore and wondering if she ought not stay and pray with him after all.

In the end she snatched up her basket, her mortar, and her pestle and left, stepped out into the wilderness with only a dim lantern as a beacon, so determined to go through with her plan that she could hardly wait out the inky dark to conceal her. She walked to the little bed of green leaves she'd come to two nights before. Their dotted surface glistened with the start of dew drops as if to greet her. With sure fingers she plucked them from the ground.

This time, though, she did not return home, turned instead to that old fall-down church, the only place she knew for certain she'd go unseen.

After the war, folks had forgotten the white folks' church, shunned it as a hated place, a place they'd been taught to submit, to bow down in the Lord's name. To hush and to surrender. Bruh Abel's church was water and sky, his Bible was a hymn and a battle cry. What use did they have for the grim gray four walls of the old Protestant church? They'd shiver just to go into it, to feel encased all in brick. They'd sooner let it crumble, but they'd never tear it down. The Northern army, too, had stopped their hellfire short of burning it—as Rue had bet they would—just as superstitious in the end as they accused black folks of being. They feared the ill luck that destroying a sacred place would bring, and who could blame them? Whatever folks believed or didn't believe there was no sense fueling the wrath of things not seen.

Now Rue came to the pews and set down her bowl and began to grind down the leaves by lantern light. A fine powder, finer than fine. She didn't dare hesitate. When she was finished she stowed the poison in a little vial and hid it in the folds of her dress.

Above her the roof creaked sharply. She glanced upward.

Up, where the slaves, when there had been slaves, had listened to those sermons, had had obedience whupped into their minds with words as sharp as any cat-o'-nine. The boards groaned again with the noise of someone shifting their weight, unsure, and from the corner of her eye Rue caught the movement of a woman's white night shift rippling back into the shadows.

"Varina," Rue said.

The woman rippled out again at the sound of her name.

"S'alright, Varina," Rue said. "You might as well come on."

Varina took the steps down from the loft slowly, taking care to step where she knew the old boards would still hold her. She creaked all the way down and then crossed the church slow, too, trailing her long white nightgown through dust, came like a reluctant child about to be scolded though she was a woman grown, and a used-to-be mistress. "Is it safe?"

"Safe as it ever is," Rue said. She put down the bowl and pestle, made room for Varina beside her on the bench. The white woman sat down next to her, so close their two dresses touched.

Varina petted Rue's hand like she wanted to make sure Rue was altogether real. She looked sallow in the lantern light, and there were black rings beneath her eyes.

"You've been gone away too long," Varina complained. She always complained no matter if it was a day or a month since Rue had last been to see her in her hiding place.

"I'm sorry, Miss Varina. I met with a bit a' trouble in town. Nothin' to worry after. Cure's in hand." Rue patted her pocket where she'd kept the poison for Bean.

"Is it Ma? She unwell?"

Rue shook her head. "No, no, ain't nothin' like that. Ma Doe's well as ever. She asks after you."

Varina looked up at the broken rafters. "May I come out soon, Rue? I'd so like to."

"Soon," Rue lied. "When all is well and settled."

Rue could go on and on putting off Varina's demands, could keep on telling the woman that it was not safe for her to venture beyond the confines of the old church. But she looked at Varina now and there was some of that old defiance starting to crackle on Varina's face, there and gone, fast like lightning.

In their hide-and-seek game, Varina kept herself well hid in the distant church, far off from the plantation. The old routes to the church had been cut off by a particularly bad swell of the river that made the woods look all turned around if a body wasn't over-familiar with traversing them.

Varina made her home in the rectory. On braver days she ghosted through the empty church aisles or up in the vaulted second story where the corpse bell swung through dust and gleaming spider webs.

Those first hard months after the fire destroyed her home, Miss Varina had near wasted away in her bedroll, her mind gone, fogged over with fear and sorrow and shame. Every shadow was sin or a Northern soldier in a war she didn't know was ending. Without Rue, Varina might have died, or lost her senses altogether. Might have hurt herself, in some final brutal way, just to be free of the torment of her own memories.

But Varina had gradually healed. And Rue knew that one of these days she was going to reclaim that old hunger. Then she wasn't going to stay satisfied eating up the simple lies that Rue kept on feeding her.

Rue's ears pricked up to some sound outside. Was that the crack of twigs beneath a quick approach? She stood from the bench. Tried to listen. There again, motion.

Varina stilled. "Rue?"

"Go." Rue took up her lantern, moved as swiftly as she could, and slipped her way out through the double doors. Shut them behind her, hard.

Bruh Abel was there in the field of the church. His eyes were arrowhead sharp in the rocking light of her lantern.

"There you are, Miss Rue." His breath smelled of brandy, but his voice was steady when he spoke. Exacting. Sober.

"You ain't drunk," Rue said.

"I poured out the brandy, boiled it up into the stew, while you wasn't lookin'." He seemed pleased with himself. "I wanted to know what it is you hide in these woods. What you ain't want me to see."

Rue glanced behind her, tried to make it look like she wasn't looking for anything. But she was looking, up at the high windows of the church and into the bellhouse, but there was no movement there, just the chill of a disused building, frozen in time.

Bruh Abel was wanting an answer. She had to give him something, she thought, one secret to keep another.

"Go on and look then."

He stepped through the doorway of the church. He took Rue's lantern from her, held it high and set it to swinging, and the shadow his body cast stretched out long and sinister over the empty room.

Rue followed close behind him, struggling in his wake to see over his shoulder. She tried to see it through his eyes, the cracked church pews and the broke-down altar and the second story that looked about ready to collapse. She tried to read the shadows for a hint of white movement.

Where had Varina hid herself?

"What is this place?" he asked. It was like his preacher voice knew it was a church house and felt at home—it echoed sharply taking up the whole of the room, made Rue's heart scud in terror.

"Nothin' but where we used to get made to worship," she told him. "Forced to worship."

"And you stay comin' here?" Bruh Abel illuminated one sharp

corner. In it was a rocking chair. There was a handkerchief draped across the seat with a half-finished bit of embroidery, lily of the valley, in neat green stitch, the flowers not bloomed in yet.

"Folks don't come here no more. Can't, I s'pose," Rue said quick. "But I do. For quiet-like."

Bruh Abel tipped back the chair, set it to rocking, but it didn't rock right and as he moved, dragging the lantern light over the stores of dry food by the altar, the chair kept rocking. Its crooked pace fell in time with Rue's wracking heartbeat.

"And this?" He'd turned his light into the farthest room of the rectory proper. Past the stove and water basin was a little back room with a bedroll on the floor, the scant covers neatly tucked.

Rue hurried in after him. The back room was all empty too, but he'd lighted on something tucked into the bed. He picked it up and turned it in his hands, studied it closely. A little black doll baby in a green dress, a crude likeness of Rue but a likeness all the same. May Belle's creation had held up all these years. Thread-bare, but it had held, and if he flipped the doll over he'd see the face of the white doll hid beneath her skirts. He did not flip it over but tossed it on the sleeping mat.

There was the one small back door. It took Bruh Abel out into the night again and Rue after him. There was no grass beyond the church but an area of hard-packed mud that looked red in the moonlight. Carved out in its center was a neat square door made of heavy wood, an entrance to a slave jail in the earth.

Bruh Abel seemed to know what it was from the moment he saw it. He recoiled from the spot, yet the circle of lantern light settled on the thick metal padlock that sat atop the door. The lock was open, Rue saw, and the chains had been disrupted, left a track in the mud from where they used to be to where they'd just been moved. Varina.

He reached down, as if he meant to pull open the heavy door.

"Don't."

Bruh Abel swung the light up at Rue, near blinding her with the sudden motion. She covered her face, spoke through her hands.

"Miss May Belle," Rue said. "Marse Charles locked her down there once. For three days. Punishment."

She let her whole body shudder with the memory of it as though it were a fresh hurt and she were overcome.

She heard the lantern clatter to the ground. Bruh Abel pulled her into a fierce embrace. Her head at his chest, Rue listened to the pounding of his heartbeat, fast as hers, like a drum on her ear.

"You punishin' yo'self by comin' here, Miss Rue," Bruh Abel said. "It ain't right. This ain't the right way to make peace."

"It's like you say," Rue spoke into his chest. "I can't seem to let go a' the old ways."

"We can set this to rights."

"Please," Rue said. "Help me."

SLAVERYTIME

1860

Before the war, they found a dead man in the woods. They'd found him on the edge of the thick trees, at the crest of a small hill, as if he'd used the last thrust of his life to get up it and had succeeded in that at least. And all the folks agreed that the rusted iron collar locked around his throat looked like a crown of thorns fit for Jesus himself.

It was the little pickaninny boy, Red Jack, that found the dead man, a mercy that, folks said, for what if it had been one of the girl children who'd come across him? You see, the dead man was full naked, stark as the day he was born, save for his collar of rusted iron.

Still Red Jack, too, was only ten years old if he was a day, and it was often said that he did not have enough wits to rub together for a fire, so when he stumbled into the thick of the wood to relieve himself and saw the dead man there, facedown in moss, Red Jack shrugged and shook dry and went to Ma Doe, who was the only thing like a mama he'd ever known, and said to her, "Ma Doe, there's a dead man in the wood."

Well, Ma Doe, who minded the children—the master's and the slave ones and the ones who didn't or couldn't know their mamas—

well, she'd heard all nature of things in her long life and she thought she had heard every last thing there was to hear 'til she heard that.

"Who is he?"

"Don't know."

"How'd you know he's dead?"

"He ain't movin' none."

"How long's he been there?"

"'Least as long as right now."

Ma Doe had a baby on either hip and one swathed up on her back, and she was in no type of place to go running off into the wood on Red Jack's half-clear declaration, but she had a sense that something dread had come to them and she knew Red Jack didn't have it in him to lie. If he said there was a dead man in the wood, then there was.

She sent Red Jack to fetch Charlie and Ol' Joel and take them to the place where the dead man lay. He did just that, and the two men and one boy came back to her, hats in hand.

"Sure 'nough he is a dead man," said Ol' Joel.

"Can't make no sense a' who he is or where he come from," said Charlie.

"Runaway," said Ma Doe, who had wisdom of such things.

Ol' Joel was for telling Marse Charles, as he always was for telling Marse Charles. Charlie, who thought himself wise because he'd been allowed to apprentice at the side of a white blacksmith, commented on the iron collar. One of the long, cruel bars was bent enough to allow the man to lie, his head propped up awkward as if on a pillow of air. But at a touch the whole thing was rusted, weak. Perhaps he'd come up through the water, from the river, risen.

It was Red Jack that came to the solution, which was as simple as saying, "Miss May Belle oughta know."

Ma Doe sent Charlie and Ol' Joel to fetch the dead man. Standing in the doorway, draped in her orphan babies, she watched as they carried him through the crossways center of the plantation. Ol' Joel with his bad knees took the legs, Charlie held the head and shoulders, and as they passed her by Ma Doe couldn't help but to say how young the dead man was, how he was surely just fresh from his first shave and how sad, how very very sad, was the world.

Rue was not there when they brought the dead man into their home. Ma Doe had had the sense to tell Red Jack to run ahead, to warn Miss May Belle of what was coming her way, and in turn Miss May Belle had sent Rue on a fool's errand—go pick some sassafras from down the road a ways, as if there wasn't sassafras sprouting up all over the place, but Rue went.

Sassafras, Rue knew, liked gaps, dwelled in drops of light where the soil was moist but not too wet, and like all good things, it came wrapped in bad. It had a way of tangling itself with poison vines, trying to hide. But Rue's hands were small and already well practiced, and she picked the two apart and came back to her mama with only the good, a whole mess of sassafras sprouting out from her arms like she was herself a garden.

They'd put the dead man on the table, drawn the curtains, hid the sun. His raised head was turned at attention, like he'd been startled by the opening door, and though his eyes were half-closed, his blue-lined lips were partways open as if he was making ready a greeting.

"Who's that, Mama?"

"Nobody know."

Nobody did know. His yellow-brown skin could have been anybody's yellow-brown skin, as could his shorn black hair, as could his broad nose, his calloused fingers, his flat, bloodied feet. He was young enough to be any mama's son and old enough to be any baby's daddy. The lash marks on his shoulders could come from any overseer's licks, and it was only the iron around his neck that made him the least bit remarkable. Sure as a brand, it meant he was trouble. It meant he had run away and been brought back and made an example and shackled. Then he had run again.

There was a quilt for his nakedness, though it seemed small on him and only covered his lower half: his raw knees to the crescent of his belly button, shrouded. Rue looked long at the quilt then up to her mama, who stood behind the stretch of the dead man the way other mamas might stand behind a supper they'd cooked.

"He ain't died of no pestilence, leastwise. Wouldn't let them have brung him here if he had. Nah, body's strong, wiry-like, sure, but strong."

Miss May Belle touched the taut skin over his calves, thick as tree trunks. She moved to the top of the body, past various scars and scratches, a short life's worth of hurts and healing. His eyes, not all closed, were hooded, so she opened one of his lids all the way for him and looked in.

"No yellowin'. No cloudin'. Nah. He just die scared." She let the eye slip back to half-shut. "See how he look afraid?"

Rue could not tell what afraid looked like on a dead man. What did he have left to fear for?

"But, Mama," she said. She was still frozen in the doorway with all her flowers. "Who is he?"

"Nobody know," said Miss May Belle, but that didn't stop folks from trying to figure it. They came through the cabin one after another to look at him, the dead man, to confirm his strangeness and to make hollow suggestions about from where he'd come.

"Young buck," said Ol' Joel. "They like 'em like that down south way. Strong, they is, but got no sense. Disobedience is his name if it's anything."

"He got some Injun in him," said Beulah, who'd seen Indian in her red-skinned daddy and so saw it everywhere. The dead man's ears, she said, were like arrowheads; he could hear danger and that's how he'd run so far, for so long.

Opal, who knew a whole mess of men, was known to know them intimately, could not make sense of him.

"I ain't never come 'cross him," she said, as if she'd come across every man since Adam. She swept her hand over the peak of his pointed cheekbone. "Woulda like to known him, though. Face like that, surely he was somethin' good to somebody."

Seemed the dead man was something to everybody. They kept coming to look him over, though it was clear no one could name him. Even folks from the neighboring plantation came by if they could get the leave, not even to speak, just to stare. They put the pennies on his eyes after a while, to respectfully weigh down the lids. They all agreed there was something shiver-stirring in the pureness of those half-mooned whites. White as they knew cotton to be, white as they'd heard snow could be.

"It's foul luck to spend the pennies off a' dead folks' eyes," Miss May Belle warned the children that came to peek, "so don't you dare go an' think it."

Rue did not think of it. What she did think was how strange his stillness was, this dead man, with his muscles still poised as if at any moment were he to hear the hounds barking or the guns firing or the footsteps of white men's boots on wooded ground, he could take off. He could run again. Rue sensed it in him, and it sent a sort of thrill through her she as yet had never known. She had never before been so close to a man, dead or alive, and it was his potential to run that thrilled her. Women, she realized then, were not built that way. Women were for crouching, for becoming heavy-bellied, for bearing down and pushing close to the earth, that different sort of running, that sedentary sort of endurance.

———

They all of them conspired to keep the dead man hid from Marse Charles. It was a dangerous folly, they knew, but a risk worth taking to bear the dead man home. He had the look of every runaway sketch hanging from any tree in the county, but still someone might come to claim him if they knew where to look. There was profit in runaway corpses. Even dead, his white folks might string him up in the center of their cotton field as a warning to the others, a scarecrow to watch rot while they worked. His white folks might conspire to have him cut up, each limb and ligament worth a silver dollar from some white doctor curious on how a black body differed from his own.

The dead man, therefore, had to be prepared, and quickly, for the homegoing. Charlie Blacksmith came through to Miss May Belle's cabin. He sent a storm of sparks into the air, but he did it— the collar and its serpentine spikes fell away, and beneath it the dead man's neck appeared, seeming small and vulnerable. When they pulled it away, the collar, once sinister, fell to pieces like so many petals. What power it had had was gone from it now, left to bits of rust and iron.

Rue and Miss May Belle had to sleep with the man; there was no better place to put him than where he already was, stretched out on their supper table. The proposition didn't seem to bother Miss May Belle much, who long ago had lost her discomfort with life and death, with other folks' bodies, if she'd ever had any discomfort to begin with. She slept deeply through the night that he was with them. Rue lay awake beside her mama in fear and in wonder both. Across the room she could not see the dead man clearly, but she could make out his bulk and the shape of him, and beneath the lighter color of the quilt, she could make out perfectly the pale white bottoms of his feet, which caught the moonlight.

Miss May Belle was as boisterous sleeping as she was awake. Her breath came in gusting stutters, a force, for certain, but so rhythmic that Rue most often found it soothing. But there was no comfort this night, and so awake, Rue listened and counted each of her mama's breaths as a way to keep time 'til it felt safe to move, whenever that might be. When she did get up she did so without telling herself she would. She was just suddenly in motion, quick but quiet to sit up and sweep the sheet from her legs and then stand so that the bed would shift slowly with her spare weight and not disturb her mama, who stayed snoring.

Rue crept across the room. She ghosted her way across the wooden floor until she reached him. The dead man waited, his head tilted toward her.

She held her hand to his open mouth, not so close as to touch his lips, but close enough to feel air. There was none to be felt and, emboldened, she hovered her hand down lower and lower still. The quilt was thin, a pattern of interlocking scenes, each block bearing little stitches of activity. Faceless black men and women— made women by the bell of their skirts—danced here and tended harvest there and bore black wings up to white misshaped stars. Rue dared. She pulled back the thickly bordered corner of the quilt and followed the taut V of the dead man's waist. She saw the dark coiled hairs surrounding the mass of flesh there, long but unmenacing. It was what made him a man, she knew; it stuck close to his left thigh, dead too. A wrongness roiled in the pit of her belly. Rue dropped the quilt back down.

Across the room Miss May Belle's breathing came steady, slower than the rhythm of Rue's nervous heartbeat. Rue slipped one foot toward the bed, another, another. She froze when she saw them, the knowing bare whites of her mama's eyes. Watching.

"You done, girl?"

Rue could scarcely remember how to nod.

"A'ight. Come on back to bed now."

Rue did as her mama said.

The suit they found him the next morning fit as best it could, being something borrowed and not meant to be returned. It was a dusky gray, and folks said he looked ready for his wedding day. Wed to death, some of the older women were saying, wed to Jesus. But no one could spare him shoes, shoes being so rare to begin with. "Where he goin'," they assured themselves desperately, "he ain't gon' need 'em."

Still, the pale white bottoms of his feet seemed accusatory in their bareness, even after they had washed the worst of the blood from between his toes and from beneath his splintered toenails. That task, too, fell to Miss May Belle, who had the most knowledge, it seemed, of what was needed to make ready the dead. She surrounded him with flowers to keep him sweet smelling and cleaned his skin, gentle, as though he were her own son. The feet she saved for last, and Rue watched as the cleaning made her strong mama finally weep.

"He look like yo' daddy," she was saying under her sorrow.

Rue nodded, but he did not. Her daddy was stronger, older, darker. Alive.

How beautiful they'd made him when it was time for him to go on. Rue knew they'd cinched the suit in the back, so it pulled about his shoulders in the right way, and she knew the coffin was nothing much more than spare bits of wood left from the repair of other things: chicken coop stake, cracked church pew, things worked together and hastily painted one hue, as if that made for belonging.

They held the funeral at night after the work was done, and though they were tired they danced and though they had sorrow they sang. They made themselves a slow procession going by him in a manner strangely similar to when he'd first appeared to them. The dead man's head was pillowed by flowers, by quilted bits of pretty fabric, the finest anybody could spare. In death he looked himself like a celebration, though surely his life had never been. But here it was, close up, freedom. He'd reached finally what he'd been running toward.

Rue lingered back with the other children, all of them giddy like it was Christmastime and overtired besides. They did their best imitation of their mourning daddies and mamas, bowed their heads when bowing was necessary, keened when others keened. So, this was grieving. Rue followed last in the line that visited the dead man's motley coffin. She was not sure what she was meant to think or feel when she touched the splintery surface as others before her had done—what message she was supposed to be imparting through her fingers. Goodbye? Sleep well?

She looked out into the wood, focused on fixing her face in solemn dignity, for the sake of others if not for the sake of the dead man—and that's when she first saw them, there amongst the dark of the trees, looming white faces watching from afar. Had the dead man's white folks come for him after all? They weren't advancing to pay their respects, only looking on, eerie-still in comparison to the commotion of all the black folks' mourning. Rue took her hand from the box, moved on. Surely she was not the only one who had seen them. For certain everyone felt their presence. Their eyes, watching.

The movement of mourning had turned to a tight circle around the coffin. The four strongest men lifted the coffin up high onto their shoulders. Rue's daddy made up the back left corner and she watched closely as he and the other men bent as one, like something they'd practiced, to heave the dead man forward. They made the lifting of it look easy, and for sure it was compared to the back-breaking labor to which those sun-blackened field hands were accustomed. It was an honor to lift this burden and so the burden was light.

They processed through the wood and someone far back kept time with just the clap of their two hands in lieu of a drum, which was surely a devilish instrument to hear white folks tell it, but those two hands were as good as one drum, thundering off the trees so that it was joined up a hundredfold in furious echo. Rue kept an eye to the white faces, tried to keep solemn sight of them. They kept an equal distance from the black mourners, but they did follow, all the way up through the trees and there they stayed as the casket borne by the black men crested up the graveyard hill, illuminated full for their audience in the big moonlight.

They laid him down in his plot slow. At the head of the grave they were meant to place his belongings so he wouldn't come out again, a hungry spirit jealous after their own belongings. But he'd come to them with nothing but the twisted collar on his neck, and so that's what they left there to mark his rest. It bloomed from the ground, rusted and bent and broken, as good as any bit of stone bearing words could be. Better.

They formed up in a final circle for him and took up singing. Rue felt strange to be part of it, to hook her arms in with folks who'd paid her little mind before. But there was a warmth there that she liked and the song they gave was easy to learn, looping through them as it did, the words simple and sharp and real. Rue thought even that the white faces could learn the song if they chose to journey up the hill, but they didn't join and they didn't sing, only watched from the black shadow of the trees as on the graveyard hill the singing rose and rose.

"Wonder where is my brother gone?" a voice would lament.

And then another would come from the night. "He is gone to the wilderness," and another would join: "He ain't comin' no more."

"Where is my brother gone?"

"He gone to wilderness, ain't comin' no more."

"Wonder where will I lie down?" Rue asked when the circle of the song came round on her. Her voice felt thin but she made it hold. "Wonder where will I lie down?"

THE RAVAGING

==

On the third day of Bruh Abel's watch, he took Rue walking. They moved through the town square on a gray rain-slicked afternoon, and though no one came out of doors, Rue knew that all of them were watching through windows as the preacher man and healing woman passed.

"They ready to forgive you," Bruh Abel said.

"Are they?"

"They will want to witness yo' redemption." Already he was planning it, like a show. "You need only to admit yo' wrongdoing."

Rue did not feel like she had committed wrongdoing that needed admitting, not yet anyway, but she walked beside Bruh Abel just the same, going where he led her, up the steep hill to where the town cemetery sat veiled in mist.

At the peak of the hill, they stopped to look down on the town below. They watched as a line of black smoke plumed from behind a cabin. The sickness wasn't gone.

"You broke my mama's spell," Rue told him.

He looked at her confused.

"Folks say before she died she laid a curse on the town, made it so's no one could come in an' no one could come out. But you come in and you come out easy. How's that?"

"Maybe I'm magic too," Bruh Abel said, "and don't even know it myself."

He spoke of magic with that amused expression that lit up his crooked dimple.

"C'mon," he said, and he took her over to her mama's grave. He knelt beside it. "She was a good 'un, yo' Miss May Belle. Glad I knew her the time I did."

Rue stayed standing, didn't speak. At the end she'd felt her mama hadn't been really happy with her. She'd always felt that, throughout her life, she'd gone up and down on the bobbing tide of Miss May Belle's esteem. That last year her mama hadn't been proud of her for choosing to hide away Varina. Wanted no part in it. Cussed Rue for a fool and worse.

It was like Bruh Abel was picking thoughts from her mind when he said, "My mama wasn't so kind always."

"Yo' Queenie?" Rue had rather liked the fanciful tales Bruh Abel had told of his mama, though she didn't half-believe them. "Thought that you was her favorite."

Bruh Abel rocked on his haunches. "Favorites come and go," he said. "First thing she did when the captain gave us our freedom? She turnt round and sold me right back to bondage."

Rue took a step back from him. Recoiled at the very idea of it. "Y'own mama? Sold you?"

"Sho' 'nuff. She had other mouths that were wantin' to be fed, how she told it. Her older sons were grown by then, no property of hers. She weren't like to sell off her daughters neither. Men do nasty stuff when they buy up pretty mulattas, she tol' me, but I was a boy, and sons is meant to leave, that was her thinkin'. Or least-wise what she said aloud. When I recollect it all now, though, I suspect it was more the eyes."

Bruh Abel tilted his head all the way back. He opened his eyes wide for Rue so that she could examine them for herself.

"Like the captain's," he explained.

Rue looked hard. He was kneeling below her still, the same height as the lesser gravestones all around him, and in the bright of high noon his eyes were the same swampy mixed-up gray of those rocks. His whites were red-rimmed, like he'd lost as much sleep as she had been losing. He blinked hard and carried on. "I was the only one that got 'em. Ain't it funny what we pass down? Her man was dead but she always said I had a haint in my eyes. Now, how could she be free with a white man looking on her from beyond?"

Rue said nothing, had nothing to say to something so hard.

"Ain't no one reason for anybody doin' anythin', is there?" Bruh Abel said. "Like as not it was just as much that I was what my new marse was lookin' for to buy. Boy, young enough to still be molded. He used to be a breaker before he got religion. Don't think they have a word for what he become."

Breakers. Rue had heard of such men. In slaverytime Marse Charles would threaten to send his more discourteous slaves to a famed breaker a few counties over, though he never had done it, perhaps more because of the prohibitive cost than the cruelty of the breaker's methods. But the threat still rang in their heads, which was just as good to keep them in line and cheaper besides, a fear on the inside of their backs, always rolling up their spines, the knowledge that they could be sent away to a place whose whole function was to leech you of your spirit, to send you back home hollowed and broken and thankful for it.

Bruh Abel pulled Rue close to him and leaned his head on the soft bottom of her stomach, buried his nose briefly in her belly button like it was meant to fit there naturally. Rue had a sudden moment of sorrow, and of wanting. A flash thought that she ought not go forward with her poison scheme. But just like that it passed in her. She did not pull away from him, not even when his grip on her hips tightened, each finger digging in with individual need.

"I ain't mad at what my mama done or what the breaker done," Bruh Abel said. "The scripture teaches forgiveness and the scripture is what my marse branded into me without even lifting a hand. There's other ways to make a boy the man you want him to be, and that's what he was after. To prove it could be done another way. Through the spirit, he said."

Bruh Abel went on, and said, "It started off as a drunken parlor bet. Can you teach a bird, teach a monkey, teach a black man how to worship so good he draws in a white crowd? Funny thing is, he never did collect on that bet, my marse. Man he laid the bet with said in the end it didn't count, didn't prove nothin' seein' as my ability might've come from my half-white side. Well, my marse, bein' white and smart hisself, he recoup in another fashion. He took me all round. To every state and out on the ocean, in trains and steamboats, and out west to wildernesses not even yet staked or named, all so that folks could look on me as an example. Of all the things a black man could and could not be. That's the part I ain't forgive, Miss Rue, that he aimed to diminish other black folk through use a' me."

Bruh Abel pulled himself up by her hips. Rue bristled but did not pull away. His truth had his body shivering, nothing eloquent about him now. Just another mama-less child.

"I've been wantin' you to know that," he said. "Didn't know how to tell it but in a story. Figure you'd understand. I don't care for what folks are expectin' a' Bean, lookin' the way he does. Layin' they burdens at his feet. Seems to me they should 'llow him to be a boy, not just an evil or a spectacle."

"You mean to go to him now?" Rue asked. "To pray over him the way you done my mama?"

"Just this minute," Bruh Abel said.

"Before all to see?" Rue pressed.

"I swear it."

Rue kissed Bruh Abel. A brief pressing of her lips to his in which neither of them moved or even breathed, the better to feel. She wound her hands down his body and lingered at his taut chest, and then at the waist of his belt, and then at his pocket, where she swapped the vial of holy water he kept there for her own plugged-up vial of poison.

When she pulled back, she was almost reluctant to leave him. It was like peeling away from a place that she belonged.

"Go on then, Bruh Abel," she said. "With my blessin'."

He moved her hair and kissed her again, easy, like he'd always had the right.

Rue waited and imagined. She was not to be seen when Bruh Abel led Bean out amongst the townspeople to be healed through prayer and singing and drinking holy water. So she had to picture it, and sit and wait, alone.

Her cabin seemed overlarge now that it was hers alone again and empty of Bruh Abel. His watch was over. He had the truth of her, or so he thought. He'd gotten the witch to promise that she would admit before everybody her misdeeds. It was to be done in the harsh light of the next day's dawn. Now he was free to minister to her changeling, to free Bean of her hold.

Bruh Abel had no sense of how well his freeing would go. He didn't know that his praying was laced, that by daybreak Bean would have the froth and the fever that had wracked the other children. Just enough sickness to silence all suspicions.

Rue had to imagine too, Varina in the old white church, imagine how she must have sat for hours in the prison she had put herself in, 'til she could be certain it was safe to return to the rectory. Rue had cautioned Varina over and over that she must never be seen, and if she were to be seen she must do everything she rightly could to appear like she was dead, only an apparition in the eyeblink of any superstitious gaze. Seemed Varina had took Rue's warnings to heart.

So Rue kept on, waiting, sat by the warm of her fire as the things she had laid unfurled. She pulled from her pocket the bottle of holy water she had stolen from Bruh Abel, replaced with her own more potent liquid. Rue pulled up the cork stopper and at the fireplace she overturned the vial and let the whiskey-water out. It hissed and sizzled where it met the heat but the fire kept on burning.

When the sickness came, they needed her, Jonah and Sarah did. They had to believe Rue had been absolved by Bruh Abel's word, because he said so. She was the only one with enough knowledge to tell them what had befallen their youngest son. They sent Bruh Abel to fetch her and he led her to their door, hovering behind her, like he was still suspect of her power for all that he had vouchsafed her coming redemption.

The poison had worked quicker even than Rue had figured. In his bed, Bean twisted and sweated against an inferno fever. They had called on her for help though they had not trusted her. What else could they do?

"Don't touch nothin'," Bruh Abel told her, and Rue did as she was told.

Rue stood beside him as he looked over the sick boy.

"He's sweatin' out somethin' awful," Bruh Abel said. Rue could see that. Could see the way the boy was succumbing to the fever. Like he was being cooked alive.

"Y'all need to cool him." Rue turned to the mama and daddy.

Jonah eyed her with suspicion but seemed to be thinking on the whole situation, deciding. Sarah's expression was drawn, like she'd gone away and left her body behind.

In the bed Bean reared up. The black in his eyes seemed to have spread. He spoke. Not sentences, not even words, just the harsh sounds of a muddy guttural language, hard tongue pangs on the back of his teeth.

"Take him to the river," Rue said.

Sarah and Rue followed behind the men as they went ahead. Bean, slung over Bruh Abel's shoulder, was a limp weight in his arms, looking back at them through half lids, an uncanny stare like an accusation.

"The cold water outta help cool his burnin'," Rue told them.

"You know he afraid a' the water," Sarah said.

Bean fought them. As Bruh Abel and Jonah both walked into the deep of the river, the little boy between them thrashed and hollered. They had to hold him in it, beneath the water made icy with night. But he did soon calm, maybe shocked by it into an eerie still. On the bank, Rue's heart ached for what she'd done to him. But she'd had to. Every wrong she'd ever done, she'd done to protect others. Bean. Varina. The whole of the town and every soul in it.

"Folks won't come after him no more at least. They can't say he ain't suffered." Sarah spoke the words of the thing that Rue had been hoping after, but to see it there before them enacted, it seemed a cruel means, hardly worth its end.

"I love him," Sarah said. They watched Bruh Abel and Jonah drag themselves out of the river, Bean hanging limp between them. "You may not think it, but I do. I love him the way anyone loves any child, because they a child. It's not like he mine. It's like he came outta me but he ain't hardly touched me."

In the silver of the light Sarah looked pale, resigned, like the haint of someone Rue used to know. "You'll know when you got one a yo' own what it's like," Sarah said. "That Bean, he don't belong to me. I can't say who he was meant for."

They took the boy back home, dripping, to shiver in his bed.

WARTIME

===

1861

Varina never did bleed. Varina had been their pacer for all those years, the girl and then the woman by whom they, her black servants, might set the clocks of their own bodies, for they had no better way of knowing their own age besides looking and guessing at their reflections in the glass they were scrubbing or in the water pails they were fetching. Then all at once Varina, who was always first, fell behind, came up dry.

Sarah bled, and then Beulah that same spring that they counted as their thirteenth year. Then Rue bled in the rainy season, the last of a crop of girls turned to women in the course of one evening, now elevated in value by the promise of their multitudes.

Varina came to Miss May Belle's cabin each time she heard that one of the black girls had become a woman. She pestered, sniffed it out of them, like a beast for the blood, and when she caught the scent she'd come knocking at Miss May Belle's door.

"Girl, ain't nothin' wrong with you," Miss May Belle would say. "It'll happen when it has cause to happen."

It was Rue that set Varina on wanting to bleed. They were where they should not have been, up in the lofted gallery of the little church, which, every Sunday, creaked and buckled under the weight of the black congregation. It seemed so much smaller, Rue realized, absent of that press of bodies. Rue and Varina lay together on their backs, the way they might've in their field. Outside the sky flashed and rocked with thunder and lightning, working itself up to a downpour.

The little church was much farther down the path outside the plantation than either of them had the right to go, but Varina had urged them one step farther and one step farther still.

"If we come across someone I'll say you mine." Varina had it all figured. "I'll tell 'em I brought you out here to give you some religion." But they did not meet anyone as they picked their way east through the wood and there was no religion to be found in the building—only below them the simple pulpit and the empty pews, important to no one on a black-cloud afternoon, for the minister lived in the next county, which was by horse hooves still a day's trip.

Still, Varina said it was better to stay hidden in the church's second story than to be caught out by the pews should anyone wander in. But they had trouble lying still on the wood floor, and Rue felt that they were only doing a gimcrack imitation of their younger selves, those carefree children who could lay about, mindless and gathering grass stains.

The passing of time was most obvious in Varina, whose round, full face had grown pointed, whose freckles had faded altogether. In Rue's memory was Varina as she'd always been, fat and thumbsucking, defiant in a calico dress bearing patterned flowers. Now Varina was growing round-chested, requiring new sets of lacy frocks and fresh fine-boned corsets seemingly every fortnight.

Rue had hardly grown. She still wore an apron of her mama's, so long it had to be hemmed. But beneath her thin, easy muslin skirt she had a secret.

"Touch here," she said, and she guided Varina's hand to her

waist and moved her fingers for her as though they were her own, letting Varina feel the smooth round shape of each bead on the ribbon hid beneath the rough fabric.

"Show me," Varina demanded.

It didn't feel as easy now to show Varina her body as it had been when they were young, back when the only real obvious difference between them was the light and dark of their skin.

On the roof, the first fat raindrops fell and sounded like knocking. Finally, Rue untied her apron, pulled up her skirt.

The beads fit close to her skin just as her mama had tied them the night prior, a pattern of red and orange and brown stones that reminded her of the earth lit up by the sun. The string of beads crossed under her belly button like a horizon. They *clicked* quietly when she moved; she'd heard that *clicking* all day.

Varina was just as drawn to the beads as she was to the red strip of fabric they held up. The strip disappeared beneath Rue's white skirt, secure between her legs. Rue tucked the skirt back into place before Varina could be bold enough to follow the bit of red fabric with her creeping, greedy fingers.

"What is that?" Varina could make even a question sound like a commandment.

"My mama gave it to me. Last night I bled."

Varina's eyes rounded. "Why?"

"What you mean, why?"

Before then it had not occurred to Rue that Varina didn't know about blood the way she did. She herself could not remember the first time she'd understood that being a woman meant being bloodied, but then she could not remember the first word she spoke, or the first time she knew herself for herself—some knowing just felt like it had always been.

"Ain't yo' mama tell you 'bout it?" Rue knew it for a foolish question as soon as it left her lips. Varina's mama, who folks knew

to be as brash-mouthed as a clarion in the keeping of her house-hold, was as mute as a fish when it came to her only trueborn child, as though the girl was nothing more than a spare room that a housemaid sometimes neglected to dust. The rearing of Varina fell most to Ma Doe, who could command the girl in schooling and dress, but lately was losing her authority in even that. But in the manners of a white woman and the matters of her body? Rue imagined Ma Doe—who easily was the most proper woman she'd ever known, slave or not—making up Varina's bed each morning, relieved to find those soft white sheets unstained another day.

It took Rue what felt like hours to set the girl right. Varina's ideas were all muddled. She supposed that the bleeding hap-pened only when the woman went to relieve herself. She sup-posed it was an unusual, unending affliction. She supposed there was shame in it.

"It's natural, my mama said," Rue explained. "There's no shame. It's beautiful. That's why my mama made me the beads to hold up the cloth."

Miss May Belle didn't believe in shame, or so she'd tell anyone who'd stop long enough to listen.

"What's the use for it?" she'd often say.

Rue knew it was no good to be ashamed when she'd had to wake her mama in the middle of the night. She knew she had to look brave holding out the front of her white sleeping gown, point-ing out the bloodstain she'd left there long enough that it had dried to brown. But she was scared. "Look, Mama."

Her mama stirred from her sleep. There was no surprise in her when she saw the blood, and Rue was used to that. Miss May Belle smiled. She knew girls and women before they even knew them-selves. Her mama crouched down beneath the bed frame to a bas-

ket of spare things she kept there: bits of fabric, tore-up trinkets, and dried posies of no particular use but to be pretty to look at. She pulled the length of beads out inch by inch, like a garden snake. She wrapped the beads around her neck to free her hands 'til she worked the end out at last.

"Do you hurt, baby?"

Rue shook her head. She couldn't feel a thing but a warm damp. It was like a new-sprung well. A thing happening without her say-so.

"Sometimes you will and sometimes you won't," her mama explained. Rue knew this already. There were folks who suffered with it, she knew, women who came to them once a month or more, wanting something to fight away their aches.

Rue had seen Miss May Belle take care of women her whole life, had done so at her side, at her command. But now, bound by the papery warm feel of her mama's work-roughened fingers, she felt something she had not known she had wanted so badly.

"These beads is special." Miss May Belle held out the belt to its full length, the whole stretch of her arms. The red rag hung in the middle like the flag of some proud country. She shook the string so that the beads *click-clacked* together loudly. "Iff'n you ever forget yo'self, let that sound be what reminds you."

She drew the beads up along Rue's body with her hands splayed, and Rue felt the thrilling spin of them all the way up her hips. Her mama pulled the ends of the string tidy so they'd lay flat beneath even something as flimsy as her nightdress.

"A man come and bother you, he can make you a mama. Now that's a good thing sometimes and a bad thing another. Depends."

Rue knew this too. She had seen new mamas collapse in their crying, brought down by all manner of tears, overjoyed or sorrowed.

Miss May Belle laid a palm on the flat of Rue's belly. "When the beads start to pull too tight, well that'll be one of yo' first signs that somethin's changin'."

Then Miss May Belle did something Rue wasn't at all expecting, something she never did with the other women who came to see her with all their needs and all their wanting. She pulled Rue close and wrapped her arms around her, spoke quiet words with her lips in her hair.

"I'm proud a' you."

Rue did not know what she had done that deserved pride but anyway she was glad she had done it.

Outside the rain had soothed itself down to beat but a few half-hearted patterings on the roof of the church.

"We ought to get back 'fore they know we gone," Rue said.

Varina was quiet as they descended the church steps. She walked down slow, over-careful in her hoop skirt, and Rue coming down behind her was impatient. Outside, steam curled up from the ground drawn out from the heat. Already the sun was returning and Rue felt very tired thinking on the work her mama would surely have waiting for her.

"Make one for me." Varina's demand came out of nothing and nowhere. She ghosted her hand over Rue's hip, where she knew the beads were hidden.

"What you need it for? You ain't bleed yet."

"But when I do. I'll for certain need one when I do."

Irritation rose in Rue the same as the tendrils of mist that came up off the rainwater. She wanted then so suddenly to slap Varina it was like a sting she already felt in her palm. Varina had pearls and brooches, bows and combs; Rue could have no one thing of her own.

Varina made her separate way up the road to the House. Rue

watched her go, watched her skip round puddles and pockets of mud, her pale hand shading her pale face, her hair glowing like a beacon fire in the growing strands of sunlight. Rue watched Varina all the way until she disappeared into the House, and then she turned and walked home herself, her beads going *click-clack-click.*

In their cabin Miss May Belle was working nutmeg, grounding it down to a fine powder. It raised up in a spicy earth smell, Rue's favorite scent.

"Where you got to?" Miss May Belle didn't need to look up to ask it.

Rue watched her mama's elbow go up and down with her grinding, and she knew she was in some kind of trouble.

"Fetched the skullcap like you asked." Rue set down the basket of damp purple flowers and knew it for a meager offering.

"Now, wasn't that near an hour ago?" It wasn't a question.

Rue picked up the flowers from the basket one by one at the stems the same way she'd picked them from the thicket. She drew the dew off the leaves and tried to look busy doing it.

"You and that Varina, y'all got different lives to live," Miss May Belle said. It wasn't the first time she'd warned it, but Rue had to be impressed at the uncanny way her mama had of knowing what was what. "You listenin'?"

"Yes, Mama."

Rue bound the skullcap stems with twine and hung the bundled posy up by the window. There were a mess of other herbs up there, waiting with their bottoms up, their stems to the sky as they dried. Rue tiptoed and stretched and added her new pickings to the others, choosing a spot where they could get the full of the heat without getting the full of the sun. The skullcaps hung awkward. To Rue it looked as if their drooping violet heads were straining to stay upright.

"You got to obey her, fine, but you don't got to follow her," Miss May Belle said. Rue was uncertain of the distinction. She wished her mama would leave off the topic. A low twisting pain had started in her stomach, not a stabbing but an ache, and she knew she had to bear it. Miss May Belle of all people wouldn't have sympathy for woman pains.

Her mama passed her the ground-up nutmeg without a word, but Rue didn't need telling. In a large jar on the shelf was where they kept the mama's milk, an extra bit of help for mamas too thin or too sickly, too overworked or just not at all able to call up any milk of their own. Rue poured out a splash from the jar and stirred in the nutmeg before it could drink up all the milk. The trick of it was to add just the right amount, make a paste not a soup, and Rue had the knack for these kinds of mixings, better, she thought, than even her own mama had.

Still, Miss May Belle kept up her faultfinding. "You takin' too long with that. It ain't Sunday supper."

Rue was bleeding. She was tired. She was thirteen, thereabouts, and a woman, thereabouts. But all her mama wanted to talk about was how she ought to stay clear of Varina.

"You ain't," Miss May Belle finally said, "friends."

The ache in Rue's stomach grew to a spasm of pain. She set the bowl down suddenly on the table like she'd lost the strength even to stir. Rue heard Miss May Belle *click* her tongue at her, presumably in disapproval. It was that small noise, that lifelong *cluck* of her mama's correction, that sparked her ire. Rue drew back her hand and slapped the bowl from the table.

The mixture of mama's milk and soothing nutmeg splattered, sent a streak across the floor and dashed along the skirt of both of their dresses. The bowl clattered and spun so long it was almost comedy, before Miss May Belle raised her foot and stepped on it to clap the bowl down into silence. She stood there like that with the bowl underfoot, like a turtle subdued, its head and limbs pulled in in fear.

Rue wanted to run. She'd done a horrible thing, she could feel it in her stomach, a pooling of shame.

"Good," said Miss May Belle in a nasty bite. "Good, you go ahead an' get it all out, girl. But don't you go an' forget it. You not a child now, so you best hear it from me an' remember it well. You can sass all you want in here. But out there"—she pointed hard in the direction of the House—"you never say no more'n, 'Yes, Miss Varina.' You hear?"

"Yes, Mama."

Miss May Belle stepped over the bowl in coming closer, stepped through the mess of their ruined tincture. She took Rue hard by the shoulders, something desperate in her grasp.

"That girl ain't yo' friend."

The slap Miss May Belle gave Rue was hard, shocking. The pain of it resonated long after, tremulous on Rue's skin like the reverberation on a drum. But it was what Miss May Belle said that was slapped into Rue's memory and stung just the same, years after: "Varina ain't yo' friend. An' I ain't either."

Rue made Varina a belt. In rare moments of baby-less, mama-less, blessed quiet, Rue drove holes through pieces of nutmeg. She'd stolen the knitting needle, just the one, straight out of Ma Doe's basket on a hot afternoon when they'd both been tasked with watching Varina dance.

It was in a back room of the House, a forgotten parlor, disused and dust-ridden, and it was its emptiness that Varina had taken a liking to when she'd developed all sorts of peculiar wants and fancies shaped by the perceived tastes of other white girls. To Rue those girls were real as haints, which was to say not real at all, and she held ghostly impressions of these playmates of Varina's, with whom Miss Varina was sent to sometimes take luncheons, a mission for her propriety, endeavored with all the purposefulness of a war campaign.

Varina was all glory on those visiting days. With her frizzed hair brushed out to an obedient shine, she'd sit beside Red Jack as he drove her to her visits like a queen on her throne. Red Jack for sure was thrilled to have the permission and the pass to leave the plantation. He had a natural way with horses, something holy in the way he yelled "Hey now," that made him safe to drive the cart that bore the master's daughter. He had a natural way with a simpleton's smile that made him safe to come back with her by nightfall.

Varina would return from these visits with, as Miss May Belle would put it, "some fool idea rattling like beans in her empty head." The white girl would make herself half-sick with wanting until she got what some other white girl possessed or something better still.

Now Christmastime was coming on and the cool season and the good harvest and the bounty of babies was making everything languid and slow, and Varina had seen to it that her Christmas present came early, a book of dancing steps that she'd ordered, come all the way from the North. She'd spied an advertisement and sent away for it and some months later the thick tome was there, spread on Ma Doe's knee. Rue could only pick at certain letters but she liked well the drawings. They were mostly intricate footprints going this way and that, trailed by dashes to mark from where they'd come to where they had to go. The gentleman's footprints were always the larger, the lady's daintily following in his wake.

"You gotta be the man," Varina had said but Rue had already figured that. She was clumsy at it, trying to lead as the book suggested, but Varina, who squirmed in her arms, wouldn't let her do the leading, and all they had for music was Ma Doe reluctantly smacking the base of her chair with the heel of her shoe, and she wasn't very good at that neither.

"No, no, no, it's all of it wrong." Varina stopped Rue right in the midst of a turn. She tugged at her curls, let them spring back to her head to mark her agony.

"Now, Miss Varina," Ma Doe petted, "you needn't learn all this foolishness to be well-liked. You have any number of fine virtues. You'd do well to remember that."

It was on Christmas Day that Varina remembered her finest virtue, and that was her wiliness. She knocked on their cabin door just after supper and grinned up at Miss May Belle.

"Fannie's took ill at the house. She's needing someone to nurse her."

Miss May Belle was not a fool. She squinted down at the white girl.

"And they sent you all the way down here, Miss?"

Varina grinned demurely. "I volunteered."

"Then I'll be up presently."

"Oh, you needn't trouble, Belle. Rue'll do just fine." Varina leaned in conspiratorially. "I suspect it's only a block of the bowels that's botherin' Fannie. Mother quite spoils her with sweets."

Rue came out sleepily, armed with a sloshing gourd of palma christi oil to soothe Fannie's complaint. She followed awhile in silence before Varina made an abrupt turn away from the House through a thin path in the woods.

"Dump that someplace." Varina waved away the oil.

"Where we goin'?"

Rue kept the gourd hugged close to her. They stepped through uneven craggy ground, over bent weeds and barren land. They walked for some time, Varina just ahead, Rue struggling behind.

"What about Fannie's bowels?"

"Don't be foolish, Rue. Ain't nothin' the matter with Fannie's bowels. Come on now, keep up."

Where they were going there was music. It snaked out at them through the trees a little at a time 'til Rue could put it together whole as a song, and closer, as someone picking a banjo, and closer, as folks keeping time with their foot stomping. Closer too there were the words, easy to pick up in their repetition, saying, "I got a right, y'all got a right, I got a right to the Tree of Life."

Red Jack had guard of the place. He was crouched atop a log like a frog, his hands hanging between his legs, and he shook his head at Varina like he'd been expecting her and was disappointed to see her all the same. Still, he gave them leave to pass. Inside the singing grew forceful. "You may hinder me here but you cannot hinder me there. God in heaven's gon' answer my prayer."

Varina and Rue came up to the weathered cabin, stood at either side of the doorway, and listened. They said nothing but watched each other's faces in the flicker of warm light leaking out. Varina smiled her thumb-worn gap-toothed smile. "Let's join 'em."

Rue followed behind Varina. She thought that the silence that hit the inside of the little cabin was for her, but of course not; it was for the white girl who'd entered, for the master's daughter, and it wasn't a whole silence at all but a hiccup, a dampening not of the sound but of the exuberance, of the joy. Black folks turned from what they were doing and faced them.

There was the seamstress Dinah, and Big and Li'l Sylvia both; there was Charlie Blacksmith and Ol' Joel, grinning toothless, with Opal and her sweet bottom sat on his lap. There was Fannie even, who should have been asleep at her mistresses' feet or else straining in some outbuilding somewhere else. Anna's daddy twanged at the banjo and Sarah sang prettily but loudest, and beyond that was folks from Marse John's plantation, and Coffey and Homer and Mary John besides, and folks Rue could not name but whose drawn faces looked familiar. And beyond all of them was Rue's own daddy.

She caught eyes with him from across the room. He didn't say anything but shook his head the way Red Jack had shook his head when they'd arrived.

Rue's daddy was playing spoons, a trick she'd never known he had, and he did not stop playing when she stood dumbstruck in the doorway watching the metal flash in his hand like the anxious metallic heartbeat of the whole of them.

"S'alright," Varina said at last over the hushed music. "Y'all carry on. We not here to stop you."

Someone provided the white girl a stool, wiped off the dust from the seat, and bade her sit a spell. Rue settled in by Varina's feet, which tapped along feverishly with the music. Sarah was singing again, joined in a lilting harmony by others.

Red Jack came in next, trading his post with one of the other young fine-armed boys. They didn't need to speak to swap the sentinel but passed a jug of something swishing clear between their two hands. Red Jack leaned his head back and drank and then passed the bottle to Ol' Joel, who thanked him with a wink of one of his clouded eyes. He released Opal, giving her three rhythmic taps on her bottom along to the music, which was fine with her. She swished her way over to the center of the cabin floor where the dancing was.

"We shouldn't be here," Rue said.

Varina said, "Huh," and continued her foot tapping.

Across the room, Rue's own daddy rested down his spoons. He took up the floor to where they danced a breakdown, their legs sawing to the beat like it was a job of work. Their whoops of laughter started out for Varina's benefit, but surely they grew genuine as the beat deepened. Rue felt it too—there was no earthly way to deny a good beat.

Marse Charles did not altogether frown at his slaves dancing. He'd been known, especially at Christmastimes, or after a particularly bountiful harvest, to encourage it, to bring certain visiting guests of his to look upon the boundless happiness of his slaves, to even clap with them if he felt so moved by their native kind of frivolity. But it seemed different when he wasn't there looking on. Like as if their amusement, for its own sake, was a waste. Now Varina clapped like her daddy might have clapped as the dance floor grew crowded.

Red Jack slid up to them. The close room was overwarm with so much activity, and a fine sheen of sweat was shining up his face. His eyes glittered too, and someone had passed him back the jug and this time the smell of whiskey wisped clear out when he swallowed. He smiled toothily and began to pass it back on down the line.

"Now wait." Miss Varina snaked out her arm and took the jug from him. He didn't resist, couldn't really. Varina took a dainty sip, grimaced, but tipped back some more. "Go on," she said and held it out to Rue.

Rue still held in her lap her bottle of unneeded castor oil and she hugged at it with one arm while she reached out for the proffered jug. Varina would not hand it over but motioned that Rue should tip back her head. Now Rue did so and Varina spilled into her a burning mouthful. Rue's tongue floated, her lips burned. A trickle escaped down her cheek as she swallowed thickly. Varina returned the jug to Red Jack, and between them they seemed to share an easy amusement that made Rue's stomach roil.

"Take a turn, Rue." Varina didn't take her eyes off Red Jack. "Rue's the finest dancer."

Red Jack raised his brows, feigning at being impressed. "That so?"

"Show him." At Varina's urgings Rue got to her feet, feeling the slosh of the whiskey and the slide of the earth as she did so.

Red Jack led her out with the briefest tap on the small of her back. The music was already at its swell and, bidding her to watch him, Red Jack strutted to the foot-stomping rhythm that was taking up the whole of the cabin. Feeling loose, she rocked with him, then bent her knees and hopped from foot to foot as he did. Their arms wheeled in large, free circles in the air like they might any minute take off into flight. They caught elbows and spun past each other, not certain where they'd end up.

Rue laughed breathlessly as Red Jack aimed to outdo her with his own enthusiasm, throwing back his elbows, launching himself forward in wild skillful imitation of a hot-footing chicken. Rue found herself clapping, dancing in improvised whirls 'til she couldn't draw a blessed bit of breath and had to break free of Red Jack and sit herself back down. She fanned herself at Varina's feet and caught her daddy smiling at her from his own side of the dance floor.

"Really such fun." Varina clapped gaily but she didn't seem to mean it. She kept her eyes on Red Jack pivoting and twirling in the midst of all the others, light as air, his two feet gifted with springs on the bottoms.

"We best get back before you missed, Miss Varina," Rue said.

Varina got reluctantly to her feet, made her way around the dancing to the door. "G'night, Miss Varina," folks were saying with ingratiating smiles stretching their faces, and they looked more than glad to see the back of her as Varina and Rue went out into the night. "An' Merry Christmas."

Full-on dark seemed to have taken over the evening. Rue could have cussed with the trouble they'd be in if anyone noted that Varina'd been gone so long.

"Oh, Jack."

Rue jumped. She hadn't known Red Jack had followed but there he was, slinking behind them. "Mightn't you escort us back?"

The boy could not be so foolish as to keep getting close to this girl so near to being a woman, and a white woman at that. Rue answered for him. "We be alright. We know the way."

Red Jack echoed her. "You be alright, Miss Varina. It ain't so far."

"Yes, if you say so," Varina said. "G'night then."

"A Happy Christmas to ya."

"And say g'night to your sweetheart."

Rue balked. Whose sweetheart?

"G'night, Rue," he obeyed.

"It's alright," Varina said. She bared her teeth. "You may kiss Rue if you like. I won't tell."

Red Jack leaned in. Rue didn't know whether she could pull away. In her face his whiskey breath was a visceral thing; it had manifested itself in the cold night air and clung between them, as good a barrier as any cloud was, 'til Red Jack got up his courage and kissed Rue through it, leading, lizard-like, with his tongue. When he pulled back, it was not to check on Rue's pleasure but on Varina's.

"Good night," their mistress said again. "And a very Merry Christmas."

Rue's lips felt wetter for the cold. She wondered then if Red Jack was so dull after all, or if he'd just devised a way early on to seem to dance to the white folks' tempo.

Varina and Rue walked side by side back to the House. Rue aimed to put the kiss far from her mind, found she was thinking instead of her daddy and the easy way he'd rattled those spoons.

"Have you ever kissed anybody before, Rue?"

"No'm." She hadn't and had never found that she'd particularly wanted to.

"I have," Varina said, dreamily.

Rue reckoned she ought to ask who but she wasn't sure she really wanted to know the answer. They were coming up onto the House, preparing to part ways.

Ahead of them came the noise of crunching footsteps on frost-hardened grass.

Illuminated by the lantern she carried, Miss May Belle was coming around the corner like a bad omen borne of light. The shadows that skittered across her face told of her displeasure better than the frown on her lips or the hardness of her words ever could. The lantern in and of itself was a bad sign. It came from the House, a place Miss May Belle never had cause to go except in the case of some unusual trouble.

"She been callin' for you, Miss Varina," Miss May Belle said. Varina stopped just behind Rue as if knowing she'd be in need of a shield. Their shoulders overlapped. Rue could feel Varina's body shiver.

"Who is?"

"Missus took ill in the night. Ain't you heard?" Miss May Belle knew full well they hadn't heard. She must've been smelling the corn whiskey on them heated up by their sweat. Rue, self-conscious, wiped at her lips, fearful they were glistening still.

"What's the matter with Mother?" Varina sounded troubled.

"Can't say. But they done called for the county doctor. They say he on his way." That was a journey of miles.

"Why won't you help her?" Varina stomped her foot same as she had when she was a child, a child still in so many ways.

"It ain't won't, Miss Varina." Miss May Belle held higher her head and her lamp. "It's can't. She won't 'llow me or anyone else to see her. Cusses and spits and foams when we get near. But she been askin' fo' you."

"For me?" said Varina. "What can I do?"

"Set with her, I s'pose. Just be with her."

Varina paled. She did not argue but followed last in line behind Miss May Belle and Rue as they hurried to the House, came out into the clearing together, purposeful, like nocturnal creatures starting their day. Varina went up to the porch. The lanterns were all lit in the windows, despite the late hour, further signaling that all was amiss. Only in the circle of their light could Rue see that it had begun to snow, white bits of nothing-ice were hanging in the air, melting before they ever hit the ground. From the depths of the House there came a high, sharp woman scream. Rue already knew death by the turn of a scream the way she knew when babies were hungry or wanting to be held by the turn of their cry. She thought, the white doctor won't come in time.

In the doorway Varina stalled at the sound her mama was making. Miss May Belle nodded her on, and the girl disappeared all the way in.

Now alone with her own mama, Rue feared a scolding but all Miss May Belle said was, "Ain't nothin' we can do here now. Best we get us some rest. Long days ahead."

Her mama reached out to her then and put her palm on Rue's cheek, a gesture that felt loving. Rue smiled, and her mama looked in her eyes. Miss May Belle licked the end of her thumb, and Rue saw there the sparkle of a silver ring that she had never seen before. It belonged to Missus. Or used to. Miss May Belle wiped the wet thumb across Rue's cheek, cleaning away something only a mama could see.

"Ain't nothin we can do," she said.

———

Missus's funeral fell in the cradle between Christmas and New Year. She'd put it in her will that her slaves ought not to mourn too heavily for her and should not be expected to cease in their work at all. Bless her heart, the black folks said, for even in death she could give them the gift of toil. They did not have the day off to attend her burial, and those of the House were put to work double, preparing for the elaborate stages of weighty mourning, black ribbons and black crepe veils, black door pulls and flowers blackened for wreaths. Black makes you blameless, folks said, makes death look the other way when it's deciding on who to chomp at next.

They'd all know the moment she was put into the ground when they'd hear the church bells ringing out her years.

"Forty?" Red Jack had asked, wide-eyed.

"Yea, forty," Ma Doe had told him, exasperated, and then she'd had to call on Rue, who wasn't strong enough to pull on the bell's thick cord to set it ringing—but she was good at keeping count. Rue had never had cause for reading, but she'd learned her figures, had to learn them well when keeping labor time for the mamas.

Rue and Red Jack crawled up in the church bell tower like thieving mice, unseen by the mourners just then pouring out from the lower levels behind the fine, heavy coffin. Red Jack was fast and agile with his climbing. Rue was slow and clumsy and had to be helped up the last few rungs. She brushed away his helping hands when she got to the top and tucked herself in the farthest corner from him.

From above they could see clearly the white mourners retreat up to the graveyard, trailing behind the coffin like black ants bearing a prize back to their hill. Rue was nervous. If they timed the bells wrong they'd surely be whupped. You didn't get between folks and their mourning. She told Red Jack as much, but he just shrugged.

"I been whupped before," he said, which was surely true and maybe explained why he was so damned slow. He seemed excited by the pull cord for the heavy brass bell. He kept running his hands over the knots in anticipation.

"Why'd you do what you done on Christmas night?" she asked. She'd never quite shook off the taste of that whiskey kiss. For days after it had come to her, swirled into her nose like it was fresh, a kiss just laid.

Red Jack shrugged again. Rue hoped his head would fall plum off with the movement. "Miss Varina said to, ain't she?"

"That all?" Rue didn't want her voice to give out or to give away her true feelings. He'd only been obeying Varina.

"Sure, I thought it might be nice to kiss you." He let go of the cord. Crossed over to her, hopping the dangerous place where the floor of the tower was opened for the ladder.

"You alright, Rue," he said. "When you ain't frownin' at every damned thing."

He kissed her again. She tried to decide if she liked it at all. It was warm and strange. Her teeth got in the way.

She let his lips go. The mourners were all on the hill.

"One," she said and Red Jack leaped back to his position and began to toll. "Two," she said.

Forty years resounded off the corpse bell loud enough to give Rue a headache. She watched Red Jack, who partway through the counting had felt it necessary to undo his shirt. His back muscles worked as he pulled, and when he was done he used his bundled shirt to wipe the sweat from his brow and then from each tuft in the red-brown coils of hair in his armpits.

"Forty," Rue said and then, "Don't never kiss me again. Iff'n you do I'll put a goopher on you, fix it so yo' lips turn black-blue and fall right off one night in yo' sleep."

Red Jack let her precede him down the ladder and through the

empty church where the bell's last echoes still pealed. He held
the double doors open for her and let her leave before him down
the way.

He said, "Uh, thank you, Rue. For the countin'," and he didn't
say one more word to her for years after that but hello and goodbye
and ain't the weather fine.

The belt for Varina was done. It clicked nutmeg shells when Rue
gave it over to her. Still swathed deep black in heavy mourning,
Varina looked pale and suspect but she took it anyway.

"I ain't yet bled, Rue," she said. She held the belt with its dark
seeds and bright red ribbon around the tapered black waist of her
mourning gown.

"I know, but I wanted to give you somethin'. Figure you still a
woman bein' that you turnin' fourteen years."

There were no invitations, no letters to mark the occasion of
this birthday. Varina, who had so longed for visitors, could receive
none, then, or for a full year after her mama's death. In that season
there was only brittle frost on trees and crepe black sheets over
mirrors in the parlor, crippling Varina's vanity. The white doctor
had come too late and said after that it was the flu that took Missus.
They'd sealed up her room right off just as tight as if it were the
tomb in which she'd been interred. Afterward, the house girls gossiped, said Varina sometimes walked the hallways at night to stand
in front of the door like she was still waiting on her mama to summon her in.

Marse Charles wore his grief as a tight black armband and nothing more. Folks said all his widower thoughts were of expansion.
The whispers of the war coming to their doorstep might've had
others making themselves smaller, less vulnerable to change, but
that was not Marse Charles's way, never had been. He was wanting
more, another acre, another wife. He'd had made a mourning

locket for Varina, woven gold from her mama's brown hair, and Rue was yet to see her wear it.

Now Varina pulled back her skirts and her petticoats, which had been all hemmed black lest anyone spy her underthings and think her lost-mama grief was not full. She held her skirts close to her skin. Beneath the flurry of fabric Rue helped her secure the belt above her small freckled hips. The bloom of color looked like a scandal and Varina laughed in giddy delight, despite her mourning, as she smoothed down the many layers of black.

THE RAVAGING

===

"Now, Sister Rue, in Jesus's name," Bruh Abel said, "renounce the Devil."

Rue's redemption, when it came, didn't feel the way she thought it might. She hadn't pictured the way that folks wouldn't look at her. They stared. They stared so hard she felt she could hear it, like a low contemptuous buzz, but when she picked out eyes from among the crowd at the river, they shifted and skittered away. They thought Bruh Abel safe to look at, it seemed—when they caught his eye, they smiled.

Rue pictured Bean, hoped thinking on him would give her strength. Bean was likely home with Jonah still boiling up with a fever, not made by nature or the displeasure of God but out of her own benevolence. She would not be ashamed of that, whatever this day brought.

Ma Doe was absent from the crowd also, though Rue hadn't truly thought the old woman would be there. Sarah had come, bringing only her eldest boy, not Bean, with her. The boy stood between his mama's legs and twisted his face into her skirts when Rue passed by, like he was scared of her, she who he had known his whole little life, she who had twisted his head and tugged him out on the end of Sarah's meager, singing thrust. There were only a handful of other children there. Most were still weakened, she knew, from the sickness she was said to have cursed them with.

As she made the long, slow walk toward Bruh Abel, he looked at her with a certainty. He strutted forward, and the crowd parted for him as he approached Rue head-on.

"Renounce the Devil," he said again.

"I do," she said loud. Murmurs shivered up from the crowd. "I wish him gone. I do."

Bruh Abel put his hand heavy on her head, as though it were an effort to do so, and he pushed her down, down, down 'til her knees and her legs and her hands were all in the dirt. Still she kept her eyes turned up to him.

"You only need tell him, 'Leave me.'"

"Leave me," she repeated.

"Louder."

"Leave me." Her voice cracked. "Leave."

"Louder for all to hear, Sister Rue."

She felt a monstrous sorrow rise up in her like a swell. She looked away from Bruh Abel, down at her hands spread out in the dirt, and she began to sob. Tears dripped clean from her face to darken the ground beneath her in fat circles that made strange patterns as they wetted the dirt—looked like stars set out on a sky below, and all the while she ground out the words, "Leave me."

The ground shook when folks started up their foot stomping to the rhythm of Bruh Abel's words raining down: "Cast off your wicked ways. Don't let them demons have no more hold on you."

She wanted it, salvation, not in the sense she'd always known—as a promise of hereafter eternity. Instead, she wanted salvation in the here and the now, for herself and for Bean, or a glimpse of it at least, a place she might feel safe and rest her head at last. Bruh Abel was beside her, his warm hand on her face.

"Out. Anything not of You," he said, "out."

In the far-off distance she felt her throat constrict and release and cry out. Her tongue flickered out words of no clear form, desperate sounds articulating something kin to wanting, kin to ravening. She seemed able to observe her own body in its flawed entirety from afar.

Then all at once the euphoria left her—a sudden depletion, like the moment after a passing gust of wind when still air seems strange and inexplicable. Someone lifted her at her armpits and set her on her feet. She swayed but stayed standing.

"Was it the spirit a' Jesus what come to you?"

"Yes," she said. "The Holy Ghost entered me."

All around her people were staring and murmuring, holding out their hands to touch her. She turned to Bruh Abel, who was now some distance away from her, though he hadn't moved at all. It was the crowd that had rushed in. Over their heads he was puzzling her out again, a slow eyeing from top to bottom and back up.

"Tongues is a sign for unbelievers." If he was speaking for the crowd or just for her she couldn't figure, but either way it sounded like something he'd snatched whole cloth from some other preacher's mouth. "Prophecy is for believers."

"In Jesus's name," she mumbled. That was what folks kept saying, wasn't it?

"What He say, Miss Rue?"

"He say, I be His. I be healed."

After, Rue took herself over to the old church. She walked the long way to be certain she was not followed, stood outside in the well-trod path, that rut made over time from years on top of years of folks going back and forth in search of worship. For Rue, faith had always flickered in and out of her consciousness like a flame on a candlewick, sometimes resilient against wind, other times extinguished easy in a sibilant hiss. She could not account for what she had felt that afternoon in the town center, any more than she could account for why Bean hadn't caught the ailing naturally while others had.

After the walk of several miles Rue was glad to push through the double doors and shut them tight behind her. The air was heavy with dancing dust motes like loosed cotton bolls. Rue sat herself down in the front row of the church where she had not been allowed to sit. It still felt wrong, after all those years, to break the white man's nonsense rules. Up above, the floorboards creaked.

"You listenin'?" she asked, staring straight at the pulpit. If anyone else were to come across her they would have thought she was arguing with God. Either way there was no answer.

"Varina," Rue called out, and her voice bounced through the vaulted ceiling and seemed to return to her tenfold.

There, a groan of wood, and summoned, Varina came out of her hiding place, behind the rectory door. She looked wan, skeletal.

"You didn't come back," Varina said.

Rue sighed. "I'm sorry, Miss Varina."

"You ought not leave me for so long." Her voice came at a warble, and Rue looked at her proper and saw fear there. "You really ought not leave me."

"Ain't I always come back?" It was like speaking to a child, but that's just what Varina looked like now, one startled from a nightmare, looking for any comfort. But there was only Rue to give it to her, and it was the threadbare sort. Varina had been raised to have a hundred black souls at her call. Rue alone must have felt like a pathetic disservice.

"That white man you came in here with. Was he a soldier?"

So Varina had seen. "Bruh Abel? He weren't white. He's colored, Miss Varina. Just real pale."

Varina rocked on the heels of her bare feet like she wished to run but had no place to go. Rue hadn't seen her mistress so agitated in an age, not since the early months of her hiding. Then Varina had prowled the rectory, fitful and crying, or euphoric in turns, and there had been only the one way to soothe her then, one awful way. Rue had made the white doctor's medicine last as long as she could. It was all she'd thought to grab from the house before it burned, a small supply, and she mixed it with wine or thinned it with water to ration it and still Varina had screamed in her agony that she was dying.

Those draughts of laudanum had run dry finally and Rue could not get hold of more. She had broke Varina of the awful addiction the long, hard way, like breaking down a wild stallion by receiving a hundred kicks to the face. The hundred and first time Varina came away clean; the only stain the poppy had left on her were the dreams. The nightmares.

"I can't sleep, Rue," Varina said now, recalling an old complaint. "I see the soldiers comin' for me."

"Ain't I say I'd keep you safe, Miss Varina?"

But her mistress seemed not to hear her, was trapped in a danger of her own imagining, and in her mind that danger was still marching toward her, as it had been three years past. Rue let her keep her nightmares. Let her think they were still real.

"When will this goddamn war be at an end?" Varina moaned.

"By God's grace, any day now."

Rue held her body still when she heard the knock at her cabin door, though she'd heard so many knocks before and more urgent ones to be sure. This one, if she could presume so much from simple knocking, sounded resigned. Rue took her time crossing the small room and opening the door. Took her time in saying, "Sarah. What's the trouble?" because she knew what the trouble was.

Sarah was weary-looking, likely from taking care of her family in the way all the women in town had grown tired on their kin-folks' behalf. If there was a sickness in the town, every woman was made weak by it, whether she had the symptoms or not. Worrying was a disease for women, and it came as a chronic ailment. By the time Rue opened the door to her, Sarah had rested her arm up on the doorway, her head cradled weak on her forearm.

"Bean," she said, lifting her eyes but not her head. "He's sicker now."

They walked in the same purposeful stride, matching their steps unconsciously, side by side. Rue had the sense they were in some kind of race where the winner had to be the first to arrive and the last to lose their composure.

The night long ago that Bean's strange crying had come to her bloomed in Rue's mind. She recollected how the sound, the pecu-liarity of it, had yanked her from a sleep with no dreams. Rue had forgotten the exact quality of the sound. She could recall only how horrifying it was, how it had set Bean apart before this trouble had even begun. She could recall only wanting to keep him quiet, like the cry would speak something she didn't want heard.

Rue let Sarah lead her inside. Jonah was there, sitting on the floor of the front room with the little girl in his lap, the little boy around his shoulders. They looked healthy, and Rue was glad to see it. They played on him like he was a tree, and Jonah was just as immobile as one, to be sure. He watched her cross the room behind Sarah, not saying a thing, and all that silence led Rue to believe that something had passed between them, some sort of dispute. He'd been the loser, Rue figured, and then Sarah had come to find her.

Rue knew what to expect from Bean, but she was still shocked to see it. The froth and fever, when she'd sought out the right mix-ture to fix the symptoms, had sounded in her head as ordinary. To her, sickness—death and birth—did have the habit of growing ordinary over the seasons, until one case cropped up to shock her. And this was it and, worse, it was of her own making.

Bean's breathing came in wet shards, a wretched sound like someone drowning. He was not fighting but lying still, as if weighted down by something only he could make sense of. He locked eyes with it, this oppression in the air, and did not stop staring it down, even when Rue and Sarah drew near.

Rue rested her palm on his forehead. She felt exactly what she knew she'd feel. Fire. She couldn't keep up the pretense long and drew her hand away, hid it in the apron of her dress as though it had been branded to tell of her guilt.

Rue slipped from the room. There was only so much she could do, and she'd done too much already.

In the outer room she found Jonah risen from the floor. He'd put the children in a rocking chair in the corner. They huddled together in the seat, fighting a doze and losing.

She could sense his distrust from across the room, as thick as though it were a thing he could hold in his hand. A stone to throw. Jonah did not like her looking at his children. Rue looked dead at him, feeling suddenly bold. *I am still your witch*, she was about to say. *So you best be scared of me.*

Rue opened her mouth to speak, to cuss, but it was Sarah's wailing that came, mournful and absolute from the other room. Rue rushed back, but Jonah was quicker, and she followed after him as close as she dared. He stopped himself in the doorframe with his hands braced against each wall. Rue had to slip beneath his arms to get past him. She near had to climb over Sarah crouched at the foot of the bed. Bean's strange eyes, Rue saw, had shut.

"What's the matter?" Jonah was asking. His voice was urgent and aggressive, like he was ready to fight with the truth if it came to it.

Rue put her hand to Bean's mouth and felt no breath. She put her hand to his neck and felt no rushing blood. She put her head to his chest, hoping, hoping to hear a distant pounding there, but there was nothing to hear and no way to hear it besides. All Rue could hear was the sound she knew well, Sarah's howl, the desperate sorrow of a mama who already knows.

Still, it fell to Rue to pronounce it like it always did. Like it always would. "Bean," she said. "He dead."

WARTIME

—

There is a new fox in the wood. Miss May Belle jokes that she's gonna go out and skin it, wear it for a coat when the season gets chill.

It's a woman. Ma Doe says the right word for a woman fox is a *vixen*. It's brown and bold, been seen prowling round the House like it thinks it belongs there, pawing at the front door trying to get an invitation in.

Miss May Belle got herself a new ring that don't belong to her, come off a bigger hand, it only fits on her thumb. Word is it used to belong to Missus, who isn't even yet cold in the ground. Did Miss May Belle thieve it? Did Marse Charles gift it?

Lord, but that Miss May Belle is uppity.

Who can say—except that a thief would never be so proud. The only time Miss May Belle's seen to take off that ring is when she's birthing. Says it's bad luck, she does.

The fox prowls. Missus's grave chills. The South divorces the North, wanting its freedom.

Mary John, the kitchen girl, her new baby comes too early, comes out feetfirst, comes out still. Makes sense, the world turned upside down the way it is. Miss May Belle and Rue see to Mary John, who's burning up, sparked with the birthbed fever.

Heard Marse Charles is looking for a new wife, a third. If you listen hard in the wood you can hear them two foxes fighting, the old one and the new, two vixens baring teeth, going at each other's throats. That's how all women are, Miss May Belle says. Territorial. Soon the woods will be flooded with foxes, before the coming war is done. Those foxes won't let black folks alone. They'll run in packs. An *earth of foxes*, that's what that's called.

Marse Charles's sons look mighty fine in them tintypes sent home. Proud with their new uniforms: epaulets, scabbard and sword, gleaming new buckles, yet untouched by dust or dirt or by blood. The House flies a proud new battle flag. They're calling it the *Stainless Banner.*

Miss May Belle finally oversteps herself. She asks for too much. Soap and candles in war times? That's one thing. Now she's begging after medicine for Mary John. Real medicine. What comes in glass vials. The birthbed fever burns, inferno.

Miss May Belle begs. Says she'll do anything. *Anything.* She pleads after Mary John's life. Marse Charles says, "What, now you niggers too good for grass?"

Varina's needing a husband. She ain't never bled yet. She's the missus now her mama's gone. The tousling foxes sound like women screaming through the night. Screaming 'cause their sons are returned to them dead, if they're lucky, or else not returned at all, left wounded and trampled on and ground up in some Northern dirt. Morning come, there's blood in the grass. Blame them foxes. The South renames their flag the *Bloodstained Banner.* Whose blood? Red-backed and blue-crossed, stars along the middle, corner to corner for every Southern state that says hell no.

Marse Charles said no, but Miss May Belle's got ahold of the medicine some other way. Mary John comes back to life like the last few mighty embers of a fire you think been full stomped out. She'll live to love lots more babies.

Now, what is that screaming? Ain't no fox. Out of the door and into the night. In the square and Marse Charles got Miss May Belle by the hair of her head. He's saying how dare you? How dare you disobey me? His strong white fist is squeezing out her curls like to make them straight. He's dragging her out and into the night, and as he goes her body spins on the end of his fist, on the twirl of her hair, over the rocks and mud and grass. She's fighting hard, yelling words that ain't even words no more. Maybe she learned them things from her African mama. Savage promises of violence. Her face is bloodied, red on her like tears.

Lord Jesus.

When Marse Charles gets tired of dragging, he throws her over his shoulder like a sack of grain. They go clear out of the plantation. It's a bleach-white moon-filled night. You can see where he's taking her to. Right off in the distance, the church looms.

Where's her girl? That Rue. Found her hid under the bed. Yes, it was Rue, not the fox, doing the screaming.

White folks planning for themselves a jubilee. Let the shooting stop for a while. Let the sons come home. Let the fox go shrill in the field. Why doesn't Marse Charles just go out and kill those foxes? Folks says he hasn't got the heart. When mourning for Missus is done in three months' time, Marse Charles says, we'll have ourselves a fete.

Three days now Miss May Belle's gone. That jail beneath the white folks' church? You ever seen it? You ever been sent to it? That's where he's locked her up, ain't it? There beneath the ground. On the inside it's five steps this way and five steps that way. No sun, no moon. All dark. All black. They say the water seeps up, down there, when the river swells. Water how high? Not high enough as you'd be hoping, by day three. Not high enough to drown you or them rats neither.

Ain't no one deserve that. Not for trying to save a dying mama's life. Not even Miss May Belle.

Do you think Miss May Belle killed Missus? Killed the first wife too? Conjuring them into foxes to haunt them woods?

Marse Charles let her out, finally. He let her keep his dead wife's ring. Miss May Belle come out from the jail afraid of the sky. North of here them Yankees win another battle. Ain't this war ever going to end? Miss May Belle come out afraid of the light.

Folks said, should we go and see to her? Nah, she'll be alright. She's a tough 'un, that Miss May Belle. Let them alone. Let her daughter see to her wounds. In the woods two foxes stay prowling.

e night,

ιug her,
ιold her
e pray?"
mess of
ugh that

ιoulders,
"Be with
must sor-

ked away

ς her own
ur instru-

ke a razed
ι continu-
ls.

right," she

ιd she was
like petals
vere sold.
ggle to say

down. Ma
ιead and it
o suck her

syrup slow motion of a dream,
r mouth thick and strange. She
repeated them, and even when
ill they did not feel like sense:

place to end up, but Rue came
standing in front of it. She shied
ng chair and brought her knees
nd tried to think of Bean. Bean
be. Now she'd have to see him
ompleted the circle she'd hesi-
her scissors raised high. Did he
s do say babies born with their

ama had called her. Ma Doe
lling her in. Rue went into Ma
ι't any children there. Ma Doe
feet resting on an overturned
alves, pockmarked and black
time of standing on the behalf

of other folks, nursing at their children in the middle
rocking them to sleep.

"Come here now." Rue was not expecting Ma Do
to kiss her on the cheek like someone's mama migh
at the end of her arms and look her over and say, "Sh

They bowed their heads as close as conspirators,
their hair mixing together at the end of their spirals as
were the way secrets were passed.

"Almighty Lord." Ma Doe had her hands on Rue
was holding herself heavy on them, weighing Rue do
Brother Jonah and Sister Sarah, for the loss of their ch
row them."

Rue felt she was holding them both up, like if she
she'd send their two bodies tumbling down.

"And, Lord, keep Miss Rue." She shuddered at hea
name. "She's done the best she could by you, for she i
ment. And Bean's death—"

Ma Doe's face fell then, sunk down on the left side
tower. Her eyes got wide and fearful. She began to hu
ation of her prayer as if she'd suddenly run short of w

"Ma?" Rue clutched her close.

Ma Doe nodded, working her lips like chewing. "
managed.

Rue had forgotten. Ma Doe was everybody's mama
nobody's. Her boys had all been stripped from her, eas
off a stem. Same age as Bean was, when each of them

"I'm alright," Ma Doe said, but she seemed to str
more.

Rue led her back to her seat and helped her settl
Doe leaned back, looking hollowed. She nodded her
reminded Rue of the mindless way Varina had used

thumb. Like Ma Doe had, in all her grief, been dumbstruck and turned into a child.

Rue's fault also. She didn't know that she was weeping. Not 'til the tears were at her neck, wetting her collar. She sat herself on the ground by Ma Doe's raised feet, buried her face in that ancient knee, and let the weeping take her.

Miss May Belle wouldn't have prayed and she'd suffer only so much weeping. When Rue would come to her as a child, snot-nosed and guilty, she would say only, "That's enough now. Fix what you've done. Or live with it quiet."

Still, Rue wept.

WARTIME

—

Their plantation held a ball. Marse Charles demanded it for himself, said he deserved a jubilee. Missus had been dead a year by then and he'd grown restless with grieving, bored already with playing the widower. Every day there was news of young Rebs fighting battles and winning to fight another. Or losing and dying of it. Marse Charles had sent his sons to those battlefields, but he was impatient on their glory. He wanted his own safe sort of victory and decided not to wait to celebrate a Northern defeat. But the black folks were whispering behind their hands calling it a Dead Man's Jubilee.

The House was made to gleam, a shining beacon of sophistication that had many of the indoor slaves' hands rubbed raw from keeping those parts of the House that were well-trod from looking like they were ever lived in at all. Even Rue and her mama had to work in a way they'd never been expected to before. Miss May Belle had for so long got by on being too busy with birthing, on giving the plantation its robust number of babies and maintaining the bodies of others. She'd been so important in that above all else, that it was almost like her own body was free. But now she scrubbed with the rest of them, tasked at cleaning the tall white pillars that wrapped around the House's porch, and it was a lofty type of falling from grace, as she was made to climb up high to remove years of dust and dirt and errant grime between each ridge, approaching immaculate.

If Rue were to keep an image of her mama in her mind it might be that: Miss May Belle on the top of a rickety stepping stool, the legs of it lodged deep in dirt to keep it steady because it was a waste of a worker to have someone hold it there, even a child.

Each day of that long, tedious week of preparation, Rue passed by her mama outside on the porch on her step stool, scrubbing. Varina had asked for Rue in the same way she'd asked for a new frock—a heavy blue gown of a certain fabric she'd seen on a rare trip to the nearest town three months prior, on a bolt that had already been sold and made into something for somebody else. Because the dress she got was not the exact shade of blue that she'd been wanting, she felt she could ask for shoes to match it. She asked for Sarah and got her too.

Rue and Sarah found themselves draping behind Varina like the two ends of a veil. She wanted to practice at being a lady and that in itself was a masque in need of spectators.

Varina's preoccupation was her red hair. It had always vexed her, made her look strange and bright and not as demure as she might have wished, what with carrying brimming locks of hellfire everywhere she went. But that had been when she was young and small and a thumb-sucker on Ma Doe's lap. Now, despite the continued arid nature of her monthly visitor, she'd decided to count herself a proper woman and, in her mind, proper women did not go about having the red cherubic hair of little children.

"We ought to darken it." This she said to Sarah, who stood stock-still and held up for her the glass so that Varina might better see herself at all angles.

It was a thin, garish space, Varina's bedroom, a place Rue did not often find herself and did not like when she did. Varina had long since moved out of the nursery in favor of one of the disused guest rooms. Her wide bed with its thick posts like tree stumps took up more of the room than made sense to Rue, and up above it a canopy hung in thick drapes that made her hot just looking at them. With three bodies and all their warm, restless breathing, the room was particularly stifling, and Rue relegated herself to the cool varnished wood of the floor, which she was tasked to scrub from end to end. It would have been an alright place to make herself invisible if not for the fact that this position, on hands and knees, put her eyeball to eyeball with the dust-mottled collection of Varina's ceramic dolls heaped all in one corner. Rue sweated under their staring, and the white gleam off their porcelain skin was like to make her blind. All the dolls were a striking straw-headed blond, unlike their owner.

Varina and Sarah were already stepping in the part of the floor Rue had just washed. Sarah's bare feet left little gray imprints of themselves, and Varina's impatient foot tapped dirt from her small dagger-hilt heel. Sarah fussed, brushing out Varina's hair. Rue could have screamed as the red spirals drifted out and down to the floor. She'd have to sweep it again when they were all through.

"Darken it like how, Miss?" Sarah, with her sweet voice, was being just as doting as Rue had ever seen her and Rue had a good sense of why. It was no secret to them that as much as the world seemed to be changing it was not changing so much, so quick. Varina would be needing to become a lady—a lady in pursuit of a husband—and a lady in pursuit of a husband would like as not be in need of her own nigra housemaid.

Fannie had been the Missus's girl for all of their lives. A perfect petted favorite, she'd oft be seen to flit all around the House in the Missus's old clothes, reminding other folks of her favored place, putting them down in theirs.

Rue watched Varina and Sarah in the mirror, didn't like how

easy they were with one another, how close. They'd just together drew the black crepe off Varina's large wall mirror and found that, beneath, the glass had been streaked black by the press of the fabric over those long months of mourning. Their doubled reflection was marred, lines over their faces like trenches through mud, and Rue just knew Varina was waiting to tell her to clean off the mirror soon as she finished the floor.

It made sense that Sarah would be chosen. That Sarah would go to the fete that night and serve drinks to fancily dressed white folks, that she'd follow behind Varina and make sure that her skirt wasn't dragging in anything dusty. It had never been said, not out loud, but it had always been meant to be Sarah, anybody with eyes could see that. She'd never had a place in the field, not with her skin smooth and light.

"Miss May Belle's likely got somethin' I can use for yo' hair. What you think, Rue?" They were both looking at Rue, their heads turned just sideways. Their mouths and noses and eyelashes in profile were strange and synchronous, and Rue could not deny that she felt a burst of foreknowledge.

She was invigorated with envy also when she stood and glanced at her own figure in the glass Sarah still held. She was small and dark-skinned and, in that moment, just as ugly-feeling as they must have imagined her, raisin black between them.

"I'll run on out and ask Mama."

Miss May Belle had not been the same after that time spent locked up in the jail hold of the church. Starvation and silence, three days of it, for disobedience, the simple sin of getting a mama some medicine.

"I done so many worse things than that," Rue's mama had said when she'd first come back, like she'd been thinking on all of those things she had done during her time locked away.

Rue didn't know what to make of her mama, come back the way she had, with nothing on her to heal. Her body had taken care of itself, the way a body can, eaten up the stored-up flesh so she was just left to sharp, angular bone. Sealed up cuts and scabbed over hurts. There was a chipped tooth far enough back in her mouth to not change her smile, unless she smiled real wide. All of it superficial, save the patch of her scalp where Marse Charles had pulled the hair clear out of her head. It was tiny, barely even there, Rue had assured her mama. It was star-shaped. Fist-shaped, Rue realized after. It didn't grow back, never would, but it was easily brushed over.

Why couldn't she magic her way out of that jail was what Rue kept wondering. A deep resentful hurt centered in her like a pit in fruit. If Miss May Belle was as powerful as folks would have you think, so mysterious, so feared, couldn't she free herself, or feed herself, turn the ground seepage in that dank cell, water to wine, hoodoo herself into one of them little fleas that had left hard red welt bites on her skin and hop on out?

Miss May Belle was still scrubbing at the balustrade when Rue came out from the House, and Rue felt her mama tracking her from deep within sunken eyes as she went past. If Marse Charles's punishment had been meant to make the slave woman obedient, then it had failed. Instead she was all the more outcast, all the more feral. And Rue always became what her mama was.

Rue had never had any intention of asking Miss May Belle after a way to darken Varina's hair. It was just that Varina could not be pleased. First Rue returned with a poultice of nettle and sage, and Varina did not fancy the color the leaf skins would make. Next Rue returned with tea, steeped to black as ink, but Varina had turned up her nose at the smell. The cure Rue returned with last was a pleasing amber-brown liquid she knew that Varina would take to, the darkness in it likely to bring out her light.

"There isn't very much," Varina complained when Rue showed the small bowl to her. "Do you think it's enough?"

Rue could see in Sarah's eyes that she recognized the stuff where Varina didn't. There was a hard-questioning look to Sarah's face, but she stayed stiff-lipped and mute. Who knew? Maybe Sarah was feeling just as vengeful against Varina as Rue was. Perhaps they could be vengeful together. Rue turned the bowl, roiling the liquid enticingly so it would not begin to settle.

"It's enough to work," Rue said. "Color's like to bring out your eyes."

"Alright then," said Varina, ever easy and trusting.

It wasn't that Rue blamed Varina for what her daddy had done to Miss May Belle. Rue didn't believe hating was transferable. But it awed her that Varina had never in her life had any reason to be distrustful of anything handed to her, even by Miss May Belle or Rue. Never thought that she could be hated for no reason, or for the simple reason of existing. The sweet smell of the gummy resin wafted up between them. Varina had not a clue and Sarah said not a word. Rue kept on turning the bowl in her hands, roiling the brown liquid. Soon it would start to set, harden; it would give the trick away.

Varina sat on her stool inspecting her hair, her nose almost up to the glass, curling a strand and uncurling it around her finger like something were going to change if she kept doing so.

"Try it on her first," Varina said, gesturing at Sarah.

Sarah and Rue looked at each other. Open-mouthed.

"Ain't enough for both," Rue said.

"So y'all will go out and fetch more. But I'd like to see how it's lookin'. We got close kinds a' hair."

It was true. Varina and Sarah were similar, especially sitting together like that in front of Rue. Both thin and drawn and pretty, pug-nosed and curly-headed; the only difference in them was a matter of wording. Varina's ringlets were red. Sarah's nappy curls were rust. Sarah, there holding the little mirror, was holding a different version of herself in the glass, or so it seemed to Rue, a different kind of life Sarah could have had.

Rue struggled to come up with a lie, an excuse that might prevent her being whupped for daring to play such a trick. But Sarah was resigned. Without a word they'd been caught out in their trick before it ever began, and now they had to see it through. Varina and Sarah traded places. Sarah took the vanity stool and Varina held the mirror, playing at being a servant. Rue raised the slow-dripping syrup to Sarah's waiting head where it would settle and harden, thick as tar.

"What were you thinkin' of?" On Miss May Belle's cabin floor Sarah's cut-off hair lay left behind, hardened like petrified bugs in amber, though Sarah herself had long since gone, sent to bed shorn and weeping. Hair grew back, Miss May Belle had assured her, saying nothing of her own hidden star-shaped scar.

"I wanted to get her back," Rue said. "Make Varina feel somethin' for what Marse Charles done to you."

That was the simple answer, the answer that Rue figured her mama, who was always juggling a hundred schemes herself, would be proud to hear. Truth was, Rue could not put simple words to her anger, just that it was anger. She'd wanted to hurt Varina for love of her and did not so much mind hurting Sarah in Varina's place.

"And see yourself whipped for it?" Miss May Belle moved about the cabin in her distress like she mistrusted the distance between walls. Even as she raved she walked up and down, smacked at one far wall then crossed the length of the room to smack at the other. "You lucky Miss Varina ain't catch on to what you was about. You wanna see yo'self hanged? Or worse, sent where they sent me? You couldn't never survive that place."

It was the only time Miss May Belle ever alluded to the three days she had been buried alive in the church's jail. Rue took her mama's scolding with her face set sullen.

"Stupid girl. Ain't you know it ain't worth it? Don't you know there's no way round it? Aiming to curse white folks is like tryna slap at a fly sittin' on yo' wound. It's never gon' do you no good. You only gon' smack yo'self, and that fly gon' go off laughin'."

Rue felt defiant. "Varina say I could go to the party tomorrow in place a' Sarah."

Marse Charles was never gonna let a bald-headed slave girl into the House, not while there were guests there, chittering on in the face of the North-brought war about the fine way they treated their slaves. Like family, they'd lie. Like beloved children needing a stern hand to be raised right.

"It's my own fault. I kept you shielded." Miss May Belle ricocheted off the far wall and sat down hard on the dirty hair-covered floor, drew her knees up to her chest. Curled in on herself. Rue didn't know what to do. "Go on then. Let Miss Varina take you."

"Take me where?" The party was being held up at the House, only a stone's throw.

"Let her take you away and show you how the world is."

Rue's mama had told her once that Cain and Abel were not brothers, not twins. They were, Miss May Belle said, two sides of the same person, good and evil warring against its own inclinations. The same struggle was borne out in every person, over and over, from the very most beginning of time, and you could only answer for yourself which brother would win. Varina had told her later that it wasn't true, that the Bible said it plain, spelled it out in those little letters Rue couldn't read. There was Cain and there was Abel. There was black and there was white. It wasn't so much that Rue didn't believe Varina, but she kept hold of what her mama said, applied it to others, held up that story to folks' faces and tried to decide which brother they had ruling them.

Varina could be good, Rue said to herself that day, as giving as Abel. They met in the clearing before the fete. Varina was lovely in her blue gown, the one she'd demanded for herself and won. Rue's dress was new also, new to her anyway, a bit of calico repurposed in a different pattern, so it almost wasn't that old rough stuff anymore. She thought it fit her fine. She thought they both were pretty.

"You can't work it," Varina said first. Not a hello or a nice thing about Rue's new dress, or her own, or even a good word about the neat coils Rue had managed to twist her own hair into with the help of some pilfered pomade—not one of her mama's ground-up oils neither, but that real patent pomade. Varina's hair blazed red as ever. "I asked for you. But Daddy's only wantin' the light girls inside servin'."

Rue could have cried, might've, she could feel the sorrow screwing up the back of her throat like a rising sickness.

"Don't you worry." Varina cupped Rue's cheek lovingly. "I've got us a solution."

The air buzzed with nightfall gnats as they walked toward the back of the House. Already they could hear the hired-out fiddler playing, little snippets of nothing that began with a flourish then scratched away to frustrated silence, then burst out again, louder. They could hear him crick his strings, 'til they whined like cats. He began anew.

Varina led Rue through the servants' entrance to an ill-lit hallway with an oilcloth floor that worked its way like a snake through the House. It was well-trod by Varina's mama's maid, Fannie, who most often had to appear in rooms throughout the House, serve a visiting guest, and then melt away again like she never even was. Rue hadn't ever quite got the lay of this trick, had never needed to.

She knew they'd come close when she could hear the fiddler again. He played a song she knew but could not place the words to. A jaunty tune that deserved a whistle. The corridor they crept through opened into the parlor, only just. The hidden door was only a parting in the heavy flower pattern of the wallpaper—the painted flowers were of a type that did not exist in any stretch of nature Rue had ever known—and the door's outward swing was hidden by a screen and hindered by a large wooden trunk set deliberately in the path of the disused servant's door.

Just beyond the screen and the trunk in the stretch of the parlor she could see the fiddler, but at this angle he could not see them. She knew he couldn't see them because he cussed at a broken string, a thing he'd never do if he knew a white woman was in his hearing.

"Only, you have to trust me," Varina whispered.

There was a little padlock on the trunk to which Varina produced a little key. With some effort she pulled the trunk open, careful not to ask too much at once of its old rusted hinges.

The inside was near empty but for a pile of old yellowed papers dotted black with little markings Rue knew signified music.

"If you hold tight to your knees," Varina suggested, kindly. "You'll fit inside just."

Rue's stomach dropped at the thought.

"Go ahead." Varina cocked her head; her curls danced.

Beyond the screen, farther into the room, someone out of sight had joined the fiddle player. Black or white? There was no way to tell from hushed, unclear conversation and it didn't matter much. If anybody caught them there'd be hell to pay no doubt. Rue pulled up her skirt and stepped into the box. She sat as Varina had suggested, pulled her knees into her chest, tried to be smaller than small. The papers beneath her cut into her thigh, and she had to bite down on a sneeze from the dust they'd roused. Varina began to shut the lid.

"What you doin'?" Rue hardly remembered to whisper.

"Can't leave it open, can I? It'll draw folks' attentions. They find you and we'll both of us be whupped bloody."

"Maybe I ought to just go home."

"And miss all this?" Varina shook her head, her eyes gleaming. "No, Rue, I want you to be here. To see."

Here in this box like a coffin? It was too horrible, too much like her mama's punishment in the church. Three days, three nights, in the cold and the dark. No food. No water but what leaked in when it rained. Why should Rue ever trust Varina? But there had been her mama's warning, a cruel thing tossed away that stuck and rang in Rue's memory: "You couldn't never survive that place."

Rue made to stand. Varina laid a laced hand on her shoulder, pushed her back down. "You can't miss this, Rue."

The lid yawned as it closed down over her head. With her back rounded she could fit into the domed roof, she found. Everything went black. She worried too late about biting spiders and tried again to stand. She heard the latch of the lock click shut, an impossibly loud doom. Then light crept back in. Varina's fingers snuck in the gap no more than two inches wide.

"If you sit up straight, you'll be able to push it open a li'l for yourself," Varina said, peering in at her. "You'll be able to see the show. Me dancin' and all the pretty folks. Go on now. Try it."

If Rue turned her head just so she could, in fact, lift the lid open for herself as far as the stretch of the lock would allow. Up close was the corner of Varina's gap-toothed smile, and beyond was the lofted stage, set up for the minstrel show. Varina raised her finger to her lip, and she was so close that Rue could make out only her knuckles and the leftmost side of her nose, but she knew what the gesture meant and already the first of the white folks were crowding in.

Rue uncraned her neck and let the box fall lightly shut. Chatter grew in a buzz about the room, and the scuffing footfalls echoed louder. Bereft of sight, Rue made her ears keen, and though she could pull no voices in particular out of the din, she did mark the high, crinkling sound of white women laughing and the deeper rumble of white men pontificating and, beneath, the hush of black folks servanting, the clink of silver, and then the first trill of a flute being played with a scattering of heavy notes on a piano, joined in artful earnest by the strings. She didn't dare peek out for much of the first few songs, but by the third, a fast, roiling tune that had the wood floor shaking with the force of it, she dared to push up the lid with her head and look awhile.

There the white folks bent their knees to each other as though in greeting, and at some command of the music that Rue could not figure they began working themselves into knots, here and there turning at sharp angles beneath each other's arms like lines of ants after some flour, and how they did not smash into one another she couldn't say. The women and girls swished past her corner in whirls of solid color. Every time she picked out a flash of blue she wondered if it was Varina, but she could not see enough of them to tell, as their skirts quivered up and down with their frantic, senseless bobbing. And here a man's pant legs and tails would come sweeping in and swing the woman away, and another flash of skirt would come and bob in the same fashion as the last. By the time she'd worked out which way the dancing ought to go, the song had come to an end and they were about the bowing again and she knew she must retreat back to her closed position like a tortoise drawn in on its own self.

The only indication she had of the time was the growing crick in her neck and the changes in the music, and she'd already lost the sense of how many songs had come and gone. The applause caught her attention, but it was when the strains of a harmonica reached her, muffled through the box, that her curiosity got to her again. She pushed open the lid and looked.

The white folks had stopped dancing, had made an audience of themselves, and though Rue could not see quite over their heads she could see their legs, the backs of which strained in their desire to watch something that was happening in the very corner of her sight on the far edge of the stage. She saw the first man that came out, an old black man she did not recognize. He walked out on the stage to the strain of the small metal mouth organ he played, his hand working, his wrist flicking as he set the notes to ripple. As he moved across the stage she quickly lost sight of him but his music remained, and she gave her sore neck a rest and let the lid fall down.

Darkness, 'til she heard a curious spring of laughter. Though she knew she shouldn't, she pushed her way up again so that she could just see who next crossed the stage. They were, she understood right off, meant to be black men. What they were instead were white men with their faces soot-smeared to a shining solid black. Their lips were reddened out to huge false smiles as gleaming and ugly as bleeding wounds. As one they skipped and tapped their way from the makeshift wings, propelling themselves out from behind the heavy red curtains like they'd been given a swift boot to the behind by some unseen foot.

The last man in that line lingered in Rue's sights as he paused to raise his white gloved hand in an enthusiastic wave. He reached up and tipped his tall black hat to reveal a crop of black wool beneath that stuck up in wild tufts. The crowd shook as one with laughter at the mottled wig. Between the pristine white gloves and the sleeve of his threadbare overcoat, Rue saw the true pink skin of his bony wrist before it disappeared again beneath the fold of cloth and he too moved on, obscured to her by the nodding heads of his captive audience. They jerked in time to the swelling music of the black fiddle player starting up again.

If she shifted her weight she could see clear only the last man, the one who'd so delighted the crowd with the unruly kink of his false black curls. He'd taken up a seat on the edge of the stage, and he sat with his legs comically wide. He leaned in now and then to watch his fellow performers or to react to their clowning by slapping his hand at his knees in an overdone imitation of mirth.

They introduced themselves with a comic lack of humility as the world-renowned Ethiop Choir, promising the crowd the most authentic Negro melodies they'd ever had occasion to hear. At this, the one on the end jumped up, stomped his foot as if a thought had hopped on him like a flea.

"Whee," he began with a low whistle through his front teeth. "Why, y'all ever hear how it came to be that us black folks gotsta be so black?"

His fellow players moaned like they'd heard this one before, but the audience chuckled, shook their heads. Some amused themselves by baldly calling out their own punch lines: Tar. Paint. Falling asleep during sunup.

"I tell you it goes back to when the good Lawd was handin' out colors." His accent was overthick. Sludgy. "The good Lawd says one day to all his peoples, 'A'ight now I'mma start handin' out colors tomorrow and y'all better come through on time if y'all want 'em, ya hear? So's the next day folks is lined up and the Lawd, he say, 'You there, y'all Chinamans? Y'all folks be yellow. And, y'all Injuns, y'all folks be red. And you there, you fine folks, you will be white.'

"And then the Lawd, he look round hisself and find one of the

groups of his people is missin'. He draw out his pocket-y watch"—
a dim laugh rose from the audience at his overdone pantomime—
"'Di'n't I tell y'all folks to be on time if you wantin' yo' colors?'"

Rue had heard this joke before. It was one her mama liked to
tell, berating the lateness of this or that person. Miss May Belle did
it better, didn't belabor the telling as a long walk for a small drink
of water. God was never angry in her version, just benignly amused
at the way things were.

"So's finally the last group come runnin' up from Africa to get
they colors and they so greedy and wantin', climbin' over each
other like that, and the Lawd say to 'em 'Get back, get back.' But
so fevered was they, all they heard was 'Get black, get black'—and
that's the truth!"

The trumpet blasted as the crowd clapped and laughed and the
end man dipped a bow so low his nose touched the waxed-up floor
of the stage. They drew further cheers as they trotted in high-
stepped kicks switching places and hats and jackets in a comedic
whirl. They plumped up their collars pretending to be black folks
who were pretending to be white dandies and, that done, they
plunked down in their original seats in slovenly postures of exhaustion.

"Lawdy," said one of them, "it sure is tiresome bein' white folk."

Rue thought to sink low again but then the raucous crowd
turned soberer as they waited on the next act, and lo the man on
the end began, without the aid of music, to sing.

He drew his cap from his head and held it over his heart. "If you
want to find God, go in de wilderness, de wilderness."

He was good, there was no denying. He sang it so sweet that
Rue wanted to take his advice. She thought if only she could rear
up that she would run away right into that wilderness he promised,
but her neck and legs stayed cramped; she shifted and the box she
was in fell shut. She listened as the other men joined him, lending

him their voices in four blending parts. She found she could pick them apart better there in the darkness.

Hours might have passed in which Rue grew drowsy the longer she remained in that damned box breathing in her own stale air. She itched, she needed to relieve herself. The revelers took their time in leaving and she heard them go one by one, asking their black footmen to bring about their carriages or going away reluctantly on foot themselves or begging a spare room in the House, stumbling away drunk and ecstatic.

Varina appeared so suddenly in the gap Rue would have jumped if she'd had the space to do so. The girl was grinning, and her curls were flattened-down ringlets matted to the sweat on her forehead. Her cheeks were rosy beneath false rouge.

"Can't you let me out now?" Rue found her voice gritty with disuse.

Varina lifted a bare finger to her lip to sign for silence again. She'd lost a glove it seemed.

"In a moment," she said in whisper. "Shh. He's coming."

"Who?" The lid slipped shut again.

Varina was giggling, Rue heard that plainly—a high, sweet giggle nothing like her usual laugh. Rue could not make out the man's words, but she did hear the deep baritone vibration in his voice, which seemed much too loud, which bounced and echoed in the suddenly emptied room. At first she made him for Marse Charles, but no, Rue knew her master's voice in her sleep and this man's voice was much too deep to match it. Varina laughed again. Rue's legs ached something awful.

The man was fixing to ask a question, Rue could tell that much in the pitch of his voice, and she strained to hear Varina's side of the conversation. There was no response, laughter or otherwise. Rue didn't quite dare peek, not with the strange man there and liable to beat her if he realized she'd been there all along. She figured him for white he sounded so sure of himself, the way he kept demanding. His voice came back in the same low rumble it had before, like he was disciplining an ill-behaved child by asking it to explain exactly what it had done. Again, there was the long, strange stretch of Varina's silence. Rue edged open the top of the chest, just the barest amount.

They were across the room from her, nearer to the stage, and all she could make out was the tight cinched waist of Varina's new dress and the man's middle in a fine suit. He wore a white glove, she saw, and he took Varina's bare hand in his, squeezed her roughly at the wrist. Varina tried to pull away but at the last minute faltered like she didn't know what to do, did not want to offend. The center of their bodies glowed in the orange of kerosene lamps, the only light left lit, and they stood there in their awkward tableau like dancers primed for the music to start.

The man's question came again, and Rue caught the very ends of it. "Wartime," he'd said.

Varina was not giggling now. The center of her body was so strangely tight and still and she said then, quite harshly, "Please." At that he twisted, reached out his other hand. He yanked up the good blue fabric of her dress as if it had offended him. He pushed her against the wall and tilted her body wholly back like a swinging bell, her thin, pale fighting legs for the clapper. There was the sharp sound of ripping fabric, of seams collapsing. Something skittered, a button perhaps, then a sharp intake of breath, and now Rue could see Varina's pink bared thighs. Rue balled herself up and disappeared.

But the image of Varina's pale hand, tensed and gripped by the pristine white glove, seemed to imprint itself wholly in Rue's dark hiding place, and she couldn't tell if her eyes were open or whether they were shut. She listened to the thudding of her blood in her ears and told herself if Miss Varina wanted to reveal her she need only call across the room. Rue reasoned there was nothing to be done, nothing she could do; she herself was still bound by the lock.

Rue began then to hum, not aloud but in her head, trying to put right the words the minstrels had sung: *the wilderness, the wilderness.* It had been lovely music, no matter the color their faces were painted. She heard Varina scream out loud just the once and thought of the wilderness, a place to run for both of them.

The abrupt turning of the lock seemed like violence, the lid cracking full open was like a trigger pulled. The dim of the room felt like too much bright and Rue squinted and there was Varina, alone, with tracks of tears ruining her rouged face.

"Varina." She reached out her hand. Varina smacked it immediately away.

With her head bowed and her legs jellied Rue stepped out of the box at Varina's command. She straightened Varina's pretty blue dress so it fell down again in the perfect circle it had held before.

"We ought to get to sleep," Varina was saying. "It's very late, isn't it?"

Rue shrugged, she didn't know. She looked around the room, suspicious of its dark corners, of what lay behind the minstrels' curtains, even suspicious of the box she'd just come out from.

"He gone?" Rue asked quietly.

Varina sniffed, choked on a sob and stifled another back. "Who?"

This time when Rue put out her hand Varina took it, and Rue was shocked with how cold Varina's hand was, and clammy. Was this the hand the man had held? Now she could not remember which it had been. It felt like the memory was slipping away from her, like she'd just sat up from sleep and tried to grasp at the tendrils of a nightmare. Who would want to remember this?

"I'm very tired." Varina did not look tired. Her eyes were red-rimmed and more aware than Rue had ever seen them, like someone had forced them open, peeled back the lids. "Take me to bed."

Rue did, if *taking* was the word for it. She followed behind Varina through the still, sleeping house, a white girl and her shadow. They moved like they were walking through a graveyard, afeared of raising the dead. Every movement felt too loud underfoot to Rue, the night seemed so fragile, the air made all of glass.

THE RAVAGING

==

In grief, the town chose to sit up with their dead. Rue did not altogether care for the idea that had rose amongst the people, that they ought to hold a town-wide wake in respect of the children that had died. Wakes were for the living, she figured. Their grief, no matter how good, would not bring the dead babies back. It would not bring Bean back.

They had chosen just three boys to serve as the symbols for all the other babies they'd lost since the sickness took hold. "The Ravaging" they called it amongst themselves, as though the illness was a swarm of locusts, a collective doom fallen on a mutual harvest, a force so great it could not be attributed to one man, or one woman neither. Give Him the glory, Rue thought darkly as she gathered death's flowers. She was careful what ones she picked, steering wholly clear of the type that grew in the graveyard, particularly wary of the pot marigolds that grew thick as head hair around her mama's stone. She didn't wish to call up the spirit of Miss May Belle, not on this occasion, as she made to decorate Bean's small body with no more special favor than she paid the other two child bodies she had been charged with. Preparing them in her cabin, she set Bean out as the one on the far left instead of the one in the center for that same reason; he was not a Christ, just some third criminal hung on a lesser cross.

Rue wept. Hard and heavy 'til she thought her body would be wrung completely dry of all its water. She was glad folks had let her alone in her work preparing the bodies so she could afford the right to cry. She was glad especially that Bruh Abel was scarce. If he suspected that she had made him her vessel, he did not show it. He did not slow down, but moved from house to house, ministering to folks, praying.

What did Bruh Abel ask for, Rue wondered, when he talked to that God of his? And did He ever give a good answer back?

Bean's body was small and waxen and fully white. With his eyes closed he was just as harmless as any child could be in sleep. His russet hair grew in tight at the root of his head, but the longer locks weighed themselves down into fine loose ringlets. Rue cut them neat and short with the thought that she'd give a piece to Sarah. But she wouldn't, for Sarah could not be trusted to weep on it as well as Rue would. No, Rue would keep the lock for herself, in the depths of her pockets.

Set in the corner was her small metal tub and she tugged it out to the center of the room in three sharp pulls, the bottom scraping at her floor in sickening squeals. When she lifted him Bean was light. She set him down inside the empty tub like a baby into a crib.

She covered him waist to knees with a washcloth but she left his face clear, didn't mask him as she sometimes did with bodies she feared might stare back at her. No, she wanted to look on him, to look upon what she had done.

She poured cold water from out of clay pots, cascaded it over the still planes of his body. First the right then the left. He'd once screamed when water touched him. It'd woken him once before. She turned him slightly to clean along his legs, his behind. Rue's hands shook through the whole of the scrubbing.

She added camphor to the water. The deliberate perfume, that flavor of hidden death, left her choking. She had to stop and gasp in acrid breaths that made her weak, cracked inhales that cut straight through her. She was sick in her guilt. There was a sharp pain in the bottom of her stomach that grew and had her suddenly bent double, spitting up yellow-tinged sorrow right there on the floor. She thought of how her mama had used to rub her back when she was a sick child, a strange rhythmic motion she didn't know the point of. Rue felt it then in the small of her back, that up-and-down love rubbing, even though she was alone with only the dead for companions.

"Bean?" His hands hung limp from the tub.

Rue stood. She wiped at her mouth and her eyes. Dried Bean's body and drew him up again in her arms. She finished all the preparations, washed the body of the middle boy, arranged the flowers in a neat wreath around the head of that boy's casket, and started in on the third. There was always something more to do, and had that not been what she'd wanted? To be needed just like this?

By the time the wake came, Rue was already a full day sleepless. Sitting up with the dead had always brought haints to the back of her tired eyes. She'd not seen so many bodies buried as others had on the plantation during slavery times. She was young then, and those last years before the war had been a relatively robust time if not an easy one. Black folks young and old still died, sure, died in numbers—of overwork and over-tiring, of having lived too old or having been born too young, of hunger or fever, of sorrow or ne-

glect, but just as many new healthy babies were being born at
Marse Charles's behest, and if there was birthing happening or liable to happen, it was that vigil Rue and her mama were tasked to
keep. Naught to do for dead bodies once they'd been cleaned, no
promise there and no profit made on mourning.

Still, Rue knew how a sitting-up went as well as anyone, and
she had always liked those nights in a sad kind of way for the simple honesty of them, just singing and wailing and reflecting in
long stretches of impenetrable quiet 'til it was time to lay the body,
and the saved up sorrow, to a final rest.

But this day it seemed none of them could raise the exuberance
that had harbored them in tragedy so many times before. Their
sitting-up was no sitting-up at all but a march of stations, the crowd
moving in a stunned roulette amongst the three houses to look in
at a child for a spell and then to move on to the next with promises
to come back round in an hour or so. They passed each other in
the square, mourners with solemn candles, crisscrossing their
lights to keen at one another's doorstep.

What singing there was came low and listless. It was orphan
Sarah who'd been the loudest, strongest singer amongst them in
all the time that Rue had been alive, as though the girl could be
possessed by the full-limbed spirit of grief on the behalf of others.
But now that little girl was a grown woman, and a mama besides,
and she sat black-veiled with both her two living children in her
lap, perched at the far end of the mismatched chairs they'd hastily
assembled in the front room of her home. Sarah kept that single
vigil for Bean, not singing or weeping or anything but just struck
still, same as her dead son, there in his open coffin. Any tune her
visitors took up, even those songs laden with love for the Lord and
his wisdom, seemed to taper off into thin scraps of nothing without Sarah's voice.

A fine red oak casket held Bean, the brass handles of which winked yellow in the low candlelight. He wore a little white calico sleep gown, the ends sewn up like a sack. His head was lofted on a white pillow, and all around him was a hedgerow growth of flowers as though he were a doll someone had left out in the yard for weeds to grow up and around.

Folks came and went as the night darkened, but after one respectful circuit Rue stayed with Bean. The men, Rue noticed, came the latest, stayed as long as they were able, which was not long at all. It reminded Rue of the birthing rooms, the anxious daddies with no stomach for the pushing or the hollering or the waiting on the water to boil.

They'd come back to carry the casket, she knew, just as they'd show up when the babies were born, washed, and snipped.

Rue had always been quietly proud of her own endurance for suffering. Being surrounded by the mamas' grief-stained faces seemed to her to be the first in a receiving line of self-inflicted punishments she might bestow upon herself.

Bruh Abel came along to Bean's wake round midnight with some of the other men. Bean's daddy, Jonah, was mute amongst them. Certain of the men passing through smelled of liquor, but the smell was miasma on them, a vapor that couldn't be husked from the group to be better assigned to one or another in particular. Bruh Abel seemed the most sure on his feet, but Rue knew him for a drunk. He'd always had strong sea legs and could keep his mask painted on just right when he had need of it. Rue kept her eyes on him as he trailed past Bean's body.

All night she'd received compliments on how well she'd made the three boys look; she could vomit again with the bile of that poor pride. But Bruh Abel didn't look like he was fixing to pay her any sort of compliment. He walked right by her, didn't even look at her, but came to settle after a time with Jonah and Sarah. He knelt before them with one hand on their daughter's head and the other as a slow-rubbing comfort on Sarah's knee.

He leaned forward and Rue watched him whisper in Sarah's ear. Didn't need to hear it to know it. He'd asked her to sing. For the first time that evening she obliged, setting down her son and daughter and starting with no preamble or pretense on the slow steady words: "Wade in the water, children. Wade in the water."

This was the part of the song they all knew well, where her call was to earn a response, but Sarah didn't stop for it, and no voice in her small, close house joined hers. She continued singing alone, her voice straining roughly on the top notes so that every time she trilled for one Rue held her breath, afraid she wouldn't make it, but she did, every time.

"Look o'er yonder, what you see? God's gon' trouble the water. The Holy Ghost a-comin' on me. God's gon' trouble the water."

In the midst of Sarah's dirge Rue let her head bow down, dug her hands in her pockets, stroked the sprig of Bean's baby hair. She tried to call up the words of the song for herself, feeling like if only she could draw the strength, if only she could sing beside Sarah, it all would be made right, or else not have happened at all, none of it. Instead she'd be back at the river where she'd last heard the hum of this particular song from that assembled earnest crowd on the day Bruh Abel had baptized her and Bean both: "God gon' trouble the water."

But Rue couldn't sing. She couldn't speak; all she could get her messed-up mind to do was pray. She was there again, under the river, gasping out bubbles, falling headlong, and there was no one to pull her up from it this time, no one to bring up her head from this dry, barren drowning on land.

"If you don't believe I've been redeemed, just follow me

down to the Jordan's stream," Sarah sang. "God's gon' trouble the water."

The silence that followed that last note of hers was filled up fast with keens and claps and folks borrowing bits of her song and humming it to themselves as they wiped in vain at their tumble of tears. Sarah had sat back down heavy, like her legs had been snatched from under her, and her man and her babies crowded around her in her swoon. Bruh Abel stood aside from them as though completing some biblical picture, but soon, without saying any more, he turned from them and made to leave.

Rue took to her feet. "Wait. Bruh Abel. Wait."

Wait for what? Her senses were far ahead of her mind. Her eyes had spied something her head hadn't even put words to yet, for there in the little coffin was a small, stirring movement. A little white hand raised itself up, grabbing at the air as though falling and looking for something to catch on to.

Rue ran over so fast she clattered past chairs and stools, tripped over her own anxious feet, but she landed at the head of Bean's coffin and grabbed on to that searching hand. With her other she began tugging at the flowers, throwing them from around his stirring head same as she'd plucked them from the dirt. She tossed them over her shoulder not caring where the stems and leaves and heads landed or who they hit, not caring when one landed smack in Bruh Abel's face—he'd come to join her kneeling on the ground. Once the casket was cleared of its bouquet she could feel for the little boy's neck and yes, there, there was the slow but steady streaming thrum she'd been looking for. In the red oak casket below Bean opened wide his black eyes and looked around, blinking away the dust of death.

Bruh Abel said, "I told 'em all it was a miracle."

Rue nodded. "It was."

They were walking from Jonah and Sarah's cabin where every-body had gathered at that sitting-up that ended like none they'd ever seen before. Rue had been the one to pluck Bean wholly from his casket. When she'd buried her face into his good clean skin, he'd wriggled in her hug and said that he was very hungry. He had fallen asleep again a few moments later, clutching a heel of bread someone had fetched. It bore only a few tiny nibbles when he fell into a doze, but his sleep was light, his breathing even. He fussed when Rue handed him over to Sarah but he did not wake again as he was carried off to the bed, safely draped on his mama's shoulder. Even then folks had tried to follow after him, an unsure parade, 'til Jonah had intervened, thanked them and shooed them all from his home.

"Bean," he said, "he need his rest." It was a funny thing to say after all that time he'd spent sleeping.

No one else slept. The town was alit with curiosity, and they just about hummed with questions they couldn't give voice to other than to say how good was God and hallelujah.

How long, Rue wondered, 'til they'd get their minds around to asking other things? Eventually they'd have to close the other boys' coffins over their still faces. Those boys hadn't woken, hadn't stirred, and with morning approaching no one had moved to put them in the ground. No one could say the words.

Going through the quarter, Rue and Bruh Abel let others linger behind or go ahead of them so that they walked side by side now as if by chance.

"Is it a miracle?" Bruh Abel asked. It was the first time she'd ever heard his voice ring with doubt, and she found she didn't like it.

"I wished it," she answered.

The lines on his forehead wrinkled at that.

"I prayed," she said instead.

"We ought to look after him," Bruh Abel said, and Rue could see his mind grinding down each thought. "Ain't Bean goin' to need us more now?"

"He got us," Rue said. She found she ached inside for leaving Bean with Jonah and Sarah. They never had known what to make of him. Would know even less now that he was "a miracle."

Bruh Abel was following her, she realized after a time, or else letting himself be led straight to her home at the far end of the town, past where all the good folks lived, close and huddled together.

"Come on in," she said at her door. "We can talk on it." The memory of Bean's black eyes opening up and seeking hers.

Inside they did not talk at all but stood facing each other. Bruh Abel hovered near the shut door like he was trying to build up a good reason to run through it. Rue stood tensed with her hip hitched up on her table, feeling she'd fall without the aid of something solid.

Bruh Abel chuckled at some joke that didn't need speaking and then his laughter grew and Rue joined him in laughing, shook her head like it might loose the shock. It didn't.

The laughing made her belly hurt. Rue crossed the room to Bruh Abel, tired of their being on separate ends of the same thing.

It was some strange affirmation from somewhere that flooded through her mind then. Want, it said, and you shall receive. She put her hands on the sides of Bruh Abel's face because she wanted to. She pulled him near because she wanted to. She kissed his open, slack-jawed mouth—usually so slick-tongued but now gaping, yielding—because she wanted him.

He regained himself in a moment, kissed her back. She moaned the words of her wanting right into his mouth with the unrelenting force of her own lips, felt the rising feeling of wanting like a swell in her whole elastic body as she reached and reached and reached 'til, short of air, they pulled apart and gasped in shallow mismatched breaths, like they'd swum across a river and come out on the opposite side together.

"Jesus," Rue said.

Bruh Abel took her by the waist, so suddenly sure, and stirred her over to her own bed. There he folded her over easy like she was a sheet so that her back was on the thin mattress and her knees were so bent they near about touched her shoulders. He scratched at her when he pulled up her dress and she might've drawn blood tugging at his pants, but they worked it together in the end, got each other free.

Rue bucked. He pressed into her like a blazing fire, and the thrill of him spread wild as one too. She felt him in even the tips of her fingers, burning. He buried himself deep and his eyes grew wide and unfocused like he'd gone over to some other place, and she put her hand to his cheek, drawing him back to her in slow, careful measures.

No tricks, now, no sprung trap, just wanting.

Simple and just the thought brought her over to that cresting pleasure she'd been after, just as Bruh Abel burrowed his face into her neck and ground out, "Rue, Rue, Rue," as desperate as a man drowning that wanted rescue.

"I'm here," she said to him. Loud and clear. "I'm here."

Rue made a visit to the church, basket in hand.

"You listenin'?" She called out to Varina, and there was no answer.

She went down the dusty aisle and up the bowing steps and, she couldn't help it, she was humming. She felt Bruh Abel's wanting in her body and Bean's rising in her heart and she would not let the shadows of the old white church despair her, even in the face of one of Varina's tempers.

"You hidin' from me, Miss Varina?"

Rue had to look up to find her. Varina sat in the bell tower, and from below Rue could only make out her legs swinging off the landing of the third floor. Rue climbed the ladder, clutching nervously on each rung, and Varina didn't reach out to help her even when Rue struggled up beside her onto the thin wood slats. The thick rope for the corpse bell hung heavy between them.

Varina had bunched her skirts round her thighs and her bare legs were pale in the moonlight, dotted with russet downy hairs. She'd put on a bonnet and wore a moth-bitten pair of evening gloves like she had someplace to be, though, of course, she did not.

"What you doin' way up here?" Rue said.

Varina did not answer, but kept on looking where she was looking, out through the arrow slit window. Rue watched her in profile, studied her harsh gaunt face. Varina's tongue darted out to lick her lips, a nervous gesture like a troubled snake.

"I saw them comin'."

"Who you saw, Miss Varina?"

The window Varina gazed out of looked over the woods and the river and beyond, to the graveyard on the hill and to the plantation that used to be. It was the whole of the world as much as either of them ever knew it.

"Soldiers," Varina said. "They've come to kill us."

"You was only dreamin'."

How many times now had Rue quieted this same fear? How many times too had Rue stoked it? For it was fear that kept Varina locked away, and fear that kept her safe.

"I wasn't sleepin'. You don't dream if you don't sleep," Varina said. Then, "There. Rue, look." She pointed her gloved finger out the window.

Rue looked and saw, or dreamed she saw, down below on the path she'd walked and walked: one pale rider on a horse. He was all white except the black holes cut out for his eyes. But then Rue blinked, and he was gone or he never was, swallowed up by the woods, made black by the midnight.

PART FOUR

PROMISE

==

1871

Have you heard about him? The boy that rose?

There was word of mouth to stretch out the news, the telling and retelling. The gossip ran upriver, so it was that people were tramping down to them from a journey of weeks, of months, from all over and kingdom come, just to come up close on a miracle.

Now a tent rose to house those multitudes. It sat on the cleared-up ruins of the old House. Gone were the broke-down balustrades of Marse Charles's plantation home, gone the ashen outlines of his grand rooms. The high, swirling stairway existed now only in memory, and who could say for sure that any of it had ever existed at all?

That tent might have been magicked, it rose up so fast. Rue could see it, just, from the one window of her cabin, its cresting top poked up higher than the tree line. She had near forgotten that the plantation had been structured around the House and not the other way around. Her home then felt like it was set in the back row of a gathering crowd, all eyes riveted on the show.

Strangers came. Rue did not like it. First they were relations of folks she knew or had known, folks dispersed to different counties, sold away or run away in slaverytime, or folks that had took their after-war freedom and fled with it.

Charlie Blacksmith was among these; he'd came on back ashamed of the money he'd stolen that had been meant to buy the town a white doctor during those dark days of the Ravaging. The money was long since spent, but Charlie's mouth was filled up with apologies like apologies were tobacco chew. They forgave him. At Bruh Abel's pious suggestion they were forgiving everybody.

The peak of the tent replicated the chimney of the fallen House. The whole tent structure, white once and quickly dust-darkened, was like a ghostly afterimage of what had been, a stain of light on closed eyes.

Bean had healed up slow, but he had healed up. The Ravaging had left them. The babies had begun being born again in earnest, and of that season two were boys, two were girls, like someone re-paying a debt by giving double. Their people had given them names, not like Joseph or Mary or Charles, but like Divinity and Freeman and Jubilation and Promise.

Folks thought Bean ought to remember something about God or heaven, but he did not. He was like any five-year-old child, really; he fussed when asked too many questions, he sucked his thumb. They all came with the idea of wanting to see him, the Wonder, the Imperishable Seed, but once they saw him and got their own glimpse of his black eyes, they were sated. They came to see Bean, but they stayed for the tent, where inside Bruh Abel was known to give great, thunderous sermons so stirring they had crowds of people falling over in stunned worship. Rue sometimes sat in the back aisle and watched Bruh Abel. There was something about his strut, his absolute confidence, that she could admit now she had always hoped to learn from him.

It was on the nights of his most impassioned sermonizing that he'd come to her cabin, lie down beside her with all of his sweat and fervor still shining on him. She always let him in, kept him 'til morning.

Rue began to heal again in fits and starts, began with visits to Bean and Ma Doe, and then just carried on, unable as she'd always been to ignore a body in need. Just as, after the war, folks had returned to Miss May Belle in gradual dregs, so now they returned to Miss Rue, first for aches and pains, then for bigger things, for matters of life or death. She had to keep telling people, there was no promising she could raise their dead. Still, they kept after her, asking.

Around town administering to folks, suddenly Rue had gone and gained herself a shadow. Bean had fixed his black eyes on her upon his waking and now it was if he could not look away.

Even when she shooed him off she'd come home to find him curled up like a sow bug at her doorstep.

There was no way to wake him then but to crouch down beside him, smooth his soft brown hair. It had grown back since she'd cut it, sprang up in wilder corkscrews.

"What you doin' here?"

"I like where it's quiet, Miss Rue." The peak of the tent loomed in his sights like a mountaintop.

"Wanna know something secret?" Rue said.

"What?"

"I don't much like that tent either."

Rue let him come inside her cabin only when he promised to let her alone, not ask so many questions. He was fond of touching things, asking what's this and what's that to every stem and leaf, asking why, before she'd hardly got round to answering the last thing he'd asked.

Still, better to have him there than amongst all them strangers, or worse, wandering on the edge of the woods. One time, Bean had wandered out of the tent in the middle of one of Bruh Abel's more fervent orations, just walked on out under all the amen-ing. Rue had chased after him only to find him standing at the place where the wilderness thickened, the place where the trees grew so mightily that it was almost always night. Bean was there, at the very edge of the sunlight, squinting in at the dark.

Rue caught up to him, breathless. "What you lookin' for?"

"My friend," he said.

He'd pointed then into the shadows, at nothing.

There came a day that a knock sounded on Rue's door. She said, "I'm comin' and comin'," and she swung it open and startled.

There in front of her was a white woman with a newborn baby, smallish and wrinkled and pink, drooling on the woman's shoulder. She could have been Varina, and for a long, bad moment Rue thought she was, and she couldn't say a word or hardly breathe.

The white woman's teeth were brown spokes in her gums. "You the conjure woman, ain't you?"

Well, when a white woman told you you were a thing, that's what you were. Rue nodded dumbly, and the white woman and her baby came right on in.

Rue knew poor and this woman was poor—she could see it, and smell it, on her. Still, the woman wasn't ashamed to make herself at home. Rue had but the one good chair, and the white woman dropped herself down in it, raised one mud-blackened foot, and rubbed at the heel.

"Come a long way, Missus?" Rue asked.

The white woman nodded, dislodging the pink body on her shoulder. "Heard this was a place a' healin'."

"Preacher's in the tent." Rue gestured through the window. The tent was so blaring white it was like a presence in the room with them. "He'll be preparin' for the night's sermon, but I can take you to him if you like."

The white woman shook her head. "I come lookin' for you."

Rue stood and waited, afraid to sit or even slouch in the presence of this white lady, no matter how poor she might seem.

"All my babies I ever had were taken from me before they first birthday."

"Taken?" Rue thought of Ma Doe, who'd had every last one of her children sold off.

"Taken to heaven," the white woman said. "All 'em doctors came and went each time and still 'em babies died, and I says to my husband I gotta find me somebody what knows what they about, that's got some divine correspondence what can save this here boy."

Rue could have laughed. If divinity was coming now in forms of correspondence, then she was more than illiterate to it; she was deaf and blind besides.

"I tell you, Miss Conjure, I do got a fear."

"Rue."

"Huh?"

"My name. It's jus' plain Rue, Missus."

The white woman put her baby to her knee and bounced both in agitation. The baby yawned and jiggled, unbothered. "You got a baby, don't you?"

Only a white woman could ask something so intimate so pointedly. Rue shook her head. The woman leaned forward, really squinted at her through a fall of grease-stiffened hair, looked at her like she didn't quite believe it, which was fair enough. It was strange, Rue supposed, hard to think of a girl, and then a woman, who'd made her whole life and livelihood from other folks' babies never having one. Not wanting one herself. Well, Rue had never thought it would or could be. But now.

"You soon to have one," said the white woman. She sat back, satisfied like she'd won an argument. "And when you do you'll know just exactly what I'm feelin', all the fear and the baby love. Every single minute a' every single day. It'll eat you up."

She leaned forward and kissed the top of her baby's creamy head. The baby crooked its mouth in pleasure; drool dribbled from his open lips and dangled down to the woman's blue-scabbed knees. She didn't seem to feel it puddle.

"Come back on Friday," Miss Rue said. It was a thing her mama often said, because magic was meant to be best on Fridays. Probably it was just to give her space to think. Friday was in two days' time.

The woman nodded and stood. She swooped up the fussing, restless baby. Rue would've liked to hold him, but she didn't.

"Y'all got some place you stayin'?" Rue wasn't offering.

"We on at my uncle John's place." It took Rue longer than a moment to remember Ol' Marse John. He'd been her daddy's old master. The Marse John who had died under his wench saying, *Goddammit goddammit god—*

"You a relation to him?" Rue did not remember any living family, but a son, Jack, who had died, not in lovemaking like his daddy, but in the war. Rue thought, it seems the dead is rising.

"I'm the daughter a' his sister what married up and lived east a' here. Government man come to me and said he was tracing up white folks' properties that were deserving. A bit a' Christian charity that. Yank devils tore Uncle John's whole house asunder but no matter," the white woman said. She was talking singsong to her baby, her voice roiling as she bobbed him in her arms. "Don't matter, no it don't. We come here for the land."

Varina's expression was haunted. "I seen 'em. A white man and a white woman. A mangy black dog. A baby."

"They ain't see you?" Rue asked.

"No, no, I stay well clear of that white man." Varina made *white man* sound like a cuss word every time she said it.

"Good." Rue walked the length of the rectory. Five steps, turned, walked the other way. It made for agitated pacing. She thought, not for the first time, how could Varina stand it here?

"They lay traps in the woods catchin' rabbits and varmint." Varina sniffed, that old plantation daughter's affectation. "They let that baby go round stark naked."

Varina still carried herself stiff with her lost wealth and station, queen of a cotton industry so mighty she could play the hostess to visiting princes and have them feel grateful to be received.

"Miss Varina," Rue said, startled. Knew then what about the room had set her so suddenly on edge. Varina had hid her bedroll, neatened her one dress, tamed down her curls. She turned her chair toward the door and there were two tea cups set out, like they were just waiting for a housegirl to run up and fill them. Sweet tea for company. "Has somebody been in here with you?"

Varina's blush rose on her pale skin like a fever tell.

" 'Course not. Whyever would you think that?"

Secrets. They had always had them.

Weren't the meek to inherit the earth? Rue felt she'd heard a preacher say that once or twice before. It was the truth. The tent near glowed in the dark as she approached it. Inside, lit lanterns and the fiery passion of all them people made the thin covering shine yellow from the outside. As Rue neared, the applause that emanated shook away the smudge of black on the tent's far side that she'd been thinking was a shadow. It was, in fact, a thick murder of crows that took flight and cawed as they did so. Such a synchronous exodus that. How'd they know? Not just to flee but to flee as one, none left behind.

Rue parted the flaps of the tent. The enthusiasm shook her, a blast of hot air. Standing before hard-hewn benches, a crowd of fifty or so folks, come from far and wide, were on their feet, praising. They needn't have bothered making the benches. This was not a place for sitting but for standing up and hollering, for rising up in ecstasy to be that much closer to the good Lord. Their hands worked in clapping and fanning and upturned exalting. They stomped and sweated, raised up whorls of dust and grass into the air, audacious on the very spot that had once been the plantation House.

Rue's man hotfooted at the front of the crowd in his usual glory, and there beside him, like a miniature in white robes, was Bean, holding out a collection basket half his size, taking in the action with the full of his big black eyes.

Bruh Abel threw Rue a wink across the crowd when she came in. Didn't miss a step. Bean moved amongst the parishioners with his little wicker basket, collecting dark-colored coins and even dirty, coiling slips of paper money that he had to tamp down with his little hand, lest they get caught up by the wind. Folks gave and gave. Here Bean was, a little miracle, or the little miracle that they had made him, five years old, and he carried himself like a man. Who had taught him that? Up in the front Bruh Abel was kissing the wrinkled hands of some reed-bent old grandmama who was moved to weeping just to see him.

Folks left in an unhurried fashion. They kissed and hugged and goodbyed each other, exuberant, congratulating themselves for worship well done. They dropped money in Bean's basket, rubbed his thick brown hair, same as if he were a rabbit's foot, a disembodied thing for other folks' luck. They streamed on past her and said, "Miss Rue," if they knew her or just cast a smile in her direction if they didn't. They knew she was someone important, leastwise, because she was important to Bruh Abel.

Rue waited as the tent all but emptied. Bean, drifting, neared her, and she caught his eye. "Miss Rue," he said politely, and she liked the way he said it. He mashed the two words together like they were one. For him, there was no distinction. She was who she was.

"Bean, I brung you somethin'."

He held out the collection basket and it made her heart hurt to see that that was what he was expecting. From her apron pocket she pulled out a little bag full of marbles. Bean's eyes narrowed down to strange black stitches of delight when he smiled. He pulled the drawstring open and spilled them right out onto the grass aisle.

"I can have 'em?" he asked. His collection basket was all but forgotten now as he plopped down to play with the marbles. Rue laughed and scooped the basket up.

"'Course you can."

"Can I take 'em to play with her?"

An ill chill ran through Rue at that. Her enthusiasm shriveled but surely he had meant Sarah, his mama. Who else?

Bruh Abel came up on her from behind and put his arm around her waist, took Bean's basket from her in the same motion.

"Y'all stayin' on to listen to the next sermon?"

Bruh Abel's services had grown so sought after, he'd lately had to double them. It was a fascinating thing to see them back-to-back. To watch the things he mirrored in himself and the words that came to him in one and not the other, the movements of his hands, the twitch of a smile in his face. It was like catching someone admiring their own reflection. "Ain't vanity one of them big sins?" she'd sometimes say to him, and sure enough he'd just grin, suck her into that sinking cheek dimple. There was no shaming him. Not there under his own big white tent, with his own Lazarus playing marbles at his feet.

"I come to speak to you in fact," Rue began. Now that she was here to say it, she didn't know quite how to put words to her urgency or the fear that was rising up inside her. "I seen a white woman."

Bruh Abel quirked his eyebrow. "What? You ain't never seen one before?"

"She come to see me about her baby."

"You help her, ain't you?"

Rue worried her lip. "I tol' her to come back. I plan to help her," she hurried to say. "But she a relation a' Ol' Marse John who owned the only other plantation near here durin' slavery times. She stayin' on at his place. Got a husband with her."

"Tell 'em to come hear some prayin'," Bruh Abel said. He busied himself adjusting the tall wood lectern he'd had made. It was where his Bible often sat, open but untouched. Already, the tent was filling up again for the second go-round.

"That ain't it," she said. She hated him a little then. How easy he was with words when she wasn't.

The last time strange white folks had come through the woods, her mama had been alive and the country had been warring. And they had come as an army.

Bruh Abel bent to start picking up Bean's marbles, ignoring the small whine of protest the little boy made. Rue couldn't understand why Bruh Abel didn't see it. That he had made Bean in his image, made him a curiosity on which the town hinged, when he'd said all along that that was what they'd been trying to avoid. For her part in it Rue felt sorry, but in a town now known for its curiosities, she had begun to fade quietly into the weave. Hadn't that fact saved both of their lives—hers and Bean's?

Sarah came in at the lead of the next flood of parishioners, heading straight for her son with a sense of duty if not of ease. She laid a kiss on Bean's forehead, one he didn't seem even to feel, then straightened up slow to greet Bruh Abel and then Rue. Her expression was tight and tired. Jonah was away working at some port, here-and-gone the way only a man could be in the name of supporting his family.

"Bean, you mindin' Bruh Abel?" she asked her son. She petted his head the same way the other faithful had. No feeling in it, just a kind of reluctant awe.

"Yes'm," Bean said.

Rue wanted nothing more than to scoop him up and run. Instead she said in a hush to Bruh Abel, outside of Sarah's hearing, "I just ain't think it's a good sign. White folks wonderin' after us. After all a' this."

Bruh Abel raised his arms wide. If he could've he would've held in his palm the very idea of all-of-this. "Ain't you heard? This our time. The time that was Promised."

He kissed her, full on the lips, there in front of Sarah and Bean and those waiting on worship. Rue extracted herself quick from his arms. She was dizzy from just the sheer force of how free he thought he was. Nothing like that could last.

"Miss Rue." "Good evening, Miss Rue." "Sister Rue." It all clattered around her brash as church bells as she forced her way out of the tent against a crowd clambering to get in.

It was never fully dark anywhere now, not with the candlelight in the tent always burning, emanating that constant soft glow of promise. The woods on the periphery were what was all dark; the distance in between stayed stuck in everlasting twilight. That's where Rue lingered, masked in shadow, with a steadying palm to her belly. She was making herself afraid, she reasoned, because it had always felt safer to her to be afraid. From the tent she heard the beginning of Bruh Abel's second sermon, thick and clear and well-rehearsed.

"Out of the land of Egypt," he was proclaiming, "out of the house of slavery. You shall have no other gods before me."

"Miss Rue," a man's voice called. There was no getting away from folks, was there? Rue stopped and put a smile on.

It was Charlie Blacksmith approaching her. His wide face was weighted down with contrition as it had been the whole time he'd been back. If anyone had killed them babies it was him, she might have said, if she were to let hard devil thoughts in. He'd run off with the money meant for the white Quaker doctor who might've healed them. Rue was not a preacher, or a Quaker, or an angel besides. She didn't have to be forgiving.

He pulled his hat from his head, showing the place where his hair was thinning, the roots coming in a startling gray. She'd known him all her life. He'd known her daddy, too, 'til he'd died.

"I got a story for you, Miss Rue, if you'll oblige an ol' fool," Charlie said. "After I left here I went searchin' for word of any relations I had still livin'. Had three sisters an' four brothers that got sold away, always wondered where they got to, what they'd grown up to be like, but I couldn't find no trace of 'em. Got round to the place I myself was born to see if I could find my mama's grave at least, but that place is all gone too. The white folks stayin' there now ran me off their land with the assistance of a shotgun.

"In the end I just roamed. Got to feelin' that everybody I'd ever known was gone. But then I recalled an ol' sweetheart a' mine by the name a' Airey. Y'all remember her, don'tchya? You was only such a little thing back then."

Rue remembered her: Airey, that pretty runaway so many of them had envied when she'd stayed and envied more when she'd gone. And Rue remembered her mama's hand in it, though the miracle at the river when Airey had taken flight, just disappeared like a bird, surely was just a wish, a muddling of Rue's childhood memories and dreams. Still, didn't miracles abound?

"I remember."

Charlie grew excited. "Weren't she beautiful?"

"She was."

"Well, I went lookin' an' askin' round an' finally I found her." He paused to grin, perhaps stirred by the memory. "She made it up to the North, she did, an' once there she hired herself out as a cook like she was always wantin'. Done real well fo' herself. Got herself a lawful husband an' a whole crop a li'l 'uns, littlest of 'em favors her mama." He moved his hand over his own arms like he was sprinkling stardust, to indicate the birthmark patterns up Airey's body. "She done named that last baby May, after yo' mama's memory."

A bubbling sadness rose up in Rue but underneath was joy. "It's a good name."

"It is," said Charlie. "But Airey, she say she missin' home, this place the onlyest one her family ever known, goin' back generations. Her daddy plant the first seed, that's what folks says. I tol' her if she can scrape together the money maybe she oughta come back to look on it like I done. I hope that she do.

"Anyhow, I got to askin' Airey how she made it north when so many others didn't or couldn't, how she escaped the patrolmen an' the swamp an' the sickness an' the dogs. Well, she set me down an' she cry a li'l for all the time an' all the years an' all them people we done lost, an' at the end a' it she tol' me how she got over. She say, 'Charlie, I just flew.'"

That night, Bruh Abel came to her, crawled to her, woke her from sleep and kissed her and worried at her chest and nipples with his teeth ravening as only a man could. He'd leave moons with his front teeth, bite marks that would remain as indents on her skin for lovely long hours after.

"Quit that," she said in the midst of her sleep. She was trying to stay angry at him.

"Can't," he said. He was cupping her breasts now in his hands

like water he was bringing to his mouth to drink. "These gon'
heavy. Like to break yo' back."

She hadn't quite noticed that. She hadn't been letting herself
notice a lot of things. But there it was: the tightening of the click-
clack beads Miss May Belle had taught her to wear, and just earlier that white woman's telling grin. Rue's brimming senses, her
full breasts teeming with promise, spreading longways and sideways across her chest, her body making ready, making room.

Rue pulled Bruh Abel's head away from her flesh-full nipples.

"That ain't for you no more."

"What?"

"Them is for the baby now."

She watched for what seemed like hours but was only one small
moment as Bruh Abel caught on to her meaning, his gray eyes
going just the littlest bit wide, his lips parting in wonderment. And
then the whole of his face brightened with revelation, with delight, and only then was it real, because it was real for him, the
whole idea, a quickening of her heart.

"You sure?"

She laughed. "I make my name on being sure when a woman's
got with child."

"Yeah, you do, but it's different when it's you, ain't it?"

"Lord." It was so different.

He pulled away from her, drawing back his weight, suddenly
careful. He inspected her naked body now like he'd never seen a
woman before in the whole of his life. It was sort of wonderful,
even just to shock him, to make Bruh Abel, of all people, care-
filled and new.

On Friday, early morning, the white woman came back, and Rue
had to see to her, like it or not. She had the vial ready, one of Bruh

Abel's empty jars, cork stopped on whiskey and water. The white woman had made herself at home again.

"I done made you three cures," Rue told her.

Her baby looked well, Rue had to admit. He was smallish, but boys she'd found were often smallish 'til they all of a sudden grew into men. She hoped she herself would have a girl.

Rue didn't know what she would say, even as she cast a handful of emptied walnut shells across the open floor, shells upon which the white woman was singularly transfixed, believing without even being told that those cast shells had the power of divination simply because they'd been cast by Rue's black hand in the close mystical quarters of a fall-down plantation house in the woods.

Next Rue brought out the necklace she'd made. It was a simple bleach-boiled bone wrapped in rough twine. The white woman tied it around her neck quick and eager. The little hooking bone sat primly on the top of her low-slung cleavage, the twine already irritating her neck, splotches of red forming.

"What is it?"

Rue struggled. "It a coon's penis, Missus."

The white woman nodded reverently, her baby cooed. "What it for?"

"Keep yo' husband virile."

"'Course."

Lastly Rue handed her the vial, held out her hand, and waited for payment. It came, one silver coin in her palm, that simple.

"It'll work?"

"It'll work," Rue lied. "This one won't be took from you."

The white woman showed again her habit, bending over and kissing on her baby's head, breathing that scalp in greedily, like that was where all the air in the world was coming from.

"Thank you, Miss Conjure," the white woman said. Rue did not correct her.

When the woman had gone Rue went walking, past the crowds, past the tent poles, past the graveyard and the creek. The knot on the tree faced north, that was how she always found it, occluded as it was by a thick matting of moss. Making sure that no one had followed, she slipped her two coins—one coin from the easy work she'd done, the other spirited out of Bean's collection plate—into her little bag of treasure hid away in the hollow.

WARTIME

===

1864

The drumming was in the sky. Marse Charles had woke the whole plantation to come and hear it. It was before sunup even, that he'd sent out the trumpet player whose bellow usually started the day. Come so early, this music had not been meant to signal work time for the field hands, or to summon house slaves who felt they'd only just rested down their heads. It was to herald doom. The trumpeter played a mournful tune, like a sad, strange accompaniment to the distant syncopation of warfare.

But who did Marse Charles think he was waking? They were all already awake, braced in their beds. Was this it now—kingdom come?

"Come on now," Miss May Belle said to Rue.

They joined the sweeping crowd of black folks being summoned by their master, a black cloud moving dazed in the first crack of morning light.

The mood was tense. They were shaken, like a whole mess of sleepwalkers startled awake to find themselves in the yard of the House, field workers on one side, house workers on another, and between them Marse Charles high on the top step of the porch, which reminded Rue of the stage he'd constructed and deconstructed in the space of a day for his fete. Six months had passed since the party, but it still made her dizzy just to think on it.

A loud bottomless boom echoed in the distance, and the house seemed to rock within their vision. Behind her daddy, Varina came out as if summoned by the cannon fire. She was dressed already for the day, looked small and pale and likely to break the next time the crashing sound came down. It shook through them all like they were the bunched leaves on the same branch of a tree. With no means of knowing from which way the echo was coming, they all of them instinctively turned their eyes to the North.

"Y'all hear that?" Marse Charles's voice was high and strained, harder than any of them had ever heard it. This man who had whupped them and cussed them and told them he was selling them off or ripping apart their families. He who had plain said no to any bit of independent hope they'd ever thought they'd found—never in any of those times did he sound so tore up as he did now. So downright sorry.

"Those vile Yankees. Those perfidious devils. They mean to snatch y'all up in yo' sleep," he warned. "They brought this feud to blood, them Northerners. To get at y'all." He leveled a shaking finger at the assembled crowd. He was so pale there in the gloaming. Did any of them believe him? "Y'all hear that? That's the stamp of their cloven feet."

What they did hear over their master's small, reedy voice was another explosion in the night, the seams of the world coming all undone. On his whim they waited there for what seemed like hours as the twilight eased to day, waited on him to release them.

"I'm to be married."

Varina had been in front of the mirror when she said it, and Rue was behind her brushing out her red curls. Everywhere about them was the heady scent of ash blown downwind from the battlefield. The fighting was miles away and yet too close; its smoke was pervasive as a plague and Varina, fool she was, seemed to think the smell was about her. She'd already taken two baths that day, made Rue carry bucketfuls of bathwater up the stairs each time and lug it away again after. Varina had stunk up the water with rose syrup enough to make herself gag. She hadn't allowed Rue or any of the house girls in to help her wash but had gotten into the hot bath alone, and there stewed herself for what seemed like hours before she'd let anyone in to dote on her. Now her hair was taking up an agitated frizz from all the washing and it wouldn't obey Rue's ministrations as she tried to gather it in a low braid. Rue never had liked white folks' hair, the way it clung wet and stringy, the way it slipped and slid and would not hold.

"Did you hear me, Rue? I said I'm to be married at last."

They caught eyes in the glass, neither one of them looking glad. It seemed to Rue that they were waiting, watching for the drama of these two people to play out before them. Who were these strange, tired little women they'd turned into? They'd lost the children they'd been—now they were grown and picking bits of war-flung ash out of their hair. The mirror told of the years, but there were things the mirror couldn't tell. The time-flattened scars from a tree branch on Rue's back, the price of a friendship she couldn't let go—and for Varina, were there marks from the minstrel show six months back? Hurts of the kind that left no earthly scar, showed no reflection?

They never spoke on it, that awful night. It was meant to have been Varina's coming out, but instead Rue felt she'd collapsed in on herself. Like a promised harvest that never came, Varina had wilted before she'd ever come to bloom.

The misery that had lately plagued Varina had little to do with her brothers turned to soldiers, brother against brother at war, or a world made suddenly bereft of men, eligible husbands slim for the picking. It seemed to Rue that there was a corruption now growing in Varina that had never quite been there before. Just because you couldn't see it or hold it or heal it didn't mean it didn't exist. The Rue of the mirror eased her face into passable excitement and said, "I heard you, Miss Varina, and I am happy for you."

"Do you want to see him?" Varina pulled herself and her hair out of Rue's grasp, pawed through her belongings. Ribbons and pins and nets and combs tumbled from in front of the mirror, and in it Rue watched herself watching Varina, watched herself trying to stay small and out of her mistress's way, lest she become just another bit of clutter to be knocked to the floor and trampled on.

"Here it is."

It was a little nothing bit of tin that Varina could hold in her two hands, and at the insistence of her fingernails it peeled open like a storybook might. It revealed no stories, only the one little picture: a man, his uniform, his gun.

"Henry is his name."

Henry peered up at Rue, and Rue had to push back on that self-saving instinct to look away from the probing eyes of a white man, real or no. He was young and thin-lipped, and someone had rosed up his cheeks in the image like they thought it would give him life. It hadn't done anything but made him look sterner. Beneath the dark shadow of his heavy brow and the flat brim of his soldier's hat, his colorless eyes seemed like empty places where something had been left out.

"Handsome Henry," Varina sung out. She wasn't even looking at his hard-tin face. She was instead waiting on Rue's expression like it held some soothsaying, reading for tea leaves in her squinting eyes and wrinkled brow.

"Handsome," Rue agreed.

Varina shut the tintype like it was a sprung trap.

———

Sarah and Rue were summoned to the parlor. Just them two. Led there by Ma Doe, who would tell them nothing of what they were about to hear.

All that week they had been in preparations, flushing the house of every single sign of mourning, searching out every inch of black and removing it in preparation for Miss Varina to receive her suitor, who, visiting temporarily from the somber northern battle lines, would not want to come to his future wife's home and find death clinging there also.

"Sit," Ma Doe told them. Neither of them moved. They'd never been asked to sit in a white person's living room a single moment of their lives. Their knees wouldn't bend that way.

Ma Doe said, "He's in a gracious mood so you best keep him that way and do as he say."

Ma Doe left and the both of them sat on the very edge of two wooden chairs like they thought comfort would lick at them from behind. Marse Charles didn't come in for nearly half an hour. That whole length of time Rue and Sarah did not speak. The sun-dense parlor grew hot from the daylight streaming in through the wide bay window. The light played tricks with the pattern of the floral lace curtain hung from the windowsill, sent an illusion of black roses across the floor to pass the time.

When Marse Charles did come, he was wearing a soldier's uniform and was trailed by a reluctant-looking Varina, her eyes downcast. There was a large desk there in front of the wide window and he sat behind it, seeming to struggle to bend at the middle in the uniform. It was not like the one Varina's beau was wearing in his little photograph. It bore no buckles or spangles. It was a ragged moth-eaten thing in a river-bottom brown. Rue thought she could make out old blood on its hem before he sat. Where did he think he was marching to in that?

Marse Charles drew out a piece of paper from the drawer.

Peeped out his tongue in a pink point and wet the nib of a pen. Began writing. To Rue the scratching sounded violent.

"I'm making a gift of them to you and your future husband," he said. "To round out your household."

"Thank you, Daddy," Varina said.

Rue didn't understand. She didn't catch on that he was referring to the two of them, to Sarah and herself, to the facts of their bodies, not 'til Sarah began suddenly to cry. It was a silent crying, just the hitch of her chest and one slow track of hushed wet down her jaw and neck. Rue doubted that Marse Charles and Varina at the other end of the room had even noticed. Sarah curled her head down so the light wouldn't catch on her tears. If he saw, Marse Charles would certainly smack her face dry.

"What this one's name. May Belle's girl?" He sighted his pen at her.

"That's Rue, Daddy."

"How many years?"

Rue didn't know if she was meant to answer or if Varina was, but no one spoke. Marse Charles grunted and scribbled something down for himself.

"And Sarah. Quadroon. Sixteen years," he added with a pen flourish. "Belongin' to you and yo' husband now."

Varina kissed her daddy dutifully on the cheek.

Miss May Belle cackled when Rue came home and asked her what it all meant. The sound wasn't laughing. It was the brittle cracking of something, some illusion Miss May Belle had let Rue have, maintained the way someone lovingly raises a pig knowing full well they plan to plate it and make a feast.

"It mean"—Miss May Belle leaned in, pausing to look around their one-room cabin like she thought that someone might be there to overhear—"that yo' new Marse Henry is gettin' hisself quite the dowry along with his new wife. Sarah's the dish, sure. But you the seasoning."

"Mama—?"

Miss May Belle wouldn't let her finish, in fact couldn't seem to stop herself. "It mean too that Marse Charles don't want Sarah round no more. Can't have her round no more. Not growin' so pretty like she's doin'. Even he won't let that kinda sin tempt him. Though Lord know he wouldn't be the first, would he? To take a drink from his own stream?

"And it mean most, Rue-baby, that they gon' take you away from me like I always knew that they would."

When Rue shut her eyes at night she'd be cast back in the darkness of the box that Varina had locked her in, like maybe she had never left it. Like maybe this Marse Henry would be the one to open up the trunk this time instead of Varina. Lay her open like she was a gift-wrapped present from one master to another. Varina had allowed it. Asked for it even.

In Rue's mind, Varina had laid for her a curse. But Rue knew well the way that curses worked, for Miss May Belle often warned against them, saying, you can tell who's got a mind to curse you by who you done wrong. A curse was a problem that could be countered. Rue would need a piece of him to do it, a lock of hair, a toenail clipping. An image to direct her curse toward.

In the midday empty, the air in Varina's bedroom was a stale outline of the mistress—it smelled of rose hip and burning hair and sweat, all a uniquely Varina scent that Rue had never been able to put words to 'til she smelled it in the air of the room without her there. It gave Rue pause, that smell—made her feel that Varina was right behind her, ghosting in her steps. She persisted despite it. Began searching under and behind things just as Varina had. She'd have secreted the photograph of her sweetheart away, no doubt.

When Rue couldn't find the photograph, she turned to the dolls, like they might hold the answer. All in a row, gorgeous doll babies that had been handmade in far distant places Rue could not even cobble up enough imagination to dream about. They were the only acceptable gifts of Varina's childhood, Rue knew, and the only real education. Varina had been taught to want to be a wife and a mama from the very day that she was born.

Rue unscrewed their heads. Ignored the plaintive squeaks their hinges made. Inside their hollow was cobwebs and disused fly parts some spider hadn't thought to eat. Nothing.

She thought about smashing them, Varina's porcelain babies, even took one by the head and raised her arm high and willed herself to do it, waiting on the satisfying crash and crunch, the sound of the porcelain skittering across the hardwood she'd just scrubbed clean. In the end she didn't do it. Couldn't. She set the doll down back in its outline of dust on the shelf, even smoothed down its hair like it was a child she was putting to sleep.

There was no use in fighting Marse Charles's commandment. Varina and Rue, they were bound to their roles, and always had been, Rue figured, by something stronger than curse and conjure — simply, they'd been raised to be the women they had become.

PROMISE

—

Ma Doe had lost her words. She had always had that slow, stately way of speaking, the deliberateness of a schoolteacher, every breath of hers a lesson. But by the summer that the tent swelled, Ma Doe's speech had slowly turned into a slurry. Worse than this—and Rue cussed herself for thinking there could be worse—Ma Doe could not write.

The pen trembled violently in her hands whenever she took it up, as if some fear of her own failure started even before she could lay the nib to paper.

It had begun when Bean had died, Rue recollected; the grief of it had sunk Ma so low. Even when he rose again, Ma Doe, who had been battered by so much loss the whole length of slaverytime and after, could not herself be resurrected to her former buoyant majesty.

The letters from the North piled up and Rue hardly knew what to make of it. She lied to Ma Doe, told her not to fret over it, but Rue fretted enough for the both of them. Varina's auntie in Boston would have to note the silence soon, and rather than take it as her due, she was liable to be sparked to action, of what type Rue dared not think on. She'd never known a white lady to leave well enough alone, and the scribbles of words on all them unanswered letters began to follow Rue everywhere she went, shading her as black clouds on the horizon.

They'd devised together a plan, Rue and Ma Doe had, but it was slow going. Every evening they'd sit at the back of the emptied classroom, and Rue would lay her hand atop Ma Doe's and together they would write. They wrote 'til their candle burned low and still only got to a sentence a night if that, had yet to finish even one letter, but they kept on.

"What's that word?" Rue asked. They'd taken a break, exhausted at the bottom of a page. Rue pointed to a word they'd just finished. It was short but she liked well the loops and swirls of it, recognized the tiny V in the center.

"That one?" Ma Doe's voice trembled, also. "That one says 'love.'"

"It's so small." Rue's hand, which ached from holding Ma's still, went straight to her belly in wonder. "'Love.'"

There were a thousand different ways to love somebody. But Rue still hadn't settled on which was the one Bruh Abel was needing. They'd never made promises. She did not know where he slept when he did not sleep with her, and she did not want to know. But with her stomach growing fat he'd been lured into her bed every night, and despite herself she made room for him.

After their lovemaking he was bound for his tent. He climbed up and out from their bed, put on his suit with quick, well-practiced movements, always did it the same way, dressed himself pants first, regimented, like if the day called for it he could go just like that, running at a moment's notice.

"You comin' to hear the sermon?"

Still naked, sheet tangled, Rue thought about saying no. She hadn't grown used to the tent, probably never would like it, and

liked less the fervor that folks felt for Bruh Abel. The way Bean
paraded down the aisle at the end of each service like some kind
of finale.

"You comin', Rue?"

Rubbing at the small, hard peak of her belly, she said, "If you
want me."

Sarah had set herself up singing, formed a little choir who
wound their music around the shape of Bruh Abel's sermonizing.
Charlie Blacksmith was forging horseshoes by the dozen for weary
travelers come at the end of their long journey from there to here.
Dinah made big quilts stuffed thick with Spanish moss, a dollar a
piece for any one of her woven stories. Li'l Sylvia sold ashcakes,
honey sweet, a secret recipe passed down from her mama. Ma
Doe had spread her schoolhouse between two cabins, employed
the knowledge of newcomer women with Northern book-learning,
and everywhere the children were beginning to scratch out their
letters and numbers too, easy as if they'd always known them. They
had all grown prosperous, as Bruh Abel had always said they
would. Sarah's choir sung on the subject of prosperity this day.
They stood on three-tiered risers, wore long gowns in baptism
white. They bellowed it—Sarah, as always chief among them and
tallest, proclaiming "This is the day the Lord has made."

Bruh Abel strutted over to the choir in step to the enabling
mhmm-ing of his audience. Rue watched as he caught eyes with
Sarah, the choirmaster of her own creation. Was there a wink
passed there that Sarah caught and received as a signal to start
singing? He looked up at her on the riser like she was the only one
he was talking to, a whisper for her ear: "What y'all go out to the
wilderness to see? This here a prophet."

The choir burst into praising ol' John the Divine. It was a good
old-fashioned, foot-stomping tune, like to get you picking cotton
faster. But just as Bruh Abel stepped away from her, Sarah's knees

began to buckle and sway, and the choir, thinking she'd been took by the spirit, sang louder. Rue watched as Sarah drew in breath but no sound came out. She crumpled and fell, hitting against each tier on the way down.

Sarah was pregnant.

"You needa rest up," Rue told her. In the new world that they'd made, maybe a black woman could afford a little rest for her own sake. "Stay in bed."

Bruh Abel carried Sarah all the way to that bed and laid her down in it.

"When's Jonah due back?" he asked and propped her pillow. Rue looked on, wary.

Sarah, still faint, could barely shake her head without making herself dizzy. "Inside a month or so. But just as soon as that he'll be off again."

"He's a good man," Bruh Abel offered.

"You go on back, tell 'em Sarah's just fine," Rue told him. Bruh Abel turned to her, seemed to see her and her belly for the first time.

"You right. I oughta leave womenfolk to womenfolk."

Bruh Abel kissed Rue's hand and took himself out. She could see in the set of his retreating shoulders that he was already re-forming himself, shape-shifting back into the preacher returning to his tent to talk of a miracle. "Let us pray for Sister Sarah," Rue could already hear him saying.

"You pregnant," Sarah said.

Her warm brown eyes looked on Rue, sharper than they had cause to be. Womenfolk to womenfolk indeed. Rue laid her hand on the slight stretch beneath her own oversized dress.

"Folks talkin'," Sarah explained.

"They always do." She sat herself down on the edge of Sarah's bed, her legs already aching. "I ain't even as far along as you is. How come you ain't say nothin'?"

"How come you ain't?"

They were both of them just passing through that strange twilight where the new feeling stirring in their bodies was pushing past simple sickness and weakness and aches and pains into being a real idea, a person, a possibility. But to say so aloud seemed over-proud, like fate itself might wend in, overhear, and intervene.

Sarah sighed. "You'd think I'd know by now, how to go about bein' with child. It don't get no easier."

"You just havin' a rough go is all. Some babies is just more difficult than others. You take it slow, like I say, you be alright."

"You too," Sarah said, easy. "Think ours will come at round the same season. Like twins. What you think?"

"That'd be nice." Rue almost meant it too.

Bean had disappeared again. They'd forgotten him in the confusion and by the time Rue got herself back to the tent no one could say where the little wonder had got to, only that he'd vanished. *Into thin air*, they were saying. *Like he Raptured.*

"Now, now." Even Bruh Abel wouldn't allow that type of gossip to start up. "Most likely the boy just wander off."

"He upset about his mama," Rue said, though she didn't think that was altogether true. She had the notion Sarah and Bean would never warm to each other, as mama and son ought to. Rue recalled what Sarah had told her the night of Bean's short death: *He don't belong to me.*

To whom did he belong then? They got up a search party. Folks went through cabins, looked in outhouses and amongst the tall, prosperous wheat in the field, but Rue went straight into the thick of the black woods, not knowing why, but just *knowing.*

It was coming on dusk, but Rue's eyes were sharp. She was just beyond the sickle-bend of the river when she first saw it, black and shining amongst the roots of a hedge of thorns: one black marble. The next one was blue and not so far from the first. Then a green marble led Rue away from the river and brought her to a grouping of three more scattered along a disused footpath.

Now Rue had strayed so far that she could no longer hear folks' cries of "Bean!"—could hear only her own urgent footfalls and the insistent hum of sunset insects. The night was their time but hers also. One more marble, there, at the end of the path.

Rue turned on her heel when she heard the low growl behind her. Slinking, the gray fox stepped out from behind a tree, its eyes glowing. Something was grasped in the fox's jaw, caught in its pointed teeth. It looked to be a bit of black and green fabric.

Her stomach lurched. She'd never known a fox to attack a human child, only livestock, hens and rabbits and smaller prey. But a mama fox might do anything to defend her babies, and Bean was only such a little boy, so naïve and curious.

The sound of a gunshot came, so close and so loud that Rue thought the bullet must've tore through her own body. But before her the fox jerked and fell in a splash of blood. The shot was true, so neatly through the spine it had near severed the fox's head.

Stunned but unhurt, Rue shivered. She shrunk down to her knees beside the fox, and from the trees a white man stepped down, heavy-footed over twigs and leaves. His shotgun still bloomed smoke and he whistled as he approached, impressed.

"Damn," he said, delighted. "That thing near got you."

Rue wouldn't look up or meet his eyes, not even when he crouched down to inspect his kill.

"Foxes is wild in this part a' the country," he was saying. "Like I ain't never seen. Distemper most like."

"Please, suh." Rue's voice came out in a warble, child-thin, like it had been in slaverytime when every white man was *sir*. "I'm lookin' for a li'l boy. He lost."

The man stood and Rue took it as permission to do the same. Her stomach ached. The dead fox lay between their feet and Rue couldn't stop watching the man's cooling gun.

"Figured somebody done run him off," he grunted. "That boy sick or somethin'? Eyes ain't right."

Rue didn't know how to answer so she didn't. The man whistled again, this time like he was calling a dog.

At the sound a white woman waddled down from the same direction he'd come. She was less sure on her feet over the vines, for she had a drooling baby on her hip. And she led Bean by the hand. Rue knew her at once.

"Miss Conjure, ain't it?" the white woman asked.

Rue was surprised when Bean ran straight over to her, hugged at her waist. He smiled up at Rue, didn't seem bothered at all by the white folks or the gun or the dead fox's unhinged neck.

"Found him wanderin' the woods," the woman said. "He belong to yer missus?"

Rue blinked. So they thought Bean was white? And Rue his good nurse? She felt something rise in her throat, maybe bile or bitter laughter.

"Yes. Thank you fo' findin' him," she said and scooped him up in her arms. Bean was heavy in a pleasant way, and his warmth calmed the thud of her heart. "I best take him on home before his mama get to missin' him."

"You oughta keep better care a' him, girl," the white man said.

Rue wondered if under his bloodstained overalls the white man was wearing the coon penis charm she'd made for his wife.

With Bean in her arms, she walked backward a ways before she felt safe turning away from them: the man, his wife, their thriving baby, the lifeless fox. Rue broke into near a run, best she could with Bean cuddled over her shoulder.

When they came close to home Rue stirred the boy, set him down to walk on his own.

"Where was you runnin' to?" she asked him.

"Wasn't runnin'. Wantin' to see my friend."

"Which friend is that?" But at the bottom of her belly Rue felt she already knew.

"The lady"—he yawned—"that lives in the woods."

"The lady what found you?"

"Not her." Bean squeezed Rue's hand. "The other lady. With the pretty red hair."

"How you come to know her? You follow me?"

Bean shrugged. Of course. He followed Rue everywhere 'til she'd shoo him off, tell him to find somewhere else to play. The other children were averse to his strangeness, all the things that made him different. Or was it that they remembered the Ravaging, when they had sickened and some had died and Bean had lived and died and lived on? Who would want to play with a miracle?

"Her name is Auntie V. I go there when I don't wanna be seen."

He told it like a riddle and Rue might've hoped he was speaking on an imaginary friend as children sometimes did, made real enough because they believed in them. But Rue knew he knew her, Varina. Easy as he'd told Rue about it, he might tell somebody else.

The tent still glowed as Rue and Bean neared it. There were voices within, joyous. Had they given up their search for Bean as soon as that? Or rather had they given up searching in favor of praying? Rue could've spat.

She took him home, or leastwise, to the place where he was born, to the very bed in fact, and there was Sarah, wide awake. Her eyes were rheumy; the weakness that had caused her swoon had only worsened while Rue had been gone, and Sarah didn't seem even to know her boy had been missing the whole of the evening.

"Don't worry," Rue said, touching Sarah's fever-warm skin. "I'll keep watch over Bean 'til you get yo' strength up."

And she would, if only to keep him from telling things better kept hidden.

Rue did as she promised, kept Bean close after the day he'd disappeared as a godmama might. Black women always had been good for caring on each other's children, even since slaverytime, a point of pride that. As Sarah's condition worsened, Rue took on Bean, especially as it became clear that even the most reverently charitable of the newly come folks would not keep him long in their houses. There was something eerie, they whispered, about his eyes. Not even the color but just the way he stared like he could see past things and through things and into things that weren't quite there.

Did he see his mama's sickness? Seven months along now and Sarah could hardly walk the length of her own room without some hand-holding. Persistent, Rue made her walk the little bit that she could. Sarah's growing baby sat low like a stone at the bottom of her belly and seemed just as strange and still. When Rue would check on Sarah, Bean insisted on following. The whole visit he'd stare at his bedbound mama, not at all upset, but like her sickness, her decline fascinated him.

"What's doin'?"

Rue steeped mint leaves in the bottom of a cup, the water still bubbling at the boil. Bean followed close, nearly underfoot as Rue brought the drink over to his mama.

"She weak is all. Carryin' the new baby."

Bean wrapped an arm around Rue's leg. Birth, sickness, death, and resurrection, it had all happened in those two slim, dark rooms of the cabin, Rue reminded herself. Was it a wonder that Bean saw things in the shadows, when all over, every cabin in that plantation, there were so many shadows to see?

"It's a girl this time, I'm thinkin'." Sarah's voice showed the weakness Rue had warned against. She wasn't doing enough eating. Holding nothing down.

"What make you say so?"

Sarah shook her head just a little. No answer then, just a feeling. "What you think fo' yours?"

Rue hid her grin by blowing the steam off Sarah's tea. She was supposed to say she just wanted one come healthy, fingers and toes. Ain't that what the mamas always said? "Girl maybe? Tryna think up good names."

Sarah breathed a laugh. "Bruh Abel's liable to pick a page out the Bible."

Rue shook her head. "Think I'll pick somethin' I ain't heard no one have before. What you thinkin' for yours?"

"S'pose I'll 'llow you to tell me when she comes out."

It was the closest they'd ever come to talking on it, the way Black-Eyed Bean had got named. No other thing had stuck to him. In the beginning Sarah had tried. Called him by his true name, Jordan. But folks that saw him had whispered in horror "Black-Eyed Bean" around him so often he'd got to thinking that was what he was called. He would answer to no other thing but Bean. Would just sit in the same mute fascination that froze his face now.

Was it meant to be a slight, what Sarah had said about Rue naming her baby? A curse? Rue could not say. Sarah had shut her eyes, grown tired maybe from that little bit of jawing, her tea gone untouched. From the other side of his mama's chair Bean was watching her sleeping, examining the rise and fall of her chest, unaware or uncaring that they'd been speaking on his origins.

———

Bruh Abel dreamed of other tents, a sky-wide spread of tents as lofty as a field of clouds. "Can't you just see it?"

Rue shrugged. "Not really."

"Girl, you ain't got no imagination."

It tired her out just to watch him moving through the wide, empty space inside his tent. The area seemed so much larger without all the worshipping bodies who'd just left it, and Bruh Abel moved like a little boy at play in it, going from stillness to sudden motion in unpredictable bursts like summer rain.

"When the baby come," he said, "we can go south first. Follow the warm in winter."

The life Bruh Abel dreamed of sounded to Rue like the exhausting up-and-down movement of migrating birds. In search of what? Everything he said lately began with *When the baby come* and ended in a kingdom of revival tents stretched the whole way from north to south. Rue couldn't begin to see how they might get from here to there, what sacrifices might hammock in between. There was Bean to think of. And Ma Doe's health. There was Varina most of all, whose existence was every day threatened by Bruh Abel's growing flock. Their trepidation about the wilderness beyond the revival tent could only so long be fueled by secondhand stories of haints.

Bruh Abel wanted to preach, he said. He wanted her to heal. Lately Rue had no stomach for healing. There was growing a sudden fear in her, a distaste of touching other folks' sickness. When the baby came, her sweet little girl as she'd lately been thinking of her, Rue didn't wish to lay hands on any skin but hers.

Still, something was coming. There was no denying that same something that had Bruh Abel spreading his wings hawk-wide and her doing the exact opposite, pulling up twigs around herself for a nest. Was it always like this? she wondered. Being with child had sent her into a hoarding up of love, like she'd got word that a hard frost was coming to befall everything, love being nourishment. Love being hope.

Bruh Abel jumped up onto the bench in front of her. Stood on it straddled and carefree like it were a log he was balancing down a creek.

"When we get down there," Bruh Abel was saying, from above. "When the baby come, we'll get ourselves good and married. What y'all think a' that?"

She made him no answer, for in the corner of her vision a ghost flickered. "Get down," she said.

Behind him through the thick of the tent she saw the black outline of the people on the other side, running. The sound of their panic came through the tent skin in muffled singular chaos. Outside someone had let out a high, feral scream. Bruh Abel jumped down from his perch. Came to wrap his arms around her, protecting her. Them.

The shadows of the crowd loomed long and large as their outlines came across the tent. They were coming closer, a few startled sweating men, Red Jack and Charlie amongst them, a few others Rue didn't know. Bruh Abel hid her behind him.

"What's happened?"

"We need yo' help," Charlie said, and Rue saw that he carried a curled-up body on his back, something as still as a carcass. He laid it down gentle in the grassy aisle and the men stepped back as if afraid to approach it. It looked like an overgrown black crow, spilling everywhere its feathers. It was only as it unfurled itself in a slow jerking fit that Rue realized what it was they'd brought her. It was a woman, and one she knew: Airey.

Oil wouldn't budge it, water neither. When Rue put either to Airey's sore, ruined skin, the woman would begin to wail and thrash. They couldn't even move her but left her down in the center of the church tent where Charlie had placed her, and as Rue worked she had amassed an audience of disturbed onlookers, all of them whispering about the haints in the woods.

"Who done this?"

"You seen 'em?"

"White faces."

"Monstrous."

"Come to kill us all."

Rue found she couldn't focus with their chittering. Her fingers kept sticking in the tar that covered Airey head to foot. It was still warm. Rue tried to get at the root of a black feather and instead set Airey to caterwauling.

"What you need?" Bruh Abel asked, kneeling beside Rue. He secreted a hand at her back and rubbed where he knew it often ached her when she was bent working like this.

"A clean new knife."

Bruh Abel asked Charlie to fetch it, but Charlie refused to leave Airey's side, kept pacing and smacking at his chest and saying, "I'm the one that done this to her. Told her to come down here. Told her her home was safe again."

Airey's home was not safe. In halting fevered confusion, she'd whispered about the monsters she'd encountered as she'd approached the town, a woman traveling foolishly alone on the road to a fabled land of Promise. She'd made the long journey back from the North, the reverse of the one she'd fled through, this one in leisure on a train and then a steamboat, but after that there was no sure way to get to their isolated strip of land except on foot, so that's what she had done, with a little money in her pocket and a lot of determination. She had wanted to come and see where her folks were buried, maybe buy them up a headstone so that no one would forget their names.

The ill spirits had come up on her from behind she said, and by the time she'd heard their horses' hoofbeats, their mangy vicious dogs barking, there was no point in running, no safe place anywhere, and she'd crumpled to the ground.

"Who was they?"

"Devils," Airey kept saying, writhing in the dirt. "They must have been devils."

They were masked. Airey could identify only the grim black of their cut-out eyeholes, bearing down on her from the white of their full-body robes. Hid beneath those sheets was surely something much more horrible, something so heinous it couldn't even be bared. Still, Airey fought as their cold, white hands had ripped off her clothes. As they poured the hot tar. As they dumped the feathers. She was still fighting.

Bean was the one that brought Rue the knife. He came quick, his chest still panting from the run he'd taken to her cabin and back, swift on his little stick legs. He'd picked just the type she needed, one good and sharp.

"What you mean to do?" Bruh Abel asked.

"Ain't no way I can see but to cut it from her. Just slice as close as I can, try not to get too much of her own skin." Rue whispered to him. "But dammit, she won't be still."

"I can help," Bruh Abel said. He got down on his knees beside Airey, careless of his own white robe, which straight away picked up mud and grass and tar and some of Airey's blood as he drew close to her and clutched her fighting hands.

Airey had never met him but she stilled and looked right at him, like she knew him and was trying to puzzle out where from.

"You ain't alone in them woods anymore, Sister Airey," he said. "And I got to tell you, you weren't never alone."

"They hurt me so bad," Airey croaked out. "They say they only gon' leave me alive to be a message to the rest a y'all."

Bruh Abel drew nearer to her, his expression placid but determined. Rue placed the knife a hair breadth shy of skin, beginning at Airey's arm, which beneath the black tar was white-speckled still, just as it had been long ago, with the force of Miss May Belle's curse.

"Oh, you a message, alright," Bruh Abel said. "One heard loud and clear."

Airey's whole body tensed like she was about to bolt.

"You a message, sister, that any devil can be fled from, can be survived no matter how pervasive. You beautiful as an angel, girl. You just sprout wings of faith and fly."

She relaxed, breathed in his words, kissed his hands to her mouth, and began to cry. And hearing his words, seeing through his eyes to his vision in the clouds, Rue, slowly, carefully, was able to make the first slice, and the first of the feathers came free.

WARTIME

===

Miss Varina's betrothed was soon to arrive. They waited. Every one of Marse Charles's colored slaves stood in the yard of the House, assembled in the same manner they'd listened to the exploding cannonballs in the distance weeks earlier, a gathered awkward collection of black folks and their two white owners. But unlike that war-torn morning, this noontime was hot and quiet, a stillness punctuated now and then by heat-drunk flies and one or the other of the slaves fidgeting, quelling the urge to swat.

Varina waited on the veranda, which offered no shade at this time of day. Rue stood beside her holding up a white lace parasol, her arms aching. Varina was not satisfied. Halfway through their waiting she'd sent Sarah into the house to run and bring to her a small white hand fan. Now Varina was working herself into a sweaty anxiousness with that fan, flapping it about her flushed face, her madness burning hotter than the sun could. Marse Charles hovered in the doorway, looked like he'd like to snatch that fan straight out of his daughter's hand.

Because of their gathered stillness they heard the carriage rumbling up through the gravel road from a great distance, but they could not see it at all through the thick of the trees, and so they were left to stand there in anticipation, listening to the horses' hooves beating the ground and the strain of the wagon rolling over craggy land. The assembled slaves had long, strange minutes to imagine their new master inside, perhaps sitting with his head in his hand and his hat in his lap and his leg across his knee, his foot tapping in nervous but eager anticipation, deep in thoughts of his new bride. Would she look like her photograph, hair tugged back tight, and center parted, cheeks pinked? Would her voice be soft and sweet when they sang at the piano at night? Would she make him lots of children, boys preferably but a girl too that they might name after his mama? Would she love him for all the rest of her God-given days, and his?

When the wagon turned the corner, it was obvious it was empty. There was only a sad, thin-looking black man at its helm, old as creation, with a straw hat and a bad limp. He said nothing but disembarked and hobbled his way over to them, looking sorry about the time it took him to cross those few yards.

"Got a letter here for the mistress a' this house?"

Varina stepped forward through the crowd of her slaves and took the letter as if the paper alone was a badge of shame that ought not see the light of day. She unfolded the letter at its crisp lines. The envelope bore an emblem of the Confederate army, and after she'd read the letter, her lips moving furiously, her gloved finger slipping and shaking over the handwritten lines, she dropped it to the ground and let the wind take it and none of them knew whether to go after it—so they didn't, just watched the emblem swirl away. The old negro messenger was watching even with his eyes downcast. Perhaps he'd been told to report back on her reaction; perhaps he was only waiting to have his pass marked, his old bones being unsure of how and where to move without being dismissed.

Varina's low keening was explanation enough. It was a sound

like a sick cow might make. She turned and fled into the house, and Marse Charles did not follow her but sighed as though this was an eventuality he'd been wise enough to see coming.

"Go and see to her."

Rue didn't know if he had meant her. She was the only slave on the veranda. She tried to look out at the crowd for her mama, but if Miss May Belle was there she was just another black sweating body, waiting and tense.

"Go on," Marse Charles hollered and Rue went, taking the stairs through the house two at a time with the aid of the folded-up parasol as a cane, all the faster to propel her.

She found Varina in her room, panting and yowling and ripping off her clothes like she couldn't get them away from herself fast enough.

"Miss?" Rue didn't know how to calm her. "Is he died in the war?"

"Better he was dead," Varina moaned. "Better we all were dead."

Rue tried to approach her, but she cussed and swung away. Varina rampaged to her vanity table and swiped at the contents on top; her perfumes and hair things and jewelry all clattered to the ground. She raised her gloved hand and slapped at the mirror, and Rue braced herself for a shattering that didn't come. The mirror held and, enraged even further by that futile gesture, Varina stumbled back into the center of the room, headed, it seemed, for her doll collection. They were looking on her calmly with their rictus smiles.

Rue didn't know why she moved to defend them. They were only dolls. But it flashed in her mind that she had always loathed the stupid things and if anyone was going to destroy them it ought to be her. She stepped in front of Varina's path and tried to soothe her.

"I don't understand what's happened."

"He ain't comin'. Ain't never comin'. Only sent the letter as a courtesy." Varina cracked out a sharp laugh. "A courtesy to tell me the engagement's broken. He's found himself a better girl. One who ain't touched. Ain't ruined."

At that one word, *ruined,* Varina ripped the parasol from Rue's hands and swung it once and hard across Rue's face.

Rue felt the angry welt already rising in a perfect line across her face and she tasted blood boiling up in her mouth.

"I don't understand," Rue said.

"Oh, don't you see?" Varina kept saying. "Don't you see? Don't you see?"

Varina backed away. She was throwing down her clothes, all her pretty things. The net she'd put her hair up in snapped in its stretch and her curls came raining down on her bare freckled shoulders. She was tugging at her gloves, angry at each individual finger as she pulled. Varina was all come undone as the world around her was, and Rue, always behind, it seemed, always fool-ish, didn't put it all together until Varina was all but naked in front of her save a thin white slip, see-through and gossamer. Still bent, cowering, Rue looked up and saw Varina's belt, the one she'd made for the courses that had never come—just as the husband had never come—and in that instant of seeing it and remember-ing it, Rue watched it snap, all the little beads of nutmeg scattered across the floor like marbles, and some broke in half and spread their dust, and Varina began, again, to cry.

Oh, Rue understood what she was seeing then and how right Miss May Belle had been, as she always was, for the belt had served its purpose and sent its message as good as any letter: Varina's little belly was protruding, the skin already rounded out in a stretch of six months.

PROMISE

====

Miss Rue had been, all her life, a liar. Over the years, in slavery-time, wartime, in freedomtime, she'd lied and said, *I know.*

When the mamas told her something was going wrong below, something they could not explain, *I know,* she'd say, to shush them. But she had never got to understand wrong from inside herself. She realized she had spent her life in kneeling, in peering in, in parting legs, touching skin, squeezing hands. In wiping brows and blood and bits of birth. In interpreting moans and sighs and vague descriptions of other folks' pain.

Ooh, Miss Rue, it's like a fire, like a stabbing, like a burning, like a gunshot, like a tearing, feels like I'm dying.

She always wanted to ask them, how you know what dying feel like if you never done it?

I ain't know nothin'.

The thought rang through her as she woke in the middle of the night to the feeling from the inside that she didn't have a name for other than wrong. The feeling persisted, grew, in the place at the bottom of her stomach, the warm round place she had been sending love feelings to for months now.

Bruh Abel was asleep beside her and she hesitated one lonely second before waking him because waking him meant that the wrong was real.

She shook him. He looked at her like he didn't know her, and she understood then that she did not know him, she could not gasp out his name or make sense of his shape in her bed. She could only keep saying, "Something's wrong." He touched her hot, flushed skin and he looked angry, spitting mad, and that's how she knew it was so much worse than wrong. Bruh Abel was never angry unless he was worried, and he was never worried unless the world was tore up, all hope come undone.

"What am I s'posed to do?" he said as he climbed up out of bed. "You the one that's s'posed to know."

He didn't say what he'd decided when he decided it; he only scooped her up in his arms, cradle style. He lifted her from the bed. The sudden, hysterical thought came to her that he meant to baptize her again and certainly it hadn't taken the first time, so why would it now?

She hid her face in the hard-pulsing hollow of his neck and his shoulder. She could feel his shifting panicked muscles with her lips, taste his salty sweat. It did not calm her to know him scared for the first time.

They walked awhile, him clutching her and her clutching herself. If she thought too hard she knew she'd break; if she thought too hard she'd lose what she was holding on to. She had to hold on.

She had her face still buried and hid and she only knew they'd gone outside by the sudden cool whip of night air. He was carrying her fast, running near as best he could with the burden of her, and each step gave a bounce and each bounce disrupted the wrong that had worked its way up from her stomach and blossomed now in her chest.

"Feels like I'm dyin'," she told Bruh Abel's neck. "We dyin'."

"Hush, girl."

Now she knew they were in Ma Doe's house by the warm, by the smell. She'd made the old woman a new gris-gris charm only days before, stuffed with all her favorite stinks. Ma Doe, for all that she was a learned woman, had always believed in asafetida as a way of warding off haints and hate alike. Miss May Belle had made them for her, and Miss Rue did the same after. And lately Rue had been making them for everybody in town, a little faith to clutch at if they glimpsed whiteness in the woods. The smell when she'd packed the bags had nearly sickened her, but now, stretched out in the empty cabin, it seemed dull, a pathetic stink.

"What's this?" she heard Ma Doe saying.

Bruh Abel's chest thumped with his every word. "The baby's comin'."

"It isn't yet time for the baby to come."

"Well, it's comin'," he said.

The wrong unfurled in Ma Doe's long silence.

"You'd best find her help then."

Bruh Abel roared, swung them round so fast she thought he meant to throw her.

"Don't know of anybody here that can safely bring an early child but Miss Rue," Ma Doe called after them.

It jarred her to hear her own name, as if Miss Rue were some other person than the one there hanging in Bruh Abel's arms and if that other person would only come, she could save them. Well, it didn't look as if she were coming.

There was that shock of the cold again and she opened her eyes to see the stars above her, swimming in trails of silver. Dizzy. She shut her eyes and the next thing she knew was the hay.

It clung to her, that hay, in her hair and nightdress, on her fever-damp skin, stuck to her fingers when she tried, weak, to pick it off. Through the wooden grates of the borrowed merchant cart she could see the world rushing by her, blending all its colors. Up ahead was the broad stretch of Bruh Abel's back. She squinted at a sweat stain on his nightshirt, a senseless expansive pattern that grew as he whipped the one tawny horse pulling them, urging it to go faster and faster, though there was everywhere the sound of its hooves beating the ground with a fury and the cart creaking after. She was all ashiver, felt the way lips felt with a hum passing through them.

Finally the wagon stopped. Bruh Abel jumped down. He came round and plucked her from the hay. She wanted to scream when he gripped her waist. He didn't know how to touch her with her stomach in the way, with the wrong big between them. Bruh Abel settled on clutching her in something like a hug.

"It's just a li'l ways down the road," he said. She felt him pointing, his fingers bending against her back. "You gotta help me, girl."

She tried to walk but her legs felt as though they'd been replaced by double-pointed needles. They stuck to the ground, they stabbed up her hips.

"Where we goin'?"

"He's gotta help you," Bruh Abel said.

She knew it was a white person's home by the size of it, though she'd never before seen it in her life, never ventured out so far in all her days. It was opulent and it was devastated. Taller than Marse Charles's House that she'd known in her youth, this one shared the familiar white balustrades but the whole thing was covered in creeping green, as if the land itself was tempted to consume it, a slow, methodical swallow.

She saw right off why Bruh Abel had left the horse and cart at the path. As he led her closer, the grass of the grounds gave way to mud that gave way to swamp. The world sank as they moved forward; the house, the trees seemed to sit on the brackish water before them, floating. Bruh Abel drew her forward as best he could, saying sweet things, saying she'd be alright, they'd be alright. He was saying it too convincingly for it to be true. Below them the ground made sucking sounds, and they stepped barefoot through the yard, bound together like some hideous four-legged creature, damned to struggle lifelong against itself.

It was strange to enter through the front of a white person's home without permission. Inside, the house was the kind of dark too tar black to see through, and Bruh Abel set her down on the floor. She rested her head on his calf, gripped the cracked wood beneath her hands as a particularly strong pang of wrongness ran through her. The bottom of her dress clung to her legs with wet and she could not think what that wet was but hoped that it was all swamp water. Above her, Bruh Abel fiddled with a book of matches and cussed, his hands too clumsy, cold and shriveled by damp.

It gave Rue a queer kind of comfort to imagine that the house was like the one she'd known in her girlhood, and in the uneasy dark she could just see the entry to the parlor, the fine furnishings, the stairs swirling up to heaven, Varina descending the steps two at a time, as unladylike as she wanted to be when she thought no one was looking.

Bruh Abel's match caught, illuminated the truth as he stretched away from her for a candle set by the door. The flame took and bobbed bigger on the wick of the wasting-away stub of wax and before them a stretch of empty beds was revealed. This was no ordinary home then. This was something like she'd never seen. The rows of beds stretched as far as her eyes would let her see, blocks of white packed even closer together than the tightest of slave quarters, tattered curtains hung on rods between them, made a meal of by moths. There was no one in those beds, though they were made up like they were waiting for someone. Me, she thought. Us, she thought again. Bruh Abel lifted her, laid her on the first bed they came to, where she let herself curl up around the pain.

The rough mattress gave up a sigh of dust, and it was with just the barest of strength that she managed to move her head away from a stiff dark stain that she only recognized as old, old blood after long minutes of staring.

There were hurried steps and then a voice that echoed. "No flame," it said, harried. "Please, no flame."

Bruh Abel put out the candle he had lit just as Rue strained to see who'd spoke. She could only make out the glaring white of his face, the anxious flapping of his mouth surrounded by a mass of dark hair, a beard that shaped the hollows of his face into something like a skull. "No flame," he kept saying, and when the dark blanketed them again she had to imagine the rest of him. His manner of speaking called to her memory the marching-up-north army that had tramped through their woods years back, as disorganized and forceful as locusts.

Bruh Abel, all dark save for the pale linen of his nightshirt, stepped between her and the white man. He matched the whisper tone of his words, and she could not make out what was passing between them any more than she could make out their expressions. They were making a deal she feared, an arrangement, perhaps a sale.

Bruh Abel stepped away and she saw the white man's hand coming at her in the dark. She feared she would die if he touched her. She reared back from him fast and slammed herself backward into the metal head of the bed. It rained down rust on her face. His hand when he reached her only settled around her wrist. His fingers, shifting along her skin, were cool and coarse.

"Help me hold her now."

She did not want to be held, not even by Bruh Abel, maybe especially not by him, not then when it seemed like it was all going wrong, inside and out. He laid his hands on her shoulders and she tried to shrug him away. She fought him to the rhythm of her pain, like the wrong was music and her fists beat the drums.

The white man brought back with him a sweet smell so weighty she thought she'd be crushed by it. She tried to draw away. Bruh Abel wouldn't let her and then her body wouldn't let her. She could only lie there, gasping, as the white man laid a sheet, white as a cloud, over her mouth and nose, over her eyes completely. It was the softest thing she'd ever felt, that sheet, and he pressed it to her face and she figured he meant to kill her with it. Her eyes searched but all she saw was the white, and the scent it bore coiled down into her, and she knew it had to be true that something so sweet must mask something full evil. Surely beneath it there was brimstone. The white cloud scudded across Rue's eyes, spread across her sky, disintegrated. In another place, another time, back when she was a child at play, she might have looked up into the wide-open sky and dreamed.

In that memory place, the trees dripped down water, though Rue couldn't remember the last time it had rained. The bed of grass beneath her was weighted with dew. It drenched her back, it greened her dress, but she didn't mind because she was the mama. And Varina was the conjure woman.

"Rue," said the cheeky little redheaded child, "it's time."

Varina was on her knees above her, smiling. Her hair was falling loose of the careful braid Ma Doe had put it in that morning, the red ribbon unspooling slow, without Varina even noticing.

"Look here, Rue."

Varina held up a knife, something like a saw with jagged teeth, the sharpness of each tooth inconsistent with the next, as if it had been used to cut something irregular and never sharpened after. It was the wood handle that made Rue's stomach buckle. It was varnished dark and looked strange in Varina's hands, which were delicately covered in her lady lace gloves, so dainty her pink skin shone through the gaps of white. The knife's wood varnish was dark, Rue knew, so the blood wouldn't tell.

"Won't it hurt?"

"This time, yes," Varina conceded. The knife bit down. "But I know better'n anybody. These'll harden so the next time and the next time it won't hurt quite so bad."

"Ain't gonna be no next time. This here's my last."

Varina gave her a knowing smile.

The cut was more a pressure than a pain, and Rue sat up a little to watch the flourishing of the pen in Varina's hand. She held it delicately by its dark varnish hilt and wrote something Rue of course could not read. She recognized the V though, it was the one letter that Varina had ever taught her, over and over, again and again, in the dirt of their childhood.

"Now," Varina said when the cutting was done, "we got the same birthmark." The baby inside of Rue was cradled in her flesh and blood. It drew up its arms through the wound propelled by instinct, its small fists grabbing already, climbing already, as though it were drawing itself up through the branches of a tree.

Varina pulled the baby out of Rue's belly. It was so small its body fit entirely on the length of her two hands. She sawed through the cord, back and forth with quick tree-felling motions. All the while the baby cried, and Rue felt she knew the sound so well it was as if she'd made it herself. Her Posy, finally come.

Varina held out the little loving thing, and Rue brought her daughter to her chest.

"I wanna show Bruh Abel what we done."

Varina looked over her shoulder into the woods. "He's a-comin'. I hear him." Rue heard nothing except for the crying of her own

baby girl, a heaven-sent sound. How simple and strange it was, to
ache and love at once.

"What we gonna do with all of this?" Varina asked. She puzzled
over the gash she'd made in Rue's belly, the spew of her innards,
the bag that had held her baby and the shriveling snakelike cord
that had nourished it. Varina had her thumb in her mouth, sucked
at the filigreed tip of her glove, heedless of the blood darkening
the lace.

Rue didn't much care about what Varina meant to do. She
wanted to touch her skin to Posy's skin, how perfect and dark it
was. She was secretly pleased that it was more like hers than Bruh
Abel's. If only he'd come along and see what they'd made.

Varina drew the ribbon out from her hair, carefully pulling it
through the more menacing snarls in her curls. When it was fully
free she set to work stitching Rue closed with it, building an intricate series of knots end over end through the loose pools of Rue's
skin. "There now," Varina kept saying, pleased with herself. "There
now."

Posy's cries had quieted to a self-comforting whimper. She had
big brown eyes that took an interest in Rue's face. She knows me,
Rue thrilled herself in thinking.

"There now."

The drape of moth-eaten leaves parted like double doors and
Rue, fool she was, expecting Bruh Abel and expecting him to be
pleased, held up her Posy. Presented her. But it was the fox that
came.

"Varina?"

Varina was too busy making her knots.

"Not me," Rue said. "Don't be worryin' about me. Help Posy."

The fox drew forward slow with the leisure of a predator. Hungry but not hungered. It trained its eyes on them. If she ran, it
would run after. She could not run, she was still weak, she was laid

open, she had her baby girl in her arms and Varina had tied her down with her wealth of red ribbon. Still she tried, Lord how she tried and tried, to run from this, to break free.

Rue saw the bunching muscles of the fox's hind legs, felt the coiling of time before the pounce. She waited 'til the very last moment to shut her eyes. She held Posy close as long as they would let her. And even when she could no longer feel her, she listened for her. As long as she could. She cradled her baby's cry 'til the very end. Such lovely, lovely crying.

WARTIME

===

Varina's pregnancy was a blight. She wished it gone. Had wished it gone for months and months before anyone had even noticed — her widening or her wishing.

"How long this been goin' on?"

She could not name the precise moment she knew that it had happened, that it was happening. Only that after her daddy's jubilee, every day her nightmares thickened, and her sleep thinned, and she woke one morning to find her mouth filling up with a volley of saliva like a flood so acrid and awful that she spat it out in her bare hands. Outside a cock crowed the morning into being and she, frantic, disentangled her legs from the covers that stuck to her like fetters, and there in the dipping valley in her mattress, between her legs, was a spot of red followed after by a darker, browner line, the whole stain fine and thin as a scripted point of exclamation. Her body heaved. She was sick onto herself and she called, high and shrill, for the housegirl Sarah, who did not come for long horrid minutes in which she shivered in the wet of her own vomit. Her body had betrayed her.

———

"You still bleedin', Miss?" Sarah had asked.

Varina sighed, sunk deeper. The water in the tub scalded at her shoulders. She bade her house girl to make it hotter and hotter still. It was not enough.

"No. The bleedin's stopped."

"It's like that for me too sometimes." The mulatta had dipped her voice low, sharing a secret as if she thought it was something Varina needed. "Like it don't want to get started. But it always comes."

Varina knew it wasn't going to come, not for her. This was not the start of her monthly courses. This was an end. Varina kept her expression steady, though inside she rocked with shame, with horror. Was that the moment she'd known? She had wished for more blood, known it wasn't enough somehow. Knew that it meant one way or the other that something was wrong. She was wrong. She'd skipped something important in her life. Gone from child to woman, violently.

"Ain't the water too hot, Miss?" Sarah warned.

In the tub Varina let her body slip down and down. Slowly. Inch by boiling inch, then she let her face sink down too and watched the strange quivering way her curls floated up above her, stretched in their effort to stay at the surface. She watched bubbles flutter from her nose and mouth. They called to her dimming mind a memory of the moths she'd chased through the yard sometime in those endless dragging days of her youth. She'd never caught a single one, had she?

Sarah yanked her upward by the arms so forcefully that half the water gushed out to splatter on the wood floor. Varina drew in air in desperate clumps and the mulatta hissed at her and Varina watched Sarah's big pretty brown eyes go wide with panic as their two hearts pounded, and then go wider still when she realized she was still gripping onto a white woman's arms with enough desperation to bruise. She let go.

"What's the matter with you?"

"I don't know," Varina had said. But she did know.

They both seemed to recall themselves in the same moment. Varina wicked the wet from her eyes. Sarah began to clean the puddles on the floor. When she was done, she stood and stared down at Varina, which was a thing she should have known better than to do, and Varina would have told her so. Would have scolded her and screamed. But Varina couldn't draw the breath.

"Can I help you outta there now, Miss Varina?" Sarah spoke like she was bargaining with a stubborn child.

"No," Varina said, the one word harsh and terrible. She couldn't bear the thought of being touched again.

Her daddy took to wearing that old dusty uniform, relic of another war, marched around the house planning a one-man campaign against the Yankees, saying how the youngbloods nowadays didn't know how to fight, had no pride in the things they were fighting for, and that was why they were losing. He'd told her of the offer of marriage as an afterthought, not even looking at her. Not even seeing.

Varina hadn't cared. Not about her daddy's hurt that he was too old to fight at the front line. Not about pride, or tradition, or ways of life. She cared about her one life and tried to ignore the new one gurgling inside her. The sooner the husband came the better. Maybe she could tell of it then. Maybe she could love it. Take pride in it. Give it a name.

She couldn't say when she first felt it move, only that it felt like moth's wings in the dip of her stomach, a sensation so strange and small it seemed like something she'd made happen by half-wishing that it would. There was so much half-wishing then when her daddy had showed her the tin countenance of the man she was to marry. A man she'd danced with only once. Hard and fast and rough and alone, a dance to no music or at least no type that she had ever imagined to hear in her life. No time for courting in wartime, he'd told her, and no time to be so shy. Varina had never been shy a moment in her life 'til then, 'til a man, a supposed-to-be-beau, had ripped up her dress and made her shy of everything, shy of her own reflection in the glass, shy of a flutter in the bottom of her stomach that should have been a good thing. Her life should have been a good thing, but there was a war to the north and there were explosions in the sky and the first time she felt it kick, really kick, it had been a musket shot come from her insides so hot and hard, she'd half-wished she were dead.

Varina asked for them for comfort, her two little nigras. She'd take them with her right to her marriage bed if she could, like a beloved childhood blanket to stick between her and her new husband, a moth-eaten shield. But Varina wasn't stupid; in fact, she felt smarter as she grew fatter, like she was filling up with a sharper, keener knowledge.

Varina knew what she saw when she looked at that mulatta girl, Sarah, and it was something like seeing her own face looking back up at her, distorted only by a ripple in the pond. Sarah was darker than Varina; that mark of Cain left by a dead black mother made them only half sisters, but if not for that they might have been twins.

Her daddy, Varina realized, was a dirty man. The fact did not surprise her like it ought to. She'd lately been introduced to the dirtiness of men, was growing heavy with it. And if she were to pack up Sarah and take her as her double, it would be all the sweeter that she might send Sarah out to her husband, a soldier for proxy.

———

"How long this been goin' on?" Rue asked.

Varina had stripped herself down to next to nothing. Had ruined her room. Had smacked Rue across the face with a parasol
handle. Dully Varina marveled at the red raising up on the nigra's
cheek even through the black, a perfect line of the parasol.

The beads off of Varina's broken belt were still rolling. She
could hear them reaching the far corners of her bedroom. Spinning. Under her bed and vanity, bouncing off the walls and edges
and corners and still spinning. What would it take to make them
come to rest? Varina didn't have an answer to Rue's question. To
her it had felt like a lifetime that she had been nursing her shameful secret.

PROMISE

==

His word. It was all Rue had. Bruh Abel kept saying, *Girl, you have my word.* She did not want his word or anything his.

"The baby come dead," he said. He said it slow each time, careful, like this was the first time she was hearing it.

Spat on the floor and said to him, "I don't believe you."

He cut her nails for her because he thought he was being kind.

"Used to do this for Queenie," he said of his mama, trying to make Rue smile. "Toes too."

She did not want to think of Bruh Abel's mama, she did not want to think of him as coming from a mama who was real, and anyway Queenie did not feel real. She waxed and waned in each story, first kind then cruel, first brilliant then flawed. Rue had it hard enough trying to believe him. So why did he keep trying to pile on more lies?

She wanted to take herself to the field, told Bruh Abel she was going to go look for some sort of quiet and he ought not to follow her. He didn't want to let her go off alone, that much she could tell from the way his eyes roved over her. He was trying to figure if she could be trusted by herself.

"Stay here," he said.

He blamed it on the danger that was thrumming through the town, the fear of the newly come whites lurking around, scheming to take their Promised Land, looking vengeful of it. But Rue knew what Bruh Abel was fearing. Rue's worst threats had always come from within her own self. She could find death in the weeds. It had always impressed her how many things could harm you just by being eaten wrongly. How many things could kill.

"It's the plant's defense against predators," Miss May Belle had explained once. That answer didn't satisfy.

"It's too late to be poison," Rue had argued. "If you already bein' eaten."

Miss May Belle had laughed at that and said no more.

Rue was not even shamed by the thought that occurred to her, which was to put Bruh Abel to sleep so she could slip free of him. She could give him something she could trust in. Lavender or valerian or lemon balm; she mixed a poison for him in her head. In the end he did it to himself. He placed the bottle of label-less liquor on the table between them as though it were a solution.

"Drink," he said. Maybe his mind was working the same way hers was. Thinking near fondly on the time he'd first wiled his way into her home. She had meant to slip free of him then in much the same way but couldn't work it. She had tried to trick him and he had tried to trick her and the two of them had known each other for what they were. Liars. She could've almost felt nostalgic after it, if it hadn't all ended up so bitter.

Rue got up from the table. Fetched two cups and ignored the pull of the stitches on her stomach as she moved. The ache of the healing wound centered from the deep cut where Bruh Abel had told her they'd taken her baby out. She didn't like to think on it, being laid open by the Quaker doctor. It didn't bear thinking about.

Rue set the cups down hard on the table in front of Bruh Abel.

Miss May Belle had used to say that you ought to pour in drink if you wanted to pour out truth. So, his cup she filled to near the brim and did the same to her own.

He took a sip and she watched to see that he swallowed it. She sipped, and he did the same. They watched each other, wary as any two creatures that knew they were well matched.

"Queenie lost her last child," he said.

It wasn't like Bruh Abel to start one of his tales in such an unfanciful way, to lay down the bare bones of a thing without a careful, purposeful arrangement of false skin to dress it up. No preamble here, no magic.

"I thought you was her last."

He shook his head. Rue took a sip and listened.

"Was after me. I was little then. I watched, though I wasn't supposed to. No men in the birthin' room was what folks used to say back then."

"Bad luck." Rue touched her stomach. Sipped. That wasn't true. It was just something folks said. Something Miss May Belle had used to say: "Where d'you think Adam was when Eve brung out Cain and Abel?"

"I was scared," Bruh Abel said.

She blinked at him. For a moment she forgot what time he was speaking on. She was all mixed up; the present was the past come again.

"I hear my mama screamin'," Bruh Abel said. "I loved her more than anythin' then. I didn't understand it. I thought they was killin' her, them strange doctorin' grandmamas that come. Them two crones who'd rid themselves of their menfolk and lived together in a one-bed cabin. Folks whispered about 'em as much as they relied on 'em.

"Queenie, laborin', was hollerin' somethin' awful when they laid her down. Me, a child, I thought, 'I'm the only one that can stop it. I'm the only one.'"

Bruh Abel could weave a tale, Rue knew, and she shut her eyes to see it, this birth, unremarkable as all the ones any woman had ever suffered before and after. But Bruh Abel transfigured it, made it sound so terrifying, his mama there sat up in bed and a pair of old prune-black women at either of her fat ankles, her dress shucked up to her thighs, her toes writhing round the ends of the metal bedpost—all that Abel could see from his vantage point.

He paused in the telling to take a long sip, like he was pushing something down. "I don't know how y'all women do it."

"I don't know either."

He was deep in his drink by now, drooping across the table already. He'd fall asleep soon, like she'd been after. Now the story wanted finishing.

"What happened to her baby?"

"Come dead." She held back on hitting him. For telling this story of all stories. But she felt too sluggish and too sick and too defeated.

"I seen him, though." Bruh Abel's voice grew thin. "Before they named him a lost cause. The baby. He was as strange a li'l thing as ever there was. Blue all over. So pale he was, it seemed strange to think he'd come from my mama, who was big and dark. But she was his mama alright."

"'Course she was." Rue was growing fed up. "He come out a' her. Ain't no question a' origin to be had there."

"What it was, though, was his skin," he ventured quietly.

"They had the same colorin'?" It always seemed to come down to a matter of coloring.

Bruh Abel scoffed, polished his glass to empty. "Not hardly.

Queenie was dark as the night is. This baby boy was lighter even than me."

Rue tried to remember what she knew of Queenie, could recall only that she'd been the figurehead on her master's boat, every detail of her fecund body chiseled out as a mahogany mermaid, the whole of the boat patterned as her flipper tail.

"So what then?" Rue asked.

"The baby was light enough to be white; that's why it looked so vivid on him and was nothin' on her." He touched his own smooth arm. "A birthmark maybe. All up the body."

"What it look like?"

"Looked something," Bruh Abel said, "like scales."

There were so many sights in the world that Rue hadn't ever seen. But what she had seen, once, was the birth of a shock-white baby with ochre black eyes. Sarah's baby, born in a caul and covered all in a birthmark that looked like scales. Just like Queenie's lost boy.

Bruh Abel had no birthmark that Rue had ever seen, but she understood now that that was how it worked sometimes. The past revealed itself in mysterious ways, and Bruh Abel it seemed had passed his mama's brand onto his own son. Bean.

Maybe Rue's girl would have had the same birthmark had she lived.

Posy, half-born and half-remembered. Rue could almost see her baby. The new dark skin, still wet. The wanting O of her little mouth, suckling at the empty air. If Posy had not been real, then nothing was.

Rue's body remembered. Inside, her muscles still ached, caught in a suspended spasm, still pushing. Her arms and fingers remembered that soft feel of baby, rich and butter smooth as flower petals.

Did all babies feel that sweet, and she had never known it? She didn't wish to touch another to find out.

What was it she thought she'd find out there in that wilderness besides singed earth and bark, same as ever? The clearing in which she'd held Posy was one from her memory, lusher, greener probably than it had been even before the war. Fertile, the way only the land in wistful memory could be. Fool she was, did she think she'd see Varina there waiting? Proud of the predictable childish trick she'd pulled—*Here's your doll baby, Rue.*

Rue had loved that stretch of empty green once, for how solitary it was. Now she felt that she'd never be alone again, that she'd be alone all her life. The shed still stood with that usual crooked perseverance at the river's edge. It was in that place that she'd found Bruh Abel, hiding from the Ravaging, the scores of dead babies. She had told him then to come into town, give the mamas balm in the form of lies.

"My baby come dead," Rue tried saying it aloud.

She was bleeding. Down below and from the neat gash in her stomach. The liquor she'd shared with Bruh Abel had made her blood rush. There was one more place still to look. Rue could have walked through those woods with her eyes closed, might have sleepwalked there, for before she knew what was what, she was tumbling through the church's double doors, expecting to be scolded by white parishioners. It was empty as always, the ground torn up, the grass poking through the old wood floor a harsh reminder of time. The woods were trying to take the space back, chew up the bricks and spit them out crooked.

Rue came to a rest on a bench in the old white folks' section, cleared a cobweb off with her hands and laid herself down across it. The high white ceiling of the church was going dim on its edges.

She put pressure to her bleeding. She could feel her heart beating under her hand.

"You listenin'?" Rue screamed or whispered. It was the way she knew to summon her haint.

"What's happened to you?"

Rue could taste blood in her mouth, metallic and tangy. There was no way of knowing if she'd bit her tongue or brought it up hot from her stomach.

"Did you take her?" Rue asked.

Varina swam into her vision. She looked pale and troubled. Not at all like she'd been in Rue's dream.

Here, alive, she was a grown woman made small by the cavern of the church. Her hair was turning muted at the roots. She looked more like her daddy than she ever had. Varina sat down on the bench beside her, and Rue felt the wood shift beneath her back for the added weight. Varina's hands hesitated over her, unsure how to help but twitching with the urge to, little birds hovering, looking to perch.

"Rue. You're bleedin'."

"Did you take her?"

"Take who?" The worry lines lately etched in her forehead deepened. "Rue, you ain't makin' a lick of sense. Here, let me help you."

Varina fussed at her, tried to make her sit, but the incision at her stomach set Rue screaming.

"Where's my baby?"

"That li'l boy with the eyes?" Varina frowned. "I only meant to watch over him."

Varina made to get up but Rue caught her arm, sunk her jagged clipped nails into the thin flesh, felt the bone roll beneath the skin as Varina struggled to move away from her.

"Posy." The name came rusted out of Rue's throat. She hadn't ever got to name her girl out loud.

"I don't know who that is. Rue, you're not well. Please, let me get you help."

Varina's arm slipped from her hand and Rue let her go, let strength leave her too, let herself lie on the cool hard bench, imagined it to be a burial slab welcome against her cheek. This had been her last hope, her last place to look for Posy. But the church was, as she was, hollowed out and empty. Gutted of its value. Sealed.

"She'll be alright now." That voice was a woman's. Far away.

"You sure?" That voice was a man's. Close up.

There was no more sound from either of them, and in the stretched-out silence Rue opened up her eyes.

Jonah. Rue almost didn't recognize him, couldn't reconcile his work-darkened skin, his shorn-short hair, or the new scar that wormed its way down from his brow line to the corner of his eye, looking like a fishing hook beneath the skin. He couldn't be real. He didn't belong inside the dank, dust-thick church that no one was meant to recollect existed.

"Easy, easy," he said. He didn't want her getting up, but she couldn't think on her back. Her head stewed and swirled. Far behind him Varina stood stock-still in a different aisle of the pews.

"What you doin' here, Jonah?"

"Just come through now. Back from workin'." He hefted up a haversack at his feet to prove it, half-filled with his traveling possessions. He handed Rue a canteen from its depth, but she felt too ill to drink. He wouldn't say more 'til she did. Rue took a few sputtering sips that made her feel sicker.

"Ran into Miss"—Jonah glanced back at her—"Varina at the side a' the river."

"I couldn't find my way to the quarters with the river up. Isn't that silly?" Varina's voice had gone high and tight in a way Rue hadn't heard in years. Her company voice.

"She said you was in need a' help. So I come runnin'," Jonah finished.

"I'm alright," Rue said, but she didn't feel alright.

"Take yo' time," Jonah said. Whether he meant in moving or explaining she couldn't figure.

Varina, never good at silences, moved to fill it. She walked around one whole bench only to settle in the next aisle, eyeing Jonah, skittish the whole time.

"Is it alright, Rue? I didn't know what to do. I thought you'd died and if you died—" She cut herself short at some horror.

"It alright, Miss Varina. Thank you."

But now that Varina had got going she couldn't seem to stop. "I knew it wasn't safe for me to be seen. But he said he ain't a soldier. I wasn't sure. Don't the North have nigger soldiers?"

Jonah seemed to flinch. "I ain't a soldier, no ma'am," he said. He wouldn't look at Varina, knew more than well enough not to, but he did stare goggle-eyed at Rue. "I let her know that I'm on the side a' the South."

"Thank you." Rue could only get herself to whisper it.

Jonah walked her back like he was escorting her on a promenade, a firm hand on her arm, another on her back. Maybe he feared she'd fall, but to Rue it felt like he feared she'd take off running. He was wanting answers.

"Miss Varina ain't even recognize you," Rue said, tried to make a joke of it. Jonah wasn't laughing.

"We wasn't long acquainted," he said. "When she come runnin' up to me I ain't know what to think. When I figured who she was, though, I did wonder if I hadn't lost all my senses, seein' for myself a woman what's supposed to be dead. Then I remembered Ol' Joel, all 'em crazy mutterin's he made through the town."

"Folks that have glimpsed her, they tell themselves she a haint."

The hand Jonah had on her back swatted dismissively, resettled at her hip. "I ain't believe in all that. I saw her, first thing I thought was she just a white woman run mad. We walked back to the church an' she kept on askin' after news from the war. Wasn't 'til she say her name that I recollect that she was Marse Charles's daughter, aged over five years since last I knew her. If there is haints in this world, they don't grow old."

Did Varina look so old? Rue couldn't tell. For her the five-odd years had passed on Varina's face gradually. To catch her aging, to really see her youth lost, it was like trying to catch the moon moving across the sky at night.

A mile on, the tent reared its white head up over the treetops. "I heard about this here tent, but I ain't half believe it," Jonah said. "All that for Bean?"

"It's grown bigger than Bean," Rue said.

The way was a steep upward struggle, and it would have been faster by half to cut straight through the woods as Rue often did. But she could sense Jonah's nervousness as a twitching hand at her side. He kept peering into the thick knit of gathered trees, double-checking every shadow he saw. Likely the white woman had given him a fright. He hadn't had any way of being sure of where she meant to lead him. Jonah'd followed her anyway, for Rue's sake.

"She went away north and come back? Miss Varina?"

Rue shook her head, no.

"Don't say she been among us all this time."

"Since the House burned," Rue admitted. "That ol' church was meant to house a minister. She got all the things she need."

Jonah let go of her hand. His face crinkled up in wonderment. "Ol' Joel. He done saw it all clear."

"Not all clear," Rue said quick. "Ain't no hoodoo involved."

"Just lies."

She shrugged. Jonah should have long ago lost the ability to make her feel the fool. She had kept him safe all these years, and everybody else too.

"You feed Miss Varina?" Jonah asked. "Clothe her? All this time? Like a li'l child?" Rue nodded.

"What if she fell sick?"

"She was sick for a long while," Rue said, and in saying she could almost smell again the acrid stink of laudanum, hear the clink of the syrup-sticky vials that Varina had sucked from the way she had used to suck at her thumb as a girl.

"She near-about died. But she come back to life." Rue looked to Jonah, but she was thinking of Bean. "And now she's wantin' after things again. It makes her bold."

"How'd you keep her hid this long?" Jonah wanted to know.

"She believed when I tol' her it wasn't safe to go out. She believed when I tol' her she'd get out of there soon. She believed in me," Rue said. "Everybody did."

Now Jonah fell dumb silent and Rue asked a question of her own, one that had been pounding at her. "Jonah. You ain't tell her the war was done when you met her?"

"No, I did not."

"Why didn't you?"

"I ain't in the business of tellin' white women they wrong," he said. "Why didn't you never tell her? Now or all them years ago?"

Rue had thought on an answer to that question for years. Chewed on the question and tossed and turned on it, sleepless at night, coming up with kindness as an answer on some days and rage as an answer on others. She could have said to Jonah that Varina didn't have any living relations save a spinster aunt up north that she'd never known. She could have said that Varina, opium-blind, had been too fragile to accept the South's surrender 'til the lie told to comfort her was too old to alter. Rue could have said that the world would not be kind to a disgraced belle who'd never been expected to even bathe herself. She could have said that Varina would have reclaimed her home, or what was left of it, would have turned her slaves into her workers, paid them in scraps and promises like nothing had ever changed, a different name for the same thing. She could have said that Varina deserved it, deserved only to see the light of day in small gasps, to prowl the woods only safely unseen at night, that Varina deserved to still have nightmares of her brothers dead on battlefields and of exploding cannonballs and of Yankee devils with cloven feet. That Varina deserved it all, deserved to be locked up, left to stay waiting and praying after a glory that wasn't ever going to come.

All of those things were true but what Rue did say to Jonah was true most of all: "I just didn't want her to leave."

PART FIVE

EXODUS

==

1872

Rue had herself some nightmares. Haunted dreams in which her dead baby was a part of a collection. A pickled curiosity on a white man's shelf, floating and ill-fitting inside a jar, preserved with whiskey, posed and primed to raise her thumb to her mouth in an aborted suck. She woke from these dreams screaming, hollering, clawing. Beside her Bruh Abel was a man she didn't know. He tried to kiss her and hold her, and she wouldn't let him. He swore to her the dreams weren't real. Swore he'd paid the white Quaker doctor, and not the other way around, to see to it that the baby got buried proper. When she got well they could go up and see the place, if she liked.

Rue wouldn't believe him, wouldn't go anywhere with him, wouldn't make love to him ever again, she swore, even though his hands were loving and soft and gentle. What was the point? He said they could start again, make another, but she knew it wouldn't take. The place inside her where she'd held Posy was gone all arid now, an earth of dry, cracked clay.

"You can't know that," he said, kissing at her neck.

"Yes, I can know."

She knew now the secret of Bean's origin, from Queenie to Bruh Abel. The secret had been as plain to see as a mark of Cain, but she had not been looking. Now she could not look away.

In her nightmares Rue would walk on over to that white man's shelf and stare. She would pick up the specimen jar in her two hands and hold up her Posy in repose and spin round the liquid in it to get a closer look. She would inspect her baby's skin and see that it was dark like hers, but with all this dream time in which to look and ponder, she could see things she hadn't had the chance to see before. Or hadn't wanted to see. Posy's skin was like Bean's. Bean's skin was like Queenie's, patterned all over with little scales.

Inside the dream, Rue threw the jar to the ground where it splintered and shattered, all the liquid gushing away like a foretold flood. But what came out was not her baby Posy. It was Black-Eyed Bean, no longer Sarah and Bruh Abel's baby, but Bean grown and freed.

When Rue woke, her eyeballs were like packed mounds of mud in their sockets, as if she'd stared into the sun unblinking and let them bake. She could see then what it was that needed doing.

As she crept up on Sarah and Jonah's house, slow going still with the pain in her gut, Rue thought she saw a baby. No, that weren't it. It wasn't a baby but a child, but still the sight made her heart gallop. When she drew closer she saw clear that it was Bean, and he held in his hands a corn-husk doll, surely one his sister had used to carry around everywhere when she herself was his age. It was a sad thing dressed in a green sack with its face muddied to make it seem black, and Rue recollected one time that she'd humored Sarah's daughter by looking over the corn-husk baby and pronounced it as thriving.

Bean stood there on the porch with the doll propped up on his shoulder the way he'd probably seen his daddy transporting wood.

He'd watched Rue coming down the path and seemed to want to be noticed in that way that children sometimes did and sometimes did not. Rue thought about picking him up, to what end she could not rightly say. She edged closer, not knowing if she meant to love on him or turn him over. Did he look like Bruh Abel in other ways? Ways she'd never known or didn't let herself know?

It was the doll baby that made Rue stop. It was not, after all, the one that had belonged to Sarah's daughter as she'd first guessed. This was far older, blacker. One made lovingly with red bow lips and a green dress and wild hair in a bramble of yarn, and there in the dead center of its head, as she had done with all her hoodooing dolls, Miss May Belle had likely put in a tuft of Rue's baby hairs. Her own signature.

Slung over Bean's shoulder just so, the doll's skirts turned and tousled and showed the black baby's underside, where the white doll ought've been, the one that Miss May Belle had made to look like Varina. But there was nothing. Only a hollow, loose fabric, and a trail of straw stuffing, come undone.

"Where'd you get that?"

Miss May Belle had made those two halves, those two dolls tied together like one soul. Conjure to keep Varina from being sent away. But Rue had misunderstood from the start, supposed Miss May Belle had made Varina tied to the land, when all along it was Rue that Varina was tied to. The two of them bundled up together and trapped for it. No feet, or knees, or thighs. No legs to run with.

"Bean. What you done with the other half a' the doll baby?" Rue knew her voice was too harsh but she couldn't temper it. Bean's eyes filled up with tears. He backed away from her, for the first time, frightened.

"I done a surgery," Bean said.

Rue stilled.

They both heard the ring of Sarah's voice coming from inside, and though Rue couldn't make out what she'd said, Bean responded to his mama's call and disappeared into the house in a hurry, like he was being pulled away from Rue on the end of a string.

Rue thought to chase after him, to snatch away the doll and make certain she had seen what she'd thought she'd seen. But from down the road a group of men ambled along slow, bearing an injured body between them, and they were coming straight at her the way folks always seemed to with their hurts. It was Jonah, she saw, who hobbled between them. He had to be supported on either side by others, but at least he was moving himself.

Rue sighed. "Take him on to my cabin," she said before they could even tell her the full story.

Way they told it, the black men in the town had grown ashamed of their own fear, and in their shame they grew belligerent. They refused to wait out the perceived white demons squatting in the woods. Would not be haunted by haints in white robes.

They'd gathered themselves into a party of the bravest amongst them to ride out and stand their ground. Jonah was a natural leader, just as he had been during slavery times when he'd been entrusted to protect the women of the plantation, the closest he'd ever been to being viewed by his white master as a man.

Bruh Abel had told them that they shouldn't go into the woods, but they'd done it anyway. They had only the one sad-sack mare between them on which Jonah rode out. Before they had even got halfway to where the danger was, the horse had sensed something it felt it had no business going near.

From deep in the darkness a black mangy dog had appeared and began to bark. The horse had run off in a spook, dragging its rider along, trampling on his leg in its haste to get away.

So with a leg badly sprained, if not all the way broken, here was Jonah at last, who Rue had wanted for so long. She had learned to want by the lines of him, his broad shoulders, yes, and the strong prominence of his brow and, yes, his dark dark skin, shining. But more than that it was his hands that had always fascinated her, marked as they were from his work by a motley pattern, a deep intersection of scars from reeling fish bare-handed, flesh healed and broken and healed over. His hands reminded Rue of her daddy's scarred back, a smaller history all in a similar brutal constellation.

"Horse drug me far," Jonah said. "Foolish I know."

Rue shook her head. "Mighta saved you. Them white folks out for blood and worse."

Now was the best chance Rue had to talk to Jonah, what with him lying across her supper table hissing softly at his hurts, and there was a lot that wanted saying. He'd kept secret his discovery of Varina; as far as Rue could tell no one else was any the wiser that their old mistress had been living amongst them hidden, trapped away thinking the war still raged. For that Rue was thankful, but now she had a favor to ask. She started off light, asked him about where he'd been when he'd been away, the things he'd seen and the money he'd made. Jonah talked between gasps as she looked him over, giving her the bare bones of a scheme he'd heard tell of in a Northern city.

"I'm of a mind to go back and take it up, permanent-like," Jonah said. "That's what I heard from the other men too. That it ain't safe here and ain't gon' never be. You right, Miss Rue, they won't never let us rest. Now more than ever."

Rue didn't disagree with him. Men were not trees, she knew, black men especially; it had always been dangerous for them to take root.

"Sarah's too far along to travel safely," Rue said.

In truth Rue had been neglecting Sarah, who had not had an easy time the whole length of this pregnancy. But even with the mama's suffering, the baby in her still thrived and Rue couldn't help thinking it was the most unfair thing she'd ever seen. That woman's big, proud high-yellow belly. To have another baby when Sarah had never claimed her last baby rightly, had wanted to cast Bean out if it came to it.

Would this baby have skin like scales too? As Bean did. As Posy might've.

"I'll send for Sarah after," Jonah said. He hadn't quite said it in a way that Rue believed. But Jonah had always been the good kind. She had to hope, and this was her chance.

She said, "When you leave you oughta take Bean with you."

"I can't do that." His answer came calm as a windless sea. "As I see it they ain't mine to take."

Rue was bracing to tell him, figuring how to put into words what she knew about Sarah and Bruh Abel. It was the same truth that she'd had such a difficult time telling for herself. Because beneath the shock of their hoodwink was the low-down hurt of an infidelity. It was base and it made Rue angrier to think on. That she had expected any different when she had named Bruh Abel as a liar with lies in her mouth also. And laid down with him just the same. It was the least original of all sinning.

But Jonah was leaning toward Rue, straining across the table, coming so close she thought he meant to kiss her. He said in her ear, "Miss Rue. You know ain't none of 'em mine." She pulled away from him like he'd scorched her. Busied herself on the other side of the room pretending she was gathering up healing things. More so she was gathering up her wits. None of them children were his?

Rue tried to figure the times that Jonah had traveled away, count up the years that Bruh Abel had been amongst their town, and came up empty. There was no way of knowing, was there, for Bruh Abel had come like a thief in the night and made a fool of them, and of Rue most of all for thinking that her trickery was the only trickery that mattered.

"Cold hands," Jonah murmured when Rue brought herself back to him. He was smiling even with his teeth gritted and there was a fond haziness to his eyes. Dark eyes, she reminded herself, dark as any she'd seen, true black African eyes. But Jonah's eyes had never been as dark as Bean's.

She'd heated a knife 'til it glowed the hot red she liked. She undid Jonah's belt without asking him, pulled it free of his belt loops in a fluid tug and handed it back to him, said, "Bite down."

He looked like a warhorse with a bridle. She surveyed the wound again on his leg, like a general taking in the land and how it lay. She eyed his pant leg and didn't hesitate.

"I'll be needing to cut the fabric away."

He didn't hesitate either. "Go 'head," he said and he didn't even remove the belt from his mouth but balanced it on his thick bottom lip. She began cutting the pants up their damaged seam.

The weak chambray pants tore away easy, worn-down as they already were. Next were his drawers, and she pulled them off fast to get over the pain of where they stuck to him in stitches of dried-up blood. He didn't even wince as she ripped them full open.

Rue couldn't help herself, she looked away. Had to. Because there in his lap she saw the real horror. The real wound.

Jonah's thighs bore the same dark skin as the rest of his body, but as they crawled higher there was the menacing singular black of old burnt skin. And the horrid snaking pink where the skin had broken clear open, like looking into tore-up earth. Above his thighs there was nothing but that black puckering made darker here and there by flashes of more horrific white boils, nothing at all there to make him a man but a few curling dark hairs that had somehow had the audacity to grow in the landscape of pink angry scar tissue, of the black cracking pattern not even worth calling skin and the strange empty nothing between his legs. He was a ruin. Jonah was ruined.

"Apologies, Miss Rue," Jonah said in that same soft, gentle way he'd sometimes say good morning or good afternoon or remark on the coolness of the day. "Only I thought you knew a' it."

Questions bubbled up with bile. "When this happen?"

"Years and years," he said but he didn't need to answer, she could tell that. Of course she knew what a fresh scar looked like and this, some distant part of her mind impressed, had healed long ago and healed quite nicely despite itself.

She still held up the knife, high up like she meant to stab him with it if he moved too sudden, and the gruesome thought came to her mind that maybe she ought to, the poor wretched man, not a man at all, and then she recalled when she'd had a similar thought, held a similar weapon aloft. She'd thought to snip away the life of little Bean when first she'd discovered the horror of him wrapped up beneath the black veil. Jonah's son. No, not Jonah's son at all.

"Miss Rue?"

"Why would I know a' it?" She put the knife down. "How could I?"

"'Cause Miss May Belle knew."

Rue took up the whiskey and sipped it and then gave it to him. He shook his head no but she pressed.

"Yo' mama knew," he qualified, like she'd forgotten who Miss May Belle was, and, well, maybe she had. Her mama been dead and gone over five years.

Then it must have happened years back in slaverytime. And Bean was soon to turn six, had been born into freedom. Into peace.

"How'd she know?"

"Well, 'course she knew." His eyes looked past her like he was trying to remember it. "Miss May Belle was the one that done it."

WARTIME

==

May 1864

I know the real story, Miss May Belle says.

"The fox didn't kill 'em chickens" is what I told Marse Charles, but he too fool to listen.

"You don't know a damned thing, May Belle," he tells me.

The slaughter of the chickens on the edge of Marse Charles's property is the first crime of the promised war that I have seen with my own two eyes. A small bit of violence done by some scheming soldier-boys, picking at the edges of King Cotton.

Marse'll shrug it off as a nothing crime, blame it on a fox at best, or a colored at worst. He don't know what I know.

A wise mouth nibbles before it bites down whole. Ain't the worst still yet to come?

I only knew of them dead chickens because I went to see my man, to meet him behind the shed, to kiss his lips in secret.

He got there before me, like he do. I seen him standing in the clearing and it made my belly do that wishful thing, that mournful tumble. I just about ran to him, 'cause walking wouldn't've got me to him fast enough.

"May." He said my name when I got near, said it like it was a warning, and that's when I knew there was something awful to know.

First thing I did was look him over. Can't help habit. Awful, in my mind, is always borne by the body. I was looking for a new lashing scar, a cut, a burn, a bruise. A loss. He caught on to what I was after and shook his head. Not the body then. The head?

He took up my hand and pulled me over the whole way to the shed by the creek. We had to step out of the safe thick of the wood to cut through the clearing, and I felt like we were stark naked there, like anyone could see us and know what we were about. He stopped me at the door and pushed it open and so I looked in.

I couldn't see rightly 'til my eyes could catch up, but it didn't matter—my nose got to it first. There's no mistaking the smell of dead things, not when you've known it as often as I have, like a oft-worn cologne. When I could see right I put it together fast. There were all the chickens, and they'd been slaughtered. Splayed-out innards and feathers made all red. Their heads were gone. Their clutch of eggs had all been smashed, the fertilized and unfertilized alike so's that the dead headless hens lay in a mess with all the possible outcomes of their purpose. Blood and yolk and blood and chicks not yet chicks, pink and small and all dead too.

"Marse Charles'll be sore," I said first.

My man shook his head. There was something I was not getting at quick enough, but he wasn't going to say it for me. That's his way. He don't ever press a thing. He lead you where you need to go then let you make up your own mind, horse to water.

"It's a message," I said, building up the thought as I spoke it. "Somebody got somethin' to say and this is how they sayin' it."

"More'n that."

"Yes, it's a message and it's punishment also."

We've heard tell of the abolitionist folks, Northerners who ain't just angry for their own sake, but on behalf of colored folk. If not heard them straight out then heard echoes of theirs, reverberating. But they'd spoken for themselves now, here, and spoken right out loud.

"More'n that too," my man had to say. He was leading me away from the shed, but I still had my eye on it, and even when I couldn't rightly see into it I still saw the no-sense slaughter behind the blink of my eye. That little meaningless massacre, them headless chickens, they had me shaken as much as any violence I've ever seen, and I seen just about every kind. Only what was the point of it?

"Tell me plain." In the shade of the trees I touched his face. He leaned his long body up against a tree and looked at me in his way, considering.

"Them Northerner soldiers ain't saints. They ain't want nothin' more than to be right. This their way of winnin'. They wanna make you hurt. Yo' marse and li'l mistress and slavefolk too. They wanna make you go hungry."

I laughed, looked up at the fecund green of the wood, yonder, persimmon and mulberry and Chickasaw plum in blossom. The eucalyptus hanging down and tickling at the top of my man's head. He swat at it like it was a bother.

"We hardly livin' on chicken offal alone out here," I said. "Why you suddenly got so much hate for some Blues you ain't even met?"

He shook loose my searching hand. Is it so wrong that I was wanting him right there? Not even a stone's throw away from the awful stink of death and I was still wanting him, wanting him more because of it. The whole length of his body was warm and alive, so broad and strong he was making the tree trunk behind him seem weak. As I snaked my arms around him, my fingers touched the wretched grouping of scars on his back. Can he even feel me there anymore? That I don't know.

"May." He undid the knot of my hands. "Marse John takin' me with him when he go to enlist. Said doin' so will make me free."

Now something in me come loose. I sat myself down hard. I beat at the earth. I pulled up grass in rough fistfuls like there was some answer to be found buried underneath if only I could get at it. My man took me in his arms and shushed me with kisses come too late to be comfort.

We sat together in the grass longer than we should have. We were watching the creek babble. That thin offshoot of the river was what divided Marse Charles's land of plenty from Marse John's small lot, and in the high heat of noon when everything was lazy, a smart slave might steal away for a quarter of an hour. That quarter hour was ours for lovemaking, but instead he let me weep softly and we let the chickens fester. He'd be wanted back there soon to take up his toil in the field. He's Marse John's favorite, a workhorse he call him.

"When he joinin' up?" I stirred up the strength to finally ask it. Marse Charles and Marse John had been jawing on it but we never thought they'd really go, old as they were. But the war's been growing desperate, running low on bodies.

"Soon" is all my man could give.

I nodded, knowing neither of us was deserving of knowing what time we had left.

"Marse John, he say the day we leave he will see rightly to give me my freedom."

"Marse John been danglin' freedom so long, sayin' it easy as passin' wind to him."

"Stinks as bad too."

I had to laugh through my melancholy at the surprise of something so wicked coming from his careful mouth. But there's a loyalty there, beneath the toil and the sweat and beneath the scars

growing ever outward. My man ever as sweet as a kicked dog, returning and returning 'til that last kick kill him. Marse John is God
to him, and how could he not be? I never seen the face of the Lord
but I have seen a white master decide who suffers and who don't.
I've seen that every goddamn day.

We could run. I thought of it while looking at the creek then,
though I've thought of it so many times it's as constant as a heartbeat. But we don't. We never do. I thought of my girl and I can't
say what my man thought of that kept him from running, but I'm
sure there's something of that too.

I done a cruel thing to him by having Rue, I know it. I could've
stopped her coming, like I'd done before and done since, every
time I feel a stirring in my stomach or a pausing to my courses. But
that was some years ago and now I don't have that worry. Now I'm
a woman where nothing's gonna grow, perhaps before my time,
but who can say how many years I've got really? Enough.

I can only say something came over me like loneliness and
when I first felt my girl, when she was nothing to me but a corn
seed, I knew her even then and a sudden thought come to me: I
swear in the shape of my long dead mama, that he and I could die
and leave nothing of our love. So I done it without asking. I let one
baby grow warm in my belly. And now I can't ever leave her.

"I mean to have my freedom on paper." My man's promise cut
off my thoughts. "And when I do," he said, "I'll come back and
make you somethin' you ain't never been."

"And what's that?"

"A wife."

I'm struck altogether silent by the thought of that.

When our time was done we both felt it in our bones. We re-
treated from each other, him going his way me going mine. No
goodbye. Every word, all the time, might as well be goodbye.

"Promise me somethin'?" I asked.

My man nodded. He don't even know what I'm fixing to say, but already he nodded.

"Promise me if ever they let you get a musket in yo' hand you shoot yo' Marse John. That's freedom."

I could deserve to die just for saying it. I expected my man to cuss at me for being so foolish. But he didn't. He nodded just once, then he disappeared into the woods like he was part of it, so easy that even I couldn't keep track of him.

White folks won't say they scared in our hearing but they show it in their actions. Marse Charles one day gets himself three new slaves just like that. We been as we were for so long I forget what it's like to change. See, Marse Charles proud that he don't need to buy new when he got me to make sure all his nigras putting out babies every season and that all his old black folks stay living and living and living whether they want to or not.

The new souls come to me in a wagon from somewhere, fit with hay for easy cleaning and chains for binding. A woman, a girl, and a boy about to be a man, and I'm bid to look them over for sickness and for louse bites or for some reason why Marse Charles might be able to barter after the price of them even though the sale is already done, the goods delivered this one hot day with nary any word of the bodies to be added to the expanding plantation.

The woman and girl are ordinary, two sisters, dark and heavy and good for the field. I take them inside, bid the boy to wait a spell. Up close they smell sweet, almost sickeningly so, and I guess rightly that their used-to-be master had them work at sugar kettles making molasses. I try to smile at them because I know they scared, and as I feel through their hair looking for nits I tell them to come to me if they find themselves bothered by a man, any man, if they need a remedy. Next I inspect the full of their bodies, my hands moving on Marse Charles's behalf, seeking out defects, roaming

gentle but persistent inside the slick wet of their low-down fear.
The older one I can tell has the kind of chest that's known a child,
that's grown engorged by wasted milk. I don't ask her where the
baby gone. They both clean and worth their price, and I'm glad at
least they have one another, that rare threadbare gift you might
pass off as benevolence.

I send them on their ways. Their new home is a cabin of single
women, three to a bed, and I don't feel guilty that I don't offer
them a place in my own bed. I've earned the whole of my greed.

Next the boy. The boy is near a man, and as men and boys often
do he's thinking how to look at me, mama or whore or both, and
when I meet his eyes he holds on to my gaze a moment then looks
down and that's how it's going to be between us. I cross to him and
feel the strength of his arms. I do it not like a master but like a
mama. Lifelong hunger's done battle with years of hard work on
his body, and I can tell he's just escaped thin by growing into lean.

"What they call you?"

He don't answer me at first and I think, Lord, don't tell me he
slow. But finally he look up and give me his name, and you can see
the smart in his eyes. Nah, he ain't slow. He too smart for his own
good, and I don't have to wonder too long what Marse Charles was
thinking when he brought this young cock to our hen house. I
only have to think—why now?

"Y'all come from the same place?"

"Yes'm. We from Marse Avis Payne's place," he say. "Out west a
ways. 'Bout five days' ride it took us."

He was paying attention then. And he know his directions.

"How'd Marse Charles come to get you?"

"Marse Payne dead in the war. We parcel of a forfeiture."

A good deal then. Marse Charles lucky, always has been, rubbing on me for luck.

I ask the boy, "You got people back there?"

Now he's turning his face back into that fool-stone and I suppose I can't blame him for it. He don't know me; far as he's concerned I could be the master's right hand. I hope fiercely that I ain't.

"Mama?" It's my girl at the door.

When my girl come in I have it figured all out, just from her look. This boy was bought for breeding. See, she's eyeing him like she someone who ain't never tasted food and he's the dish being brought into a feast. But my girl is shy and given over to thinking on things too hard. That child is so like her daddy and she don't even know it.

"Rue-baby," I say to her. "This Jonah."

After I sent Jonah on his way to the men's cabin Rue takes me aside and says to me that thing that all mamas long to hear and horror after, too: "Mama, I need yo' help."

I done forgot the way to the old white folks' church. I ain't been there in so long and the last time I was took there it was through nightfall and I was being dragged, clawing and grasping at the root of trees as I went. I don't wanna go out that way, not at all, but Rue says there's something I need to see, something she can't speak aloud no how, so I bundle up my fear like a sack of spikes and sling it over my shoulder and follow her through them miles.

When we get there the double doors are slight-ways open, like someone just went through them, and it makes me so nervous I stop and shy like a wary dog that's sniffed up trouble on ahead of itself. I nearly whine in fear from down in the thick of my throat. My girl Rue beckons me forward. What can she be thinkin'? What could be so urgent? I have a bone-deep feeling that this might be my very worst fear come real, that they finally turnt her against me, that she's the one that's gon' drag me back there, put me in that jail, that hole in the ground. She's gon' turn the key for them.

"Please hurry, Mama." So I do.

Little Miss Varina is sat up by the pew looking anxious in a dress too flimsy for propriety, and I don't have to go all the way up to her to see it. Her big round pregnant belly.

"No."

"But, Mama."

"I said no."

I turn right around and drag my daughter after me saying no no no.

Varina's hefted herself to her feet and she's yelling stop but I don't have to listen. Not as if she can chase me down in that state. Let them kill me later, but I'm leaving with my girl right now.

"Mama, she need you," Rue says, chasing after me as I clatter through the grass and around the trees, wheeling so fast I almost can't remember which way home is. "She ain't got a husband now. She can't have that baby."

I grab Rue by the hair and drag her after me the same way Marse Charles done to me so many times. No no no.

"We will not. I won't and you won't. That's death you talkin' about. Killin' a white woman's baby for her."

I smack at her back. Stupid soft-hearted darling. Push her further into the woods 'til we're far from there.

"But she need our help," Rue is saying and stumbling. She wants to turn back. After how far we come, she's still trying to turn back.

"I'll kill you myself first."

She stops. She looks at me and knows I'm speaking the truth. Rue don't argue after that.

I'm dreaming pure mad and I know it. I burnt up a leaf meant to give me sweet-nothing sleep but breathed too deep it seems, came up on the other side of silence, where the nightmares gallop. In this dream I am the headless chickens and I am the fox snapping their necks. That's all wrong. That weren't how it happened. There's a *tap tap tap* that I wake to and my girl Rue's in my arms, thank the Lord, sleeping undisturbed. She ain't forgive me for leaving Varina, and I don't care if she never do.

"Who there?"

I hear the *tap tap tap* again and I know who it is right off. It's Ol' Joel and his goddamn cane. The one Marse Charles give him. The one he think as good as Moses's own staff. He's rapping it at my door, impatient.

I open the door to him, not caring I'm in my nightclothes, and the old filthy man has a long, slow look from my bare feet on up, before he finally gets to the reason he's woke me up while the moon is still shining.

"It's the new 'un," he says.

And I say, "Which?" fearing it's one of them sisters.

"Jonah," he say and I bristle at it. Surprised he's even bothered to get the boy's name.

I throw on a shawl against the cold night air and Ol' Joel looks disappointed at the loss of my pricked-up chest.

"He hurt?"

"Bleedin' bad."

I grab the healing things, ones good for when there's no fore-warning what the danger might be: yarrow and oak bark and com-frey root come to hand. I have one tallow candle left to light, and I can see Ol' Joel looking at it with envy as I draw it out and set the wick afire. The shadows writhe something sinister. I all of a sud-den want to stop and kiss my girl, but there's no time for that. She doesn't stir even as I draw the light from the room. Outside, Ol' Joel moves slow with his cane and I'm too frustrated to wait on him to lead.

"Where's the boy?"

"By the creek," he say and I run off in the direction of his crooked, pointed finger. The night's set in too deep to see the water, which runs black as ink in the thicker parts of the wood. I follow its lapping sound awhile and I feel it the moment I've left the bounds of Marse Charles's lands, though I can't say how. Still, Jonah ain't too far from home when I do find him and I gotta wonder who put the whisper in Ol' Joel's ear that this would be the place the boy would be.

The nighttime screeching of wild hogs is a strange, awful thing, for they ain't nighttime animals and they know it, but the poor starved creatures ain't stupid neither. They know a feast when they see it, and this boy is the feast, doused as he is in bacon grease. Somebody's tied him to a tree by his wrists, covered him in hog fat and offal. Them wild beasts is eating the remains of their captive cousins with feral glee and eating up Jonah along with it. He struggled I can see by the deep red gashes the rope made on his wrists, rubbed raw down to the bone. Now he's suffered so long, he ain't even making a sound no more. He dead?

I swing my candle at the hogs—it's the only weapon I've got— and they scream and grunt and hiss at me awhile and I worry that they're so ravenous they'll turn on me next but they don't. They trudge back into the wood as my flame swings near, and they take their awful grunting with them so that finally I can hear the low whimper coming from the boy.

"Jonah." I speak to him to keep him hearing sense. "Jonah. Boy. Jonah."

He chatters his teeth and looks at me like I'm hollow, like he's seeing through me to some other place. "Stay here now, Jonah."

It seems like forever 'til Ol' Joel catch up, like he took his time. He's brought with him two other sturdy men and I suspect the delay was in waking the overseer, in asking permission. They pick up Jonah like he's nothing at all and I'm left to trail by his side, to hold his hand, to say his name over and over. I make them take him to the House, as it's nearest. We go in the back hall through the servants' quarters, and Fannie, our dead mistress's house maid, is up, looking scared, her arms crossed over her breasts. How dare she have time for propriety?

They lay Jonah down right on the ground on a threadbare bit of rug. There's nowhere else left to put him. I go down with him, afraid to pull my hand out of his firm grip, the only thing about him holding on.

"Mama?" he ask me, like to make my heart break.

"Yes, baby," I say. Lying comes easy. "I'm with you now."

I'm looking round the kitchen and in my meager basket thinking, what can I use? How can I save him? I can barely catch my breath, never mind my thoughts. The men are watching, the housemaid is watching; I can see the horror lilting off their faces as shadows in the night. That's when I remember my candle, the single flame, all mine. Yeah, I know what needs doing to close up those wounds.

"I'll be needin' somebody to hold down his arms," I tell the room. "And someone to hold closed his mouth. Mind he don't bite his tongue, now. Muffle him. He will scream. And we don't need to wake no more white folks."

When it's over I am weary. I walk to my cabin slow because I have to drag all my gathered sorrow along with me. I push open the door, wanting only my sleeping girl, wanting only to rest my head. But I can't 'cause I'm not alone. I walk in and sniff the air and know that he's been waiting on me and that he's been waiting awhile. I always know him by his smoke, white-man smoke too thick and fine for the likes of us. It's in my clean air, still curling.

I ignore him. Sit on the bed by my sleeping girl, watch the breath come in and out of her easy, like he must have been doing this long while. She sleeps so deep, my baby. She don't know how cruel real life is. My own fault. I want so bad to touch her but my hands are stained. I look at my palms in what little light the moon gives out.

"You know you too pale to hide in the shadows, don't you?" I whisper-speak.

He chuckles out a breath of that smoke. "You take care of that boy?"

"Jonah."

"Yeah, him," he say. "Y'all fix him up?"

"He'll survive it. Can't take no drink 'til it heals. Can't pass no water. If the thirst don't kill him, he'll survive it."

"Good," he say. "Knew you'd save him. It's a waste but we'll have to make a good use of him elsewise now that he's a eunuch."

When he says "we" I don't know if he means me and him, but there's a thrill in his voice like maybe that's what he'd intended for Jonah all along from the moment he bought him, his mind on how he'd keep his henhouse safe when he gallops off to war.

It's a greedy shame, but I can't help but touch Rue's thick dark hair. So much thicker than mine too, resilient. She's been sticking flowers in her hair again and I pick out the petals. Fool girl. Wasteful little sweetheart.

"Belle," he says from behind me. I keep my eyes on my girl just a little while longer. Now, where did she get that warm, dark skin so much like her daddy's? I gave her everything else but that's all his doing.

"Come along now, Belle," he says and I know my defiance has gotta run short sometime. I kiss her, my girl. Not her face but the air above it and I'm so sure that she feels it, even through his smoke. She smiles in her sleep.

I go outside with Marse Charles but I don't have to go where he's wanting to take me. He's a fool, doesn't even know what's happening to his own daughter, to his own land.

I'm always free to leave, you see, to run away in my mind. And every time Marse Charles touches me, in my head I am gone. I go and meet my man by the river. In my freedom, I make it daytime 'cause I love to see his body in that light with no fear of being seen or found out or stolen back again. We can love in the daytime, take every moment the sun has to give, pull off all our clothes, no sinful shucking up of dresses here, Lord no, we can know each other like man and wife do, stretched out beneath the trees. And I can touch every inch of my man, claim him, even the sweat behind his kneecaps is mine, the small seashell curve of his ear or the field of his back, timber brown and rippling with muscle but here in my mind, and here only, he is unblemished, unscarred, unhurt. I can howl at the thrill of loving him and him me, and when we're done we can wash each other clean in the river, safe with the feeling that the rocks under our toes are as steady as the shore.

"Belle," he say and I flinch away because my man doesn't never call me that, not here, not anywhere.

"Shh," I say to him. I press my finger on his lips. The water moves around my waist and his arms snake up around my neck. I can feel the slow, steady lacing of his fingers against my spine, slipping against the wet. North is the way the river flows here and it could sweep us away if I let it.

"I love you, Belle," he say.

And I say, "Hush, hush," because in my mind I'm only May. And my man's hands break free of my neck and different hands appear.

Marse Charles's voice breaks into my mind, says, "Do what I tol' you now, Belle," and he grabs roughly onto my face, his fingers dig deep into my cheekbones like as if they wish to rip them out. And he has me again, there in the moonlight and the worst of it, the very worst of it is, beneath all of it is the stench of his white fingers that smell so hotly of bacon grease. Even my springtime river can't wash that stink away.

Marse Charles goes his way and I go mine.

In the bed my girl is safe, hasn't even rolled over. I love her so, love how dark she is like her daddy. I lay down beside her hardly rippling her sleep. I shouldn't have had her, but I did. Kept her hid no matter how big she grew in my belly, and when it was time for her to come on out I stole away to a clearing in the woods and birthed her all by my lonesome.

I tell that tale all the time, about how I brung my own baby out into the world alone. But I ain't never tell it true. For if my Rue-baby had been born into this cruel life half-black, half–Marse Charles's child, I would have dashed her head in on the rocks myself.

"Rue-baby," I say to my sweet dozing child. Almost a woman grown. "Rue. You listenin'?"

Sleepy and slow her voice comes out like it had far to travel.

"Yes, Mama?" she say.

EXODUS

—

"It's almost time," Sarah said.

Over the top of her pregnant belly, she stared blearily as Rue looked her over.

"Oh, we got a while yet."

In the front room of Sarah's cabin Rue settled in, Bean right beside her. She looked around regretfully at the empty house. Jonah had took up his things and left, chasing prosperity up north, and there were empty places on the walls where a man's belongings used to hang. His hat. His axe. The painted walls had not faded even, left outlines of what wasn't there.

She sat herself down at the table where she saw there were leaves spread in orderly lines like they were marching in. She recognized their various patterns.

"What's all this?"

"I got 'em for Mama," Bean said.

Rue looked closer. She saw what Bean had gathered, leaves and stems of various uses, heaped together by type and color and shape, things he'd seen her bring to Sarah over the months. He'd gone and got them himself.

"Let me see you." She pulled him into her lap and he didn't

squirm but let her look him over, his hands down to his legs. She had a fear that he'd troubled into some poison while he foraged. He didn't know what to avoid. But as Rue looked at the uneven crag of his skin she saw that there was not a scratch on him.

"How'd you do all that?"

He shrugged, a warm easy weight in her arms.

"I watch you," he said.

What else did he know? What else had he seen but every little thing they'd all done up to now, every lie and hid truth? Every sickness and every worship. Bean with his big, smart watchful eyes.

He let himself be cuddled closer and Rue rubbed her face in the thread of his hair. An oiled-leather brown, so much like Bruh Abel's. Why hadn't she seen it? She'd never bothered to look past his eyes.

"And she helped me some," Bean admitted, like he wasn't really wanting to share the credit. "Auntie V. She nice."

"You friendly with her, ain't you?"

"Sure. I like her plenty. She look like Mama."

Rue squeezed him in her arms like to say sorry with her squeezing. It was folly to think that she was the only one that had ever had any secrets.

Bean told her of the woman who'd let him call her "Auntie V," how she'd been kind to him and spoke to him and kept him safe from the white demons riding through, and as he told it Rue settled it all in her mind, muddled together a bittersweet solution but a solution all the same.

"Yo' mama gon' be alright," she said to Bean.

"How you know?"

"'Cause I'm gon' stay here. I'm gon' watch for you."

"Miss Rue? Where am I goin'?" he had the sense to ask.

———

Rue told Bean a story to remember her by. It was what Miss May Belle would have done, she reckoned.

This is a story, she said, of how Bruh Rabbit done fooled God. He went up to the sky, straight up to God, and said, God, I'mma bring you one hundred slaves and all you need give me to do it is one kernel of corn. God laughed. Said, you can't make one hundred slaves out of a kernel, but he gave the seed to Bruh Rabbit anyway just to see what would happen.

Well, Bruh Rabbit took that seed and he planted it and it did grow up into a mighty cornstalk, and when it had grown tall he picked the ear and traveled on to the next town over. There Bruh Rabbit begged a room, told the innkeeper, this here corn is special. This is God's corn. Don't let no harm come to it. But Bruh Rabbit was clever. In the middle of the night he hopped out to where he'd left the corn and he plucked every kernel from it and, unseen, took himself back to bed.

Come the morning he pretended like he didn't know nothin' 'bout it. Screamed to the townspeople, some chicken must've ate God's corn. You best replace it or you'll be sorry. Afeared of God's wrath the townsfolk gave to him the chicken they thought must have done the eating.

Now he took the chicken on to the next town. Told the folks there, this here is God's chicken. Don't let no harm come to it. But in the night he crept to it and killed that chicken also. And when morning come he hollered at the people, said, that's God chicken. You best replace it. Just then some workers passed by carting after them dead bodies fresh from the war. So Bruh Rabbit took himself the littlest amongst them as payment and went on to the next town.

There he dressed up the body like a child and he moved him and spoke for him and told the folks there, this here's God's child.

Don't let no harm come to him. But come mornin' Bruh Rabbit cried at what he'd found. Somebody done killed God's child. Now the townsfolk were aggrieved and didn't know what all they could do but to replace the child one hundredfold with their finest, strongest men of good stock.

Bruh Rabbit marched those men to heaven, right up to God's veranda, and proclaimed, here I have done it. From one corn kernel to one hundred slaves.

And God did have to admit that Bruh Rabbit was the most cunning of all creatures.

WARTIME

==

Varina sucked her thumb. She hadn't done it in years, but there she was, sixteen, her body worming with pain, and she put her thumb in her mouth because it was the only thing she had at hand to keep herself from screaming. She sucked hard at it 'til it was red and sore, the nail down to the quick, the skin puckered and wrinkled and raw. When she put it in her mouth she tasted only the acrid lye-white bubbles that she had held in her hands when she'd prepared the flush of soapy water to do what needed doing. To clean out her baby, root and stem.

Now she curled around her aching middle like someone had put a sawed-off shotgun to her belly button and pulled the trigger. She rolled on the varnished wood floor of her bedroom, her body sliding and twitching. Stuck her thumb in her mouth as the pain rose and rose, bit down on her thumb to try to hold in the mounting scream, because she knew if anybody came upon her, if they came too soon, their first thought would be to save the baby.

But the scream broke loose and came out jagged, tearing at her insides as it carved its way up and out of her throat, a mournful cry against her will.

———

Miss May Belle rolled back her sleeves. Didn't know truly where
to begin. It was a poor sight to see Varina as she was, shaking and
screaming, foam coming from her lips like she'd swallowed the
soap instead of the truth, which was that she'd stuck it between her
lily-white legs. Marse Charles had sent for Miss May Belle reluctantly but it was better than the alternative, which was to send for
the doctor, who, miles and miles off, might not come in time and
upon seeing Varina would know instantly the nature of the shame
she'd brought down on them, on her own good name—once for
conceiving and again for committing such a foul, twisted act as
trying to end that conception.

Well, the girl was paying for it now. She might not make it to
sunup. And there was a part of Miss May Belle that thought, now
maybe that would be the better ending for all of their stories to say
she'd tried her damnedest but there was no saving neither of them,
mama nor child.

Miss May Belle kneeled and held her hands in a rictus of un-
certainty, and beneath her Varina curled and cried, looking like a
salted-over slug. Miss May Belle had brought with her everything
she had, every type of healing she knew of. It wasn't the first time
she'd seen a woman in such a state, though the slaves down there
on the plantation had different ways and different reasons. Varina
had chosen a hard-chemical death for her baby and to that end
Miss May Belle brought with her harder medicines, tinctures in
bottles saved up from Varina's mama's sickness that had come too
late to be used.

"Calm her with the laudanum," Marse Charles had told Miss
May Belle. "Don't give my daughter any a' yo' shit black grass."

The bottle held enough, Miss May Belle knew, to put Varina to
a dreamless forever sleep, and she did think on serving it to her for
a long dark while. In the end, Miss May Belle administered Varina
only a taste, decided soul-deep that she simply didn't have it in her

to let any woman die, especially not for the mere sake of taking her fate into her own two hands after the world of men had shackled those hands behind her.

Rue ran. Out through the slave quarters of the House, a labyrinth of tight dank corners, underground rooms, not hardly fit for habitation but lived in all the same, and she came up gasping on the other side of the slaves' entrance with the little bundle in her arms wrapped and wrapped and wrapped in cloth. If she encountered anybody she was meant to lie, tell them what she held was a bundle of kindling or a sack of root medicine or a collection of rusty bloodied knives, whatever lie needed telling to get her fast away because the baby needed to be buried and it needed to be buried quick.

Don't even think on it as a baby, Miss May Belle had said when she'd passed off the little strange bundle, already swathed and hid from Rue's curious eyes. It ain't a baby really. It's just a shame.

Rue took Varina's shame to the river, as far as she could go without being thought of as running away, the very edge of Marse Charles's vast territory so large he probably had never even strolled the half of it. There she dug deep with use of little more than a piece of slanted rock that cut and bruised her palms, but the mud was yielding, softened by a slow-falling rain.

She laid the shame down in the hole, and there she could just make out the baby's figure through the dried blood on the thin blanket. There, his little arms and his little legs, his twisted-up chest and sunken stomach. There the outline of his shock white face. She looked on him so long that the rain collected in the hollow of his skull, pooled on the blanket in black, where his eyes should have been. All black.

Rue plugged up the hole with mud, packed it in deep. She buried him and prayed the whole while. That the shame would stay hid. That the creek wouldn't ever rise and bring the dead baby back again.

Varina wouldn't speak. When her daddy came to see her, his fellow want-to-be soldiers were in his company, bedraggled and obviously drunk. Ruddy and heavy with it, they'd called her down to the parlor because her bedroom, the whole upper floor of the House it seemed, was a tainted place in Marse Charles's estimation. She had stained it all over with a womanly sin.

Her legs would barely take her down the stairs, her head rocked and flipped and did not settle. On the long walk she saw ghosts of women, translucent spirits, all of them with babies to their bared breasts, laughing. She was lost in her own home and it took two slave girls to find her and lead her back, and when she did finally reach the parlor she lay shriveled and pale on a stiff-backed chaise. The men were automatic and polite in her presence, but they were ready. They had their dogs and their guns and their whiskey and their rope. All they needed was the name, they kept saying, and the hungry dogs kept barking, and the ghost women with their babies stood over Varina and let themselves be sucked dry. A name. A name.

"May Belle," she said to quiet them. "May Belle, she ought to have helped me."

"May Belle?" Marse Charles said. "May Belle's man? He's the beast that attacked you?"

The question echoed. Above her the ghost women leered. A name.

EXODUS

==

Rue had smacked Bruh Abel. Once and hard and across the face. Named him a cheat and a liar and told him to get gone. She had never hit anybody before, let alone a man, let alone one she might have loved.

Bruh Abel had still been grinning, even when blood bloomed from his split lip, but there was sorrow in that grin. It had been there awhile, Rue knew, since her baby died. Their baby.

"Guess I was deserving that," Bruh Abel said and rubbed his swollen cheek.

She'd made him a poultice to soothe the red mark her hand had left on his fair skin.

Deserving? What did she herself deserve? She thought on it now as she sat on a pew in the white church as though it were the subject of a sermon.

Across from Rue, Varina held Bean in her lap.

"How long?" Varina bit out.

She'd already asked. Rue answered again. "Comin' up on seven years that the war's been over."

"We lost?" Varina said.

Rue didn't know if she counted as "we," but she nodded.

"You never told me. You never said."

"I thought I was helpin'," Rue said and that much had been true at the start.

That first year Varina had been delirious, her body half-poisoned from the lye, half-poisoned from the laudanum she'd sipped and sipped.

Rue hadn't known what to use to cure Varina of the addiction. She'd never had to counter white medicine with her own, and Varina seemed so content to die in her dreams. By the second year, if Varina had cared enough about the war to ask after it, it was easy for Ma Doe to arm Rue with scraps of old newspaper. Varina'd lost her sense of dates, quickly lost her appetite for news entirely. After that she'd simply waited and trusted and believed.

She'd believed that the South's glory and the life she'd been promised would rise up from the war ash resurrected and recon-structed, as if by magic. Faith in magic was far more potent than magic itself—hadn't Miss May Belle said that all along?

Rue held out her hands like she meant to give Varina some-thing, but her hands were empty and her right palm stung. "I thought you were safe here."

"Safe? When was I ever safe here?" Varina moaned, and it echoed off the church walls. In her arms Bean snuggled close to her, unaware of what they were speaking on but keen to hurt just the same.

Rue figured Varina would rail against her, would scream, would haul off and hit her, same as Rue herself had hit Bruh Abel. Or worse, Varina would drag her off to the middle of the used-to-be plantation and whip Rue raw.

But Varina was not the girl she had been or the mistress she might have become.

She was a woman like a flower that had lived in a dark, dark place and tried her best, if not to flourish, then to survive—and that sort of thing made a body grateful, Rue well knew.

"So it's over?" Varina asked again. "I can go?"

"Yes."

Varina kissed Bean's head, then looked up to the church rafters. She said, "Thank God."

IN THE BEGINNING . . .

====

There was the ship hold. The early swirling motion of the sea, sickening. The heat of fever, the heat of fear, the only thing cold the new chains, and even those warmed quick and rusted over with rubbing with sores, with blood, with futile struggle. The darkness, the void of that black ship bottom, the darkness on the face of the deep, and then someone said unto them let there be light, piercing light, did you know light could hurt so bad? On the deck above they were made to dance under that brightness. So much light—the light of the heavens, and also the light of the heavens reflected on the sea, and then a few black bodies that got somehow free of the dance went jumping into that sea, blind, perhaps confusing the sea they'd never seen before for heaven, God's face in the waters. Waste that. False profits. The rest of them were sent back to the dark void 'til the ship reached firmament.

She had no words for then; they hadn't given them to her yet. But if she thought back and tried to give words to the memories of the ship and after, there was the one that had rung out when they'd stood her up before the curious white faces and made her hold out her arms and then hold open her mouth and then hold open her legs. Sold.

And was a mama the warm body that made you in a time and a place and a land you couldn't remember? Or was a mama what you made for yourself—the good warm body, the first kind memory of the older woman who slept beside you in the hayloft, who let you fold into her warmth that first evening that you were owned? And she hummed to you because she couldn't speak what you spoke. And that first sense of love, the earth still for the first time beneath your back, and for the first time, through an opening in the roof, the evening sky. You can make due with unspoken kindness and the stars also.

There were signs and seasons and days and years. After a time she was called Dorothea, named in the mistress's own image. They whupped the name into her, but it couldn't stick right. "No," she could say. And then "Doe" for the rhyme. In the end, they tied the two together, called her Doe—and it was good.

EXODUS

═

If anyone had ever loved Varina, Ma Doe had. Rue knew that. Had sometimes envied that, but now she made good on it, or as good as good might ever get leastwise.

Rue walked slowly between her two prizes like she was the juncture between the beginning and the end of time—Ma Doe on her right, Bean on her left, a march for penance.

The new school building wasn't all the way erected but it had four walls. In Rue's estimation that was enough to make a room or a home, a permanence, that one could start to feel safe with for a time, never mind that the roof was not quite finished and the rain came blustering in.

"It's dangerous," Ma Doe kept warning. She knew as well as anyone the danger the night could hold.

"I want you to see her 'fore she goes."

Inside Varina had made a seat for herself out of a fat leather case, crafted for her special some years ago for a trip she'd never taken. She sat in the corner as nervous and hair-raised as a wet cat, but she was alert. Ready. She troubled on the finer details of Rue's plan, seemed to not understand at times the things Rue was asking forgiveness after, but she was not angry to learn that blacks were freed, was only relieved to hear that no hurt was coming after her. Varina was ever fierce after her own survival and she was fierce after the things she loved and now Bean had become one of them.

Ma Doe broke into a shudder when she saw the little baby girl she'd raised from birth. All these years and Ma Doe had been protecting Varina like a jewel in a box she could not open, for there was hardly any safe time that they could meet where others mightn't discover the secret. Rue hadn't ever understood how you could love something you couldn't have and hold, not 'til she'd loved and lost her own baby, loved hard on empty air and an idea.

Ma Doe moved faster than Rue had ever known her to and wrapped her ancient arms around Varina. They hugged and whispered to each other, ignoring the hard-falling rain. Rue looked on, her hands tight on Bean's little shoulders, rubbing to keep him warm, keep his spirits up. He didn't seem afraid, though, only curious to see Ma Doe, who he'd known all his small life as a fine marbled rock of a woman, moved to such tears.

Every other bosom baby of hers was gone to meet their maker by various hard means. Marse Charles's boys had marched away, had not even sent her a letter before the war ended them, she who had taught them their first stumbling words. Marse Charles had followed after, gone out to fight in the last pathetic dredging battles and had gotten not much farther than the next county before he'd surveyed all they'd lost and put a pistol to his mouth, frowned on the metallic taste, and drunk down a bottle of strychnine instead, or so the story went.

At least they had stories. Ma Doe's trueborn baby boys all had been torn from her arms, not one word to say what had become of them. Rue could, in some ways, sympathize, could understand the way a losing and not knowing was the only thing in the world worse than simple out and out losing. This was the gift she could give before Varina and Bean's departure. Knowing.

Rue had done the same for Sarah, had asked the bedbound woman permission to disappear her son away.

"A mama'll suffer just about any heartbreak," Sarah had said, through sweat and sorrow. "If it means her child is someplace safe."

When Ma Doe and Varina had finally pulled apart, Varina turned to look on the boy that was Black-Eyed Bean, Sarah's baby and, Rue supposed, Varina's nephew if the tangle of rumors surrounding Sarah's origins was finally to be named true. Marse Charles had prided himself on his sons, but here were his two daughters, Sarah and Varina, planted in the same season, and like to overgrow the world if the world would only let them.

In the little schoolhouse, Varina and Bean took the measure of each other, and then Varina crouched down to match his height.

"I like your hair," she said, easy and familiar.

"Me too."

He'd fidgeted and fussed when Rue had spread the calendula and carrot juice mixture through his hair to lighten it. All it took, a simple change of coloring, of wording, russet to redheaded, and there he was, a white boy before her like she'd laid magic on his head. The color had come out just right, that was clear to see with the two of them face-to-face, close as kin.

Bean looked to Rue and rubbed his big black eyes with both fists in the loving little way of his. "Miss Rue say Mama gon' be alright."

"Yes," Varina said. "Miss Rue has the care of everybody in hand."

Rue only waited out the rain. There were things that wanted doing and night was coming on with the intention of blackening out the sky, though the sun still had the edges.

She walked Ma Doe halfway back 'til she knew she was safe in the center of the old plantation where folks were still milling about in a hurry to finish what needed finishing before the threat of nightfall. There was something hanging in the air around them, call it foretelling, call it inevitability. Rue kissed Ma Doe's cheek and said goodbye.

"Where you off to?"

"Goin' to grab a li'l magic."

Ma Doe frowned, not catching her meaning, and Rue rubbed her fingers together to indicate coin.

"Thought you gave 'em what they needed." Ma Doe turned her head in the direction they'd left Varina and Bean, like she could see them going. Between them they carried the satchel of letters that had turned brittle waiting all those years in Ma Doe's locked desk. The correspondence to the Northern auntie to whom they now were headed had been taken up in two thick bundles: letters received, and, in Ma Doe's meticulous hand, copies of the letters sent. Two sides of the story. Varina'd read up on the facts of her life. She was like to add embellishments. Hadn't that always been her way?

"They'll do just fine," Rue told Ma Doe.

No dark back roads for a white lady and her white son. Bean with his shock-white skin and his new orange hair would pass as easy as folks had always told Bruh Abel that he could. Why the man had never chose to do so Rue couldn't rightly say. There were so many things about loving him she'd formed whole cloth in her mind and wouldn't now ever get the chance to turn over and examine proper in the light.

"This money ain't for Varina. It's for someone else."

Ma Doe *mhmm*ed a smart rolling sound from the back of her throat, like to say she'd lived so long, she'd heard everything before. "And what are you fixin' to tell him when you give it?"

"Don't know, Ma," Rue said. "Maybe somethin' like goodbye?"

SURRENDER

=

1865

They hanged Rue's daddy from a tree. He'd been named the cause of Varina's shame. That was all it took to enact Varina's curse upon Miss May Belle, revenge for her refusal to heal her of the baby she did not want. Lily-white conjure. Simple as pointing a finger.

Rue hadn't been there when they'd done it but she could see how it went. It was an oft-enough told tale. They'd come upon him up the road, on his way to join up with the Rebs. Hadn't his marse freed him after all and everything? So there he was when Death came upon him, a black man with the flimsy protection of freedom papers.

Maybe they'd been brutal and rough, beat him to bloodied before they'd done it, though Lord knew they didn't have to. They could just have easily bade him string himself up.

Fetch the rope, nigger.

Miss May Belle had not been witness, either, when they'd killed her man. But she knew what they'd done the moment they'd done it. Sat in their cabin, Rue watched her mama's body twitch and bend like she was bearing an assault of unseen hands. Then she went all-over rigid, her neck overextended, her head tilted too far back. Inside her skull her eyes rolled to all white and a gasp shuddered out of her mouth with such force as to be her last. Just like that it was over, and Miss May Belle was herself again, sullen but dry-eyed. *He ain't gone,* she kept saying like saying could make it so.

They'd left him to swing. Said the darkie-loving Northerners could cut him down if they felt so inclined. But the truth of it was his slow-spinning body, big and strong and heavy enough to bow the branch he dangled from, was meant to serve as a reminder in the master's absence. That they would be back once the war was won.

Marse Charles had left Jonah in charge. Who better than a clipped cock to guard a henhouse? With Ol' Joel beside him, overseeing, things didn't hardly change. Miss Varina was like a ghost watching from her bedroom window, searching outward. From that height she could just see the tree they'd hanged Rue's daddy from. She told them the next day to cut him down.

Folks said the Union army was creeping closer. They'd taken Marse John's plantation for themselves, eaten up all the goods left in the stores, drank and sang their Northern songs, trampled on the fledgling crops, smashed things in Marse John's parlor that weren't worth the trouble to steal. Did they have horns, hoofed feet, like they'd all been hearing? They'd disappeared away with the slaves left there, it was said, marched them away not as free but as contraband. Better maybe the devil you know.

By then Miss May Belle had took to her bed with something worse than grief, which was denial. Said, *He ain't gone,* of her man and Rue knew she'd find no help from her mama, maybe never would again.

Time was drawing to a close, it felt like, and there was a bristled-up anticipation amongst the people they couldn't name, precisely, because it was tinged in fear. They'd led their whole slave lives waiting on *someday,* singing *a day will come,* promising *on that day* that they would be ready. Rue never had been good at singing along. She had decided not to wait on the Day but to act in the Night.

The moon lit the way for her, and Rue took herself right on in through the front door of the House, straight up the spinning stairs and down the gilded hall to Varina's door, went in without knocking, without seeking permission or needing it.

Varina was deep asleep. One of her slave girls had tucked her neatly in her bed like a body laid out for burial, and all her earthly belongings surrounded her. Rue watched Varina for a moment in her repose knowing the moment she woke everything would change.

Rue shook the girl by the shoulders like to snap her neck. What had come over her, Rue could not say, only she knew it needed doing. Had to happen now.

The white girl shocked awake, saw Rue wild in her bed, and seemed to think it was her judgment day, started confessing.

"I didn't know they meant to kill him," Varina hollered.

Rue didn't follow her meaning at first.

"Your daddy," Varina said. She clutched her bedsheets close and shook. "I swear I didn't know what they were asking when they asked it. I didn't know."

Maybe it was so. But the trouble was that Varina had never had to know anything up there in the House; she could close the blinds if she didn't like what she was seeing, could turn away in her featherbed.

"It alright." Rue began with a lie. "Come with me now. It ain't safe for you. The army is a-comin'."

Varina grabbed at Rue. Hid her face in Rue's little chest, and Rue could feel Varina's tears and snot and sorrow soaking through her own muslin dress.

"I can't bear it," Varina said.

Rue knew that for all her life the little white mistress had been told the bedtime stories where the black man was the brute, the creature to fear in the darkness. Now the world was all turned over and at Rue's suggestion Varina could just hear the boot stomps of a hundred Northern men, none of them a savior, every one of them like the gentleman Rue had glimpsed defiling Varina's innocence the day of the Dead Man's Jubilee. A white-gloved monster. Rue never had been good at comfort, but she comforted Varina's fears then, laid a kiss on her forehead, said, "Ain't I gon' keep you safe?"

It was likely when the Blues came through that they'd be kind to Varina, send her on to wherever disgraced women went to be hid away from the fighting with others of their station, to write letters and sing songs and wait out the new dawn. But it was just as possible that those Northern soldiers, hungry and vengeful, would swoop in and see her as part of what her opulent house stood tall for, just another room in which to plunder. And Varina still had Rue's name and Sarah's name on a spirited away bit of paper that promised her ownership of her nigras should she ever take a husband. Any day now the world might right itself and the old laws would hold. Rue had never seen that thing the Yankees were promising—freedom—and she did not trust in what she could not see.

There'd always been rumors of what lay beneath the white church, and in the end the rumors held true. The little locked room under root and earth was not a room at all but a pit, a grave, and Miss Varina, mistress-made, had the key.

"But, Rue," Varina kept on saying, even as she eased her way into the dark. When her feet landed in the mud down below there was the sound of it sucking, the earth swallowing. Looking up at Rue from down below, Varina shivered.

"It's the only way." Lie two. How quick they grew and strengthened and tangled.

"You'll come back for me, won't you? Please?"

Rue slid closed the lid. Turned the key hard in the lock.

Day started dawning, and Rue met it. Everybody on the plantation was sleeping still, dredging the last of their resting hours, for normal folks toiled all day, slept at night. Not Rue, never Rue. She was all opposite, a nighttime creature. She could see through the darkness and she had seen what was coming from way off.

Rue stood on the porch of the House alone, little, thin and nothing to her. When they came she faced them down, an army. She had her hand on the pillar for strength, laced her fingers in the etched grooves and rubbed so hard, feeling like it was the only thing left that was real. If she didn't hold on here she would float away—that was her thinking, as she drew her breath on the next lie.

The leader of them walked up, no uniform on him, but just an air of command. He talked to her slow like he thought maybe she wouldn't understand.

"Step away from there now, girl." Already he was snapping orders at one of his men to come and grab her away.

She held, gripped. Spoke: "Only I need to tell you, suh. Miss Varina, our mistress, is dead. Died of the pox just late last night."

It was the best lie to tell. She saw the effect it had, the way the men shivered and stepped back afeared of the House as if she'd painted a curse on it, and in a way she had, the conjure of contagion. The only course they had was fire, that one true final cure.

The crackling, popping, hissing of the House going up in flames seemed to speak to the slavefolk in a forgotten language they hadn't known they'd lost. When they heard it talking they came out of their quarters, out from by the river, out from the cotton fields, to hear what the fire had to say, to watch it devour all they'd known, turn that white House black, sunder it all to a thin wind-swept ash. When it had eaten up all it could, the fire, still hungry, went after the trees.

Miss May Belle came out amongst the gathered people, strange and stumbling in the light, like somebody just drawn out from the depths of a cave. Rue ran to her, wanted to whisper to only her mama the truth of what she'd done. Let the rest of them mourn after Miss Varina or dance on her grave if they liked. Rue held the truth of her trick to her like treasure. The key was in her pocket.

But when Rue reached her mama the woman was not smiling; instead she was collapsing, falling like her knees were where the fire was, all her bones popping and snapping.

Rue held her mama, hugged at her, tried to understand where her grief came from. Miss May Belle was pointing at the trees, to one in particular, a tall white birch where the flames had caught the very top, blazed all orange like a new type of leaf.

"My man," Miss May Belle cried. "My man. Lord, Rue, what you done? Ain't you know I made him safe? Ain't you know I turnt him to a tree?"

EXODUS

===

"You wanna see her 'fore you go?"

"You think there's time?"

Rue did not.

"You think she mine?" Bruh Abel said "she" because Rue had said "she." There was really no telling what a baby meant to be 'til it had come.

"Don't you know?"

"Even Adam wasn't sure a' Eve an' they was the only two in the garden."

Save the snake. Rue shrugged. "Won't know 'til she come out. An' even then." Even then.

Bruh Abel smelled of his faith, the bold, beautiful kerosene lights that illuminated his church's tent like a lone star in the night sky. Did the moon see it and envy? Most likely, and if it did not, he'd only go on and build that light bigger. The scent of the burning oil clung to his clothes, traveling clothes of a type Rue'd never seen him in. Unadorned and ordinary, they fit close to his lithe body like extra skin. Running clothes.

"It was done with long ago, me an' Sarah was. Rue, I swear it."

Rue had never asked him to swear. And maybe that had been her failing. She didn't know how to ask. Or how to believe.

They were in the front room of Sarah's house, looking on water boiling in a pot. When it was time to go Bruh Abel had nothing with him but the tied-up bundle of his suit wrapped around his Bible and whatever he could hold in its smaller pockets, as if he'd accumulated nothing in all those years. That couldn't at all be true. Rue kissed him while the water bubbled and popped and hissed.

Their plan, like all the plans they'd ever formed together in the rut of their shared bed, between the optimism of flesh to flesh, was simple. Bruh Abel would lead his people out in the early threads of morning light, march sure through the gathered dew, wind up northward, away from the legacy of danger, all of them that wanted gone, going together. Those that would stay would stay, the old, the infirm, those tied to the land they found too beloved to leave, it being theirs by bitter rights, a home where they'd sweated and bled and lost as much as it was a place they'd planted seeds and watched things flourish. Miss Rue was among those staying. She felt rooted here.

"What if folks change they mind, if things get too bad?" Rue asked. "Wanna follow after you?"

From inside his bundled suit, from inside the fluttering pages of his Bible, Bruh Abel conjured. Paper. Pen. He wetted the pen on his tongue. With a swirl of ease and grace he began to write. The words blossomed black out of his pen like fast, elegant little miracles, and Rue was astonished to see his agility—and with his left hand no less.

"You can write," she said.

He smiled.

"You can read."

"The two things go together nicely I'm told."

She was too shocked to slap his smart mouth. "I didn't know you could read."

"When did I ever say I couldn't? 'Sides, some knowledge is better kept hid."

Rue would keep that. It was the truest thing he'd ever told her.

Ma Doe would read it, tell the others the direction they'd run if they were wanting to know it. Rue herself found she didn't want to know. Rue had told Bruh Abel that Bean was gone but safe, spirited off to a trusted location, though she did not tell Bruh Abel the color of his son's escape. The gift of one last lie.

"You sure you gon' be safe here?" he asked.

"They was always after you," Rue told him, "yo' faith and yo' freedom. The power you and Bean had made here. Them white men, they ain't heard tell a' me."

Bruh Abel grinned for her a final time and went.

Rue sang when Sarah sang as they made their way in a slow march around her bedroom waiting on the baby, that last leaving of Bruh Abel's, to come on out and greet the world. The song was a simple sweet appeal to God, and when the pain got so great that Sarah could not grind out the words, Rue hummed with her too, felt the squeezing of her hand and squeezed back.

When the hooves beat in the distance, when the dogs barked, when they heard the gunshots and the whooping and the hollering, all the telling signs that the white demons had come down from the trees, Sarah and Rue quieted.

Sarah labored in terrified silence as they listened to the night fall all around them. Rue laid her down, not in the bed but on the ground, where they were as well hid as they could be, far from the windows, the white robed men, and the malevolent light they bore, a skittering glow from their passing torches. Rue told Sarah to be brave, to close her eyes and pray. To bear down close in her crouch, push all she could toward the ground.

"Easy, easy," Rue whispered. She stroked Sarah's face, tried to pass comfort through the tips of her fingers.

When she looked up she spied him, the white man in the window. He stared down at them, watched Sarah push and twist and scream all from inside the hollow of his draped white disguise, no expression painted there, just the crooked point of his hood, the deep pool black where he'd cut for eyes.

Rue said one, small word. "Please."

Just like that, the man was swallowed back up by the night.

An hour or an eternity had passed by the time the baby came on out in three forceful pushes and Rue was there to catch her, to pull her into her arms and to hear that first powerful cry, afraid that cry would call back the demons, but loving it too much to ever quiet it.

"Sarah," Rue told her. "You got yo'self a baby girl."

The baby blinked up at Rue, gray-eyed as Bruh Abel was, and perfect, as promising as any fresh day.

In the quiet of the morning Rue woke. Sarah was beside her, watching her. In her arms the baby suckled with delight. The dawn was still. The air smelled of smoke. Rue rose from the ground where they'd survived the night and made her way to the door.

"You ain't tell me what her name is, Miss Rue."

She turned to look back at Sarah, who stood and pulled herself and her baby into the bed. Mama and child settled in, looked safe and small.

"I think her name is Posy."

"Posy," Sarah said.

Outside, the town was a mess of toppled houses, of scorched grass and bitter smells, the work of the white-hooded demons.

"Miss Rue," folks said as she passed. Their voices were rough from smoke and from grief. "Them that left with Bruh Abel? You think they got away safe?"

"'Course," Miss Rue told folks, and they were appeased. "I gave them a charm, best that I got, to see them safely north. Root a' High John the Conqueror."

She walked on, through the town square, out from what had used to be the plantation up to the clearing where the House had stood and fallen, where the tent had stood and fallen also. Now there was nothing there to mark either, no words on a grave, just the lone thing the white devils had left standing to say that they had come and gone, burning itself out to black: two planks of tall wood formed perfect in the shape of a cross.

GILEAD

===

1929

Rue walks. If she doesn't keep walking the pain catches up on her, settles round the low of her stomach and burns. The thing is, there isn't much place to walk in the hospital room. She amuses herself by fitting her bare feet full in the tiles, avoiding the sharp black lines delineating the edges. The tile is cold beneath her feet, unyielding beneath her uncut toenails, and it takes only ten of those tile steps lengthwise to take her from one side of the room to the other, and then she has to turn round and start back again. But it takes only these next ten steps for her to grow nearly so weary that she can't stand. And she has a notion that soon it will take less, and less still.

One day, today, whatever day it may be, a doctor comes. He is not the first doctor, let's say he is the third, who seeks to cure what can't be cured. Now the first doctor said, "Miss Rue, we will try to cut it from you, to cut your body clear of it." And he took her to a place he called a theater where they watched from above what was done to her. That doctor, a small mustached man who spoke in a voice like her old master, made an incision where an incision had been already made, tried to take something out of her that had been put in long ago, a curse, she liked to think of it. A bitter taste in her mouth. But it grew again and bigger. The affliction would not leave her.

Then came the second doctor, big and ruddy and from the North, though the country was one borderless place now, or so they told her. That doctor came and said to her, "Miss Rue, we will try a course of poisoning." But her sin-sick soul worsened while the affliction fed on the poison they put to her and multiplied.

Now the third doctor comes to her. There's no door to her room but he knocks politely at her doorframe.

"Miss Rue," says he.

She stops in her walking, paused on the sixth and seventh tile, turns to him and squints to see him better. She is twice forty now and failing. He is a white blur at her threshold.

"Come in," she gets to say, and there's power in that at least.

Up close he's as handsome as any doctor she's seen. The freckles on his nose make him appear boyish; the slicked-back brown of his hair suggests a root that would coil if it had half the chance. He's carrying a chart he doesn't need to read from, but he puts on thick-paned glasses anyway and it's through that glass that she notices his eyes, big and all glossy black as spilt oil. He looks at Rue then like he knows her. Looks at her like he knows.

But quickly he fiddles with the heavy folio in his hands, flutters open the pages to their well-worn center, and the moment's broken. He clears his throat to speak. He has a lovely voice, she notices, like music to be heard. "Miss Rue, how are you feelin' this mornin'?"

They always start off that way, the doctors, like someone has told them they ought to. Rue nods to him politely, the way she'd nod to any white man asking her something. But inside she does wonder.

"Alright, thank you," says she.

"Any advanced discomfort? Any pain?"

There is always pain, but you don't tell a man that nor a white man besides. "No, suh."

He sighs, shuts his papers. "I think we'll try a different course today if you don't mind, Miss Rue."

She does mind, very much, their cold metal and their bright lights in her eyes, their nods and their note-taking. She can't figure why they don't know what she knows. There is no help for it. She's dying.

"What course is that, suh?"

He smiles, as bright a smile as any balm.

"Well, Miss Rue," says he, "I thought we'd go walkin'."

AUTHOR'S NOTE

Immeasurable recognition is owed to the people whose real histories informed the fictional stories that make up *Conjure Women*. I drew largely from *Slave Narratives: A Folk History of Slavery in the United States from Interviews*, as conducted in the 1930s by the Work Projects Administration, to find voice and flavor, curses and cures. So, too, is great recognition owed to Lucy Zimmerman, Anarcha Westcott, and Betsey Harris, as well as countless unnamed, unknown women whose indignities and suffering under the medical "care" of J. Marion Sims were detailed in his own *The Story of My Life*. I offer gratitude to the African American men and women who, through their own written narratives, through interview or amanuensis, willingly and at times unwillingly, shared their experiences within the horrors of the transatlantic slave trade and its long-lasting aftermath.

ACKNOWLEDGMENTS

Raising *Conjure Women* was a village-wide undertaking. I am immensely grateful to all those who aided in ways great and small in this novel's conception, labor, and birth. Thank you:

To my mother, Diana Okyere Atakora, who offered great insight into matters pertaining to medicine and motherhood and everything in between—who taught me, always, that I could do anything, and then helped me to do it.

And to my grandmother Dora Akua Akomaah, "Ma Doe," who relayed a hundred years' worth of memories, stories, and proverbs all the way from Ghana and did not let the language barrier, the Atlantic Ocean, or her dwindling cellphone battery keep her from inspiring her granddaughter.

To all those at ICM who advocated both at home and abroad. Most especially to the amazing Amelia Atlas, who saw this novel's potential long, long before I did and who tirelessly guided me in every step of the journey.

To the incomparable Kate Medina, who is in possession of that singular skill of extraordinary editors (and midwives) to ask for one more push and one push more, and under whose immeasurable guidance this story thrived.

In the United States, to the team at Penguin Random House—most especially Erica Gonzalez, who warmly read and reread, and in so doing re-sparked my enthusiasm at every turn.

And in the United Kingdom, to the team at Fourth Estate, HarperCollins—most especially Helen Garnons-Williams, who believed early on that the magic of *Conjure Women* could cross all borders.

I am indebted to the many teachers, mentors, and friends who supported early drafts. At the Tin House workshop: to Elissa Schappell, Dana Spiotta, and the lifelong cohort I formed there over one wild week. And at Columbia University: to Binnie Kirshenbaum, Chinelo Okparanta, Rebecca Godfrey, and the group of daring, witchy women writers who studied and conjured alongside me. Heartfelt thanks to Joni Marie Iraci, who offered wisdom and wit in equal measure.

Thank you to my beloved literary sisters Janet Matthews-Derrico and Rosemary Santarelli, who read every crazy incarnation and only ever asked for more crazy.

And to the "biddies," my best friends and chosen family, for celebrating the successes and celebrating the failures, for making celebrating a lifelong pursuit.

Lastly, thank you to my husband, Sean, my best friend and partner in every way, who kept me fed and watered, who heard me say a million times, "I'm going to do the thing," and answered, every single time, "I know you will."

About the Author

AFIA ATAKORA was born in the United Kingdom and raised in New Jersey. She graduated from New York University and has an MFA from Columbia University, where she was the recipient of the De Alba Fellowship. Her fiction has been nominated for a Pushcart Prize and she was a finalist for the Hurston/Wright Award for college writers. *Conjure Women* is her first novel.

About the Type

This book was set in Electra, a typeface designed for Linotype by W. A. Dwiggins, the renowned type designer (1880–1956). Electra is a fluid typeface, avoiding the contrasts of thick and thin strokes that are prevalent in most modern typefaces.